# A NOTE TO READERS

Rebekah Cunningham and her brother are fictional characters, but they represent real children who came to America from England and Holland. The hardships they faced, both on board ship and in their new home, helped make our country a place where all can worship God in whatever way they choose.

Although the main characters are fictional, this book is filled with incidents that actually happened. Many of the minor characters are true as well: Governor William Bradford, Captain Myles Standish, John Alden, and others. If not for Samoset, Squanto, and Chief Massasoit, the real-life American Indians who helped the Pilgrims, the colony at Plymouth would never have survived their first long and tragic year in the New World.

SISTERS IN TIME

# Rebekah
## in Danger
### PERIL AT PLYMOUTH COLONY

COLLEEN L. REECE

BARBOUR
PUBLISHING

SISTERS IN TIME

# Rebekah
## in Danger

ISBN 1-59310-352-2

Cover design by Lookout Design Group, Inc.

Published by Barbour Publishing, Inc., P.O. Box 719, Uhrichsville, Ohio 44683, www.barbourbooks.com

*Our mission is to publish and distribute inspirational products offering exceptional value and biblical encouragement to the masses.*

Member of the
Evangelical Christian
Publishers Association

Printed in the United States of America.
5 4 3 2 1

*For all those, young and old, who read this book. May you enjoy reading it as much as I enjoyed writing it. What a thrill to relive those long-ago days, both bright and dark, and realize what the courageous Pilgrims who wanted freedom to worship went though so we could live and serve God without fear in this country today. It is my prayer that we may never take that freedom for granted.*

*Colleen L. Reece*

# CONTENTS

# CHAPTER 1

# A New Land

*The New World, November 1620*

"I'm tired of working," eleven-year-old Rebekah Cunningham muttered to herself as she crawled into her familiar hiding place under the chicken coops on the *Mayflower*'s deck. On the long trip across the Atlantic, this cramped little corner had been her refuge when she needed a few minutes alone. Now she heaved a sigh of relief as she crept back into the tight nook.

*Mend this stocking, Rebekah. . . . Stir the pot. . .milk the goats. . . sweep the floor, Rebekah. . . . Mend this mattress. . . . Don't forget to keep an eye on your brother, Rebekah. . . . Have you done your sewing yet, Rebekah?. . .* The list of chores never seemed to end. By the time she had one day's worth of work done, it was nighttime—and then the next morning, she had to start all over again. She had been so excited about reaching land, thinking that once they were no longer at sea, life would be easier. Instead, things were just the same. If only they could all move off of the *Mayflower*. Rebekah was tired of the stinky old ship. She wanted room to run. She was tired of tripping over someone every time she moved.

When they had first set sail from Holland, it had all seemed like such a grand adventure. Rebekah knew that her parents had lived most of their lives in England, but she had been born in Holland, and she was both excited and terrified at the thought of seeing somewhere new. Her parents and the other Separatists had come to Holland so they could worship God the way they wanted, without the king forcing them to meet secretly.

Rebekah had been happy in Holland. It was the only home she had ever known, and she had hated to leave all her friends. She worried about what it would be like to live somewhere ruled only by the strict Separatist leaders. The Dutch had sung and danced and laughed, and Rebekah had enjoyed visiting her friends' homes, where everyone seemed to always be having a good time.

But she knew this was the very thing that had worried the church leaders. The Separatists' children were no longer separate. They were beginning to dress like the Dutch and act like the Dutch. They even talked like the Dutch. Meanwhile, the Separatist adults had such a hard time fitting in with the Dutch that it was difficult for them to find jobs and earn a living. The church elders also worried that Spain might conquer Holland, turning it into a Catholic nation. If that happened, the Protestant Separatists might face the same persecution they had endured in England.

And so the Separatists had found English merchants who were willing to take them on board their ship to the New World. First, they had to travel to England, though. The whole thing had involved lots of complicated, grown-up arrangements that seemed to take forever.

When they finally set sail from England, Rebekah and her brother, Will, could hardly keep still. They had run from one side of the *Mayflower*'s deck to the other, trying to see everything at once. The rise and fall of the deck beneath their feet, the sight of fish leaping from the waves, the way the moon looked sinking into the sea—each new experience filled them with wonder.

But as their journey went on week after week, the wonder wore off. Their sleeping quarters were so cramped that there was never any room to move around below deck. Many people became sick, and the dark quarters smelled of vomit, diarrhea, and too many unwashed human beings packed into too small a space. The children grew tired of the meager meals, and their stomachs hurt. The exciting adventure had turned into long, dreary weeks that seemed as though they would never end.

But now at last they were here in the New World. The *Mayflower* was anchored off the shore, and soon they would have a chance to go on land. But first they had to hear the news from Captain Standish, who had gone with a few other men to see what the land was like. Rebekah could hardly wait until she could finally go on shore. She longed to feel solid land beneath her feet. When she thought about eating fresh food again, her stomach growled with anticipation.

She moved deeper into the shadows beneath the old coops. The chickens that had survived their journey clucked gently, eyeing Rebekah sideways from their beady eyes. She knew that soon one of the men would move the coops onto the land. But in the meantime, Rebekah was going to take refuge here one more time. She pushed back the curly wisps from her dark brown braids that poked out from her hood and tickled her nose. Then she snuggled her wool cloak more tightly around her shoulders and wrapped her arms around her knees. With a sigh, she let her mind drift into a daydream.

"Captain Standish!" She recognized her ten-year-old brother Will's voice, and she heard his feet race across the deck. Rebekah peeked out from a crack between the coops and saw the red-faced, mean-looking man who had been chosen chief military officer for the new colony in America. Her brother saluted smartly as he skidded to a stop in front of the captain. Rebekah pressed back deeper into the shadowy recess. She would be in big trouble if Captain Standish caught her shirking her duties.

"What do you want, Cunningham?" Standish gruffly demanded. "Can't you see I'm busy? The people are waiting to hear what our scouting party discovered. Step out of my way. I have to enlist volunteers for a longer exploration." The corners of the captain's mouth turned down. "I suppose it will have to be after the Sabbath. Anyway, we have to find a place for our permanent settlement. I don't have time to waste standing here talking to you." Standish waved his hand, as if to brush Will aside like a troublesome insect, and Rebekah's blood boiled.

Rebekah leaned forward to glimpse the pale November sunlight shining on Will's short dark hair.

"I know, sir. That's why I stopped you. I want to go with the exploring party," announced Will.

Rebekah was proud to hear Will keep his voice steady.

"You?" Standish laughed unpleasantly. "I need men, not lads. Try again in a few years, if we survive that long in this godforsaken land." The corners of his mouth turned down. "We'll be lucky if any of us are alive by the end of next year."

"Sir, I am almost eleven," Will persisted. "I'm strong. I can also outrun every boy and most of the men on board ship." Rebekah saw her brother flex his right arm and grin.

Captain Standish planted his feet apart, his hands on his hips. He gave Will a sour, unconvinced look. "You're a cocky one, aren't you? I thought you Separatists were taught it's a sin to boast."

"Is it boasting if you know you can do something well?" Will asked. "I only told you because I thought you might need a swift runner to carry messages."

Reluctance crossed the captain's hard face. He looked Will over from the top of his head to the tips of his worn boots. "Hmm. You are tall for your age. Wiry, too." He hesitated and tilted his head to one side. "I might be able to use you, at that." Standish drew his brows together in a ferocious scowl. "Very well. You may go if your father agrees and—"

"He plans to volunteer."

"Quiet, whelp!" Standish roared. "If you go, you are under my command. You will obey my orders, keep your mouth shut, and stay close to your father. Understand me?"

"Yes, sir," Will mumbled.

"Dismissed." The captain marched across the ship's deck, his boots thumping loudly on the wood.

Captain Standish barked, "I know you're all waiting to hear what those of us who first stepped foot on the New World discovered in the brief time we were ashore. We saw no signs of habitation. The sand hills here are similar to the downs in Holland but better and wooded. We suspect there are miles of forests. We saw an abundance of oak and sassafras, pine and juniper. We saw birch and holly, some walnut and ash. Near the swamps are cedar and red maple." His dour voice brightened. "Although we didn't find any good water, we dug into the earth. It is rich, black, and good for planting."

A murmur of approval swept through the people on board. The first sight of the rocky coast had been less than promising. Rebekah knew that rich, black earth meant abundant crops.

"I suppose it is too much to ask that any of you Separatists will consent to be part of an exploring party until Monday," Standish continued, and Rebekah heard the sneer in his voice.

"Monday will be time enough," Governor John Carver quietly told him. "Tomorrow will be given over to preaching, praise, and prayer, as is our custom. Monday we will begin our work." He cleared his throat gently. "My wife, Katherine, and the other women are eager to wash clothes. Did you find a place suitable for such a long-postponed purpose?"

"Yes. There is a small pond not far away. The water isn't good for drinking, but it will serve well for washing."

"Good. While the women and girls are scrubbing the stink of the voyage from our clothing, we men will separate into groups." Governor Carver looked over their number. "I suggest that those who are too sick to be among the exploring party use the time searching for food."

"I agree." Captain Standish took charge once more. "Cunningham," he said, "if you consent to go with me, bring your son. He may prove useful, if he can live up to his boasting as to speed!" Loud laughter came from the group of people; then several men stepped forward to volunteer, Rebekah and Will's father among them.

Rebekah knew that she had best leave her hiding place now, while everyone was distracted. She quickly crawled out and stood up, smoothing her skirts. When she turned, she caught her mother's eye, but Mother only smiled, and Rebekah hoped her mother hadn't been watching her daughter creeping on her hands and knees from under the chickens.

*Lucky Will,* Rebekah thought. *He will get to go exploring, while I have to scrub mountains of laundry.* Then her envy turned to worry. Would her brother and father be safe out in the wilderness? What if they were attacked by wild animals? What if something dreadful happened and they never came back?

Rebekah always worried about her brother's safety. Although he was only a year younger than she was, she had always been the more sensible of the two. Will had a habit of flying off the handle—and then he ended up in trouble. She knew their parents counted on her to watch over him and do her best to keep him out of trouble. Sometimes the responsibility seemed like a heavy load to carry.

"Please, may I go?" she heard her brother ask their father, and she knew Will felt not even a tinge of fear.

Father looked him over, much as Myles Standish had done earlier. "I see no reason why not, especially as Captain Standish has requested it." Rebekah saw that a twinkle lurked in their father's eyes, though his mouth stayed solemn. "How is it that he knows so much of your running skills? And what is this about boasting?"

Will's face turned dark red from embarrassment. "Uh, I didn't know whether he knew I could run fast, so I told him. I didn't think it was wrong to do so, when God has given me long legs that have learned to travel swiftly."

"I see." Father folded his arms across his chest and grinned. In that moment, his expression was almost identical to Will's. Father turned to Mother. "Well, shall we let this son of ours go?"

Perfect trust showed in Mother's eyes. "So long as he promises to stay close beside you," she agreed.

Before Will could holler with delight, Rebekah asked, "Why must you go? There are plenty of men. I know you're almost a man, but you don't know how to fire a musket. What would happen if you crossed paths with a bear or wolf? What good would you be to the scouting party?"

"If Captain Standish thinks I am man enough to go, I am, Rebekah Cunningham. Oh, what's the use? You're a girl, and girls are always afraid!"

"That is enough, Will." Father's smile vanished. "Your mother was a girl herself not long ago, and I don't know any man braver than she. Did you not see how she cared for the sick and weathered the hardest storms on the Atlantic without a word of complaint?"

Father's hand lightly touched Mother's shoulder, then came to rest on Rebekah's head. "This one is just like her. There is no fear for herself in your sister. Only for you, and with just cause. In the past, there have been occasions when you were careless and fell into trouble. Rebekah has truly been her brother's keeper. It is well for you to remember this and show her more respect."

Father's stinging criticism made Will hang his head. "I'm sorry," he told his sister. "Forgive me?" He grinned. "If I find any curious or pretty things ashore, I will fill my pockets for you."

Rebekah rewarded him with a smile. "Thank you, but be careful, please."

"I will," Will added with a sigh. "I only wish we could go tomorrow and not have to wait until Monday."

"Explore on the Sabbath?" Rebekah frowned at him. "You sound like a heathen." She proudly raised her chin. "Elder Brewster says we must always set a good example for the crew, the London Strangers, and the Indians. What kind of example would it be to have you go tearing off on the Lord's Day?"

"She is right," Mother put in. "It is God's own commandment. 'Remember the Sabbath day, to keep it holy. Six days shalt thou labour, and do all thy work: but the seventh day is the sabbath of the LORD thy God. . . . For in six days the LORD made heaven and earth, the sea, and all that in them is, and rested the seventh day.' "

"Mother, why did God need to rest?" Rebekah asked. Her forehead wrinkled. "I wouldn't think God would ever get tired."

"I have always felt God set aside that time to simply appreciate and enjoy all the beautiful things He created," Mother said. A little smile played about her lips. "Perhaps He felt a little like you do when you slip into your hiding place beneath the coops—as though He needed some quiet time." Mother laughed at the expression of embarrassment on Rebekah's face, and then she continued, "God also set an example for us. So did Jesus. Setting aside one day out of every seven to remember Him and spend time being glad for all He has given us is not too much to ask, is it?"

"No, Mother."

But Rebekah couldn't help but squirm a little, thinking of the endless services they held each week. If God was trying to be nice to them, surely He could have thought of a better way for people to spend their quiet time than sitting in stuffy, boring services. Many times in Holland, she and Will had envied the Dutch children, especially on Sunday. The Dutch boys and girls laughed and sang and played games just outside the church door. The deaconess who sat with the Separatist children in a special section watched them with a sharp eye. She made sure they never whispered, and they certainly never laughed. If they did, they were sorry.

Rebekah made a face as she remembered. A few times she and Will had forgotten the strict rules against talking and laughing. The deaconess promptly boxed their ears. One time she whipped Will with a birch rod. When they weren't listening to sermons or singing hymns on Sundays, Will and Rebekah were expected to sit quietly. Sabbath days seemed to never end.

"I don't understand how it can be wrong to be joyful," Rebekah had complained to Will more than once. "God must have been happy when He finished His world." Now Rebekah secretly sighed. She loved God. Yet how could she live through another long, long Sunday knowing that on Monday they would finally step onto the shores of the New World, land of freedom? Even if she had to do laundry all day, it would be better than being on board the ship.

# CHAPTER 2

# Laundry

To Rebekah's joy and Will's dismay, the scouting party from the *Mayflower* did not go on Monday, after all. While the women and girls waded, small children ran on the sands. How good it felt to be out in the fresh air after the long days and nights huddled in their smelly quarters!

Some of the men walked the beach. Excitement spread when they found mussels and clams. For nine weeks, the travelers had been without fresh food. The Pilgrims had never seen clams or mussels before and didn't know anything about eating them. Many of them stuffed themselves and ended up sick. Fortunately, Father and Mother cautioned Will and Rebekah not to be greedy. They escaped the stomach upsets that followed.

Meanwhile, carpenters examined pieces of the damaged shallop. "Sorry," they told Governor Carver and Captain Standish. "The boat has been battered so badly by the crossing it will take us some time to get it ready for use."

Standish scowled. Rebekah knew the captain hated for things to come up and make him change his plans. Rebekah suspected that Will secretly sympathized with the captain. Surely Will was as eager as the new military leader to explore the New World!

Tuesday passed with Will so impatient he worked off his extra energy by racing up and down the deck. A cold Wednesday morning dawned. Standish, privately called "Captain Shrimp" by some, announced, "We will go on foot." He glanced south toward what appeared to be the mouth of a river, then shook his head. "That can come later. For now, we will go northeast." He strutted to the head of the scouting party. "Muskets ready?"

"Ready," came the answer.

Rebekah looked at the gun her father carried. She hoped he would know how to use it correctly. Only this morning she had watched Captain Standish demonstrate how to use a musket for the benefit of those who didn't know. It took time to load. First, Standish poured black powder down the muzzle and then tamped and wadded it. Next, he dropped in a lead ball and shoved it down with a thick pad. When the captain completed his preparations and released the trigger, Rebekah nearly jumped in the air at the yard-long burst of flame, a deafening roar, and a cloud of smoke.

*If it takes all that time to get ready,* she wondered, *won't the Indians or bears or deer already be gone by the time anyone gets around to shooting?*

Rebekah watched as her brother fell into step at the end of the line, close behind his father. She hoped he could manage to stay out of trouble. If there was one false move on his part, she knew the captain would order the youngest member of the party to return to the *Mayflower.*

A gruff voice said in her ear, "Your brother best step lively, lass. 'Cause I plan on being right b'hind him."

Rebekah turned and a grin spread over her face as she looked up at Jake, the big sailor she and Will had made friends with on their voyage. "You're going, too?" she asked him.

"Came t' see the New World, didn't I?" Jake snapped, face grim as ever. Only a flicker of light in his small dark eyes showed the friendship he felt for Rebekah and her brother. "I best be catchin' up or I'll be left behind."

Rebekah gave the sailor a smile. "I'm glad you will be going along." She eyed the wicked knife stuck in Jake's belt and the way the seaman rested one hand on its hilt. He had fought pirates and had a long scar on his shoulder to prove it. If the explorers ran into danger, Jake would be a good man to have with them.

She waved until her father, Will, and Jake had at last disappeared between the thick trees. With a sigh, she turned away.

"There's work to be done," her mother reminded, her voice gentle.

Rebekah heaved yet another long sigh, this one even louder and wearier than the last. "Mother, don't you ever wish you could go off with the men sometimes instead of doing women's work?"

Her mother shook her head. "Nay, Rebekah, I can't say I do. I have to confess, I would like to go along just to keep an eye on my menfolk. But otherwise, I'm content to stay behind. In fact, I'm eager to be scrubbing all that dirty laundry. It will be good to have everything clean again." She put her hand under Rebekah's chin and lifted her face so she could look into her daughter's eyes. "You'll see. It will be fun to be up to our elbows in sudsy water. And it will be good to be on solid land for a change. There may even be time for you and your friends to play hopscotch and tag in the evenings."

Comforted, Rebekah returned her mother's smile.

In the days that followed, Rebekah followed her mother's example, while her father and brother roamed the beach and forests. Always a good helper, Rebekah worked alongside Mother, scrubbing clothes and dirty blankets. She won approving looks and high praise from the other women for her hard work.

"Mercy, she is as good as a full-grown woman," some said. Mother only smiled, but the pride in her face made Rebekah feel good. She thanked God that she was strong, in spite of being short and petite. She flew from task to task, green eyes shining and curly dark brown braids tossing. Mother was right. The work was hard—but it was also fun. It felt good just to be off the ship, with room to run and breathe.

During the days of hard work, Rebekah had a precious memory she kept treasured in her heart, like a rare jewel in a box. It helped a lot during the anxious time of waiting for Father and Will to return. Each time fear for their safety sneaked up and grabbed at her, Rebekah whispered what Father had told Will: "There is no fear for herself in your sister. Only for you. . ."

Once Rebekah asked her mother, "Do you think Father was right? About me, I mean. That I don't really worry about me. Just about Will."

"You are a loving sister," Mother said. "Any boy would be proud to have you care for him as you do Will. Even though he teases you, always know how much he cares about you. You are also a joy to your father and me."

Rebekah blushed until the red dimmed her freckles.

As the days went by, though, Rebekah's back began to ache

from bending over to scrub the dirty clothing. Her arms ached from carrying the heavy wet blankets and stretching up on tiptoe to hang them to dry. By evening, she was too tired to play with her friends. She wondered what the men were doing.

"Mother," she said with a sigh, "I'm starting to wish again that I were Will so I could go exploring, too. I want to see more of the New World than what we can from here, and I'm getting tired of cleaning these smelly old blankets." She looked with loathing at a pile of blankets waiting to be washed. They were stiff from dried saltwater and the vomit of sick passengers.

Mother's eyebrows raised, and Rebekah hurried on. "I know it's silly. Goodness, Will barely got to go, and he's a boy." She giggled. "Can you imagine what Captain Standish would look like if I begged to go scouting? I can just see him." Rebekah placed her feet apart, squared her shoulders, and made fists of her hands. She put them on her hips, tucked her chin into her neck, and said in a deep, unnatural voice, "Be gone with you! Girls are made for tea parties, not exploring parties!"

Mother's green eyes sparkled with laughter. "Respect your elders, Rebekah."

"I do. It's just that Captain Standish acts like he is more important than anyone else." Rebekah dropped her imitation. A troubled look crossed her face. "He isn't a believer, is he?"

"Nay, but we pray he may become one of us." Mother sighed. "We must also appreciate what he is doing for us. Father says he feels Captain Standish will be faithful to his duties, no matter what happens."

"I'm sorry I made fun of him."

"As am I sorry for laughing at your nonsense," Mother admitted.

*Boom! Boom, boom, boom!*

"The signal!" Rebekah joyfully shouted. "The men are back!" She ran, shading her eyes with one hand. "Will promised to bring me whatever he found," she cried. "I wonder what it will be!"

She caught sight of Jake, marching near the front of the company this time, and she moved back. Friend he might be, but the sailor's scowl sent shivers through Rebekah sometimes.

"Jake is not a believer, either, is he, Mother?"

Her mother shook her head. "I doubt it. But he has been a good friend to you children. I was grateful for his watchful eye while we were on board ship."

Rebekah nodded, but her green eyes were cloudy. She knew the church leaders preached that not everyone was chosen by God to go to heaven. But she hated to think that God might not love Jake. Surely God would see past the sailor's ferocious exterior to the kindness she knew lived inside him.

"Does God love Jake, do you think?" she asked her mother. "Is he one of the elect?" She bit her lip, looking troubled. "He won't send Jake to hell, will he?"

Her mother glanced down at her daughter's face. "I believe God loves everyone," she said softly but firmly. "The Bible says that God is not willing that anyone should perish. He wants us all to have eternal life." She smiled. "We must pray that Jake will come to know how much God loves him."

Rebekah puzzled over her mother's words for a moment. Was her mother saying she did not agree with the teachings of the church?

Then Rebekah recognized her father's hat, and she forgot about her worries. Father and Will were walking toward her and Mother, their eyes bright with eagerness. Rebekah dashed forward and flung herself at them.

"You're home!"

# CHAPTER 3

# Joy and Tragedy

Rebekah danced around Will. "I am so glad you are safe!"

He grinned at her. "Aren't you glad to see Father, too?"

"Of course I am," Rebekah replied indignantly.

"You worry more about me, though, don't you?" Will teased.

Her freckled nose went into the air. "With good reason." When he started to protest, she laughed and said, "Never mind. What did you bring me?"

"Just you wait and see!" Will's eyes sparkled, and his hands crept toward his pockets. "Hold out your hands and make a cup of them."

Rebekah started to obey, then put her hands behind her back and demanded, "You won't give me something squishy, like a worm, will you?"

"Where would I get a worm this time of year? C'mon, Rebekah. You can trust me. Honest. Put your hands out and close your eyes."

Rebekah slowly did as her brother asked. All the time he had been gone, she'd tried to think what he might bring her. Cones from the evergreen trees? Pretty shells? She felt a shower of small objects pour into her cupped palms, then something long and rough. Her eyes popped open.

She looked at what she held. Dried seeds. They were hard yellow kernels and an ear that was bigger than any grain she had ever seen. "Oh, Will!" she whispered. "It's the best present in the whole world. What is it?"

Will laughed. "It's the Indians' grain. We've been calling it corn, though it's not like anything we've seen at home. We're going to plant it come spring. And in the meantime, we will eat it."

"Where did you get it?"

"We got it from the Indians."

"Real Indians? What were they like? Were they frightening?"

A shadow passed over Will's face. "We never saw them. We found the corn near a grave. There was an abandoned house there, as well."

Rebekah frowned. "How did you know the Indians wouldn't come back for their corn?"

Will shrugged. "Captain Standish commanded us to take it all."

Rebekah's eyebrows pulled together. "Isn't that stealing? What if the Indians come back for their corn and find it gone?"

Will looked unhappy. "I know. That's what I said. But Captain Standish wouldn't listen to me."

Rebekah shook her head. "Well, of course not, Will. You're just a boy. What did Father say?"

"He said we had to obey the captain's orders. We need the food desperately, after all. Father said we will pray that God will show us how to make things right with the Indians."

Rebekah let go of her worries and closed her fingers around the corn. "What will it taste like, do you suppose?" Suddenly, she wanted to hug her brother and dance, even though the Separatists permitted no such foolishness. Real Indian corn, here, in her hands! And her brother and her father had returned to them safely.

"Mother, just see what Will has brought!" Rebekah said when she could finally tear her gaze away from her gift.

"I know. Isn't it wonderful? William, how glad we are to have more food," Mother said to Father with a grateful look. "Our stores were perilously low."

"I want to hear every single thing that happened," Rebekah told Will. "But first, we have some news for you. While you were gone, we had a visitor."

Will, who had wearily dropped to a pallet on the floor, sat up straight. His eyes opened wide enough to satisfy even Rebekah. "A visitor? Don't tell me an Indian came when we didn't see any!" Disappointment spread over his face.

Rebekah laughed. "I didn't say it was an Indian."

"There's no other ship in the harbor, and we're miles from any other white people." Will looked puzzled. "Who else could it be? Did he come in a canoe?"

"No." Rebekah giggled again. For once she had news before Will. It was fun to keep him guessing.

"Then he must have walked," Will figured out. "Is he still here?"

"He's still here, but he didn't walk." Rebekah burst into laughter. So did Mother.

"Go ahead and tell him," Mother finally said.

"Susanna White had her baby," Rebekah explained. "The first white child born in New England. Susanna and William named their new son Peregrine."

"Peregrine! I thought the Hopkins family had already chosen

the worst possible name when they called their son Oceanus," Will protested.

"Peregrine means *pilgrim* or *wanderer*," Mother put in.

Will grinned. "You were right, Rebekah. He isn't an Indian. He didn't come in a canoe, he didn't walk, and he's still here. Now will you listen to what happened to us?"

"Of course." She scooted closer to Will, propped her elbows on her knees and her chin in her hands, and prepared to hear Will's and Father's adventures.

An hour later, Will finally finished his exciting stories of everything that had happened on the trip. Rebekah solemnly said, "I want to see the New World, but I don't want to be so thirsty I don't know what to do like you were. Or have to fight my way out of thorn thickets. You and Father will be in danger whenever you go on one of those expeditions."

"God will protect us," Will told her.

Rebekah shook her head. "Not if you do foolish things. You'd better stay close to Father."

"I have to." Will made an awful face. "Captain Standish will have my hide if I don't. So will Jake." He grinned. "That is, if Father doesn't get to me first!"

Rebekah wasn't satisfied with the answer but didn't want to nag. She touched a torn place on her brother's jacket. "Tomorrow when it's lighter, I'll mend that for you."

"Thank you." Will yawned. "I don't know when the next scouting party is going out. I hope I get to go along."

"Don't plan on it," Father warned. "I heard Captain Jones say he planned to lead the next party. I suspect it will be after the shallop is ready. Captain Jones wants to explore the river we saw close to where we found the corn. The river's mouth is swampy, but it's wide enough for the shallop."

"Do you think Captain Standish might speak a good word for me?" Will asked. Rebekah noticed how round and anxious his eyes looked.

"Perhaps." Father's brown eyes twinkled. He yawned. "It's been a long trip. Time to say good night."

Rebekah lay wide-eyed and sleepless long after her family fell asleep. When she did close her eyes, visions of Indian graves, Indian corn, and angry Indians ran through her head.

"Lord," she prayed, "You know I wish Will would be happy just to stay here with me. He isn't, though. He will be terribly disappointed if he can't go again. Please keep him safe, and help me to be brave."

Comforted at last, Rebekah fell into a deep and restful sleep.

Ten days later, the shallop was repaired enough for use, although more work needed to be done on it. Thirty men climbed aboard, but not Will. Captain Jones chose those he wanted and scoffed at the idea a mere lad could be useful to him. "Stay here and protect the ship," Jones said.

Rebekah knew he was mocking her brother. She was glad Will was wise enough to realize that showing disappointment or arguing with the captain would merely strengthen the older man's opinion that Will was too young to go.

"Aye, aye, sir." Will put on as cheerful a grin as he could and saluted. The surprise in Captain Jones's face made Rebekah proud of her brother.

"Good fer ye, lad," Jake hissed before ambling down the deck in the rolling sailor's walk the crew used in order to stay upright during storms.

Father echoed the words. "Taking disappointment like a man is important," he told Will. "Each time we do this, it makes us stronger for the next time." He glanced at the sky. "It may be well you were left behind, son. I don't like the looks of those clouds."

Father's fears proved correct. The scouting party ran into terrible weather. The shallop had to turn back. Some of the Pilgrims refused to do so. They waded through icy, waist-deep water to get to shore. Up hills and down valleys through six inches of snow they went. The wind blew. It snowed all that day and night. When they finally returned to the ship, many of them were so sick that they never recovered.

When the weather improved, the scouting party tried again and found a few deserted wigwams, built of bent sapling trees with the ends stuck in the ground. Thick mats covered the wigwams both inside and out. A mat also covered the wide hole used as a chimney. Another mat made a low door. Even more mats served as beds.

The scouting party found wooden bowls, earthenware pots, many baskets, deer feet and heads, eagle claws, and other curious things.

At Corn Hill, where they had first discovered the corn, they dug in the frozen earth and discovered more corn to eat as well as some beans. Again, the settlers vowed to pay the Indians for what they took. They triumphantly carried their treasures back to the *Mayflower*.

"This is a real find," the leaders told the people when they returned to the ship. "Indian corn is well known by the explorers from the Caribbean and the Carolinas, as well as here. It gives two harvests a year and makes into good bread. We are fortunate, indeed, to have found it."

Rebekah wasn't sure how she felt about the corn. They needed the food desperately, but if they took the Indians' corn, what would the brown-skinned people do for food? She put the worry out of her mind when the scouts reported they'd seen a plentiful supply of game: deer, partridges, wild geese, and ducks. Will would be happy to go hunting with the men, and the fresh meat would be a welcome addition to their diet. And it would be their own food, fairly earned, not stolen.

Edward Winslow described seeing whales in the bay. "One lay above water. We thought she was dead. One of the men shot, to see if she would stir. His musket flew into pieces, both stock and barrel! Thanks be to God, no one was hurt, although many stood nearby. The whale gave a sniff and swam away."

Rebekah was glad the whale had not been hurt. But Captain Jones and others more experienced in fishing decided they would try whaling the next winter. They could make three thousand to four thousand pounds in whale oil, a fortune indeed!

To Will's delight, as soon as the shallop was completely repaired, another expedition set out. This time Captain Standish was in charge. He took the same group that had gone with him on his earlier expedition. Will waved good-bye to Mother and Rebekah, then huddled between Father and Jake. Later he told Rebekah that the cold was so intense that the spray froze on their coats. Two men fainted from the cold.

While Will and Father were away, Rebekah kept busy helping Mother and the other women. They were still sleeping at night on the *Mayflower* and spending most of their time during the day there, too, and Rebekah was heartily sick of the cramped quarters. She longed for the day when their family could once more live alone in their own home, rather than sharing every moment with many other families. She yearned for the freedom to run and run, without tripping over the belongings and stretched-out legs of the others in their group. Once more, she could not keep herself from envying Will and the freedom he had simply because he was a boy.

One night she lay awake, listening to the familiar sounds of snores, fussy babies, and soft murmurings all around her in the crowded sleeping quarters. The air was thick with the odor of many unwashed bodies, but Rebekah barely noticed, being used to breathing the heavy air. But she was tired of listening to so many other families settling down for the night. Two women were arguing nearby, their whispers hissing like angry wasps. Someone else was crying softly, long shuddering sobs that Rebekah knew belonged to a grown woman rather than a child. The sound made her uneasy, and she held her hands over her ears, trying to shut out the noise. If only she could fall asleep so that she could wake up and it would be morning, time to get up and go up on the deck in the fresh air.

"Hush now, Dorothy." Rebekah recognized her mother's voice,

speaking softly to William Bradford's wife. Rebekah took her hands away from her ears so that she could hear better. "I know it's hard to be so far from your little son," Mother was saying, "but you must trust him to our Lord. God is with your son across the ocean in Holland, just as He is here with us in this new world. In God, you and your son are not separated at all. Think of it like that."

"I cannot." The words sounded more like a moan, as though Dorothy Bradford were in pain. "My little son. My baby. . ." Her voice dissolved into sobs. "I should never have left him."

"Little John will be safe there in Holland, Dorothy," Mother answered quietly. "You know that's what you and William decided. Think of how hard the voyage was. So many of us fell ill, including you yourself. You know it's hardest on the children. And now with winter coming, we know hard times may lie ahead, as well. Your little boy is safe and warm and well fed, and you shall see him again by and by, when you and William have built a good home here."

"I should never have come to this terrible place," Dorothy choked out.

"But you are here now, Dorothy, and William needs you by his side."

"I am no use to William," Dorothy sobbed. "I am too ill. I will never be well again."

"Of course you shall be well. You are already far better than you were."

But Rebekah could tell that Dorothy Bradford was crying too hard to listen to the reason in her mother's voice. "I cannot bear it," she wept. "I cannot bear to live without him. I will never see him again. I hate this place. I shall die here, I know, and never see my little John again."

"Hush, Dorothy." Mother's voice was gentle but firm. "You must have faith. You will make yourself more ill if you continue crying like this. Our men need us to be strong."

"I cannot be strong," Dorothy Bradford wailed.

"Rely on God," Rebekah's mother replied, "and He will be your strength."

But Dorothy Bradford would not listen. She was still crying when Rebekah finally fell asleep.

The next day, the early morning hush was split by the sound of a scream. Rebekah sprang up from her mattress, her heart pounding. "What is it?"

Mother pushed the hair back from her face as she scrambled to her feet. "I don't know. I'll go see."

She disappeared up the ladder to the upper deck. Rebekah waited, her blanket clutched around her against the morning chill, her heart pounding with a terrible foreboding.

From the deck above, she heard the sounds of agitated voices. A man shouted something. Rebekah thought she heard the word "overboard," and then there was the *thump-thump-thump* of running feet, followed by a splash. Rebekah dropped the blanket and yanked on her skirt and waistcoat. Not bothering with her stockings, she ran barefoot up the ladder.

Mother and several other women were leaning over the ship railing. "What happened?" Rebekah asked.

Her mother glanced at her, but she seemed to barely see Rebekah. "A woman has fallen overboard," she said, her voice trembling. Her face was very white.

The women huddled together, waiting while one of the sailors climbed back on board the *Mayflower*, the limp and dripping body of a woman clutched in his arms. As he threw his leg over the railing, Rebekah saw it was Jake. His face was grim as he gently laid the woman down on the deck.

"Oh, Dorothy," Mother whispered.

Rebekah stared down at the pale, quiet face of Dorothy Bradford. She looked more peaceful than Rebekah had ever seen her since they left Holland.

She was too quiet, though. With a gasp of fear, Rebekah looked up at her mother's face. The look in Mother's eyes told Rebekah the truth.

Dorothy Bradford was dead.

CHAPTER 4
# More Trouble

All day, Rebekah huddled in her spot between the chicken coops. No one called her name, bidding her to do some chore. An awful hush hung over the *Mayflower*. Even the sailors went about their business quietly. The sound of weeping floated up from the sleeping quarters below. Rebekah had cried, too, but now she had no more tears left to cry.

She watched the hens shift their silly heads from side to side. Their soft, gossipy voices comforted her a little, but her heart felt heavy and strange inside her. She kept remembering the conversation she had overheard the night before between her mother and Dorothy Bradford. Dorothy had been right: She would never see her son again. Why had God let her die?

The question went around and around inside her mind, until at last, tired from lack of sleep, her head slipped sideways against the chicken coop. With a shuddering sigh, she slid into a shallow sleep.

"I wonder where our womenfolk are." The sound of Father's puzzled voice made Rebekah raise her head.

"Why would they all be below deck in the middle of the day?" That was Will's voice now. "Mother? Rebekah?"

"Here." Rebekah scrambled out from between the chicken coops and lifted her woebegone face to her brother. "Oh, Will, the awfulest thing has happened!"

Will's face turned white. "Not Mother!" The terror in his voice drove the fog from Rebekah's mind.

"No," she reassured her brother. "It's not Mother."

"I am fine, son." Their mother's muffled voice came from the hatchway.

Father ran to put his arms around Mother. "What is it, Abigail?"

Mother's words fell as heavy as hailstones. "Dorothy Bradford has drowned."

"It can't be true!" Will looked more astonished than distressed, and Rebekah knew he truly couldn't believe what had happened.

Rebekah remembered the way William Bradford had looked when he said good-bye to his young wife. She had seen the tenderness in his eyes, and the memory made her choke with fresh tears.

"How did it happen?" asked Father.

"A tragic accident." Mother sounded as if she had wept so many tears there were no more left in her. "Apparently, she fell overboard when no one was around to hear her cries and save her." She took a deep breath. "Will, stay here with your sister on deck and tell her about your journey. I wish to speak with your father below."

"Of course." Will put his hand on Rebekah's shoulder. He peered into her tearstained face and asked, "Why is Mother acting so strange? She isn't like herself at all."

Rebekah looked down at the deck. She gulped and twisted her apron front into ugly wrinkled knots, but she could not find the words to answer her brother's question.

"What's the big secret?" he demanded.

She looked at him, afraid to put into words the awful thing she had heard earlier. "Promise you won't tell?" she said at last. "Mother doesn't know I heard her talking with some of the other women. I don't believe it, anyway!"

"Don't believe what?" She could hear that Will's patience was slipping, and for a moment she could not understand how he could sound so annoyed in the midst of such sorrow. Then she realized that he still did not truly believe that Dorothy Bradford could be dead.

Rebekah stood on tiptoe and whispered in his ear. "Some people are saying Dorothy Bradford's drowning wasn't an accident!"

Will jerked back from his sister so quickly she nearly lost her balance. "Rebekah Cunningham, what did you say?"

"Shh!" She placed a finger over her lips and leaned close again. "Some of the people say Dorothy Bradford did not drown from an accident."

"You don't mean somebody pushed her?" Will looked sick. "That's impossible!"

"No, but it's just as bad." Fresh tears came to Rebekah's eyes. "They say she leaped into the sea, that she hates it here and went crazy because she won't ever see her little son in Holland, and—"

"It's wicked gossip, and I don't believe a word of it!" Will cried, keeping his voice low. "She was only twenty-three years old. I know she's been sick, but so have a lot of others."

Rebekah's stomach churned, and it felt like a heavy rock lay in the bottom of it.

"Mother doesn't think it's true, does she?" Will asked.

"Nay, son." Father had come up to them so quietly that neither had heard him. "Neither do I. This is a sad thing, and the least said about it, the better. William Bradford will need all our friendship. Don't mention his wife to him. He has already shown he prefers silence in the matter." Father put an arm around each of them. "Mother and I are counting on you to be loyal."

"What if people talk to us about it?" Rebekah asked.

"Simply tell them you have been asked not to speak of it." He sighed and looked across the bay. "Only ninety-nine of our number will sail to our new home. God grant that we do not lose many more."

Long after Father went below, the children stayed on deck. Will quietly told Rebekah that there had been a storm and the explorers had seen some Indians. He quickly described the area where they would settle. Rebekah asked a few questions, and then they fell silent. Neither made any attempt to seek out friends, even Jake. They had known Dorothy Bradford since they were small. They still found it hard to believe the frail, white-faced woman had drowned.

"It will be many months before the news travels across the ocean," Will said at last.

Rebekah thought of Holland where a small boy waited for a mother who would never come back to him. Her eyes stung. *Please, God,* Rebekah silently prayed, *take care of William Bradford and his son. Keep little John safe.* She wondered if Dorothy Bradford would be able to see her son from heaven.

"Will?" Rebekah asked quietly. "How can people who don't

believe in God stand it when someone they care about dies?"

"I don't know." Her brother stared out into the growing darkness. "We feel sad enough even though we know we will see them again in heaven." He fiercely added, "It will be a lot better place than this! Just think of it, Rebekah. God and Jesus will be there, and no one will ever get sick or die again. Or be hungry. Or sad."

Rebekah pulled her cloak closer around her. "If Father or Mother die, how will we find them when we go to heaven?"

"Don't worry about it. They aren't going to die for a long, long time," Will told her.

"They're lots older than we are, so they probably will die first," Rebekah said.

"I never thought much about it." Will paused. "I guess Jesus will make sure we find each other. It's like Mother and Father are always saying: We just have to trust Him. No matter what happens—even if we die—we'll be all right."

He shrugged, as though he were trying to shake such serious thoughts off his shoulders. "It's getting dark, and we have to go below," he said, changing the subject.

"I wonder how long it will be until we set sail."

That Friday, four days after the return of the explorers, the ship hauled up its anchor and sailed into the bay. Neither Will nor Rebekah looked back at Provincetown Harbor. The spot held too much sadness. Strong headwinds slowed the *Mayflower*'s progress. It took until Saturday to cover roughly thirty miles across the bay. The ship anchored about a mile and a half from shore because the water was shallow.

A foot of snow lay on the ground. Women shivered and stood close to their husbands and children. Children stared round-eyed. "We shall continue to live on board ship until we build shelters," Governor Carver announced. "It will be necessary to take people and cargo ashore in the smaller boats."

Captain Jones looked sour. Jake had told Will and Rebekah that Jones wanted to get the Pilgrims off his ship as soon as possible. "Tired of yer company, he is, and wants to save his vittles," Jake said.

Now the children exchanged delighted glances. Their friend Jake would remain with them, at least for a time.

The Sabbath passed in the usual manner, with prayers, psalms, and songs of praise. On Monday a band of armed men marched away to explore. Will wasn't included this time, but he and Rebekah listened eagerly to their report when they returned.

"It's a good land," one said. "The soil looks promising. Great sections are already cleared. There are signs that huge cornfields once existed, although they don't appear to have been planted for at least a year. It looks like the Indians just up and abandoned them for no reason at all."

Rebekah couldn't help asking, "Why would they do that?" She was glad when her father repeated her question loud enough for everyone to hear.

A puzzled look crossed the speaker's face, and he rubbed his bearded chin. "Your guess is as good as mine."

Another man eagerly put in, "We discovered berry bushes, timber, clay, and gravel. There is a high hill well suited to the building of a fort. From it, we can see the harbor and the country all around. It's ideal for defense, with a place for our cannon. We also found a clear, running stream of good water."

Governor Carver looked around the assembly. "What more can we ask for than already-cleared land, sweet water, and a fine view of the surrounding area?" He hesitated and spread his arms wide. "We are ill prepared to meet the many challenges of this land. Yet we have all that is needed."

His voice rang out, and he counted on his fingers. "First, we have faith: in Almighty God and in ourselves. Second, we have courage. Did we not cross an ocean known for claiming ships and passengers? Third, we have good sense. Fourth, we have determination. Here, by the grace of God, we will build our colony, our home—and we shall call it New Plymouth."

Mighty cheers rose from the company, Will's and Rebekah's among them.

Governor Carver immediately ordered twenty of the strongest men to go ashore in the shallop and begin cutting wood. When a wild storm blew in, Rebekah knew that this time Will wasn't at all disappointed that he had to stay on ship. The anchored *Mayflower* tossed violently. The waves were so high the shallop could not get back. Those in the woodcutting party found themselves marooned and miserable for a few days.

One day, as Rebekah and Mother were mending clothes with the other women, Mary Allerton gasped.

Mother gave her a knowing look. "Is it time?" she asked.

"Aye," said Mary.

"Quick, Rebekah," Mother instructed. "Clear out a corner for us in the sleeping quarters. Tell anyone who asks that it's time for Mary's baby to be born. Then get a bucket of water and some clean rags." Without waiting for an answer, Mother quickly turned to one of the other women, asking her to help get Mary safely down the ship's ladder.

Rebekah hurried to obey Mother. As soon as the other passengers understood what was happening, they created a private corner for Mary. One of the men went off to let Isaac Allerton know his wife was about to give birth.

When Rebekah returned with the water and rags, she could see that Mother was worried. Something wasn't right. Rebekah stood beside Mary and wiped the young woman's face with a cool cloth. The birth seemed to be taking forever.

Finally, a beautiful baby was born—but it never opened its eyes or took a breath.

As Mary hugged her lifeless baby and cried, Rebekah quietly stroked Mary's back, trying to comfort her. Everyone had been looking forward to the birth of another baby. But instead of feeling joy, they were now full of sorrow.

Soon, Christmas Day came. The Pilgrims considered Christmas a pagan holiday and did not celebrate it, but the others on ship had a small feast. They invited the Pilgrims to join them.

Knowing the weather would soon become even colder, people worked harder than ever. Some cut trees. Others split the logs. The first thing to be built was a twenty-foot-square "common house" to store tools and house the workmen, as well as serve as a shelter for the sick and a church.

Rebekah again felt as though all she did was work, work, work. From before daylight until long after dark, there were jobs to be done. Will was as busy as she was. Everyone needed food and shelter. Muscles that had gotten little exercise during the months on the *Mayflower* quickly grew sore from the hard work.

"At least everyone being so busy keeps them from arguing and quarreling with each other," Rebekah whispered to Will one night.

He moved his sore shoulders and yawned. "That's 'cause if everyone doesn't work together, none of us will survive," he told her. "There are a few who complain about our leaders. They say they were better off under the king of England's rule than starving in America."

He sighed and patted his growling stomach. "I know we need to finish the common house, but how I wish some of us could go hunting or fishing! We'll have to wait until next year for ripe berries and fruit and nuts, but scouts say there's a lot of seafood and waterfowl." He licked his lips. "I'd give anything for the leg of a roasted duck."

"So would I." Rebekah shifted position and rubbed her aching back. "I am tired, tired, tired. Sometimes I think if I have to carry another bucket of water for cooking, bathing, or washing clothes, I'll scream! I won't, though. Mother stays so cheerful and always has such a sweet smile, I can't complain to her. Just to you."

"That's good." Will yawned again, opening his mouth so wide Rebekah wondered if he'd dislocated his jaw. "Father and Mother are working even harder than we are. Besides, what good would complaining do? The work still has to be done."

"It never ends." Rebekah drooped against her brother's shoulder. "When Mother and I aren't cooking and washing and mending clothing for our own family, we help those who are too sick from scurvy and pneumonia to take care of their families. There's no time to spin and weave cloth for more clothing."

She put a rough hand to her mouth to nurse a sore finger. "Ow! Making torches from pine logs leaves my hands full of splinters. We have to have something to see by, though. I can hardly wait for spring, so we can dip wicks into melted fat and make candles. We're also running low on soap." She made a face. "I hate making soap. It's so hot stirring the lye and fat in the big kettles over the fire."

"Poor Rebekah. I'm tired, too."

Rebekah looked at the dark circles under her brother's eyes and knew he was speaking the truth. If only they didn't have to work so hard! Yet if everyone didn't do all that they could, their small group would never survive the winter.

Once the common house was built, families built their own homes. Father built a simple thatched hut that looked like an Indian lodge. Some of the settlers made dugout caves in the hillside. Single men lived with families to cut down on the need for houses, and plot sizes were determined by family sizes. New Plymouth was laid out in the shape of a cross to make it easier to defend. A sturdy stockade surrounded it.

Will and Rebekah soon learned how unforgiving their new home could be. Peter Browne and Will Goodman took their dogs when they went to collect reeds for thatching. They didn't return that afternoon, so Myles Standish sent out a search party. No trace of the two men could be found.

That night, everyone in New Plymouth wondered where the two men were. The next day, the men returned and told their story. Their dogs had scared up a deer. Eager to bring in fresh meat, the two men followed. They got lost in the woods. Noises like the howling of wolves terrified them, and they wandered all night in the forest. Will Goodman's shoes had to be cut off his frostbitten feet. He died a few days later.

When Rebekah learned what had happened, she tried to be brave. Yet her heart filled with fear every time Father or Will left New Plymouth. The only way she could bear their leaving was to remind herself how much God loved them. Rebekah tried to hide her worries, but she felt sure Will suspected her secret. He never said anything, but almost every time he returned, he brought her a pinecone, a curious shell, or a funny story. They made her feel a little better.

But it was hard to be brave when so many in their company were falling sick. . .and many were dying. Sometimes, Rebekah wondered if this new world was trying to punish them for invading its shores. When she looked at the cold, rocky ground, she felt as though it were an enemy. Thoughts like that made her shiver. Her only comfort was to whisper a prayer, knowing that God understood her fears.

Will never seemed to be afraid. He loved to go out with the men. All the strangeness, all the adventures, still excited him. But the day came that Captain Standish said Will had to stay behind when the men went out hunting. "It is growing too cold," Captain

Standish said, "and we do not know what dangers the weather will bring. Too many of you are sick, and we cannot risk losing more of our company. Only the strongest men can accompany me."

Rebekah was relieved. She did not like knowing both her brother and father were facing unknown dangers. She would sleep better if at least Will were home with her and Mother.

But Will was furious. "I am not a child," he said between his teeth. "I am as strong as any of those men."

Rebekah giggled. "No, you're not, Will. You're only a boy."

Will's face grew red, and his eyes were bright with anger. Rebekah's heart sank. She knew that look. It was the look Will always wore when he was filled with rebellion.

Right before he got in trouble.

CHAPTER 5

# Where Is Will?

"I'm going to follow the men," Will told Rebekah when they were alone. "I'll catch up with them, and then they'll have to let me go along with them. I'll show them I'm strong enough to be one of them."

"Don't, Will," Rebekah begged.

But her brother would not listen. "Promise me you won't tell Mother," he said. "Not until I'm gone."

Reluctantly, Rebekah nodded. With a curious feeling of foreboding, she watched Will march away. She already regretted her promise not to tell Mother where he was headed.

*He's been good,* she tried to tell herself. *This is the first time in ages he's done something he knows he shouldn't.* She sighed. *But I would feel better if I knew for sure that Will found the hunting party. Then even if he got in trouble, I'd know he was safe.*

Rebekah stared into space, deciding what to do. With Mother, Father, and Will busy around the new settlement, she was responsible for most of the home chores. She had more than enough work to get done that afternoon without worrying about Will. Suddenly, a smile crossed her face. She reached for her cloak that was hanging on a peg by the door and quickly stepped outside.

With hurried steps, she headed toward the sentry.

"Where be ye off to in such a hurry, little Miss Rebekah?" asked the guard.

"I was wondering if you saw my brother, Will," Rebekah said.

"Aye, he left a few minutes ago to catch up with the hunting party. With those long legs of his, he's probably with them right now. Did you need to get a message to him?"

"Oh, no," Rebekah said, a relieved smile crossing her face. "I just wasn't sure if he had left yet. Thank you for your help."

With a nod of her head, she turned back to the small hut Father had built for their family. Removing her cloak, she quickly began catching up on her work.

Rebekah and Will slept in a loft above the one main room where the family cooked and lived. Each night, the children climbed a ladder and slept on beds made from straw mattresses on the floor. Now Rebekah climbed up to the loft to shake the mattresses and smooth them out. She also tidied the sheets, blankets, and rugs they had brought from Holland. They never put the rugs on the earth floor. Instead, they kept them on the beds for added warmth.

Scrambling down the ladder again, Rebekah shook out Father and Mother's straw mattress. As soon as he had time, Father would make rope springs so they could have better beds, but Rebekah wished they could someday have featherbeds. The linen bags filled with goose feathers made soft mattresses in summer and warm coverlets in winter.

"I should be thankful for what we have," she told the warm room. Father had laid wooden boards across two wooden sawhorses for their table. At night, he put the boards against the wall to make room for the mattress. They had no chairs. Father always said, "When there is only one chair in a household, the man sits in it while his wife and children stand. I cannot be like them. Nay. Will and I shall make a bench, and we will all sit together. One day we shall have enough chairs for all."

A quick glance at the fireplace that provided light, warmth, and a place to cook showed it needed wood. The corners of Rebekah's mouth turned down. It always needed wood. Sometimes she felt the fireplace was a greedy beast that sulked when she didn't feed it enough.

The thought made her laugh, a pleasant sound in the small room. How hard they had worked to gather their wood! She and Mother picked up fallen branches. Will and Father split and sawed. The whole family had carried the split wood to their home and built a great mound just outside the rough wooden door.

After Rebekah had added wood to the fire, she straightened the everyday clothing hanging on wooden pegs on the wall. Their Sabbath clothing lay in a chest, along with extra bedclothes. Mother often warned them about being careful of their clothes. What they had brought with them would have to last for a long, long time.

Rebekah was so involved in her work that she didn't notice how late it was getting. A sharp gust of wind at the corner of the hut reminded her. She ran outside.

An army of storm clouds played tag across the sky. Rebekah shivered from the cold. "At least Will had sense enough not to go off hunting by himself," she whispered. "Surely the hunting party will start for home when they see the dark sky." But in the deep woods, would the men notice how dark it was getting?

Rebekah shook her head and went back inside. She stood by the fireplace to get warm and wondered if Father and Will would return before the storm hit. Memories of Will Goodman dying so soon after he got lost in the woods troubled Rebekah. But what could she do?

"I can pray," Rebekah told the crackling fire. She plopped down on her knees before the blazing fire.

"Dear God, please be with Will and Father and the other men. Will did wrong to run after the hunting party, but You know how he gets sometimes. You understand him even better than I do." Rebekah stayed on her knees for a long time, and when she got up, she felt better. Now if only Will and Father would come home soon!

"We may have venison stew for supper," Will had promised her before he left. Rebekah's mouth watered. Yet as each minute passed, a cold knot of fear grew in the pit of her stomach. Three times she wrapped up in her cloak, went outdoors, and peered into the worsening storm. But she saw no sign of Will or the hunting party.

Again and again, she wondered what to do. Another hour went by. Rebekah's smile had long since vanished. She continued to wait for her father and brother, a prayer on her lips, fear in her heart.

At last, Mother arrived, rosy-faced and chilled. "Ah, that is good, child!" She hung her wet cloak on the peg closest to the fireplace and held her hands out to warm them. Then she looked around the little room. "Where is Will?"

Rebekah hesitated. She would not lie, but the faint hope that Will would come soon made her say, "I don't know. He went out." *All true,* she told herself.

"Where can he be? I didn't see him." Mother looked worried.

"Do you think Father will come home soon?" Rebekah ventured to ask. "I hate it when he is gone. Especially after what happened to Will Goodman." Her voice sank to a whisper. "So many people have died since we left Holland. . . ."

"I know, dear." Her mother held out her arms, and Rebekah ran into their warm circle. "But we shall all meet again—and then we will be together forever."

Rebekah's arms tightened around her mother. If only she could hold her close and keep her safe from sickness and death. She longed to tell Mother that each time someone died, the fear of losing her or Father got worse.

*Be brave,* she told herself. *Don't make Mother more worried than she already is.*

Mother sat down on the bench Will and Father had made, pulling Rebekah down beside her. Shadows from the fire flickered on her tired face. "Life is hard here, harder than any of us imagined." Her eyes glistened, and Rebekah knew she was close to tears. "I do all I can, knowing the next time I go to the common house, one or more will be missing."

Rebekah had never felt closer to Mother. "Why do our men bury the dead at night?" she asked in a low voice.

Mother held Rebekah so close the girl could hear the steady beat of her mother's heart. "We dare not let the Indians know how many of our people have died," Mother said huskily. "Once they realize our numbers are small and that we are so weak, they may become bold enough to attack."

Rebekah and Mother silently huddled together on the bench until a sound came above the storm. "It's Will!" Rebekah felt weak with relief. She sprang up and flung wide the door. Father entered, empty-handed and with a set look on his face, but there was no sign of Will. A furious blast of wind sent a cloud of smoke from the fire through the hut.

Father slammed the door shut. "We found no game, but at least we got home before the worst of the storm." He smiled at his wife and daughter but only with his lips. His eyes held no hint of their usual sparkle. "I'll change into dry clothing." He shrugged out of his wet coat and looked around. "Where's Will?"

"Isn't he with you?" Rebekah asked, fear filling her heart.

"With me? Why would he be with me? You know Captain Standish didn't want Will in our hunting party today."

"But Will left, and the sentry said he was headed toward the hunting party," Rebekah explained.

"Left?" Father's eyebrows met in a frown. "When?"

"He went a long time ago."

"You mean Will is somewhere out in this storm?" Father's face turned whiter than snow. "Abigail, did you know about this?"

"Nay." Mother turned to Rebekah. "How could you let him go?"

"I tried to stop him!" Rebekah cried. She covered her face with her apron and burst into sobs. "I'm so tired of trying to be a brother's keeper! Will won't listen to me, and I get blamed for what he does!"

Shocked silence filled the hut. Rebekah cried harder. She knew the church elders taught that children should always speak to their elders, especially their parents, with respect. It truly wasn't fair for her to have to always bear the burden of Will's mischief—but now she feared she would be in more trouble than ever.

"Daughter, I spoke too hastily," Mother said.

"As did I." Father picked up Rebekah and hugged her. "We know your brother can be a trial, and you are to be praised for your love and patience. We also appreciate how much you have grown up. It is not your fault he is rebellious. You cannot change Will. All you can do is continue to set a good example. Will must decide for himself how he will behave. Forgive us, Rebekah."

The humbleness in Father's voice surprised Rebekah. "I. . .it's all right. I know you are worried. So am I." She buried her face in her father's shoulder. "I've waited and prayed and waited and prayed all afternoon."

Father set her down. "I'll get a few neighbors and see if I can find him." He put his wet coat back on and slipped outside.

The waiting went on, and Mother tried to help time pass quickly by having Rebekah eat some food. Less than an hour later, Father returned. "The storm has increased. We can do nothing until morning," he said heavily. "Rebekah, go on up to bed."

She reluctantly obeyed, feeling Father had things to say to Mother he didn't want her to hear. For once, her curiosity matched Will's. When she reached the loft, she crouched near the top of the ladder. Spying it might be, but she could never sleep without knowing what Father had to say. She had to listen hard, but she did manage to catch his words.

"I pray to God the rain doesn't wash out Will's tracks. I also pray Will is wise enough to remember what he's been taught, which is to find cover and stay there. If he wanders around, it will make our search a lot harder."

Rebekah crept to her bed and buried herself in her blankets under the rug. She lay sleepless, praying for her brother until the first rays of light crept into the sky.

Just as she slipped into sleep, a loud pounding on the door startled her awake. She sat up on her mattress and listened, her heart pounding. After a moment, she recognized Jake's loud, gruff voice. . .and then Will's. With a glad cry, Rebekah leapt to her feet and tumbled down the ladder.

"Look what I found," Jake was saying.

Mother and Father wrapped their arms around Will. They looked as though they might never let go.

"He's all right," Jake said. "Just a mite hungry and cold. I'll leave ye to yer breakfast now."

He ducked out of the low doorway. Mother and Father stepped back from Will, and the joy and gratitude on their faces faded into something sterner. "I'll let your mother get you something to eat," Father said. "And then, son, you and I shall have a talk."

That was one talk Rebekah had no desire to hear. She did not envy her brother one bit today.

In the days that followed, Will was unusually quiet and obedient. Rebekah knew he was trying hard to prove to Father and the other men that he had learned from his mistake. She also knew how embarrassed and ashamed he always felt once his rebellious feelings died down. Rebekah felt sorry for Will—but she was relieved to have him safe inside the stockade.

The days slipped past, one after another. More and more people fell ill, but Mother, Father, Will, and Rebekah stayed well. Rebekah began to feel more comfortable in their new home.

Then one cold night in the middle of January, the cry, "Fire! Fire!" echoed throughout New Plymouth. The Cunningham family jumped up from their sleeping mats and snatched more clothes. Even in the dim light of a pine torch, Rebekah could see the terror on her parents' faces.

CHAPTER 6

# Fire!

A dozen voices took up the cry. "Fire! The common house is on fire!"

Rebekah and Will raced toward the common house. Rebekah was more frightened than she had ever been in her life. She knew that the common house was filled with the sick, including William Bradford, who had collapsed while working, Governor Carver, and many others. "Please, God, help them!" Rebekah prayed under her breath.

Someone shouted words as she dashed past, but she could not make out their meaning. Cries of terror came from the gathering crowd.

Rebekah put on a burst of speed and caught up with a man running in front of her. Frantically, she snatched at the man's rough sleeve. "What is it?" she gasped.

"Gunpowder," the man panted. Sweat and fear covered his face. "Barrels of it. Some open. Stored in the common house!"

"No!" Rebekah's hand fell away. The new danger threatened not only those who lay ill, but all of New Plymouth. It was far more deadly than the flames that burned the common house's thatched roof and spread to its walls. If the fire ignited the gunpowder, it would explode. Rebekah and Will exchanged terrified glances.

"Here! You, boy! And you, lass." A man coming toward them from the common house thrust wooden buckets into their hands. "Fetch water, and be quick about it!"

Rebekah had felt as though she were frozen stiff with fear, but the man's order released her from her horror. She turned and raced after Will toward the water. Would the spark that set the common house on fire destroy everything they had worked so hard to build? Would it claim victims from the rows of sick inside the burning building?

"God, save them!" she heard Will yell, never slowing his pace. He filled his bucket and dashed back to the burning building. Rebekah did the same, being careful not to spill the precious water. When she got there and passed the bucket to eager, waiting hands, a great sob of relief tore from her throat.

The barrels of gunpowder sat away from the common house, safe from harm.

"Who got the powder out?" Will demanded of a breathless, soot-streaked man standing nearby.

The man slapped at stray sparks on his clothing. "God, I reckon." He coughed. A river of tears poured down his grimy face. "I never saw such a thing." He coughed again. "Even the weakest among us somehow managed to help! They tottered up from their sickbeds, grabbed those barrels as if they were feathers, and hauled them out." He mopped at his face and put out a spark greedily burning yet another hole in his already-tattered garment. "We lost a lot of clothing we can ill afford to spare, but praise be to God, no one was killed, at least so far." A shadow darkened the speaker's face. As if suddenly aware of his own weakness, he slumped to the ground and lay there panting.

Rebekah bit her lip, understanding only too well what the man meant. The fire and gunpowder had been cheated of their victims. But from the looks of those who had staggered from the common house and stood shaking with chills, their efforts could bring more death to the settlers. She had nursed enough patients on the voyage across the Atlantic to know how people looked when they were seriously ill.

All through the night, Rebekah and Will continued hauling buckets of water to the common house. Everyone was fighting the fire, but the people who were sick eventually collapsed in the snow. Rebekah noticed that Mother was busy helping them get up and leading them to small homes where at least they could stay dry. Father was pouring water on the roofs of nearby homes to keep them from catching fire.

Finally, the fire was put out. As the tired group looked at the steaming roof, they knew even more work lay ahead. The roof needed to be repaired and the common house cleaned before the sick could return to their shelter.

Will and Rebekah looked at each other. As she wiped her nose with the handkerchief a Dutch friend had given her so long ago, Rebekah said, "Will, don't you sometimes long to be back in Holland where at least we had time to play with friends?"

"Do I ever," Will said. "And we weren't so tired or hungry, either."

Rebekah let go of her gloom with a determined shake of her head. "Well," she said, "we certainly can't go back now. And if we're going to survive, we need to keep working. I'd best go help Mother cook up some porridge for everyone."

Sickness and death continued to haunt the colony. Sometimes, Rebekah hated the New World, with its cold and hunger. What good was it to be free to worship as they pleased when so many people in the colony lay sick and helpless? How many more would they lose in this harsh land?

Rebekah was especially sad when Captain Standish's wife, Rose, died. She had grown to admire the gruff captain as she saw him work among the sick with Elder Brewster. "After what I've seen him do," Will confided to Rebekah one day, "I'll never call him Captain Shrimp again."

The Cunningham family was alarmed one morning when Will woke up flushed with fever. Having seen so many people die, Rebekah was terrified her brother would be next. For days, she did everything she could to help Mother take care of Will. She helped with the cooking and washing, and she stayed by Will's side every chance she had, wiping his forehead with a cold wet rag. "God, please help my brother get better," she prayed over and over beneath her breath. She did not think she could bear to lose Will.

When Father, Mother, and Rebekah were so tired they could no longer keep their eyes open, Jake stayed at Will's side. The sailor's big hands proved surprisingly gentle as he wiped Will's hot face with the cloth dipped in cool water. Jake also managed to secretly bring Will small portions of food. The family never asked, but they suspected Jake saved it from his own rations.

Finally, Will was able to get up, although he was so weak he could barely walk across the room. His eyes looked enormous in his thin face, and his freckles stood out as if painted on his nose and cheeks.

The first afternoon he was able to sit up, Will peppered Rebekah with questions about what had been happening. "At least there hasn't been any trouble with the Indians," he said.

Rebekah sniffed. "Depends on what you call trouble. No one can leave any kind of tool lying around or it mysteriously disappears. One of our men went out for ducks and saw Indians coming this way. The men working in the forest left their tools and came back after their guns. When they got back, both the Indians and the tools had vanished." The corners of Rebekah's mouth turned down. "Now the Indians are getting bolder. One day they stole tools from some of our people who left them just long enough for the midday meal!"

"We need our tools or we can't cut wood and make crops," Will protested.

"Don't judge them too harshly," Mother told the children. "This was their land before we came."

"It's ours now. The king gave it to us," Will protested.

Mother sighed. "I wonder how we would have felt if someone came to our house in Holland and told us it no longer belonged to us. The king means nothing to the people who were born here across the ocean."

"Elder Brewster said it's for their own good," Father spoke quietly. "He says when we tell the Indians about God and Jesus they will be happier."

Rebekah was glad the Indians would have a chance to learn about Jesus. But she wondered if the Pilgrims were using that as an excuse to make them feel better about stealing what rightfully belonged to the Indians. The thoughts that filled her head were strange, uneasy ones, and she tried to push them away.

When the Pilgrims who were still living aboard the *Mayflower* fell ill, Captain Jones insisted most of them be taken ashore. "I can't risk having my men take your sickness," he barked. "It's bad enough we couldn't leave and go back to England as we planned. We don't intend to get your consumption and pneumonia."

Some of those who had been passengers on the *Mayflower* weren't much kinder.

"One man fixed meat a few times for a friend who said he would leave him everything," Rebekah whispered to Will. She knew Father and Mother didn't approve of telling tales, but she was so angry she just couldn't keep it to herself. "The man didn't die right away, and you know what?" Rebekah clenched her hands into fists. "The man who was supposed to be his friend called the sick man an ungrateful cheat! He said he wouldn't fix him anything more. The sick man died that very night."

Rebekah's mouth turned down at the corners. "Why are some of our own people acting this way? How can they, when we so badly need to help each other?"

"From fear." Will sadly shook his head. "The crew on the *Mayflower* is said to be even worse. They snarl at one another like dogs. Jake says they think they're all good fellows when they're well. But once sickness strikes, the healthy crew members absolutely refuse to help those who are ill. They are afraid to go in the cabins and risk infection."

"That's terrible!" Rebekah exclaimed.

"Well," Will said, "at least one good thing happened. Remember the boatswain who never missed a chance to curse us and tell us how worthless we are?"

"How could I forget him?" Rebekah rolled her eyes. "He was awful! He never said anything nice about any of us."

"He has now." Will took in a deep breath. "The few people from our group who were allowed to remain on board the *Mayflower* are pitching in to help the sick crew members. Our people refuse to just let the sailors die. Hard as it is to believe, the same boatswain who couldn't stand us told our people before he died, 'You, I now see, show your love like Christians one to another, but we let one another lie and die like dogs.' Can you imagine that?"

Rebekah blinked hard. "I'm glad, but I wish he hadn't died. I hope he knew Jesus."

"I do, too."

Rebekah felt sadness shoot through her like an arrow. "Not just him, but all the others. More than half the crew is dead. I don't know if any of them knew Jesus." A great lump came to her throat. "I hope so." Rebekah took in a deep breath, held it, then slowly let it out. "Will, do you know what I want almost more than anything in the whole world?"

"Enough food to feel really full?" her brother asked and patted his flat stomach.

"More than that. More than anything except for you and Father and Mother not to die." Rebekah swallowed hard at the thought. There had already been too many deaths. Some whole families were wiped out, although no girls and only a few boys had died.

"What do you want?" Will asked.

"To have Jake know Jesus. I think maybe he's starting to. The last time I talked to him, he said, 'Somethin' fer a man to think about, how ye Pilgrims are kind to everyone.'"

"What did you say?" Will leaned forward eagerly.

Rebekah shrugged. "I told him it was 'cause that's what Jesus would do if He were here and folks were sick, even folks who cursed Him."

Will's face glowed with pride. "Good for you! I don't think I'd have had the courage to say that, but, oh, I'm glad you did!"

"So am I." Rebekah grinned, the first real smile that had settled on her face since before Will got sick and worried them half to death.

"What did Jake say then?"

"Nothing." The disappointment she had felt when she talked with Jake came back. "He just cocked his head to one side and raised a shaggy eyebrow like he does when he's tired of talking, and then he mumbled that he had to get back to work."

"Maybe he will think about it," Will comforted. "I love telling people about Jesus. He's the best thing in the world. I wish everyone could understand about how much He loves us. If they did, people wouldn't be so crabby and scared and mean to each other. They would know that God would keep them safe, no matter what—so then they wouldn't feel as though they had to fight and snatch for the things they want."

Rebekah liked the way her brother put her own thoughts into words. She looked into Will's face. "Will, someday when you grow up, you might be a preacher, like Elder Brewster. You could, you know."

Will shook his head. "I can't imagine being a preacher. A carpenter, maybe, or a fisherman, or explorer. Besides, you know you don't have to be a preacher to tell people about Jesus."

"Perhaps not, but you'd make a good one." Rebekah's faith in her brother remained unshaken.

"Well, you were the one who told Jake, not me."

Rebekah giggled. "Silly, girls can't be preachers. And I just wish I had said more."

The next day she wished it even harder. Father brought terrible news. Jake was violently ill and lay burning with fever and freezing with chills aboard the *Mayflower*.

"I feel it's only fair to warn you he will probably die," Father added sadly, "although our people are doing everything they can for him."

"No!" Rebekah cried. Tears burned behind her eyes, but she shut her lips tight to keep back her sobs. She ran away to the new hideaway she had found, between two stacks of firewood. Curled up tight, with her chin resting on her knees and her cloak snugged around her elbows, she began to pray harder than she had prayed in her whole life.

# CHAPTER 7

# The Promise

For a full week, Jake hung onto life with every ounce of his strength. Those who cared for him shook their heads and said he should have died days before. They marveled that a man so sick still lived.

For a full week, Rebekah, Will, and their parents prayed for the seaman. Rough and without polish though he was, Jake had proven himself to be their friend again and again. Rebekah couldn't think of him without crying. When she remembered the food he had brought them so many times, she wept bitter tears. "If he had eaten it instead of giving it to us, he might not be sick."

"Hush, child." Mother's stern command shocked Rebekah. Their mother sometimes scolded Will, but she seldom raised her voice to her obedient, even-tempered daughter. "Jake chose to give you the food. Don't spoil his gift by feeling guilty. You know he would not want it so."

Rebekah sniffled, and Will sent her a weak smile. She knew her brother wanted to think of something to cheer her up, but he couldn't. How could anyone laugh or think of funny stories when Jake and so many others lay close to death?

"Father, may I go see him?" Rebekah pleaded.

"You mustn't!" Will cried. "You could become sick and die!" For once, Will was the fearful one.

Rebekah looked into Will's face and read there the terrible fear that haunted her as well: Who else would they lose to death's dark grip? She smiled at him, trying to chase away her own terror as much as his.

"Jake didn't let that stop him from coming when you were so sick," she reminded her brother.

Fresh horror sprang to Will's eyes. "Did Jake catch his illness from me?" He ducked his head and tears ran down his cheeks. "It's my fault. It's all my fault!"

"William Cunningham, stop that this minute!" Father thundered. "I will not have you carrying on in this manner. It is unbecoming to a child of God. We have put Jake in our heavenly Father's hands. It is not for us to place blame on ourselves or on others." His white, set face showed no trace of his usual kindly expression.

The children gasped. Father had never spoken to them in that tone. Will raised his tear-streaked face and stared at their father.

"It hurts me to have to speak to you this way, but I must." Father looked weary. "God has blessed you both with loving, tender hearts. He sees and is pleased that you care when others are sick or in trouble. However, you need to remember something. God does not expect you to carry the burden of all the sins and hurts of the world on your small shoulders." A gentler look crept into Father's face, and he stroked Rebekah's tousled braids. "That's why Jesus came. To carry all the hurt for us."

"Father is right," Mother said in a low tone. "Jesus took those

74

burdens to the cross. Our part is simply to trust and serve Him. Don't fret, Will. Nor you, Rebekah. It has taken your father and me many years to learn this." Mother smiled at Father. "Many times, we still feel like we need to take a hand in whatever life brings—to control it—instead of waiting for God to do His perfect work, as He has commanded."

"We must learn to be patient," Father added. "The Bible tells us this over and over. The prophet Isaiah said, 'But they that wait upon the LORD shall renew their strength; they shall mount up with wings as eagles; they shall run, and not be weary; and they shall walk, and not faint.'"

"It's hard," Will muttered.

Father lowered his voice and whispered, "That's where the promise comes in."

"The promise?" The children's ears perked up. For a moment, the excitement of a possible mystery took their thoughts away from death and dying.

"The Bible is filled with promises, such as in Psalm 23," Father told them.

"I know that one," Rebekah cried. "David said the Lord was his Shepherd and would take care of him—"

"Even in the valley of the shadow of death," Will quickly finished. "Is that the promise you meant?" He looked at Father.

"It's a good one but not the one I was thinking about." A faraway look came into Father's eyes. "When your mother and I fled from England to Holland, we didn't know what would happen. What if we were stopped by the authorities, beaten, or put in jail? I could bear it for myself, but I felt I could not stand it if your mother suffered at the hands of King James's men."

A look of gratitude came to his dark eyes when he looked at Mother. "I finally shared my struggles with your mother. She reminded me of the promise, a single verse. We claimed it as our own. It has kept us going all through the years. Each time life becomes unbearable, we repeat the Scripture."

"What is it?" Rebekah and Will asked at the same time.

"In Paul's first letter to the Corinthians," Father said quietly, "the great apostle promises we shall never be given more than we can bear, and that God will make a way for us to escape."

"Always?" Rebekah left her mother and crept into her father's welcoming arms.

"Always, Rebekah." His face shadowed. "This doesn't mean God answers every prayer the way we think He should or that He gives us all the things we ask for. It does mean He answers in the best way."

Rebekah felt her heart pound with fear. Her throat felt dry. Surely the best way wasn't for Jake to die without knowing Jesus! Her nails dug into his hands. "Father, I just have to see Jake," she choked out.

Father looked down into Rebekah's face. She felt as though she were being carefully weighed. "Are you strong enough to see your friend close to death, perhaps dying? To smell the poison that is taking lives? The stink of sickness that clings in spite of what all those who are able to help can do?"

"I am." Rebekah raised her head and looked her father straight in the eye. "Haven't I already carried slops for those in the common house and helped clean up when they have been sick?"

She saw Father look at Mother, and Rebekah's heart leapt when she saw her mother's nod.

"Aye, lass," Father said with a sigh. "So be it."

"May I come, too?" Will asked. His face was pale but determined. "Jake is my friend, too."

"Very well," Father said. He gently put Rebekah aside. "Come with me, but mind what you say." He paused. "Let the Spirit of God guard and guide your tongues."

Rebekah didn't fully understand what Father said, but she nodded, anyway. They boarded the *Mayflower* and walked toward where Jake lay. She tried not to gag. The stench of sickness and death on the ship made her want to head for the rail.

*Oh, God,* she prayed, *help me.* Taking small breaths in the hopes of keeping from heaving, she followed her father's sure steps down the deck she and Will had so often walked with Jake. Would they ever stride that deck together again?

"Jake, it's William Cunningham," Father said in a loud, clear voice when they reached the tossing, turning man. "I have young Will and his sister Rebekah with me."

The seaman's restless fingers picked at the blanket on which they lay. He opened his eyes, but Rebekah knew he didn't recognize them.

Could this gray-faced man really be Jake? It seemed to be impossible. Where had all his magnificent strength gone, his way of showing without a word he could control any situation?

But it was Jake, for the sick man turned eagerly toward the sound of Father's voice. A broken whisper came from between his parched lips. "Tell th' lass. . ."

"The lass? Do you mean Rebekah? Tell her what, Jake?" Father asked.

Jake stared straight ahead, and Rebekah knew the sailor could not see Father, though Father was leaning close to him. Jake lifted a trembling hand to his mouth. "Tell th' lass. . ." He made a mighty effort to raise himself but fell back to his pallet, breathing heavily, moving his body as if seeking a comfortable spot to rest. Sweat clouded his face.

"Is he dying?" Will whispered.

Rebekah's heart gave a mighty lurch.

"He's very close to it." Father put a hand on Jake's shoulder, then turned to the children. "Stay with him, and I'll fetch water."

One of the hardest things Rebekah ever had to do was sit with their friend while the seconds limped into minutes. She tried twice to speak, but she could not find her voice. At last, she managed to say, "Jake, we're here. It's Rebekah. And Will is here, too." She hesitated, and then she added, "So is Jesus. He's here with you, as well."

A slight change came over Jake's still figure. His breathing slowed, and his thrashing body grew quiet. Rebekah pressed her lips tight together. Was this the end?

"Keep talking to him, Rebekah," Father instructed as he placed a bucket on the floor and dipped a cloth into the cool water to bathe the seaman's face. "One of the workers just told me that ever since Jake fell ill, he has been repeating, 'Tell th' lass' over and over. Let him know you hear him."

Rebekah leaned closer, being careful not to get in Father's way. "I'm here, Jake. It's Rebekah. Remember all the things we did together? Remember the long voyage we had together and all the stories you told Will and me?"

Rebekah searched her mind for things that might help her reach their friend. Or had Jake already gone so far down into the deep, dark valley of death that only God could help him?

"That's it!" Rebekah whispered. "Listen to me, Jake." She placed her hands on the big man's shoulders and gently shook him. " 'Yea, though I walk through the valley of the shadow of death, I will fear no evil.' David said that. He knew God was with him and he didn't have to be afraid. You don't have to be scared, either."

Jake didn't open his eyes, but something in the way he turned his head toward Rebekah's direction gave her hope. Again and again she repeated Psalm 23. Each time she came to the part about the valley of the shadow of death, Jake quieted, until he lay like one dead.

At last, Rebekah grew so hoarse, she could barely whisper. Father laid a hand on her shoulder. "Come, lass. We have done all we can. Now he is in the Father's hands."

Despair filled Rebekah. Why hadn't God heard her prayer? If only they had come sooner! Perhaps Jake would have asked Jesus to forgive and save him. She slowly stood, feeling like someone had kicked her in the stomach. "He's dead."

"No, Rebekah. Just sleeping."

A stubborn hope sprang up inside her heart. "Will he live?"

Father shook his head. "I cannot say. I do know your words reached him and stilled his tossing and turning. Now all we can do is wait."

"Let me stay with him," Rebekah begged. "Mother needs you,

but Will and I could stay here. It may be the last thing we can do for him."

"You know the risks." Father's keen gaze studied Rebekah's face. "You, too, may fall ill."

Rebekah thought of those who had died, many who had fallen ill after caring for others. "Father, Jake would do it for us. You know he would."

Tears sprang to Father's eyes. "Aye. Stay then," he said in a low voice. "And don't forget that when we serve others, we serve our Master." He touched Rebekah's cheek and then Will's uncombed hair. Rebekah felt they had been given a blessing.

One of the strangest nights Rebekah would ever know began when Father left. Neither she nor Will spoke, and Jake was silent except for his heavy breathing. For the first time in many days, Rebekah had time to think. Midnight came, followed by the early morning hours.

"Our bodies are at our lowest point after the midnight hour, before the dawn," Father had warned before he wearily trudged away. "Then also comes the greatest danger of loved ones slipping from this world into the next."

Would that happen to Jake? What had the sailor wanted to tell Rebekah so badly that even in his fever he continued to call out for her? Perhaps he had only wanted to say good-bye.

But maybe. . . Another possibility occurred to her, and it was so wonderful that she felt fresh strength flow through her as she silently kept watch. What if during the time of sickness Jake had remembered what she had told him about Jesus? What if he had cried out to the Lord in his heart, asking to be forgiven and saved?

Wouldn't he want the one who had told him about Jesus to know?

Rebekah scrunched up her knees, rested her elbows on them, and laid her head on her folded arms. *Please, God, I have to know.* It took all her courage to add, *If it be Your will.* She prayed the words again. And again.

Only this time she couldn't finish the prayer. Her eyes closed. Her breathing slowed. Her head still resting on her arms, Rebekah slept.

A slight sound roused her. She opened her still-tired eyes and saw that Will was sleeping, too. And it was daylight.

Oh, no! Some guards they were, sleeping the hours away instead of keeping watch. If they were sentries posted outside the stockade, they would be severely punished.

Rebekah was afraid to look at the pallet on the floor beside her. With a deep breath, she gritted her teeth and looked down at Jake.

## CHAPTER 8
# You Can't Stop Me!

When Rebekah looked down at Jake, she expected to see a corpse. Instead, the sailor's small eyes twinkled. The shadow of a grin touched his lips. He licked them and croaked in a hoarse, unnatural voice, "Ye stayed with me?"

"Yes."

Their voices made Will raise a sleepy face, and his face exploded into a grin when he saw that Jake was still alive.

"I be thinkin' yer a brave lass." Jake laid one big paw on Rebekah's hand, then turned to Will. "And you, too, lad." His grin grew a bit wider before his mouth settled into its familiar stern expression. "Now git, afore ye catches the fever."

Rebekah knew better than to argue. "I'll come back later. You'll be better then." She and Will stood and turned to go.

Jake's low voice stopped her where she stood. "Mayhap I will be better by and by. But no need to fret if I ain't. That Friend of yers, Jesus. . . He fergive me." A look of wonder came into the sailor's face. "Me, who's sailed the seven seas and done black things! And all I had to do was ask."

Rebekah ran back to Jake's pallet and knelt next to him. She grabbed Jake's hand and squeezed it tight. "This is the best present anyone ever gave me!" she cried.

"Aye, mate." Jake smiled again. It softened his face until he looked like a different man. "I be chartin' a new course now." Some of his old fierceness came back. "But didn't I tell ye to run along? Now git, the two of ye!"

Rebekah and Will laughed at the scowl that no longer hid Jake's tender heart. Jake's eyes shone steady and true, showing how much he had already changed in the short time since he signed on with a new Master.

Proud to be the bearers of such good news, Rebekah and Will raced back to their parents.

"Now all he needs is rest and good food," Rebekah announced. A frown chased away her joy. "Where are we going to get food for him?"

Father smiled. "Captain Standish is sending a few men for game." He laughed at Will's obvious excitement. "A good meat broth will help Jake and the others."

"May I go?"

Rebekah knew Will was holding his breath. Ever since the time Will had tried to catch up with the men by himself, Captain Standish had ordered the boy to stay behind.

To Will's disgust, Captain Standish did not relent. Rebekah watched while Will bit his tongue to hold back hasty words that might mean he'd be left out of future hunting parties. She knew disappointment burned inside him when Father and two other men left with Captain Standish.

"I'm needed at the common house," Mother told Will and Rebekah. She put on her warm cloak and bonnet and told Will,

"Cheer up. I know it's hard being left behind, but next time you will probably get to go. Besides, after staying with Jake last night, you two need some rest." A moment later she was on her way, leaving the two children alone. Father had forbidden them to go back to the *Mayflower*.

"Jake sent word that you were to stay away," Father said. "When I get back, I'll go see that all is well. I want to tell him how glad we all are over his decision to accept Jesus."

Will sat and glared at Rebekah, who had done nothing to deserve his ill will. "It's our duty to help Jake," he said. "Besides, I'm tired of people thinking I'm only a child."

His expression changed. Rebekah watched his face uneasily, wondering what thoughts were taking shape in his mind. "Rebekah," he burst out, "I'm going to show them I'm not a child. All of them!" He hastily collected the warmest clothing he owned.

"Where are you going?" she gasped. "Father told you to stay off the *Mayflower*. And if you try to follow the hunting party again, you'll end up in trouble just like last time. If you do something silly, you won't be proving how grown-up you are. Just the opposite!"

But her brother's lips were set as though he had made up his mind.

"Will, you're going to get in trouble." She stamped her foot. "Well, I won't let you do it." Sparks flew from her eyes. "You're tired from being up all night, and you need to rest. Besides, you're still weak from being sick. I'm going right to the common house and tell Mother you're planning something you know you aren't supposed to do!"

Will whirled around to face her. "If you do, I'll never forgive you!" A black scowl appeared on his face, but then he smiled at her, his eyes full of pleading. "C'mon, Rebekah. You never tell on me, and I've been good for weeks now!"

"All the more reason you shouldn't disobey now," she told him. But some of the anger left her eyes.

Will added layers of clothing. He carefully took down a musket from the rough wall of their home and went through the slow process of loading it. Rebekah watched with anxious eyes. She heaved a sigh of relief when he finished. "Be careful," she warned.

"I will. I just want to be ready when I see a deer."

"Then you are going after the hunting party! Will Cunningham, you know what's going to happen. Father will be so upset with you, and what if you get lost? Remember what happened last time? I'm not going to let you go!"

"I'm going, and you can't stop me," he told her. "We don't know that Father and the hunting party will find game. I might. I'll head a different direction from the one they take. That way, if they don't find deer, I may. Jake needs broth, and later, he'll need the meat. So do we. You're so thin that when you stand sideways, you hardly cast a shadow!"

Rebekah couldn't keep back a small giggle.

Will went on. "Do you think Jake would stay home with the women and children if we needed food? Don't be a goose, Rebekah, and don't tell anyone."

Rebekah's giggle changed, and she sounded hurt. "You don't have to be so cross."

Will looked ashamed. "I'm sorry. But I need to get out of this place."

Rebekah searched his face. "Why, Will? Why are you so eager to run off all alone in the woods?"

Will looked down at the ground. "I'm not sure," he said slowly. "I just have to." He lifted his head and looked at his sister. Then he said in a rush of words, "Last night when we were sitting beside Jake, I felt so helpless. Jake could have died while we were sitting there with him—and there was absolutely nothing I could do to stop it from happening."

He flung his hands out wide, and Rebekah heard the frustration and fear in his voice. "I still feel helpless. As though I'm just sitting here waiting for death to sneak up and take someone I love. I can't just sit here doing nothing. It's driving me mad. I have to do something."

Rebekah studied her brother's face. She understood his feelings. But their long night at Jake's side had made her feel calmer somehow, more sure that God was in control of their lives. It seemed to have had just the opposite effect on Will. His eyes were wild, and she could see he was breathing fast.

This was apparently another one of those moments when Will seemed bound and determined to get in trouble. And this time, there would be no Jake to find him and bring him home. All too often, when Will was determined to have his own way, someone got hurt—usually Will himself. Rebekah had learned that if she could keep him from going off on his own when he was in one of his moods, she could usually curb his more foolish impulses.

"All right," she said suddenly. "But I'm going with you."

Will looked startled. "You can't."

"Oh, yes, I can. If you're going, then so am I."

Will hesitated. Then he shrugged. "Put some warm clothes on, then. And let's get going."

Rebekah and Will had a bad moment at the gate. The sentry challenged them. "Who goes there?" he shouted.

"We'll never get past him," Rebekah whispered, feeling relieved.

But then the sentry recognized them, and his face relaxed into a smile. "Where are you two children going?"

"I saw some rabbits on the hillside by the woods," Will said. "We thought we'd try to snare some for our supper. Some rabbit stew would taste awfully good."

"That it would," the sentry agreed. He raised an eyebrow at the musket Will carried. "And if you should see a deer, you're all ready, I see."

Will grinned and nodded. He shifted the weight of the musket and stood straight and tall.

"Well, don't go far, children," the sentry said. "You don't want to get lost."

Rebekah nodded, and she and Will hurried on their way. "Children!" Will hissed under his breath. "I'm sick to death of being called a child."

"You shouldn't have lied to him about the rabbits," Rebekah said, her voice laced with disapproval.

"I couldn't very well tell him we were hunting deer, could I?"

"He suspected it, anyway."

A faint trail led off into the woods, and the children followed it, bickering all the way. A half mile down the trail, though, Will found deer tracks and droppings. "These look no more than a few hours old." His voice was full of excitement. "Father and the others will be happy to see us when we come back with all the meat we can carry. We'll have to figure out a way to hide it so animals and Indians don't find it before someone comes for the rest of the meat."

Rebekah gave him a skeptical glance. Will was already planning what they would do with meat they hadn't even found yet.

But Rebekah, too, soon became caught up in the excitement of tracking the deer. The children stopped arguing and instead discussed how much the fresh meat would help Jake and the others. They were so intent on watching the ground that they failed to notice the storm swooping toward them. Huge clouds joined others, but not until they hid the pale winter sun did Rebekah notice and look up at the sky.

"There's going to be a storm!"

Will shifted his gaze between the tracks and the sky a half-dozen times. "Deer seek shelter from bad weather," he said slowly. "The one we're tracking might be just ahead. It might be hunched down in a bed beneath the trees to protect itself from the storm." Will plunged ahead, scanning both sides of the trail. No deer.

"Might as well turn back," he muttered in disgust. "It's getting so dark I couldn't see a deer unless it jumped up in front of me, and then I probably couldn't kill it. Of all the days for a storm, it would have to be this one. Let's go home."

The children turned around and strode back down the trail the way they had come. Their feet felt heavier now, almost as heavy as their spirits. Going home with meat was one thing. Neither of them looked forward to arriving empty-handed!

"How far did we come, anyway?" Will asked. He came to an abrupt stop and stared around at the gathering darkness. Rebekah also peered at the path, trying to recognize some landmark that would tell her how far from the stockade they were.

"That's funny," she said after a moment. "I don't remember stepping over a fallen tree in the trail before." She pointed to the downed log that blocked their path ahead.

Will suddenly looked uneasy. "Maybe we took the wrong fork back where the trail branched."

Rebekah nodded. "That must be it."

They turned, retraced their footsteps, and tried the other path. It led directly to a huge, uprooted tree and ended.

Thoroughly confused, Rebekah and Will went from one promising trail to another, only to become more hopelessly lost than ever. Worse, Will stumbled and fell. The musket flew out of his hands. They searched on their hands and knees in the darkness, but they could not find it.

Rebekah felt sweaty and cold by turns. The growing gloom soon hid any landmarks she might have recognized. All she could see in every direction was endless forest. The only way they could keep on the faint trail was to kick out with their legs as they walked. When they hit brush, they knew they had strayed from the path.

Rebekah's stomach growled loudly, reminding her that the last time she had eaten was too long ago. "Why didn't we bring some food?" she complained.

Will didn't answer. The rising wind bit through their clothing. Rebekah stamped her feet to get them warm.

"I guess I thought I could get a deer and be home before anyone knew we were gone," Will said at last. "If we only had a fire! No chance of that without the musket." He waved his arms to warm himself. "I wonder what Father would do if he were caught out like this?"

*Plop.* A large wet drop fell onto Rebekah's face. *Plop, plop, plop.* Others followed. From the look of the angry clouds, an icy downpour had overtaken the children.

Rebekah and Will dove beneath a tree with thick drooping limbs. Its overlapping branches grew so close together they protected the children from the rain, but Rebekah knew their problem wasn't solved. Huddled against the rough tree trunk, she tried to think. "We should pray," she said. "We should ask God to help us."

"Why would God want to help us?" Will's voice sounded sullen, but Rebekah knew he was feeling guilty. Will always felt guilty after one of his rebellious moods was over. "If I were God, I might want to help you. It's not your fault you're out here, not really. It's all my fault. I knew you were right. I knew it was wrong to go. And now that we're here, it doesn't seem like there's much point in asking God to get us out of a mess that I created all by myself."

"You might as well ask why God would want to send Jesus to die for us," Rebekah said. "I don't think God only helps people who never make mistakes. The Bible always sounds as though God is willing to help whenever someone asks Him. Beside, I don't think we have a choice." She looked around at the thick darkness, and her voice wavered. "No one knows where we are. We can't just stumble around in the dark all night. We'd better pray."

Will still didn't seem convinced that God would want to listen to him. After a moment, though, he sighed. "All right, then. I'll pray." He hesitated for a long moment. Then he bowed his head and said softly, "God, you helped Daniel in the lions' den, but he got thrown in. He didn't just walk in by himself." Will sighed again. "I should have listened to Rebekah. Forgive me, please, God. We sure can't help ourselves, and no one knows we're here but You."

"Please help us, God," Rebekah added. Then they both said together, "Amen."

Rebekah felt a little better now that they had asked God for help, but Will still seemed discouraged and angry with himself. "Why am I so foolish?" he asked, hitting his forehead with his palm. "No wonder Captain Standish and Father don't believe I'm a man."

Will and Rebekah huddled together beneath the tree's meager shelter. Exhausted from the long night at Jake's side, Rebekah finally fell into an uneasy sleep.

Later, she awoke stiff and half frozen. The slight warmth the branches offered could not keep back the increasing cold. She sat shivering, thinking about her brother, who still slept at her side.

Even the tossing storms of the wild Atlantic Ocean had not been able to drown Will's spirit of adventure. She had never seen him as shaken as he was now. She knew he bitterly regretted leaving the settlement without permission.

When she was shivering so hard that her teeth rattled, she poked Will awake. "We can't stay under here. I'm freezing."

Will jumped up and hit his head on a branch. "Ow!" Rubbing the sore spot, he turned back toward Rebekah. "If we walk to keep warm, we may be getting farther from the settlement. But what else can we do? We're in an awful mess."

"God," Rebekah whispered, "please help us."

Suddenly, she grinned at her brother.

"I know what to do."

CHAPTER 9

# Left. Right. Left. Right.

Left. Right. Left. Right. Rebekah and Will swung their arms and marched. Cold, hungry, and miserable, they wanted to run, but they dared not. Rebekah knew that Will's head was throbbing, a painful reminder to him to keep a steady pace. If they crashed into a low-hanging branch, they could be knocked senseless. They might freeze to death before they recovered.

Left. Right. It was getting harder now. How could a person keep going when her legs felt weaker than water? Could she starve to death in just one night? *Don't be a goose,* she ordered herself.

"Have to keep moving," Will mumbled. "Jake needs broth. Meat."

But Rebekah was so tired. Perhaps they should stop this endless marching and rest.

"No!" The sound of her own sharp cry alerted her to the dangerous state into which she had fallen. She scrubbed at her eyes.

"We can't stop," Will muttered.

Rebekah remembered every horrible story she had heard of those who rested in the freezing cold and never woke up again. The stories also kept her walking long after she felt she could not keep on.

Left. Right. Left. Right. Was she going mad? Rebekah giggled wildly. Dangerous or not, she had to stop.

"I won't sit down," she panted. She leaned against a tree trunk to catch her breath, and after a moment, Will joined her. If she closed her eyes for just a moment, would sleep keep them shut? Will might fall asleep, too. She couldn't chance it.

Left. Right. On and on and on. Was this how a beast of burden who walked in a circle turning a mill wheel felt? She and Will leaned against a tree again. *What are Father and Mother doing right now?* Rebekah wondered. *Will we ever see them again?*

Left. Right. Left. Right. Her feet felt like two anchors, weighing her down when she must keep moving.

"God, forgive me," she heard Will whisper. She reached for his hand with her numb fingers. Their hands clung together, warming each other.

After what felt like a lifetime, Rebekah knew she couldn't walk another step. She leaned against a tree, as she had been forced to do so many times throughout the long dark night. Her eyes closed. She felt the rough bark of the tree on her hands when she slid to the ground, but she was too tired to care. Beside her, Will slumped to the ground, as well. They leaned against each other, too exhausted to go on. Dimly, Rebekah realized they dared not sleep, or death would take them, as it had taken so many others. But she was too tired to fight the sleepiness that swept over her.

"Will? Rebekah?"

Rebekah stirred. "God, is that You?" she asked sleepily. Had she and Will died and gone to heaven?

"Will! Rebekah!" The cry came again. Strange. It sounded like Father. What was he doing in heaven? Or were they all back in Holland? Had everything been a dream: the *Mayflower,* Jake, the terrible night of walking? Rebekah struggled to understand.

When a third cry came, she felt Will struggle to his feet. He shouted, "Here! We're here."

His shout was so weak that Rebekah feared Father would never hear it.

"Son, where are you?"

Rebekah forced her eyes open, got to her feet, and called, "Father?" Her voice was barely more than a whisper. She swallowed, licked her lips, then screamed at the top of her lungs, "Father, we're here!"

A crashing of brush and heavy, thudding footsteps told her she had been heard. She sagged with relief against the tree. A heartbeat later, Father burst into view. He raced toward them and gathered them both in his arms.

The others of the rescue party followed close behind. "How'd you manage to keep from freezing?" one wanted to know.

"We prayed," Will said. He looked at his sister and grinned. "Then Rebekah remembered a story Jake told us once about a man who got trapped by a blizzard and didn't have any food or a way to make a fire. He knew he had to keep walking, or he'd freeze, but he couldn't see where he was going. Neither could we, so we did what he did." Will stopped for breath.

"What was that, son?" Father asked. His arms tightened, sending warmth through the children's shivering bodies.

"We walked around the same tree all night. It kept us warm,

and we didn't wander any farther from the settlement." Will yawned.

After a moment of stunned silence, relieved laughter came from the rescue party. One man slapped his leg, chuckled, and said, "Well, I never! Cunningham, those are mighty clever young ones you have."

Rebekah's heart thumped with pride. "It wasn't me," she said. "God made me think of the story." She looked at the men's faces. Some looked convinced. Others did not.

"I still say it's mighty clever," the man said again.

Father quietly added, "If Will had done as he was told, he and his sister wouldn't have been in trouble at all."

"That's right, lad. Listen to your father from now on."

"I will." Will looked at the ground. "I guess this is my last hunting expedition for a long time."

"It could have been your last forever," Father reminded him. "Now, let's get you home where you belong. There you will stay until you learn to act like a man instead of a child who goes running off when he doesn't get his own way."

Rebekah knew Will deserved everything Father said, but she also knew how much he must hurt to be corrected in front of the men. Captain Standish's judgment would be far harsher than Father's. She hoped her brother would take it like a man. Neither of them would ever forget what could have happened to them without the love of God to protect and help them.

Afterward, Rebekah didn't remember much of the trip home. At one point someone spotted Will's musket and rescued it from the snow, but Will barely noticed. One weary step after another, the children managed to keep going until just outside the settlement. Left. Right.

When the stockade gate swung open, Rebekah's knees buckled. Father slung her over his shoulder and carried her. If she hadn't been so tired, she might have been embarrassed to be hauled home like a sack of grain. As it was, she was just glad not to have to walk anymore.

"Abigail," Father called as he opened the door to their little home, "the children are safe and unharmed. They need food and rest. Bring warm, dry clothes and broth. We'll talk later."

The last thing Rebekah remembered clearly was the sensation that the ice inside her was melting as she drank her mother's broth. Then she vaguely remembered her father's strong arms helping her up the ladder to bed. After that, she remembered nothing at all.

Rebekah awakened to pitch darkness. Had she only dreamed that Father and the others had come for them? Was she still in the woods? She cautiously shifted her body. The straw in her mattress crackled, telling her she was safely home. She turned over and fell asleep again.

The next time Rebekah woke, daylight had come. She glanced sideways at her brother's sleeping shape and then slid farther under her covers. The day was likely to bring hard moments for her brother. Captain Standish would certainly kill any hope of future hunting expeditions. Others in the colony might laugh at the boy who wanted to be a man but sneaked off like a sulky child.

"Lord, help him to bear whatever scolding we get," Rebekah

whispered. "Help me to be a good big sister."

"Will. Rebekah. Dress and come down quickly," Father's ragged voice called.

Something in Father's voice frightened Rebekah. She had an uneasy feeling that he was not calling them down to scold them for their adventure. Her muscles stiff and aching from their night in the forest, Rebekah managed to get into her clothes and down the ladder. She left Will still fumbling his way into his wool pants.

Rebekah ran to the fireplace and warmed her cold hands at the blaze. Its cheerful glow felt good, but even the fire could not melt the icy fear in her heart. When she looked at Mother's face, she saw that her mother's lips trembled.

Father waited until Will stood beside Rebekah before the fire. Sadness lined Father's face as he said, "Children, you must be brave."

"What is it?" Rebekah clenched her hands until she felt the nails bite deep into her palms.

"Word just came from the *Mayflower*. Our friend Jake died in the night."

Rebekah buried her face in her apron.

"No," Will said hoarsely. "No, no, no! Jake was getting better. You know he was. That's why I went for the deer. He couldn't have died. It must be another crew member." He started for the door.

Father caught him halfway there. "Running isn't going to help."

"Let me go!" Will twisted and turned. "It isn't true." He stared up into Father's face. "Did he know we were lost?" When Father looked blank, Will shouted, "That's it, isn't it? He knew and tried to come for us." He buried his face in his hand. "What have I done?"

"Stop this, Will." Father shook his son, not hard, but enough to get his attention. Father's eyes blazed. "You had nothing to do with Jake's death. Plague took him, as it has taken many others and will take more. Jake never knew you were missing." Father pulled Will to him in a big hug.

Rebekah wiped away her hot tears. Her mother's arm went around her and held her tight.

Father looked over Will's head at his daughter. "We grieve, yet we praise Almighty God that our friend met Jesus, our Savior, before it was too late. The bearer of the news said Jake died with a smile on his face and the words 'Tell th' lass' on his lips."

A great sob tore free from Will's throat. He jerked from Father's arms and bolted up the ladder. Rebekah heard the crackle of the straw as he threw himself on his bed.

After a moment, she followed him up the ladder into the dim loft. "I loved him, too," she whispered. "I thought he was going to get better. I thought God had healed him." Her voice broke. "Sometimes I don't understand God."

The two children were silent for a long moment. Finally, Rebekah sighed. "Father and Mother are so sure of their faith. Maybe someday we'll be as strong as they are."

Will sat up and looked at his sister. With a sob, he put his arms around her, and the two children clung together. Perhaps later they would have more to say to each other, and they would find a way to comfort each other's hearts. Right now, Rebekah was just glad they still had Father, Mother, and each other.

Just thinking that made Rebekah's mouth go dry with fear. All she could do was cling to the promise that God would never send more than they could stand but would always make a way of escape.

# CHAPTER 10

# What Is a Samoset?

A few weeks later, as Rebekah trotted alongside her little brother, she suddenly noticed that he was no longer so little. In fact, he was taller than she was. The realization made her giggle. She clapped her hand to her mouth and quickly looked around to make sure no one had heard her laughing on the Sabbath—but it felt good to laugh again after so many days of sadness.

They had just come from Sunday meeting, and Father and Mother were walking ahead of them. Rebekah looked sideways at Will. "My, that was a good sermon." She laughed again. "Elder Brewster's Scripture was about you."

Will stopped dead still. "Whatever are you talking about?"

"The Scripture," Rebekah patiently repeated. Her green eyes twinkled with fun. "Weren't you listening?"

"Not very well," Will confessed. He was staring at the *Mayflower*, and Rebekah knew he still ached inside each time he saw the ship where Jake had died.

"You should have been," Rebekah told him. "It just fits the way you are now."

Curiosity seemed to finally pull Will's attention from his sad thoughts. "Really? What Scripture was it? What did it say?"

"First Corinthians, chapter 13, verse 11." She smothered another giggle, and her face lit up with fun. "You know. The one where Paul says when he was a child, he spoke and understood as a child, but when he became a man—"

"He put away childish things," Will soberly finished for her. "Do you really think I'm like that?"

"Oh, yes." Her cap-covered braids bobbed up and down. "You're ever so much more grown-up. You're kinder to me, and I heard Father tell Mother he was proud of the way you took your punishment like a man."

She slid her hand into the crook his elbow made. "Father said even when Captain Standish roared like the wind, you held your tongue and looked straight at him. Mother's awfully proud. So am I." She hesitated, then whispered, "God must be proud, too."

"I hope so." Will scuffed his boot on the hard ground. "I'm trying."

"I know," she said sympathetically.

They walked in silence. For the first time in many days, Rebekah was filled with contentment. The cold winter could not last forever. On days like this, when the sun shone, she felt spring must soon be on its way.

Then suddenly, as she looked up ahead at her parents, she gave a little cry and sprang forward. Mother had fallen to the ground. When Rebekah reached her, she saw her mother was as white and still as a dead person. Rebekah's heart pounded with terror.

Father snatched up Mother in his arms and raced toward their hut. "Will, fetch Dr. Fuller," he ordered. "Tell him she collapsed for no apparent reason. Rebekah, run ahead and spread the mattress."

Will looked up at his father's ashen face. "Shouldn't you take her to the common house?"

"Nay. Home is closer. Go, lad, and don't stop to argue!"

Will turned and ran as if pursued by a thousand howling wolves. Rebekah hurried ahead to get her mother's bed ready. Dread kept time with her flying steps. Would Mother be taken next? "Please, God, spare her. Not just for our sake, but for the sake of others who need her so much." Rebekah's prayer came out in little gasps as she ran.

Minutes felt like a lifetime before Dr. Fuller reached the Cunninghams. Will had delivered his message and flown home without waiting for the physician. The kindly, overworked doctor bustled in. "Eh, what's all this? Is my best helper giving out on me?" He quickly examined Mother. She didn't even move.

Rebekah held her breath, waiting. Will was standing more still than a mouse that suspects a cat may be nearby. Father sat on the homemade bench, head bowed. Rebekah knew he was praying. Finally, Dr. Fuller finished his examination, rose from beside the straw mattress, and smiled. His expression filled Rebekah's heart with hope.

"Now, now, nothing to worry about." The doctor's face crinkled into laugh wrinkles. "She's just plain worn out. Our bodies keep going and going when we push them. How well I know!" He yawned mightily. "But eventually they give out. If we don't give them the rest they need, then they take it for themselves. That's why your mother collapsed."

The doctor turned to Father. "Your wife has no fever," Dr. Fuller said. "She has no signs that foretell illness. I'd say what she needs is a good night's sleep. Don't wake her, even for food. Her body needs rest." He yawned again. "In fact, that's what I'm going to do: rest. All my other patients have either died or are mending."

He shook hands with Father and Will, then tugged on a braid that showed beneath Rebekah's cap. "It's your turn to play nurse, Mistress Cunningham. See that you do a good job."

"I will," Rebekah promised.

Dr. Fuller went out, leaving the others to follow his orders.

The rest of the day, Mother lay without moving. Once when Father and Will weren't looking, Rebekah bent low to make sure she still breathed. She felt her mother's slow, steady breath against her cheek and sighed in relief. But when evening came and the Sabbath ended, Mother still slept.

"Should we ask Dr. Fuller to come again?" Rebekah anxiously asked Father.

"I hate to disturb him when he is so tired." Father knelt and touched Mother's forehead. "Her skin is cool and dry. She has no sign of fever. We will let her rest."

"Shall I stay up with her?" Rebekah volunteered.

"Should Dr. Fuller be wrong, although I have no reason to believe this is the case, you will be needed more on the morrow. Go to bed, child. I will watch."

All through the long night hours, Mother slept. Neither did she waken when morning came. Thoroughly alarmed, Rebekah coaxed Father into letting Will fetch the doctor again.

After Dr. Fuller examined Mother, he assured them again that she would be fine. "I expect her to wake before night," he told them. "If she should not, then is time enough to be concerned."

Shortly after he left, a sound from the mattress brought all three watchers to Mother's side. She opened her eyes, yawned, stretched, and looked around. "Mercy, what am I doing here at this time of day?" She looked confused, and then her face cleared. "My goodness, I fell asleep walking home, didn't I? I never heard of such a thing." She glanced around the hut. "I hope you ate without me." A frown wrinkled her forehead. "I smell something cooking. Surely you are not breaking the Sabbath by cooking food?"

"It's no longer the Sabbath!" Will shouted. A broad grin spread over his face. Matching smiles covered Rebekah's and Father's faces.

Father reached down a hand to help Mother get up. "It's Monday and time for dinner. You have slept ever since the meeting yesterday."

"Dr. Fuller said we weren't to disturb you unless you didn't wake before dark," Rebekah explained. She clasped her arms around her mother's waist. "I'm glad you're awake. It frightened me when you stayed asleep for so long."

Mother began to laugh. She laughed so hard the others joined in. "A grown woman, sleeping all the hours on the clock twice around! I do feel rested, though." She looked ashamed. "I hope no one needed me."

Father shook his head. "Not even Dr. Fuller. He says the worst is over and his patients are mending." The laughter in his eyes died. "Almost every family but ours lost at least one person."

A lump came to Rebekah's throat. "We lost Jake."

"Indeed we did, although we haven't actually lost him. We've just parted for a time." Father looked with joy at Mother. "Let us give thanks for your mother's recovery."

Signs of spring began to appear at Plymouth Colony like a long-awaited guest. They brought a wave of relief and hope. Surely things would be better now that the harsh winter was slowly retreating. The little band of surviving settlers prayed for good weather, asking the Lord to bless the land.

Yet many of those who survived were still weak. How could the few strong ones left in the settlement take on extra duties and provide for everyone? There was also the ever-present fear of Indian attack.

One day in mid-March, Will burst into the Cunningham home as if chased by a whole tribe of unfriendly Indians. Eyes wide with excitement, he cried, "Mother, Father, Rebekah, come quick. Just come see!"

Will frightened Rebekah so badly, she dropped her knitting. "Father and Mother are at the common house. Will Cunningham, is this another of your tricks? Just when you've been good for such a long time?"

"It's not a trick," he indignantly told her. "Are you coming, or aren't you? If you don't, you'll miss all the excitement." He placed his hands on his hips and glared at Rebekah. "C'mon, will you? Father and Mother will have heard the news. They'll be there before I get back with you." He hurried out the door and started up the lane.

Rebekah quickly took care of her knitting and ran after him toward a cluster of people on the road a little way ahead. The children headed straight for Father and Mother, who stood at one side of a small, gaping crowd.

"What is it?" Rebekah stood on tiptoe, trying to see.

"Him!" Will stepped out of her way and pointed to a tall, black-haired Indian halfway across the clearing between the settlement and the woods. The Indian carried bow and arrows and steadily walked toward the nearest group of men.

"Is he going to scalp us?" Rebekah squeaked.

The men reached for their muskets. The Indian never faltered. He was close enough now so the settlers could get a good look. Rebekah knew her eyes grew large as cartwheels. She felt herself blush and quickly looked away. So did the other girls and women. The unexpected visitor wore no clothes. Just a little war paint and a leather apron that hung down from his belly! Who was this bold Indian who marched into the colony instead of skulking in the woods?

He reached the men. "Welcome." The word sounded strange on the lips of the nearly naked man. "Samoset."

"Did you hear that?" Will whispered. "He speaks English!"

"What is a samoset?" Rebekah whispered back.

Will choked back a laugh. "Not *a* samoset. Samoset. That must be his name."

Rebekah risked another look, making sure she kept her gaze on the stranger's face. "Why did he come here, and what does he want?" she wondered.

"That's what we need to find out," Father said.

CHAPTER 11
# Hair-Raising Stories

The first thing Samoset did was ask for something to drink. The settlers quickly took on their roles of hosts, and once his thirst was satisfied, Samoset told his story.

He explained he wasn't from the area but came from Monhegan, an island off the coast farther north. He said in broken English that he had learned the white man's language from English fishermen there. To prove he told the truth, Samoset mentioned the names of many captains who fished there.

He'd come to Cape Cod the year before and remained eight months. He added he could reach his home with one day of good sea breeze, but it took five days to go by land.

Fascinated by the visitor, the Pilgrims brought out a long, red, horseman's coat. Samoset wrapped himself in it, grunted, and talked on. The settlers brought food: butter, cheese, a slice of duck, and pudding. He ate and ate and talked and talked. It appeared Samoset had no intention of leaving.

"What will we do with him?" Will whispered. Even in the red coat that covered his nakedness, Samoset was a frightening figure.

Others wondered the same thing. The Pilgrims decided to take

Samoset to the *Mayflower*, but they ran into trouble. A headwind and low water made it impossible to get the shallop across the flats to the ship. Stephen Hopkins at last agreed to keep Samoset overnight and guard him without seeming to do so.

"I wish we could have quartered Samoset," Will grumbled to Rebekah later. "Think of all the stories he could tell us! Now we'll have to hear them from the Hopkins family."

Rebekah's mouth turned down. "I'm glad we don't have to keep him. He might tell us stories of how the Indians scalp people."

Will grinned mischievously. "I guess you could say they would be hair-raising tales, couldn't you?"

Rebekah's green eyes flashed. Her freckled nose went into the air. "Humph! You won't think it's so funny if we wake up murdered in our beds."

"If we're murdered in our beds, we won't wake up," Will answered. When his sister's face turned red, he quickly added, "Don't be mad, Rebekah. I was just joking. Besides, if Samoset were unfriendly, he would never have come right into the settlement. He'd have brought a band of warriors."

Rebekah finally agreed, and Will said no more about hair-raising tales.

The next day Samoset left, the proud possessor of a ring, knife, and bracelet. He promised to come back with some of the Wampanoag Indians, who would bring beaver furs for trade.

The next time Samoset came, he arrived on a Sunday with five tall Indians wearing deerskin clothes.

"It's too bad they came today," Rebekah said. "We can't trade on Sunday."

"It is awkward," Father admitted. "Our leaders will just have to explain we don't trade on Sunday."

Will ran up to his family, bursting with news. "Wait till you hear what's happened!" he shouted. "You'd never guess, not in a million years!" He didn't give them even a minute to answer but said, "The tools. The Indians brought back the tools they stole from us."

Mother clapped her hands, and Rebekah cried, "Then they must be honest." She stopped and wrinkled up her face. "If they are honest, why did they take our tools in the first place?" Then she remembered something, and the same funny feeling she had known weeks earlier came back. She lowered her voice so no one else could hear. "What's the difference between our taking their corn and them stealing our tools?"

"Your mother and I have never felt comfortable about that," Father quietly said. "Even though our leaders have vowed to repay the Indians when the crops are harvested."

Samoset soon brought someone else to the settlement, an Indian named Tisquantum, or Squanto. Squanto's life had been hard. Rebekah listened in wonder as Squanto told his story. Years ago, a captain named Weymouth had explored the northern New England coast. He took Squanto back to England with him. There the Indian learned to speak the white man's language.

Nine years later, Squanto sailed back across the Atlantic as interpreter to Captain John Smith. A man named Hunt commanded one of the ships. Hunt persuaded twenty Indians, including Squanto, to board his ship.

Rebekah burned with anger when she learned what happened next. Hunt kidnapped the Indians, took them to Spain, and sold them for twenty pounds each. Pride filled Squanto's face, and he drew himself up with great dignity. "No Patuxet shall be slave to a white man. I escaped to England, lived with a merchant, then sailed to Newfoundland as a guide and interpreter." Two years ago, Squanto had returned to his home of Patuxet.

A sad look came into the Indian's dark eyes. He placed one hand over his heart. "Plague had killed all but a few of my tribe. Those who yet lived had joined the Wampanoag and their mighty warrior chief, Massasoit. I found them and also stayed with the Wampanoag."

Governor Carver asked, "Squanto, will you not stay and help us? You have lost most of your people. So have we. Sickness and starvation have taken more than half our number since we came a few months ago. Our food is almost gone. We want no trouble with your people."

Squanto turned his glittering gaze on the governor and crossed his arms over his chest. His voice rolled out like a judgment. "Chief Massasoit and the Wampanoag are very angry. The white men stole their corn."

"We did that, and it was wrong," Governor Carver admitted. "Our people were starving and needed food. We will replace the corn when we harvest our fields."

Squanto grunted. Rebekah had the feeling he admired Governor Carver for being so honest. She remembered her father telling her that Indians respected courage, and it surely took courage to confess to stealing the corn and to admit it wasn't right.

"I will stay. First, I will talk with Chief Massasoit. If he will come, I will bring him to you so our tribes might have peace." He turned and marched away.

Samoset and Squanto had been bold but friendly. Chief Massasoit and his twenty scantily clad warriors, however, strode into New Plymouth as if it belonged to them! Massasoit appeared to be a few years older than Squanto and stood as tall and straight as one of the arrows he carried. Chief Massasoit kept his kingly air all through the hearty meal and gifts brought to him by the Pilgrims. At last, the time came to talk about peace. Squanto interpreted.

After a brief battle with her conscience, Rebekah followed Will. The children tucked themselves into a good place where they could see and hear without being noticed. Missing the meeting between Chief Massasoit and the governor was unthinkable, but they knew better than to ask Myles Standish for permission to be present. Every time the captain looked at Will, the captain's glare shouted he hadn't forgotten a certain Will Cunningham's disobedience.

Massasoit, king of the Indians, was indeed a fearsome sight. He sat on cushions. Sweat and grease covered his head and red-painted face. White bone beads, a knife on a string, and a tobacco pouch hung from his neck. His warriors also had painted faces: red, white, black, yellow. Rebekah was relieved that they had come on friendly terms. She would hate to have the men meet up with them in the woods otherwise!

Governor Carver and Massasoit talked for a long time. At last, they made a treaty. Rebekah listened carefully to Squanto's explanation of the agreement. Neither Massasoit nor any of his people would hurt the Pilgrims. If any of his people did hurt them, Chief Massasoit would send the guilty person to the Pilgrims for punishment. If any of the Pilgrims harmed an Indian, they would turn the person over to Chief Massasoit. If any tools were taken, the chief would see they were restored. If anyone made war unjustly against either the Pilgrims or the Indians, the other group would provide protection.

Chief Massasoit also promised to send word of the treaty to his neighboring tribes, so they would follow it, as well. The Indians would leave behind their bows and arrows when they visited the Pilgrims. The settlers would do the same with their muskets when they were in the Indians' presence. Through this treaty, King James would recognize and honor Massasoit as his ally and friend.

After the meeting, Governor Carver, with great ceremony, escorted Massasoit to the brook and bid him a courteous good-bye. Then they put their arms around each other and hugged. Rebekah watched with wide eyes, hardly believing what she was seeing.

Will threw his cap into the spring air. "At last, things are better, Rebekah. The best thing is that Squanto and Samoset have agreed to help us plant corn and will spend the summer nearby."

Soon the Pilgrims found it hard to remember when Squanto had not been among them. He knew so much! He showed them how to raise the finest corn, beans, and pumpkins by planting dead herring with the seeds. He taught them the best places to fish and how to catch eels. The children were delighted by their improved diet. Mealtimes were much more interesting now.

Everyone who could worked hard. Rebekah, Will, and Mother, along with the other women and children, spent long hours in the fields. Father and the rest of the men cleared and tilled land. What little time they had at home was gobbled up by other tasks. Furniture making, candle making, spinning, weaving, sewing, shoe-making, and a hundred other duties cried out to be done.

Father and Will stole what time they could to fish. Although they both enjoyed fishing, they needed to catch lots of fish to help make a living. Dried fish shipped to markets in Europe could be traded for cloth and other needed supplies.

Other men caught whales so they could send whale oil to Europe. John Alden continued his cooper business. A blacksmith also served as a dentist.

In early April, a silent group of settlers stood on shore watching the *Mayflower* set sail for England. Not one Pilgrim had accepted Captain Jones's offer to take anyone who wanted to sail back with him. Rebekah winked back a tear. Would she ever see Holland again? Or the Dutch friends she and Will had skated and played with? She sighed. "Father, will we ever go ho—back?"

Father watched a strong breeze fill the sails of the *Mayflower* and move her out of the harbor toward the wide Atlantic. "Nay, child. This is our home now." He placed one arm around her shoulders, his other around Mother, and smiled at Will. "God is good. He has brought us safely through the winter. We are at peace with Chief Massasoit and his tribes. We have much to be thank-ful for."

"We mustn't forget Squanto," Mother said. "Surely God sent

him to us, that we might learn to live in this new land."

Will said nothing. Rebekah knew he wouldn't go back to Holland if he could. Seeing the *Mayflower* move toward the horizon where it would dip out of sight brought back memories. The crossing. The poor food and lack of good water. The storms that threatened to tear the ship apart at the seams. Most of all, their good friend Jake.

Rebekah hadn't been back on the *Mayflower* since their friend died. Would Captain Jones and the small crew who must battle their way across the heaving seas miss the rough seaman? Rebekah turned away to hide her tears. Better to do as Father said and be glad that life was not as hard as it had been during the winter.

But the peace of New Plymouth exploded a few days later. Will and Rebekah were working together in the fields near Governor Carver. Suddenly, he clutched his head and groaned. He staggered toward his home.

Will and Rebekah continued working, but they watched anxiously as Dr. Fuller hurried to Governor Carver's home. It seemed like the doctor stayed with the governor for an eternity. When he finally left the governor's home, Dr. Fuller's face was grim.

Rebekah and Will looked at each other. Was Governor Carver only the first? Were any in the colony strong enough to survive a second round of sickness?

## CHAPTER 12
# Danger for Squanto!

The Cunningham family and all the other Pilgrims prayed for Governor Carver to get well, but just a few days after he fell ill, he died. The whole colony mourned.

"Pray for me, Rebekah," Will confided as he solemnly prepared his musket. All the men and boys who had muskets were going to fire off volleys of shot in honor of Governor Carver. "I don't want to shoot at the wrong time or do something stupid," he admitted to his older sister.

Rebekah gave his arm an encouraging squeeze. "I know you'll do fine," she said, "but I'll pray for you, anyway."

Somberly, the Cunningham family joined their neighbors outside in the warm spring air. When the time came for the muskets to be fired, Will fell into line. Rebekah saw he was paying careful attention to the orders that were given. His hands must have been sweaty from nervousness, for he quickly wiped them on his pants. Rebekah knew he didn't want his finger to slip off the trigger.

*Boom! Boom!* The sounds of the shots echoed across the settlement.

Rebekah sighed in relief when it was over. Her brother threw her a grateful look. He'd managed to stay out of trouble ever since that terrible night in the woods, and Rebekah was glad nothing he'd done during this important event had drawn attention to her brother.

Shortly after Governor Carver was buried, the men of New Plymouth voted for a new governor. Rebekah and Will knew better than to try to sneak into that meeting, but they were glad to learn from Father that William Bradford would be their next governor.

Now that spring had arrived, Sunday meetings were more pleasant. No longer did they have to bundle up in all the clothing they possessed to keep from freezing in the unheated meetinghouse.

"I wish the tithingman would go away," Will complained to Rebekah one Sunday. He rubbed his head. The tithingman's rod had feathers on one end to tickle those who nodded, a knob on the other to whack those who fell asleep. He walked up and down checking on people and had given Will a smart *whack!* Rebekah took care to sit up straight on the hard wooden pew and concentrate on the elder in the high pulpit. Yet even she found it hard to pay attention. Sometimes the sermons lasted five hours.

"At least I didn't have my neck and heels tied together and get left without food for a whole day," Will soberly said. "That's what the governor ordered when Will Billington refused to take his turn standing guard at night. He would have carried it out, too. It's a good thing Mr. Billington said he was sorry and would keep watch for strange Indians and fire, like the rest of the men."

"Let's talk about happier things," Rebekah pleaded. She didn't like to think of people breaking the rules and being punished. "Did you know Edward Winslow and Susanna White are getting married?"

"Yes. I heard they have both been lonely since Mistress Winslow and William White died." Will squinted his eyes against the bright sun. "Rebekah, if Mother or Father died, do you think the other one would get married again?"

Rebekah thought for a moment. "Perhaps. They'd want us to still have a mother and father."

Will shrugged. "I'm not sure I like the idea. Can you imagine anyone ever taking Mother and Father's place?"

"I don't want to think about it," Rebekah said. "I'm so tired of death and dying. I hope all of us who are left live to be as old as the mountains!"

"Maybe we will." He flexed his right arm, and Rebekah knew he was proud of the muscle that popped up. "Now that Squanto has taught us how to fish and plant, we shan't go hungry." He laughed. "Do you want to hear something funny?"

"Of course."

"I asked Squanto how he knew the very best time to plant maize and the seed we brought with us," Will explained.

"What did he say?" Rebekah promptly forgot to be sad. Over time, she had learned not to be afraid of Squanto.

"He told me the time of planting must always be 'when the leaves of the white oak are as large as a mouse's ear.' "

Rebekah chuckled. "A big mouse's ear or a little mouse's ear?"

"Can you imagine Squanto's face if I asked him that?" Will demanded. He crossed his arms over his chest, planted his feet apart, and deepened his voice. "White boys ask too many questions."

"You sound just like him!"

"I know." Will went back to his normal voice. "I like Squanto.

He has been so good to us. He. . .he's almost as good a storyteller as Jake." A shadow crossed his face and he quickly added, "We have to go back to hoeing. Now that the maize is growing so well, it's hoe, hoe, hoe." He bent over his work.

"I think it's pretty, all green and in rows." Rebekah looked over the large cleared space. "Father said we prepared ninety-six-thousand hillocks and trapped and carried forty tons of dead fish to make the crops grow!" She looked at her small hands. Calluses from hard work marred the pink palms. Her short nails were rimmed with earth. "I guess it will be worth it when the harvest comes."

Because friendly relations had been established with the Indians, a new problem arose. Throughout the spring and into the summer, groups of visitors came regularly, always expecting food. In desperation, two ambassadors were chosen to go see Massasoit and ask him to call a halt to the frequent visits. The Pilgrims simply didn't have food to spare. Edward Winslow and Will Hopkins served as ambassadors, with Squanto as guide and interpreter. Will wanted to go with them and longingly watched the three set out.

To the travelers' dismay, Massasoit had very little food, for he had only recently arrived at his home. What little the visitors were given and a few bits of fish on the way home barely provided strength enough for them to again reach New Plymouth.

Rebekah listened when Edward Winslow told the story.

"We had nothing to eat the first day. The next morning was used in sports and shooting. About one o'clock Massasoit brought two boiled fishes that were supposed to feed forty people!" He groaned and patted his stomach. "If we had not had a partridge, I fear we should have starved. Swarms of mosquitoes meant we could not stay outdoors. Being crammed together with Massasoit, his wife, and two other chiefs on bare planks on the floor, to say nothing of the fleas and lice, made sleep impossible. We knew Massasoit felt ashamed he could offer us nothing better. We told him we wished to keep the Sabbath at home and departed on Friday before the sun rose."

Rebekah hugged her knees, glad Father hadn't gone. Adventuring was fine. Being hungry and eaten alive by insects was not!

Another Indian came to live with the settlers. Hobomok was a member of Massasoit's council. Captain Standish made a special point of winning his friendship, but Squanto loyally served Governor Bradford.

One day Hobomok and Squanto went to Nemasket, an Indian camp about fifteen miles to the west. There they hoped to arrange for trade between the colonists and the Indians.

A few days later, Hobomok raced into the settlement. "Squanto has been murdered!" he gasped. His long hair hung in strings. Sweat beaded his frightened face. "The Nemasket chief Corbitant hates the English. He started a quarrel with us. He tried to stab me, but I escaped. It is said Corbitant has also helped the mighty Narragansetts take Massasoit." His chest rose and fell from his hard run.

Governor Bradford immediately said, "I need volunteers to go with Captain Standish. We cannot allow this thing to go unpunished. Doing so would encourage more such incidents. No Indians would ever again dare be friendly with us. Corbitant and others like him will first kill them, then massacre the colonists. Men, who will go?"

Rebekah watched her brother bite his lip to keep from shouting, "I will!" Such childish behavior would immediately bar him from the expedition. Instead, he hurried to his father, who had already stepped forward. "Take me with you," he said. "Please?"

Father hesitated. He gave Will a measuring look, then turned to Captain Standish. "The lad's wiry body and fleetness of foot might be of use."

Standish looked at Will with cold eyes. "That it might. Has he learned to obey orders, and will you be responsible for him?"

Rebekah saw Will squirm and look guilty, but Father said in a clear, ringing voice, "He has and I will." Rebekah hoped her brother would prove himself worthy of his father's faith.

"See that he stays out of the way," Standish ordered. "If I need him, I'll say so. Otherwise, he's to keep back." A somber look came to his face. He wheeled toward Will. "I do not expect that those of us who bear arms and attack shall all be killed. If we are, you must run as you have never run before and carry the news to Governor Bradford. Should the Indians kill us, they will be wild with triumph, perhaps crazy enough to launch an attack on the colony."

"Yes, sir." Although Will's face was pale with fear at Standish's words, he kept his gaze level, and he saluted.

Rebekah's heart thudded against her ribs as she watched her father and brother fall into line. It had been months since they had ventured outside the stockade, and then it had been to explore and discover food. Going into the night for the purpose of finding and destroying Indians was far different. Would any of the men, even Father, come back alive? Yet the murder of Squanto could not be ignored. *Please, God,* she silently prayed, *keep them safe.* No other words would come to her mind. Even though Corbitant and his followers were the enemy, Rebekah could not pray for their deaths.

With Hobomok as guide, the party set out for Corbitant's camp. Rebekah sighed and turned away. She took her mother's hand as they walked back to their hut. Now all they could do was pray.

Rebekah's heart leapt when the men finally returned. While the gathering of adults buzzed with news, she grabbed Will by his sleeve and pulled him aside. "Tell me everything that happened," she commanded.

Will told her how he knew he would never forget that August night. Every rustle of brush had rung in his ears. The muffled steps of his companions sounded like thunderclaps. Surely any listening Indian could hear the hard beating of his heart.

At last they reached their destination. The rescue party fired their muskets into the air. A wave of terror filled the Indian village. Men, women, and children were ordered not to stir, and Captain Standish marched into Corbitant's hut.

"Corbitant isn't here," Captain Standish called minutes later.

The next instant, some braves made a dash for the woods, straight toward the spot where Father had pushed Will down behind a log and ordered him to stay! Will flattened himself on the ground and shoved his face in his arms. Shots rang out, followed by cries. Will burrowed deeper behind the log. Then a shout brought him to his feet.

"Come, Will. The danger is past." Father reached for Will's hand and then pointed to a tall figure.

"Why, it's Squanto," Will gasped. "I thought he was dead!"

"Neither dead nor injured," Father explained. "The people here know nothing of Corbitant's wicked doings. See, they are bringing food."

"But the shots!" Will protested. "Men cried out."

"Some of the Indians were frightened by us and were afraid we had come to harm them. They tried to run away, and our men, thinking those who were fleeing were working with Corbitant, started shooting. Three of the Indians were injured by musket fire, but they will be fine," Father assured him. "Thank God, there was no more bloodshed than this. The rumor about Massasoit appears to be just that—a rumor. Captain Standish says we shall take the wounded braves back to the settlement and dress their wounds. We will keep and care for them until they are able to travel back to their own people. This will bring goodwill between us and the Indians."

Will suddenly felt weak in the knees. At last, he had been in an actual raid. But Indian braves had been injured in the attack. He decided that fighting the Indians was not as exciting as he had thought. It was terrible!

"Were you frightened?" Rebekah asked.

"Yes, I was," he confessed.

She didn't answer for a time. Finally, she asked him quietly, "Do you still want to go adventuring?"

"Yes, but not on Indian raids. I'd rather be a fisherman than an Indian fighter. Does that make you happy?"

Her green eyes shone. "More than I can say."

"All the time I was lying behind that log, I thought how awful it would be to have to run back with news of a massacre! Or how you'd feel if Father or I got killed. I still like adventuring—hunting animals for food and discovering new things. I don't like hunting people. Perhaps we have to in order to protect our settlement, but if we could just have peace, I'd be happy."

"So would I." Rebekah slipped her hand in his, then ran off to help their mother. She couldn't help but wonder what would happen next in Plymouth Colony.

# CHAPTER 13

# Thanksgiving and Good Fortune

For the next month, many of the Indian chiefs praised the settlers for the way they had handled the incident. Some sent messengers from many miles away to offer their tribes' friendship. Others claimed themselves to be loyal subjects of King James. To everyone's surprise, even Corbitant offered peace through King Massasoit.

Autumn brought more work: Will and Rebekah spent hours with their neighbors, preserving and drying as much food as possible from their small harvest. They had already dried berries and fruit that had ripened earlier in the year. The settlers did not intend to go hungry this winter. The men explored more of the country around them, made treaties with other tribes, and traded trinkets to the Indians for beaver skins.

Then great news came. Will burst into the Cunningham home and shouted, "Mother, Rebekah, Governor Bradford has declared a celebration, and it is to last three whole days!"

"When?" Rebekah demanded. "Why? Who is it for?"

"Soon," Will told her. "It's a time for giving thanks that God has brought us through our first hard months in the New World. Everyone in New Plymouth will join together and. . ." Will hesitated, and then burst out, "Massasoit and his tribe are to be our honored guests!"

A broad grin spread over his face, making him look more like the mischievous boy who had boarded the *Mayflower* than the young man he was starting to become. "Squanto says we may have ninety Indians here for the feast."

"Ninety? Mercy on us," Mother gasped. "Think how much time it will take to prepare enough food for one meal, let alone three days of celebration!"

"Governor Bradford says everyone in the colony must help." Rebekah could see that Will was thoroughly enjoying himself. "The Indians have promised to bring deer and wild turkeys. Four of the men have been sent to kill wild ducks and geese. Father and I will join others in fishing, plus gathering shellfish and eels."

"I suppose the girls and women will have to cook all this." Rebekah made a face. "Well, someone else can take care of the eels, slimy old things."

"You don't have to do all the cooking," Will promised. "Governor Bradford says the younger children are to turn the great spits over the open fires where the meat roasts. They also will gather nuts and watercress."

"We will have to make great kettles of corn and beans," Mother planned. "Oh, my. Think of the baking. We will need journeycake and cornmeal bread and—"

"Be sure to make enough food," Will interrupted. "Indians are always hungry." He grinned. "Me, too." His mouth watered. "I hope they don't eat up all the good things before I get a chance at them."

"Remember, son, they are our guests and will naturally be served first," Mother said firmly, but her eyes sparkled with fun. "However, I can't imagine there not being enough food for all."

"There isn't room in the common house or any of the other houses," Rebekah pointed out. "How can we feed so many people?"

"The men will lay planks on sawhorses," Will said. "We'll eat outside."

Rebekah peered out the open door at the warm, mid-October sunshine. "God has already decorated for our feast, hasn't He?" She smiled.

"Indeed He has," Mother agreed. "I have never seen a more beautiful sight than the colored leaves against the dark green forest. There were times when I wondered if we would all be here to see them together."

"Why, Mother! You never told us you were afraid," Rebekah said in wonder.

Mother wiped her eyes with one corner of her apron. "Every time I cared for the sick, it was as though I cared for one of you or Father."

Will and Rebekah looked at each other. How hard it had been for Mother, who had bravely kept her fears to herself for the sake of her family. Rebekah put her arm around her mother's waist and whispered, "It's all over now."

"Yes, child." Mother's beautiful smile bloomed like a flower after rain. "Now is a time for giving thanks to our heavenly Father. Come. There is much to be done."

"Mother spoke well," Will told Rebekah days later when the feast began. "I never, ever saw so much food, not even in Holland."

"That's 'cause we didn't have almost a hundred hungry Indians coming for dinner!" Rebekah giggled. She nodded toward the brown-skinned people who had swarmed into the settlement. "Does Massasoit ever laugh? I'm not afraid of Squanto now, but Chief Massasoit makes me feel a little strange when he comes. He's so serious—perhaps because he is the king."

"He is serious, but look at his people. They're really having a good time."

Rebekah couldn't help staring. The tribes chattered away in their own language. They laughed and poked one another in the ribs, evidently sharing private jokes. And how they ate!

"Are you sure there will be any food left for us?" Will questioned. "You'd think the Indians hadn't eaten for months."

Rebekah rolled her eyes. "If you had helped prepare as much food as Mother and I did, you wouldn't ask such a question. If I never see a dish of succotash again, it will be all right with me."

Rebekah liked the games and contests almost as much as the food. She was pleased when Will won some of the races, while she enjoyed playing stool ball, a game in which a leather ball stuffed with feathers was driven from stool to stool. But she liked the parade best. One man blew a trumpet. Another beat a drum. Men marched and fired their guns.

Rebekah wasn't sure what she thought of the Indian dancing. Their dances were beautiful to watch, but their chants made chills race up and down her spine. After she got used to the strange noises, though, she decided they were beautiful, too.

At last, the three-day celebration ended. The great mounds of food were no more. Thanks and praise to God for His goodness still echoed throughout New Plymouth. Will patted his full stomach and watched the Indians prepare to leave. "I hope we have another feast next year," he told Rebekah.

"It was hard work, but so do I," she said. "I don't know if we will, though." She sighed. "If only all the Indians were our friends, we could eat together and have peace. They aren't. The Narragansetts hate us. Remember the snakeskin tied to the bundle of arrows they sent? Squanto said it was a challenge that meant they wanted war."

"It didn't frighten Governor Bradford and his counselors," Will proudly reminded her. "They refused to back down and returned the snakeskin with powder and shot and the message we had done no wrong. The message also said if the Narragansetts would rather have war than peace, they'd find us ready to fight. The arrow came back, but there has been no attack. Don't worry, Rebekah. A strong fence surrounds our settlement, and every night a man stands guard. Our men are ready to fight at the first cry of fire or attack." He smiled at his hardworking sister. "Besides, God has taken care of us so far. Perhaps war will never come."

Rebekah already knew all those things, but hearing Will repeat them made her feel better.

Early in November, the Pilgrims took stock of their harvest. Their high spirits fell with a thud. The small harvest simply had not produced enough to see them through another winter. Governor

Bradford called the people together. "We planned for much larger crops," he soberly said. "Since this did not happen, we must take harsh measures. The ration of meal to each person must be cut in half."

A ripple of protest swept through the assembly. "There is no other way," he told them. "Otherwise, we shall be no better off than we were last year." The people reluctantly agreed they had no choice, but many looked at one another in fear. How could they get by on a half ration of meal?

A few days later, everyone forgot their troubles for a time. Will brought the news to Mother and Rebekah. "A ship is on the horizon," he shouted. "It is coming nearer and will soon anchor in the harbor!"

"Is it the *Mayflower*?" Rebekah asked.

Will shook his head. "This looks like a much smaller ship. Mother, Rebekah, do you think any of our friends from Leiden will be aboard?" His brown eyes sparkled at the idea.

A little worry frown creased Mother's forehead. "Perhaps. I do hope the ship's hold is filled with food supplies. Even by going on half rations, we barely have enough for those already here."

When the *Fortune* anchored and its passengers came ashore, every person in New Plymouth eagerly awaited them. Fourteen long months had passed since the Pilgrims had left England. Now, new, strong people had come to help settle the colony. Supplies from the ship would give strength to continue with the task.

But joy over greeting friends from Leiden soon changed to dismay. Although young and strong, the newcomers were terribly unprepared. They didn't have any food—not even biscuits. They also didn't bring bedding and pots and pans, and most of them had very few clothes. Many of them had sold their coats and cloaks at Plymouth in order to get money for the voyage from England.

"It's not fair," Rebekah complained. "They should have brought supplies. Everyone here is tired. Now we have to take these people in and care for them!"

"Didn't God send Samoset, Squanto, and Massasoit to help us?" Father asked. "We will share what we have."

Will said, "Those on the *Fortune* felt the same way we did when we first saw Cape Cod. They were afraid we had all been killed in an Indian massacre or died of hunger. The captain said he had just enough food to take the crew on to Virginia. No provisions were sent for the settlers."

Rebekah watched her brother's face flush with anger. "Will Weston sent a letter bawling us out for not sending cargo back to England on the *Mayflower*. He said the Adventurers are furious and would never have lent us money if they'd known they wouldn't start getting some back soon." Will scowled. "More than half of us died, and all they can think of is their precious money. And Will Weston dared to sign himself our very loving friend!"

"I hope Governor Bradford sends a message back telling those people all we have gone through," Rebekah indignantly added.

"I am sure he will reply in a manner suited to a godly man," Father quietly told his family. "Just because others are ill-mannered and judge us unfairly does not mean we are to answer in anger."

Rebekah hung her head. Would she ever be as patient and good as Father?

By mid-December the *Fortune* was ready to sail back to England.

It was loaded with cargo, including many beaver and otter skins that would begin paying off the money that the Pilgrims owed. Robert Cushman also traveled on the *Fortune,* carrying a contract signed by the Pilgrims. Although the terms were harsh, the colonists had their charter and for the first time were legal owners of New Plymouth.

Will and Rebekah watched the ship until it disappeared over the horizon. "So much has happened, I wonder what is ahead," Rebekah mused.

Will gently tugged on one of her dark braids. "Whatever it is, we know God loves us and will take care of us." He proudly raised his head. "Governor Bradford says, 'As one small candle may light a thousand, so the light here kindled has shone unto many, yes, in some sense to our whole nation.'"

"As long as the world lasts," Rebekah mused, "do you think people will learn about the Pilgrims and how we came to a land where we could worship God in the way we believed right? Even more of our people will come, but I'm glad we were the first."

Will nodded. "I love the New World, don't you, Rebekah?"

Rebekah thought hard before she answered. Did she feel it had all been worth it? All the hardship and misery, sickness and death, starvation, and fear of attack? She glanced at the dark, ever-mysterious forest and shivered. She turned toward the sea. Sometimes it danced and sparkled, but it often roared with wind and storm. Last of all, she looked at her brother. He had grown up so much in the past months. She knew the day was coming when she would no longer feel so responsible for him, when she could trust him to make wise decisions for himself.

"Well?" She could see on his face that he was hoping with all his heart that in spite of everything, Rebekah shared his love for their new home.

A smile tipped her lips up and a happy laugh rang out in the cold December air. "I love our new home, too," she said. "I wouldn't want to live anywhere else in the whole wide world." Her words hung in the cold December air, and mischief came into her face. "Race you home!" She took off in a whirl of skirts, happy laughter floating back over her cloaked shoulder.

*Thank You, God,* she prayed while she ran. *Thank You for keeping us safe. Thank You for blessing us here in our new home.*

# OFFICIAL

## SISTERS IN TIME

# WEBSITE!

# Your Adventure
# Doesn't Stop Here—

LOG ON AND ENJOY...

### The Characters:
Get to know your favorite characters
even better.

### Fun Stuff:
Have fun solving puzzles, playing
games, and getting stumped with
trivia questions.

### Learning More:
Improve your vocabulary and
knowledge of history.

*Plus*

you'll find links to other history sites,
previews of upcoming *Sisters in Time*
titles, and more.

## *Don't miss*

# www.SistersInTime.com!

If you enjoyed

# Rebekah
## in Danger

be sure to read other

# SISTERS IN TIME

books from BARBOUR PUBLISHING

- Perfect for Girls Ages Eight to Twelve

- History and Faith in Intriguing Stories

- Lead Character Overcomes Personal Challenge

- Covers Seventeenth to Twentieth Centuries

- Collectible Series of Titles

6" x 8 ¼" / Paperback / 144 pages / $3.97

# TUMBLEWEED
*Weddings*

*Love Overcomes a Mountain of Doubt in*

*Three Contemporary Wyoming Novels*

## DONNA REIMEL
## ROBINSON

BARBOUR
PUBLISHING

Dear Readers,

In Tumbleweed Weddings, you'll meet the Brandt siblings—Callie, Tonya, and Derek—who live on a sheep ranch with their parents near Fort Lob, Wyoming. That part of the country has rolling hills, a sparse population, and tumbling tumbleweeds when the wind blows.

Callie thinks she's going to live her life as a spinster librarian, like old Miss Penwell.

Tonya dreams of marrying a handsome man, but she doesn't know what her secret admirer even looks like.

Derek doesn't plan to marry at all—at least, not until he's forty.

But the Lord has a plan for each of their lives, as well as a special someone. They might be single at the beginning of their stories, but each finds their one true love by the end. I hope you enjoy getting to know the Brandt family.

I love to hear from my readers! Please write to me at Donna@DonnaRobinsonBooks.com, or through the post office at P.O. Box 963, Eastlake, Colorado 80614. You can also visit my website at DonnaRobinsonBooks.com.

May the Lord bless you abundantly as you follow Him.

Donna

# FOR THE LOVE OF BOOKS

# *Dedication*

This book is dedicated to my wonderful husband, Richard, who always knew I would get published, and to my Savior, Jesus Christ, who called me to write according to His own purpose.

A special thanks to my JOY Writer critique partners: Kathy Kovach, Paula Moldenhauer, Holly Armstrong, Margie Vawter, Bonnie Doran, Lynnette Horner, Heather Tipton, Jill Hups, and Marla Benroth. Also, thanks to Nancy Jo Jenkins for your prayers. And thank you, JoAnne Simmons, Rachel Overton, and April Frazier, for your hard work in making this book a reality.

# Chapter 1

I loved this book when I was your age." Callie turned over a worn copy of *Go, Dog. Go!* and ran the bar code under the computer's scanner. "It's due back in two weeks, on Friday, August fifteenth." She smiled at six-year-old Tiffany as she handed her the slim volume.

"Thanths, Callie," Tiffany lisped. One of her front teeth was missing.

Callie watched the girl's braids bounce as she skipped out the front door of the Henry Dorsey-Smythe Memorial Library. *That was me twenty years ago.* She sighed. Her love of books had probably ruined her eyes—just as Grandma had warned her—and now she wore thick glasses. But she still read every chance she could get.

Pulling the tail of her green Dorsey-Smythe polo shirt over her jeans, Callie perched on the tall stool behind the checkout counter. The library was housed in an old Victorian mansion, and the wooden front door had a beveled oval window that Callie loved. She often gazed through it at the main street of Fort Lob, Wyoming.

The door closed behind Tiffany and opened a moment later as Agatha Collingsworth stepped inside. Agatha was tall, and her pink-tinted beehive hairdo barely cleared the horizontal beam of the door frame. She wore her usual outfit—stonewashed jeans, which puffed out at her thighs, and an oversize T-shirt. DON'T MESS WITH TEXAS was emblazoned across her ample bosom.

"Howdy, Callie!" Agatha's husky voice resounded against the high ceiling as she approached the checkout counter. "How ya'll doing, sugar? I'm here to collect my book."

"Okay, Aggie." Callie turned to the shelf of reserved books behind her. "Your order came in yesterday."

"Yeah, Lucille called last night after I got home from the Beauty Spot and told me to pick up that booger as soon as possible. She don't like folks leaving their books."

"Here it is." Callie pulled it off the shelf and glanced at the title—*Fixing Big Hair the Texas Way*. The model on the cover, who had hair bigger than Aggie's, must have posed for that picture in the mid-1960s. "Looks like your kind of book."

"Oh, I was so excited when I noticed this book in an old catalog." Aggie's gold bangle bracelets clinked as she handed Callie her library card. "Folks around here have such flat hair, and I never could get anyone interested in real style. When I saw this little gem, I had Lucille call the Casper library right away. Wouldn't you know it? They had a copy in their old books section."

Callie ran the bar code under the scanner. Not many people could get away with calling the head librarian *Lucille*. A person had to be at least sixty. "I'm glad Miss Penwell found it for you."

"Lucille can find anything." Aggie took her book. "I have to hustle back to the Beauty Spot. I left your sister minding the store all by her lonesome, and we usually have a crowd on Friday afternoons."

Callie tried to keep a straight face. "I bet you'll have two or three customers wanting their hair done for the weekend."

Aggie's dark eyes danced as she let out a throaty chuckle. "Oh, Callie! Sometimes we have eight! And that's almost more than Tonya and I can handle in one afternoon." She strode back outside, her big hair safely clearing the doorway.

Smiling, Callie placed her chin in her hand. She loved working at the library. When she was a little girl, she'd pretended this mansion was her home. Mildred Dorsey-Smythe, the maiden daughter of Henry, had willed the house to the town of Fort Lob for the specific purpose of providing a library for the residents. The front entrance alcove made a perfect place for the tall wooden counter that served as a checkout desk. It was tucked next to the sweeping staircase that accessed the reference rooms upstairs.

But Mildred had died almost fifty years ago, and now the house was over a hundred. The wooden stairs, scuffed by generations of children, competed with the old chipped banisters, which had been repainted a dozen times.

Grabbing the cart laden with books to be reshelved, Callie wheeled it past the staircase into the main room of the library. She glanced up at the ceiling molding that ran around the perimeter of the room. A chunk had fallen out last week. Even though Chance Bixby, the janitor, had cleaned it up, he had not fixed the hole yet. If only the town council would spend some money on this place, they could restore the mansion to its former glory.

Passing several rows of bookshelves, she counted seven patrons. Miss Penwell's voice played through Callie's mind. *"You should know how many people are in the library at all times."*

Mrs. Anderson looked up from her reading. "Hello, Callie, dear."

Callie smiled and waved at the older woman then moved her cart to the gigantic fireplace. The white limestone hearth had been blackened with soot when the fireplace was used years ago, but now skeletal radiators heated the room in the winter. Those radiators sometimes clicked and hissed alarmingly, making more noise in the library than a group of excited schoolchildren.

Callie selected a book from the cart called *Cowboys of the Old West* and displayed it on the wide mantel. She had just finished it last night. *Such a great read.* No wonder the author, Herbert Dreyfuss, was so famous. Of course, having a weekly syndicated newspaper column that was read all over the nation helped his fame, too.

She glanced at the other volumes on display. Two history books and three fiction, all published years ago. She sighed. If only she could fulfill her dream of owning a bookstore, she could have new books all the time. *And I would read every single one of them.*

Behind the main room, the former dining area had been remodeled as a children's book nook. Callie wheeled her cart through the wide archway. She greeted a young mother with two children who were seated at one of the small tables.

After reshelving a dozen books in the children's section, Callie pushed the empty cart back to the front of the library. On the other side of the mansion through double-wide french doors, she glanced into the conservatory. It ran the width of the house, with tall windows and plants—a comfy place with sofas where people liked to sit and read.

A loud guffaw drew her attention.

She frowned. Bruce MacKinnon and Vern Snyder were making way too much noise. *"You must keep the patrons quiet so others are not disturbed."* Miss Penwell's voice again.

Callie walked into the conservatory, folded her arms, and stared at the two old men. They didn't notice her scowl. It was probably because her glasses, which her sister called "Coke-bottle bottoms," made her eyes look big and round. Tonya said Callie looked like she was always about to say *Huh?*

She did not appreciate her sister's opinion.

Bruce held an open newspaper and pointed to the article he was reading. "Listen to what Herbert Dreyfuss says." His *r*'s rolled slightly. "Wyoming is the best place in the United States to raise kids."

"Now ain't that a hoot?" Vern had a thin, high voice, but it was loud—probably because he seldom wore his hearing aid. "That Dreyfuss is a smart one."

"Aye, that he is."

"He's so famous, and here he says Wyoming, our grand old state, is the best. Too bad his column's only in the paper once a week."

Bruce turned a page. "I enjoyed that article last Friday on the history of golf. Dreyfuss does good research. Made me feel like a boy again, before I left bonny Scotland."

Callie cleared her throat. "Excuse me, but you two need to keep your voices down." She motioned around the conservatory to the other library patrons—ten of them, some sitting on sofas and others studying at tables near the back of the room.

Vern looked at Bruce. "What'd she say?"

"Are you trying to tell us how to live, Callie Brandt?" Bruce spoke in a loud voice. "Why, I remember the day you were born, and here you are, repri-manding me about talking too loud in the library."

Vern laughed. "Shoot! I remember when her daddy was born."

Callie rolled her eyes. "If you want to talk, go upstairs to one of the conference rooms." Several of the bedrooms had been modified into study rooms with soft lighting, tables, and chairs.

"A conference room!" Vern patted the sofa. "But the chairs up there are hard. We want to be comfortable."

"That's the truth." Bruce shook the paper with a rattle. "All right, Callie, we'll be good."

Vern perused his paper. "You won't hear another peep from us."

Callie stood there a moment, but the two men didn't move. Bruce MacKinnon had always reminded her of Clark Gable. He had a commanding presence and was still a handsome man, even in his seventies. As president of the town council, folks looked up to him.

She walked to the checkout counter, remembering another pet saying from the head librarian. *"I would love this job if it weren't for the people!"*

Callie moved behind the counter and turned her back to look at the reserved books on the shelves. If some of these people didn't pick up their interlibrary loans, she would have to send them back to Casper.

Behind her, a patron placed books on the desk. "I'll be right with you," she said, shoving a reserved book back in place.

"Take your time."

Callie didn't recognize the bass voice. Must belong to that new guy in town. What was his name? It was an unusual name, nothing common like John or Tom. He had visited the library yesterday, and Miss Penwell informed her the man was an insurance salesman.

*What is he doing in a little town like Fort Lob?* Young people didn't move in—they moved out. The shrinking population, now fewer than five hundred, was predominantly made up of older folks, many retired.

She turned around. "Hello. Thanks for waiting."

He smiled. "Sure."

*My goodness, he's handsome!* She adjusted her glasses. This was the first time she had seen him up close.

Callie pulled the stack of five books toward her. His library card lay on top, and she glanced at his name before she flashed it under the scanner. *Lane Hutchins.*

While she checked out Lane's books, Callie checked *him* out. He was tall—at least six feet—with brown hair and brown eyes and no glasses to cover his good looks. Nice hands—tanned and clean with trim nails—and no wedding ring.

*No wedding ring!* Her heart leaped at the implications. But as she slid another book under the scanner's laser, her shoulders drooped. Why should she get her hopes up? Her sister would probably snag him. Tonya just glanced at a man with her beautiful twenty-twenty-vision eyes, batted her thick lashes a few times, and he would ask her out.

Callie pasted a smile on her face, determined to be friendly. "There you go, Mr. Hutchins." She pushed the books across the counter toward him.

"Thank you."

"You're new in town. Didn't you just move here?"

"Uh, yes." He picked up the heavy volumes and stowed them under one arm. "About three days ago."

"I've lived here all my life, except the few years I was in college. The University of Wyoming, of course."

He nodded and moved toward the door.

Callie didn't want him to leave. "Do you have family here in Wyoming?"

He turned. "I grew up in Cheyenne. Have a good day."

"So, where are you staying right now?"

He pulled on the doorknob. "Down the street." The door shut behind him.

Callie frowned. "Down the street" could be anywhere in this small town. He must be renting an apartment at the Stables, Mrs. Wimple's place. Didn't she have an extra one available? Callie would ask her at church on Sunday.

She turned back to the reserved books. Evidently Lane Hutchins was the type who kept to himself. But time would tell why he was here. A person couldn't hide in a small town like Fort Lob, Wyoming.

∽

Lane blew out a breath. *What a nosy girl.* A warm, dry breeze lifted his hair as he walked the four blocks to the Stables. Why couldn't he move to a small town without people asking questions? He had lived in other small towns, and most people didn't pay any attention to him.

But Fort Lob, Wyoming, was the smallest town he had lived in during the past five years. It was number sixteen in his venture to live in a small town in every state in the Union. The thing that surprised him about this town was its fantastic library. *What a find!*

The rumble of a muffler sounded behind him, and he turned as a black 1972 Ford Mustang thundered by. The kid behind the wheel bopped to loud music. His car backfired twice as he hit the brakes at a stop sign, and when he took off, the Mustang protested with a screech of tires.

Lane shook his head. Had he ever craved that much attention when he was sixteen?

Arriving at his new place, Lane opened the door beside the garage and took the inside stairs two at a time to his second-floor apartment. Mrs. Wimple had informed him that her apartment building used to be a horse stable, built by James Thomas Lob himself in 1878. Now the stables on the first floor formed the garage for the residents' cars, and the rooms upstairs had been divided into apartments.

*That's what I like—living history.*

In the tiny kitchen, he set his books on the table and looked out the window. From here he could see Main Street, which dead-ended at the imposing Victorian mansion that housed the Dorsey-Smythe Library. The mansion was built on a small hill and towered over Fort Lob. Between the library at one end and the post office at the other, Main Street was lined with shops, including a grocery, a Laundromat, a hardware store, a newspaper office, and two restaurants. The residential streets—with names like Elk, Bison, and Bighorn—spread out from Main.

And that was the extent of Fort Lob, Wyoming.

A smile touched his lips as he thought back to the conversation he overheard in the library's conservatory. Those old men sure liked Herbert Dreyfuss. In fact, everywhere Lane stayed in America, people spoke highly of the author and his articles in the newspaper.

He took a seat at the table and opened one of the books. "People enjoy your writing, Uncle Herb. Especially the old people." He chuckled.

Then his mind drifted to the girl with the curly dark hair who had checked out his books. She certainly asked a lot of questions. But she had a pretty smile, and he liked the way her mouth moved when she talked. She might be attractive if she didn't wear those thick glasses that magnified her eyes.

One of the old men had called her Callie. Callie Brandt. *Pretty name.*

Lane sighed, thinking of the lonely life he led. It was nice to have someone take an interest in him for a change. Maybe he would spend more time at the library. . . .

But no, he should avoid Callie Brandt and her questions. He planned to stay only three months in Fort Lob gathering information, and then he would move on. Hopefully, no one would find out who he really was.

# Chapter 2

Callie stacked the older woman's three books and slid them across the counter. "Two weeks, Mrs. Nielsen. They're due on Saturday, August sixteenth."

"Thank you, dear." She placed the books in her bag and tottered toward the library's entrance. Just as she reached for the handle, the door burst open, and Murray Twichell, dressed in his patrolman uniform, strode inside and almost trampled the woman with his polished black boots.

"Whoa!" Murray caught Mrs. Nielsen's arms before she fell down. "Sorry, Mrs. Nielsen. Didn't mean to run you over."

Callie rushed to the door. "Mrs. Nielsen! Are you okay?"

"Oh, I'm fine, dear." She placed her hand over her heart. "Just startled, that's all."

"I'm so sorry." Murray looked concerned and then seemed to remember he was part of the Wyoming Highway Patrol. He straightened, stretching as tall as his five-foot, six-inch frame would allow him. Placing his left hand over his patrolman's badge and his right hand on the gun holster residing on his hip, he bowed slightly. "I sincerely hope you will accept my most humble apology, ma'am."

"Oh, Murray." Mrs. Nielsen laughed. "I'm all right. Really."

Callie took her elbow. "Let me walk you home."

"No, dear. You have work to do." She exited through the doorway. "No harm done."

Murray closed the door, and a puff of warm air wafted the strong scent of his Stetson aftershave toward Callie. He brushed a hand over his reddish-brown crew cut. "Whew! Every time I come to the library, I run into someone I know. This time I literally ran into someone."

"You need to be more careful, Murray." Callie walked back to the checkout desk, away from his overpowering fragrance. "The last place a person expects to be injured is at a library." She pulled a book from the Reserved shelf. "Your reservation came in from Casper. *A History of Gunfights in America* by Herbert Dreyfuss." She shook her head as she laid the book on the counter. "Well, if that's what you want to read..."

"Hey, this is going to be interesting." Murray picked it up. "Have you ever read anything by Dreyfuss?"

"Of course. I've read all his books except this one. It was just published.

I'll read it because I love history, but gunfights are not my favorite subject."

"His research is amazing." He pointed the book at her. "When you read history by Herbert Dreyfuss, you know this is not some piece of fiction. It really happened."

"True." She held out her hand. "Your library card, please."

Murray unfastened the brass button on his uniform shirt pocket. "Why do you need my card? You know who I am."

"I know *everyone* in this town, but it's one of Miss Penwell's rules. 'All patrons must present their library card at time of checkout.'"

"Oh, brother." Murray fished the card from his pocket and handed it to her. "By the way, Callie. . ." He lowered his voice. "I have some business over in Lusk this evening. Thought maybe you and me could have dinner and catch a movie." He raised his reddish eyebrows then jiggled them up and down.

Callie looked straight across the counter into his blue eyes. She had always thought Murray Twichell looked like a leprechaun. All he needed was a green suit. "Not this week, Murray, but thanks for asking." She scanned his book.

"Come on, Callie. It's Saturday night. We need an evening in the big city." *In Lusk?* "I have to work until six o'clock."

"So? I'll pick you up at six. I'm so busy with my highway duties, you hardly ever see me. When was the last time you saw my handsome face at this library? Three weeks ago?" He placed his right hand over his badge. "My heart yearns within me for time spent alone with you, my darling, and only you."

Callie rolled her eyes. "You've been reading those poetry books again, haven't you?"

"I don't read poetry," he scoffed. "I check those books out for my mother in the nursing home. Now come on, Callie. Let's make it an evening on the town."

She pushed his library card across the counter. Murray Twichell was the only guy who ever asked her out. They had grown up together, and when they were twelve years old, he declared he was going to marry her someday. But Murray was not *the one*, and she was tired of dating him every three or four weeks. "Sorry, not this weekend. I don't. . ."

Her words died as the front door opened and a man walked in. Lane Hutchins? He was here yesterday—and the day before.

Callie smiled. "Hi, Mr. Hutchins. Back at the library so soon?"

"I'm returning these." He set down the five books she had checked out yesterday. "I also need to research something and was wondering if you could help me."

"I'd be glad to." She motioned to Murray. "This is one of Wyoming's patrolmen, Murray Twichell, and—"

"You new in town?" Murray stuck out his hand. He wasn't smiling.

14

Lane shook hands. "Lane Hutchins. I just moved here a few days ago. I'm staying at the Stables."

*So, he does live there.*

Murray frowned. "What's your business in Fort Lob, Hutchins? It better be legitimate."

"Murray!" Callie felt like slapping him across the nose. "A person has a right to live in Fort Lob if he wants to, or anywhere else for that matter."

"Just doing my job." Murray stretched to his full height, which still fell short of Lane's by six inches. "The townspeople count on their cops to keep law and order. We don't want any unsavory characters moving in."

"I understand, sir, and my business is quite legitimate." Lane had a serious expression on his handsome face. "People in a small town are protective of their community, and rightly so."

"That's right." Murray looked at Callie. "Smart man." He picked up his book and walked to the door. "Welcome to Fort Lob, Hutchins. See you later, Callie." He exited the library.

Lane turned to Callie. "Was he carrying a Herbert Dreyfuss book?"

"Yes, the new one about gunfights. I had to order it on reserve from the Casper library."

He nodded. "It's only been out a few weeks. I guess you haven't had time to buy a copy for the Dorsey-Smythe Library."

"Well, that's not the problem." Callie looked down, shuffling some papers into a neat pile. It was hard to concentrate with Lane's brown eyes staring at her. "Usually Miss Penwell buys all the bestsellers for our library—in fact, we bought all the other Dreyfuss books—but the town council put a cap on our spending."

"Oh?" Lane folded his arms. "Does that mean you won't be able to buy any new books?"

"That's exactly what it means. They cut our funding, and we haven't bought a new book in four months." She motioned behind her at the thirty or so volumes on reserve. "I have to order books from Casper all the time now. And if they don't have it, I call the library in Cheyenne."

He nodded. "I grew up in Cheyenne with my aunt and uncle, but I've lived in other places more recently."

"Oh." *His aunt and uncle?* Maybe he was an orphan. "So were you—"

"Say, I need your help." He glanced up the wide staircase. "Are your reference books upstairs?"

"Yes, let me show you." She walked to the stairway. "What's your topic?"

"I'm interested in Yellowstone National Park."

Callie ascended the stairs. "In that case, I'll show you the Wyoming Heritage Room. There's lots of information about Yellowstone in there, and unlike the reference books, you can check them out."

"Good." Lane moved up to walk beside her. "I figured a library in Wyoming would carry a number of volumes on Yellowstone, and this is one of the best libraries I've ever visited."

"Thanks to Mildred Dorsey-Smythe." She didn't mention how fast the library was going downhill—thanks to the town council.

They entered the former master bedroom that was packed with shelves of geographical books and local history tomes. Callie scanned the volumes as she walked down the aisles. Lane followed her.

"Here we are." She pointed to four shelves. "Yellowstone National Park. You have a lot to choose from."

"Wow." A spark jumped into his eyes. "This is great."

Callie wished she could stay with him, but her job of pointing out the books was done. "Let me know if you need more help."

"I will." Lane pulled a book from the shelf. "Thanks, Callie." He opened the volume and began perusing it.

Her heart did a little flip as she left the room. *He said my name.* She almost floated down the stairs.

A redheaded blur, in the form of eight-year-old Kincaid Watson, barreled into her as she turned toward the checkout counter. Her daydream disappeared with the impact.

"Sorry, Callie." Kincaid dashed out the front door.

Callie trudged to the desk. Who was she kidding? Lane would never be attracted to her with her ugly glasses. She would probably end up like Miss Penwell, working in the library her whole life as an unmarried librarian. Even if she saved up the resources to begin her dream bookstore, she would do it single-handedly—and single.

But Lane had never answered Murray's question about what he was doing here. Was it to sell insurance? If so, wouldn't he be handing his business card to every patron in the library? On the other hand, the citizens of Fort Lob didn't need an insurance man in town. Everyone got their insurance over the phone through agents in Casper or Cheyenne.

*So why did Lane Hutchins move here?*

# Chapter 3

At exactly two o'clock, Callie heard the regimented tap of sensible shoes striding toward her. *I could set my watch by her arrival.*

Miss Lucille Penwell marched into the library.

Callie moved to let the head librarian take her place behind the counter. "Good afternoon, Miss Penwell."

The older woman pursed her lips, causing the skin above them to pucker into ripples. Her thin face and high cheekbones made her look like a skeleton, and the short-cropped gray hair did not soften her angular features. "How many reserved books were picked up?"

"Six or seven, I think."

Miss Penwell adjusted her wire-rimmed glasses. "You should know exactly, Miss Brandt. Did you make any phone calls to remind people about their books?" She pressed a few keys on the computer.

"Yes, Miss Penwell."

The head librarian kept her eyes on the computer screen. "And how many patrons are in the building right now?"

Callie had counted five minutes ago, knowing Miss Penwell would ask. "Eight people are in the main room, four children in the book nook, eleven people in the conservatory, and one person upstairs." She wondered how long Lane Hutchins would stay. He had been in the Wyoming Heritage Room almost two hours.

Miss Penwell scanned down the list of those who had checked out. "Only seven books from Casper were picked up. Why don't these people come and pick up their books? Don't they understand we have to order these from somewhere else? We have to send them back."

Callie shrugged, knowing it was useless to answer.

Outside, a car backfired.

"Oh, that awful Spencer boy is here." Miss Penwell glared at Callie as if it was her fault. "I hope he didn't bring any of his friends with him. The last time they were in the library, they made so much noise that I kicked them out."

Chance Bixby, the janitor, ambled toward the conservatory. He held a mop in one hand, and the front of his shirt was soaked, emphasizing his potbelly. He glanced at the two women and lifted his baseball cap an inch. "Hey there, Callie." The light cast a glint on his gold front tooth.

"Mr. Bixby!" Miss Penwell folded her arms across her thin chest and stared at him.

"Well, hello there, Lucille. Nice day, eh?" He moseyed toward the conservatory.

Miss Penwell huffed out a breath. "A word with you, Mr. Bixby."

He stopped and frowned at her.

"Have you fixed that hole in the ceiling of the main room?"

"No, I haven't." He began to walk away.

"Why not? It's not going to fix itself. That hole is a danger to our library patrons. More plaster could fall and hurt someone."

*Oh no.* Callie let a sigh escape. Miss Penwell was looking for a fight.

Chance stopped. "No money. That's why."

"What do you mean? We have a repair fund."

"It's empty—as if you didn't know." Chance headed toward the conservatory.

"Mr. Bixby, come back here! I'm not finished speaking with you!"

Chance sighed and walked back to the checkout counter. "Well, I'm done. If there's no money in the repair fund, how can I fix anything? No money, no repair. Even *you* should be able to understand that."

Miss Penwell ignored the insult. "Then talk to the town council—"

"I've talked to them!" His voice increased a decibel. "And they're taking their good old time trying to decide if the library's worth repairing."

"What?" Miss Penwell's gaunt face paled. "Of course it's worth repairing. Use your own money! Plaster can't cost that much."

"My own money?" Chance eyed her. "Do you know the little pittance I make at this job? If I didn't have my pension from the army, I'd be on the street!" He looked at Callie. "You know it's true."

Callie didn't want to get involved in the argument, even though she agreed with Chance. Her librarian's salary was too low to live on by herself, which was why she still lived at home with Mom and Dad.

Chance looked back at Miss Penwell. "You're the head librarian. Maybe *you* should pay for it."

Miss Penwell pursed her lips. "I'm sure the town council will pay you back for—"

"Pay me back? Oh sure." He slapped his hand on the counter. "In five years, they might get around to voting on it."

"What seems to be the problem here?"

The three of them turned toward the voice coming from the conservatory.

Bruce MacKinnon strode up to the checkout counter. "The entire library can hear you two." He kept his voice low. "I suggest you take your fight outside."

Miss Penwell scowled. "We are not fighting. I merely suggested—"

"We are too fighting, Lucille!" Chance thumped his mop handle on the floor as he turned to Bruce. "She's being ridiculous, telling me to use my own money to make repairs. Now where is *that* going to end, I ask you."

Bruce's eyebrows dipped. "But the library has a fund for repairs."

"We have zero money in our fund, Mr. Town Councilman, but a certain town council is too stingy to—"

"Did you put in a request?"

"Yes! Last week! I talked to Ralph Little, since he's the treasurer." Chance shook his head. "Haven't heard a word."

Bruce sighed. "Ralph said nothing to me. But we have a council meeting tonight, and I'll be sure to bring it up. In the meantime. . ." Bruce took his wallet from his back pocket. "Here's some money to buy plaster." He handed Chance a crisp fifty-dollar bill.

Miss Penwell's eyebrows shot up. "Bruce! You shouldn't give him your own money."

"Aha!" Chance waved a thick finger in her face. "He shouldn't spend his money to fix the library, but I can spend mine. Is that it?"

"I never said that."

"That's exactly what you said."

"You are putting words in my mouth!"

"Hold on, you two!" Bruce clapped his hand on Chance's shoulder. "Let's stop this foolishness. Buy the plaster and fix the hole."

Chance nodded and stomped toward the back of the building.

Bruce leaned across the counter. "Now, Lucille, you have to stop these arguments." His voice was low as he took her hand in his. "No one wants to hear you bickering."

Miss Penwell snatched her hand away. "This is *my* library, and I'll do as I please."

He shrugged. "Suit yourself, Lucille, but someday—someday *soon*—you may discover that someone else is running this library." He glanced at Callie. "And that is the town council speaking."

Miss Penwell's eyes narrowed. "Are you threatening me?"

He cleared his throat. "Guess I'll gallivant over to the Cattlemen's Diner for a good supper. T-bone steak is the Saturday night special." He moved toward the door. "See you later, ladies."

"Good-bye, Bruce." Callie was glad another infamous Chance-Lucille argument was over. They always ended one of two ways: Either Chance would stalk off and Miss Penwell would purse her lips for a half hour, or Bruce MacKinnon would stop it. Callie was caught in the middle—she had to stay on Miss Penwell's good side, but she liked Chance. He was a good janitor, and he was usually right.

She sighed as she stacked books on a cart to reshelve. Catching a movement from the corner of her eye, she glanced toward the stairway. Lane Hutchins descended, a huge stack of books in his arms.

He approached the desk and set the volumes on the counter.

Miss Penwell frowned. "You're checking out all those books?"

He grinned. "I have more." He ran back up the stairs and disappeared around the corner.

"He can't check out all these." Miss Penwell counted the books with her pencil. "He has eleven books here, and he's going to get more?"

Callie winced. Lane was going to catch the wake of Miss Penwell's bad mood. "But we don't have a rule about how many books a person can check out."

"We do for him! This man is a stranger, and who knows where he came from? My intuitions often prove correct, you know."

*No, I didn't know.*

Lane descended the stairs with an equally tall stack of books. "This should do it." He set them beside the other books.

"Young man." Miss Penwell pursed her lips. "You may either go upstairs and study these in one of the conference rooms, or you may check out five books."

Callie's mouth dropped open. "Five books? But, Miss Penwell—"

"Miss Brandt!" The head librarian turned her frown on Callie. "You stay out of this. I believe you have some reshelving to do."

Callie folded her arms. *I'm staying right here.*

"Now then." Miss Penwell raised an eyebrow at Lane. "What will it be?"

Lane tapped his fingers on his chin. "I didn't realize I could only check out five." He looked at the two stacks. "Guess I'll take five out and put the rest back." He lifted the top five books from the first pile.

"Good." Miss Penwell looked at the computer. "Your library card." She held out her thin palm.

Lane's eyes met Callie's as he took out his wallet. She shook her head. She wished Bruce MacKinnon was still here to talk some sense into Miss Penwell.

He handed over his card. "I'll take the rest upstairs while you're checking these out."

"And I'll help you." Callie grabbed an armful of books before Miss Penwell could stop her. She marched up the stairs behind Lane.

As they entered the Wyoming room, she glanced around to make sure no one was there. "Lane, I'm so sorry." She looked at the call number on a book spine. "Miss Penwell seems to thrive on being mean."

He put back one of his volumes. "That's one thing I've learned about living in small towns. The townspeople don't trust strangers."

"Miss Penwell doesn't trust anyone!"

"It's okay. I'll come back on Monday and get the information I need."

Callie shelved another book. "If I were you, I'd come in the mornings. Miss Penwell works from two o'clock until the library closes at nine."

"And you work in the mornings?" He leaned against a bookshelf and thrust his hands into his pockets.

Callie gazed at his tall, relaxed stance and closed her mouth to keep in a wistful sigh. "I work from when we open at ten until six at night."

"Six days a week?" He looked concerned.

"We're closed on Wednesdays—and Sundays, of course."

He raised his eyebrows. "Oh, closed on Wednesdays. I'm glad you told me." He smiled at her before moving toward the door. "I guess we should face the music, as the saying goes."

They descended the stairs. Lane took his five books and thanked Miss Penwell for her time. His sweet attitude didn't improve her sour disposition.

Callie watched him walk out the door. She probably wouldn't see him again until Monday morning.

It was a depressing thought.

# Chapter 4

Lane glanced at the vintage sunburst clock on the kitchen wall. Six o'clock. He wasn't fond of the decor in his little yellow and orange kitchen, but it didn't matter. At least the clock worked. What mattered was that it was supper time, and he had nothing to eat.

He had a sudden craving for a frozen dinner—something quick and easy. That was how he defined good food when he had to make it himself. Good thing he brought his microwave. As with most furnished apartments in small towns, that appliance was missing. And a microwave was a necessity for Lane Hutchins.

It took him all of three minutes to walk across Main Street to the grocery store. A bell tinkled overhead as he pushed the door open.

"Hello there!" The man behind the cash register had a booming voice. His barrel-like chest, covered with a white shirt and green grocer apron, had plenty of lung power. "Welcome to Wilkins Grocery."

"Thanks." Lane glanced down the long, narrow aisles that extended all the way to the back of the building. The shelves were crowded with boxes and produce. "Uh, do you have any frozen dinners?"

"Sure thing!" The man nodded his full head of gray hair and moved down one of the aisles.

Lane followed him.

"By the way, the name's Jim Wilkins." He stuck out his meaty hand.

Lane shook it, which was difficult since the man kept walking. "Nice to meet you, Mr. Wilkins. I'm Lane Hutchins."

"Call me Jim. I hear you're new in town."

"Yes, sir. Just moved here a few days ago."

"You'll love Fort Lob. It's a great place to live." At the back wall, Jim stopped at a row of upright freezers with glass doors. "All the frozen stuff is back here. If you need milk, the dairy case is over there to the left against the wall. Help yourself."

"Thanks."

Jim walked to the front of the store as Lane glanced over the frozen dinners. He seemed to be the only customer. Probably everyone was at home eating supper. He picked out three dinners and stowed them under one arm, then he meandered to the dairy case.

The bell over the door jangled.

"Hey there, Callie!" Jim's voice boomed out.

Lane froze.

"Hi, Jim. I need to pick up a gallon of milk and a few other things for Mom before I go home. Be right back."

Yep, that was Callie's voice. *And she's headed straight toward me!* Lane sneaked over to the aisle of canned vegetables, hoping she wouldn't see him.

The dairy case door opened.

*This is too close.* Lane turned, and his elbow bumped a can of green beans. It fell to the floor with a *thud*.

Callie peered into the vegetable aisle, her magnified eyes widening behind her glasses. "Lane?"

"Oh, uh, hi, Callie." He picked up the can and placed it on the shelf. "Fancy meeting you here."

"Well, it *is* a small town." She glanced at the frozen dinners under his arm. "Are you, um, shopping?"

He shrugged. "Just picking up something to eat tonight."

Her eyebrows lifted. "Well, you know, if you'd like a home-cooked meal, you're welcome to come over to our house. Mom always has plenty of food. She wouldn't mind at all if you popped in."

*Just what I need. . . .* "Uh, no thanks. I have some work to do tonight."

"Are you sure? My mom's a great cook. One of the best in Fort Lob, in fact."

He chuckled. "Thanks for the offer, but I'd better turn you down." He strode off to the front of the store. "See you later."

"Lane, wait!"

He stopped and turned toward her.

"I was just wondering. . . ." She bit her lip. "Are you going anywhere to church tomorrow?"

"Church?" That was right, tomorrow was Sunday. He hadn't been inside a church since his uncle died. "I don't know of any churches around here, so—"

"Then I'll invite you to ours!" She smiled. "We have a great fellowship, and all the folks are real friendly."

Lane hadn't noticed any churches in the area. "Where is it located?"

"On Bighorn Avenue, two blocks west of here. Turn south on Bighorn and go about a half mile. It's a little white church with a thin steeple. You can't miss it."

He nodded, intrigued again with the way her mouth moved when she spoke. "So there's more to this little town than just the businesses on Main Street?"

Callie huffed out a breath. "Of course! We have three churches, a school—even a jail! Fort Lob is way bigger than it looks."

Lane grinned. "Don't get your dander up, Callie. I was just teasing."

"Oh." She adjusted her glasses. "Well, anyway, our church service starts at eleven o'clock. Of course, if you want to come to Sunday school at ten, you're more than welcome. My brother teaches the singles' class. We have fifteen members right now—every single adult in the congregation."

Overwhelmed, Lane shook his head. "I'll just go to church maybe. Thanks for the info."

"Hope you can make it. I'll keep an eye out for you."

"Yeah. See you." Lane walked to the cash register. *Church?* He didn't want to go to church, and he wasn't about to go just because Callie invited him. He set down the frozen dinners at the checkout.

"Is this it?" Jim ran the first box over the scanner. "We do have a great church. You should come and meet some of the town folks. You'll enjoy it."

Lane sighed. He should have known that Jim, with the booming voice, would have good hearing, too. And of course, ironically, he would attend the same church as Callie in this little town.

Jim packed the dinners in a grocery sack. "That'll be nine dollars and forty-two cents."

Lane pulled his wallet from his back pocket and handed over a ten-dollar bill.

"We have a great preacher." Jim took the money and opened the cash drawer. "Every Sunday he feeds us with the Word. I've learned more under Pastor Reilly's teaching than any other man of God. A Christian can really grow in our church." He handed Lane his change. "Hope to see you tomorrow."

Lane nodded. "Yeah, thanks." He took the bag, and the bell jingled as he left the store.

Crossing Main Street, he mused over Jim's words. They awakened memories Lane hadn't thought of in seven years. A sudden longing came over him—a longing to hear a good sermon. A longing to get back in fellowship with God.

*I think I'll go tomorrow.* He could sneak in just as the service was starting and sit in the back. No one would even know he was there.

~~~

Callie paced in front of the church building, looking down the road. Where was he? She had spent a half hour in prayer last night, specifically praying that Lane would come to church today. *Oh, Lord, please make him come. Push him, Lord!*

The strains of the organ floated outside, playing the introduction to "All Hail the Power of Jesus' Name." The congregation started singing.

A warm summer breeze blew a strand of hair across her glasses. She brushed it away then smoothed her skirt down with both hands, hoping the wind wouldn't pick it up.

A motorcycle rumbled down the street toward her.

Callie shrank against the building. She didn't like motorcyclists and didn't want this one to see her. She had known a few boys in college who roared through the streets of Laramie on their cycles. They seemed to have a penchant for black leather jackets and earrings.

The motorcycle slowed. The driver wasn't wearing a helmet.

Callie's mouth dropped open. *Lane?*

He pulled into the parking lot across from the church. He wasn't wearing a black leather jacket and earrings; he was wearing a short-sleeved shirt and tie.

He looked *good*.

The congregation was on the third verse as Lane approached the church. He ascended the stairs and stopped short when he saw Callie.

She stepped forward. "Good morning, Lane."

"Callie." He hesitated, a question in his brown eyes. "I didn't think anyone would be out here. Thought I'd just sneak in the back."

"I was waiting for you, and I'm glad you came." She looked down, suddenly feeling like a love-struck girl in junior high. But it was too late to backtrack. "Would you like to sit with me?"

He shrugged. "Sure. Lead the way."

She opened the door. The congregation was standing, sustaining the last note. She led Lane down the side aisle.

Halfway down, the song leader seated the congregation. The air rustled as they took their seats. Callie saw her parents in the middle of the fourth pew from the front. She slid into place next to Mom. Lane settled beside her.

❧

Lane glanced around, feeling conspicuous. Callie *would* have to sit way up here in the front. The auditorium was crowded, but it was a small room. He estimated there couldn't be more than seventy people in attendance.

A man with stooped shoulders welcomed the crowd. He looked fragile, probably in his sixties, but he had a strong voice.

Callie leaned toward Lane and whispered, "That's Pastor Reilly."

She looked back at the pastor, and Lane took a moment to study her. From this angle, he could see her eyes in profile behind her glasses. They looked like pretty eyes, and her lashes were long. He wished he could see what she looked like without those awful spectacles.

"And I see we have a visitor." Pastor Reilly looked straight at Lane. "Introduce yourself, young man!"

Startled, Lane glanced around. Was he the only visitor?

"Stand up!" Callie whispered.

He stood, restraining the desire to straighten his tie, and looked at the sea of expectant faces. "I'm Lane Hutchins."

"Lane Hutchins," the pastor repeated. "Where are you from?"

"I just moved here from Gridley, Illinois."

"Ah, Illinois! I'm from the Chicago area myself."

Lane nodded and sat down. Fortunately, after a few comments about Chicago, Pastor Reilly moved on to the announcements.

"Illinois?" Callie whispered. She gazed up at him, but as the light reflected off her glasses, he couldn't see her eyes.

He gave her a nod. *What am I doing here?* He wished he had stayed in his apartment. The town of Fort Lob was too tiny for his venture; the people were too nosy. Perhaps he should move to a larger town in Wyoming. Either Pinedale or Lusk, each with a population of fourteen hundred or so, would be better suited for his purposes.

While he was musing, the ushers came forward to collect the offering. As they passed the plates down each row, piano music began—a rendition of "Onward, Christian Soldiers."

Lane glanced at the piano player and drew in a sharp breath. What a beautiful girl!

With dark hair that was fashionably messy, the girl looked to be in her early twenties. She had an oval face with perfect skin and full lips.

She played with passion, concentrating on the music, weaving about on the piano bench. One moment she leaned into the piano, her eyes never leaving the music. The next moment she leaned away, her eyes still glued to the notes. After striking a chord, she would lift her left hand—with manicured red nails—in the air and crash it back down, amazingly, on the right keys. Despite all her theatrics and the fact that the music sounded difficult, she played the piece to perfection.

At the end, the audience gave her an enthusiastic round of applause. Lane joined in.

The girl smiled and nodded at the audience. Her beautiful dark-blue eyes glanced around and then stopped at Lane's. She locked her gaze with his until he looked away.

As the pastor came back to the podium, Lane leaned over to whisper to Callie. "That piano player's really good."

Callie stared straight ahead. "That's my sister, Tonya."

⬥

After the service, Callie introduced Lane to Mom and Dad, and Mom invited him over for lunch. For the next twenty minutes, the church people surrounded him, introducing themselves. He shook hands with them, one by one, until his smile began to falter. Callie felt sorry for him.

"Come on, Lane." She pulled him away from old Edna Beazer. That woman would be talking nonstop on her deathbed. "We'll see you later, Edna. Mom invited Lane over for dinner, so we'd better get going."

"Well, my goodness!" The older woman stopped to suck in her dentures.

"I was going to invite him myself, but I know your mother is a good cook. She always brings something wonderful to our church potlucks."

Callie nodded, wiping a drop of Mrs. Beazer's spit from her arm. "Maybe some other time." She pulled Lane toward the door.

The church building was empty, and most of the cars had left. But several people were still talking in the parking lot, including Callie's brother, Derek.

She walked down the steps with Lane. "I noticed you were riding a motorcycle."

The church door slammed shut behind them. "Callie! Wait for me!"

*Oh no!* Callie pivoted at her sister's voice.

Tonya, in her tight knee-length skirt, gracefully descended the stairs. She looked at Lane. "Hi there! I didn't get to meet you earlier. I had to attend a meeting after the service."

Lane smiled and stuck out his hand. "Lane Hutchins."

Callie sighed. He looked entirely too interested.

"I'm Tonya Brandt." She shook his hand, moving closer to him. "I've heard all about you, Lane. You just can't keep a secret in a small town like Fort Lob." She twittered her signature laugh—the one she used for impressing guys.

He grinned. "Great to meet you, Tonya."

Callie noticed they were still shaking hands.

Lane continued. "I enjoyed your piano playing. Not many people can play that well. It sounded like a difficult piece."

"Thank you so much!" Tonya finally released his hand. "I love playing the piano for our church services. It's such a joy."

*Such a joy?* Callie wanted to throw up. Instead she jumped into the conversation. "We'd better get going. Mom invited Lane for dinner."

"Oh, that's wonderful!" Tonya batted her thick, dark lashes. "Why don't I ride over with you, Lane?"

"Well. . ." He glanced down at her skirt.

"He has a motorcycle." Callie turned to Lane. "You can follow our pickup truck. We're riding home with Derek—our brother."

He nodded. "Okay."

Tonya pouted. "Oh, I wish I could ride over with you. We live seven miles east of Fort Lob on Antelope Road. My dad's a sheep rancher."

Lane raised his eyebrows. "Sounds interesting."

Tonya laid her hand on his arm. "I'm glad you're coming over. We'll have all afternoon to get to know each other."

Callie grabbed her by the elbow. "See you there, Lane." She walked with Tonya to Derek's truck while Lane strode to his motorcycle. Tonya climbed into the cab. Callie followed and settled beside her sister. As she closed the passenger door, she felt her opportunity with Lane slamming shut as well.

The thing she feared had come to pass.

# Chapter 5

*Ah! The open road.*

Lane enjoyed the seven-mile motorcycle ride out to the Brandt family ranch. He followed the pickup as it rattled down the paved two-lane road. They passed a few other houses that were set way back from the road and were usually surrounded by trees. Small groups of cattle munched contentedly on tufts of wild grass. Besides those few signs of civilization, the road cut a path through barren rolling hills dotted with sagebrush.

He could see the three Brandt siblings through the back window of the truck's cab. Tonya sat in the middle, talking nonstop to her brother. Lane had been impressed with Derek Brandt. Taller than Lane, Derek looked to be in his midtwenties, with dark hair the same color as his sisters'. And that Tonya—what a beauty! She reminded Lane of a Hollywood actress, with her perfect facial features and flawless skin.

Derek slowed and turned left onto a narrow blacktopped drive. Lane followed on his cycle, passing under a wrought-iron archway with the words THE ROCKING B RANCH in the middle. The driveway was long, possibly five hundred feet, with a row of evergreen trees marching up the left side. Over a small hill, a farmhouse came into view down in the valley. The front porch ran the entire width of the place, with a swing suspended on the left side near the door. Several wicker chairs sat on the opposite side of the porch. It would be nice to sit there in the shade, sipping a tall glass of lemonade.

The pickup stopped beside the house, and Lane parked his motorcycle behind it. He had barely dismounted before Tonya appeared at his side.

"Come into the house, Lane. I'm sure Mom has the meal all ready. She's made a beef roast today. I know it will be great, and her mashed potatoes are to die for."

"Sounds good." He gazed into her eyes—those dark-blue eyes surrounded by thick black lashes. Definitely Hollywood material.

They ascended the porch steps together. Jake Brandt, Tonya's father, held the door open for them. Like his son, he was tall. He wore glasses, but unlike Callie's, the glasses didn't magnify his eyes.

"Welcome to The Rocking B!" Jake shook his hand. "Come on in."

"Thanks." Lane motioned for Tonya to precede him into the house. As he walked in, the savory aroma of roast beef surrounded him. "Boy! That smells delicious."

# FOR THE LOVE OF BOOKS

"Doesn't it, though?" Tonya agreed. "I'm starving."

Lane followed her into a spacious living room. They passed a pink-flowered sofa sprinkled with pillows, and an upright piano with framed pictures on the top. In the dining room, a large oak table was set with six green and tan place settings. Several steaming bowls of food made his mouth water.

Mrs. Brandt came out from the kitchen. "We're all ready to eat. Hi, Lane. Welcome to our home."

"Thanks." He smiled, trying to remember her first name. "The food smells great." He could see where Tonya got her beauty. Even though Mrs. Brandt looked in her midfifties, she still had a beautiful face. Just like Tonya's, her eyes were dark blue with thick, dark lashes.

"Have a seat, Lane." Jake motioned to the chair on his left as he took the seat at the head of the table.

Tonya slipped into the chair across from Lane. "It's going to taste as good as it smells. This is a feast fit for a king." She twittered a little laugh.

He smiled. This promised to be an enjoyable meal just because he could drink in her beauty. A saying from Uncle Herb popped into his mind. *"Marry a pretty gal, Lane. You'll have to look at her across the table every morning."*

Mrs. Brandt took a seat at the other end of the table while Derek sat down next to Tonya. Callie slid into the seat beside Lane. Jake asked the blessing, and they passed the food. The next twenty minutes were filled with pleasant conversation and fine dining.

It had been years since Lane had enjoyed such a good home-cooked meal, probably not since he had eaten Aunt Betty's cooking. And she had died ten years ago, when Lane was nineteen. He took second helpings of everything and was actually full. That hadn't happened in a long time, either.

He glanced at his hostess. "That was a delicious meal, Mrs. Brandt."

"Thank you, Lane, but please call me Yvette. Everyone does."

He nodded. "Yvette."

Across the table, Tonya leaned forward. "I hope you liked the homemade rolls."

"Homemade?" He raised his eyebrows. "They were fantastic. I've never tasted such good dinner rolls."

She sat back. "I made them—from scratch, of course."

"So, you have cooking talent as well as musical talent."

Her beautiful eyes widened. "Oh, I have a lot of talents. Not only can I cook and play the piano, but I'm also artistic, I love to sew, I'm athletic, and I'm a hairstylist, too. I work at the Beauty Spot over on Elk Road."

"Really?" He grinned, teasing. "Is there anything you can't do?" Lane expected her to lower her beautiful eyes in modesty.

Instead, she looked thoughtful. "Not really. I can do almost anything."

Derek folded his arms. "She's especially good at boasting."

29

"I am not!" Tonya frowned at her brother.

Derek shrugged. "Then what do you call it?"

Yvette scooted her chair back. "Now, you two. Don't get into an argument. We have company today." She stood. "Girls, help me clear the table, and then we'll have dessert."

Callie stood, and a sigh escaped her lips.

Lane wondered if she was living in Tonya's beautiful shadow. "Do you only have two siblings, Callie?"

She turned toward him. "Actually there are six of us, and I'm in the middle."

"Yep." Jake laid his napkin beside his plate. "We have two married children. Ryan lives in Denver with his wife and sons, and Melissa lives in Colorado Springs with her husband."

Tonya picked up Derek's plate. "Melissa just got married last summer. I fixed her hair, and she looked absolutely gorgeous at her wedding. Molly is her identical twin, and she's a nurse. She works at the Pine River Nursing Home in Douglas."

Lane leaned back as Callie took his plate. "So Ryan is the oldest sibling?" He looked at Jake, but Tonya answered.

"Yes, he's thirty-one." She set down her dishes and counted off her fingers. "It's Ryan, Molly and Melissa, Callie, Derek, and me. I just turned twenty-three last week." She shrugged slightly as she gave Lane a little smile. "I'm the baby of the family."

Jake adjusted his glasses. "I wish my three oldest hadn't moved away. Seems all the young people leave Fort Lob sooner or later, and I don't understand it."

"Well, duh!" Tonya picked up her stack of dishes again. "Fort Lob, Wyoming, is not exactly the hot spot of America, Dad."

He grinned at his daughter. "It gets pretty hot in the summer. Near a hundred degrees most days in July."

She looked at Lane and then rolled her eyes. "That's not what I mean." She giggled as she grabbed some silverware. "I like Fort Lob. I'll probably spend my life here, married to a wonderful man someday." She paused to give Lane a significant look. "But if my husband wants to leave, I'd have to leave, too." She glanced at her dad. "That's just the way it is."

Callie came back from the kitchen and picked up several more dishes.

Lane glanced at her as she took the potato dish from the table. "How long have you worked at the Dorsey-Smythe Library?"

"I got the job right after college graduation four years ago."

"Do you like working there?"

Callie nodded. "I love it. I've always loved to read and—"

"Which is why she wears glasses," Tonya put in. "When the rest of us kids were playing, Callie was sitting in some secluded corner with a book. Absolutely ruined her eyes." Toting her dirty dishes, she walked to the kitchen.

Lane was glad she was gone. His infatuation with Tonya faded the more she talked. "Tell me about the library, Callie. With a name like the Henry Dorsey-Smythe Memorial Library, it must have quite a history behind it."

"It does." Setting the dishes down, she took her seat beside him. "The history goes back to James Thomas Lob, the founder of our town. For several years in the 1800s, he was a scout for settlers who moved west. But scouting was dangerous work."

Derek leaned back in his chair. "But James Lob wasn't of the same caliber as Kit Carson or Buffalo Bill or Jim Bridger. He never made a name for himself like those other guys."

"I always admired Buffalo Bill Cody," Jake put in. "He was a fascinating man. When the U.S. Army was fighting the Indians, he'd hunt buffalo so they'd have something to eat. That's how he got his nickname."

"Not the army, Dad," Callie said. "He supplied buffalo meat for the men who were building the transcontinental railroad."

Lane didn't want to get off the subject. "So Lob quit scouting and built this town?"

Callie nodded. "But it wasn't much of a town when he was living."

Jake laughed. "It was more like a few buildings with a big fence around them to keep out the Indians."

"Where does Henry Dorsey-Smythe come in?"

Tonya walked back into the room. "Okay, everyone. Mom is ready to cut the pies." She looked at Lane. "Do you want cherry or apple?"

"Uh. . .cherry would be great."

Tonya smiled. "Whipped cream?"

"Sure." Lane smiled back.

Tonya gazed at him another moment before she took the other orders.

Lane drummed his fingers on the table. As soon as he ate his pie, he would make some excuse to leave. Tomorrow he could ask Callie at the library about the history of Fort Lob. He wondered if there were any books about its founder. Fort Lob seemed to be one of those overlooked towns in the United States with a fascinating history.

On a more personal note, he had to think of some way to get Callie to remove her glasses. She might be as beautiful as her sister.

And a lot less suffocating.

# Chapter 6

On Monday morning, Callie reached beneath the library's checkout desk and pulled out a book to read. Business had been slow this morning. Only twelve people had entered the library, and ten had left. Of the two remaining people, Mrs. Anderson had settled in the conservatory. The other person was Cheyenne Wilkins, Callie's best friend since first grade. Cheyenne worked at the post office, but Monday was her day off.

Removing the bookmark from *Hearts Joined Together*, Callie began reading. This was a new romance novel she had ordered from Casper, and she was already in chapter nine. In a few minutes, she was deep into the story, but every time the library's front door opened, she looked up and noted who came in and who left. After a half hour, she had tallied seven people who had come and gone. Somehow she kept her mind on her book.

"Morning, Callie." Lane Hutchins closed the door and walked toward her.

"Oh!" She shoved the novel under the desk, not bothering with the bookmark, and hoped Lane hadn't noticed the title. She didn't want him to think she was interested in romance.

The sleeves of his blue denim shirt were rolled up to his elbows, and he held two hardcover books in one hand.

"Uh, hi, Lane. I guess you're back to finish your research on Yellowstone."

"Yeah, I should work on that." He laid the two volumes on the desk. "I went down to Cheyenne this morning and got a couple books for the library."

Callie looked at them—two new copies of *A History of Gunfights in America* by Herbert Dreyfuss. "Wow! These are expensive!" He must have bought them at a bookstore, and the retail price was $27.99 each.

He grinned. "It was nothing. Since the town council put a limit on the library's spending, I thought I'd donate these. At least the library will have two new books in its possession."

"Thank you, this is great. I'll have to catalog them." She hoped Miss Penwell would show more favor to Lane for his generous donation. Hmm. . . maybe that was why he bought them in the first place.

Lane folded his arms on the desk and leaned forward. "I'd like to learn more about the history of Fort Lob and this library. Are there any books on the subject?"

"A few." Callie found it hard to breathe with Lane this close. His muscled arms rested on the counter, and she stared at them. "Uh, there are some books in the Wyoming room upstairs, and we also have information on the Dorsey-Smythe family on the third floor."

"The third floor?" Lane stood up straight. "I didn't realize you had a reference room up there."

"We don't." Callie dropped her voice. "It's not open to the public. But if you're interested in the history of the library, we have some old documents, letters, and photographs."

His eyes opened wide. "I'd love to see those."

She glanced around. "Let me make sure no one needs me."

Cheyenne walked in from the conservatory. The green and orange broomstick skirt she wore swirled around her sandaled feet. "Are you busy, girlfriend?" She laid four books on the desk. "I want to check these out."

Callie had always thought Cheyenne was pretty with her blond hair and blue eyes, and her round face sported two deep dimples. Her dad called her "pleasingly plump," but Cheyenne moaned that she was fat.

"Hi, Lane." Cheyenne's eyes were almost level with his. "Nice to see you again."

"Uh, hi." His brow furrowed.

Callie motioned to her friend. "This is Cheyenne Wilkins. You met her yesterday at church. Her dad owns the grocery store."

"Oh yeah." Recognition dawned on his face. "I think I met the whole town yesterday. So, Cheyenne. . .were you named after the city?"

"Yeah, my mom liked the name. Of course, there was hippie blood in her family, so she had to name me something different." She laughed.

"You're looking rather *hip* yourself today." Callie pointed to Cheyenne's big hoop earrings and the psychedelic headband surrounding her blond hair. Topping her skirt, she wore a neon orange T-shirt.

Cheyenne laughed. "Last night I was cleaning out Mom's old sewing room and found a whole bunch of hippie stuff." She touched the headband. "This belonged to my aunt Vera. She was totally immersed in the hippie culture in the sixties."

Picking up the first of Cheyenne's books, Callie ran it under the scanner. Lane stood at the corner of the desk, perusing the cover of *A History of Gunfights in America*.

Callie picked up Cheyenne's second book. "I'll check these out and then take you upstairs, Lane. Today has been quiet, so I should have plenty of time to show you some things."

As if to prove her wrong, the door burst open and two moms with a passel of kids trooped in. The noise level rose ten decibels. They greeted Callie and Cheyenne. Right behind them, five teen girls walked in and ascended the stairs.

Callie's heart sank. "I'd better stick around the desk for a while, Lane. I'm the only librarian, so—"

"I'll watch the desk for you." Cheyenne turned to Lane. "I used to work here during high school. It'll be fun to check out books again."

Callie cocked her head toward the noisy children's section. "Do you think you can handle all the ragamuffins? Sometimes they check out lots of books."

"Sure." Cheyenne walked behind the desk. "Piece of cake."

"Okay, I'll try to hurry." Callie looked at Lane. "Follow me."

❧

Lane trailed behind Callie, his heart picking up its pace. *Herbert Dreyfuss might get a book out of this research.*

She led him up to the second floor then unlocked a door that held a sign reading EMPLOYEES ONLY. Another set of stairs took them to the third floor, where Callie opened a door into a small room with a slanted ceiling.

"It's warm up here." Lane walked to the window and looked out over the town of Fort Lob. "What a great view!"

"You can see for miles." Callie walked around old furniture, covered with sheets, and stopped in front of a cabinet with glass doors. She took a set of keys from her jeans pocket and unlocked it. Pulling out a large box, she set it on a nearby table. "These are old town documents and photos." She took another box from the cabinet and glanced at a label on the top. "These are letters written by the Lobs and Dorsey-Smythes."

"True history." A thrill ran through him as he opened the lid of the first box. Neatly packed inside were thick envelopes, yellowed with age, and old sepia photographs of Fort Lob in the early 1900s. "Wow, what a gold mine."

Callie went back to the cabinet, and Lane wondered what else that cabinet held. His gaze swung around, and he pointed to three trunks sitting on the floor. "What's in those trunks, Callie?"

"Those belonged to Mildred Dorsey-Smythe. She was the granddaughter of James Thomas Lob."

"And who was Henry Dorsey-Smythe?"

"Mildred's father. She turned the house into a library and named it after him. She felt her father never got any recognition in this town since her grandfather was so famous."

Lane nodded. When Callie left, he would take a look in those trunks. They might hold some valuable stuff. "When did Mildred die?"

"Almost fifty years ago. And let me tell you, Lane, this house is falling apart. I wish the town council would do something about it."

"Don't they have money to repair it?"

"They have money." She pulled another box from the cabinet then locked it and faced him. "But they *want* it to fall apart. Mildred willed the house to the town to use as a library, and according to her will, it must remain a library unless the town can't keep it in repair." She huffed out a breath. "I think the town council wants to condemn this place."

*Fascinating.* Lane watched Callie's mouth move as she talked, hardly hearing a word she said. But he heard enough. "This is a great library. I don't know why they want to get rid of it."

"They don't want to get rid of the library itself, but some of the towns-people think the mansion is an eyesore. They want to tear it down and build a modern building."

He nodded. "Progress, I suppose. Some people have no use for living history."

"I know. I've always loved this old house, and I love history."

"Me, too." He gazed at Callie, wishing he could see what was under that pair of glasses. What if she had a beautiful face like her sister? He liked her personality.

With a sigh, he turned to the table. "Is there a chair around here? I'd like to read these documents."

⁓

Callie checked out Mrs. Anderson's books and watched as she walked out the door. "We sure have been busy for a Monday."

"I'm glad I was here to help." Cheyenne perched on the stool behind the desk, pulling the edge of her orange T-shirt over her skirt. "You need more librarians, girl. Why doesn't the town council hire more people?"

"That's Miss Penwell's fault. She wants to be in control." Callie sighed. "I do wish I could get away sometimes. I love this place, but I live here for eight hours every day. Even though I get a lunch break, Miss Penwell makes me stay in the library. Sometimes I feel chained to this job."

"Well, I'm going to help you—at least on Mondays. You should get out of the building for an hour."

Lane walked up to the checkout counter. "I agree."

"Oh! Uh, hi, Lane." Callie felt her face heat up. How much had he over-heard? "Are you finished on the third floor?"

"No, but I needed a break." He glanced at his watch. "It's twelve thirty, and I feel...chained to the library." He grinned. "Why don't I take you out to lunch, Callie? We can visit that diner on Main Street."

*Is he asking me out?* A quiet excitement filled Callie, but at the same time, she knew she couldn't leave the premises. "I'd love to go with you, Lane, but I have to watch the desk here. My lunch break doesn't start until two, when Miss Penwell arrives."

Cheyenne studied Lane for a moment before her eyes cut to Callie. "Cool idea." She turned her back to Lane and winked at Callie. "You definitely need a break."

Callie opened her mouth, but Cheyenne turned toward Lane and contin-ued. "But you shouldn't take her to the Cattlemen's Diner, Lane—or anywhere else on Main Street, for that matter—unless you want all the locals to listen to your conversation and gossip about you."

He raised an eyebrow. "That bad, huh?"

Cheyenne flipped her blond hair behind her shoulder. "Oh, the gossips in this town are notorious. I could name several in our Main Street eating establishments, but I wouldn't want it to get back to them." She grinned.

"Okay, then. Where could we go for lunch?"

"I've got it!" Cheyenne slapped her hand on the desk. "Why don't you two go to Ray's?"

"Is that a restaurant?" Lane asked.

"Yep. Ray's Burger Retreat. It's a little hamburger place on Rattlesnake Road."

His lips parted. "Rattlesnake?"

Cheyenne laughed. "I never thought of it being located on Rattlesnake—that doesn't sound too appetizing, does it? But Ray has the best burgers around."

Callie placed a restraining hand on Cheyenne's arm. "Listen, I appreciate this, but I can't leave. I'm the only librarian—"

"Now, Callie." Cheyenne folded her arms. "We were just talking about that. Let me watch the library for you. I'm having the time of my life."

"Cheyenne. . ." Callie raised her hands then let them drop. "Your life must be totally boring."

Cheyenne ignored her. "You *know* you want a hamburger. Do something daring for once in your life."

Callie bit her lip. "Well, just so Miss Penwell doesn't find out."

"Who's going to tell her?" Cheyenne laid her hand on Callie's shoulder. "Take a break, girl. Remember how the old song goes. . ." She began to sing softly. "You deserve a break today, so get up and get away. . .to Ray's."

Lane grinned. "Is that how it goes?"

"Well, at least it rhymes. Now shoo!" Cheyenne waved her hand toward the door. "I can hold down the fort for an hour."

Callie breathed a sigh. "Thanks, Cheyenne. I owe you one."

"Oh, you'll owe me more than one."

Lane opened the door for her, and they walked outside. "Do you want to ride on my motorcycle, or do you have a car?"

"Well. . ." Callie pondered as they walked around the library to the back parking lot. She had never liked motorcycles. In fact, the fatalities on motorcycles were high in Wyoming. But Cheyenne's words whizzed through her mind. *Do something daring for once in your life.* "Um, let's take your motorcycle. That sounds fun." She was glad she was wearing jeans.

When she saw the huge motorcycle with HARLEY-DAVIDSON printed on the side, Callie took a deep breath and prayed for safety.

Lane straddled the bike and motioned to her. "Hop on. You can hang on to me if you want."

Callie managed to get on behind Lane, throwing her arms around his waist as he started the motorcycle. The powerful engine roared to life.

She tightened her grip, feeling his solid muscles beneath her arms.

He looked back at her with a grin. "You're not scared, are you?" he yelled.

"Um, not too much."

He laughed. "Don't worry, just lean when I lean, okay?" Not waiting for an answer, he squeezed something on the left handle, twisted the right handle, and they roared out of the parking lot and down Main Street.

A thrill raced through Callie as she hung on, trying to lean with him. Then reality hit.

*I'm going on a date with Lane Hutchins!*

# Chapter 7

Lane drove his Harley down the main street of Fort Lob, relishing the feel of Callie's arms around his waist. Neither wore a helmet, and he could imagine Callie's dark hair flying out behind her. *I want to get to know this girl.* Something about her attracted him. Must be the way her mouth moved. On the other hand, spending Sunday with the Brandt family made him realize how lonely he was.

When they arrived at Ray's Burger Retreat, he parked the bike and helped Callie dismount. He thought of how nervous she had looked when she got on. "You okay?" he asked.

She grinned. "That was fun. But I can't imagine riding all the way down to Cheyenne on this thing. It must get tiring."

"It does." They walked toward the small restaurant building that had huge plate glass windows on either side of the door. "I always wear my helmet when I get on the freeway, and that gets hot. So I'm hot and tired by the time I get to Cheyenne." He opened the door for her.

Callie introduced him to everyone in the restaurant, including Ray, who was surprisingly thin for being a chef, and the waitress named Beverly—a dowdy, middle-aged woman who wore rubber-soled shoes. He even met a dozen customers who were eating lunch. Lane shook hands all around. *You'd think we were at a family reunion.*

They finally settled at a corner booth and ordered the hamburger special. Beverly brought their drink order to the table and left.

For a few minutes, Callie talked about the motorcycle ride. "I always thought motorcycles were so dangerous. Only daredevils rode them."

He grinned. "Do I look like a daredevil?"

"Definitely not!" She smiled as she played with her straw paper. "I suppose it's a cheap form of transportation, although I can't believe what a huge motorcycle you have. It must have cost you a pretty penny."

He shrugged. "I wanted to get those saddlebags in the back for traveling, so I needed a bigger bike." Lane took a sip of his iced tea. He didn't tell her he had two cars, a Lexus and a Mazda, parked in his garage in Cheyenne. "What I can't believe is how you know everyone in this town." He nodded at the other customers.

Callie raised her eyebrows. "That's what happens when you grow up in a small place. But you said you grew up in Cheyenne with your aunt and uncle.

38

Are you an orphan?"

He nodded. "My parents were killed in a plane crash when I was six years old."

"Oh, Lane." Callie knit her brows. "I'm so sorry to hear that. Do your aunt and uncle still live in Cheyenne?"

"No, both of them are dead now." He didn't want to talk about his past. She might start asking questions that he didn't want to answer. "Tell me about yourself, Callie. Do you have any hopes and dreams for the future?"

A tiny smile tugged at her lips. "I do have a dream, but I've never told anyone about it."

Beverly, holding two large platters, approached their table. "Here's your order." She set a plate in front of each of them. "The mustard and ketchup are right there on the table. Do you need anything else?"

"This should do it for me." Lane glanced at the thick hamburger stacked with lettuce, onions, and tomato slices. "Smells delicious."

Callie nodded. "Thanks, Beverly." As soon as the waitress left, Callie leaned across the table. "Lane? Would you mind saying grace for us?"

*Grace?* He hadn't prayed over his food in seven years. He cleared his throat. "Sure."

She bowed her head.

He looked down at his plate. "Uh, Lord, thank You for this food." He kept his voice low, almost to a mumble. "Bless it to our bodies. Amen."

"Amen," Callie echoed. She took her napkin and placed it in her lap then grabbed the ketchup bottle.

Lane picked up the mustard, wondering what she thought of his prayer. At the family dinner yesterday, her dad had prayed for seven or eight minutes. Lane thought the man would never stop, but at the same time, Jake Brandt seemed to know God personally—the way Lane used to.

But he didn't want to think about his spiritual problems. The safest thing to do was change the subject. "So, Callie, what's this dream you have?"

She picked up her knife and cut her hamburger in half. "Well, I love to read, as you know, and I've always wanted to—" She glanced around and lowered her voice. "I've always wanted to have my own bookstore. It's been my desire for years, and I've been saving up to rent a storefront in town."

"That's great." He smiled at her. "Dream big, Callie."

She shrugged. "I don't know if it will happen, but I feel in my heart that it's the Lord's will. I already know what the name of my bookstore will be, and the idea came straight from the Lord, too." She leaned forward, and the light from the window reflected off her glasses. "For the Love of Books. That's the name of it." She sat back. "It's an acronym."

"An acronym?"

"Think about it." She smiled, biting her bottom lip at the same time.

"For the Love of Books." Lane pronounced it slowly. "Oh. *Ft. Lob*. That's cool."

With a nod, she picked up her hamburger. "I'm especially interested in history. I'd like to sell books about Wyoming. Our state has such a fascinating past—the scouts and trailblazers, the battles between the army and the Indians, the Oregon Trail, the Pony Express, the transcontinental railroad...."

He laughed. "You're a walking encyclopedia."

Her face tinged pink, and she took a bite of her hamburger.

For the next few minutes, they ate in silence. As Lane chewed on his burger, he also chewed on what Callie wanted to do. He wished he could help her. But a bookstore in Fort Lob? Would she have enough customers?

He set his half-eaten hamburger on the plate. "You know, Callie, I'm wondering if you should tweak your dream a bit."

She frowned. "What do you mean?"

"I like the bookstore idea, but I think you should expand it to include a museum."

"A museum? But Wyoming has lots of museums."

"Not about James Thomas Lob." He leaned forward. "Look at all that stuff in the library. It's just sitting there, collecting dust. You could bring it to life, Callie."

He noticed a shiver run over her. "I would love to do that."

"You could set up a museum and sell Wyoming books in the gift shop." He shrugged. "You'd still have your bookstore."

"That would be a fantastic project—if I could save enough money." She shook her head. "But that might be too big of a dream for me."

～

*I can't afford a museum!*

Callie sighed under her breath. She wasn't sure she could afford a bookstore. But a museum would have to be housed in a building by itself on its own property, and she didn't have that kind of money. Then she'd have to get permission from the town council since Fort Lob owned all those things in the library, and she didn't want a job where she would be accountable to them.

Beverly came to their table. "How about some dessert? Our special today is hot peach cobbler with a scoop of ice cream."

Callie shook her head. "I'm so full, I can't—"

"How about just the ice cream, in a cone?" Lane raised his eyebrows at Callie then turned to Beverly. "We'll take two cones. A large vanilla for me."

They both looked at Callie.

"Uh, okay. I'll take a chocolate cone—small."

Beverly nodded. "One large vanilla and one small chocolate. Be right back."

While they waited, Lane waxed eloquent about the museum. He talked about the photos of the town, the family's history, the old furniture. Callie listened, resting her chin in her hand and enjoying his enthusiasm. Enjoying *him*. But at the same time, she knew the museum idea would never happen. That was certainly a pipe dream, if ever there was one.

Beverly came back with their cones and left.

Lane took a few licks. "This is really good ice cream."

"Ray makes his own. He's famous for it, actually." Callie took a bite and adjusted her glasses. "This has been a wonderful break, Lane." Spending time with Lane and getting to know him was the best part.

"My pleasure." He licked his ice cream into a point. "Like Cheyenne said, you deserved a break." He leaned across the table and lowered his voice. "You needed to rest those eyes."

Lane poked the point of his ice cream at her glasses. Suddenly she saw nothing through the left lens but a big white spot.

"Hey!" She whipped them off and glanced at the damage before looking up at him. "You did that on purpose."

He grinned. "Yep. Just wanted to see your pretty face." His smile faded. "And you are pretty, Callie—even prettier than I thought."

Heat rose in her face. She wasn't sure if she should thank him for the compliment or yell at him for smudging her glasses. But even though he was blurry and out of focus, the look he gave her as their eyes met stopped her heart and stilled her tongue.

Flustered, she glanced around. "I need something to clean my glasses, but. . ." She scooted to the end of the booth. "Guess I'll have to go to the ladies' room."

"Wait!" Lane held out his hand. "Give them to me. I messed them up; I should fix them."

Callie handed her glasses over. Lane looked at the splotch of ice cream residing on the left lens and pulled a napkin from the holder at the end of the table.

"No, Lane, don't use a napkin. Paper will scratch the lens. I'll ask Beverly to get us—"

"Don't bother." He swiped his thumb across the glass, smearing the ice cream. "I'll just mess it up good, and we'll clean it later." He grinned as he dropped her glasses into his shirt pocket.

She raised her eyebrows. "You're not giving them back?"

"Not yet." Lane folded his arms on the table and leaned toward her. "Why don't you get contacts? You have such pretty eyes, and those glasses are hiding your beauty."

She drew in a surprised breath. Did he say *"beauty"*?

A warm feeling stirred inside Callie. No one had ever told her that before, especially not a handsome, single guy like Lane Hutchins. She leaned across the table toward him. "Well, I, uh. . ." She gazed into his eyes.

He gazed back.

Finally she blinked. Several times. "Um. . .what was the question?"

He cleared his throat and sat back. "Contacts? For your eyes?"

"Oh yeah, contacts." Looking down, she sighed. "My eye doctor said they wouldn't work for me."

"So you're stuck with glasses forever?" Lane did not look happy.

"Not necessarily." She shrugged. "Although I might as well be stuck. He said laser eye surgery would work and I could have twenty-twenty vision, but my medical insurance won't pay for it."

Beverly came by the table. "Here's your bill. Well, my goodness, Callie. I've never seen you without your glasses. Don't you look pretty." She picked up their plates. "I never realized how much you look like Tonya."

As she left, Lane winked at Callie. "I was thinking the same thing. But you're even prettier."

Did he say *"prettier"*? Feeling warmth rise in her face, she squinted at her watch. "Oh no! It's after one thirty. Cheyenne is going to have my head."

"I doubt that." Lane stood, took out his wallet, and threw a couple of bills on the table. "She seemed to be enjoying her stint as librarian."

They walked out the door and straddled Lane's motorcycle.

"Are you going to give my glasses back?" Callie circled her arms around his waist.

"Maybe. Someday." He started the cycle, and it thundered to life.

They flew down Rattlesnake Road. Callie held on to Lane tightly, loving the feel of the wind blowing her hair back. And now it fluttered against her eyelashes. Her heart gave a happy leap. Lane thought she was pretty, even prettier than her sister.

*Oh Lord,* she prayed, *please let something good come from this.* Did she dare pray that Lane would want to marry her?

But was he a Christian? She just assumed he was, but his prayer for the food didn't give her any confidence about his relationship with God.

Lane slowed down to turn onto Main Street, and Callie smiled at the tall spots of color on the sidewalk who waved to her, even though she wasn't sure who those people were. The entire population of Fort Lob was probably gossiping about them. After all, a person could hardly sneak through town on a motorcycle, especially on Main Street.

When they arrived at the library, Lane pulled up before the door. "I'll drop you off here, and you can let Cheyenne leave."

Callie dismounted. "*Now* will you give my glasses back?"

He gazed at her eyes a moment before he winked. "Not yet." Revving the motor, he guided the cycle to the back parking lot.

Callie laughed out loud as she walked up the library steps using the handrail as a guide and pulled open the front door. She stepped inside, and her smile froze.

The navy blue blob standing behind the checkout desk couldn't be Cheyenne. For one thing, Cheyenne had been wearing an orange T-shirt, and for another thing, this blob was as thin as a skeleton.

"Miss Brandt!" Miss Penwell's voice rang out across the entryway, grating on Callie's nerves. "Where in the world have you been?"

Even without her glasses, Callie knew Miss Penwell's lips were pursed.

# Chapter 8

Lane jogged up the library steps. Callie's glasses jiggled in his shirt pocket, and he smiled. *She doesn't even realize how pretty she is.* He reached for the library's door handle. How could he give Callie the money for laser eye surgery without offending her? It couldn't be that expensive, probably a few thousand dollars. *I'll think of something.*

He stepped inside and stopped short.

"I should have you fired!" Miss Penwell's arms were folded against her thin chest.

Callie stood in front of the checkout counter, her head bowed.

"You are not to leave this building during your shift, Miss Brandt, and you know that."

Lane strode up to the desk. "Now just a minute." He kept his voice low.

"You!" Miss Penwell's gray eyes widened. "You are the reason! It's because of you that Miss Brandt is in trouble. She knows better than to leave the premises, and you were the devil's agent to cause her to—"

"Listen!" Lane held up both hands, feeling his ire rise. He glanced at Callie's profile. Her head was still bowed, her face pale. Obviously she wasn't going to defend herself.

He took a deep breath. "Miss Penwell, we need to discuss this calmly, like three rational human beings."

"There is nothing to discuss. You dragged my employee to Ray's—"

"All right, Miss Penwell, I apologize. This whole thing was my fault. Please don't fire Callie over it."

Callie looked up at him. "Lane—"

"No, Callie. I shouldn't have asked you to leave your job." He glanced at Miss Penwell, noting that her lips were pressed together. "It won't happen again; you have my word on that."

"No, it won't happen, young man, because you will not set foot in my library again. I forbid you to come here. No more books for you. I won't have my employees—" She stopped as two older men walked up to the desk. "Bruce! Vern." She frowned. "How long have you two been standing there?"

Lane recognized the men who had liked the article by Herbert Dreyfuss the first time he had seen Callie. *I hope they're on my side.*

The more dignified man, the one from Scotland, stepped forward. "We've been here all afternoon, Lucille. We heard you dismiss Cheyenne—"

"The whole library heard you." The other man pointed to his hearing aid. "Even me."

Callie winced.

The Scottish man drummed his fingers on the desk. "Lucille, I've already discussed this issue with you."

"What issue?" Miss Penwell frowned at him. "As I recall, Bruce, I have never had to deal with an errant employee who left the premises because some boy—"

"Lucille." Bruce lowered his voice as he leaned toward her. "I'm talking about your temper. You cannot prohibit people from using the library." He motioned toward Lane. "And this is not the first time I've heard you doing that. The town council discussed your behavior at our last—"

"My behavior! Why, Bruce MacKinnon! How dare you say that my behavior is anything but outstanding? In fact, exemplary. I've been running this library for thirty-nine years."

The other man spoke up. "And the council thinks it's time you retire."

"Vern, I'll handle this." Bruce turned to Miss Penwell.

"Retire?" Miss Penwell's voice rose with her words. "And just what would I do if I retired? Sit around my house twiddling my thumbs?"

Bruce sighed. "Lucille, you're seventy-two years old—"

"I am not!"

He raised his eyebrows. "You're the same age as me."

Miss Penwell pursed her lips before she spoke. "I'm seventy-one."

"Okay, seventy-one."

"And I'm in excellent health. Excellent, I tell you!" She waved her hands in the air as if she could stop the discussion. "I do not need to retire. Now, if you'll excuse me, gentlemen, I'll let Miss Brandt take over." She stalked toward the main room.

"But, Lucille—" Bruce stalked after her. "We are not through discussing this."

Without a word, Miss Penwell rounded the corner, and a few seconds later a door slammed behind her.

Bruce strode into the main room. "Now, Lucille, just a minute. Open this door." His voice faded.

Vern shook his head. "We'll never get rid of her." He walked to the main entrance. "Someone will have to kill her before she stops working at this library." He exited.

Callie turned her beautiful eyes up to Lane. "Thanks for defending me, but you didn't need to apologize. I made the decision to go with you."

"And I'm glad you did, no matter what Miss Penwell says."

She sighed. "Poor Cheyenne. I'm going to have to call her."

Lane reached into his shirt pocket. "Here are your glasses. Sorry I didn't clean them."

She gave him a faint smile. "Thanks, Lane. And thanks for lunch. It was fun, even though I had to pay the piper."

He frowned. "Does Miss Penwell have the authority to fire you?"

"No. The town council hired me, and I know they won't fire me. Actually, they've been trying to get rid of Miss Penwell for a couple months. She's been so nasty lately." Callie shrugged. "I don't know what will happen now."

"Well, she's digging her own grave, if you ask me." He glanced up the stairs. "I should finish that research on Yellowstone. Can I check out five books on my card?"

Callie walked behind the desk. "You can check out as many books as you want."

⁓

"Cheyenne, I'm so sorry you had to go through that." Callie spoke into the library phone. "That must have been embarrassing when Miss Penwell yelled at you."

"No problem. Besides, it was my bad. I practically pushed you two out the door." Cheyenne paused. "Are you sure it's okay to talk right now?"

"Yeah, no one's in the building except Lane, and he's upstairs in the Wyoming room."

"I bet Miss Penwell scared off all the patrons with her tantrum." Cheyenne laughed. "By the way, how did lunch go?"

Callie smiled for the first time since she entered the library. "It was wonderful." She lowered her voice. "I'll call you when I get home after work and tell you all about it, but I think he likes me."

"Oh, Callie!" Cheyenne squealed into the phone. *She* didn't have to keep her voice down. "I'm so excited! I can't wait until you give me the entire scoop. I just *know* you two were made for each other, and I'm already praying."

"Thanks." Callie took a deep breath. "I hope we do end up together, but I want to make sure it's the Lord's will. Right now I don't have a perfect peace about it because I'm not sure if he's a Christian." She adjusted her glasses, which she had cleaned. "I think—"

Lane descended the stairs, his arms stacked with books.

"Oh, I have to go, Cheyenne. Talk to you later." She hung up the phone as Lane approached the desk.

"Seven books, Callie." He set the pile down and placed his library card on top. "We'll show that old Miss Penwell who's boss."

Several people entered the library as Callie checked out his books. She greeted them, hoping they hadn't heard about the afternoon fiasco.

Lane made a trip to his motorcycle to place the books in the saddlebags. Coming back inside, he folded his arms on the counter and leaned toward her. "Callie, I want to apologize for getting you in trouble."

She waved away his apology. "It wasn't your fault."

"Yes, it was. I shouldn't have asked you out for lunch. In fact, I'm going to make amends. Would you go out to dinner with me on Friday night?"

Her heart leaped into her throat. "I'd love to."

"Good." He grinned then reached up and pulled off her glasses.

Startled, Callie stepped back. "Lane—"

"Just wanted one more look." His smile faded as he gazed into her eyes.

She gazed back, a wistful sigh escaping her lips.

The front door opened, and a group of kids walked in.

Lane set her glasses on the desk. "Until Friday." He strode to the door, then he turned and winked at her before stepping outside.

At least she thought he winked. His face was so blurry she could barely make out his eyes.

*Friday night.* Callie hugged herself. But this was only Monday, and Friday seemed to stretch into eternity. *Oh Lord, please give me peace about Lane.*

Donning her glasses, Callie reached for the phone and dialed Cheyenne's number. This was too good to keep until after work.

# Chapter 9

It was a trying week for Callie.

She didn't see Lane at all, but she saw plenty of Miss Penwell. Instead of arriving each day at two o'clock as she normally did, the head librarian came in at one o'clock on Tuesday and criticized everything Callie did. Fortunately, the library was closed on Wednesday, but on Thursday, Miss Penwell arrived at noon, spewing out more criticisms until Callie left at six.

Before going to the library on Friday morning, Callie decided to fortify herself with a cup of coffee at the Trailblazer Café on Main Street. It wouldn't surprise her if Miss Penwell arrived at ten o'clock today. She probably heard that Callie had a date with Lane after work. In fact, Callie expected the whole town knew about their date by now, thanks to Tonya and her big mouth.

A lot of the locals, mainly retired men, met at the Trailblazer for breakfast every morning. Today, eight of them—old-timers she had known her entire life, including Bruce and Vern—sat at two tables in the corner. Along with swilling coffee refills, most of the men perused a copy of *The Scout*, Fort Lob's newspaper.

Vern spotted her as she walked by. "Hey, Callie! Did you see the column in today's paper by Herbert Dreyfuss?"

She stopped beside their table. "I haven't read this week's column yet."

"Another great article about Wyoming."

"Yeah." Floyd DeWitt pointed to the paper. "We've been discussing it all morning."

"Really?" Callie folded her arms. "What's it about?"

"Yellowstone National Park."

"Yellowstone?"

Vern nodded. "Would you believe, Dreyfuss says it's one of the best vacation spots in the country. And he tells you all about it." He chuckled. "That Dreyfuss is a smart one, just like I always said."

Callie bid the men good day and left to get her coffee.

*Yellowstone*. What a coincidence.

❧

At 6:30 that evening, Lane guided his rumbling motorcycle down the long driveway toward the Brandt farmhouse. He and Callie had agreed to leave his cycle at her house and drive her car to Lusk for dinner. Even though Lusk was a good half hour away, it was closer than any other town, and they certainly didn't want to eat in Fort Lob, where everyone could watch them.

To be honest, he was tired of Fort Lob's gossip. If it weren't for Callie, he would have moved to Lusk or Pinedale by now.

Approaching the farmhouse, he noticed Jake Brandt sitting on the porch. Lane's stomach lurched. *He's going to grill me about dating his daughter.* After all, what did Mr. Brandt know about Lane Hutchins?

Except for taking Callie out to lunch on Monday, Lane hadn't been on a date in years. He'd forgotten how much parents could worry about their daughters. He parked his motorcycle beside the house and dismounted.

"Howdy, Lane!" Jake called from one of the wicker chairs. "Come on up and have a seat. Callie should be out in a few minutes."

Lane climbed the three steps to the porch. "Thanks." He took the other wicker chair and drummed his fingers on the arms. *This is it.*

"Great weather for a Friday night, ain't it?" Jake stretched his long legs in front of him and crossed them at the ankles. "I like to sit here most evenings and watch the sunset. Course, it doesn't set until eight or eight thirty this time of year, but every sunset is spectacular. God's handiwork."

Lane relaxed. Maybe Jake wouldn't grill him after all. "I hear you're a sheep rancher."

"Yep, fifth generation. My great-great-grandparents were homesteaders in the 1880s. I have a good spread here—two thousand acres and five hundred sheep."

"Wow! That's huge."

Jake seemed pleased. "Aw, that's nothing. My grandfather owned eight thousand acres with horses, sheep, and cattle. But it's hard to care for such a large ranch. My dad sold most of the land and animals, concentrating only on sheep. I still have a few horses."

Lane gazed at the rolling hills that stretched toward the horizon. "So, all this land is yours?"

"As far as your eye can see. I plan to pass the ranch on to my son Derek. He has a college degree in range management, you know, and he's helped me with some new methods."

The front door opened, and Callie stepped onto the porch.

Lane's heartbeat quickened. She was beautiful. The summery yellow print dress she wore emphasized her soft curves and made her dark, curly hair look even darker. He hardly noticed her glasses.

Lane felt underdressed in his shirt and jeans. Good thing he hadn't worn his I Visited Devil's Tower T-shirt, which he had considered doing. But he'd decided against it since he wanted to have a shirt pocket available. . . .

She closed the door behind her. "Sorry you had to wait, Lane."

"No problem." He stood, wanting to tell her how nice she looked, but her dad's presence stopped him.

"Here's the key to my car." She handed him a set of keys, and a whiff of sweet fragrance drifted toward him. "It's around the back." She descended the porch stairs.

Jake got to his feet. "Have a good time, you two."

"Thanks." Lane smiled as he shook the older man's hand. He liked Jake.

"We will, Dad." Callie rounded the corner of the house. "And don't wait up for me," she called.

*Hmm. . . .* Lane followed her to the car. The evening looked bright.

∽

"You move to a different state every three months?" Callie's head spun.

She sat on the passenger side of her car, secretly thrilled to see Lane behind the wheel. Since he obviously didn't own a car, she pictured this little Honda as their family car when they got married—*if* they got married.

"But, Lane, how can you move so often? I always thought military people had it rough moving every three years. But three months?" Only fugitives did that.

*Fugitives?* Callie glanced at his profile. What if he *was* a fugitive trying to escape the law? She knew so little about him.

"I love moving." He grinned. "I've lived in sixteen states in the past five years, and every place was in a small town. It's been an interesting adventure, and I enjoy the change of scenery." He shrugged. "If I cover all fifty states, I figure it will take me another eight or nine years, at least."

Callie's buoyant spirit sank. *I hate moving.* "Is there a method to your madness?"

Lane's expression turned serious. "It's research, actually. By the time that fiftieth state is covered, I plan to write a book about my experiences. I'm going to call it *Living in Small-Town America.*" He glanced at her. "How does that title grab you?"

"Sounds interesting. . . ." *He sure has big dreams.* "But I've heard it's really hard to get published. Of course, you have to write the book first, and that's a lot of work."

"Oh? Do you have personal experience?"

"Well. . ." She thought about that half-finished novel in the notebook on her closet shelf, languishing next to the manuscript she had started five years ago about Fort Lob's history. "Nothing to speak of."

They entered the town of Lusk, and Callie pointed ahead. "Turn left at that stop sign. I love the Italian restaurant on West Second Street." She was glad to change the subject and decided she would enjoy this evening with Lane, whether she married him or not. "It's called Mama's Kitchen, and it has great Italian food."

∽

"You know what? This restaurant has great Italian food." Lane took another bite. He had never tasted such good lasagna in his life.

A mural of Italy's wine country covered the wall beside their two-person table, and a tiny lamp, set on the edge, shed a circle of yellow light on the white linen tablecloth.

"I guess 'Mama' is a good cook." Callie adjusted her glasses. "They always give their customers such big portions. I have enough Eggplant Parmigiana on my plate for three people, and we *have* to save room for dessert. Mama's Kitchen has the most delicious desserts."

"Ice cream cones?"

A blush spread over her face. "Much better than that, but please don't throw a spoonful of tiramisu at my left lens."

He grinned. "If you recall, I don't use that ploy anymore." He reached across the table and snatched off her glasses.

"Lane!" She covered her face with both hands and peeked at him through her fingers.

He dropped her glasses in his shirt pocket. "Much better." He gazed into her eyes, startled again by how pretty she was. *I have to get her that laser eye surgery.*

She sighed as she dropped her hands back to the table, and he could tell she was trying not to smile. "What am I going to do with you?"

*Kiss me?* "Uh, I don't know. . . .I'll think of something."

⁓

Callie felt completely lost without her glasses. Everything was a blur, even her food.

She swallowed a bite of her eggplant. "Could I ask you a personal question?" She glanced up and blinked a couple times, unsuccessfully trying to bring his face into focus.

He gazed a moment at her eyes. "Anything."

Callie hesitated. *The power of a woman's eyelashes*—one of her sister's pet phrases. No wonder Tonya batted her eyes at every new guy she met. "Um, first of all, could I have my glasses back? I really can't see anything."

"Oh." He dipped into his pocket and pulled them out. "Sorry to tease you. Guess I'm just an insensitive cad."

She smiled as she took her glasses. "No, you're not." Noticing a smudge, she wiped the lenses with the hem of her dress.

Lane leaned forward. "So, what's the personal question?"

"I was wondering about your job. What do you do for a living?" There, she asked him. His job status had bothered her since she'd met him. "When you first came to the library, Miss Penwell asked what you did, and you told her you were an insurance salesman."

He frowned. "I did?"

"That's what she told me." Callie put her glasses back on, thankful Lane was in focus once again.

He pushed a bite of lasagna around on his plate. "Oh, I remember now. I told her I was an *agent*." He laid his fork down. "But an agent can be anything—a manager, an investment broker, a real estate person, an insurance man, a book agent, a spy. . . ." He tapped his chin thoughtfully. "I'll let you guess which one I am."

"You're definitely a spy."

He threw back his head and laughed so loud that other diners turned to look at him. "Right you are, Callie."

"Oh sure." She couldn't help but smile. "But really, Lane, tell me about yourself. You know so much about me. I've told you about my family, my church, my job, and even my dreams, but I hardly know anything about you." She touched his hand, which was resting on the table across from her own. "Tell me all about Lane Hutchins."

He shrugged, and his smile faded to a frown. "I have no family, no friends. I'm just a drifter, Callie." He looked down, picked up her hand, and cradled it in both of his own. "When my parents died, my aunt and uncle raised me." He looked up. "I've already told you that."

She nodded. "How did the accident happen?"

"My dad owned a Cessna, a small airplane. He had a pilot's license, and he was always jetting my mom around the country. They took a lot of vacations—without me."

Callie pictured the young couple, too busy with their own lives to take care of the little boy who needed them. She squeezed his hand. "That's sad."

"It would have been, except for Aunt Betty and Uncle Herb. I stayed with them so often, they might as well have been my parents. When the plane crashed, I was actually excited I could live with them permanently." He paused. "I've often wondered what would have happened to me if my parents had lived."

"What do you mean?"

"Uncle Herb, my mother's brother, married Aunt Betty late in his life, so they were too old to have kids. But Aunt Betty was so motherly. She loved children, and whenever I was with her, I was her son."

Callie smiled, nodding for him to continue.

"The most important thing was that she was a Christian, and she led Uncle Herb to the Lord before they married. Then, when I was nine years old, Uncle Herb led me to the Lord."

Relief flooded through her. "That's wonderful!"

Lane squeezed her hand. "I still remember him sitting on my bed that night. I was scared for some reason, scared to die. He told me about Jesus, who died in my place so I could go to heaven. And I believed."

"I'm so glad, Lane." Callie bit her bottom lip, willing the tears not to come.

"Me, too." He gazed at her. "But if I had grown up with my parents, I doubt if I would be saved today." He sighed. "Not that it's made much of a difference lately."

Callie widened her eyes. "How can you say that? Being saved makes all the difference in the world. It's going from death to life."

"I know." He looked down at their hands. "I used to be on fire for God. Back in high school, I was the student leader of our youth group, and I led a prayer meeting after school. But when Aunt Betty got cancer, I started cooling off toward spiritual things."

It looked like he would say more, but he stopped.

Callie spoke softly. "How old were you when she passed away?"

"Nineteen. For thirteen years, she'd been my mom, and it really hurt when she died. Uncle Herb told me not to blame God, but God could have healed her, and He didn't." Lane paused. "I started drifting away from the Lord. At least that's what Uncle Herb told me. And then, three years later, he died. Very suddenly."

"How did he—"

"Heart attack." Lane blew out a breath. "Like I told you, I'm all alone in the world, Callie." A resentful tone crept into his voice. "You have your parents, grandparents, aunts and uncles, brothers and sisters—I have no one. And I've always asked, *Why?* Why did God take every single relative I had, leaving me to navigate through life alone?"

Callie laid her other hand on top of his. "I wish I knew, Lane."

"At my uncle's funeral, someone told me that God was trying to get my attention." For a moment, he pressed his lips into a firm line. When he spoke, his voice was bitter. "Well, if that's the way God is—if He has to kill all my loved ones to get my attention, I don't want anything to do with a God like that."

She caught her breath. *How can he believe that?* At the same time, she prayed for God's guidance in saying the right thing to help him. "Lane, the Lord doesn't work that way. He has a plan and a purpose for each life. Evidently your aunt's and uncle's work on earth were finished, so He took them home. God didn't cut their lives short just to punish you or to get your attention."

"Well, maybe not." He caressed the back of her hand with his thumb.

She clamped her hands on his to stop the motion. "The Lord has a reason for everything He does, Lane. The Bible says, 'It is God which worketh in you both to will and to do of his good pleasure.' He loves you, and He wants to guide your life." She shook her head. "Whatever you do, don't become bitter against God."

"Bitter." Lane almost spat out the word. "I never thought about that before, but yeah, I guess I'm bitter at God."

The more Callie found out about Lane, the more she realized she didn't know him at all. She withdrew her hands from his and slipped them in her lap. "I'll pray for you, Lane. Only the Lord can heal your heart."

He gazed at her a moment. "You're a good woman, Callie." Sighing, he pushed his plate away. "I know I have a bad attitude. Sometimes I have such a longing to get over it and get right with God."

"Then get it right." She leaned forward. "The Lord is waiting for you to come back to Him. He'll welcome you with open arms."

"Like the prodigal son?"

She nodded. "Yes, just like that."

He stared at his plate a moment before he looked up at her. Finally he smiled. "How about if we order some of that tiramisu?"

As Lane drove Callie home, he couldn't get rid of the heavy feeling in the pit of his stomach. She had managed to churn up the bitter feelings he had buried in the deepest part of his heart. He ground his teeth together. *This is not the time to think about my problems.*

He glanced at Callie. She sat on the passenger side, looking out at the rolling hills of Wyoming as they drove north on Highway 270. She'd been quiet on the way home, and he wanted to draw her out again. He loved to hear her talk. Somehow her smooth voice made him forget about the emptiness in his heart. And tonight, when he dropped her off at her front door. . .

In the west, the sun lit the expansive sky in a spectacular array of reds and oranges, and the subject of the next article he wanted to write popped into his mind. "Give me your opinion, Callie."

She turned toward him. "My opinion on what?"

He frowned, trying to strike a thoughtful pose. "What do you think about overpopulation in the world?"

"Overpopulation?" She squinted at him like she thought he was crazy. "Where did that thought come from?"

"I was looking out at all this barren land, these hills covered with nothing but sagebrush and scraggly grass. It got me thinking how some folks are screaming about overpopulation. They say the world is too crowded."

She laughed. "You don't have to worry about that here. You could fit an entire third-world country in the state of Wyoming and still have room to spare."

"Hey, that's good." He grinned at her. "I'll remember that. You know, I like these western states. They're huge compared to the ones out East."

"Wyoming is the ninth-largest state in the Union, and it has the fewest people per square mile, except for Alaska."

"Why, thank you for that tidbit of information, Miss Librarian. Maybe I should pick your brain instead of doing research."

She blushed. "I'm really not a walking encyclopedia."

"Close enough." He drove past the sign that read WELCOME TO FORT LOB; POPULATION 576. "Are there really more than five hundred people in Fort Lob?"

Callie shook her head. "Not anymore. That sign is at least twenty years old."

"Why don't they put up a new sign?"

She shrugged. "The town council never saw the need. Most of the people on the council are old, retired men who grew up here, although every once in a while a woman will get elected." She looked at him. "Miss Penwell served on the council for eight years."

"Really?" He smirked. "I can just imagine the arguments she sparked in their meetings."

"I don't know about that, but the library thrived while she was sitting on the council. The mansion was in great shape, and we had plenty of new books. In fact, Miss Penwell bought a lot of the books in the Wyoming room. She even talked the council into getting that state-of-the-art computerized circulation system."

"You worked at the library then?"

"I was in high school and worked during the summers with Cheyenne." She grinned. "We had a lot of fun."

"Cheyenne seems to be a fun person."

Callie nodded. "She's a rascal. And she's not afraid of anything."

"Not even Miss Penwell?"

"Nope. Cheyenne got us in trouble a few times while we were working at the library, and to be honest, Miss Penwell doesn't like her. Of course, Miss Penwell has very few friends, but that's the way she wants it, evidently."

"Is she dating anyone?"

Callie looked at him. "Miss Penwell? She probably hasn't had a date in fifty years."

"No, I meant Cheyenne."

Her eyes widened. "Are you interested?"

He laughed. "Would it make any difference to you?" He winked, letting her know he was teasing.

A faint blush stole across her cheeks. "Actually, Cheyenne has been absolutely in love with my brother Derek since she was a senior in high school."

"Absolutely?"

"Oh yes." She sighed. "I wish Derek would marry her, but he's never been interested in girls. He's only dated five times in his life, with five different girls, and every time it's been because one of his four sisters pushed a girl his way."

Lane threw back his head and laughed. "You'll probably have to push him to the altar."

"We've been trying! But personally, I think he has a commitment phobia.

He says he's not getting married until he's forty."

Lane couldn't imagine waiting that long himself. Then again, the age of forty was only eleven years away. He might as well wait since he wanted to live in every state in the Union. On the other hand. . .he glanced at Callie. *"When you meet the right girl, you'll know."* Another piece of advice from Uncle Herb. And Callie seemed more right than any other girl he had ever met. But would she be willing to marry him and move every three months?

Continuing their pleasant small talk, Lane drove through town and turned right on Antelope Road, driving the seven miles out to the Brandt sheep ranch. At THE ROCKING B archway, he drove down the long drive toward the house and pulled to a stop beside his motorcycle. They ascended the three porch steps together.

Callie turned to him. "Thanks so much, Lane. I had a wonderful evening."

"So did I." He faced her, standing close. When the moment was right, he planned to take her into his arms and kiss her.

She placed her hand on his arm. "I hope you think about getting back into fellowship with God. Having the right relationship with the Lord is so important."

He raised his eyebrows. At the moment, thoughts about God were the furthest thing from his mind. "Uh, sure. I appreciate all your advice. Um, you know, Callie. . ." He moved closer, reached up, and touched her face—just as the front door burst open.

"Callie!" Tonya stood framed in the doorway. "You're finally home!"

Startled, Lane took a step back. Callie folded her arms, looking perturbed.

Tonya continued, a worried frown on her beautiful face. "Oh, Callie, you need to comfort Mom. Aunt Sara called, and Grandma took a fall."

Immediately Callie looked concerned. "What happened?"

"They think she broke her hip. She's in the hospital." Tonya's porcelain skin was pale. "Mom's packing to leave right now."

"Tonight? But Casper's a hundred miles away." Callie glanced at Lane before looking back at Tonya. "Well, she can't go by herself. I'll go with her."

"No, Mom doesn't want either of us to go since we both have to work tomorrow. Derek is going to drive her." Tonya glanced at Lane for the first time. "Sorry to bother you two, but they're leaving in the next few minutes." She went back in the house, closing the door behind her.

An awkward moment followed.

Lane was struck again with Callie's huge family and how they took care of each other. A seed of jealousy sprouted in his heart. "Sorry to hear about your grandmother. I hope she's okay."

Callie nodded. "I need to talk to Mom." She turned the door handle. "Would you like to come in?"

This was certainly not the way he had envisioned the end of the evening.

"Uh, I think I'd better be going." He walked down the steps.

"Lane, are you sure?" Her eyes widened behind her glasses. "I just want to see Mom off, and then we can talk out here on the porch."

He shook his head. "You need to be with your family. See you later, Callie. Thanks for a great evening." He jogged to his motorcycle.

His soul was in turmoil as he started the engine. He wished he were part of a big family like this one. Of course if he married Callie. . . He shook his head. She'd never marry him unless he got rid of his bitterness and got right with God. And he wasn't ready to do that. At least, not yet.

Making a U-turn, he glanced back at the house. Callie stood in the doorway. She waved. He waved back then fed the cycle with gas and gunned down the driveway—away from Callie and back to his empty, lonely life.

# Chapter 10

When Callie drove past the front of the library on Monday morning, she noticed Bruce MacKinnon and Vern Snyder talking outside with another man. The man wore a uniform with his name embroidered on his shirt pocket, but she couldn't read it from her car. He pointed to a clipboard as he talked.

*He must not be from around here.*

Driving to the parking lot in the back, she spotted a white utility truck parked under the oak tree. On the side panel were painted the words WILSON AND JEFFRIES, BUILDING INSPECTIONS, DOUGLAS, WYOMING.

A building inspector!

Callie parked her car and entered the library through the back door. As she approached the checkout desk, the front door opened. Evidently, Bruce had unlocked the door for the building inspector early this morning. Now Bruce and Vern walked in, deep in conversation.

Callie placed her purse under the counter. "What's up?"

Bruce glanced at her. "Good morning, Callie."

Vern nodded. "Howdy, Callie."

They moved into the conservatory, still talking in low tones.

She followed them. "What's going on? Why was a building inspector here?"

The two men turned toward her, and Vern folded his arms. "He has just condemned the Henry Dorsey-Smythe mansion."

"Condemned!" She raised her eyebrows. "You can't be serious!"

"Vern, I'll handle this." Bruce cleared his throat. "I'm afraid it's true, Callie. This old place needs to be torn down. It's dangerous to the town's citizens."

She sighed. "I knew this day was coming, but I was hoping for a few more years. So you're going to demolish the mansion and build a new building in its place?"

"Nope, no new building." Vern smirked. "Fort Lob won't have a library anymore. This place is going flat in two months, and that will be the end of Dorsey-Smythe."

Callie's mouth dropped open.

"Vern!" Bruce gave him a stern look before he turned to Callie. "The town council has already voted not to rebuild."

"But what about our patrons?" *What about my job?*

"The townspeople can drive to the Niobrara County Library."

"But that's in Lusk."

Bruce nodded. "Our citizens drive to Lusk for a lot of things. I guess everyone can use their library, too."

Vern grinned. "You can have a big book sale, Callie. It'll be fun."

*Fun?* That was not the way she wanted to sell books.

An hour later, Callie sat at the checkout desk, her chin in her hand, thinking depressing thoughts. Bruce and Vern had left the premises with Vern muttering something about raising all the councilmen's salaries. *He just wants the town's money for himself.*

Another depressing thought pierced her mind. Thanks to Tonya's interruption on Friday night, Lane had not kissed her after their date. And it sure looked like he wanted to.

Tonya could have waited a few minutes to tell her about Grandma. Mom and Derek hadn't left for another half hour.

But Callie wondered if she should get involved with Lane. She still didn't know what he did for a living. Sure, he said he was an agent—but what kind? Besides, she hadn't seen him since he roared off on his motorcycle Friday night. He hadn't come to the library on Saturday, and he wasn't in church on Sunday. The fact that he had skipped church really bothered her. All she could do was pray that he would get his heart right with God.

The front door opened to admit Agatha Collingsworth. "Howdy, Callie! Brought back that big-hair book."

Aggie's own hair looked bigger than ever. Today it was tinted green and teased into a swirl in the back. A green butterfly barrette resided in the fluffy nest above her right ear.

"Oh, I wish I could keep this book!" Aggie laid *Fixing Big Hair the Texas Way* on the counter. "I tried all the hairstyles I liked. Course some are a little out-of-date."

*A little?* Callie pulled the book toward her. "Do you want to renew it?"

"Nah, I'm done with it, but I had so much fun whipping up the styles." Agatha brushed bejeweled fingers lightly against her hair. "Actually, Lucille found me another book about hair. It's one of your own here at Dorsey-Smythe." She pointed at the reserved books. "Look behind ya, sugar. She said she'd hold it for me."

It only took Callie a few seconds to find the volume. She pulled it out. "Must be this one. *Beauty Tricks and Tips*." The model on the front cover looked like she was from the 1980s.

"Oh, look at this!" Aggie gazed at the cover. "I love it already! Wish I could buy books like this, but they just don't sell these good ones nowadays."

"If you wait a couple weeks, you could buy this one."

Aggie looked at her with an arched brow. "So it's true about this place being torn down?"

Now Callie quirked a brow. "You heard about it?"

"I heard through the grapevine about the building inspector. And now that uppity town council says they ain't gonna build a new library."

"The inspector has already come and condemned this place."

"No!" Aggie's eyes widened. "The mansion ain't that bad off."

Callie shrugged. "I guess it is, Aggie. According to Bruce and Vern, the council wants to sell off all the books, flatten the building in two months, and have everyone patronize the county library in Lusk."

"Well, if that don't beat all!" Agatha hit her fist on the counter. "It ain't going to happen, I tell you. We'll protest."

"Aggie. . ." Callie shook her head.

"Besides, if the building was falling down around our ears, why would the inspector give us two months to vacate? I tell you, sugar, it ain't that bad."

"Maybe you're right."

"Course I'm right. This building can be fixed. How many people are in here right now?" She looked around as if expecting them to materialize. "Let's get everybody together and have a good old town protest."

Before Callie could argue with Aggie's plan, the older woman tramped into the conservatory. "Yoo-hoo, ya'll come upstairs to the conference room. We have a problem to settle." She strode to the main room and hollered the same words.

Callie rolled her eyes. Agatha Collingsworth was one of a kind, but a little hope seeped back into Callie's soul. Maybe they could save the Dorsey-Smythe library from extinction.

❧

"I can't believe it!"

"They can't tear down this library!"

"Why, this library has been here since I was a kid!"

Callie jumped up on a step stool, which was used to get to the higher shelves, and motioned with her hands. "Everyone, calm down!"

The talk died as Callie glanced around the conference room. If only Aggie hadn't blurted out the news about the library's demise, Callie could have explained everything in a calm way. The crowd looked at her expectantly.

The library patrons ranged from a few moms with children to several teenagers and a number of older people. She estimated at least twenty-five people filled the room. Most stood clustered in groups, although several sat at the tables.

"Okay." She expelled a breath. "All we know is that a building inspector was here this morning. He condemned the mansion, and Bruce MacKinnon said the council has already voted not to build a new building. We'll sell off all the books before they tear down this place."

"How long before they tear it down?" Horace Frankenberg asked.

"Two months."

A murmur went through the crowd.

"But, Callie." Mrs. Anderson, seated at one of the tables, raised her thin hand. "What are we going to do without a library in Fort Lob?" Her head of snow-white hair quivered slightly as her blue eyes gazed up.

"I'm afraid we'll have to drive to Lusk and—"

"What goes on here?" Vern Snyder stepped into the room.

Agatha placed her hands on her ample hips. "This is a protest meeting, Vern! You town-council people think ya'll are so high and mighty! Well, we are protesting your decision to close down our library."

"You think so, do you?" Vern glanced around. "Huh! Don't look like much of a protest to me."

Callie sighed. "We're just giving out information right now. Some of the—"

"No! We're protesting!" Agatha looked around. "Who wants this library to close down?"

She waited a split second, but no one moved. "See? Everybody's in favor of keeping the library open, just as is."

"But, Aggie, the building has been condemned." Vern folded his arms. "The inspector said the floors are bad, the electricity should be replaced, the plumbing is old. The whole place is a disaster waiting to happen. Someone could get hurt."

"So the town needs to spend some money on repairs." Aggie touched the barrette in her hair. "What's a little money? We could all throw in a few bucks, don't ya'll think?"

The crowd glanced around before a murmur of voices broke out and got louder.

Callie raised her hands. "Listen, everyone!" She waited for the crowd to quiet. "We need to know what the general consensus is about this. How many want to keep the library open at Fort Lob?"

Everyone began talking at once, and several people raised their hands.

Vern pulled out a chair and hopped up on it. "Folks! You can't vote on this." He glared at Callie. "What do you think you're doing? The town council has already decided to shut down the library and not build another one."

Once more Mrs. Anderson raised her hand. "But what will we do without a library in town?" She glanced around before continuing in a small, quivery voice. "I come here every Monday and Friday—Callie knows. It takes me eight minutes to walk from my house. But I don't own a car, so how can I drive to Lusk every week?"

"Am I hearing you right, Shirley?" Vern stuck his finger in his ear and twirled it around. "You want the council to keep this library open just to support your book habit?"

"Vern!" Aggie glared at him. "That ain't nice."

"The town council is supposed to represent the citizens!" said one of the men.

"Where will the children go in the summer?" asked a mother.

Aggie folded her arms. "See? Ya'll can't close it down."

For the third time, Callie raised her hands as a babble of voices broke out. "Let's work something out, folks! Who would like to meet with the town council to discuss this?"

Hands shot up all over the room.

"Aha!" Aggie had both hands in the air. "Looky here, Vern, we are in protest mode. How about we meet tomorrow night at the Elks lodge on Pronghorn Avenue? Everyone in favor say 'Aye.'"

The ayes resounded throughout the room.

"Now, Aggie." Vern stepped down from the chair. "You're not following *Robert's Rules of Order*."

Agatha ignored him. "Tomorrow night, citizens! Seven o'clock at the Elks lodge. Ya'll spread the word. Let's go!"

The library patrons filed out amid a low hum of conversation.

Aggie thumped her finger against Vern's chest. "You, Mr. Vern Snyder, can tell the town council about the protest meeting. And if they don't show, our protest just might turn into a town riot." She cackled a laugh as she waltzed from the room.

Callie stepped off the stool. She and Vern were the only ones left.

"Really now, Callie. You can't seriously think you can change the council's mind."

"I guess we'll find out tomorrow night, won't we?"

Vern shook his head. "Bruce is not going to like this."

Callie smiled. For once she was glad Bruce was not here to intervene.

# Chapter 11

On Tuesday night, Callie stood beside Cheyenne at the back of the Elks lodge meeting room. The open windows and two fans circling above did little to move the stifling air. Both young and old citizens of Fort Lob filled row after row of folding chairs set on the dusty wooden floor. It looked like the entire town had turned out. Not one chair remained empty, and about fifty people stood in the aisles.

Murray Twichell strutted back and forth at the front of the room before taking a position near the platform with his arms folded. He surveyed the crowd.

Chance Bixby sat halfway back on the south side of the building, and Agatha Collingsworth's green-tinted hair could be seen above the crowd on the north side. Miss Penwell was missing since she had elected to keep the library open during the meeting.

Lane Hutchins was not there, either. Callie had called him that afternoon, but he seemed reluctant to come.

Callie sighed as Ralph Little, the balding treasurer of the town council, droned on about the need to close the library. A few heads in the crowd nodded when he spoke of the low taxes the citizens paid.

"Now, unless you want us to raise those taxes—" He stepped back as the microphone emitted a high-pitched whine. "We need to shut down the Dorsey-Smythe permanently."

He took his seat amid a spattering of applause. Most of the hand clapping came from the front row, where the nine members of the town council sat. Some of the other citizens looked like they had been lulled into a stupor.

Bruce MacKinnon ascended the wooden platform and took the mic off its stand. "For the past hour and a half, your town council has spoken. It is clear why we need to close the library. If there are no questions or comments, we will close this meeting." He glanced around. "Is there anyone from the floor who wishes to speak?"

*Finally!* Callie strode down the middle aisle, waving her hand, hoping Bruce wouldn't change his mind and close the meeting anyway. Frowning, he handed her the microphone.

Callie took a deep breath. "Citizens of Fort Lob." She paused as the back door opened and Lane slipped in. *Oh, thank You, Lord!* For the space of a heartbeat, their eyes met, and she smiled.

People began to turn around, craning their necks to see what she was staring at.

Callie cleared her throat and turned her attention to the men seated in the front row. "The town council is unanimous about shutting down the Henry Dorsey-Smythe Library. However, many of our citizens, including me, do not want to close it." She looked out over the crowd. "Now, I ask you folks—isn't the town council supposed to vote according to the wants and needs of the people they represent?"

Fortunately, the citizenry came to life, and several people shouted out affirmations.

"Let me tell you something." Callie spoke softly into the mic, and the room quieted. "Four months ago, the town council cut the library's spending to zero. We couldn't buy any new books. That's why we have to order them from Casper on the interlibrary loan system."

Several men in the front row folded their arms.

"Not only that but the council let the library's repair fund run completely dry."

"That's right!" Chance shouted. "I didn't have money to fix nothing. No wonder the building is condemned."

A murmur ran through the crowd as Bruce stood. "Callie has the floor right now, Mr. Bixby. Please wait your turn." He sat down and nodded for her to continue.

"Here's my point." She took a deep breath. "I believe the council decided several months ago to close down the library, and—"

Vern jumped up. "Now just a doggone minute!" His face tinged red as he glanced at Bruce and then sat down. "I'll refute that when you're finished."

Callie rushed on. "They have also wanted Miss Penwell to retire, but she has refused to step down from her position as head librarian."

The councilmen exchanged wary glances.

Callie caught Lane's eye. He grinned and raised his thumb in the air. She continued, more confident. "So, I believe the council's decision to tear down our library and not build a new one stems from two reasons. First, they claim this will save the town money, but they really want to raise their own salaries."

A buzz of conversation went through the lodge. Callie glanced at Vern, who folded his arms and glared at her.

"Second, they'll be able to get rid of Miss Penwell."

"Just fire her!" someone shouted. "We want our library!"

A chorus of voices broke out with similar sentiments, and several people stood to shout out their convictions. Callie replaced the mic and stepped off the platform.

Murray strode to the platform and grabbed the mic stand. "We will not have this meeting erupt into a riot! All of you—sit down!" The microphone responded with a loud high-pitched whine.

Amid the noise, Callie made her way to the back, where Lane stood beside Cheyenne.

He smiled and placed his arm around Callie's shoulders, giving her a quick friendly squeeze. "Great job, Callie."

She expelled a happy sigh. "Thanks."

Cheyenne gave her a high five. "What a speech, girl. I can't believe how calm you were. You really told them like it is."

Callie shrugged. "I hope it did some good."

The three of them stood in the back as one townsperson after another came forward to add their support for the library. After each speech, one of the councilmen took the mic and refuted what had just been said.

After a particularly scathing rebuke from Vern Snyder, Callie gave a frustrated sigh. "The council won't budge," she whispered to Lane. "They have their minds made up, and it doesn't matter what the people want."

He folded his arms. "That's the danger of power. Sometimes it goes to people's heads."

Cheyenne tapped Lane on the shoulder. "You should give a speech."

"Me?" He looked startled.

Callie smiled. "That's a great idea."

He shook his head. "I'm not good at that kind of thing."

"But, Lane. . ." Callie placed her hand on his arm. "You told me this was one of the best libraries in the country. Most of our people have never been to another library. We need your input."

"I don't like speaking in public, Callie." He kept his voice low. "Besides, I don't think it would do any good."

"I think it would." She moved a little closer and stared up at him. "Won't you do it for your new hometown? Or maybe, for me?" She whispered the last two words and realized she was acting just like Tonya. But she stood still, waiting for his response.

Lane returned her stare then reached over and slid her glasses down her nose. His face went out of focus, but Callie stared at his eyes and blinked a few times.

He leaned down to whisper in her ear, "Okay, Callie, I'll do it for you." He straightened and winked.

A little thrill ran through her.

The microphone whined again. "Is there anyone else?" Bruce scanned the crowd.

Most of the people looked worn down. Several children had fallen asleep in their mothers' arms. Many older citizens fanned themselves with pieces of paper.

Callie gave Lane a little push, and he took off toward the front of the room. She adjusted her glasses so she could watch him.

The crowd stirred as he walked forward. Bruce handed him the mic and sat down.

Lane took a deep breath. "Uh, I'm new in town. The name is Lane Hutchins."

He paused, seemingly surveying the crowd, but Callie thought he looked nervous—like he was about to bolt off the stage. She gave him a thumbs-up, just as he had for her.

Clearing his throat, he nodded. "I've lived in a number of states during the past few years, all in small towns. Every one of those towns had its own library, but none of them were as good as the Dorsey-Smythe."

A murmur ran through the crowd.

"When I first visited the library here at Fort Lob, I couldn't believe the excellent reference section. Here was a library that had books about Wyoming in its own room. And I heard that Miss Penwell, who was on the town council for eight years—" He nodded to the men in the front row. "Evidently Miss Penwell was instrumental in buying the books in that room." He smiled, seeming to relax a bit. "The history of Wyoming is fascinating, and you have a great collection at your fingertips. It's a wealth of information. Don't let it go! We need to fight to keep the Dorsey-Smythe Library open."

The crowd broke out in applause. Lane replaced the mic and stepped off the platform. The applause accompanied him all the way to the back of the room, with a few whistles and shouts of "Bravo!" thrown in.

Bruce took the microphone. "It is now ten o'clock, and we will dismiss the meeting. Be assured that the town council will convene to discuss this, um, problem."

Conversation filled the room as the crowd rose and began flowing toward the exits.

Callie shared a smile with Lane. "I'm glad you spoke, Lane. You did a great job."

"Thanks." He gazed at her.

Agatha Collingsworth strode toward Callie. "Oh, Callie, sugar! I must speak to ya'll. Got a minute?" Not waiting for an answer, Aggie pulled her to a corner of the room, away from Lane and the milling crowd. "I don't like the way this meeting went tonight. Do you?" Her dark eyes, usually dancing with fun, were serious for once.

Callie shrugged. "It's hard to say how it affected the council."

"Hard to say?" Aggie lightly smoothed back her hair. "Those stubborn men are going to do *nothing* about keeping our library open. But I got an idea." She glanced around and lowered her voice. "We need a petition, ya know? If we get enough townspeople to sign a petition to keep the library open, the town council will have to honor it."

"But what are the laws about presenting a petition?"

Aggie cackled. "I'm one step ahead of ya, girl! I talked to Bertram Lilly this morning over at the county courthouse, and he told me exactly how to get that council to sit up and take notice." She pulled a piece of paper from her purse. "I already made a mock-up to collect names and addresses. Look it over and see what ya'll think."

After some discussion, they agreed on a plan. Finally Aggie left the Elks lodge, which was empty now except for five people clustered near the platform, deep in conversation. Cheyenne sat by herself in the second row from the back of the room.

Callie realized she'd been standing for more than three hours. She sank into a chair in the row behind Cheyenne. "Where's Lane?"

Cheyenne swiveled around. "He didn't stay long."

"He left?" Callie sighed, tired from the emotional roller-coaster ride she'd taken in the past few days. "I don't know what to do about him, Cheyenne."

"What do you mean?"

"I really like him, but I don't think we're meant for each other."

"Don't say that. He likes you. Why, just look at the way he acted toward you tonight—staring in your eyes and whispering in your ear. I bet he'll be at the library tomorrow morning when you open."

"The library's closed on Wednesdays."

"Oh, that's right."

Callie removed her glasses and rubbed her eyes. "He's so reclusive, and I still don't know what kind of agent he is. Sometimes I wonder if it's God's will for us to get together."

"Oh, Callie." Cheyenne placed her hand on Callie's arm. "I have a strong feeling about you and Lane."

"I don't. I don't have any peace at all. He hasn't called or tried to see me." Callie shrugged. "Maybe I should just forget him."

Cheyenne's blue eyes widened. "Don't do that! I thought you wanted to marry him."

"Well, yeah. . ." Lane's handsome face popped into Callie's mind, and she thought how easy he was to talk to. "But he's so bitter toward God. And besides that, something is going on in his life that he doesn't want me to know about."

Cheyenne shrugged. "If that's the case, God knows what it is. Personally, I think the Lord brought him to Fort Lob just for you." The dimples in her cheeks deepened with her smile. "You have to trust the Lord, not worry about the future. Take your burden to the Lord and leave it there."

"You're right." Callie sighed. "I'll pray and let the Lord take care of it." She put her arms around her friend and hugged her, which was difficult with a chair between them. "Thanks for your advice. I don't know what I'd do without you."

"You keep owing me more and more, but I know how the debt can be paid."

Callie raised her eyebrows. "How?"

Cheyenne grinned. "Make me a bridesmaid in your wedding."

# Chapter 12

I'm checking this book out, Callie." Vern Snyder laid a slim volume on the checkout desk and slapped his library card on top of it.

It was eleven o'clock on Friday morning, and Callie hadn't seen Lane since Tuesday night at the meeting. But she'd seen plenty of Vern.

She picked up his card. "Seems like you're spending a lot of time at the library, even though you want the building to be demolished." She glanced at the title of his book—*How to Become a Millionaire in Twelve Weeks*.

"Yeah, well, you know." Vern shrugged. "It's a place to hang out. Once the library closes, I aim to spend my time at the Trailblazer Café."

She ran the book under the scanner. "Has the town council met to discuss the protests about tearing down the library?"

"Nah, we don't need to do that. This building will be gone in two months."

"Aggie Collingsworth still thinks we can keep the library open. She's circulating a petition for a revote."

"A petition?" Vern's bushy eyebrows met between his eyes. "That woman don't know when to stop. How does she know what's good for this town? Well, she don't. That's why we have a town council." He picked up the book. "This library has got to go, Callie. It's for the good of Fort Lob. Remember that."

Callie sighed as he left. Why were they bothering to petition?

The door opened to admit Cheyenne, dressed in her US Postal uniform, a mailbag slung over her shoulder. "Here's the mail for the library." She placed a letter, several magazines, and a newspaper on the checkout desk.

Callie smiled. "You're delivering the mail today, Cheyenne?"

"Yeah, Bernie's sick. But I like doing delivery. Gets me out of the building. It gets so hot in there without air-conditioning." She tapped the newspaper. "You should read today's article by Herbert Dreyfuss."

Callie picked up *The Scout*. "What's the subject?"

"The danger of power in city halls." Cheyenne smirked. "It was awfully quiet over at the Trailblazer Café—you know all those men who meet there for breakfast every morning? Most of them are on the council, and I don't think they appreciated Mr. Dreyfuss's opinion."

Callie found the column on page eight beside the familiar picture of Dreyfuss—a handsome man in his sixties with graying temples. She spread the paper on the desk. The article was called "City Hall and the Dangers of a Political Machine." Silently she read the first few sentences. "But Cheyenne, this is about New York City and the history of Tammany Hall."

Cheyenne leaned over and pointed to a paragraph near the bottom of the page. "Read this—out loud."

Callie focused on the words. " 'The political machine that wields power doesn't have to be in a big city. Sometimes small towns have a group with great influence over their citizens. A town council often runs the town, making decisions without any input from the populace. In effect, it's the old problem of taxation without representation.' " She looked up. "Wow, he put his finger on Fort Lob's problem."

"Isn't that an amazing coincidence?" Cheyenne hefted her mailbag over her shoulder. "You'd think old Herbert knew what had happened Tuesday night." She turned to the door. "Gotta run. Later, girlfriend."

"Bye." Callie perched on the stool behind her and read the entire article. Except for that one paragraph, the article didn't have a remote resemblance to Fort Lob, but the mention of the town council was certainly a strong coincidence.

Just like the Yellowstone article.

Turning to the computer, she pressed a few keys. Lane's name popped up with a list of books he had recently checked out.

Callie's jaw dropped. "I can't believe this," she muttered.

Two children brought their books to the desk, interrupting her. She checked them out then helped a young mother find some books on child rearing. Ten minutes later, she got back to Lane's name on the computer, hoping no one else would need her.

She remembered calling Lane on Tuesday afternoon about the protest meeting. She called around four o'clock, but then he was late to the meeting, not arriving until eight thirty. According to the computer, he had checked out two books at 7:15. She stared at the titles.

*William Tweed: Boss of Tammany Hall.*
*New York City and the Political Machine.*

She took a deep breath. Lane definitely had something to do with Herbert Dreyfuss. But what?

The door opened, and Aggie swept into the library. She held a clipboard in her bejeweled hand. "Oh, sugar! You wouldn't believe all the signatures I'm collecting."

Callie sighed. "Do you think it will do any good? Vern seems to think the library is history."

"Of course Vern would think that! He doesn't come up for reelection for another three years. But we'll show him!" Her husky voice sounded confident. "I just got back from Bruce MacKinnon's ranch. We had a good talk."

Callie raised her eyebrows. "Did Bruce sign it?"

Aggie sobered. "Well, no. But he did agree to a meeting with the citizens. After all, his reelection is coming up in November. He has to consider the popular vote." She brushed her fingers against her hair. Today it was back to pink and looked like spun cotton candy. "I'm so excited! We have a date."

"You and Bruce?"

"No, no!" Aggie cackled out a laugh. "As if he would want to date an old hen like me." Her smile faded. "A date for the meeting, girl, held at the Elks lodge on Saturday, August 30, seven o'clock." She tapped a red-manicured fingernail on the desk. "Write it down, sugar. We'll beat the pants off those old councilmen!"

"Really, Aggie." Callie tried to hide her smile but didn't quite succeed. "So we need all those signatures by the thirtieth?"

"Oh, I'll have them long before then. Why, that's two weeks away. Plenty of time." She placed the clipboard in front of Callie. "And I need to get your John Hancock, Miss Callie Brandt. Sign right here." She pointed to the next available line.

After Callie wrote her name and address, Aggie picked up the clipboard. "By the way, sugar, did you see that article by Herb Dreyfuss this morning?"

"Yep. Looks like we have a political machine right here in Fort Lob."

"I know!" Aggie knit her brows together. "Ya'll don't think Herbert Dreyfuss snuck into our protest meeting, do ya?"

"Well. . .I don't think so."

Aggie brayed out a laugh. "Just kidding." She glanced around. "Think I'll take a little traipse through the library and have everyone sign up." She ambled into the conservatory and soon struck up a conversation with Mrs. Anderson.

Shaking her head, Callie pulled out a reserved book. That Aggie was a real character. But. . .could she be right? Was Herbert Dreyfuss actually at the meeting Tuesday night?

Callie sank down on the stool. First the Yellowstone article—after Lane had checked out all those books about Yellowstone. Then the one about New York, Tammany Hall, and the political machine—after he had checked out books on those subjects. And he *did* have an uncle Herb.

But that must be a true coincidence. His uncle had been dead for seven years. However, a rumor had circulated a few years ago that Herbert Dreyfuss was dead. Everyone thought it was speculation, and Callie herself had never believed it.

Maybe Lane was Herbert Dreyfuss's agent. Yes—a *book* agent. That must be the type of agent he was. And perhaps. . .perhaps Lane did the man's research for him.

"That's it!" She jumped up from the stool just as two teen girls walked by the desk. She smiled at them sheepishly before looking again at the reserved books.

Probably Lane looked through dozens of books for each article, found good material, then called Dreyfuss and talked it over with him. Maybe he e-mailed him through the Wi-Fi at the Trailblazer Café. She once saw Lane at a table in there with a laptop sitting in front of him.

With a smile, Callie nodded. She'd figured it out. And she felt 100 percent better knowing Lane's secret.

A week later, Aggie breezed into the library. Callie stood at the checkout desk beside Miss Penwell, who had just arrived.

"We did it!" Aggie laid down the clipboard, stuffed with a sheaf of messy papers. "Girls, we have collected enough signatures. I am so excited I could scream!"

Miss Penwell pursed her lips. "Please don't do it here, Agatha. Take your screams elsewhere."

"Oh, Lucille!" Aggie cackled out a laugh. "Ya'll are a riot! I'm gonna drive out to Bruce MacKinnon's ranch and throw this petition in his lap. Why, practically the whole town signed the thing!"

Callie folded her arms on the desk. "I sure hope it saves our library."

"It won't." Miss Penwell turned to the computer. "This building will be gone before you know it."

A cloud of depression settled over Callie. Miss Penwell was right. The library was history, and so was Callie's relationship with Lane Hutchins. She had tried to call his apartment several times in the past four days, but there was no answer. Finally, in desperation, she had called Mrs. Wimple who informed her that Lane was out of town. He said he wouldn't be back until the end of the month.

She couldn't believe how much she missed him.

But Aggie had no such reason to dampen her spirits. "Now, Lucille, don't be such a wet blanket. I think this petition will do a world of good. And don't forget that Bruce agreed to a meeting on the thirtieth. That's only eight days away."

Miss Penwell glanced at Aggie before looking back at the computer. "Bruce may well be impressed with the number of signatures you've collected, Agatha, but some of the other men on the council won't be swayed. They have no use for Fort Lob's history. They would tear down every old building in this town if they could."

Aggie patted Miss Penwell's hand. "That's not true, hon. Besides, some of them are up for reelection this year, and they'll probably agree to give it time. At least they'll fix the electrical or something. I think—"

"You don't know the councilmen like I do." Miss Penwell wagged her finger at Aggie. "These old buildings are expensive to maintain, and they don't want to spend the town's money. They'd rather put it in their pockets."

"But, Lucille—"

"Do you know what kind of books Vern, Ralph, and some of those other men check out? They're all about finance and investing and making money. That's all they care about."

Aggie sighed, her good mood seeming to deflate for the first time. "I guess some of them men are greedy, Lucille, but that don't mean we can't persuade them to see our side." She tapped the papers on the clipboard, her voice lifting with each word. "Look at all these signatures! Why, when the men see all these names representing people—the people of our town—who want to save our library, the idea will take wings and fly."

"It will never get off the ground." Miss Penwell pursed her lips.

Aggie ignored her. "Callie, hon, why don't you go with me to see Bruce? He likes you, and maybe you can add your two cents. Ya'll can represent the younger crowd." She turned to Miss Penwell. "That okay, Lucille? You won't need Callie for a few minutes, will ya, sugar?"

Callie looked at Miss Penwell, knowing *that* petition would never fly.

The older librarian adjusted her wire rims. "Well—"

"Oh, you're such a sweetie!" Aggie leaned over and gave Miss Penwell a quick hug. "We'll be back as soon as we can."

❧

Callie hung on for dear life as Aggie's open Jeep bounced over the dirt road to Bruce's ranch, which was four miles southwest of town. Even though Aggie hit every pothole in the road, she managed to talk the entire time she was driving. Callie kept her mouth tightly shut, hoping to keep the dust and bugs out. When they finally pulled up in front of Bruce's two-story farmhouse, she prayed she wouldn't look as disheveled as she felt.

Aggie parked the Jeep in front of the porch.

Callie got out, hot and covered with a thin layer of dust. She couldn't wait to get into Bruce's air-conditioned house.

"Oh, look at these roses!" With her clipboard, Aggie pointed to the red flowers growing profusely on trellises beside the porch. "How Bruce can keep his roses growing like that in August, I'll never know."

They ascended the steps to the front door. Before Aggie could knock, Bruce opened the screen door for them. "Come on in. I heard through the grapevine that you'd collected enough signatures, Aggie." His *r*'s rolled with the lilt of his voice. "Thought you might be over today."

"Now isn't this the most gossipy town ever? I only told one or two people." Aggie walked past him into the house. "Maybe three."

Callie smiled when Bruce winked at her.

Aggie took a large blue easy chair in the living room. "I brought Callie with me to represent the younger set, Bruce." She dropped her voice and nodded at Callie. "Now ya'll be sure to jump into the conversation, sugar."

Thankful for the cooler air, Callie took a seat on the comfortable blue-and-white-plaid sofa. "Well, I—"

"Oh, Bruce." Aggie glanced around. "Every time I come to your house, I'm impressed all over again! I just love the way ya'll decorate."

"Why, thank you, Aggie." Bruce handed her a glass. "Iced tea? I remember that you like plenty of sugar."

"Oh, ya'll are just the sweetest thing!" Aggie smiled up at him as she took the glass.

Callie stared at Aggie's face. *She really likes him!* Callie had never thought of old Agatha Collingsworth falling in love with someone. But this was too funny—a down-home, overweight Texas gal falling for a sophisticated and staid Scotsman. Aggie had mentioned that Bruce wouldn't want to date an old hen like her. Evidently she had no hope for a relationship with him. *Just like me with Lane.*

Callie thanked Bruce for the glass he handed her, grateful for something cold. Taking a sip, she glanced around. She had always loved his spacious home. Instead of carpet, the highly polished wood floor was partially covered with a large, braided blue rug. A nautical theme, in blue and white, dominated the room with lighthouses on the fireplace mantel and a ship's wheel attached to the white-paneled wall.

Aggie talked on about nothing while Bruce took a seat in a wooden rocking chair. After ten minutes of her blabber, he glanced at his watch. "Don't you have a petition to give me?"

"Oh, land's sake! Course I do!" She plucked the clipboard from her lap and thrust it at him. "Now don't forget about our meeting at the Elks lodge. Just one week away, Bruce."

"Yes." He glanced through the sheaf of papers. "I plan to call some of these petitioners—random calls, of course—to make sure they signed willingly." He looked at Aggie. "I'm simply satisfying my curiosity. Did all of these people sign the petition because they want to keep the library open, or did you talk them into it?"

"Well, in all my days!" Aggie sputtered the words out. "Everyone who signed that thing wants it open, and some were stubborn as a mule about it." She glared at Bruce. "Ya'll on the council do not give a hoot for the pulse of Fort Lob. Only twelve people in the whole town refused to sign, and most of them were councilmen!"

Callie glanced between the two. So much for falling in love! She cleared her throat. "Uh, Bruce, I have a question. If the council does decide to keep the library open, will they demolish the mansion and build a new building?"

"No, I believe we'll try to renovate the Dorsey-Smythe house."

"Oh good." Callie let out a relieved sigh. "I've always loved that old place. It has so much history in it, and I would hate to see it torn down."

Bruce grunted his agreement. "But some of the council members don't see eye to eye on restoring the mansion. They don't value our town's history."

"Like that Vern Snyder!" Aggie folded her arms. "He certainly has a mind of his own."

Bruce smiled. "Like a number of our citizens, Aggie. But you realize, of course, that in renovating the property, we will be forced to increase local taxes."

"So what's a few more bucks? It's like that nice young fella, Lane Hutchins, said. The Dorsey-Smythe is one of the best libraries in the country with a great collection of Wyoming books." Aggie glanced at Callie. "Remember when Lucille went on that spending spree to get all them books?" Barely waiting for a nod, she turned back to Bruce. "And did ya'll see the column by Herb Dreyfuss in this morning's paper? 'The Influence of Libraries in America.' You'd think old Herbert knew what our citizens have been going through."

Bruce nodded. "I read it. In fact, it convinced me to be more open about keeping a library right here in our town. Our children and young people need it." He looked at Callie. "And I suppose you want to keep your job."

"I certainly do!" Callie smiled, but her smile was for Herbert Dreyfuss.

# Chapter 13

It was good to be back.

Lane rode his Harley down Main Street and turned in at the Stables parking lot. The sun was high overhead, warming the air to ninety-seven degrees. He had removed his helmet as soon as he left the interstate, and he enjoyed the warm wind hitting his sunglasses and whipping through his hair.

For the past two weeks, he'd stayed in his house in Cheyenne, writing two magazine articles and feverishly trying to beat his publisher's deadline on a new book. He knew he'd never make the deadline if he stayed in Fort Lob. The people here were too...friendly. Even though he should move to a bigger town, he didn't want to. The suffocating small-town feel was growing on him.

Besides, he missed one particular person in this town—a twenty-something girl who hid her beauty behind a pair of glasses. Tomorrow would mark three weeks since their date, and he needed to give her a call.

He parked the Harley but didn't bother going to his apartment. Whistling, he sauntered across the street to Wilkins Grocery.

The bell above the door jangled as he entered, and he relished the cool air. Removing his sunglasses, he dropped them in his shirt pocket.

Jim Wilkins was checking out an old lady's groceries. "Hey there, Lane!" he boomed out with a grin. "Haven't seen you around these parts for a couple weeks."

"Uh, no, I was out of town." Lane rushed on, not wanting Jim to ask questions. "But it's great to be back, and I need some groceries. Do you have any fresh fruit, like strawberries?"

"Of course we have strawberries. That will be twenty-seven dollars and forty-three cents, Mrs. Babcock. The strawberries are full price right now, but the watermelons are a steal. And a few of our apples are on sale, too. Thanks so much, Mrs. Babcock." Jim's loud voice never varied between the two conversations.

Lane moved toward the produce section. "Thanks."

Twenty minutes later, he left the store with a carton of strawberries, a quart of milk, a box of cereal, and five frozen dinners. He walked back to the Stables and climbed the stairs to his apartment, ready to eat lunch.

He was getting tired of frozen dinners.

At six o'clock that evening, as he microwaved yet another frozen entrée, he realized he had left a book in his motorcycle saddlebag. He bounded down the stairs and out into the sunshine. After retrieving the book, he walked back to the apartment building.

The blast from a car horn made him jump. He turned toward the sound.

Callie rolled down her car window as she pulled into the parking lot and stopped. "Hey, Lane! I heard you were out of town. Welcome back!"

Lane jogged over to her car. He hadn't realized how much he had missed Callie until this moment. A deep contentment settled over him just hearing her voice.

He placed his arm above her car door and peered inside. "Hi." Why should he eat that tasteless frozen dinner when he could have a hot steak with company? "Hey, if you're not doing anything right now, how about eating with me at the Cattlemen's Diner?" He pointed down the street toward the restaurant.

"Sure! Let me park the car."

He held up his book. "I'll run this up to my apartment. Meet you here in a few minutes."

&

Callie glanced around the crowded diner, knowing every person in this place. If only she and Lane could have gone to Lusk for dinner. But she was so happy he asked her to eat with him that she'd just have to make the best of it.

They settled across from each other in a booth by the front window. It wasn't the best place for a quiet romantic dinner—in fact, it was in the middle of everything. In the booth across the aisle, a baby was crying. The old jukebox in the corner was playing "The Candy Man," competing with the sounds of clashing dinnerware and loud conversation. Two waitresses swished back and forth from table to table, taking and fulfilling orders.

Sara Stine, Ralph Little's teenage granddaughter, brought Lane's and Callie's drinks to the table, took their order, and left.

"I hate eating alone in a restaurant." Lane sipped his iced tea. "And I'm really getting tired of frozen dinners, so I'm glad you agreed to eat with me."

Feeling like a flirt, Callie peered over her glasses at him. "Are those the only reasons?"

He laughed. "I might have another reason."

He gazed at her eyes, and Callie gazed back. A feeling of peace settled over her. *Thank You, Lord.* In that moment, she knew that marrying Lane was God's will for her. She didn't know if he was still bitter at God, or if he was really Herbert Dreyfuss's agent, or how long it would take for them to get together, but she knew without a doubt that she wanted to share his life someday.

When their food arrived, Lane stared down at his plate for a moment before looking up at her.

Callie adjusted her glasses. "Would you like me to say grace?" She realized—too late—that she had embarrassed him at Ray's.

He half smiled. "Sure, that would be fine."

Twenty-five minutes later, after the family with the crying baby had left, they had a few moments of quiet as they ate their dessert—a brownie sundae for Lane and New York cheesecake for Callie.

Vern Snyder and his wife, Blanche, settled into the booth across the aisle. *Oh great!* Callie looked out the window, hoping Vern and Blanche wouldn't notice them. But of course they had good eyesight. In fact, Blanche had small dark eyes that darted around like a bird's, seeming to take in everything at once. And she was one of the worst gossips in Fort Lob. She would strain to hear every tidbit of conversation between Callie and Lane.

Callie took the last bite of cheesecake and looked up. "Ready to go, Lane?"

"Already?" He looked puzzled. "I thought it would be nice to sit here with a cup of coffee and talk for a while."

"Well. . ." That *would* be nice if Blanche Snyder wasn't sitting three feet away. "I really should get home—"

"Hey, Hutchins!" Vern turned in his booth toward Lane. "Where have you been the past few weeks?"

His voice was loud, and Callie noticed that Vern wasn't wearing his hearing aid.

Lane paused before smiling. "Oh, hi!" He reached out and shook Vern's hand. "Mr. Snyder, isn't it? Good to see you."

Now Vern looked surprised. "Uh, you, too. But you haven't been around. Was wondering what happened to you."

"I had to go out of town for a couple weeks on some business, but I'm back now." Lane grinned. "A person can't stay away from Fort Lob for long. This small-town atmosphere just gets in your blood."

"Huh!" Vern grunted, his glance bouncing to Callie before it settled back on Lane. "So, Hutchins. . ." He folded his arms. "How did your business survive while you were out of town? I hear you're an insurance agent, but you don't seem to have any customers."

Blanche nodded. "How can you sell insurance when you don't have an office in town? No one has ever seen your office or gotten a business card from you."

Lane frowned. "But I don't sell insurance. I'm not—"

"Then why did you say you did?" Blanche's voice rose. "Did you lie to our people?"

"No, certainly not." Lane held up both hands as if to fend her off. "I never said I sold insurance."

"That's what Eloise Riddell told me, and she heard it from Iva Hockett who heard it from Lucille Penwell, and you know Lucille don't talk idle."

"I told Miss Penwell I was an *agent*. That's all I said. I never mentioned one thing about insurance."

"Then what kind of agent? What was this business that took you away?" Her voice got louder with each sentence. "Fort Lob is a very small town, young man. You just can't go gallivanting around the country without telling folks why you're leaving. We want to know what you do for a living."

By this time, several people from nearby tables were listening in on the conversation.

Lane's mouth dropped open. "Well, I—"

"Wouldn't be surprising if you was some kind of crook." Vern squinted at Lane. "A man who don't hold a job in Fort Lob looks mighty suspicious. You have to get your money from somewhere. I bet you're an agent with the black market, selling stolen jewels under the table or some such thing."

"Vern!" Callie banged her fist on the table. "How can you say that? You and Blanche are smearing Lane's reputation in front of all these people with your gossip."

"Gossip!" Blanche lifted her chin. "I have never gossiped in my life."

Callie wanted to roll her eyes, but she didn't since Sara, the waitress, came by the table to fill up her water glass. The pitcher shook, and a little water spilled as Sara poured it. The teenager gave a furtive glance at the Snyders before she left.

*Poor girl.* "Well, Lane isn't a crook." Callie folded her arms. "And he certainly doesn't work for the black market, so—"

"Then what kind of agent are you, Hutchins?" Vern glared at Lane. "Speak up, boy! Don't make Callie defend you."

Lane raised his hands in exasperation. "I don't know why I have to defend myself. I'm a law-abiding citizen."

Vern jabbed his finger at Lane's face. "We just want to know where you come from. You gave that speech about the library, and you said you've lived in a lot of places and the Dorsey-Smythe is one of the best libraries in the country."

Lane nodded. "It is."

"Then how come you know so much about all these libraries? How come you've lived in so many places? Only men running from the law move from place to place like that."

"Mr. Snyder, I've done nothing illegal—"

"You're lying! How do we know we can trust you?"

"Vern!" Callie jumped up. "This is ridiculous. What Lane does is none of your business. You men on the town council think you can rule everyone's life. You have too much power, just like Herbert Dreyfuss said in his column. Stick with your own business and quit bothering Lane."

"Well!" Blanche turned her face away from Callie. "You certainly are high-and-mighty, Miss Brandt. I might speak with your father about this."

"That's fine with me." Callie knew she had nothing to fear there. She motioned to Lane. "Let's go."

He followed her to the cash register.

Sara had their bill ready. She fumbled with the money Lane gave her but smiled when he handed her a ten-dollar tip.

Silently Callie and Lane left the diner. In the twilight, a warm wind whispered about them as they walked down the street to her car.

Lane opened the driver-side door for her, but she didn't get in. Instead she turned to him. "Lane, I'm so sorry. I don't know what got into Vern. I've never seen him act so mean."

"It wasn't your fault."

"Well, it makes me mad that he embarrassed you in front of all those people."

Lane shrugged and opened his mouth to speak just as Jamie Spencer rumbled by in his Mustang. The car backfired twice, making Callie jump.

She grimaced. "I wish Jamie would fix that old car of his."

"He probably likes it that way." Lane glanced at her. "Speaking of old things, could you do me a favor, Callie?"

*Anything.* "What is it?"

"I'd like to look at those documents again—you know, the ones on the third floor of the library." He paused. "Could you let me up there for a few hours?"

She winced as she shook her head. "Not right now. Miss Penwell is working. Unfortunately someone told her you saw some of those old letters. I don't know who it was, but Miss Penwell was really upset."

He cringed as he moved a step closer to her. "Do you mean to tell me I got you in trouble again?"

"That's okay." She looked up at Lane's handsome face, wishing they could go someplace where no one knew them. Even right here on the street, people were probably watching their every move. She sighed. "I managed to smooth things over, but Miss Penwell is very regimented. If anything different happens, she gets all bent out of shape." An idea popped into her mind. "But you know what? You wouldn't have to look at those documents on the third floor. You can look at them in one of the conference rooms."

He raised his eyebrows. "But how would I get the box?"

"I'll get it for you." She climbed into the driver's seat. "Hop in. I'll give you a lift to the library."

⌖

At eight o'clock, Lane sat alone at a conference table, reading a town document from 1936. He had entered the library through the front door and walked upstairs past the circulation desk. Miss Penwell did not return his greeting. In the meantime, Callie entered through the back door, somehow procured a box of old letters for him, and left the library without Miss Penwell discovering her. Lane felt uneasy about deceiving the old librarian, but he couldn't get the documents out of his mind. When he was finished, Callie had told him to stow the box on top of a cabinet behind two displayed books. She would return it to the third floor in the morning.

Now, unable to concentrate, he sat back with a sigh. He kept thinking about the animosity in Vern Snyder's eyes. Why did that man think Lane was such a threat to Fort Lob? It couldn't be just because of the library. That didn't make sense.

Well, no matter. Lane would do his best to live for two more months in this town—for Callie's sake.

He folded the document and took out a letter. It was dated April 8, 1899, and was written by James Thomas Lob himself.

Lane gave a soft whistle. This was just the type of thing he wanted to put in Callie's museum. He was determined to get that organization going for her. It would be privately funded—by his money. And if Fort Lob—meaning the town council—didn't want to donate all that stuff on the library's third floor to Callie, Lane would offer to buy it all, no matter how much they asked.

As he began reading, the door opened. He looked up.

Miss Penwell, wearing a bright green dress with large white polka dots, stood framed in the doorway. "Please keep this door open."

"Uh, yes, ma'am." He smiled, hoping she would go away.

She didn't return his smile. Instead she took a step into the room, her glance taking in the opened box on the table and the letter in his hand. She folded her arms over her gaunt polka-dotted frame.

"Where did you get that box?"

# Chapter 14

The next morning, Callie decided to go to work early—really early. It was only six thirty. Last night, after she had managed to sneak the box of old documents to Lane without Miss Penwell's knowledge, he asked if she had thought anymore about his museum idea. Callie had to admit that she hadn't; in fact, it was the furthest thing from her mind. But his question piqued her interest. Was that why he wanted to look at those old documents?

Before she opened the library at ten this morning, she would spend a few hours upstairs, seeing what was suitable. Even though a museum still seemed like an impossible dream, it wouldn't hurt to organize the paraphernalia up there.

As was her custom on Friday morning, she stopped by the Trailblazer Café for a cup of coffee. After last night's run-in with Vern and Blanche, she was almost afraid to be seen in public, but then her determination kicked in. Vern Snyder was not going to run her life.

However, she was still embarrassed by last evening's fiasco.

Hmm. . .another fiasco. Maybe she should tell Lane to have Herbert Dreyfuss write a new book called *The Fiascoes of Fort Lob*. She smiled to herself. It would be a runaway bestseller.

She stepped through the door of the café and glanced around. Good. Vern wasn't sitting with the other old men. Of course, this was a lot earlier than she usually arrived. Today only three men—Bruce, Ralph, and Floyd—sat at a table, eating hearty plates of bacon and eggs with a side order of toast or oatmeal.

She walked past their table toward the order window. Bruce nodded a greeting to her, and she wondered how many people in the café knew about Vern's accusations last night.

Probably all of them.

Floyd had his nose in the morning newspaper. "Did you fellows see today's article by Dreyfuss?"

"What's it about?" Bruce took a sip of coffee.

"Overpopulation."

Callie stopped at the order window.

Ralph chuckled. "We don't have that problem in Wyoming."

"That's what Dreyfuss says." Floyd folded the paper back. "Listen to this:

'Of course, there are places on this earth that have no problem with overpopulation. As one Western citizen told me, "You could fit an entire third world country in the state of Wyoming and still have room to spare."'"

*I said that.* Callie spun around as the men laughed and expressed their agreement. She marched to the table. "May I see that article, Floyd?"

"Sure." He was still laughing as he handed her the paper.

While the men went back to their breakfasts, Callie glanced down at the newspaper and stared at the words. *"As one Western citizen told me. . ."* She had said that to Lane, not Herbert Dreyfuss. *Why would he say "told me"?*

Callie folded the paper and handed it back. "Thanks, Floyd."

She left the Trailblazer without her coffee.

⚭

Callie drove down Main Street toward the library.

Was Lane writing those articles? Could he actually be Herbert Dreyfuss? "That's impossible," she muttered.

A scene popped into her mind—something that happened when she was in the eighth grade, twelve years ago. She was sitting at the dining room table at home, writing a report on Abraham Lincoln. Dad sat in the living room watching TV, and one of those talk shows came on. The special guest for the show was Herbert Dreyfuss.

Callie listened to the interview for a few moments, then she left the table and cuddled up beside Dad on the sofa to watch the program with him. He had put his arm around her shoulders and pulled her close. Herbert Dreyfuss wore a suit and tie and must have been in his fifties back then. Although from Callie's fourteen-year-old perspective, he looked old. He sat in an easy chair talking to the television host, and they discussed his syndicated newspaper column. Callie remembered because she had asked Dad what *syndicated* meant.

So Herbert Dreyfuss was writing his newspaper column at least twelve years ago, and he was still writing it now. Obviously Lane would have been a teenager himself back then, so it was impossible for him to be writing under the Dreyfuss name. Unless. . .

Maybe Mr. Dreyfuss was incapacitated and Lane was ghostwriting the articles for him. Or maybe the old man was too busy writing his books to write a newspaper column, too. Or maybe Lane actually was his agent.

"It could be anything!" Callie blew out a frustrated breath as she approached the library. Lane seemed to be adept at evading questions, but she would ask what his relationship was to Dreyfuss; she hoped he gave her a straight answer.

She drove into the library's entrance and noticed a bright green lump lying at the bottom of the steps. A green lump covered with big white polka dots.

"What in the world is that?" she muttered as she pressed the brakes.

Throwing the gears into PARK, she got out and ran around the car to the bottom of the stairs. She stopped with a gasp.

"Miss Penwell?"

# *Chapter 15*

Callie knelt beside Miss Penwell. The older woman was lying facedown with her right arm thrown above her head. Her hand rested in the flower bed between the marigolds. Her left hand, along with her purse, was pinned beneath her stomach. Callie grasped the wrist beside the flowers and felt a faint pulse. "Oh, thank the Lord."

She laid Miss Penwell's hand down and noticed that her index finger was covered with dirt. But Callie had no time to think about that now. She had to call an ambulance.

Wishing she owned a cell phone, Callie dashed up the library steps, unlocked the front door, and raced to the phone behind the desk. A minute later, the sound of sirens came from the direction of the fire station on Rattlesnake Road.

Outside, Callie sat on the step beside Miss Penwell. She barely had time to wonder what had happened before the ambulance arrived. Callie knew the two paramedics, having gone to high school with Joe Fonsino and attending the same church as Davin Traxler. They busied themselves—one checking Miss Penwell's vital signs while the other wheeled the gurney to the front of the library.

"Oh my," a woman's voice spoke in Callie's ear.

Mrs. Wimple, the landlady at the Stables, stood beside her. Pink sponge curlers dotted the woman's gray hair, and she wore a faded blue housedress. Come to think of it, Callie had never seen Mrs. Wimple in anything but a housedress, even at church. Mrs. Wimple's face was pale. She wore no makeup, except for bright-red lipstick. Callie had never seen her without that, either.

"Hi, Mrs. Wimple. I guess you heard the sirens."

Mrs. Wimple worked her red lips around into a pucker. "What happened to Lucille?"

Callie shrugged. "She must have had a heart attack or something when she was locking up last night. That's the only thing I can figure."

Joe looked up. "She was shot."

"Shot?" Callie stared at him.

By this time, the men had Miss Penwell on the gurney with a gray blanket pulled up to her chin.

"Davin called the sheriff." Joe held up an IV bag, and the plastic cord trailed down.

Another siren screamed in the distance, and a moment later, Sheriff Fred

Krause pulled his patrol car into the library's entrance. The red and blue lights flashed across Miss Penwell's ashen face as he parked by the ambulance.

Sheriff Krause hauled his large body from the vehicle. "Move along, now." He glared at Callie and Mrs. Wimple—the only two people standing there. "We don't need any gawkers."

"We're not gawking, Fred." Mrs. Wimple's curlers quivered. "Callie here found poor Lucille."

The sheriff ignored them. As he strode toward the paramedics, a tan Buick pulled up and stopped beside them. Bruce, Ralph, and Floyd climbed out. They nodded to the women and then all stared at Miss Penwell.

"What happened here?" Bruce placed his hands on his hips as he frowned.

Callie hugged herself. "We're not sure, but Miss Penwell was shot."

Ralph raised his eyebrows. "Shot? In Fort Lob?"

Sheriff Krause whirled around, which was quite a feat for such a big man. "Yep. Looks like the bullet's still in there, too, but it must not have hit any vital organs."

A shiver ran through Callie. "Is she going to be okay?"

"Sure hope so." The sheriff grabbed the waistband of his pants and hiked them up. They immediately slid back a few inches. "Right now she's unconscious, but the boys will take her to the county hospital in Lusk." He seemed to be enjoying this. "Don't worry. We'll find the culprit."

Joe and Davin rolled the gurney to the ambulance.

"But will she survive?" Mrs. Wimple directed her question to Davin and Joe.

"Her vital signs are good." Davin moved out of the way while Joe slid the gurney into the back. "Fortunately, she had the good sense to stick her purse beneath her, stanching the flow of blood from the bullet." Davin waited while Joe climbed in the back before he shut the ambulance doors and strode to the driver's side. "It probably saved her life."

He drove the ambulance out to the road and then roared down Main Street toward Highway 270, sirens wailing.

Ralph grunted. "Lucille's a tough old bird. She'll make it."

Mrs. Wimple put her hand to her throat. "Ralph! The way you talk."

Even though the August sun warmed the morning air, Callie couldn't stop shivering. "I can't believe someone shot her. Poor Miss Penwell!"

"Yes, poor Lucille!" Mrs. Wimple's pale face turned a shade paler. "There hasn't been a murder in Fort Lob since the early 1900s. The very idea that someone would attempt such a thing. . ." She shook her head.

By this time, a number of other townspeople had joined them.

Sheriff Krause planted himself in front of the group and produced a notepad from somewhere behind him. "Now, before you all leave. . ." He pulled a pen from his uniform pocket. "Let me ask a few questions." With his brows drawn down, he gazed intently at the crowd, as if looking for a criminal.

Callie waved her hand. "Sheriff, when I found Miss Penwell lying at the bottom of the steps, her hand was in the flower bed, and her finger was all—"

"Yes, yes, we'll get to that. . . ." He cleared his throat as he wrote on the pad. "The boys think Lucille was shot late last night. Did anyone hear a gun-shot around ten or eleven?"

A murmur went through the crowd as Ralph nodded. "Come to think of it, I heard a shot last night but thought it was Jamie's car." He looked around. "Just one loud backfire from the direction of the library."

Several people voiced their agreement. Callie stepped to the side. She had been home last night and too far from town to hear Jamie's car or anything else. Evidently, the sheriff didn't think her information was important anyway.

He wrote something on the notepad. "Did anyone see Lucille last night before that time?"

"I saw her." George Whitmore shouldered his way to the front until he stood by the sheriff. He brushed back his salt-and-pepper hair. "I was at the library last night, and I tell you, Lucille was in an awful temper."

The sheriff tapped his face with a thick finger. "Did something happen to put her in a bad mood?"

George nodded. "She had a loud disagreement with one of the patrons. Of course, that ain't too rare—especially right before closing time."

"Who was it, George?" The sheriff's pen poised over the paper.

"It was that new fella, uh, Hutchins."

Callie's lips parted. "Lane?"

George glanced at her. "He and Lucille were up in one of the conference rooms, and I heard her yelling at him something fierce."

*Uh-oh.* Callie pressed her fingers against her mouth.

"And Hutchins got mad as a hornet at her. They were really having a row, I tell you."

*This is terrible!* Callie's heart sank to her toes. After she had left the library last night, her conscience bothered her. Why hadn't she insisted that Lane wait until the morning? Instead, she had sneaked up the library's back stairs and given Lane a box of old letters without Miss Penwell's knowledge.

*"Be sure your sin will find you out."*

The Bible verse flew through her mind. Now, because of her poor judg-ment, Lane was in trouble.

"Guess I'll pay Hutchins a little visit." Sheriff Krause turned to Mrs. Wimple. "Doesn't he live at the Stables, Adelaide?"

"Yes, but he's not there." The red lips worked around in a circle. "He left town last night. Don't know what time it was, but it was late."

"He left town?" Callie became concerned. "Did he say where he was going?"

"No, but he took all his stuff—what little he had." She pulled on a sponge curler that was falling out. "It's a furnished apartment, you know."

"So he left town." The sheriff wrote on his pad.

George nodded. "Rather incriminating evidence, I'd say."

A murmur buzzed through the crowd.

"Lane didn't do it." Callie pressed her lips in a firm line.

Ralph leaned toward her. "You must admit, Callie, no one knows where this man came from or who he really is."

George nodded. "I bet he shot Lucille last night and skipped town."

Bruce held up his hand. "Let's not jump to conclusions. He seems to be an even-tempered sort of fellow. What motive would he have to kill her?"

"Well. . ." George shrugged. "They certainly were quarreling about something."

"I think we're finished here." The sheriff waved his hand toward the crowd like he was brushing away a pesky fly. "Go home, folks. The library will be closed today and tomorrow so we can investigate the scene of the crime. And if any of you see Hutchins, call me immediately."

Callie folded her arms. *She* would not be the one to betray Lane.

~

Driving her Honda out of the library's parking lot, Callie headed toward Antelope Road. If the library was going to be closed for two days, she might as well go home. Sheriff Krause had cordoned off the front of the building with yellow police tape. He had searched the grounds and covered every room inside, but his investigation led nowhere. Not one clue pointed to the assailant.

She gave a helpless sigh. Who would have shot Miss Penwell? Maybe one of the council members shot her because she wouldn't retire. *That's no reason.* Unless it was a cold-blooded killer.

If only she had read more murder mysteries instead of so many history and romance books. Maybe she would be more intuitive in the psychology of the human mind and she could figure out whodunit.

Unfortunately, Lane was still under suspicion, especially by Sheriff Krause, and the townspeople seemed ready to blame him. Callie wouldn't be surprised if *The Scout* had banner headlines tomorrow morning saying, Librarian Shot by Transient Citizen.

She knew Lane did not kill—or attempt to kill—Miss Penwell. But the librarian must have discovered Lane reading the town documents, and that was Callie's fault.

*Lord, please forgive me,* she prayed. She hoped Lane would forgive her. She couldn't blame him for leaving town.

But where did he go?

A sudden thought made her gasp, and she hit the brakes. Making a

U-turn in the middle of Antelope Road, she raced back toward Fort Lob. When she arrived at the library, she pulled around to the back parking lot and let herself in the back door.

She paused inside. *Lord, am I doing something wrong again?* But the sheriff hadn't banned her from the building. After all, the crime had occurred outside, not inside, the library.

Callie ascended the stairs to the second floor and entered the reference rooms. A row of metropolitan phone books from cities and towns in Wyoming, Nebraska, South Dakota, and Colorado lined the shelf. She found the Cheyenne phone book and looked up *Hutchins*.

"There he is." *Hutchins, Lane.* She grabbed a scrap of paper from the little box beside the computer and scribbled down his address and phone number.

Callie stuck the paper in her jeans pocket. Then she went into the conference room where Lane had been last night. Nothing was on the table. She looked on top of the cabinet where she had told him to put the box last night when he finished. The two books were displayed as they had been last night, but the box was gone—Miss Penwell must have confiscated it. Behind the books lay a folded piece of paper.

She picked it up. Her name was written on the outside. With trembling fingers, she opened the note and glanced down to Lane's signature at the bottom.

> *Callie, thanks for helping me with my research during the past month, but I've decided to move out of Fort Lob. It's too small for my object in small-town living, and some of the people here don't trust me.*

Callie knew exactly whom he meant. She kept reading.

> *Thanks for all you've done for me. Sorry things didn't work out for us. I'll always remember you. Lane.*

"Sorry things didn't work out for us?" Callie drew in a shaky breath that was almost a sob. *No!* Things couldn't be over between them. They had barely gotten started. What about the peace she felt when they were eating together last night? She had never felt that way about Murray Twichell, who declared his love for her in the sixth grade and still wanted to date her.

Callie gritted her teeth. Lane was not going to quietly disappear, never to be seen again. She was going to find him.

# Chapter 16

Lane paced the tan Persian rug in the living room of his house in Cheyenne. "I am such a coward!"

With a moan, he plopped down on the brown sofa and dropped his head in his hands. For a few moments, he just sat there, regretting the turn of events. "How could I have done such a thing?"

He could never show his face in Fort Lob again.

After a few moments, he sat back. He had closed the drapes on the tall floor-to-ceiling windows, and the room's darkness complemented his mood. The tiled fireplace, with three framed pictures resting on the mantel, was cloaked in shadows.

With a sigh, he walked to the fireplace and picked up the photograph of Herbert Dreyfuss—the same picture, taken eight years ago, that graced Lane's syndicated column in thousands of newspapers every Friday, the same one that was on the back cover of every book Lane wrote.

He wished his uncle were here to give him advice. But even though Herbert Dreyfuss couldn't help him anymore, there was Someone who could, if only Lane would humble himself enough to ask.

Replacing the picture, he turned back to the room. Aunt Betty's old King James Bible lay on the end table where it had lain for years. Lane remembered her sitting on this sofa, reading it every morning.

Taking a seat, he lifted the old book and blew off the dust that had accumulated on its cover. The Bible fell open to a bookmark in Philippians, and Lane glanced at an underlined verse. *"For it is God which worketh in you both to will and to do of his good pleasure."*

This was the same verse Callie had mentioned. He thought back to what she said. *"The Lord has a reason for everything He does, Lane."*

So God had a reason for taking Aunt Betty and Uncle Herb, even though He knew it would make Lane bitter?

*Bitter.* Yep. That was Lane Hutchins to the core. Bitter at God.

*"Only the Lord can heal your heart, Lane."*

He thought back to his high school days—those happy, carefree days before Aunt Betty got sick. Lane had truly loved Jesus Christ and wanted to serve Him. But when things in his world started falling apart. . .

*"The Lord is waiting for you to come back to Him."*

He knelt by the sofa. "Okay, Lord, I'm coming back. You've got my attention, even though Callie says You don't work that way." He let out a deep sigh. "I've taken charge of my life for the past seven years, and I've failed. Please forgive me for my bitterness and for running away from You. Cleanse my heart, Lord. I surrender it to You. I need You, and I'll need Your guidance for the rest of my life."

$\approx$

The sun was shining as Callie took to the open road early Saturday morning. She had prayed long and hard about her decision to visit Lane. Of course, he might not even be in Cheyenne, but she had to try something.

She wasn't going to let him slip out of her life.

But she didn't want to stay in Cheyenne too long. The town meeting about keeping the library open was scheduled for tonight at seven, and she couldn't miss it.

Lane would be surprised to hear what had happened to Miss Penwell. The old librarian was still in a coma, which was another thing Callie was praying about. If only Miss Penwell would wake up, she could tell them who shot her. Then all the rumors about Lane would die.

Pushing the car's accelerator to sixty-five miles an hour, Callie drove south on the two-lane, paved road known as Highway 270. In the last ten minutes, only one car had passed her. Humming along with the air conditioner, she knew God would work everything out between her and Lane.

She felt a bump and glanced in the rearview mirror. Something small, like a piece of wood, lay near the side of the road behind her. *I must have run over that.* She didn't think too much about it until a minute later when she heard a *thwump, thwump* noise. The back right tire began to pull with each *thwump*.

"Oh no!"

Slowing down, she pulled the car to the edge of the road and stopped. A steady warm breeze lifted her hair as she got out and walked around the back to look at the tire. It was totally flat.

Callie slapped her hand to her forehead. "Great! Just great." With a sigh, she unlocked the trunk. She hadn't changed a tire since she was sixteen. Dad had taught her when she was learning to drive, but that was ten years ago. She had never changed a real flat tire and never by herself.

*Now I know why people carry cell phones.* Not that a cell phone would do her any good on this barren highway. Signals didn't reach out here. She would just have to change the tire herself and pray that it stayed on until she reached Cheyenne.

She got out the jack and looked at it then looked at the car. Didn't this thing come with directions? *Lord, send me help!*

Peace flooded her heart. The Lord would be her Helper. After all, He was the Great Mechanic—He knew how to change a flat tire.

She thought about the owner's manual in the glove compartment and pulled it out. Flipping through the book, she found the section on changing a flat tire. Standing beside the car, she read the instructions as a vehicle pulled up behind her. Whirling around, she breathed out a sigh of relief.

Tom Shoemacher climbed down from his tow truck. "Hey there, Callie! Got a flat, I see."

"Oh, Tom! Am I glad to see you!" She laughed, inwardly thanking the Lord for sending Fort Lob's only full-service gas station owner. "I ran over something a few miles back, and it must have punctured the tire." She pointed to the jack. "I'm not sure if I'm doing this right."

"Well, no worries." Tom smiled, wreathing his face in wrinkles. "I'll have this fixed in two shakes of a lamb's tail. Let me get my own tools from the truck."

"Thanks so much." *Thank You, Lord. You're so good to me.*

Tom came back and set his tools on the ground. He adjusted the jack under the side of the car in front of the back tire and pumped it up.

Callie watched him. "I was afraid I wouldn't see one car on this lonesome highway. You're a real answer to prayer."

"We do have a sparse population. It's like old Herbert Dreyfuss wrote yesterday about being able to fit a whole third world country in Wyoming." He laughed as he glanced at her. "Did you read it?"

She nodded. *I said it.*

"And isn't that the truth!" Taking a wrench, he twisted off the lug nuts before lifting the flat tire from the axle.

Callie sighed, thankful she didn't have to worry about those lug nuts. It probably would have taken her an hour to get them off.

"I'm on my way to Torrington to pick up my wife." Tom took the spare tire from the trunk and rolled it to the side of the car. "She's been visiting her sister this week."

Callie smiled. "Your wife was my Sunday school teacher in fifth grade."

Tom lifted the spare up on the axle. "Lila was pert near everyone's teacher in Fort Lob who's under thirty-five. Hasn't missed a Sunday for twenty-four years." He lifted the hubcap back in place and tightened the wheel nuts. "There you go, Callie. All fixed."

"I appreciate that so much. What do I owe you, Tom?"

"Nothing." He picked up his tools. "Although I wouldn't mind one of those good Sunday dinners your mom makes."

Callie laughed. "I'll talk to Mom, and we'll have you and Lila over one of these Sundays."

After Tom pumped down the jack and put everything away, he followed her car down to the end of Highway 270, where she turned right toward the freeway. He turned left toward Lusk and Torrington. She waved her hand out the window as they parted ways.

Callie glanced at the map lying on the passenger's seat, and her stomach clenched. It would probably take an hour or more before she arrived at Lane's house, but she hadn't given a thought to what she would say when he opened the door.

*Why did you run away?* No, that was no good.

*Come back to Fort Lob—I miss you.* That sounded lovesick.

*I'm stalking you, mister!* Too flirty.

She sighed. "Lord, You helped me once today. Please help me again."

A verse of scripture popped into her mind. It was a verse in Hebrews about coming boldly to God's throne of grace. She finished the verse out loud. " 'That we may obtain mercy, and find grace to help in time of need.' "

The Lord would give her grace, just when she needed it. She smiled. She had learned that verse in Lila Shoemacher's Sunday school class.

❧

*Finally!*

Callie slowly drove past number 736, then she turned around and pulled up in front of the two-story brick house. Her stomach growled. She had thought she would arrive way before lunch, but the morning had not gone as planned. First the flat tire, and then she drove around Cheyenne for a while, unable to find Lane's street.

Sitting in the car, she took a moment to pray and look at her surroundings. The house resided in an older neighborhood, with a maple tree towering in the small front yard and a long driveway leading back to a detached three-car garage. Two tall windows on the left and a large bay window on the right flanked the front door of the house. There was no porch except for two steps that led up to the door. Low bushes grew on either side. The place looked inviting.

*Then why am I so nervous?*

With a final prayer, Callie got out and trudged up the front walk, still not sure what she would say when Lane opened the door.

❧

Lane opened his refrigerator and looked at the frozen dinners stacked in the freezer. It was one o'clock, and he hadn't eaten lunch. But he had gotten his heart right with God, and he felt good. No, he felt *clean*. With a happy sigh, he pulled out the Mexican fiesta dinner.

The doorbell rang, the sound echoing through the house. Lane frowned. No one ever visited him. It must be a salesman. *I'll just ignore it.* He turned the frozen dinner over and read the directions on the back of the box.

*Ding-dong!*

Lane pulled the tray out of the box and opened the door of the microwave.

*Ding-dong! Ding-dong! Ding-dong!*

With a frustrated sigh, Lane set down the dinner and walked to the front of the house. The entryway formed an alcove between the living room on one side and the dining room on the other. He passed the flight of stairs leading upstairs before he opened the door.

Callie stood outside, a tentative smile on her face. The wind tugged at her dark curly hair. She adjusted her glasses with one hand while the other clung to the purse strap over her shoulder.

Lane's mouth dropped open. "Callie?"

"Hi, Lane." She cleared her throat. "May I come in?"

"Oh, uh, sure." Stepping back, he motioned toward the living room. His heart pounded. Why was she here? She must have heard about what happened at the library Thursday night. *That's not good.* In fact, it was downright embarrassing.

She walked past him but stopped beneath the archway into the living room. "Nice place you have. I love a formal front room."

"Aunt Betty decorated it." He strode across the Persian rug, glad he had dusted and vacuumed after his prayer time with the Lord. The light from the afternoon sun filtered into the room since he had opened the drapes, but he turned on the lamp beside the sofa—just for something to do. He motioned to a wingback chair. "Have a seat."

"Thanks." Callie glanced around as she slipped down to the chair. She couldn't believe how big this room was. The smell of lemon polish hung in the air. A brown sofa faced the two wingback chairs in front of a massive fireplace. Even though it was so formal, the room felt cozy. Homey.

On the mantel rested a framed photograph of Herbert Dreyfuss. It was the same picture that was in the newspaper and on the back cover of his books. A few weeks ago, Callie would have been surprised to see his picture in Lane's house but not now.

Across from her, Lane perched on the sofa's edge. His green T-shirt stretched across solid muscles underneath. She had never seen him wearing anything but a tailored shirt with a pocket. . . .

"So, Callie." He ran his hand through his hair before he gave her a weak smile. "What brings you down to Cheyenne?"

*He's more nervous than I am.*

She still wasn't sure what to say, so she blurted out the first thing that came to her mind. "You're writing those newspaper articles for Herbert Dreyfuss, aren't you?" It was more a statement than a question.

He lifted his eyebrows. "Well, yes, I am." He clasped his hands in front of him then unclasped them. "I, uh. . ." Jumping up, he walked to the mantel and picked up the picture of Dreyfuss. "This was my uncle Herb."

Callie's lips parted. "But he's been dead for seven years."

He nodded.

"So. . .the rumor is true? Herbert Dreyfuss is dead?"

Lane sighed. "Unfortunately, yes."

"And you're writing everything? Even the history books?"

"Yep." He smiled, seeming relieved to admit it. He motioned for her to follow him to the opposite side of the room, stopping at a narrow bookcase that Callie had not noticed before. Rows of books, all by Herbert Dreyfuss, filled the shelves.

She paused by his side. "Wow, Lane. This is amazing."

He pulled out *A History of Gunfights in America* from a shelf that held six more books, all with the same spine. "When I donated those two books to the library, I got them right here. These are my author's copies." He grinned. "So when you said they were expensive and I said it was nothing, I meant that literally."

Callie shook her head. "I just can't believe this."

He handed the book to her. "For you."

"Oh, how sweet." She took it. "Thank you, Lane. You'll have to sign it for me."

"I'll do that."

She studied the cover with the author's name blazoned across the top. "But, Lane, why are you writing under your uncle's name and not your own?"

His smile faded. "That's a long story." He motioned toward the chairs, and she took her seat.

Lane lowered himself to the sofa, again perching on the edge. "Uncle Herb was a prolific writer, but he struggled with his writing. He never gained the fame he wanted."

Callie adjusted her glasses. "I remember seeing him interviewed on TV when I was fourteen."

"Really?" He smiled. "I was seventeen. That was his only TV interview, and it was live. Aunt Betty and I were glued to the television."

"My dad and I were the only ones who saw it at our house." Hmm. . .she had been watching Lane's *uncle* those many years ago. "So how did you start writing under your uncle's name?"

He lifted his hands then let them drop. "I used to help Uncle Herb edit his articles, especially after Aunt Betty passed away. He taught me everything he knew about writing. Just before he died, he signed a book contract—his first one." He gave her a rueful smile. "He was so excited. We sketched out the book together, and then he suddenly passed away."

"That must have been a terrible shock for you."

"It was." Lane took a deep breath. "I wrote to his editor, Mr. Porterfield, and told him my uncle died. I thought he would cancel the contract, but he asked me to write the book and send it in." He shrugged. "I thought it would honor Uncle Herb's memory if I fulfilled the contract with a book under his byline."

Lane walked to the fireplace and picked up his uncle's photo. "That book sold so well that it was on the *New York Times* bestseller list for thirty-six weeks. No one was more surprised than Mr. Porterfield."

"So you wanted to keep writing books under your uncle's name."

Lane turned to her. "No, I wanted to write them under my own name, but the editor wouldn't let me." He shook his head. "I was so naive about publishing. Mr. Porterfield talked me into signing an eight-book contract as a ghostwriter for Uncle Herb. So I did."

Callie's eyes widened. "Eight books?"

He nodded. "I just sent in the eighth one last week." He perched again on the sofa, clasping his hands between his knees. "Since the books sold so well, Mr. Porterfield has become very unscrupulous. Over and over, he's denied the fact that Herbert Dreyfuss is dead. Now most people, especially the general populace, think Herbert Dreyfuss is alive and well, and I haven't been able to do a thing about it."

Callie shook her head. "And you've kept this to yourself for seven years?"

"It's nice that I can finally tell someone." He gave her a sad smile. "I'm glad it was you."

"Oh, Lane." Callie gazed at his handsome face.

"And another thing. . ." He bowed his head, pausing, as if he was struggling for words. "I finally had a good talk with God, Callie." He looked her in the eye. "I got it right and came back, just like you told me. I have such an incredible peace in my heart I can hardly believe it."

"Praise God," Callie whispered.

Lane stood and paced behind the sofa. "I've been praying about what to do. First of all, I'm going to get a good agent who can advise me. Mr. Porterfield has been pestering me to sign another contract, but I'd like to part company with him. Then I plan to tell the world my name is not Herbert Dreyfuss, no matter what the fallout."

She nodded. "You need to publish books under your own name."

"That's been my dream for years." He stopped pacing to face her. "Hopefully a good editor will accept me."

"I think the publishing world will welcome you, Lane. After all, you're a bestselling author. You could write that book about living in small-town America under your own name."

"I'm not sure if I should keep moving to small towns in America." He started pacing again. "That was something I decided to do without considering God's will. Now I think He wants me to settle down—somewhere. I don't know what my future holds, but I want to follow His leading."

Callie's heart took an unexpected leap. She walked to where he stood.

"I'm so glad to hear you talk like that. God will show you His will because He's working in your heart. You just have to trust Him."

He stepped toward her until they were only a few inches apart. "Callie, if God hadn't brought you into my life. . ." Leaving the sentence dangling, he removed her glasses and set them on the end table.

For a moment, he gazed into her eyes and Callie gazed right back. He pulled her into his arms. "You're so beautiful."

He kissed her, briefly and hesitantly, as if he weren't sure what her reaction would be. Lifting his head, he looked at her.

"Kiss me again, Lane," she whispered.

He did—several times, with his kisses becoming more passionate and ending with one slow, deep kiss.

When they finally parted, Callie rested her head against his shoulder. They stood in each other's arms for a long time.

Callie gave a contented sigh. *This is where I belong.*

## Chapter 17

*I'm falling in love with Callie Brandt!*
Nothing had prepared Lane for the feelings that coursed through him when he kissed her. He wanted her in his arms forever—or at least for the rest of his life.

His stomach growled.

"Oh!" He dropped his arms. "Excuse me." How embarrassing.

Callie stood back and giggled. "You must be hungry. Me, too."

"You are? Hey, let's go out to eat."

"Okay." She gazed up at him, a smile playing on her lips. "You'll have to pick out the restaurant because I have no idea what's in Cheyenne."

Lane thought for a moment. Fast food? Or should they go to a nice sit-down restaurant with a quiet, romantic atmosphere? "I know just the one." He picked up her glasses from the end table and handed them to her.

She raised them to her face. "Thanks."

"Wait!" Lane caught her wrist.

She paused with her glasses in midair and looked up at him.

"Just wanted one more look."

"Oh, Lane." She gazed back into his eyes.

He bent over and brushed a kiss against her lips. "Ready to go?"

                               ❧

Callie could not believe the events that had transpired or the peace in her heart. *Thank You, Lord!* He had worked everything out for good—far better than she could have asked or imagined.

Arriving at a fancy restaurant on the outskirts of Cheyenne, Callie felt underdressed in her jeans and T-shirt, even though that was what Lane was wearing. They were seated at a quiet table in the back corner, given menus, and, fifteen minutes later, ordered their food. He ordered a rib-eye steak that was twice the price of any entrée at Mama's Kitchen. She ordered one of the least-expensive items—baked chicken.

After the waiter left, Callie leaned across the small two-person table. "This is an expensive place, Lane."

"Being rich has its perks." He winked at her.

The realization that Lane was rich—probably a millionaire—made her sit back in silence. She had always thought of him as poor and starving. After all, he lived in a cheap apartment in Fort Lob and ate frozen dinners.

Fortunately, he saved her from commenting. "I thought you'd be working at the library today, Callie. Don't you always work on Saturday?"

"Oh!" Her eyes widened as another realization hit her. "I completely forgot!"

He frowned. "You forgot to work today?"

"No, not that." Callie folded her arms on the table and leaned forward. "The reason I drove down here was to tell you about Miss Penwell. On Thursday night, something terrible happened to her."

"Thursday night?" Lane looked wary. "What happened?"

"Someone shot her and left her for dead. Sheriff Krause has no idea who did it. But she survived, and she's in the hospital right now, in a coma."

Lane stared at her a moment before he breathed out a heavy sigh. "Oh, that's just great!" He ran his hand through his hair. "My doom is sealed. I suppose there's a warrant out for my arrest." His eyes darted around the room.

Callie's scalp prickled. "Lane? Did you—" She pushed her chair away from the table. "*You* didn't shoot Miss Penwell, did you?"

"What?" His confused look disappeared as he focused on her. "No! No, of course not. It's just that she found me reading that stuff from the box Thursday night, and I totally lost it."

Callie bumped her chair back up to the table. "You lost the box?"

"No, I lost my temper." He pressed his lips into a firm line before he spoke. "I have never yelled at another human being like I yelled at Miss Penwell." He pounded his fist on the table. "The things I accused her of—even *I* can't believe some of the things I said." His voice softened. "I'm so ashamed."

Callie placed her hand over Lane's fist. "Everyone knows what Miss Penwell's like. I'm sure she provoked you to anger."

He gave a rough laugh. "She provoked me, all right. The whole library heard me. It was so embarrassing." He picked up her hand and cradled it in his. "I'll never be able to go back to Fort Lob now."

"Don't say that." She squeezed his fingers.

"Callie, you're the only good thing in that town. The only true friend I have." He shrugged. "Some of the townspeople are friendly—in a nosy, curious way. But I never made friends with any of them." He sighed. "And then there are those who don't like me at all."

"There are good and bad people in every town, but you have as much right to live there as anyone else. The town council is having that meeting tonight about the library." She gave his hand another squeeze. "I was hoping, especially after what happened this afternoon between us, that you'd come back with me." She cocked an eyebrow.

He looked at her thoughtfully for a moment. "Well. . ." He lifted her hand to his lips and kissed it. "I'll go with you, Callie, but I'm not sure what's going to happen to me."

She smiled. "What could possibly happen?"

Lane decided to drive his Mazda to Fort Lob. He parked Callie's Honda in the garage at his house while she stood beside his car on the street and waited for him.

After closing the garage door, he walked down the driveway. "We can come back and get your car tomorrow after church. Then I'll ride my motorcycle back to Fort Lob."

She leaned against the black Mazda. "Okay, but let's make that after church and after Sunday dinner at my parents' house. Then we'll drive down here."

He grinned as he stopped in front of her. "I'm all for Sunday dinner."

Even with her glasses on, Callie looked beautiful to him. Impulsively he took her in his arms and kissed her.

Callie breathed out a wistful sigh when they parted. "Why, Lane Hutchins, that's the first time you've kissed me with my glasses on."

He laughed. "It works." He leaned down and kissed her again lightly.

"What will the neighbors think?" Callie tried to give him a stern look.

He grinned. "They'll think that Lane has finally fallen in love."

Callie gasped. "You—you have?"

Lane gazed into her magnified eyes. "I've never felt for another woman what I feel for you, Callie. I love you."

She breathed out another sigh. "I love you, too."

After that exchange, he had to kiss her again.

They finally got on the road.

The closer Lane drove to Fort Lob, the more nervous he became. He exited the freeway at Highway 20. "Who do you think shot Miss Penwell?"

Callie shook her head. "I have no idea. Miss Penwell didn't have many friends, and she had a tendency to argue about the least little thing with anyone who crossed her." She folded her arms. "It could have been anyone."

Lane glanced at her. "Remember what Vern Snyder said to us after we ate lunch at Ray's?"

Callie knit her brows. "What?"

"He said someone would have to kill Miss Penwell before she'd quit her job."

"Oh." Callie's eyebrows shot up. "Yes, I do remember that." She looked at Lane. "And he was so mean to you. I wouldn't put it past Vern to get in an argument with Miss Penwell and shoot her. She was good at provoking people."

"How well I know," Lane muttered. *But thank God, He forgave me.*

She gasped. "I just thought of something. Vern didn't show up yesterday morning at the library when the ambulance came." She looked at Lane. "He's usually right in the middle of everything. I wonder why he wasn't there."

Lane shrugged. "Looks suspicious if you ask me."

They drove past the Fort Lob population sign and down Main Street.

"Wow, this place is deserted." Callie looked from one side of the street to the other.

All the stores had CLOSED signs in their windows, and not one person walked down the sidewalks. Only a few cars were parked at the edge of the street.

"It's a ghost town." Lane turned onto Pronghorn Avenue. The Elks lodge parking lot was packed with cars and trucks. "Looks like everyone in the town is here."

"I wouldn't be surprised." She glanced at her watch. "It's 7:03. We're only a couple minutes late."

Lane pulled his Mazda into an empty space between two cars. "I don't know if I'm ready for this."

"Ready for what?" Callie touched the door handle. "It's just a meeting, even though it's very important. I'm praying the town council will keep the library open."

He was praying, too, although he had a different petition.

&

Callie slipped her hand into Lane's as they walked through the open doorway. The building was so full they could barely step inside. Dozens of people stood at the back. She and Lane took up a spot near the back wall behind Arnold Steiner and Lester Griggs. The two men effectively blocked her view, and the room was stiflingly hot. She glanced at Lane. He was taller and didn't seem to have any problem seeing the front.

Callie took a step to the left, closer to Lane, and peered between Arnold and Lester. The chairs were filled with older men and women. Aggie's big hair—tinted purple—stuck up above the crowd. Murray Twichell, dressed in his dark green uniform, paced at the front with his arms folded.

Standing on the platform, Bruce MacKinnon spoke into a microphone. Callie stood on tiptoe so she could see him. After speaking for several minutes, he let a couple of council members speak. The men had formulated a plan for renovating the library.

Finally Bruce spoke again. "Let us sum up our meeting thus far. In November, an addendum will be added to the ballot concerning the Dorsey-Smythe Library. If you as townspeople are willing to raise your taxes, we can renovate the old building."

Ralph Little moved behind the mic. "Now if the vote passes. . ." He glanced at some notes in his hand. "With the number of citizens in Fort Lob and the amount of money needed to renovate the library, each family will have their local taxes raised about 300 percent."

"Three hundred percent!" someone shouted.

"That's an outrage!" another man said.

People jumped to their feet in protest. The noise in the room grew like a tidal wave until everyone was talking at once.

Lane frowned and leaned toward Callie, speaking in her ear. "Can you believe they're milking the townspeople like this? The council doesn't want to keep the library open, and they're hitting people in their wallet so they'll vote against refurbishing the library."

"I think you're right." Callie's spirits sank. They were going to lose the library after all.

"Quiet, everyone!" Murray stood at the microphone and waited until the noise settled down. "If you have something to say, come to the mic. We will proceed in an orderly fashion." He stepped to the side as Bruce came back.

"Thank you, Murray." Bruce surveyed the room. "Does anyone wish to voice their opinion?"

With a determined glint in his eye, Lane huffed out a breath. "Come on." He pulled Callie's hand as he excused himself between the people standing in front of them.

The crowd at the back parted. Lane and Callie reached the middle aisle between the crowded chairs, and Lane strode down to the front, pulling her along behind him. She heard a gasp from some of the women and wondered if it was because Lane had reappeared after Miss Penwell was shot. But maybe it was because she and Lane were holding hands in public.

As Lane reached the front, Murray's mouth dropped open. But he clamped it shut as he stepped forward. When he opened it again, he declared, "Lane Hutchins, you are under arrest for the shooting of Miss Lucille Penwell."

# Chapter 18

After another gasp from the audience, the room became as silent as a cemetery.

*Oh that Murray!* Callie stepped forward. "Just a minute, Murray. Lane has something to say on behalf of the library."

Murray glanced between the two of them, and his eyes dropped to their entwined hands. "Okay. I'll give you five minutes, Hutchins. But there's a warrant out for your arrest, and as a duly authorized peace officer of Wyoming, I am taking you into custody so Sheriff Krause can question you. Just remember that anything you say can be used against you in a court of law."

Callie rolled her eyes.

Lane just nodded. Still holding her hand, he mounted the steps to the platform where they stood together.

He left the mic on its stand. "Uh, hello, I'm Lane Hutchins. I spoke at the last meeting about the Dorsey-Smythe Library. As I said before, it's one of the best in the country."

He glanced at Callie, and his face was pale. She smiled at him, squeezing his hand. She wasn't sure what he wanted to say, but she would support him, no matter what it was.

Lane cleared his throat. "All of you know about Herbert Dreyfuss, the famous author." He paused. "He's my uncle."

A murmur flitted through the crowd.

"What you might not know is that Herbert Dreyfuss has been dead for seven years."

This comment caused more than a murmur. Callie looked at the faces in the audience, some registering shock and others hardening into disbelief. A few people nodded their heads as if they had heard the rumor.

"It's true." Lane raised his free hand to stop the chatter. "Seven years ago, my uncle had a heart attack and died. But I had been editing his writing, so I kept his syndicated newspaper column going, and I wrote his books."

"So you're Herbert Dreyfuss?" a man shouted out.

A tiny smile graced his lips, and he nodded. "I'm the author behind his name."

"Wow." The man stood, and Callie saw that it was Glen Massey, a middle-aged rancher who lived near the Brandts. "We have a famous person in our midst, folks."

This comment caused an outbreak of more conversation. Callie saw a lot of smiles, and she smiled back, squeezing Lane's hand.

He glanced at her with his own smile, and she was glad to see his color had returned.

"As you can imagine..." Lane spoke into the microphone, and the crowd quieted. "Being a bestselling author brings in quite a bit of revenue."

He paused as the audience laughed.

"Therefore, in order to save all of you from having to pay higher taxes, I'd like to donate $500,000 to renovate the Dorsey-Smythe mansion."

New exclamations burst out along with a round of applause, and the audience seemed to rise as one and move toward the front. As Lane and Callie stepped off the platform, they were surrounded by townspeople. One after another pumped Lane's hand.

Callie stood back. She had never seen Lane so happy. He was finally getting the recognition he deserved.

Murray walked up to Lane's side. "All right, folks. Step back. Give us room here."

The crowd melted back at his authoritative voice.

"There is still the matter of Miss Penwell's shooting." Murray turned to Lane. "You are under arrest, Hutchins. You have the right to remain silent." He drew a pair of handcuffs from his back pocket. "Anything you say can be used against you in a court of law." Pulling Lane's arms behind him, Murray snapped the handcuffs on his wrists.

"Murray..." Callie couldn't believe this was happening. "Lane is innocent. He didn't shoot Miss Penwell."

"Sorry, Callie. I'm taking him over to the sheriff's office for questioning." He glanced around at the silent crowd. "No one needs to follow us." He gave a pointed look at Callie before grabbing Lane's arm and pulling him to the door.

With his head bowed, Lane walked away. He didn't look back.

Callie's shoulders drooped. She couldn't imagine what Lane was feeling at this moment. He must be so embarrassed. She stood by the platform as the crowd dispersed. Even though Bruce hadn't dismissed the meeting, people left the building, talking with each other in low tones until the hall was almost empty.

In a few minutes, the sound of sirens screamed outside. Listening, Callie breathed out a frustrated sigh. Of course Murray would have to turn on the siren. The sound faded as the car traveled down Main Street and Rattlesnake Road, all the way to the sheriff's office. She closed her eyes. *Lord, please work this out according to Your will. Give Lane peace—*

"Well, Callie." Vern Snyder strode up with his wife, Blanche, trailing behind him. "Guess Hutchins thought he could buy his way out of this one."

Callie frowned. "That's not true, Vern."

"Huh! He's just sweet-talking you, Callie. Do you really think he's Herbert Dreyfuss? He's lying through his teeth."

Callie folded her arms. "But he *is* Herbert—"

"That half million dollars will never show up. You watch."

Blanche clicked her tongue. "That man don't look rich to me."

"Everyone knows he shot Lucille." Vern smirked. "The way he was arguing with her on Thursday night, then he ups and leaves town. Of course he shot her."

"Who else would have done it?" Blanche shook her head. "We've known everyone in Fort Lob for years, but he's a total stranger."

Callie knew it wouldn't do any good to argue with them. "Lane will be proven innocent."

"Says you." Vern waggled his finger at her. "You'd better stay away from him, Callie. He's a dangerous criminal."

She gritted her teeth. "I wouldn't be surprised if you shot Miss Penwell, Vern."

"Me?" Raising his eyebrows, he pointed to his chest.

"You said someone would have to kill Miss Penwell before she stopped working at the library. Remember?"

"Huh!" Vern squinted at her. "It just so happens I have an alibi. After me and Blanche ate at the Cattlemen's Diner, we went to Blanche's brother's house near Douglas and spent the night there."

Blanche raised her chin. "We are innocent of the frightful goings-on that happened to poor Lucille."

Vern took his wife's elbow. "I hope Hutchins can cool his heels in jail for a few years."

Gritting her teeth, Callie watched them walk away. Okay, so it wasn't Vern. But it also wasn't Lane.

She followed the Snyders at a discreet distance out the door. She was going to find out who shot Miss Penwell if it took her all week.

☙

Callie knocked on the door of the small white clapboard house on Bison Road. She had called George Whitmore, who gave her a list of everyone he could remember at the library Thursday night. One by one she visited them, and one by one she crossed off their names.

It was Sunday afternoon, and that depressed Callie. She and Lane should have been on their way to Cheyenne by now to pick up her car. Instead, she was talking to townspeople, trying to figure out who shot Miss Penwell so Lane could get out of jail.

Glen Massey had given her a ride home last night, and Murray had brought Lane's car keys to their house this morning. Now she was driving

Lane's Mazda around, thankful she had some wheels.

She knocked again. *Isn't he home?* She walked down the porch and looked in the living room window, cupping her hands around her face. Yep, there he was, sitting on a La-Z-Boy recliner, watching television.

*He probably didn't hear the door.* She knocked on the window. Startled, he looked up. She smiled and waved. He got up, and she noticed a gun cabinet on the other side of the room. *Hmm...*

Chance Bixby opened the door, wearing a white T-shirt and blue shorts.

"Hi, Chance." She smiled. "I was wondering if I could come in and talk to you for a minute."

He frowned. "What about?"

Callie paused. Chance was usually so nice to her, always relaxed and friendly. But today he looked tired, and the stubble on his face told her he hadn't shaved for a few days.

"You're not sick, are you, Chance?" Come to think of it, she hadn't seen him at the meeting last night.

"I feel fine. Now what do you want?"

Callie stepped back, surprised at his curt tone. "I'm, um, trying to find out who shot Miss Penwell, and I heard you were at the library Thursday night."

"So you're blaming me? Is that why you're here, Callie?"

"No..." She smiled, softening her voice. "I was just wondering if you heard or saw anything suspicious when you were leaving the building."

He stared at her.

"The fact is..." She swallowed as Lane's arrest hit her anew. "Lane argued with Miss Penwell Thursday night, and then he left town. So Murray arrested him on circumstantial evidence." Tears filled her eyes. "He didn't do it, Chance! Someone else shot Miss Penwell, but Lane is being held in jail until the police figure out who's responsible."

Chance opened his mouth then closed it. He shrugged. "I can't help you. Sorry." He stepped back and shut the door in her face.

Stunned, Callie walked back to the car. Either Chance didn't want her interrupting his television program, or he was hiding something.

# Chapter 19

*I* *only want to see one person in this world.*

But visiting Lane at the jail would have to wait.

From Chance's house, Callie drove down Bison Road to Main Street, turned right, and drove three miles to Highway 270. She would visit the county hospital in Lusk. Perhaps Miss Penwell had awoken from her coma. At least, Callie prayed so. That would certainly speed things up as far as arresting the correct assailant was concerned.

After parking the Mazda near the hospital entrance, she took the elevator to the third floor. While the elevator slowly made its way up, Callie had time to reflect. She wished Cheyenne were in town, but she and her dad were visiting relatives in North Dakota. Tonya had driven to Casper yesterday to pick Mom up at Grandma's house. Dad and Derek were the only ones at home. They sympathized with Callie, but it wasn't the same kind of empathy a woman would give her.

The elevator jerked open at the third floor, framing Murray Twichell.

He smiled. "Hey, Callie!" The smell of his aftershave floated around him.

Frowning, she stepped out of the elevator. Murray was the *last* person she wanted to see. "Is Miss Penwell still in a coma?"

"Afraid so." He motioned down the hallway. "She's in Room 312, only two doors down."

"Thanks." Callie took a few steps toward the room before she realized Murray was striding beside her.

"I'll warn you—she doesn't look good." Murray pushed open the door to Room 312. "She might not make it."

A single bed took up the small space. Callie walked in, and Murray followed her. Tears filled Callie's eyes as she stood at the bed rail and gazed at the woman she had worked with for ten years. Miss Penwell's cheeks had sunken in below her cheekbones, making her look even more like a skeleton. Dark circles puffed below her closed eyes. Several tubes fed into her arms, and a monitor beeped in the corner.

Murray stood beside her. "She looks bad, doesn't she?"

Callie nodded. "I've always wondered if she was a Christian, but I never talked to her about it. I wish I had." She sighed. "Now all I can do is pray."

He put his arm around Callie's shoulders. "You could witness to her now. They say patients in comas can sometimes hear people talking."

Callie leaned over the bed and felt Murray's hand slip off her shoulder. "Miss Penwell? It's me, Callie. I'm praying for you, and I'm especially praying that you've accepted Jesus as your Savior. He loves you, Miss Penwell. He's waiting with open arms for you to come to Him as a little child. Please accept Him." She bit her lip as she stood upright and glanced at Murray. "It seems like too little too late."

Murray shrugged. "We can pray for God to work."

"Oh, I thought of something else." She leaned over Miss Penwell. "Lane apologizes for what he said to you Thursday night. He said he's so ashamed. If he were here, I'm sure he would ask your forgiveness."

Murray walked to the door and stood there with his arms folded while Callie continued.

"Lane is being held in custody in jail. The police think he shot you, Miss Penwell, but we both know that isn't true." Callie grabbed the older woman's thin hand. It was surprisingly warm. "I'm praying that you'll come out of your coma. We all want you to get better. You need to fight, Miss Penwell. Fight! With God's help, you can make it. You can be as good as new."

She looked at Miss Penwell's hand, so thin with blue veins crossing under the skin. Her fingernails looked dry, and her index finger—

"Murray, I just remembered something."

"What is it?" He strode to her side.

Callie showed him Miss Penwell's hand. "When I picked up her wrist to check her pulse, there was a lot of dirt on her index finger."

"Wasn't her hand resting in the flower bed?" He raised his eyebrows. "That's why it was dirty."

"But, Murray, I think she dug this finger in the dirt." She looked at him. "We should go to the library and see what that soil looks like."

He shrugged. "Sure, we can look, but the sheriff already combed the entire area. He didn't find a thing."

Callie laid Miss Penwell's hand down on the bed. "I'm going back."

⁓

At the library, Callie ducked under the yellow police tape that crossed the front of the building. She knelt beside the marigolds. "Her hand was right here." She parted the flowers carefully.

Murray hunched down beside her. "I doubt if you'll find anything suspicious."

She looked at him. "That's the trouble with you, Murray. You've never had any imagination. You were always content to just look at the surface of things instead of digging deeper—like Miss Penwell evidently did."

His blue eyes widened, and he spread out his hands. "What have I done now?"

"I'm sorry." She breathed out a sigh. "I'm just frustrated, I guess." But it did feel good to vent. "I'd better keep my mind on our investigation." Peering beneath the marigolds, she caught her breath.

"What is it?" He leaned closer.

"It looks like two initials." Callie studied the tiny furrows in the soil. "This first one is definitely a *C*, and this one is a—"

"*D*, maybe?"

"I think it's a *B*. Yep, that's it. *C. B.* I bet Miss Penwell thought she was going to die, and she was pointing out the murderer."

Murray sat back on his haunches. "Why, Callie Brandt! Those are your initials." A stern gleam pierced his eye. "And you had a good motive to kill her, too. Once she was out of the way, you would become the head librarian by default."

"Murray! I didn't shoot her!" She couldn't believe he would even consider that.

"Okay, maybe not." He grinned. "But who else has those initials?"

Callie thought for a moment before she grabbed Murray's arm. "Chance Bixby! And I visited him this afternoon. He was acting awfully strange."

"I can't imagine Chance shooting Miss Penwell." He glanced at Callie. "But maybe I should use my imagination for once."

She laughed. "That's the idea." Then she thought of something else. "He has a gun collection. I saw it in his living room."

Murray stood. "I'll radio Sheriff Krause and see if he wants me to visit Chance."

"And I'm going to the jail to visit Lane." Standing, she dusted her hands off. He cocked his head. "You really like him, don't you?"

She smiled, thinking of the few kisses Lane had shared with her. "Yes, I do."

"Remember when we were kids and I told you I'd marry you someday?" He gazed at her a moment. "I tried, Callie, but it looks like you're going to end up with Hutchins. And so. . ." He shrugged. "I wish you all the best."

"Oh, Murray!" She threw her arms around his neck and gave him a quick hug. "That's the sweetest thing you've ever said to me."

"Yeah, well. . ." His face turned red, and the color crept all the way up to his red hair. He straightened up to his full height and sniffed. "Guess I'd better crack down on Bixby. Have to uphold the law, you know." He strode off toward his patrol car.

A smile lingered on Callie's lips as she watched him go. *I wish you all the best, too, Murray.*

# Chapter 20

Lane paced his jail cell, which was hard to do since it was so small. Of the four walls, three were made of bars, and a hard cot was anchored into the cement-block wall at the back. The only other cell was unoccupied. His supper, which consisted of a cold chicken leg, Styrofoam mashed potatoes, and waxy green beans, lay untouched on a tray on the cot.

The other half of the building contained a small office. Sheriff Krause sat behind his desk. Lane had never seen such a strange specimen of humanity. The sheriff's head sported a few hairs slicked down, and his sagging jowls resembled those of a bloodhound. He was a huge man who looked like he wore a life preserver around his waist. He'd probably eaten one too many doughnuts through the years. Right now he was leaning back in his chair, his hands folded over his wide girth.

*He's certainly no Andy Taylor.*

The front door opened, interrupting Lane's musings.

"Lane!" Callie burst into the office and ran up to his cell.

He gripped the bars. "Callie! Man, am I glad to see you."

"Now, Callie." The sheriff's chair groaned as he sat up. "If you want to visit one of the prisoners, you have to sign in." He stared at them.

"In a minute, Sheriff." Callie laid her hand over Lane's. "I've missed you."

"You wouldn't believe how much I've missed you. I'm so bored—and depressed, too." He might as well admit it.

"I'm sorry, Lane." She gripped his hand. "I have some good news." She glanced at the sheriff. "Did Murray call you about the flower bed?"

"Yep, he told me." The sheriff got up from his chair, which creaked in protest. He stood beside Callie, making her look like a little girl, and hiked up his pants.

Lane frowned. "What does a flower bed have to do with anything?"

"Well, I visited Miss Penwell, and—"

"Did she come out of the coma?" Sheriff Krause placed his hands on his hips—or, at least, somewhere below the middle of the life preserver.

"She hasn't snapped out of it yet." Callie gazed up at Lane. "Really, I don't know if she's going to make it. But I remembered when I picked up her hand to check her pulse that there was a lot of dirt on her index finger. Murray Twichell accompanied me to the library this afternoon, and Miss Penwell had dug the initials *C. B.* in the flower bed where she was shot. Murray and I think she was trying to point out the shooter."

"*C. B.*?" Lane frowned. "Those are your initials, Callie."

"Yes, but also Chance Bixby's." She glanced at Fred. "Did Murray tell you about my visit to Chance?"

The sheriff shook his head. "What happened?"

She related the curt reception Chance had given her. "So it could be that Chance is the culprit."

"That don't prove anything, Callie." The sheriff walked back to his chair and sat down. "I'll admit that maybe—*maybe*—Lucille was trying to write something in the dirt, but you've got to have better evidence than that."

Callie folded her arms. "You don't have much evidence to hold Lane."

A siren sounded in the distance, coming closer.

The sheriff glanced out the window. "That's a highway patrol car. Must be Murray."

The siren's wail died. A few moments later, the front door opened. Chance Bixby, his wrists handcuffed behind him, walked in. He scowled at the sheriff before he spotted Lane and Callie.

Murray was right behind him. "Here's another suspect, Sheriff." He took out his keys and unlocked the cuffs. "Okay, Mr. Bixby." He placed a chair in the middle of the room. "Sit down. We need to ask you some questions."

Chance fell into the chair. He folded his arms and glared at his captors.

The sheriff stood, hiking up his pants from several places at the waistband. "Chance Bixby, where were you Thursday night, August 28?"

"Working at the library." His answer came out as a snarl.

"Did you see who shot Lucille Penwell?"

Chance opened his mouth and then closed it. He pointed at Lane. "Lucille and that man there had a real fight, Sheriff. They were yelling at each other at the top of their lungs."

Lane bowed his head. *How long will I have to relive that night?*

Callie squeezed his hand, and he looked up. *I love you,* she mouthed.

That brought a smile to his face. Someday he would marry Callie—if he didn't spend the next fifty years in jail.

The sheriff hiked up his stubborn pants. "I asked if you saw who shot Lucille."

Chance glanced around the group. "Well, I don't know. . ."

Callie left Lane's side and knelt in front of the janitor. "Chance, please, if you know anything, tell us." She motioned back to the cell. "Lane is an innocent man." She paused. "If you saw someone shoot her, we need to know."

He stared at Callie for a few seconds. "Okay, I admit it." He looked at the sheriff. "I shot Lucille."

Callie sat back on her heels with a gasp. "You did?"

The sheriff and Murray seemed as surprised as Lane felt. *That was an easy confession.*

Chance glanced around. "Yeah. Well, I'm only admitting it 'cause my conscience is bothering me terrible and 'cause of Callie." He motioned toward Lane. "I can see you like this boy, and he's suffering for something he didn't do."

"Thank you, Chance." Callie squeezed his arm, right on his anchor tattoo. "You've always been a good friend to me."

He blushed. "Aw, Callie. . ."

"You did the right thing, Bixby," the sheriff said.

Callie stepped back to Lane's side.

He grabbed her hands through the bars. "Callie, you're wonderful," he whispered. "I love you."

Wistfully, she gazed into his eyes. "I love you, too."

". . .a very serious charge," the sheriff was saying. "If Lucille dies, you will be a murderer."

Chance ran his finger around the inside of his T-shirt collar.

The sheriff nodded to Murray. "Take a few notes, Twichell."

Murray pulled out his notebook and flipped it open. "Tell us what happened, Mr. Bixby."

"If I have to." He sighed. "Lucille was in a bad mood. Probably because. . ." Chance motioned toward Lane. "When it was time to close up shop, I told her I was staying for a few hours to clean."

"Do you do that often?" The sheriff paced in front of him.

"Yeah, about once a week, and it's usually on Thursday night." He blew out a breath. "But Lucille wouldn't stand for it. She said she didn't trust me alone in the building." Chance spread his hands out. "What was I gonna do? Steal a bunch of books?"

Sheriff Krause folded his arms. "So you shot her?"

"Well, not then. We kept arguing, and she forced me out the door." Chance slapped his leg. "I got so mad—I had it up to here with that woman. I took out my pistol and pulled the trigger."

Callie leaned closer to Lane, even though the bars were in the way. He snaked his hand through the bars and patted her shoulder. He was breathing easy now.

"Do you have a permit to carry a concealed weapon, Mr. Bixby?" Murray never looked up as he continued writing.

"Sure thing! And I got it legally from the attorney general several years ago. I double as a security guard at the library, you know."

"Tell me, Bixby." Sheriff Krause stepped forward. "Did you feel any remorse for shooting Lucille Penwell?"

"Not on Thursday night. When she fell, I thought she got what she deserved."

Callie shook her head.

"But later, Friday morning, I felt bad, real bad. What had I done?" Chance's shoulders slumped. "And now I can't even sleep at night. I hope she doesn't die."

Lane actually felt sorry for the man.

The sheriff took a large ring of keys from the wall. "Okay, Bixby. Let's get in the cell." He paraded Chance past Lane's cell and opened the other one. When the door clanged shut, Chance slumped to the cot and dropped his face in his hands.

The sheriff's keys jingled as he opened Lane's cell door. "You're free to go, Mr. Hutchins."

"Thank you, sir." Feeling magnanimous, Lane shook his hand. Then he stopped to shake Murray's hand as they made their way to the door.

"Sorry about that, Hutchins—uh, Lane." Murray nodded toward Callie. "Hope everything works out for the two of you."

She smiled. "Thanks, Murray."

They walked outside. The sun was just beginning its descent in the early evening sky. Lane drew in a deep breath. "Oh, Callie, it's great to be free. Liberty is not praised enough."

She dug in her purse. "I can't believe you had to go through all that." Pulling out his car keys, she handed them to him. "It's sad that you had to suffer because of Chance's hot temper."

"I'm glad it happened."

She stared at him, her eyes wide. "You're glad you ended up in jail?"

"Sure." He threw his arm around her shoulders as they walked to the car, and she looped her arm around his waist. "I can get some good book material out of this experience. Maybe I'll write a book about the history of jails in America."

"Oh, Lane." She laughed. "That's worse than the *Gunfights* book."

He grinned as they stopped at the car. "Maybe I could interview every inmate in America who's been incarcerated on false charges." He drew his brows together. "You know, all those men who claim to be innocent?"

"There are probably a million of them." She smiled, shaking her head. "You're crazy."

"Crazy about you." He pulled her into his arms and hugged her. The sweet scent of her hair wafted under his nose. "Ah, Callie. I'm so glad God brought you into my life."

She looked up at him. "Me, too."

He kissed her lightly before opening the car door for her. In such a short time, God had changed his entire life. But there was one more thing he needed to discuss with Callie.

# Chapter 21

Callie sat on the passenger's seat in Lane's Mazda, thankful he was once again behind the wheel. They had eaten a good Italian dinner at Mama's Kitchen in Lusk—since Lane had not been particularly fond of jail food—and lingered at the table, discussing the entire arrest episode and talking about their childhoods. Now they were on their way back to Fort Lob. The sun had slipped below the horizon an hour ago, and the stars were out. She closed her eyes and leaned back in the seat with a contented sigh.

"You're not falling asleep, are you?"

She opened her eyes and gazed at him. The dials on the dashboard softly illuminated his face. "I'm just happy with how everything turned out. The Lord is so good."

"He certainly is." Lane grinned. "And better things are ahead, Callie. In fact, I want to discuss something with you."

Her heart leaped in her throat. She wondered how long she would have to wait before Lane proposed marriage. A few days? A few weeks? Or maybe only a few minutes. She gave a happy sigh. It didn't matter; it was in God's hands, and He had given her perfect peace about marrying Lane.

"I want to talk about the museum."

Callie's heart sank. "The museum?" Was that the *better thing* ahead? Maybe he wasn't even thinking about marriage.

He nodded. "I hope you don't mind if we make it a joint project. I'm really excited about displaying all those artifacts, all that history, to the public."

"I'd love to work with you, Lane. After all, I kind of. . .well, I really need. . . your money."

Lane threw back his head and laughed. The sound filled the car. "No problem there. Money is no object."

Callie sighed. "Must be nice when you have plenty of money to do what you want."

"True, although I've never had anything to spend my money on before." He glanced at her. "I've just been saving it and investing some of it. That's why I can afford to pay for the renovations at the library and build you a new museum building."

"Wow, that's so amazing." She closed her eyes again.

"There's another thing I want to discuss with you."

Her eyes flew open. "Yes?"

"Tomorrow I'm going to call Mr. Porterfield."

"Oh."

"I've been talking to a book agent I met a few years ago. He didn't know I was writing as Herbert Dreyfuss back then, which is a good thing."

"Why would that be good?"

"He liked my writing and wanted to represent me when I was a nobody."

"So you trust him."

"Right you are, Callie." He grinned at her. "Along those lines, I have a book idea I'd like to bounce off you." He grew serious. "I've never had anyone I could bounce ideas off before. I usually e-mail Mr. Porterfield and tell him what I want to write for my next book, and he okays it." Lane looked at her. "If I wanted to write about the history of garbage, he would tell me to go ahead."

Callie held her nose. "That's a smelly idea."

He laughed. "See? I need someone to tell me when my ideas stink."

She couldn't help but laugh. "So what's your new book idea?"

"It would be a type of autobiography about Uncle Herb and me, with lots of photos of our family and all the things that happened in my childhood and how I started writing for him."

"Oh, I like that."

He nodded. "I'm going to title it *The Herbert Dreyfuss Story*."

She raised her eyebrows. "Not *The Lane Hutchins Story*?"

"I'll be the author." He shrugged. "My name is not even recognized in America right now. After this book gets published, I hope it is."

She laid her hand on his arm. "It will be. I have a feeling you're going to be a very famous man someday."

⁂

Twenty minutes later, they drove under THE ROCKING B archway and down the long driveway.

Callie spotted Tonya's car parked beside the house. "Oh good. Mom and Tonya are back from Casper."

Lane pulled up behind Tonya's car and parked. "Your mom's been in Casper all these weeks?"

"Yep." Callie shrugged. "Grandma can't get around with a broken hip. Someone has to help her. My aunt is taking over for the next few weeks."

He pushed the button to roll down the front windows before turning off the ignition. "It's nice to have such a big family."

"It is." She opened the car door, and the inside light came on. "I love this summer weather. Want to sit on the porch and talk?"

"Nope." He leaned over the console between the two seats and pulled her into his arms. "I don't want to sit there because we might get interrupted like we did before, and I think we've talked enough this evening." As he said the words, he drew closer until his lips touched hers.

That kiss made Callie's toes curl in her shoes.

This was where she belonged, right here in Lane's arms. She hoped he didn't have a commitment phobia like her brother.

When they parted, he gazed at her in the twilight. "You've helped me so much, Callie. I can't begin to repay you."

She raised her eyebrows. "But you are repaying me. Remember? The library and the museum?"

"That's kid stuff. Actually, I can't imagine my life without you now."

Callie felt like her heart would burst. "Oh, neither can I, Lane." A warm breeze blew through the open door, lifting her hair across her face.

Lane brushed it back and drew in a deep breath. "I can't get on my knees in the car, and I don't have a ring—but will you marry me, Callie?"

*Yes!* "Oh, Lane." Unexpected tears filled her eyes. "I wanted to marry you the first day I met you at the library."

He lifted his brows. "Really?"

"I know now that I couldn't marry just anybody who walked in off the street, but God planted that desire for you in my heart." She gazed into his eyes. "Yes, Lane, I want to marry you."

He leaned over and kissed her again then lifted his head. "You know, this would be a lot easier if we weren't sitting in the car."

She laughed and grabbed his hand. "Come in the house. Mom and Dad think you're still in jail." She gave a happy sigh. "We have so much to tell them."

# *Epilogue*

O h, Callie!" Agatha Collingsworth stood by the big plate glass windows of the Beauty Spot and looked out on Elk Road. "It's snowing, sugar. Ya'll are gonna have a white wedding."

"It's snowing?" Callie swiveled in the beautician's chair to look outside. "Wow! It's really coming down. And I can *see* those snowflakes."

Tonya pulled a curl from the top of her sister's head. "Callie, turn back and face the mirror."

"Sorry." Callie gazed back at her reflection. Tonya stood behind her, piling her hair on top of her head and pinning it, one curl at a time. "I still can't believe how well I can see without my glasses."

Watching Tonya work, Aggie plopped down in the other beautician's chair. "That was so nice of Lane to give ya that laser eye surgery as a wedding present."

"Isn't the Lord good?" Callie gave a wistful sigh. "I always wanted to have laser surgery but never thought it would be a reality." She frowned. "Now I feel bad. All I gave him for a wedding gift was a tie clasp."

Aggie cackled out a laugh. "Hon, he could buy himself a hundred tie clasps, but this one was from you. He'll treasure it always."

"It's the thought that counts." Tonya pinned another curl.

"I guess so."

Aggie stood, frowning. "Now, sugar, look at your lips. They need some color." She opened a drawer beneath the mirror. "Here, try this one. Radiant Sunset."

"But I haven't even put on my makeup yet."

"Won't hurt to test it." Aggie handed her the lipstick tube.

Callie dutifully opened the tube and painted her lips. Aggie had already given her a free manicure and had applied two coats of Dusty Rose polish to her nails. *Now she's going to work on my face.*

Callie looked in the mirror. Her lips were orange. "I don't think this is my color."

Tonya's hands stilled as she glanced at Callie's reflection. "It's too orange, Aggie. She needs something lighter and more pink."

"Looks good to me," Aggie muttered. She rummaged in the drawer.

"A lot lighter." Callie sighed under her breath. Aggie was being a little too helpful.

The bell over the door jangled, and all three women turned. A blast of cold air accompanied Cheyenne as she entered the small waiting area.

"Hi, girls!" She removed her coat and shook off the snow. "We were praying for snow for your wedding day, and look how God answered prayer."

Callie smiled. Her wedding day. She liked the sound of those words.

Cheyenne sat down in the other chair. "Wow, Callie, you are going to be one beautiful bride."

"Except for her orange lips." Tonya laughed.

"Here, hon." Aggie handed Callie a tissue. "Blot that one off and try this. It's called Blushing Rose."

Aggie turned back to the drawer, and Callie rolled her eyes.

Cheyenne grinned. "Are you nervous, girlfriend?"

"Not too much. I still have so much to do before tonight. Mom and I are picking up the cake at three—Alice is making it—and the flowers are supposed to arrive at the church at five."

"I hope this snow doesn't turn into a blizzard." Tonya pulled on Callie's hair. "That would be terrible if the florist couldn't get over to the church from Douglas."

*No flowers!* "That would be terrible." Callie sent up a silent prayer for the florist deliveryman.

"It'll be something to tell your grandchildren someday." Cheyenne crossed her legs, and her jeans were wet on the bottom edges. "Fifty years ago on December 5, we had a huge blizzard! Why, the snow just swirled and whirled around the florist's delivery van. We never thought he'd make it."

Callie groaned. "Save the theatrics, Cheyenne."

Tonya laughed. "The weather can change fast in Wyoming. Last night it was so clear, even though it was cold."

"Yeah, cold and clear." Aggie handed Callie another lipstick tube. "Try this, sugar. Pink Carnation."

Thinking back to the clear skies last night, Callie couldn't help but smile as she applied the lipstick. When Lane had kissed her good night, he said, "This is the last night I'm going to leave you." Tonight they planned to spend their wedding night in a fancy hotel in Douglas. In a few days, they would drive to Yellowstone National Park for their honeymoon. Lane had rented a cozy cabin for them, and Callie couldn't wait.

Aggie peered at her. "That's your color, sugar." She grinned. "You'll be a beautiful bride, hon, just like Cheyenne said."

Tonya sighed. "I wish I was getting married. You're so lucky, Callie."

"Luck had nothing to do with it." Callie met her sister's eyes in the mirror. "God brought us together."

"Now Tonya. . ." Aggie cackled. "Don't you worry none. God will bring your man along soon enough."

Cheyenne folded her arms. "At least you have guys who ask you out, Tonya. Look at me." She stood. "Almost six feet tall and pudgy all over. Who would want to date an Amazon?"

"Don't say that, Chey." Callie bit her lip, wishing she could wipe the lipstick off. "We're still praying about you and Derek."

Cheyenne took her seat. "I've given up on Derek."

"What?" In unison, Callie and Tonya stared at her.

"It's impossible. He's never going to marry me."

"Yes, he is." Callie glanced back at her reflection. "If God could give me Lane, He can give you Derek. You need to have faith." She smiled. "Besides, I've always wanted you to be my sister-in-law."

"All finished." Tonya twirled Callie's chair around so she faced Cheyenne and Aggie. "What do you think?"

"Cool 'do." Cheyenne smiled. "You did a great job, Tonya. I wish I could fix hair like that."

Aggie frowned, tapping a lipstick tube against her double chin. "That color is still not right." She thrust the tube under Callie's nose. "Try this one. Light Fuchsia."

At exactly seven o'clock that evening, Lane followed Pastor Reilly from a side room to the front of the church auditorium. Derek and his brother, Ryan, plus two cousins whom Lane had just met yesterday, followed behind him.

The men stood at the front of the church, waiting. The strains of the organ played in the background, but Lane barely heard the music. The church was filled with hundreds of lit candles—the only light in the room—and an abundance of red and white roses surrounded the altar. A few stragglers were seated in the back row of the packed auditorium.

Lane looked over the congregation. There was Vern Snyder and his wife. The man was actually civil now, but Lane was still surprised he had come. It was probably one of those situations where the Snyders were friends of the Brandt family and had been for years. Weddings and funerals seemed to draw people together, especially in small towns.

Near the front, Lane spotted Lucille Penwell. She had awoken from her comatose state five days after the shooting and made a rapid recovery. While she was still in the hospital, Callie talked to her several times about her eternal destiny, and Miss Penwell accepted Christ as her Savior. God had totally changed that woman. Now she actually liked Lane.

Bruce MacKinnon sat a few rows behind Miss Penwell, and Lane couldn't stop the rush of gratitude that flowed through him. In the last three months, Bruce had convinced the town council to give Lane and Callie ten acres of property on the outskirts of Fort Lob for the museum. They also voted—unanimously—to donate everything from the library's third floor.

Plans were on the drawing board for the building. Lane planned to supervise the construction, and he had already purchased a house in town on Little Deer Road for himself and his bride. They had spent the past three weeks buying furniture, and Callie had a blast decorating the house.

As far as telling the world that he was Herbert Dreyfuss, Lane finally confessed it in his newspaper column a month ago. He had given his e-mail address and had been flooded with thousands of letters supporting him. God had worked everything out for good.

Lane pulled his wandering thoughts back to his wedding and glanced down at the front row. Yvette Brandt, his future mother-in-law, sat by an empty space reserved for Jake. Callie's grandmother, healed from her broken hip, sat beside Yvette. A host of relatives filled the first seven pews, and Lane was still trying to keep everyone straight.

Yvette caught his eye and gave a little wave. Lane smiled back. He finally belonged to a family.

The organ music changed, and Melissa, Callie's oldest sister, started down the aisle. The audience turned in their pews, craning their necks to watch her. She wore a deep-red velvet dress with a white fur collar and carried a small bouquet of red and white roses.

Lane watched Melissa ascend the platform, then he turned to wait for Molly, her twin. He thought the twins looked just like their dad, Jake. Callie and Tonya looked more like their mom, and of course, Callie was the most beautiful of the sisters.

*She's the most beautiful woman in this church—no, in the world.*

Cheyenne walked down the aisle next, and she winked at Lane as she ascended the steps. He grinned, knowing that Cheyenne had wanted him to marry Callie from the beginning.

Tonya, the maid of honor, followed Cheyenne down the aisle. Then the music changed to "Here Comes the Bride." Lane didn't recognize any of the other music, but he knew that song. He could see Callie and her dad standing at the entrance of the auditorium. She looked beautiful in her white bridal gown, which Lane had helped her pick out. Even now he remembered how bored he was, waiting for Callie to pop out of the dressing room in yet another wedding gown. As far as he was concerned, she could have worn a gunnysack and she would be beautiful. But now he gazed at her, drinking in her beauty in yards of white satin with a shiny tiara nestled in her hair.

Callie's eyes met his—those beautiful eyes, unshackled from her glasses. In a few minutes, she and her dad were at the front, and Jake was giving his daughter away—to him.

Lane drew a deep breath, hardly able to believe this was happening. He was getting married!

Callie stood beside Lane, pledging her life to him. Her flowers quivered a little, and she hoped she wouldn't cry. She had dreamed of this day for years but didn't think it would ever happen. She always figured she would end up like Miss Penwell, still single in her seventies, working in the library.

But God had other plans.

As Callie gazed into Lane's eyes, she knew God's purpose for her life was right here by his side. She repeated the wedding vows, meaning every word, amazed how God had orchestrated everything to bring them together. They had met at the library, and it seemed all that happened in the past four months revolved around that old mansion and their mutual love of books.

Now Lane would be a celebrated author in his own right, and she would be able, finally, to realize her dream of having a bookstore, plus a museum for the town of Fort Lob.

She wiped a tear from her eye as Pastor Reilly pronounced them man and wife. Lane pulled her into his arms and kissed her, and that kiss held the promise of a lifetime.

The pastor cleared his throat. "I now introduce to you Mr. and Mrs. Lane Hutchins."

The refrain of "The Wedding March" burst from the organ, and applause erupted from the audience as Callie and Lane walked down the aisle.

Alone in the lobby, Callie threw her arms around his neck. "I can't believe we're married!"

"This is just the beginning, Callie." His arms tightened around her. "I expect to cherish you my whole life."

She breathed a happy sigh. "God is so good."

"Yes, He is." Lane leaned back to look her in the eye. "Far better than I deserve. But it's like that verse in Philippians says—'It is God which worketh in you both to will and to do of his good pleasure.'"

As Callie laid her head against his shoulder, she glanced out the glass door of the church. Snow drifted down outside against the streetlight, and she felt God's peace fill her.

*Lord, You gave me a love of books. Thank You for also giving me the love of my life.*

# THE THING ABOUT BEAUTY

# Dedication

This book is dedicated to my Savior, Jesus Christ,
who called me to write according to His own purpose.
Also in memory of Arlene Reimel (1921–2009).
Thanks for your prayers, Mom. I miss you.

# Chapter 1

"Aggie is going to kill me."

Tonya pushed down on the accelerator, driving her little red Hyundai as fast as she dared on snowy Main Street. Despite her best effort, she was going to be late for work—again.

It didn't matter that the Beauty Spot probably had zero customers on this cold Friday morning. Aggie was a stickler for promptness. So Tonya had promised to leave the house much earlier than she did yesterday.

But yesterday it wasn't snowing.

Tonya's tires slipped on a patch of ice, and she let up on the gas pedal. Why didn't Fort Lob clear the streets? They had plow trucks, and this was December in Wyoming for goodness' sake. Main Street was reduced to two sets of snowy tire tracks.

As she passed the buildings in town, the snowfall tapered off. Jim Wilkins stood outside Wilkins Grocery in his green apron, shoveling snow off the sidewalk. He waved at her. She sped past the Cattlemen's Diner and then the Trailblazer Café. Both restaurants were booming with business on this winter morning.

Horace Frankenberg, bundled in an overcoat, black gloves, and heavy boots, stood at the curb, waiting to cross the street. A blue toboggan hat covered his thinning hair. As Tonya's Hyundai approached, it looked like he would attempt the fifty-yard dash right in front of her car.

"No, Horace!" She'd never be able to stop in time.

As if he heard her, Horace took a step back and waited. She waved as she sped past. That little wave would cost her on Sunday. The fifty-year-old resident bachelor of Fort Lob would corner her at church and give her a lecture about safe driving habits.

Passing *The Scout* newspaper office, she accelerated toward Elk Road. A few revolutions of her tires slipped in rebellion, but she pressed on. The clock on the dashboard signaled two minutes to nine. She was going to make it!

A blue light flashed in her eyes, and she glanced in the rearview mirror. "Oh no!"

A Wyoming highway patrol car, lights flashing, drove behind her. With a sinking feeling in the pit of her stomach, Tonya turned right onto Bighorn Avenue and stopped, letting the engine idle. The state trooper pulled up behind her.

Tonya expelled a breath. Now she'd be late for sure. She glanced at her reflection in the rearview mirror and fluffed her hair. Her gaze roved her face, noting the perfect eyebrows she had tweezed an hour ago, the twilight shadow that shimmered on her lids and brought out the blue in her dark eyes, and the midnight mascara that separated her eyelashes perfectly. The state trooper would probably be an old married guy, but even married men gave her face a second glance.

Hopefully she could use her beauty to full advantage and get out of a speeding ticket.

Behind her the patrol car's door opened. Tonya grabbed her purse and rummaged inside for her driver's license. When a tap sounded on the tinted window, she pushed the button to roll it down. A dark-green uniform came into view, and she looked up into the homely face of Murray Twichell.

"Murray!" She swiveled left to face him. "Please don't give me a ticket! I'm already late for work, and Aggie threatened to dock my pay if I was late one more day."

He raised reddish-brown eyebrows. "Maybe you should get up earlier, Tonya."

Her face grew warm. "I got up early! But it was really snowing this morning, in case you didn't notice, and it slowed me down. It's seven miles from our ranch into town, and the road was barely plowed."

Murray leaned over, folding his arms on the edge of her window and effectively blocking the cold air that tried to swirl in. "You were going forty-eight in a thirty-five zone. On a sunny day, that would be breaking the law. On slippery, snowy roads, that's downright dangerous."

Clamping her lips shut, Tonya stared at Murray. She had always thought his blue eyes, surrounded by those reddish-brown eyelashes, were much too close together, and his nose was too big for his face. Her sister, Callie, said Murray looked like a leprechaun, but Tonya thought he looked more like a weasel.

"Furthermore," he continued, "you almost hit Horace Frankenberg."

"I did not! You should give him a ticket for jaywalking."

Murray shook his head. "I've watched you speed down Main Street for the past two weeks. I decided this morning would be the last day." He paused. "I need your driver's license, registration, and proof of insurance."

She glared at him. "Are you saying this ticket was premeditated? Kind of like premeditated murder?"

He grinned. She had never noticed how white and straight his teeth were before now. "Premeditated? You could say that." His smile faded. "Main Street is a state highway, so it's part of my duty to watch this road. Yesterday, in good weather, you must have been doing at least fifty-five. But I wasn't near my patrol car, so I couldn't chase you down." Murray shook his head. "That kind of speed could land you in court."

Yesterday she was going closer to sixty, and if it hadn't been snowing today. . . *Thank You, Lord, for the snow!* But she couldn't afford a ticket; it would increase her insurance payment.

Leaning toward him, she placed her hand on his arm, hoping Murray would notice her perfectly manicured dusty rose fingernails. "Must you give me a ticket? I've learned my lesson." She fluttered her eyelashes, trying to look pathetic and beautiful at the same time. Knowing the power of a woman's eyelashes, she was confident her charm would persuade even Murray to relent.

His gaze roamed her face a second before he straightened, pulling his arm away from her grasp. "Stop trying to act so innocent, Tonya. In the eyes of the law, you're guilty, and you've been guilty for several days. I really should give you ten speeding tickets, but I guess one will have to do."

The eyelashes didn't work! That man didn't have a romantic bone in his body. "Okay, let's make a deal."

Murray's eyebrows scrunched up. "This isn't a game show."

She spread out her hands. "If I promise to drive within the speed limit, will you let me go? And I do promise. Sincerely, I do." She glanced up at him and tried the eyelashes one more time. "Come on, Murray, you've known me since I was born."

He folded his arms. "I was only three years old when you were born, and neither one of us was driving a car back then, as I recall. Now hand over your license."

With a sigh she complied.

He took it. "You can get your registration and insurance while I process this." He walked back to his patrol car, where the lights were still flashing, announcing to the entire town that she had broken the law.

Tonya hit the window button to push it up and turned the heater's fan to full blast. She wished she could blast Murray with a barrage of words. This ticket was another incident in the long list of terrible things he had done to her during her twenty-three years of life.

Well, maybe that list wasn't so long, but it had to be at least the third bad thing. She wasn't going to forgive him either.

≈

Man, that girl irked him!

With a shiver, Murray slipped into the driver's seat of his black Chevy Impala patrol car. Turning up the heater, he wished he could tell Tonya Brandt what he really thought about her. Who did she think she was—trying to use her beauty to get out of paying a speeding ticket?

*Her beauty.* Yep, she sure was beautiful, he had to admit that. When she leaned toward him, her face only inches from his own, and batted those thick black eyelashes, he almost relented. Tonya rivaled most Hollywood actresses with her silky black hair, dark blue eyes, and flawless skin.

Murray had never thought much about her beauty before. Having known Tonya since childhood, he always thought of her as Callie's baby sister, the little pest who tagged after them. But now men stood in line to ask for one evening of her company. She must have dated every guy in Niobrara County.

*And I can't get a date to save my life.*

But what did it matter? He wasn't about to stand in line and grovel at her feet. And he wasn't going to let her get out of this speeding ticket either. She deserved it.

Picking up a clipboard, he positioned the ticket and began filling in the lines with his neat, square printing.

❧

"Eighty-five dollars!" Tonya sat in one of the two beautician chairs at the Beauty Spot. "Can you believe this, Aggie? Just because I drove a few miles over the speed limit, I have to pay eighty-five bucks. And I can't write out a check—no, I have to get a money order at the bank and mail it to the county courthouse in Cheyenne."

Agatha Collingsworth swept a broom under the other chair, cleaning up after their one and only customer of the morning. "Now, sugar, it's what I've been telling you for weeks." Her gold bangle bracelets clinked together as she continued sweeping. "Get your bod out of the bed when you're supposed to, and the day'll go much smoother."

"I did get up early, but Murray had determined to give me a ticket. It was premeditated."

Aggie let out a throaty chuckle as she smoothed down her pink beehive hairdo. "Premeditated, eh? More likely Murray was just doing his job."

Tonya raised her chin an inch. "I do not appreciate him watching me like that—sitting in his patrol car waiting for me to drive by and hoping I'd go a few miles over the speed limit so he could ticket me."

"Don't take it so personal." Aggie finished sweeping.

"I can't help it. I never liked Murray Twichell."

"What's wrong with him, sugar?" Aggie's dark brown eyes stared at her. "He's a nice boy."

"Nice? He's not nice. He threw a snake—a real snake—at me."

Aggie leaned on the broom handle. "He didn't!"

"Yes he did. It was a garter snake—but still, he threw it at me, and it got tangled up in my hair." A shiver ran over Tonya just thinking about it.

"That's awful, hon! When did this happen?"

Tonya tapped her lips. "I think I was seven—"

"Seven!" Aggie placed her hands on her wide hips. "Land sakes, girl. This happened when you two was little kids, and you're still holding it against him?"

Tonya felt her temper flare. "I had nightmares for weeks! If Callie hadn't managed to get that scaly thing untangled from my braids, it might still be there."

"If that don't beat all." Aggie chuckled as she waddled to the back of the store. Her tight jeans puffed out at her thighs, straining the seams.

Tonya followed her boss. "But that wasn't the only time Murray was mean to me. The summer after that, he and my brother were catching toads in the pond down at the end of our property."

Aggie chortled as she closed the storage room door. "I bet he threw a toad at you."

"It's not funny! He chased me with several toads and then stuck one down the back of my shirt."

Aggie's laughter pealed out as they made their way to the front. "He thought you were cute. It was just his boyish way of getting your attention."

"Oh, he had my attention all right." Tonya folded her arms as she dropped into a chair. "I had nightmares about that one, too."

"Don't let it eat at you." Aggie ambled toward the front door. "You have to forgive and forget."

Tonya sighed. "That won't be easy. Do you know that I had warts all over my hands when I was in the fifth grade? I think it was because of that toad." She splayed her fingers and scrutinized them. Sometimes a wart would still pop up.

Aggie looked out the large plate-glass windows. "Don't know if we'll have too many customers today. It sure is snowing." Aggie seemed ready to close the subject about Murray.

*Forgive and forget.* Why did Tonya still resent what he did those many years ago? Maybe what Aggie said was true—he thought she was a cute little girl and wanted her attention. Tonya had never looked at it from his point of view before.

Joining Aggie at the window, Tonya gazed out at the bleak snowy day. The snowflakes were falling hard, and the wind often swept them sideways. "We might get snowed in and have to spend the night at the Beauty Spot."

"Hope not." Aggie walked behind the cash register. "Course, it's Friday, and I need to do my bookkeeping. A couple bills to pay and your salary check to make out." Her dark eyes twinkled as she glanced at Tonya. "Do you think ya can handle the thousands of customers who'll flock to our beauty shop while I work on the books?"

Tonya smiled. "I've got it covered, Aggie. You write out those checks. Tomorrow I plan to go shopping."

"Now don't spend all your money, sugar. Remember that speeding ticket."

"You had to remind me." Tonya sighed.

The morning and afternoon dragged by with only two more customers. At four o'clock, the bell over the door jangled. Both women turned as Murray Twichell strode inside.

Tonya placed her hands on her hips. "Murray! What are you doing here?" He never came to the Beauty Spot.

Aggie had a sudden coughing fit.

His small, closely spaced eyes widened. "I need a haircut." He shook the snow off his heavy jacket and hung it on one of the hooks on the wall.

Of all the people to want a haircut! The overpowering fragrance of his aftershave wafted toward her, and Tonya resisted the urge to sneeze. He must have just splashed some on his face before he walked in. His reddish-brown hair was growing down the back of his neck, but the top seemed kind of short, almost like a crew cut. *He wouldn't look so bad if he let his hair grow in the front.* But she wasn't going to argue about cutting his hair. After all, he was a paying customer.

Murray turned around and cracked his knuckles. "Clint's Barbershop is closed today. Must be the snow."

Without replying, Tonya walked back to her workstation. She pulled the vinyl cape off the chair and waited as he approached.

Obviously Murray was off duty. His state trooper uniform had been exchanged for old jeans and a navy T-shirt that stretched across his chest. His biceps bulged out of the short sleeves.

*Wow, he's really bulked up.* She remembered him as the skinny kid catching toads with Derek. Murray had towered over her back then, but now he seemed short and stocky. Callie said he was only five feet six inches. Tonya was an inch taller.

He took a seat, and Tonya threw the cape around his shoulders. With the slight movement of air, the overpowering aftershave floated toward her. She grabbed her nose so she wouldn't sneeze, taking a deep breath through her mouth. When the feeling passed, she snapped the cape together at the back of his neck. "Don't blame me if I nip your ear or—or accidentally cut off your head."

Aggie had another coughing fit.

"Still upset about that ticket?" Murray's eyes met Tonya's in the mirror. "I'm a professional who did my job, Tonya. Now you need to do yours."

"You could have let me go." She took her spray bottle and doused his hair with water, wishing she could wash the aftershave off his face. "That would have been the Christian thing to do, in my humble opinion."

"Are you sure it's humble?" He closed his eyes against the onslaught of water.

As the water dripped from his head, Tonya's conscience hit her. *This is ridiculous.* She was a professional, as Murray said, but she was acting like a spoiled child.

It was all that toad's fault.

*Forgive and forget.* Grabbing a towel, she mopped up some of the water. "Okay, how do you want your hair cut?" She would give Murray the best haircut he ever had, and somehow—but only with a divine miracle—she would improve his looks in the process.

# Chapter 2

With a flourish, Tonya wrote her name on the 3 x 5 card. She added, *I love old movies, the colors blue and purple, and classical music.* She handed the card to her brother, Derek, who collected a card from each member of the Sunday school class. The single people of the church, comprised mainly of women, attended this class, known as the Single Servings. Most of the members were in their twenties or thirties, although Horace Frankenberg attended, as did Aggie, Tonya's boss. Aggie must be over sixty-five. She was always threatening to retire.

"Do I have everyone's card?" Derek's eyes circled the seventeen chairs. "Now here's the reason I'm collecting this information. Our class has been studying Christian charity and friendship during the past two months, and for the next six weeks, from Christmas until Valentine's Day, we're going to show some of that friendship by doing something totally different." He cleared his throat. "Everyone is going to get a secret pal."

"Secret pal?" several voices asked in unison, followed by moans—mainly in the bass timbre—and an outbreak of conversation.

A little thrill shot through Tonya at Derek's great idea. She looked around. Why all the complaining? She loved secrets, and what could be more fun than secret pals? Smoothing her red skirt, she crossed her legs, letting her black stiletto-heeled boot swing back and forth. She looked at her brother, thankful that once he made up his mind, he usually didn't change it.

Derek held up his hand. "Yes, we're going to do this. Sometimes single people get lonely and need encouragement, especially over the holidays. That's where Christian charity comes in."

"But I don't get it." Corey Henning folded his arms across his lanky torso. "Are we supposed to send flowers to the other person or something?"

"Yeah." Matthew Werth slid down an inch in his seat. "What do we have to do?"

Derek straightened his tie. "Send that person a card in the mail to encourage him or her. Pray for that person every day, and let them know you're praying. You could even send a gift, or several gifts, if you want."

Corey smirked. "What if we don't want?"

Tonya glared at him. "Don't be a party pooper, Corey. It's only for six weeks."

She hoped she didn't get Corey or Matthew as a secret pal. She had dated each of them one time, and once was enough. All Corey wanted to do was kiss her, and Matthew had barely said a word.

On the other hand. . .Tonya glanced across the room at Reed Dickens—the hottest guy in the Single Servings, and she had never dated him. Of course, he had only been attending their church a few weeks. He worked at the county hospital in Lusk and, she wasn't sure, but he might be a doctor.

"All right." Derek lifted his hand to stop the undercurrent of chitchat. "Let's try it out and see what happens. This week I'll select—at random—a secret pal for everyone. I'll give these cards back next week, and remember to keep that person's name to yourself. As a secret pal, you need to encourage and pray for your, uh, person." He grinned. "I'm not sure what the recipient of a secret pal is called."

"How about your chosen one?" Horace called out.

Tonya rolled her eyes. She sure hoped she didn't get Horace. Of course, some unfortunate person would get the fifty-year-old bachelor.

"I don't know, Horace." Derek scratched his clean-shaven chin. "In this case, you're not choosing the other person. And remember, if you happen to get someone of the opposite gender, there's nothing romantic about being secret pals. We're doing this as friends." He looked at Tonya as if he wanted to make sure she got the point.

She did not appreciate her brother's unspoken message.

"What about a receiver?" Wearing a suit and tie, Reed Dickens looked like a model in a men's fashion magazine.

Derek raised his eyebrows. "A receiver?"

"Like a football receiver." Reed pantomimed catching a football. With those broad shoulders filling out his suit, he was definitely football-player material. "The person is on the receiving end of the encouragement or gifts of the secret pal, so he or she would be called a receiver." He looked around, his green eyes stopping at Tonya.

She smiled at him. *What a gorgeous guy!*

Cheyenne Wilkins, sitting three seats from Tonya, raised her hand. "Derek, the recipient is called a secret pal also."

"But that doesn't make sense." Reed frowned. "I think the recipient should be called a receiver."

Derek shrugged. "It doesn't matter to me, but for the sake of being clear, maybe we should take Reed's suggestion. All in favor?" He waited while a few heads bobbed. "So you'll all be secret pals and receivers." He wrote something down. "Don't forget about our Christmas party on the twenty-third. Everyone needs to come. For the gift exchange, each receiver will get a present from his or her secret pal. So don't put your name on your gift."

A murmur of conversation broke out. Tonya glanced from Reed to Murray Twichell, who was also wearing a suit and tie. He looked at her with his close-set eyes and smiled, showing his straight white teeth.

Returning a faint smile, she looked away. His haircut made him look better than usual, if she must say so herself. But seeing Murray reminded her of his childhood pranks.

*Forgive and forget.* She sighed. *I'm trying, Lord!*

While Derek answered a few more questions, Tonya glanced over her crimson-red fingernail polish and noticed a bump on her left thumb. She drew in a quick breath. A wart? How had she missed that? She would have to make a quick trip to the dermatologist tomorrow.

The Sunday school bell rang, signaling an end to class. As soon as Derek closed in prayer, Tonya stood, determined to talk to Reed.

Cheyenne touched her arm. "Hey, girlfriend! What do you think about the secret pal thing?"

"Oh, I love it!" Tonya looked up into Cheyenne's clear blue eyes. "I can't believe Derek got an idea like that, can you?"

"It wasn't his idea." Cheyenne grinned as she smoothed a strand of blond hair behind her ear. "Callie and I came up with it a couple months ago. I thought he'd completely forgotten about it."

"Evidently you girls made an impression." Tonya leaned toward Cheyenne. "I'm sure that makes *you* happy."

Cheyenne had been in love with Derek since high school. Almost six feet tall, she looked good standing beside Derek, who was six-three. Of course, he had never noticed girls. He was more interested in working on the ranch than going out on a date.

"Well..." Cheyenne lowered her voice. "I wouldn't mind being his secret pal."

Tonya giggled. "I'm going to be the best secret pal ever. My receiver guy is going to be the happiest man in the world."

"How do you know it's going to be a guy?"

"Well, I don't, but I'm praying for a certain person." Tonya glanced at Reed. He was deep in conversation with Laurie Smullens, and they were standing awfully close. *No!* She couldn't lose Reed before she even had him. "Excuse me, Cheyenne. I need to talk to someone."

Tonya strode toward Reed like a well-thrown football but was intercepted by Murray Twichell. His aftershave tackled her senses, and she sneezed.

⁂

Murray took a step back. "Gesundheit."

"Murray!" Tonya's eyes flashed as she sniffed. "You really shouldn't wear such strong aftershave. It's overpowering."

He clenched his jaw. "Sorry. Just wanted to thank you for the great haircut." He'd actually gotten a few compliments, and that had never happened before.

"You're welcome." Her perfectly shaped eyebrows formed a *V* in the middle of her forehead. She stepped to the side of him. "Now if you'll excuse me..."

"Don't mean to keep you, Tonya." He gazed into her beautiful dark-blue eyes, which were level with his own. Too bad she had such a prickly personality. "I know what an important job you have—playing the piano for the morning church service."

"It *is* important." Her eyes flashed again—like dark lightning.

"I suppose you're right." He felt the tension between them and couldn't keep the sarcasm from his voice. "No one else can play the piano like you."

She planted her hands on her thin hips. "Mrs. Langston is out of town, so we won't have an organist today."

"Ah!" Tilting back his head, he studied her. "So it's just you in all your glory."

She turned her back on him. "Later, Murray."

He watched her stride out of the now-empty room. She sure had a good figure. Amazing how he had never noticed before. Of course he had always wanted to marry Callie, but now that she was married to someone else, Murray was beginning to view Tonya as more than Callie's younger sister. And he liked the view.

As he exited the Sunday school room, a scrap of scripture popped into his mind. *"Man looketh on the outward appearance, but the Lord looketh on the heart."* Tonya's outward appearance was fantastic, but did anyone know the real Tonya? For some reason she brought out the worst in him, and he seemed to bring out the worst in her, too. He wondered what she was really like—in her heart.

It would be intriguing to find out.

Tonya's fingers swept over the piano keys as the parishioners entered the sanctuary. A low buzz of conversation accompanied her playing of "Nothing but the Blood of Jesus." Keeping one eye on her music, she glanced out at the audience every few measures.

Her eyes paused at Reed Dickens. His brown hair was cut perfectly, and Tonya wondered who had styled it. He must have gone somewhere besides Clint's Barbershop. He sat on the back pew—next to Laurie Smullens. Tonya pressed her lips together, determined that Dickens-Smullens would not be a couple for long. *Not if I can help it!*

"No other fount I know. . ." The wavery soprano voice with the slow vibrato could only belong to old Edna Beazer. Her singing got louder as she walked to her spot on the second pew.

Tonya took a deep breath, trying to quell her irritation. Mrs. Beazer used to have a good singing voice, but it had taken a dive with her increasing age. Every Sunday as Tonya played the prelude, however, Mrs. Beazer sang along, loud enough for the entire church to hear. *Amazing that her dentures don't fall out.*

Pastor Reilly strode to the piano, his wrinkled face pale. He leaned toward her and lowered his voice to a stage whisper. "Tonya, we have a problem."

Since she couldn't talk and play at the same time, her fingers stopped. Self-consciously she covered her left thumb with her right hand. She would have to hide that wart until she got rid of it.

She looked up at the pastor's concerned face. "What's wrong?"

"Wayne Holland's wife just called. He's really sick and won't make it. Who can I get to lead the singing?"

"I have no idea." Few of the church members were musical, and Pastor Reilly was completely tone-deaf. She hoped *he* wouldn't have to lead the singing.

The pastor twisted the lapel on his suit coat. "I'll find someone." He dropped his voice. "I have to—we have a visitor this morning."

Tonya watched him walk down the aisle of the crowded auditorium. She switched to another hymn, hoping Mrs. Beazer wouldn't know this one. Before she started verse two, the pastor came back.

"Okay, we're all set." He rubbed his hands together, seemingly more relaxed. "Do you have a list of hymns for the song leader, Tonya?"

Again she stopped playing. "Who's leading the—"

"So what are we singing?"

*Not again.* Tonya would recognize that baritone voice anywhere—and the aftershave fragrance that accompanied it. She had to admit that Murray knew music. Every few months he sang a solo in church. Secretly she had always loved his singing voice—and that was the *only* thing she loved about him.

She handed him a service schedule. "Just follow this."

He cracked his knuckles before he took the paper. "Oh, these hymns are easy."

Tonya sighed. Murray needed a lesson in humility.

Five minutes later, he stood behind the pulpit and welcomed everyone to the service.

"Let's all turn to number 496 in your hymnbooks. Number 496." He smiled, exuding confidence. " 'Victory in Jesus.' "

From his chair on the platform, Pastor Reilly leaned forward. "Have the congregation stand, Murray."

"Oh." Murray flashed another smile. "Let's all stand, please."

The audience rustled to their feet as Tonya played a rousing introduction, clipping along at a fast tempo. She ended the intro with a bouncing run up the keys.

Murray looked at her as if he wasn't sure she was finished. She raised her eyebrows and nodded.

"Okay." He lifted his right hand. "All together now on verse one." He waved his hand as he began singing.

Tonya took off at a brisk pace, but by the third measure Murray lagged behind. The people followed him. She slowed down her playing and then—fuming—slowed down some more until the music dragged at a slow tempo.

Only Murray could turn "Victory in Jesus" into a funeral dirge.

At the chorus, she gritted her teeth and sped up the pace, hitting the keys as hard as she could. A few voices in the crowd followed her, while the rest stayed with Murray.

At the end of the first chorus, he stopped the music. "Let's all stay together." He looked pointedly at Tonya. "A little slower on the tempo."

She expelled a hot breath. How slow did they have to go? She played the second verse at a quicker pace than she usually did. Murray glanced at her a few times and she mouthed, "Faster!" At the end of the second chorus, he seated the audience.

What? He wasn't going to sing the third verse?

Murray took a seat on the platform. He set his hymnbook on the little table beside his chair, then looked toward the piano. His eyes narrowed as he glared at her. Now she knew what that phrase *if looks could kill* meant.

～

"Would you set the table, Tonya?" Mom opened the oven, and the delicious smell of roast beef wafted out.

Tonya knew exactly what she would look like when she was fifty-five years old. Yvette Brandt was still beautiful with her dark-blue eyes, perfect facial features, and dark hair, and Tonya looked just like her mother.

Mom straightened up. "We'll have five for Sunday dinner."

"Five? Who's the fifth person?" Since Callie had married Lane Hutchins more than a week ago, the family only included Mom and Dad, Derek, and herself.

Tiny crow's-feet edged her mother's eyes as she smiled. "I invited Murray to eat with us."

"Mom! Did you have to invite *him*?"

Her mother raised her eyebrows. "What's wrong with Murray?"

Tonya opened the silverware drawer more forcefully than necessary. "I've seen an awful lot of him this weekend." *Awful* being the key word.

"Now don't blame Murray for your speeding ticket." Mom took the roast out of the oven. "Actually, I feel sorry for him. With his father dead and his mom in a nursing home, he's really all alone in the world. He has a lot of responsibility for a young person."

"He's twenty-six. That's not so young."

"Yes it is, Tonya." Mom took the meat platter from the cupboard. "It's too bad he doesn't have any siblings. He must be lonely, living in his parents' house all by himself." She speared the meat and lifted it from the pan. "Some of the women at church are taking turns inviting him for dinner when he's not working on Sunday. Today it's our turn."

Tonya selected five forks from the silverware drawer. How could she argue with Christian charity?

⁂

Murray glanced around the large oval dining room table. Jake Brandt, as patriarch of the family, sat at the head with Tonya and Derek seated on his right. On the left, Murray sat beside Mrs. Brandt—Yvette. She insisted he use her first name, but habits were hard to break. He enjoyed eating with other church families, but his favorite place was right here, at the Brandts' table. Passing the food around, he half listened as Jake told about the rare visitor at church that morning.

"He lives up in Canada—Saskatchewan, just over the border from Montana." Jake took a helping of mashed potatoes and passed the dish to Murray. "I invited him for dinner, but he's driving down to Denver this afternoon."

As the conversation flowed around him, Murray took a spoonful of potatoes from the dish and passed it on to Yvette. He was content to eat and listen—and reminisce.

He sat in this very spot one summer as a ten-year-old boy. Callie, who was also ten, sat across the table beside Derek, a year younger. Their twin sisters, Molly and Melissa—whom he could never tell apart—must have been around thirteen, and joined them at the table for warm cookies and milk.

And then there was Tonya, who turned seven years old that July. Her sisters called her *baby sis*, and she was still the spoiled baby of the family.

Murray took a bite of potatoes, glancing up at Tonya as she elaborated about the secret pal idea.

"So I wrote on the card that I was interested in old movies and classical music and that I like the colors blue and purple." She thought for a moment. "I should have put down that I love poetry, too, and also cooking and sewing but—oh well." She raised one shoulder in a slight shrug. "So some guy—or girl—will send me gifts and encouragement, and even pray for me, but that person will remain a secret for six weeks. Isn't that a great idea? I just love surprises."

Murray stopped chewing. *It's all about her.*

Tonya's dark eyes glowed. "I already have some thoughts on what I'm going to do for my secret pal." She turned to her brother. "I'm surprised you thought up that idea, Derek."

He shrugged. "I had a little help."

Tonya giggled. "I know. Cheyenne told me."

Murray popped a piece of roast beef in his mouth. As Tonya continued to dominate the conversation, he thought back to the way she had dominated the song service that morning. Instead of following his lead, Tonya insisted on having her own way, playing the tempo way too fast. It shouldn't be surprising that she'd break the speed limit and then try to argue her way out of a ticket.

He took another bite of meat, savoring the flavor. He had always wanted to belong to this family. Maybe that was why he wanted to marry Callie. But Tonya was the only girl left, so he'd never belong to the Brandt family now. No way would he marry Tonya, no matter how beautiful her face was.

# Chapter 3

On Friday evening, Tonya glanced out the living room window. Two headlight beams cut through the darkness, lighting up the snowflakes that floated down to the long driveway. "Mom? Are we expecting company?"

Her mother's voice wafted from the kitchen, along with the aroma of chocolate chip cookies. "Oh, that must be Molly. The nursing home hired a couple extra nurses, so she got the weekend off."

"Really?" A spark of excitement surged through Tonya. "I'll help her with her stuff." She ran to the front closet and pulled on her boots. Grabbing a coat, she threw it on as she sprinted down the snowy steps of the front porch.

Molly parked her car by the door and got out. Long auburn hair flowed over the shoulders of her gray winter coat.

"Molly! Welcome home!"

Her sister looked up. Tiny pricks of the porch light shone in her brown eyes. "Baby sis!"

Tonya hugged her. "You were just here two weeks ago for Callie's wedding. I can't believe you're back so soon. That's a long drive in this weather."

"Yeah, sixty miles on icy, snowy roads. I'm exhausted."

"You do sound tired." Tonya shivered in the cold evening air.

Molly opened the trunk and took out a suitcase. "I'm glad I could get away this weekend. After all, I have my own wedding to plan."

"Oh, Molly, I'm so excited for you." Tonya hugged her again, suitcase and all.

"Thanks. I thought Jonathan would *never* ask me. But when he said he thought it would be nice to get married on Valentine's Day, since it's on a Saturday, I agreed before the words were out of his mouth." Molly giggled. "I think I shocked him."

Tonya took the suitcase from her sister, and they clomped up the front steps together. "You've sure been patient. Haven't you two been going out for five years?"

"Six. At least, it's going to be six years on Valentine's Day." Molly opened the front door. "Our first date was for a Valentine's party at the church in Douglas."

"I didn't know that. So now you've come full circle. Your first date was in the same church where you plan to tie the knot."

"Yep." Molly took off her coat. "And that knot is going to be really tight."

❧

"How can you plan a wedding in two months?" Tonya sat across from her sister at the dining room table. Both she and Molly flipped through bridal magazines looking at bridesmaid dresses.

"A girl has to do what a girl has to do." Molly grinned. "Of course, I've been thinking about my wedding for years just in case he popped the question. But Jonathan always wanted to wait and get his medical degree first."

"I wonder what changed his mind."

"Callie's wedding. He said when he saw me walk down that aisle as a bridesmaid something hit him."

Tonya smiled. "Must have been one of Cupid's arrows. Callie's wedding was so beautiful, I got hit myself." Her smile faded. "But I have no idea who my groom will be."

Molly reached across the table and patted her hand. "All in good time, baby sis. You have plenty of time."

"No I don't." Tonya pulled her lips into a pout. "I'm twenty-three—practically an old maid."

"So what does that make me? No one else in the family hit twenty-nine before they got married." Molly flipped a page. "That's another reason I jumped at the chance to marry in two months. I want to have six kids, just like Mom."

"At least you had someone to marry all these years." Tonya sighed. "I've had plenty of dates, but no one sticks." She thought of Reed Dickens. "Although I have my eye on someone—a really hot guy. I think he's a doctor, Molly. Wouldn't that be something if we both ended up marrying doctors?"

Molly turned another page. "He and Jonathan will probably talk shop at every family reunion. Hey, here's a pretty dress." She turned the magazine around to show Tonya. "What do you think about this one in pink?"

Tonya gazed at the sleeveless gown. "That would be beautiful and perfect for a Valentine's wedding. But maybe it should be a darker pink or even a fuchsia."

"Good idea—if we can find satin fabric in purplish-red. Do you think we could get fuchsia flowers for the bouquets?"

"Maybe, but that color would look great with a bouquet of light pink roses." Tonya gave the magazine back. "I'm not going to have a winter wedding. I always wanted to get married in June, with pastel dresses for my bridesmaids. Each one will wear a different color."

"Ooh, pastels. I like that. How many bridesmaids will you have? Just the sisters?"

"Plus five or six more. I'd really like ten or twelve girls."

"Ten or twelve?" Molly shook her head. "Really, Tonya—"

"The wedding pictures will be fabulous."

Molly laughed. "Dream on, baby sis."

Tonya sighed. Right now her wedding was nothing *but* a distant dream.

∼∾

Ten minutes later Tonya opened the front door with the sound of the doorbell still reverberating through the house. Callie and Lane stood on the snowy porch.

"Hey!" Tonya pulled Callie into the house with a hug. "When did you guys get back from your honeymoon?"

"Yesterday."

"Yesterday?" Tonya took a step back. She still couldn't get used to Callie without her glasses, which she had worn almost all her life. Her husband, Lane, had paid for laser eye surgery as a wedding gift. "You got back yesterday? Why didn't you call us? Are you staying at Lane's house in Cheyenne?"

"Nope." Callie glanced up at her husband and smiled. "We spent the night at our new house on Little Deer Road."

Tonya didn't miss the look of love that passed between the newlyweds. But before she could even give a wistful sigh, Mom and Molly were there, hugging Callie and Lane. As Callie exclaimed over Molly's new engagement, Dad and Derek joined the group.

"Derek and I are watching an old rerun of *Columbo*." Dad slapped Lane on the shoulder. "Why don't you come on back, Lane? I'm sure the girls will only talk about wedding plans."

"*Columbo* sounds good to me." Lane winked at Callie. "I guess I've spent enough time with my wife this week."

Callie's face tinged pink as she smiled back at him.

*The blushing bride.* Tonya hoped she would be next.

Soon Tonya joined her sisters and her mom around the kitchen table where they feasted on warm chocolate chip cookies. Callie described the wonders of Yellowstone National Park in the wintertime and the snug cabin they had rented.

Tonya propped her chin in her hand with a wistful sigh. "I can't wait to have my own wedding."

Molly nodded. "Tonya said she's going to have ten or twelve bridesmaids."

Mom raised her eyebrows. "That many, Tonya?"

"Well. . ." She shrugged, not wanting to change her girlhood dreams. "I want to include everyone. Besides, think of how it would look—my husband and I flanked by a dozen girls in beautiful pastel colors. Like a flower garden."

Molly laughed. "That's just like you, baby sis. My three sisters will be enough for me." She picked up the magazine and showed the picture to Mom. "Do you think you could sew three bridesmaid dresses like this in fuchsia for Tonya, Callie, and Melissa?"

Mom studied the picture. "If Tonya helps me, we should have plenty of time to finish them." She picked up her teacup. "But what about your dress, Molly? Are you going to sew it yourself?"

Molly shook her head. "No time. Melissa is going to let me borrow hers. We did some planning last night over the phone."

"Don't you want your own dress?" Tonya couldn't imagine borrowing someone else's bridal gown, even if it was her sister's.

"I love Melissa's dress. We picked it out together, and she doesn't mind sharing."

Mom nodded. "You two always liked the exact same styles."

"That's what happens when you're twins." Callie grinned. "Tonya and I have the opposite tastes in clothes."

"That's for sure." Tonya picked up another cookie. "By the way, Molly, who are we walking down the aisle with?"

Molly counted on her fingers. "Melissa is my matron of honor, and Derek will be the best man."

"Derek?" Mom, Callie, and Tonya said his name in unison.

"What about Jonathan's brother?" Mom took a bite of her cookie.

"He's not coming. It was too hard for him to get away from his mission in India." Molly paused. "I've always wanted to have all my siblings in our wedding, and since Jon's brother couldn't come, he decided on one of my brothers as his best man."

"Why didn't he pick Ryan?" Mom asked. "He's the oldest."

"Jon doesn't know Ryan that well. On the other hand, he and Derek are good friends." Molly resumed her counting. "So, it's Melissa and Derek, Callie and Ryan, and Tonya and Murray."

Tonya's mouth dropped open. "Do you mean Murray Twichell?"

Molly raised her eyebrows. "What other Murray is there? He's Jonathan's cousin, so Jon wants him in the bridal party." She looked concerned. "Is something wrong?"

Tonya dropped her head in her hands. "I cannot get rid of that guy."

Mom placed her arm around Tonya's shoulders. "He gave her a speeding ticket last week, so she's upset with him."

Tonya folded her arms. "Besides that, he's an inch shorter than me, and I know you'll want us girls to wear heels. The pictures will look terrible." Of all the people in Wyoming, she had to get stuck with Murray!

"Jon and I talked about that." Molly rested her chin in her hand. "After all, Jon and my two brothers are all over six feet tall, and Murray is. . .what?"

"Five-six," Callie supplied.

"Right. But Jonathan has a plan." Molly grinned. "His uncle has a pair of elevator shoes from the '70s that he wore in college, and Jon asked if Murray could wear them."

Tonya frowned. "Elevator shoes?"

"I remember those." Mom spread her thumb and index finger about two inches apart. "The entire sole is two to three inches deep, so it makes the man taller. Some people call them platform shoes."

Molly giggled. "Murray will be at least two inches taller than you, baby sis."

"Great!" Tonya rolled her eyes. "Just what I need—Murray looking down his big nose at me during the entire wedding." A sudden thought hit her. "Hey, why don't you make Lane Callie's partner, and then I can walk down the aisle with Ryan?"

Callie shook her head. "Lane is not the groomsman type. He told me that our wedding was the last one he wanted to be in for a while."

"Well, he'll have to be in *mine*." Tonya threw her hands up in the air. "If I'm going to have ten or twelve bridesmaids, I'll need all the guys I can get."

Molly smirked. "Yeah, who knows? You might even have to enlist Murray."

Tonya rolled her eyes. "No way! I can guarantee that Murray Twichell will *never* be in my wedding."

# Chapter 4

O n Sunday morning, Tonya's fingers shook as she opened her secret pal
envelope. *Please let it be Reed Dickens!* Derek had given each member
of the Single Servings an envelope with the 3 x 5 card inside. She
furtively glanced around the circle of chairs. Everyone pulled out the card,
read it, and tucked it back in the envelope. Cheyenne, who sat next to Tonya,
pulled her card up to her face and squinted her eyes, as if the writing was
hard to read.

*She must have gotten Horace.*

"Okay." Derek rubbed his hands together. "Now you know the name of
your receiver and what he or she likes. And remember, don't trade cards with
anyone." He paused a moment to look at Tonya. "This is the person the Lord
wants *you* to encourage." He went on to reiterate his ideas for encouragement,
and above all, he admonished everyone to keep it secret.

While he talked, Tonya took a deep breath and pulled her card halfway
out. Her shoulders slumped as she read the neat, blocky printing. *Murray
Twichell. Brown is my favorite color. I enjoy singing, fixing computers as a hobby,
and watching football games.* She sighed as she put the card back. *And giving
speeding tickets, throwing toads down little girls' shirts. . .*

Cheyenne elbowed her, leaning closer to whisper. "Who'd you get?"

Tonya handed over her envelope. Pulling out the card, Cheyenne peeked
at it and raised her eyebrows before giving it back. A moment later Tonya
pulled out Cheyenne's card. The writing was so terrible she could barely make
out the name.

*Reed Dickens.*

Tonya's lips parted. Reed went on to describe his favorite things in an
entire paragraph of scribbled writing. He *must* be a doctor if his writing was
this bad. She held the card close to her face, as Cheyenne had done, and tried
to decipher the message.

*Reed Dickens. I live in Lusk and work at the hospital as a registered nurse.*

Tonya whipped her head toward Cheyenne. "A nurse?" she mouthed.

Cheyenne shrugged. Her attention went back to Derek as he began to
teach the Sunday school lesson.

It took another five minutes for Tonya to finish reading the card. Reed
not only mentioned his job, but where he had moved from, his favorite foods,
his favorite pastimes, his favorite movies, and the name of his ex-girlfriend.

Tonya handed the card back and leaned toward Cheyenne. "That guy is really stuck on himself."

"I'll say," Cheyenne whispered. "No wonder Nicole is his *ex*-girlfriend."

Well, that was one good thing. Tonya still wasn't ready to dismiss Reed as a potential husband. He was too good-looking—*really hot,* that's what he was. And after reading his card about his favorite pastimes, she had an idea. . . .

⁓

Murray tried to keep his mind on Derek's lesson, but his eyes kept wandering over to Tonya. He couldn't believe her name was on his card. *From the Lord,* according to Derek. Why did he keep getting stuck with her? His cousin, Jonathan, asked him to be in his wedding, and when Murray agreed, Jon said he would be walking down the aisle with Tonya. Murray could just imagine how she took that news.

However, this secret pal thing might prove to be an interesting situation. At least she would be easy to buy gifts for—old movies, classical music, and the colors blue and purple. He also remembered that she loved poetry, cooking, and sewing.

He watched as Tonya and Cheyenne put their heads together and whispered, showing each other their cards. Murray smirked. So much for keeping their secret pals a secret.

⁓

*Where is he?* Tonya looked out the front window for the fifth time on Monday evening, but no car drove up the long driveway.

Yesterday at church Tonya had invited Reed Dickens to watch the Monday night football game with her family. According to his card, watching the Denver Broncos play football was one of his favorite things. So Tonya invited him to come, made a batch of brownies—her special recipe that the men in her family raved about—and prepared to question him about his life. She had accepted the fact that he was a registered nurse. After all, those female nurses probably needed a strong, buff guy like him to lift the patients.

Now Tonya sat sideways on the sofa so she could look out the window. *Lord, I pray that Reed won't forget about our date.* It would be terrible if he stood her up! She would be so embarrassed. Of course, Dad and Derek would watch the game anyway. *And Lord, I need to pray about my relationship with Reed.* Actually, they had no relationship to speak of, but she hoped this would be "the beginning of a beautiful friendship," to quote Rick in *Casablanca.*

Headlight beams appeared over the hill of the driveway. Tonya jumped up and smoothed her blue and orange Broncos sweatshirt. She was thankful the snow had melted. Opening the door, she ran down the porch steps and out into the cold air but stopped at the same time as the vehicle.

It was a silver SUV, which she recognized as Murray Twichell's new car. The driver's door opened, and Murray stepped out.

Tonya's heart sank down to her tennis shoes. "Murray, what are you doing here?"

He raised his eyebrows as he shrugged. "Is there a law that I can't drive onto your property? I decided to stop by and help your dad fix his computer. He asked me to come over sometime, and I thought we could watch the Broncos-Raiders game while we worked on it."

"This is not a good night, Murray." She took a step back. He wore that powerful aftershave again, and she didn't want to sneeze. "I'm waiting for my date to show up, and he's going to watch the football game with our family."

"Oh, with the family." Murray's mouth quirked. "Sounds like a hot and heavy social engagement, eh, Tonya?"

She reined in her rising temper. "Would you just leave, Murray? He's going to be here any minute."

He held a palm out toward her. "Okay, I'm leaving." He opened the car door. "By the way, who is this nameless *he*?"

"It's none of your business. Good-bye, Murray." She stomped toward the house. Of all the nerve! Dad had been complaining about his computer for two weeks, and Murray decides to show up tonight.

It didn't help Tonya's mood that Reed was twenty minutes late. The game had started by the time he arrived, but Tonya graciously led him to the den. After exchanging greetings with Dad and Derek, Reed settled on the end of the sofa. Derek was on the other end, and Tonya plopped down between them.

"Wow, what a pass!" Reed perched on the edge of the sofa. "This is going to be a great game."

Derek slipped his arm on the sofa behind Tonya. "Yeah, the Broncos are doing good this year. Ten and four isn't a bad record."

Dad sat back in his recliner. "I doubt if they'll make it to the Super Bowl, though."

Tonya glanced at Reed's handsome profile. Still perched on the sofa's edge, he wasn't paying the least bit of attention to her. She picked up the tray of brownies from the coffee table and held it in front of him, hoping he would notice the artful display. The brownies swirled around in a circle, each one perched on the corner of the next. "Would you like a brownie, Reed?"

She gazed at his brown hair, perfectly styled as usual. His emerald-green eyes—such a perfect color to complement his strong facial features—stared at the big-screen TV for a moment before turning to stare at her.

"Uh, what did you say?"

She lifted the tray an inch. "Brownie?"

"No thanks. I'm on a diet. Do you have any popcorn? And something to drink would be nice, too."

Dad motioned to a small table next to his recliner. "We have soda over here, Reed, and a couple empty glasses. Help yourself."

With a small and hopefully undetected sigh, Tonya set the tray down and stood. "I'll microwave some popcorn."

"Light on the butter." Reed rose to get some soda. "And light on the salt, too."

Tonya nodded. "Be right back." She exited to the kitchen.

Mom rinsed a pan in the sink. "How's the game, Tonya?"

She heaved a huge sigh, which had been trying to get out since Reed arrived. "The *game* is fine, but Reed is on a diet, so he wants popcorn."

"We have some." Mom motioned toward the cupboard.

"Do we have any with no taste?" Tonya rolled her eyes. "I wanted Reed to try my special brownies, but now I made them for nothing."

"No you didn't." Mom chuckled as she wiped the counter with her dishrag. "Dad and Derek will polish them off. You'd better get one while you can."

"I don't want a brownie." Tonya pulled a microwavable bag from the popcorn box. "I wanted Reed to try one. He's hardly looked at me since he arrived." She placed the bag in the microwave and pushed a couple of buttons. "All he's talked about so far is the game."

Mom shrugged. "Football's a guy thing. Maybe you can have a nice conversation with him at halftime."

"Maybe." A tiny spark of hope ignited inside. Watching a Broncos game was one of Reed's favorite things to do, so perhaps he would associate good memories with her sitting next to him. It was a start anyway.

She took the big white bowl from the cupboard with the word POPCORN painted in blue cursive. "Do you think I should get individual bowls for the guys?"

Mom shook her head. "They can just grab a handful from the big bowl. Men are not particular when it comes to food."

The popping stopped, and Tonya poured the popcorn into the bowl. When she entered the den, the three men shouted out a cheer of victory.

But the cheer was not for her or the popcorn. All three had their eyes glued to the television, although Dad looked up and smiled at her.

Reed fisted the air. "We have 'em now! The Broncos have it in the bag."

"Here's your popcorn." Tonya made what she hoped was a graceful entrance. She handed the bowl to Reed, making sure the word POPCORN faced him before she took her seat between him and Derek.

Reed took the bowl, his eyes still on the game. "Aww! I can't believe he missed the extra point!"

Derek took a brownie from the tray. "This is only half the game. Even with a twenty-seven-point lead, the Broncos could still lose."

"No way." Reed munched on the popcorn, keeping the bowl between his knees. "The Raiders are playing lousy."

During halftime Reed and Derek talked about stats like they were on a post-game show. Tonya tried to break into the conversation several times, but to no avail.

Finally she leaned a little closer to Reed. "I was a cheerleader for our football team in high school. We had a winning team when I was a senior—state champs."

Reed didn't even look at her as he pointed to the TV. "Hey, this is a great commercial—real creative. Nicole loved it. She'd always start laughing when it came on."

"Is Nicole your sister?" Dad asked.

Reed pulled his attention away from the screen to look at Dad. "My ex-girlfriend. We once attended a Broncos game in Denver. The game went into overtime, and we won by a field goal. It was cool."

With a sigh, Tonya sat back and folded her arms. It didn't matter how handsome Reed Dickens was—she was ready to cross him off her list as a potential husband.

❧

The rest of the evening only confirmed Tonya's decision. When the score narrowed down to six points between the teams, Reed yelled at each loss and whooped at every gain. But finally Denver lost.

Tonya shrugged. "Win a few, lose a few."

Reed shook his finger at her. "Yeah, but Denver will come back. You'll see." He stood. "Guess I'll be shoving off. Thanks for the invite." He reached over to shake Dad's hand.

Tonya bit her lip. *She* had invited him, not Dad.

"Glad you could come, Reed." Dad smiled, ever the congenial host. "It was good to make your acquaintance."

"Same here." He turned to Derek. "See you on Sunday."

Derek stood. "Actually, I'll see you tomorrow night. We're having the Single Servings Christmas party, remember? The secret pal gift exchange, and all that?"

Reed snapped his fingers. "That's right. Yeah, I'll be there."

"I'll walk you to your car, Reed." Tonya followed him from the room, miffed that he had ignored her all evening. Maybe they could have a decent conversation outside.

But before they even made it to the front door, Reed turned to her. "I think the Broncos lost in the third quarter, don't you? When that long pass was intercepted, it completely turned the game."

She sighed, tired of football. "I'm sure you're right."

"And then when Stokley fumbled the ball. . ." He opened the front door and exited, not even waiting for her.

She slipped outside, closing the door behind her. The cold air smacked her, and she was thankful she was wearing a sweatshirt. "I must admit, I'm not really that big on football."

"Some girls are." He stopped at the door of his car. "Nicole loved it. We could talk football for hours."

*I bet.* "You never told me much about your family, Reed. Aren't you from Casper?"

"Yeah. Lived there all my life. Nicole is from there, too, but she moved to California—right after we broke up. She moved in with her grandmother."

*Forget Nicole, you jerk!* "So your parents still live in Casper?"

"Yep. My grandparents settled there after emigrating from England." He grinned. "Did you know that Charles Dickens was my great-great grandfather?"

Tonya's eyes widened. "Wow! That's amazing to be in the direct line of someone so famous."

"Not!" Bending over, Reed actually slapped his knee as he guffawed. "I really pulled one over on you!" He continued chuckling as he pointed at her. "And you believed me!"

Tonya folded her arms. "Very funny, Reed."

"I told Nicole the same thing when we first started dating. She believed me so much she asked my dad about it." He laughed again, big belly laughs, as if it was the funniest thing in the world.

Tonya took a step back, willing to make a quick end of this date. "Thanks for coming. See you tomorrow night at the party." She turned toward the house.

"Uh, yeah. Tomorrow. And thanks, Tonya. I had fun."

She didn't even look back.

# Chapter 5

On Tuesday evening, Murray stepped inside the Sunday school classroom at church, which had been transformed for the Single Servings Christmas party. Like a wagon train, four sofas circled around a large flowered rug that covered the linoleum, and a few wingback chairs were positioned between the sofas. By the door, a tall Christmas tree guarded several presents that peeked out beneath the branches.

Murray scanned the room. Derek, Tonya, and Cheyenne stood at the food table talking. Several other people stood in small groups or sat on the sofas. Everyone held a plate of food.

Shoving his secret pal gift under the tree, Murray removed his jacket, then found an empty hook along the wall already crowded with coats.

"Hey, Twitch!"

Murray grinned. Derek Brandt was the only person who still called him by his old football nickname. Murray still remembered the euphoric feeling of catching a long pass thrown from Derek's arm and running down the field for a touchdown.

Derek motioned to him. "Come over and get some food before we start."

"I'm always game for food." Murray hadn't eaten supper, and he was starving. He nodded a greeting to Cheyenne and Tonya as he picked up a red paper plate decorated with jingle bells.

Derek looked around the room. "Who are we still missing?"

Cheyenne laid her plate on the table. "Corey isn't here yet."

"Neither is Aggie." Tonya nibbled on a cookie. "She told me she might be late."

Murray looked at the array of food, which was mostly in the dessert category. But a tray of small meatballs with a toothpick stuck in each one caught his attention. He grabbed a meatball and popped it into his mouth. "Wow, these are good." He glanced up at Cheyenne. "Who made them?"

"Tonya." Cheyenne smiled, and her dimples creased. "Aren't they wonderful?"

"They really are." Murray looked at Tonya as he placed another meatball on his plate. "Good job, Tonya."

"Thank you." Without smiling, she walked away.

*Prickly.* Murray took five more meatballs. Why couldn't Tonya be civil to him? He remembered when she had sneezed on Sunday and blamed his aftershave. Maybe she didn't like the smell of his aftershave, although he loved the scent. Before attending the party, he had doused himself liberally.

By the time everyone arrived, Murray felt full, having finished his meatballs as well as three brownies and a piece of cake. He chose a comfortable blue chair that he recognized from the Brandts' living room. Some of the other chairs and sofas were from their home, too, and every seat was occupied. Tonya sat on a sofa between Cheyenne and Aggie, who did indeed arrive late, but that didn't keep her from scarfing down the food on her mounded plate. Aggie's hairstyle was tinted green and whipped up like a Christmas tree. Murray leaned forward for a closer look. Little ornaments nestled in her hair, and a tiny gold star crowned the top. Her ears sported huge earrings that resembled Christmas presents.

*Presents under the tree.* With a shake of his head, Murray sat back.

Derek opened the party in prayer, and then Tonya and Cheyenne led the group in a few party games. Murray thought they were childish, but that's how these parties always went. After three games, Tonya and Cheyenne took their seats.

"Thanks, girls." Derek looked relieved that the games were over. "The next thing on the agenda is opening the present from your secret pal."

Corey fisted the air. "Woo! Presents!"

A tittering of laughter followed his outburst.

Derek smiled. "Since Cheyenne works at the post office, I figured she'd be a natural at passing out the packages." He nodded to Cheyenne. "The floor is all yours."

"Thanks, Derek." Cheyenne walked to the Christmas tree and began pulling out the gifts. "By the way, if anyone wants more food, feel free to get some. There's plenty left."

Murray remembered how good the brownies were—chocolate with bits of chocolate chunks and some kind of cream cheese mixture in the center. Approaching the table, he sought out the tray. Only one brownie remained, and he watched in disappointment as Aggie's bejeweled fingers closed around it.

"Oh, Tonya, hon." Aggie bit into it and chewed as she talked. "These brownies are just scrumptious. You'll have to give me the recipe."

Tonya turned from her place on the sofa. "Sorry, it's one of my secret recipes. I made it up myself, and I'm not giving it away." She smiled at Aggie. "But I'm glad you like them."

"Oh, sugar, they're simply delicious." Aggie polished off the brownie and licked two of her fingers.

"They are good, Tonya." Murray nodded to her, hoping she couldn't smell his aftershave from this distance. "Just like the meatballs. You're a good cook."

"Thanks." A little smile curved her lips before she turned back.

Grabbing a cookie, Murray grinned with a feeling of triumph. At least

Tonya was thawing out toward him. He took his seat.

Cheyenne stood on the rug in the middle of the wagon train with colorful gifts of various sizes surrounding her feet. She picked up a clipboard from among the packages. "Before you open your present, each receiver must answer a question. If you don't get the answer right, we'll have to skip you until later."

Several groans followed this announcement.

Cheyenne selected a gift and looked at the tag. "This one is for Reed Dickens."

Reed sat next to Laurie Smullens on a love seat, and they seemed rather cozy, in Murray's opinion. Leaning forward, Reed looked confident. "All right. What's my question?"

Cheyenne consulted her clipboard. "This question is from the book *A Christmas Carol* by Charles Dickens. What was the name of Ebenezer Scrooge's employee?"

"Bob Cratchit, of course." Reed sat back with a chuckle. "You have to know your Dickens like the dickens, and that's me." He looked at Laurie and laughed at his own joke. She giggled.

Murray glanced across the room in time to see Tonya roll her eyes.

Cheyenne handed Reed a small rectangular package. He tore off the paper and looked at his gift. "Oh, a Mr. Bean DVD. How cool."

Grabbing another gift, Cheyenne read Corey's name. "Here's your question: What is the translation of Santa Claus?"

Corey frowned. "The translation?"

Cheyenne nodded. "*Santa Claus* is German. What does it mean in English?"

"Who knows?" He shrugged. "Uh, Merry Christmas?"

"Sorry, Corey. We'll have to skip you."

"What?" He raised his hands and dropped them.

Tonya smirked. "The answer is Saint Nicholas. Better luck next time, Corey."

Cheyenne picked up the gift Murray had brought and looked at the tag. "Tonya Brandt."

Trying to present a cool demeanor, Murray glanced at Tonya with nonchalant eyes, but his palms began to sweat.

"Okay, Tonya." Cheyenne looked at her clipboard. "What were the three gifts that the wise men brought to the baby Jesus?"

A beautiful smile lit Tonya's face as she reached for her gift. "Gold, frankincense, and myrrh."

"That's not fair." Corey folded his arms. "Everyone else gets easy questions."

Murray watched Tonya tear off the bright-red and gold Christmas paper he had so meticulously wrapped just an hour ago.

"Ooh, I can't believe it!" She held up the DVD he had purchased. "Twenty old movies from the '40s and '50s. I love it! Thank you, secret pal—whoever you are."

He suppressed a grin as he watched Tonya and Aggie bend their heads together to read the box.

What made Tonya tick? It didn't take much to make her happy. But then again, it didn't take much to make her angry.

An old memory, when Murray and Callie were high school seniors, jumped into his mind. Tonya, a ninth grader, wanted to hang out with them, whining that she didn't have any friends.

"Well. . ." Callie had stuck her hands on her thin hips and stared at Tonya through her thick glasses. "You'd have more friends if you weren't so selfish."

*True sibling honesty.* Murray watched Tonya and Aggie take the DVDs from the case. Tonya seemed to have some good friends now, but she was still self-centered. On the outside she was beautiful, but what was she really like on the inside? If only he could get to know her—not the Tonya she presented to the world, but the real Tonya deep in her heart.

But how could he do that?

Dating her was out of the question. She'd turn him down flat. Maybe he could correspond with her somehow, but that would only work if she didn't know who he was. She said she loved secrets. He thought about that for a moment, and a plan formed in his mind.

Murray smiled to himself. It just might work, but only if Tonya never discovered his identity.

# Chapter 6

On Christmas morning, Tonya watched her nephews, Peter and Paul, play with the empty boxes on the living room floor. "Why do little kids always like the boxes more than the toys?"

Holly, her sister-in-law, sat cross-legged on the carpet. "Those boxes are big building blocks to one- and two-year-olds." She pushed a strand of brown hair behind her ear. "When our family goes back to Denver, we'll leave the boxes here. Then they'll play with the toys at home."

Tonya gathered up the wrapping paper that had been tossed aside when the family opened their gifts early that morning. Right now Mom, Molly, Melissa, and Callie were in the kitchen preparing Christmas dinner. Dad, Ryan, Jonathan, and Lane, along with Philip, Melissa's husband, had already disappeared into the den to watch the football game.

"I wish Derek were here." Holly stacked her sons' toys in a pile.

Tonya sat down on the blue chair, thankful all their furniture was back in the living room. "You know how community-oriented Derek is. He had to help out at the soup kitchen in downtown Casper." Tonya shook her head. "Personally, I think he should have stayed here with the family, but he decided the Lord wanted him to help the homeless on Christmas day."

"That's very admirable."

"I guess." Tonya leaned her head back and wondered who sat in this chair at the Single Servings Christmas party the other night. A face popped into her mind—a face with a big nose and blue eyes set too close together, framed with reddish-brown hair. Usually she would emit a groan, but she remembered how Murray had complimented her cooking. In that area, he was a lot nicer than Reed Dickens. Murray was probably spending a quiet day with his mom at the nursing home in Douglas. With all the siblings Tonya had, she couldn't imagine what a quiet Christmas would be like.

"Tonya?" Callie called from the dining room. "Come help me set the table."

Tonya rose and made her way to the dining table. "How many are we having for dinner?" She glanced at herself in the mirror above the fireplace mantel as she walked by. Holly and Callie hadn't even bothered to put on makeup this morning, but Tonya paused to make sure hers still looked good.

"We have thirteen people, but only ten will fit around the table." Callie set the silverware box on the sideboard and opened it. "Mom said we could stick Peter and Paul at the little card table with one of the adults."

Holly walked into the dining room. "I'll sit with them."

Tonya looked at her sister-in-law, who never seemed to have a moment to herself. "I'll sit with the boys, Holly. You sit with Ryan and the rest of the family."

"Are you sure, Tonya? You don't know what you're getting into. They need a lot of help."

"It will be good experience for the future."

"If you're sure." Holly smiled. "It will be nice to eat a quiet dinner for once."

Tonya smiled back. "Hey, I can handle this. Besides, Peter and Paul and I are the only single people here today, so we'll sit at the singles' table."

An hour later, after cutting up Peter's turkey into small pieces, stopping Paul from throwing his sippy cup at her, and wiping mashed potatoes off both boys' fingers, Tonya wished she could eat her dinner at the other table. She still had mashed potatoes in her hair where Paul grabbed it. That must look real good—white clumps of potatoes in her dark hair. She should run upstairs after dinner and wash it.

Wiping the scalloped corn from Peter's face, she listened to the conversation and laughter from the big table, wishing she could join in. She sighed. Everyone here, all twelve of them, had a partner. Even her two little nephews had each other. But Tonya was the thirteenth person, the unlucky one. . .the lonely one.

*Lord, I want a man!*

The doorbell rang, and the room quieted.

Dad placed his napkin on the table as he stood. "Now who could that be?"

"It must be someone we know, Dad." Tonya popped a forkful of mashed potatoes into her mouth. Living out in the country, the Brandts didn't get many visitors.

Dad left the dining room. "It's probably someone from the church wishing our family a merry Christmas."

The conversation picked up again as Tonya wiped Paul's hands for the third time.

A few minutes later Dad came back, carrying a long thin box. "Well, well. We have a special delivery for Miss Tonya Brandt."

She looked up. "For me?"

Dad grinned. "Is your name Tonya Brandt?"

"It sure is." She jumped up as a thrill buzzed through her.

The family crowded around as she took the long box from Dad and sat on the blue chair in the living room.

"Must be a rifle," Ryan quipped.

Tonya opened the lid and gasped, staring at a mass of long-stemmed red roses. Her sisters broke out in exclamations.

Mom placed her hand around Tonya's shoulders and gave her a squeeze. "A dozen red roses, Tonya. And there's a card." She pointed at the envelope nestled among the stems.

Tonya picked it up. *Miss Tonya Brandt* was scripted in beautiful penmanship on the outside of the envelope. She pulled out an old-fashioned Christmas card—a Currier and Ives engraving of a couple ice-skating on a pond. Inside a preprinted message wished her a happy holiday, and then the sender wrote in his perfect penmanship, *Merry Christmas from Your Secret Admirer.*

"Well, who is it, Tonya?" Dad asked.

She glanced around at the curious faces. "It's from a secret admirer!"

This announcement precipitated a cloudburst of conversation. When the speculations died down, the men of the family exited to the dining room, but her sisters and mom stayed to discuss the situation.

Tonya couldn't keep the smile from her face. "Wow, I can't imagine who sent this."

Molly tossed her hair over her shoulder. "Do you think it's that doctor you told me about?"

"Reed? No way. He has terrible handwriting. Besides, he's not interested in me." *And the feeling is mutual.*

"On the other hand. . ." Callie pointed toward the signature with a stick of celery. "Maybe that's not his handwriting. He could have had the salesgirl at the florist sign the card."

Mom nodded. "You wouldn't think a man would have such beautiful penmanship."

Melissa leaned over and picked up the box's lid, which had fallen to the floor. "It was sent from Blooms and Buds Florist, Douglas, Wyoming."

Callie sat down on the ottoman. "That's where we all got our wedding flowers since Fort Lob doesn't have a florist. That's the closest one."

Melissa knit her brows together. "No clues there."

"Who cares who sent them?" Joy bubbled up inside Tonya, but she didn't want to act like a desperate teenager. "This is probably a one-time thing. Most likely I'll never hear from him again."

"But what a nice surprise for you." Mom gave Tonya a quick kiss on her forehead before turning back to the dining room. "Let's get dessert on the table, girls. Tonya, you need to put those roses in water."

Tonya was the last to leave the living room. "Thank you, Lord," she whispered. So what if this was a one-time thing? She would always be thankful for it. Carrying the box out to the kitchen, a feeling of peace enveloped her.

Later, as she helped her sisters finish the dishes, the doorbell rang again. Tonya ran to answer it. A uniformed deliveryman stood on the porch, holding a square box in one hand, a clipboard and pen in the other.

He raised his eyebrows. "Tonya Brandt?"

"Yes, that's me."

He thrust the clipboard toward her. "Sign on the next line, please."

Tonya's hand shook as she wrote her name, then exchanged the clipboard for the package. "Thank you."

With a smile, she brushed back her hair, and her fingers ran into something gooey. Oh great—she had forgotten about the mashed potatoes. *How embarrassing.*

The man grinned, gazing at her face a moment before he turned back to his truck. Tonya closed the door, annoyed that her looks were not perfect. She would have gone upstairs to wash her hair right then if not for receiving a second mysterious gift.

Again she took a seat on the blue chair, and again the family crowded around her. This time her secret admirer had sent a huge box of chocolates.

"Hey, candy!" Ryan grabbed the box. "You're gonna share, aren't you, sis?"

"Help yourself." She felt generous, even though the candy might be gone by the time the men got finished with it.

An envelope lay at the bottom of the package with that same beautiful penmanship. This time it said, *For Tonya.*

"Ooh." Molly winked at her. "He's getting more intimate."

Tonya held her breath as she opened the envelope. The card had a winter scene with an old-fashioned Victorian house decorated for Christmas. The inside was blank, except for what was written in flowing cursive: *Sweets for the Sweet. May you have a blessed Christmas, Tonya. Your Secret Admirer.*

"Wow, two gifts on Christmas Day." Callie dug her cell phone from her purse. "I have to call Cheyenne. She's not going to believe this."

Tonya giggled. "I'll call Aggie. She always told me if I wait, I'll find my man."

"Sounds like he found you." Melissa cocked an eyebrow.

Tonya breathed out a happy sigh. God had sent her a man, even if he was only temporary.

# Chapter 7

Early Friday morning Murray entered the Trailblazer Café. Usually the restaurant bustled with breakfast customers, but today only two couples, the Whitneys and the Pipers, sat in booths by the large windows that looked out on Main Street. Bruce MacKinnon was the sole customer sitting at the long counter.

Murray took the seat next to Bruce. "Morning, Bruce." He laid his patrol hat on the empty stool beside him. "I'm surprised you're not eating at a table full of your old cronies." He grinned at the dignified Scotsman.

Bruce shrugged. "It's the day after Christmas." His *r*'s rolled slightly with his brogue. "Everyone is still celebrating with their families, but my son and his family left for Salt Lake City early this morning." He glanced at Murray's patrolman uniform. "I see there's no more holiday for you."

"Nope, it's back to work. Someone has to keep law and order in this sleepy town."

"Aye." With a smile, Bruce set his coffee cup on the saucer. "There's so much crime in Fort Lob. Who knows? You might catch a madman speeding down Main Street."

"Hey, you're right." Murray glanced at his watch. "It's 7:18. I need to be sitting in my patrol car at 8:45, just in case Tonya Brandt decides to break the sound barrier." He laughed, thinking of the expensive gifts he had sent her yesterday. He had paid almost double to get them delivered on Christmas Day.

"Say, speaking of Tonya. . ." Bruce lowered his voice. "I heard she has a secret admirer."

Murray raised his eyebrows. "No joking?" *That didn't take long.* "Where'd you hear that from?"

"Agatha Collingsworth called me last night. Word is that Tonya received a couple packages yesterday from some man who is admiring her from a distance." Bruce chuckled. "The poor boy is probably too scared to ask her out for a date."

Murray hadn't thought how others would perceive his actions. "Well, she's so pretty. You have to give the guy credit for trying."

Coffeepot in hand, Joyce Hediger approached Murray from the other side of the counter. Her ample white waitress uniform already had stains on it. "Are you discussing Tonya Brandt's secret admirer? Isn't that a hoot?" She gave a toothy smile as she poured Murray a cup of coffee.

If Joyce knew about it, the whole town must know. "Where did you hear it, Joyce?"

"Barb Lathrop told me. She heard it from Cheyenne Wilkins. Sounds like Tonya was on cloud nine last night."

So Tonya was excited. Murray tried not to smile too broadly. "I suppose nothing like that ever happened to her before."

Joyce laughed as she took three little creamers from her pocket and set them beside Murray's cup. "Tonya has so many boyfriends, this guy is just one of the many. I bet she's adding him to her list. She always liked attention, you know."

Murray's initial happiness faded.

Joyce set the coffeepot on the counter. "The usual, Murray? Scrambled eggs with toast?"

"Sure." He watched Joyce waddle away before he turned to Bruce. "Does, uh, Tonya know who her secret admirer is?" He dumped a creamer into his cup.

Bruce shook his head. "Not that I'm aware. Agatha didn't say."

Murray stirred his coffee. He couldn't ask too many questions or people would get suspicious. But now he *definitely* didn't want Tonya—or anyone else for that matter—to discover his identity. Bruce thought he was too scared to ask her out, and Joyce thought Tonya didn't care who he was.

Of course, Bruce was right. Murray was afraid to ask Tonya out. But then, his purpose was to find out what she was really like. There was an end to his means, and Murray intended to see it through.

He was glad the post office was open today.

The phone rang at the Beauty Spot on Saturday morning, just as Tonya finished sweeping up from the last haircut. Aggie was at the other beauty station, giving Gloria Schutzenhofer a perm.

"I'll get the phone, Aggie." Tonya walked to the cash register and plucked the receiver from the wall phone after the third ring. "The Beauty Spot, this is Tonya."

"Hi, girlfriend!" Cheyenne's voice came over the line. "You're just the person I want to talk to. Your secret admirer has been busy, and let me tell you— that guy gets around. I have a slew of letters here at the post office for you."

Tonya's heart leaped into her throat. "Really?"

"They're all addressed to Miss Tonya Brandt." Cheyenne chuckled. "For a man, he sure has beautiful handwriting."

"Wow, this is so exciting!"

"What's going on, hon?" Aggie called from her station.

Tonya held up a *one moment* finger to Aggie. "How many are there, Cheyenne?"

"Let's see. . . . There's two letters postmarked from Lusk, three from

Douglas, one from Cheyenne, and two that were mailed here in Fort Lob."

Tonya counted silently. "Eight letters! I can't believe it."

"Believe it, girl. Do you want Bernie to deliver them to your house with the rest of the mail, or do you want to swing by the P.O. and pick them up?"

"I'll be there in five minutes!" She laughed. "Thanks, Cheyenne."

Hanging up the phone, Tonya turned to Aggie and Gloria. "My secret admirer sent me eight letters in the mail!" She pulled her purse from under the counter. "I'm going to run to the post office and get them, Aggie. Is that okay?" She grabbed her coat from the hook near the door.

"Only if you let me read them, too." Aggie cackled out a laugh. "This will fuel the town gossip for weeks to come, and we'll do our part. Right, Gloria?"

Gloria's thin eyebrows formed a *V* in the middle of her forehead. "I never gossip."

Tonya turned away so Gloria wouldn't see her laughing. That woman was such a gossip that some people called her *Gloria the Grapevine*.

Pushing open the door, Tonya walked out into the chilly December weather. An inch of snow covered the ground. But even if the weather were warm, she wouldn't walk the three blocks to the post office. She climbed into her red Hyundai and started the engine.

Maybe, after she read these eight letters, she could figure out this guy's identity.

❧

On Monday Murray sat in his SUV at police headquarters in Cheyenne, Wyoming. He'd been off duty for fifteen minutes, but he wanted to stay in the city to mail a few cards to Tonya. The clipboard rested on his steering wheel, and he tapped a pen thoughtfully against his lips.

He read over the words he had written on a piece of notebook paper.

*In the winter of my discontent,*
*Your beautiful face rivals the brilliance of the sun,*
*The beauty of roses at their peak. . . .*

"Nah." He crossed out some of the words and rewrote the poem.

*In the winter of my discontent,*
*Your face brightens my day like a multihued rainbow,*
*Rivaling the brilliance of the sun,*
*And the beauty of a rose garden at summer's peak.*

He sat back and read over the revision. "That stinks."

Crumpling the paper, he threw it with the other wadded papers on the passenger's seat. "Okay, I'll take one more stab at it." He thought a few minutes before writing. Maybe he would send this one to Tonya.

He wrote carefully, making sure his penmanship was perfect. In seventh grade he had won an award for best handwriting in the entire school, and he had been proud of his ability—until a couple of ninth-grade boys laughed at

158

him and called him a sissy. He never wrote in cursive again.

*In the winter of my discontent,*
*One look at your beautiful face,*
*Like a beam of brilliant sunshine in a dark place,*
*Lifts my countenance, warming my entire being.*

"Hmmm. . ." Was this any good? Well, no matter. He would send it anyway. After all, Tonya liked poetry. Tomorrow he would visit the library and check out some of the classics—some of the poets he loved himself. Maybe he'd copy something by Henry Longfellow or Lord Tennyson. He snapped his fingers as a name hit him. *Elizabeth Barrett Browning!* Perfect.

Now it was on to the jewelry store.

∽

That week Tonya made a run to the post office every day during her lunch hour. And every day at least four letters from her secret admirer waited for her. But as she entered the post office on Wednesday, she frowned, chewing on her bottom lip. She wasn't any closer to guessing who this man was than she had been on Christmas Day.

Tonya waited in line while Mrs. Hochstetler bought a book of stamps at the counter.

"I just don't know which ones to buy." Mrs. Hochstetler's white hair quivered slightly as she looked over the selection of stamps that Cheyenne held in front of her. "I liked the Christmas stamps this year. I can't believe it's already New Year's Eve. Another year begins tomorrow."

"Time flies." Cheyenne smiled. "Are you going to stay up until midnight to bring in the New Year?"

"Oh, I can't stay awake that late." Mrs. Hochstetler gave a little laugh. "I'll be in bed at nine o'clock."

While Cheyenne was busy helping the elderly woman decide which stamps to purchase, Murray Twichell walked through the door. A gun holster rested at the right hip of his uniform.

"Hi." He nodded at Tonya, stopped at the row of post office boxes, and thrust a key in one of them.

Mrs. Hochstetler finally settled on the stamps. She toddled outside, wishing Cheyenne and Tonya a happy New Year. The door closed behind her.

"Tonya, guess what?" Cheyenne pulled a box from beneath the counter. "You have a package today."

"A package!" Tonya almost squealed. Even though everyone in town knew about her secret admirer, she was glad no one else waited in line at the post office. Murray was the only other person in the building. "Is it from *him*?"

"I don't know—there's no return address." Cheyenne laughed as she pushed a small priority mail box toward her. "But that's his handwriting." She pointed to Tonya's name in perfect cursive on the label.

Tonya bit her lip as she opened it and pulled out a small black cardboard box. The words RED MESA JEWELRY CO. were embossed in gold letters on the top. She sucked in a breath. "He bought me jewelry."

"Wow." Cheyenne leaned forward, her arms folded on the counter. "I never heard of the Red Mesa Jewelry Company before." She picked up the mailing box and looked at the postmark. "Fort Collins, Colorado. Your secret admirer sure likes to travel."

"This is so exciting." Tonya was about to lift the lid from the box when she felt someone beside her. She glanced to her right.

Murray peered at the jewelry box before meeting her eyes. "Sorry to interrupt, but it looks like you might be here awhile." He spoke to Cheyenne. "I need to buy a book of stamps."

"Okay." Cheyenne opened a drawer. "We have flag stamps, forever stamps—"

"Flags are good." Murray pulled his wallet from his back pocket.

Tonya didn't wait for their transaction. Opening the box, she gazed at the jewelry case covered in black velvet and raised the hinged lid. A pendant necklace reposed on creamy silk. The chain disappeared underneath, but silver scrollwork held a blue stone.

"Oh. . ." She breathed out a wondrous sigh as she lifted the necklace from the box. "This is beautiful."

Cheyenne handed Murray some change. "Let's see it, girlfriend."

Tonya held it out for her inspection.

"Tonya! This must be a real sapphire." Cheyenne held it close to her face. "At least it looks real to me."

"Let me see it." Murray took the necklace and studied it a moment. "Yep. Definitely real. Of course, you wouldn't expect your boyfriend to give you some fake rhinestone." He grinned as he handed it back.

Normally Murray's comment would aggravate her, but Tonya was too happy to be bothered by him today. "I want to wear this." She took off her coat and laid it on the counter. Brushing her hair out of the way, she pulled the pendant up to her neck and tried to fasten the clasp in the back but couldn't feel the hook. She turned her back to Murray. "Fasten this for me."

"Oh, uh, sure."

Out of the corner of her eye, she saw him lay his stamps and a set of keys on the counter. Then she felt his fingers behind her neck. It took a little longer than she thought it should, but she stood still while he worked on it.

"Okay, there you go." Murray picked up his keys and stamps.

"Thanks." Tonya turned toward Cheyenne. "What do you think?"

"Looks great." Cheyenne leaned her chin in the palm of her hand and gave a wistful sigh. "I wish a certain someone would become *my* secret admirer."

Tonya shook her head. "I'm afraid my brother doesn't have a romantic bone in his body. He would never think of sending you cards and jewelry."

She sighed. "I sure wish I knew who sent me this. I can't believe the money he's spent. This sapphire must have cost him a bundle."

"Don't forget postage. He's going through stamps like crazy."

Murray pivoted and walked out the door. "Have a good day, ladies."

"Happy New Year, Murray." Cheyenne stood up straight. "I'm glad tomorrow is New Year's Day. I can sleep in."

"But the post office will be closed, and I won't get any mail from my secret admirer." Tonya fingered the necklace.

Cheyenne reached under the counter and pulled out a small stack of envelopes. "You have mail today. Five letters."

"Wow." Tonya smiled as she took them. "Would you believe he wrote a poem for me? He's so sweet. I'm saving all the cards, and it's quite a collection. I wish I could thank him."

Cheyenne grinned. "I have a feeling you'll find out who he is—eventually."

∾

Murray glanced at the clock above his desk. Nine o'clock on New Year's Eve. Just enough time to write a few cards to Tonya before he had to go to work tonight. He sighed, not relishing all the arrests he'd probably have to make in the early morning hours or the drunken parties he might have to crash.

He creased down the page of the library book and carefully copied the poem on a piece of notebook paper. He had selected "How Do I Love Thee? Let Me Count the Ways" by Elizabeth Barrett Browning. It certainly had a better cadence than his poor attempts at poetry, and the subject matter seemed appropriate, even though he didn't love Tonya.

But. . .what if that happened? What if they fell in love?

His lips curved into a smile as he thought back to her little squeal at the post office. He had waited for her daily visit, hanging out at Gilman's Pharmacy across the street and then entering the post office after she did. Her reaction was more than he had hoped for. He couldn't believe she asked him to hook the necklace clasp. Fastening a necklace was something husbands did for their wives, and it gave him a strange feeling.

Her skin was so soft.

Sitting back, he recalled the girls' conversation about the amount of money he had spent. *I guess I am spending a lot on her.* But what else did he have to spend his salary on? Medicare paid for Mom's nursing home bill, and the house had been paid off years ago. Actually, buying expensive gifts for Tonya was fun.

Picking up the library book, he went back to "How Do I Love Thee." When he finished, he folded the paper and placed it inside the card. Too bad the post office would be closed tomorrow. He read through the preprinted poem that started, "I thought of you today." His eyes traveled to the words he had penned at the bottom of the card, and he smiled to himself.

Tonya would be surprised.

# Chapter 8

On Friday afternoon, January second, Tonya stared at Cheyenne as she stood in the post office. "Only one card?" Since the post office was closed yesterday, Tonya thought a dozen envelopes would be waiting for her today.

Her friend shrugged. "Sorry. That's it."

Tonya had decided to pick up her mail after work, and now several people queued behind her. She turned and left the building. Walking out into the chilly parking lot, she glanced across the street. Murray Twichell strode toward the Cattlemen's Diner. He gave her a little salute before entering the restaurant.

Tonya waved back. Murray was going to the diner for supper. When he wasn't traveling through the state for the Wyoming highway patrol, he always ate there.

She stopped beside her car. *Hmmm. . .he travels a lot.* Her eyes widened, but almost in the same second, she dismissed the thought. Her secret admirer couldn't be Murray—of all people. He had never even liked her. Besides, he wrote in blocky printing. At least, that's how he wrote her speeding ticket.

She sighed. *Precious memories, how they linger.*

Opening the car door, she laid the card on the passenger seat. She would savor it when she got home. But what if her secret admirer was tired of sending letters to her? Or perhaps he had lost interest, and this would be his last one.

*Or maybe he's running out of money.*

Well, it was fun while it lasted. Starting the engine, she looked down at the lone envelope on the passenger's seat.

It couldn't be the last one!

Grabbing the envelope, she tore it open and pulled out the card. A piece of paper fell into her lap, and she unfolded it. Her eyes traveled across the poem in his perfect handwriting.

*How do I love thee? Let me count the ways.*
*I love thee to the depth and breadth and height*
*My soul can reach. . . .*

Tonya gave a wistful sigh as she read on. Her secret admirer loved her! He wasn't ending their relationship.

She looked at the front of the card—a Norman Rockwell reprint of a cozy couple. *He's so romantic.* She read the poem on the inside and then read what he wrote at the bottom. Jerking upright, she gasped. "I can't believe it!"

Throwing the gears into DRIVE, she peeled out of the parking lot and roared down Main Street.

~~~

"Mom, I'm home!" Tonya raced up the stairs and entered her bedroom. Her computer waited on the desk by the window. She paced the room while it booted up.

Mom appeared at the doorway. "Tonya, what's going on? I've never seen you in such a hurry."

"Read this." Picking up the card, she pointed to his handwriting at the bottom.

Mom's dark blue eyes shifted from left to right over the words. "Oh, he gave you his e-mail address."

Tonya grinned. "Now I can write to him. And he calls himself Poetry Lover Guy. Isn't that funny? His e-mail address is poetryloverguy@sweetmail.com." She picked up the poem. "And look at this. He copied a poem by Elizabeth Barrett Browning."

Mom glanced at it. " 'How Do I Love Thee? Let Me Count the Ways.' That's very famous."

"What's really cool is that Elizabeth Barrett and Robert Browning corresponded with each other, and when they finally met, Robert asked her to marry him." Tonya plopped down on her desk chair. "I hope that happens with this guy and me."

"Now, Tonya. . ." Mom took a seat on the bed. "You need to be careful. It's one thing to have a secret admirer, but quite another thing to correspond over the Internet with a stranger. A lot of young women have gotten into dangerous situations doing that very thing."

"I know." Tonya eyed her mother. "I won't do anything foolish. Do you think I'm going to run away and meet him somewhere by myself?"

"I certainly hope not."

"Here's the plan." Tonya giggled, feeling a bubble of excitement. "I'm going to invite him over for dinner with the family. After all, he can't keep his identity a secret forever. Then you can meet him at the same time and judge him for yourself."

Mom stood. "Please wait a couple weeks before you ask him for dinner. Let's see what he says on the e-mail first."

Tonya gave an exasperated sigh. "Oh, all right. I'll wait."

"Good." Mom started toward the door. "Supper will be ready in twenty minutes."

Tonya opened her e-mail program. "I'm going to write and thank him for all the cards he sent me." She clicked on the NEW tab.

"Don't forget the roses, candy, and sapphire necklace." Mom's voice faded down the stairway.

"How could I?" Tonya fingered the necklace she'd worn for the past two days. She paused to think before she began typing.

*Dear Poetry Lover Guy...*

⸾⸾⸾

The front door to Murray's house squeaked open as he turned the key in the lock. Walking into the living room, he glanced at the computer sitting on the desk in the corner. It wouldn't surprise him if Tonya had already written him.

But he would wait.

He trudged up the creaky wooden stairs to his bedroom. He had been on patrol for two straight days, since New Year's Eve, and he wanted to get out of his uniform, take a shower, and don a pair of jeans and a T-shirt. Amazingly, he had both Saturday and Sunday off. That seldom happened, and the thought of who might invite him over for Sunday dinner drifted through his mind.

But right now he was tired. The New Year festivities had taken their toll while he helped keep law and order on the streets of Cheyenne. Tonight he would relax, microwave a bag of popcorn, and dig out one of Mom's old romantic movies to watch.

His thoughts jumped to Tonya. Sitting by a window at the Cattlemen's Diner, he watched her tear out of the post office parking lot. It almost made him angry. But her irresponsible driving was most likely his fault. She had read his card and wanted to e-mail him. He shook his head. That girl was so impulsive, so unlike him in every way.

*Opposites attract.*

That's what his mom always told him. Mom had been a quiet, demure Irish woman in her thirties when she met Anson Twichell—a loud, outgoing lawyer and the life of every party. Murray grinned, remembering how jolly Dad could be. He lived life to the full—until the day it was cut short by a heart attack. Murray had been fourteen.

He wished for the millionth time his father was still living.

Walking downstairs, Murray booted up the computer and clicked on his e-mail. Sure enough, an e-mail from Tonya Brandt waited for him. A spark of curiosity flew through him, and he leaned forward.

> *Dear Poetry Lover Guy,*
> *Thank you so much for all the cards you've sent me, as well as the roses, candy, and the sapphire necklace. I wear the necklace every day—it's beautiful, and I love it! The cards have been wonderful. I love receiving mail from you, and I'm so glad you gave me your e-mail address so I could write back and thank you.*
> *Who are you? Tell me all about yourself. Do I know you? Do you go to our church? Are you a resident of Fort Lob, or do you live in Lusk or*

*Cheyenne? What do you do for a living? How old are you? Nothing like
this has ever happened to me before, and I really want to meet you.*

> *Please reply, and thanks again.*
>
> *Love ya, Tonya.*

Murray read the letter once more. She certainly asked a lot of questions—most of which he wouldn't answer. As for meeting him, she would be
waiting into eternity if he had his way.

✎

"I hope he wrote back." On Saturday morning, Tonya tapped her fingernails
on the desk, waiting for her e-mail to load. She didn't have to work today.
Saturday was usually the busiest day at the Beauty Spot, but Aggie had hired a
new beautician, Connie, who would help handle the customers this weekend.

Tonya had checked her e-mail several times last night, but there was
nothing. Now as her inbox opened, a post from Poetry Lover Guy appeared.
Her heart gave a leap, and she clicked it open.

*Hi Tonya,*

> *I'm glad you enjoyed all the letters and gifts I sent. It was fun to
> send them to someone so beautiful. But admiring you from a distance is
> one thing. I thought it would be better if we could correspond with each
> other. I want to get to know you.*

An arrow of fear pierced her heart. Could Mom be right? Was this a
stranger with evil motives? Some Internet fiend?

Tonya took a deep breath. *Calm down, girl.* After all, he couldn't reach out
of the monitor and grab her by the throat. She continued reading.

> *I'll answer some of your questions. Who am I? Well, let's just say
> I'm a guy who likes poetry and old movies. Where do I live? Somewhere
> in Wyoming. How old am I? Hmm. . .between the ages of eighteen and
> eighty-eight.*

Tonya huffed out a breath. He wasn't answering her questions at all! She
read the next line.

> *I watched* Singing in the Rain *last night. Great movie!*

Tonya's irritation melted. That movie was one of her favorites, too.

The rest of the letter talked about five other old movies he loved. Tonya
grinned. She had seen them all and couldn't wait to discuss them with him.
At the bottom, he signed off.

*Your secret admirer,*
*Poetry Lover Guy*

*P.S. My friends call me "Poe" for short.*

Tonya laughed out loud. *Poe?* What kind of name was that? But she had to admit it was better than calling him *Poetry Lover Guy* or *Mr. Guy.*

If only she knew his real name.

≈

The days flew by for Murray. Every evening an e-mail waited for him from Tonya, and every evening he replied—unless he had to work. Some nights he couldn't get on a computer, especially when he was out in the boondocks in the middle of Wyoming.

Tonya wrote lengthy letters, but it was all surface talk about her job, her family, her friends. He was not getting to know the real Tonya at all, which had been his objective.

One Thursday evening, Murray grabbed a can of cola and settled in front of his computer. Since he was off work that day, he'd had plenty of time to think about their relationship. If he took a risk and revealed his heart, perhaps she would do the same.

*Dear Tonya,*

After three paragraphs of the usual chatter, he delved into exposing his heart.

*I live by myself in a big old house, and tonight I stood by the window for a half hour watching the snowflakes drift down. I'm an introspective person and ponder a lot about my life. Sometimes loneliness overwhelms me. I'm corresponding with you—I must admit—for my own sake as well as for yours. I look forward to reading your e-mails every evening. Reading about your life and sharing things about mine causes the loneliness to disappear.*

He read over the lines. Was he revealing his heart too much or not enough? He thought of his birthday coming up next Monday on January twenty-sixth. Would anyone remember it? Did anyone even know?

Sure, his mom would remember, and he would visit her in the nursing home that day. But even though he loved his mom, a quiet visit with her wasn't the way he wanted to celebrate his birthday. What he really wanted to do was to ask Tonya out—not as "Poe," but as Murray. If only he could take her to a nice restaurant to celebrate, then he wouldn't have to eat alone.

Stifling a sigh, he continued typing.

*Thanks, Tonya, for writing to me. You make my day with every letter. Ever yours, Poe.*

He hit the SEND button before he lost his nerve and deleted the whole thing.

Sitting at the desk, he took a few moments to pray, which made him feel better. He wasn't really alone. The Lord knew what was going on in his life, and He had a plan. Murray would just have to wait for it.

He stood and stretched. Time for another old movie.

❧

Tears formed in Tonya's eyes. Poe sounded so sad. In the back of her mind the thought niggled that perhaps this guy *was* a predator, trying to pluck at her heartstrings with his talk of loneliness. The next step would be for him to invite her to meet him in some dark alley.

She grimaced.

On the other hand, two could play this game. With a determined mind-set, she began typing.

A few minutes later, Mom entered the room. "Are you still at the computer, Tonya?"

"I'm writing a letter to Poe."

"I figured that." Mom stood behind Tonya as she continued typing. "What does LOL mean?"

Tonya grinned. "You're so computer illiterate, Mom. It's an abbreviation that means 'laughing out loud' or, as some people say, 'lots of laughs.' You write it at the end of a sentence when you're joking. Or you could write JK instead. That means 'just kidding.'"

"Oh." Mom nodded. "Kind of like the old 'ha!' that Grandma writes in her letters."

"Exactly." The keyboard buttons clicked as Tonya continued her sentence.

Mom leaned over her. "What does BTW mean?"

"By the way." Tonya stopped typing. She had written her opening comments to Poe and wanted to say something more personal, but she didn't want her mother to read it. "Do you mind, Mom? I can't concentrate when you're reading over my shoulder."

"I was on my way to bed." Mom bent to kiss her daughter's forehead. "It's almost eleven, and you have to get up early for work tomorrow morning."

"I know. And don't worry, I won't be up late. Since it's been snowing, I plan to get up a half hour earlier tomorrow morning and take my time driving to work. I sure don't want Murray to give me a ticket."

"Good for you." Mom walked to the door. "Good night."

"Night, Mom." Tonya turned back to the computer, ready to pour out her heart to Poetry Lover Guy.

# Chapter 9

On Friday morning, Tonya watched Crystal Larsen walk out of the Beauty Spot, sporting her new hair color. The blond highlights looked great on Crystal, and Tonya silently congratulated herself on her good fashion advice.

"This morning's been so busy." With a broom, Aggie swept hair into a dustpan. "But I'm glad. Seems like we have more customers when the snow stops." She leaned on the broom handle. "You sure have been quiet today, Tonya."

"I've been thinking about Poe."

"Who else?" Aggie laughed. "The whole town knows about that secret admirer of yours. So, what did he write last night?"

"I feel so sorry for him. He's lonely."

"Aren't we all?" Aggie plopped down in the beautician chair, and her brown eyes turned serious. "You know who really helps curb my loneliness?" She glanced toward the door, as if checking to make sure no customers were entering.

*Aggie, lonely?* Tonya raised her eyebrows. "Who?"

"Bruce MacKinnon, that's who." With a sigh, Aggie brushed her fingers against her beehive hairdo, tinted purple this week. "I've been attracted to that man ever since his wife died, and we're good friends. I call him a lot, and sometimes he calls me. He's such a good listener. When we're talking together, my loneliness just melts away like butter in the hot sun." She paused. "But he never pays me no mind in a romantic way. I'm just his good friend—like a sister." Another sigh escaped her tangerine-painted lips.

Tonya already knew Aggie was smitten with Bruce. Last summer Callie had enlightened her about Aggie's interest, and most of the town knew Aggie pestered the man.

The bell jingled above the door, and they both turned as Murray Twichell walked in.

Tonya frowned. *What's he doing here?*

Aggie rose from her chair. "Hey there, Murray. Did Clint close the barbershop today?"

"Not that I know of." Murray hung his coat on a hook by the door. "I'm a repeat customer. I liked the way Tonya cut my hair last month, so I thought I'd come back."

"Good thing you didn't preface it with a speeding ticket." Aggie cackled at her own joke. "But you're right on, Murray. Tonya's the best in the business."

Tonya didn't know whether to thank Aggie for the compliment or yell at her for bringing up her shortcomings. She pulled the cape from her chair and waited as Murray took a seat. As she pumped up the chair with her foot, she noticed that he wasn't wearing any aftershave. Instead he smelled clean, like soap.

Her eyes met his in the mirror. "So you want the same cut I gave you last time?"

Murray smiled. "That would be great, Tonya. You're the best, just like Aggie said."

*Why is he being so nice?*

As Tonya spritzed his hair with water, Aggie sat down on the other chair. "How's your mother, sugar?" The older woman leaned toward him. "Is the Parkinson's getting any worse?"

Murray shrugged. "She's about the same. She has that jumpy type of Parkinson's, and sometimes she's more nervous than at other times."

Picking up her shears, Tonya only half-listened as Aggie and Murray conversed about Priscilla Twichell's medications, the nursing home in Douglas, and the snowy weather. Tonya's thoughts kept drifting to Poe. What was he doing right now? What did he look like? She pictured him as a tall, handsome man—like Cary Grant. In her mind Tonya reviewed Poe's e-mails, which she'd read so many times she had them memorized. What had he thought about her comments last night?

Aggie sat back in her chair. "Thanks for updating me on your mother, Murray. Hope I'm not being too nosy. Sometimes Bruce says I'm just a mite too curious."

Tonya's attention shot back to the conversation. "We have to get you and Bruce together, Aggie."

Frowning, Aggie folded her arms. "I told you about that in confidence, Tonya Brandt."

Murray grinned. "About you and Bruce? Come on, Aggie, the entire town knows you like him." He glanced at Tonya in the mirror. "You're right. It's time those two got together."

"Well I never!" Aggie sputtered. "We're just good friends, that's all."

"But Aggie. . ." Tonya clipped the hair around Murray's right ear. "Don't you want to be more than good friends?"

"Hey, I could talk to Bruce." Murray raised his eyebrows. "Maybe he just needs a push in the right direction."

"Murray's right, Aggie. Bruce is very laid-back. You two will be friends forever—and friends only—if someone doesn't nudge him toward you."

Aggie's chubby face flushed. "But, you see. . .it's just that. . ." Her bracelets clinked together as she raised her hands, then dropped them. "I don't want him to think I'm *pushy* or anything."

Murray grinned, and Tonya felt his shoulders shake in silent laughter. Biting her lower lip, Tonya tried to hide her own smile and concentrate on the haircut.

Aggie, oblivious to their amusement, paced behind Tonya. "What if Bruce don't want a closer friendship? And if I push him—why, he might never speak to me again!"

Tonya shook her head. "He probably knows how you feel already. If he's truly your friend, he's not going to suddenly hate you if you want to get closer."

"I agree with Tonya." Murray's eyes followed the pacing Aggie in the mirror. "If you want me to, I'll put a bug in his ear. I see him most mornings at the Trailblazer Café. On the other hand, if you're dead set against it. . ." He shrugged.

Twisting her hands, Aggie stopped and threw a desperate look at Tonya.

"Go for it, Aggie!" Tonya grinned. "This might be the chance of a lifetime."

"Oh okay." She pursed her orange lips. "Just promise me, Murray, that you'll talk to him in private. I don't want the whole place to know I'm pining after him."

"You have my word."

Tonya unfastened the cape and pulled it from Murray's neck. "All finished."

"I'll meet you up at the front, Murray." Aggie waddled to the cash register. "Do you want to buy any other products? Shampoo? Conditioner?" She seemed ready to dismiss Bruce as a topic of conversation.

He stood. "No thanks." Smiling at Tonya, he pulled his wallet from his back pocket. "Thanks for the great job, Tonya."

Grabbing a broom, she nodded. She had left the top a little longer, and it made him look good. Not handsome, of course—Murray would never be handsome.

After he left the shop, Tonya gazed at Murray's hair in the dustpan before she threw it in the trash. "You know, Aggie, I always thought Murray's hair was red, but it's really auburn. Almost brown."

"Growing darker with his age, I reckon. That kid used to be a carrottop, just like his mother. He's the spitting image of Priscilla." Aggie sighed as she took a seat in the other chair. "I feel so sorry for her with that Parkinson's. When I moved to Fort Lob, she was the first person who befriended me in this town. She prayed with me and helped me through some hard trials."

Tonya opened the closet door to put the broom away. "Did you have problems when you lived in Texas, Aggie?"

"Oh, hon, you don't want to know. Suffice it to say, I was running from a bad situation." She sighed. "But Priscilla—bless her heart. She soon had her own share of troubles, and I was comforting *her*."

"I remember when Murray's dad died."

"That ain't the half of it, sugar! So many people died in their family, one right after the other." Aggie counted off on her fingers. "Her father, his mother, her sister, her mother, his uncle—why, I believe we were going to a funeral for the Twichell family every month there for a while."

"How sad!" Tonya sank down on the other chair. "And then Murray's dad died, too."

"Yeah, a few years after all them other relatives died. Anson was quite a bit older than Priscilla, you know."

"I always liked Mrs. Twichell." Tonya reached back in her memory. "Sometimes Callie and I played at Murray's house, and Mrs. Twichell always had cookies for us. She was so nice to me, especially when Murray and Callie ignored me. I was a little pest to them since I was three years younger."

Aggie smiled. "And now you kids are all grown-up." She glanced out the big plate-glass windows. "It's snowing again. Why don't you hightail it home, Tonya? We probably won't have much business between now and five."

"Thanks, Aggie." Tonya stood. "I want to see if Poe wrote to me, and the sooner the better."

*Wow.* Murray's jaw dropped as he read the e-mail. It worked! He had written a few sentences about his loneliness, and Tonya peeled back her heart for three pages.

He reread the lines that caught him off guard.

> *My sisters, Melissa and Callie, are both married, and Molly is getting married in a few weeks. I'm the only single sister now, with no prospect for a husband on the horizon. Sometimes I worry that I'll never get married. Sure, I can get a date in a heartbeat, but of all the guys I know, I can't find a kindred spirit—someone who wants to know the real me, someone who will love me for who I am.*

Murray sat back. Strange she should mention the very thing he wanted to do—get to know the real Tonya underneath all that outward beauty.

But Tonya never getting married? That was crazy.

He highlighted that paragraph in his reply.

> *Tonya, you're so beautiful. Why do you think you'll never marry? There are probably a thousand guys out there who would love to marry you.*

His fingers paused above the keys. Did that include him? Would he love to marry Tonya Brandt, the spoiled baby of the Brandt family?

He deleted the word *thousand* and replaced it with *dozen*.

> *There are probably a dozen guys out there who would love to marry you.*

He nodded. Now if she had money and fame, a thousand guys might be standing on her doorstep.

With a grin, he finished the letter and shut down his computer. He had to get up early tomorrow. It was back to work for the weekend, and he had to be in Cheyenne at seven in the morning. At least he had Monday off.

His twenty-seventh birthday.

# Chapter 10

Murray sat at the kitchen table on Monday morning and finished his breakfast—a bowl of toasted oats with a few raspberries thrown in. As he ate, he perused *The Scout*, Fort Lob's newspaper.

It didn't seem like his birthday, although on Friday he had received a card from his secret pal along with a devotional book. He wasn't sure who his secret pal was, but the writing was definitely feminine.

He wished his mom were here to pamper him and bake him a cake, but after lunch he planned to visit her at the Pine River Nursing Home in Douglas. Maybe the nurses would sing "Happy Birthday." At least they did last year.

The wall phone above the counter rang.

He lifted his eyes from the paper. Who could that be? The landline rang so seldom. After the second ring, he stood and grabbed the receiver. "Hello?"

"Hey, Twitch!" Derek Brandt's voice sounded in his ear. "We missed you at church yesterday."

"I had to work all weekend, which really bummed me out. I hate missing church."

"I figured that must be the culprit. Just wanted to tell you about the Single Servings Valentine's party. Originally we planned it for February fourteenth, but as you know, my sister's getting married on that day."

Murray took a seat at the table. "Yeah, I have to go to Douglas and get fitted for my tux."

"Me, too—unfortunately." Derek laughed. "Anyway, the class decided to move the party up to February seventh, and we're going to reveal the secret pals then. I hope you can come."

Murray nodded. "I'll see if I can get a couple hours off that day."

"Are you off today?"

"Yeah." Murray held in a sigh, thinking of the slow day ahead of him.

"Mom wanted me to invite you over for supper tonight—for your birthday." Derek chuckled. "Happy birthday, Twitch!"

"Oh thanks! I'm surprised someone remembered." His mood ratcheted up a notch.

"Mom's a walking calendar—she remembers every birthday and anniversary of everyone we know." Derek paused. "After supper Dad and I are planning to watch the playoff game from last night. Since we were in church,

173

Dad recorded it. You're welcome to stay and watch it with us if you want."

"Sure, that would be great!" Murray glanced at the newspaper. "I already know who won, but I'll watch it anyway."

"Hey, don't give it away!" Derek laughed. "Dad and I refuse to look at a paper or turn on the radio until we see the game on the DVR tonight."

Murray chuckled. "Okay." This would be a good birthday after all.

Tonya entered the den holding a plate of brownies. She stopped in the doorway to survey the three men watching the football game. Dad sat in the recliner, his feet up. Derek and Murray sat on either end of the couch, each holding a can of soda. All three had their eyes glued to the action on the big-screen TV. Memories of Reed Dickens—sitting in the exact spot Murray now occupied—filled her mind, and she was glad she wasn't trying to impress anyone tonight.

"Here are the brownies." She set the plate on the coffee table.

"Brownies?" Dad pulled a fake frown. "We just celebrated Murray's birthday with cake and ice cream. How do you expect us to eat brownies?"

Tonya shrugged. "It's a tradition. I always make brownies when you guys watch football."

"I'll eat one." Derek snatched it off the plate. "I love these."

Murray leaned forward and picked up a brownie. "Are these the same kind you made for the Christmas party?"

"Yep, my secret recipe with chocolate chunks and cream cheese."

"These are fantastic! I wanted to take the last one at the party, but Aggie beat me to it." Murray took a bite and chewed a moment. "You should call them Tonya's Terrific Brownies."

A warm feeling filled Tonya at his praise. "Well, you don't have to worry about Aggie eating them up tonight." She turned to the door. "Enjoy."

"Hey!" Dad called after her. "Aren't you going to watch the game with us?"

Tonya turned back. "I'm not really into football, Dad." *And I don't want to sit beside Murray.*

"Come on." Murray moved over and patted the sofa cushion between him and Derek.

"Yeah, sis." Derek motioned to her. "Come watch the game with us. The more the merrier."

Tonya raised her eyebrows, then shrugged. She had nothing else to do and was soon settled between her brother and Murray.

This promised to be a boring evening.

"Did you see that, Twitch?" Derek pointed to the screen. "We did that exact same play one time against Northern."

Murray laughed. "I was thinking the same thing. And remember that game we played against Pinedale? Fourteen to twenty with only a half minute left, and you threw me that Hail Mary right down the middle of the field."

"Oh, that was a great game." Derek's shoulder brushed Tonya's as he leaned forward. "You made the touchdown with fifteen seconds to spare, and then we got the extra point and beat 'em by one point."

Tonya looked back and forth between the two men. "How do you guys remember all that? You played those games eight or nine years ago."

"You were there, Tonya." Murray's close-set blue eyes met hers. "Don't you remember? That was one of our biggest wins."

She smirked. "I was a cheerleader, not a statistician."

"I still remember the scores of all our games, especially during my senior year." Murray raised his eyebrows. "Don't you remember stuff from high school?"

"Well, I remember what I wore to the prom my senior year." She thought back to the dark-blue sequined dress she had made herself. "And I loved my shoes." Whatever happened to those strappy blue shoes?

Murray pointed to the screen. "Hey, watch that guy go. He's fast!"

Tonya studied Murray's hand until he dropped it back to his leg. She had never noticed his hands before—strong, masculine hands with just a hint of dark-red hair across the back, thick fingers, and clean, square nails.

The men discussed the game on TV before the talk turned once again to high school football.

"You were good, Murray." Dad reached over and grabbed a brownie. "In fact, you were probably the best wide receiver the school ever had."

"Well, I don't know. . . ."

"MVP your senior year." Derek glanced at him. "Don't be so humble, Twitch."

*Humble?* Tonya rolled her eyes. The words *humble* and *Murray* did not belong in the same sentence.

"What about you?" Murray motioned toward Derek. "You were voted MVP the next year. That school never had such a good quarterback."

Tonya looked straight ahead. "Let's just pat each other on the back."

"We are, Tonya." Murray leaned into her shoulder and lowered his voice. "And we can't forget the cheerleaders. Some of them were really pretty—especially that Brandt girl."

She tried not to smile, but didn't quite succeed. "Thanks."

He grinned at her, flashing those straight white teeth. Then, leaning forward, he looked at the screen.

She took a moment to study his profile. His eyelashes seemed darker than they used to be—the same dark auburn as his hair—and she had never noticed how long they were. His nose didn't look so big in profile, and his hair, which she had cut, was growing out nicely. A hint of beard showed beneath his cheeks, ending in a strong chin. Maybe he wasn't as homely as she had always thought.

He turned and looked at her. "Something wrong?"

*Caught staring!* Warmth crept up her neck, and she focused on the TV. "Nothing."

Murray picked up another brownie. "Why are you keeping this recipe a secret? These are the best brownies I've ever tasted."

She shrugged. He didn't need to know her dream about publishing her own cookbook someday.

As a football player ran in for a touchdown, both Murray and Derek shot to their feet.

"Great play!" Derek high-fived Murray. "Now the Cardinals are in the lead."

Murray resumed his seat. "According to the paper, that play was a turning point."

"Don't tell us!" Derek laughed.

As the men settled back on the sofa, Tonya stood. "I think I'll see what Mom is doing."

Derek swallowed a sip of soda. "Tell her to come in here and watch the game with us."

"Huh!" Dad reached for another brownie. "Fat chance of that. Your mother thinks football is a waste of time."

*Like mother, like daughter.* Leaving the room, Tonya's thoughts lingered on Murray. At least he hadn't ignored her all evening as Reed Dickens had. Murray liked her brownies, and, she admitted, she enjoyed his company.

Passing the mirror hanging in the hallway, she stopped to study her reflection. Her dark hair still looked good, but her lipstick had faded and some of her eyelashes were sticking together. How did that happen?

But it didn't matter. Tonya planned to talk to Mom and then go to bed—after she checked her e-mail. Inexplicably, she hadn't heard from Poe all weekend. What if he had lost interest in her? That thought stopped her in her tracks, and she determined to write him every day until he replied.

As she made her way to the kitchen, she mused about Poe. Who was he? What did he look like? Murray's profile came to her mind. From the side, his face was almost handsome. If only his eyes weren't so close-set.

❦

Murray booted up his computer. It was after midnight, but he didn't have to report to police headquarters in Cheyenne until three o'clock tomorrow afternoon. Tonya hadn't returned after she left the den, but maybe she wrote him an e-mail.

Folding his hands behind his head, he sat back in his chair. He hadn't enjoyed an evening like tonight in a long time. And on his birthday, too! He'd have to write a thank-you note to the Brandts, making sure to print, of course.

His mail popped up with three new letters, all from Tonya Brandt. He forgot that he hadn't written her since Friday evening. And it never entered his mind to write this morning.

Clicking open the first letter, Murray skimmed through the first two pages—Tonya's usual surface talk. On page three, she finally commented on his letter from Friday night.

> *Thanks for the compliment that I'm beautiful, Poe. I've had a lot of dates in my life, but a dozen guys wanting to marry me? Oh sure—LOL.*
>
> *The men I've dated could be separated into two camps: the trophy-date types and the smoochers. Either a guy wants to show me off (a beautiful woman hanging on his arm), or he just wants to kiss me (and usually the feeling is not mutual). No one cares about my mind or talents—what makes me tick on the inside. \*sigh\* It's hard to be beautiful.*

Murray frowned. He couldn't begin to fathom her predicament—good looks had never been his problem. But here was the real Tonya, revealing her heart, and he had no idea what to say.

His mind wandered back to the evening, sitting next to her on the sofa. He could understand why men would want to kiss her. When he had leaned toward her and gazed into her beautiful dark-blue eyes, kissing her was the first thought that popped into his mind.

But he wasn't going to toy with her emotions. If he ever kissed Tonya, it would be because he loved her for who she was on the inside, and he would know that she loved him and wanted to kiss him back.

*When I fall in love, it will be forever.*

The words of the old song ran through his mind, and he hummed a few lines before he expelled a long sigh. It would never be with Tonya.

# Chapter 11

Sitting at the kitchen table on Tuesday morning, Tonya carefully applied a coat of fuchsia rose to her fingernails. "If only I could grow them longer, but it's hard to play the piano with long nails. They have a tendency to click on the keys."

Mom looked up from the letter she penned to Grandma. "You have such pretty hands, honey."

"Yeah, as long as I don't have any warts." Splaying her fingers, Tonya inspected them but didn't see any telltale bumps.

The back door opened, and Derek walked in. "Here's the mail."

Mom stopped writing. "It came this early?" She glanced at the clock above the stove. "It's only eight fifteen."

"No, this is yesterday's mail. I forgot to pick it up before supper last night since Twitch was here." He set several envelopes and a magazine beside Mom, then threw an envelope toward Tonya. It landed near her nail polish bottle. "A letter for you, sis."

Leaning over, she looked at the envelope as she waved her hands back and forth. "There's no return address, but it's not from Poe. The handwriting is too wavery." She glanced up at Derek. "Could you open it for me?"

"Women and their fingernails," he muttered. Tearing open the envelope, he pulled out a card and began reading silently.

"Derek! You were supposed to open it, not read it." Tonya grabbed the card, hoping her nails were dry.

Her brother grinned as he left the room. "It's from your secret pal."

As Tonya opened the card, a bookmark fell to the table. She picked it up. "I love bookmarks. It says, 'Tonya: praiseworthy. A woman that feareth the Lord, she shall be praised. Proverbs 31:30.'" Silently she read the spidery penmanship. *I'm praying for you. Have a wonderful day. Your secret pal.* She passed the card to her mom. "Who do you think wrote this? It looks like my secret pal is eighty years old."

Mom studied it. "Hmmm. . .maybe Horace Frankenberg. He has shaky handwriting."

"Horace? I hope not."

Her mother smiled at her. "You'll have to wait until next week when you find out at the party." She folded the letter she'd been writing.

Tonya took the card and bookmark. "Well, it doesn't matter if that old bachelor is my secret pal. I have Poe now."

Mom frowned. "Have you sent anything to your secret pal? Isn't it Murray?"

She nodded. "Murray's my *receiver*—which is a stupid label, but Reed Dickens made it up. I've sent Murray several cards, plus I sent him that devotional book through the mail for his birthday. Remember? And I already bought his gift for the Valentine's party." Standing, she grabbed the nail polish bottle. "I'd better hurry. Don't want to be late for work."

∽

Two hours later Tonya closed the cash register at the Beauty Spot. "Thanks, Charlotte. See you in six weeks."

Charlotte Eschbach touched her newly permed coiffure. "Good job, as usual, Tonya."

As Charlotte left the building, Tonya took a seat on the stool behind the cash register, thankful for a moment's rest. It had been another busy morning. Aggie stood at her workstation, positioning curlers into Gloria Schutzenhofer's weekly set, and the two of them chatted away, oblivious to anything else.

The bell above the door jingled, and Murray strode in. He glanced once at Aggie, then motioned for Tonya to come to the door.

She walked to the waiting area.

Turning his back to the room, he dropped his voice. "I talked to Bruce this morning about dating Aggie."

Tonya's eyebrows lifted. "And?"

"He's open to it." Murray leaned closer, and his breath fanned her face. It smelled sweet, like mint. "But he doesn't like her outdated hairstyle and loud makeup. He said if she would change a few things, he might ask her out."

Tonya glanced back at the two women. Still deep in conversation, they didn't notice the tête-à-tête going on by the door. "I'll talk to her."

"People don't change easily, but I suppose it's worth a try. I'll work on Bruce."

"Okay." She smiled. "This might be fun."

Murray grinned. "It'll be interesting, to say the least. See you later." He strode out the door.

A feeling of peace settled over Tonya as she watched him get in his patrol car and drive away. Murray was no longer the boy who tormented her; he was actually a very nice guy. And he must be a romantic at heart, wanting to get Bruce and Aggie together. That thought surprised her. He always tried to act so macho, but maybe she didn't know the real Murray.

As she walked back to the cash register, Poe entered her thoughts. Now there was a true romantic soul. Did he know Aggie and Bruce? She would tell Poe about them and ask his advice on the best way to convince Aggie to change.

*I thought it might be fun if we could instant message each other every evening. Say nine o'clock?*

Excitement buzzed through Tonya as she read Poe's e-mail. Instant messaging with him would almost be like talking on the phone. But then she frowned. How did someone do instant messaging? She was on Facebook, and she exchanged text messages with a few friends from her cell phone, but she'd never tried to instant message.

Dashing downstairs, she found her mother in the laundry room. "Mom, where's Derek?"

"In the barn with Dad." Mom scattered laundry soap in the washer. "What do you need?"

"Instant messaging."

Mom's eyebrows dipped in a frown. "Never heard of it."

Tonya grinned. "I figured you wouldn't know."

"What is it?"

"Tell you later." Tonya left the room. "I'll get Derek to help me."

Making her way through the kitchen, she paused to open the oven door. The smell of roasted chicken greeted her, and her stomach growled in return. Hopefully Derek could show her how to instant message before supper.

She entered the mudroom. Mom's old winter coat hung on a hook beside the door, and Tonya slipped it on before making her way outside.

Low clouds hung heavy with snow in the coming twilight. The wind whistled past her ears, and she hunched her shoulders as she walked the hard dirt path that led to the barn.

The large sliding doors were shut, so Tonya opened the side door to enter. The warmth of the barn enveloped her, along with the smells of leather and horses.

Derek exited one of the horse stalls. "Hey, sis. What are you doing here?"

"Do you know how to instant message?"

"On a computer?"

"Yeah." Tonya moved toward him. "Poe wants to instant message every evening at nine o'clock, but I don't know how to do it."

Derek shrugged. "You need an account. Ask Dad to help you."

"Ask me what?" Dad's heavy boots clomped around the corner on the concrete floor.

Tonya turned to him. "Do you have an instant message account, Dad?"

"A what?" Dad looked as perplexed as Mom had.

Tonya sighed. "This family is so computer illiterate."

"Call Twitch." Derek walked back to the stall. "He'll explain it to you."

"Yep." Dad nodded. "If it's about computers, Murray will know."

Murray placed his supper dishes in the kitchen sink just as the phone rang. He raised his eyebrows. Two phone calls in two days. How amazing was that?

He picked up the receiver. "Hello?"

"Murray, this is Tonya."

*Tonya is calling me?* The force of the surprise pushed him back against the counter. "Oh, um, hi, Tonya. How are you?"

"Murray, I need to instant message someone, but no one in my family has a clue how it's done, and I really need to find out before this evening."

He grinned. "Instant messaging, huh? Do you have an account?"

"I don't think so." She sounded perplexed. "How long does it take to get one?"

"Oh, three minutes at the most. I could walk you through it. Do you want me to come over?"

"That would be great." Relief poured through her words. "The sooner, the better."

"I'll be there in ten minutes." He hung up the phone—and laughed.

Tonya: *So how should I approach Aggie about changing her hairstyle? She's been wearing her hair in this whipped-up beehive for years. Being a beautician, she thinks she has a corner on style, and she can be very stubborn.*

Tonya hit the RETURN button, then sat back to wait for Poe's reply. Glancing at the clock beside her bed, she was surprised that it was almost eleven. They'd been instant messaging, which Poe called "IMing," for almost two hours.

And she had to get up early for work tomorrow. She threw on her *I Love Lucy* pajamas. By that time Poe had replied.

Poe: *It sounds like Bruce doesn't want to have a 1960s fashion queen hanging on his arm. LOL He wants his date to live in the twenty-first century, and in that case, Aggie could either win or lose Bruce on her hairstyle alone. If you convinced her of that, she would probably be willing to try something new.*

Positioning her fingers on the keyboard, Tonya started typing.

Tonya: *You are one smart guy! I'll try to convince her. Thanks for the advice!*

Poe: *You're welcome.*

Tonya: *I hate to end our first conversation, but I need to get to bed. Tomorrow is a workday for me.*

> Poe: *I have off tomorrow. You certainly don't need your "beauty sleep" since you are extremely beautiful, but I'll let you go. Good night.*
> Tonya: *Wait! What do you do for a living?*
> Poe: *Haha! Wouldn't you like to know?*
> Tonya: *Yes, I would!*
> Poe: *Sorry, classified information. Let's IM tomorrow night at nine. Good night.*
> Tonya: *Good night, Poe.*

With a sigh, she shut down her computer. Who in the world was this guy? And how many days or weeks would pass before she found out?

"Change my hairstyle?" Aggie's ultra-blue eyelids widened as she stared at Tonya. "Do you know how ugly I am with flat hair? Why, the birds would stop singing, the stars would stop shining if I were to let my hair down. No, no, no." She ambled to the broom closet. "If Bruce don't like me the way I am, he can go fish for someone else."

Tonya rolled her eyes. *Stubborn woman!* "Listen, let me fix your hair and do your makeup for one date—just for one evening. Then the next morning, you can style your hair any way you want."

The broom swished as Aggie swept up after their last customer. Tonya stepped back so she wouldn't inhale the tiny curls that were flying through the air. When Aggie said nothing, Tonya made another attempt to appeal to her reason.

"Don't you think Bruce is worth it, Aggie? I mean, look at him—such a handsome, dignified man. I'm sure you'd love to be hanging on his arm at some sophisticated restaurant. And you'll want to look like you belong in the twenty-first century, cultured and refined—"

"Instead of looking like the hick that I am." Aggie's eyes spit fire as she stared at Tonya.

"That's not what I meant." Tonya sank down on a chair. "But Bruce has very particular tastes. You, of all people, should know that."

The broom handle hit the floor as Aggie dropped into the other chair. "Oh, I suppose you're right." Her shoulders drooped. "Maybe it ain't gonna work out between us after all. We just come from two different worlds."

"It can work, Aggie." Tonya leaned forward. "Bruce only wants you to tone down your makeup a bit, and. . .and step out of the '60s with your hairstyle. He's a very reserved gentleman, and he doesn't want to be noticed." She thought on that a moment. "Although he's so dignified and good-looking, people notice him anyway."

"Don't I know it!" Aggie paused. "I suppose I could change for him." The stubborn glint returned to her eyes. "But only for one date, mind you."

"That's all he's asking." Tonya gave an inward sigh of relief.

Now to talk to Murray.

# Chapter 12

At the Valentine's party on Saturday, Murray unwrapped his gift as the Single Servings watched. They were taking turns opening their gifts, and after the gift was opened, the secret pal would reveal his or her identity.

Derek had told Murray that he wanted a comfortable place to have the Valentine's party, but he didn't want to move all the furniture to the church again. So here they were, crowded into the Brandts' living room. Murray sat on the same blue chair as before. Most of the men sat on straight chairs they had dragged in from the dining room. Across from Murray, Tonya sat on the sofa between Cheyenne and Laurie Smullens. Laurie and Reed had recently broken up as a couple, and Reed seemed to be scouting out other possibilities. Near the fireplace, he sat beside Gretchen Hughes, the quietest woman ever born, and tried to engage her in conversation.

Murray finally pulled the gift wrap off his present, revealing an atomic watch. "Wow, this is nice!" Raising his eyebrows, he glanced around the room.

Tonya smiled. "It's from me, Murray. I was your secret pal."

His lips parted. Tonya was his secret pal, and he was hers? "Thanks for the watch, Tonya. This is great. I really like it."

Nodding, she looked down and her face tinged pink.

Murray gazed at her. *Tonya—embarrassed?* Or was it humility? She didn't realize how much humility complemented her beauty.

Derek sat on a straight chair near the fireplace. "Okay, Tonya. Why don't you open your gift now?"

As Tonya savagely tore the paper from the gift Murray had painstakingly wrapped, he glanced at Derek. Had Tonya's brother purposely set them up as each other's secret pal? Murray would ask Derek later how that came about. He couldn't picture Derek trying to play matchmaker.

"Oh!" Tonya's pretty eyes widened. "It's a book of hymn arrangements for the piano. Oh, I love it!" She glanced around, her eyes landing on the men near the dining room. "Horace, did you give this to me?"

*Horace?* Murray looked across the room at the man in question.

Horace looked just as surprised. "No, my secret pal is, um, well, he didn't open his gift yet, so I can't say."

Tonya's face reddened once more. "Sorry, I was just guessing, but evidently I guessed wrong." She looked around the room. "Anyone?"

Trying to hide his grin, Murray wished he could make her squirm a few more minutes, but he spoke up. "It's from me, Tonya."

"You?" Tonya's mouth dropped open. Then she clamped it shut and looked at her brother. "Derek! How come I was Murray's secret pal and he was mine? Did you do that on purpose?"

Derek raised his hands as if trying to fend her off. "Hey, don't blame me! The identity of everyone's secret pal is a surprise to me, too. Mom put all the secret pals together, and she was the only one who knew who they were."

"Mom, huh? Okay."

Tonya looked back at Murray, and he could almost read her mind. He wouldn't put it past Mrs. Brandt to play the matchmaker role either.

Tonya sighed. "Well, thanks for the piano book, Murray." She smiled, and her entire demeanor changed. "This looks like a great book. I can't wait to play these songs."

He nodded. "You're welcome."

As someone else took a turn unwrapping a gift, Murray kept his eyes on Tonya. She opened the piano book and studied the table of contents, then spoke to Cheyenne in low tones.

Murray thought about the letters they had e-mailed each other, about their own matchmaking efforts for Aggie and Bruce, about working with her on her computer, and the instant messaging they had done that week.

A strange realization hit him. *I really care for her.* He wasn't sure if it was love, but his feelings for her were definitely changing.

$\backsim$

On Monday morning, Tonya wielded her shears on seven-year-old Kylie Ewing's long blond hair. She smiled, thinking how cute Kylie would look once her hair was cut to frame her heart-shaped face.

Aggie stood at the other chair, working on Kylie's mom's hair. The bell above the door jingled, and both Tonya and Aggie looked up as Murray entered. He was dressed in his uniform, so Tonya knew he hadn't come in for a haircut.

"Hey, Murray," Aggie called. "What can we do for you?"

He hesitated. "I see you're both busy. I'll come back."

"Just a minute." Leaving her station, Tonya joined Murray, dropping her voice to a whisper. "Is this about Aggie and Bruce?"

He grinned, lowering his voice as well. "He agreed to take her out."

"Really?" She bit back a smile.

"I'll call you later about the details." Murray backed toward the door, now speaking in a normal voice. "Say, a half hour?"

Tonya nodded. "That would be fine."

He left, and she went back to Kylie's hair. Aggie kept glancing at her but didn't ask any questions. Tonya just smiled.

By the time the Ewing ladies left, Aggie had another customer. As Tonya swept the floor, the phone rang.

"I'll get it, Aggie." Walking behind the cash register, she picked up the receiver. "The Beauty Spot, this is Tonya."

"Hey, Tonya, it's Murray."

With a wistful sigh, she sank on the stool behind the counter. His voice was amazing. Every time they spoke on the phone, she thought again of how much she loved that baritone. Too bad he didn't have an ultra-handsome face to go with it. "What's the news?"

"If Aggie tones down the makeup and changes her hairstyle, Bruce agreed to take her to Phoebe's."

"Phoebe's? In Lusk?" Tonya's shoulders slumped. "But that's a diner—with a counter and stools. I wanted him to take her to some sophisticated restaurant in Cheyenne with linen tablecloths and good silverware."

"It's a start, okay? You wouldn't believe how much I had to talk him into this. And we settled on Tuesday night, mainly so he couldn't change his mind."

"Tuesday? You mean tomorrow night?"

"Exactly. Do you think she can be ready by then?"

Tonya glanced at Aggie's green teased-up hair, her green eyelids decorated with silver sparkles, her wrinkled rouged cheeks and orange lips. Dropping her voice, Tonya spoke into the phone. "She'll be ready. I'll make sure of that."

"Good. Uh, Tonya—Bruce has a stipulation for this date. He wants you and me to go along."

Tonya frowned. "Why? Do they need chaperones?"

Murray chuckled. "Not as chaperones, Tonya—as a double date. You know—Aggie and Bruce, you and me." He paused. "Would you be willing to be my date tomorrow night?"

Tonya's lips parted. A date with Murray Twichell?

"It was Bruce's idea," he continued. "I think he's nervous about dating Aggie—or *Agatha,* as he calls her. He probably wants us to be there in case he runs out of things to say."

Listening to Murray's smooth baritone voice in her ear, Tonya's defenses weakened. Why shouldn't she go on a date with him? They were good friends now. "Sure, Murray, I'll be your date."

"Thanks." He sounded relieved. "Bruce and I already talked about the car situation. At first he wanted to drive his Buick so he'd have something to do while we traveled, but I talked him out of it. Now I'm going to drive my SUV, and Bruce will sit in the back with Aggie."

"That's good." Tonya couldn't imagine sitting with Murray in the back-seat for a half hour with nothing to do.

"Here's another stipulation Bruce wants—I'm to pick you up first, then we'll drive to his house to pick him up, and then go to Aggie's house. So we'll pick her up last and drop her off first."

Tonya puffed out a laugh. "Boy, he must be nervous." But if Bruce had stipulations, why couldn't she? "Um, Murray, if you want me to go with you, I don't want to go to Phoebe's. Let's go to the Four Seasons in Cheyenne."

"Are you crazy? That's the most expensive restaurant in the city."

"Which is exactly why we should go there." She took a deep breath. "Bruce needs to show Aggie that she's worth spending money on." *And so am I.*

"I don't know if Bruce will agree to that."

Tonya raised her eyebrows. "We'll surprise him. After all, Murray, you're the driver."

"A surprise, huh?" She heard the smile in his voice. "All right, Tonya. We'll do it. Could I pick you up at five?"

"How about five thirty? I have to work until five, although I have a feeling I'll spend most of the day working on Aggie's hair and makeup."

"Five thirty, then, at your house. Be sure to tell Aggie."

"I'll give her the message. Uh, Murray, now I have a question for you."

"What's up?"

"It's about the secret pal thing. You sent me a card last week with very wavery handwriting." She gave a little laugh. "I thought it was from Horace Frankenberg, but it must have been from you."

"So that's why you thought Horace was your secret pal."

"Did you write that card, Murray?"

"No, I was visiting my mom in the nursing home, and I asked her to sign it."

"Oh." No wonder it looked like it was written by an eighty-year-old person. Mrs. Twichell must not be eighty yet, but she had Parkinson's, which made her hands shake.

A strong desire came over Tonya to see Mrs. Twichell again. Perhaps she could talk Derek into letting the Single Servings visit the nursing home in Douglas one of these days. "That was nice of your mom to write the card. Thank her for me."

"I'll do that." He paused. "Well, I'll pick you up at five thirty tomorrow, and you don't have to change a thing for me. I mean—don't whip your hair up into a honeycomb."

She laughed. "It's a *beehive*, but don't worry. I would never tease up my hair like that."

He chuckled. "Until tomorrow then."

Bidding him good-bye, Tonya hung up and glanced at Aggie. She already knew how she would change Aggie's hairstyle and makeup. This date with

Bruce was so important. It might even be a turning point for them.

Tonya was glad she would be along. Now she could witness Bruce's reaction to the new and improved Aggie firsthand. And she and Murray hadn't argued for weeks.

It would be an interesting evening.

# Chapter 13

That evening Tonya stood to stretch in front of her computer as she waited for Poe's next comment to pop up. They had been IMing for an hour already.

Poe: *Let's share a secret or two that we want to keep private. OK?*

Tonya took her seat. A secret? Well, why not? She began to type.

Tonya: *OK, you go first.*

Poe: *My mom taught me to crochet when I was a kid, and to be honest, I really like it. Sometimes I'll grab a ball of yarn and a crochet hook while I'm watching an old movie, just to have something to do with my hands.*

Tonya: *You're kidding!*

Poe: *Don't tell anyone! It will ruin my macho image.*

With a laugh, she shook her head.

Tonya: *How can I tell anyone? No one knows who you are.*

Poe: *I do have that advantage. What's your secret?*

Tonya: *Warts! When I was a little girl, someone threw a toad down my shirt, and that toad gave me warts on my fingers.*

Poe: *Warts, huh? Was this "someone" a little boy who wanted the attention of a pretty little girl?*

Tonya frowned. That's exactly what Aggie had said in Murray's defense.

Tonya: *How did you know?*

Poe: *It's a common pastime of young boys—tormenting little girls they like. Ten years later, they change their tactics and give flowers.*

Tonya: *LOL. Now I want you to share another secret. What do you look like? Describe your face to me.*

Smiling, she sat back. It would be interesting to see him get out of this one.

Poe: *I am seven shades of ugly.*

Tonya: *No you're not. Who do you look like?*

Poe: *Reed Dickens.*

Tonya's eyes widened. Was Poe actually Reed Dickens in disguise? That would be horrible! *I don't even like Reed!*

Tonya: *Tell me the truth—R U Reed?*
Poe: *You asked me who I looked like.*
Tonya: *Do you really look like him?*
Poe: *Hey, I'm seven shades of ugly, remember? But Reed can't help it if he's handsome. He's a great guy, too. Don't you think?*
Tonya: *No! I invited him to our house once, and he totally ignored me.*
Poe: *How could he ignore a beautiful woman like you?*
Tonya: *All he talked about was his ex-girlfriend. Then he claimed to be the great-grandson of Charles Dickens, and I believed him!*
Poe: *Haha! You should have beat the dickens out of him.*
Tonya: *Very funny.*
Poe: *Did I tell you I'm the great-grandson of Edgar Allan Poe?*
Tonya: *Very big LOL! I don't believe you for a second.*
Poe: *Smart gal.*

Five minutes later Poe signed off. Tonya was sorry to see him go, but she had to get to bed. Tomorrow was a big day. Aggie needed to look perfect for Bruce, and Tonya couldn't wait to visit the Four Seasons restaurant. A buzz of excitement ran through her. Tomorrow night would be not only interesting, but also fun.

❧

Murray picked up the crochet hook from the end table. Why had he told Tonya he liked to crochet? No one knew about that hidden talent. But it didn't matter. She'd never find out he was her secret admirer.

He turned off the lamp beside the sofa. He couldn't believe Tonya still held that toad incident against him. They were just kids!

With a shake of his head, he trudged up the stairs to his bedroom. Work started at seven in the morning with road patrol. And then he had a hot date tomorrow night.

❧

The next morning Tonya pushed the accelerator as she raced along Antelope Road. Why didn't she get up the minute her alarm clock rang? Instead she hit the SNOOZE button—only it wasn't the SNOOZE button. She shut the thing off. If Mom hadn't woken her, she'd probably still be sleeping.

She glanced at the clock on the dashboard. Already ten minutes after nine and she needed to fix Aggie's hair and makeup today besides taking care of any customers who might wander into the Beauty Spot.

Good thing it wasn't snowing.

Pressing her lips together, Tonya tightened her grip on the steering wheel and pushed her right foot closer to the floorboard. As she sped past Road 334, the dirt road that led to the Carltons' ranch, she noticed a car in her peripheral vision.

A Wyoming highway patrol car.

A sinking feeling hit her stomach, and she glanced in the rearview mirror. Sure enough, red and blue lights began flashing as the car pulled onto Antelope Road.

*Not again!*

Slowing down, she pulled off to the side. The patrol car stopped behind her, the lights still flashing. Through the rearview mirror, she watched the patrolman exit his car, and her jaw dropped. She would recognize that auburn hair anywhere—hair she had cut!

Clamping her lips together, she hit the window button. She would give Murray a piece of her mind. How dare he give her a ticket when they were going out tonight!

But as he approached, she reconsidered. Truthfully, she had been going way too fast, and Murray was just doing his job, as he told her before. With a humble attitude, perhaps she could talk him out of a ticket.

Tonya leaned out the window. "Murray, I'm sorry! Please don't ticket me. I accidentally overslept this morning, and I need to get to the Beauty Spot to work on Aggie's hair for tonight. So please, *please* let me go. Have mercy on me!"

Murray leaned one arm on the top of her car and gazed down at her. "I seem to recall this exact scene happening last December over on Main Street, but I don't think you learned your lesson, Tonya. Just now you were going eighty-one in a sixty-five zone." He raised his eyebrows. "In other words, you were breaking the law."

Folding her arms, all repentance fled. "I'm sorry, okay?"

"You don't sound sorry."

"Come on, Murray! Can't you let me off today? Please? I've already donated to the state of Wyoming."

"That was last year. As I said before, you've deserved a ticket many times when I've let you go." He held out his palm. "Now hand over your driver's license and registration."

⤎⤏

"And then, after he gave me that stupid ticket, he had the audacity to say, 'I'll pick you up at five thirty. I'm looking forward to our date tonight.'" Tonya squirted dark-blond hair dye on Aggie's wet hair. "Can you believe that? As if I'm looking forward to dating *him* after he tickets me. And now I have to pay another eighty-five dollars to the state of Wyoming."

Sitting in the beautician chair, Aggie looked at Tonya in the mirror. "You just forget about that ticket, sugar. We'll all have a good time tonight."

"Easy for you to say." Tonya huffed out a breath. "You'd better keep an eye on me, Aggie. I might pull a butter knife on Murray and end up behind bars."

Aggie cackled out a laugh. "Oh, sugar, you'll have fun. Just like me. I'm praying for a wonderful time—in fact, a life-changing time with my Bruce."

"*Your* Bruce, is it?" In spite of her bad mood, Tonya smiled. "Don't you think you're jumping the gun a bit?"

"Not at all." Aggie's pale lips, devoid of lipstick, pulled into a frown. "I've been praying about Bruce and me for years. Waiting on the Lord—and on Bruce, too. And see how God has answered?" She laughed again. "We'll have so much fun, Bruce will be shocked. He'll see what he's been missing all these years. And it will be the same for you and your Murray."

"He's not my Murray." Tonya set the bottle of hair solution down, thankful she didn't have to breathe those ammonia fumes anymore.

Aggie gave her a knowing look. "Maybe someday."

"No way. This will be my one and only date with Murray Twichell. After tonight you and Bruce are on your own." She lifted the timer and set it. "Forty minutes, Aggie. While we're waiting, I'll do your nails."

Picking up a nail file, Tonya pushed Murray from her mind. At least she didn't have to deal with him until five thirty.

# Chapter 14

Sitting behind the steering wheel of his SUV, Murray glanced sideways at his date. Tonya had not smiled once since he arrived at her house. Now they were driving to Bruce's ranch, which was four miles southwest of town, and she sat on the passenger side with her arms folded, holding a grudge.

The silence was awkward.

"Uh, Tonya, I know I'll see Aggie in a little while, but how did you fix her hair and makeup? Do you think Bruce will like it?"

Tonya's own makeup was flawless, as usual, and her dark hair looked perfect. She wore a blue dress that shimmered when she moved, along with the sapphire necklace he had given her. Murray certainly enjoyed the view of his date, although the conversation was less than stellar.

"Bruce will love her style." Tonya kept her eyes on the windshield, but the hint of a smile graced her rosebud lips. "You won't believe she's the same person when you see her. I permed her hair and teased it a few inches—instead of a foot, like she does." She turned toward him. "But it's the makeup that really improves her looks. I chose a foundation that matched her skin tone exactly, with deeper rouge for her cheeks and a dark-plum lipstick. Then I worked on her eyes—much more subtle than the way she paints them. No sparkles or loud colors. Instead I chose a tan for her lids with a light mauve under her brows to highlight and a dark-brown mascara."

Murray had no idea what she was talking about, and furthermore, he didn't care. He was just thankful she was talking. "That's great, Tonya. You must be good at that sort of thing."

" 'That sort of thing' is very important, Murray. A woman's makeup can make a real difference in her looks."

He grinned. "I bet you're just as beautiful without any makeup at all."

"Ha!" A pleased expression crossed her face before she turned to the window. "You'll never see me without makeup. I refuse to leave home without it."

Their conversation continued as Murray drove to Bruce's ranch and pulled into his driveway. He stopped beside the two-story farmhouse.

Tonya glanced at her watch. "We're early. I'd rather wait in Bruce's living room than out here in the car." She touched the door handle.

Murray leaned toward her. "Hang on, Tonya. I'll get your door."

❧

Tonya raised her eyebrows as she watched him walk around the front of the car. Murray was taking this date seriously. She sighed, asking God to forgive her for being selfish. *I'm not going to think about that stupid ticket.* She would have a good time tonight—for Aggie's sake.

She smiled as he held open her door. "Thank you, Murray."

Together they ascended the steps to the farmhouse and crossed the wide wooden porch. Murray lifted the brass knocker and rapped twice.

Bruce opened the door. "Good evening. Come on in." He grabbed a bouquet of yellow roses from the end table near the door. The roses were wrapped in clear cellophane.

Tonya smiled at him. "What pretty flowers, and yellow is Aggie's favorite color."

Bruce's handsome face looked a little pale. "To be honest, I'm a bit rusty on dating protocol." His Scottish burr sounded thicker than usual. "My hope is that Agatha will enjoy the flowers, and the evening."

"She will." Tonya's sister, Callie, always said Bruce MacKinnon reminded her of Clark Gable. Tonya saw a resemblance, although Bruce didn't have a mustache. But he stood straight and tall with a commanding presence. No wonder Aggie was attracted to him. If he were forty years younger, Tonya might be attracted to the man herself.

They talked together for a few minutes before Bruce looked at his watch. "Are we ready to go?"

Murray cracked his knuckles. "We're all set, Bruce. Let's pick up Aggie."

A cloud of annoyance settled over Tonya, threatening to rain on her good mood. She hated Murray cracking his knuckles, and it brought all his faults to her mind. He was so stubborn about upholding the law, and then there was that strong aftershave he always wore.

They walked to the SUV. Opening the door behind the driver's seat, Bruce disappeared into the back. Murray and Tonya stopped beside the front passenger door, and she felt Murray place his hand on the small of her back as he leaned over to open it.

His face was close to hers, and she took a deep breath. *Hmmm. . .no strong fragrance.*

"Murray, you're not wearing aftershave." The words tumbled out of her mouth before she even thought. *What a stupid thing to say!*

His eyes met hers. "It made you sneeze, so I stopped wearing it—about a month ago."

"Oh." She thought back, realizing it was true. "That was thoughtful of you. Thanks."

He gave a little nod as his eyes held hers. "You're welcome." Then he opened the car door and waited while she got in.

Bruce cleared his throat. "I wish Murray had let me drive my car."

Tonya swiveled to face him. "Don't be nervous, Bruce. Aggie will talk enough for both of you."

"True." He looked out the window as Murray settled behind the steering wheel.

Within ten minutes, they were at Aggie's doorstep. Tonya watched Bruce knock on her door and then enter the house. She turned to Murray. "I wonder why Bruce is so nervous. He and Aggie talk on the phone all the time. They're good friends."

Murray shrugged. "Maybe Bruce doesn't like change, and he's afraid their platonic relationship will turn into something more." He glanced toward the house. "I think he feels—whoa!" His jaw dropped. "Is that Aggie?"

Tonya looked toward the house in time to see Bruce and Aggie descend the porch steps. Aggie was wearing a green dress with a long jacket that had a slimming effect. Her light hair was still styled the way Tonya had fixed it, although Aggie had added a tiara that sparkled when she moved.

Tonya grinned. "Yep, that's her. She *would* have to add her own signature in her hairstyle with that tiara."

"Wow, you were right. She looks like a different person. Good job, Tonya!"

A warm feeling flowed through her at his praise. "Thanks."

Bruce opened the back door and Aggie slipped inside. "Good evening, ya'll!" There was a definite lilt in her voice.

Murray nodded at her. "Aggie, you look fantastic. You should wear your hair like that all the time."

With a smile she looked down, a faint blush spreading across her cheeks. "Aw, thanks, Murray. But I can't take any credit. Tonya's the expert on beauty and style."

"I know." Murray looked at Tonya and winked. "She looks great, too."

An unexpected flutter hit Tonya's stomach. But she didn't have time to dwell on the implications. Bruce got in, and Aggie started up the conversation as Murray started up the car. Tonya and Aggie did most of the talking while Murray and Bruce did most of the listening. Twice Tonya caught Bruce appraising Aggie with a slight smile on his face. Tonya drew in a satisfied breath.

When Murray turned onto the interstate, Bruce sat forward. "Murray, where are we going?"

"It's a surprise." Murray grinned at Tonya before glancing into the back-seat. "I realize we agreed on a restaurant, Bruce, but Tonya and I decided on a better one in Cheyenne."

Bruce cocked an eyebrow at Tonya. "Well, all right."

She smiled. "You'll like it, Bruce." *I hope you don't mind paying twice as much!*

∽

Murray exited the freeway and found the Four Seasons. As they entered the restaurant, the women decided to make a pit stop in the powder room, leaving

Murray alone with Bruce in the lobby. With shiny marble floors and a chandelier hanging from the ceiling, it looked like they had stepped into a beautiful mansion. A sweeping staircase ascended to the second floor with a balcony overlooking the lobby.

"Sorry about the switch in restaurants, Bruce." Murray stuck his hands in his pockets, trying for a nonchalant look. "Since it was Tonya's and my idea, I'll pick up the tab."

"No, no." Bruce glanced around the lobby. "I'm glad we came here. I'll be more than happy to pay for Agatha and myself."

The ladies emerged from the restroom, and the waiter showed them to a table for four with a snowy linen tablecloth and good silverware.

Murray pulled out Tonya's chair and seated her while Bruce did the same for Aggie. *This is certainly better than Phoebe's.*

Sitting across the table from Tonya was the highlight of his evening— excellent food with beautiful company. The four of them talked about their mutual friends and families. Bruce told stories about his boyhood in Scotland, and Aggie regaled them with stories from Texas. Tonya even laughingly told them how Murray had chased her with a toad when they were children, although she didn't mention anything about warts.

Murray hadn't enjoyed himself so much for months. Not even his birthday at the Brandts' home could compare with dating Tonya. Could they possibly have a romantic relationship?

Leaving the restaurant a little after nine, they dropped Aggie off at her house. Murray drove Bruce home, and the man couldn't stop talking about the wonderful evening.

"I'm glad you insisted on that restaurant, Murray." Bruce sat back, relaxed. "The Four Seasons was an excellent choice."

"Actually, it was Tonya's idea." Murray winked at her. "And don't you think those two women are worth it?"

"Oh, most definitely. We had such an enjoyable evening."

Tonya just smiled.

A few minutes later Murray pulled the SUV into Bruce's driveway, and they bade him good-bye. On the way home, Tonya discussed the date, particularly how much Bruce enjoyed Aggie's new look.

"I think they're perfect together, don't you?"

He grinned. "Yeah, perfect." *Just like us.* He reveled in this side of Tonya, enjoying her enthusiasm in someone else's success.

They traveled in a comfortable silence for a mile before Tonya spoke up.

"Murray, I have a question to ask you."

He glanced at her. "What?"

"Could you please cancel my speeding ticket from this morning?" She leaned toward him and fluttered her eyelashes. "I learned my lesson. Honest.

From now on, even if I'm late to work, I'll drive the speed limit."

With a sigh, he concentrated on his driving. She was so tempting. He wished he could pull her into his arms and kiss her and that she would passionately kiss him back. But he was just fooling himself. Tonya would never kiss him back.

He shrugged. "It's too late. The ticket's out of my hands now. But there is one thing you could try."

"What's that?" She leaned a little closer.

He glanced at her beautiful face, so close to his. "You could go to court and plead not guilty."

"Really?" A look of hope filled her eyes.

"But then, since you're guilty, I'd have to go and testify against you, and they would take my word over yours."

"Murray!" Folding her arms, she slumped back in her seat. "I thought we were friends. Why do you have to be so hard-hearted?"

"I'm upholding the law, Tonya. Just because you're my friend doesn't mean I'll let you off the hook when you break the law."

"I bet you would ticket your own mother."

Murray chuckled. "Yep—haul her to jail if I had to, but I can't imagine my mom breaking the speed limit. Her personality is different than yours, and I've discovered that people drive according to their personality."

"I suppose that's true." She sat up a little straighter. "Did you know that people play the piano according to their personalities?"

He grinned. "I've noticed that about you, too."

She raised her perfectly shaped eyebrows. "What is that supposed to mean?"

"You drive a car the same way you play the piano." Murray turned right on Antelope Road. "Just from listening to your piano playing, I can tell what kind of personality you have."

"So what kind is it?"

*Self-confident. Aggressive. Proud.* But he couldn't say that. "Uh, let's look at it this way. Right now I'm driving sixty-five miles per hour, which is the speed limit on this road." He glanced at her. "Do you think we're going too slow?"

She shrugged. "Not really."

"No, this is the correct speed you should drive on Antelope Road, just as you should play the piano at the correct speed on a hymn, such as 'Victory in Jesus.'"

Her eyes widened. "You were *dragging* that hymn, Murray. It sounded like the congregation was at a funeral."

"A funeral?" He felt his ire rise. "You were *racing* the tempo. The people couldn't even spit the words out."

"That's not true!" Tonya's voice rose a notch. "No one sang fast enough to have a problem with the words. The tempo on that hymn should be allegro, but half the congregation didn't know whether to follow you or me."

"Wasn't I the song leader?" Anger simmered as he thumped his chest. "You were supposed to follow me, not vice versa. If you had followed my leading, everything would have been fine."

"You were singing way too slow."

"That doesn't matter!" He glared at her before looking back at the road. "I was the song director—the person the congregation was supposed to follow. Why can't you understand that?"

"Wayne Holland never leads the hymns that slow." Folding her arms tightly, she turned toward the passenger window.

Murray glanced at her stiff back. Like air releasing from a balloon, his temper went flat. This argument was causing their relationship to race toward nonexistent. "All right, never mind."

A thick silence pervaded the car as he drove down the Brandts' driveway. As soon as he stopped, Tonya opened the passenger door.

"Thanks for the dinner." She didn't smile, and she didn't look at him. Instead she slammed the door and walked to the house.

Murray watched her disappear inside before releasing a long breath, which turned into a prayer. *Lord, why can't we get along?*

Tonya closed the front door gently, hoping no one would hear her. She was in no mood to discuss her date with Murray. From the noise emanating from the den, Mom and Dad must be watching TV. Fortunately it would cover up any sounds she might make.

As she trudged up the stairs, her heart seemed to get heavier with each step. What a horrible end to the evening! She entered her bedroom and glanced at her computer. *Poe.* That's who she wanted to pour out her heart to. But she'd have to wait until eleven o'clock, their agreed-on time, since she had told him she would be out tonight. If only she could call him, or better yet, talk face-to-face.

With a sigh, she dropped into the desk chair. Her Bible sat next to the computer, and her conscience hit her. She hadn't read God's Word for two days.

*No wonder I'm a mess.*

Glancing at the clock, she calculated forty-five minutes before Poe would get on his computer. She would read until then. Last week she had discovered that Poe was a Christian, which made her feel two hundred percent better about their relationship. And from some of the things they had discussed, she could tell he had an intimate relationship with the Lord. Poe would give her good advice about Murray.

Opening the Bible at the marker in First Samuel chapter sixteen, she read the story of Samuel seeking a new king among Jesse's sons. The words soon spoke to her.

Samuel looked at Eliab, the tall and handsome eldest son, and figured this was God's anointed. But the Lord told Samuel not to look on the man's countenance or his height because He had refused him. The Lord didn't see Eliab the way Samuel saw him. *"For man looketh on the outward appearance, but the* LORD *looketh on the heart."*

Tonya sat back. *The outward appearance.* To her that was the most important thing. Didn't she want a tall, handsome man to marry? But she had dated all the handsome men she knew, and they only cared about her beautiful face and good figure, not her heart. The only man who cared about her heart was Poe.

*And Murray.*

Tonya frowned. Murray? But she had to acknowledge it was true.

She thought back over the past few hours. Bruce was right—it was an enjoyable evening. The food was delicious, the atmosphere was perfect, and Tonya had enjoyed sitting across the table from Murray. He was a good conversationalist and seemed genuinely interested in her as a person. He never stared at her or made snide comments, as some of her past dates had done. Instead he was a gentleman in the best sense of the word.

She bowed her head. *Lord, please forgive me for only looking at the outward appearance.* How could she condemn those who were less than beautiful, as if it were their fault? God had created Murray's close-set eyes and long nose, but she hadn't thought about his looks one time while they were eating.

And what about Poe? Despite everyone's predictions about a predator who wanted to meet her in a dark alley, Poe didn't want to meet her at all. Since they had begun instant messaging, she had invited him over for dinner three times, but he turned her down every time.

There had to be a reason.

With a sigh, she removed the sapphire necklace and gazed at it. She was falling in love with Poetry Lover Guy—a man who knew her heart better than anyone else. A man who loved the Lord and who cared about her. And she cared about him, no matter who he was.

If only she knew.

## Chapter 15

At the wedding rehearsal on Friday night, the pastor at the Douglas church looked up from his little black notebook to Molly and Jonathan. "Who has the ring?"

Standing on the far left side of the church platform, Tonya gave a silent sigh, wishing she were the bride instead of a bridesmaid. She fingered her sapphire necklace.

Callie and Melissa stood beside her, and all three faced Molly and Jonathan. The sisters had decided to wear floor-length skirts to practice for their bridesmaid dresses tomorrow. Tonya glanced down at the creamy-yellow dress she wore. She loved the way the silky fabric swirled around her legs when she walked. Tomorrow the bridesmaids would wear the fuchsia dresses she and Mom had sewn, with pearl necklaces Molly had given them.

Derek, Ryan, and Murray comprised the groomsmen. Murray stood on the far right and wore the elevator shoes. He was three inches taller than usual, but still, he only came up to Ryan's chin.

Tonya hadn't seen Murray since their "disastrous date" on Tuesday night. That's what she called it, even though the only disastrous part was at the end. When she had poured out her heart to Poe about Murray's law-abiding stubbornness, Poe sympathized and then sided with Murray. In his opinion if she broke the speed limit, she should accept her punishment and pay the fine instead of complaining about it. That was the gist of his thoughts, but he wrote each sentence in a sweet way. Before they parted, Poe softened the entire conversation by saying, "I wish we could talk all night and then watch the sun come over the horizon together."

It was so romantic that she immediately forgave him for siding with Murray.

Tonya dragged her attention back to the rehearsal.

The pastor closed his notebook. "Then I'll say, 'You may kiss the bride.'" He grinned at Jon. "I suppose you could practice that right now."

Jon shyly pecked Molly on the cheek. Callie looked at Tonya and giggled.

"Okay. Now you need to turn toward the audience." The pastor waited while Molly and Jon complied. He raised his voice. "I present to you Mr. and Mrs. Jonathan Hunt."

The opening chords of Mendelssohn's "Wedding March" burst from the organ. Tonya watched Molly and Jonathan leave the platform, followed by

Derek and Melissa, and then Callie and Ryan.

Murray smiled as he moved toward her and held out his elbow. Averting her eyes, she crossed to the middle of the platform. He wore a short-sleeve shirt, and she linked her hand through his arm, feeling the strength of his muscle. Together they descended the steps and joined the others. It felt strange to walk beside a taller Murray.

At the back of the auditorium, Jonathan grinned at his bride. "That's a wrap. We went through it twice, so we're finished until tomorrow. Right?"

Adoration lit Molly's eyes as she gazed up at him. "I guess so."

Tonya gave another wistful sigh.

The wedding party, plus parents and extended family, left the church for the rehearsal dinner. At the restaurant, Tonya ended up sitting between Murray and Callie in the crowded room. Derek and Melissa sat across the table from them.

The hum of pleasant conversation surrounded Tonya as she ate her salad. She wished she was sitting next to Poe. Murray made a few comments to her until Derek brought up the recently played Super Bowl. Play by play, he and Murray discussed the entire game. She tuned them out as she conversed with her sisters.

&

Murray was stuffed. He shouldn't have eaten those last three bites of dessert, although the french silk pie was delicious. If only his partner had been more amiable, but Tonya ignored him during the rehearsal and the dinner.

*Still holding a grudge.*

Since most of the wedding party and relatives didn't live in Douglas, they formed a carpool to a nearby hotel. Murray entered the hotel lobby behind the Brandt and Hunt families, which comprised at least thirty people. The relatives clumped down the long arm of the first-floor hallway, all rolling their suitcases behind them. Pulling his own suitcase, Murray walked beside Derek, his roommate for the night. Just a few more steps, and he could take off these pinching elevator shoes. He didn't relish the thought of wearing them all day tomorrow.

Following a noisy passel of women, Murray spotted Tonya talking to Melissa. Soon small groups broke off as people found their rooms. Derek stopped at room 127 and slid the card key in the lockbox.

Murray spoke in a low voice. "I'll join you in a few minutes, Brandt. I have to talk to Tonya."

"Sure, Twitch." Derek opened the door and pulled both of their suitcases inside.

Murray walked down the hall as Tonya disappeared into a room with two other women. He strode to the door and knocked.

Opening the door, Tonya looked up at him. "Need something, Murray?"

*Only you.* "Uh, could I talk to you for a few minutes?"

"Okay." She leaned back in the room to tell her roommates she was leaving, then entered the hallway and closed the door. "What did you want?" She folded her arms.

He glanced down the hallway. Several travelers still looked for their rooms. "We can't talk here, and it's too cold to walk outside."

"Let's go to the breakfast room."

Tonya took off with her long yellow skirt flowing behind her. Murray caught up and strode by her side, ignoring the pain in his feet. They passed the front counter and then the outside doors to the hotel. She entered the breakfast room and led him to a small table in the back. No one else was around.

He took a seat across from her. "This is perfect."

"What do you need to talk about?" She folded her arms on the table. Her entire manner seemed resigned, as if she was at the dentist's office waiting for a root canal.

Murray glanced at the sapphire necklace that resided against the fabric of her dress before he gazed into her beautiful dark eyes. "I just wanted to apologize for the way our date ended on Tuesday night. I realize I was too hard on you."

Surprise swept across her features before she looked down. "I'm the one who should apologize. I talked to. . .a friend. . .about the situation, and he told me to accept the consequences of my speeding ticket instead of complaining about it." She looked into his eyes. "So, I'm sorry."

He tried not to grin, knowing that "friend" was Poe, aka Murray Twichell. "I'll forgive you if you forgive me."

She smiled. "Done. And I really did learn my lesson, Murray. I'm not going to speed down the road anymore."

"I'm glad to hear it." He wouldn't even mention her piano playing. "Can we be friends again?"

"Sure." Instead of getting up, as he thought she'd do, she seemed to relax. "I thought the wedding rehearsal went well, didn't you?"

"Uh, I guess so." Murray shrugged. "Actually, this is the first wedding I've been in, but you're an old pro at weddings."

"Yeah, lucky me. Always the bridesmaid and never the bride."

"You'll have your turn someday." *Maybe I'll be the groom!* That thought startled him. It seemed impossible that they would ever get that far in their relationship.

"Well. . ." She leaned across the table as if sharing a secret. "When I get married, I'm planning to have ten bridesmaids, and I know exactly what they're going to wear. Of course, I must have a June wedding so their dresses will be in the right season." Her voice softened. "I've always wanted to be a June bride."

He grinned, again enjoying this side she seldom revealed. "Maybe next summer, Tonya."

Her eyes widened. "No, *this* summer, Murray. I know June is only four months away, but I'm ready to go. And my dress is going to be beautiful." With a contented sigh, she cradled her chin in her palm. "I designed it myself, and all I have to do is sew it up. Would you believe that Molly is wearing Melissa's bridal gown tomorrow? It's pretty, but I wouldn't want to wear someone else's dress."

"I could finally tell your twin sisters apart tonight." He shook his head. "Never could keep them straight, but tonight I knew who Molly was."

"The one who couldn't keep her eyes off Jonathan Hunt." Tonya stood and pushed her chair under the table. "That's the way it will be with my groom and me—if I find him before June. I might have to get married without him."

Murray laughed as he stood. "I'm afraid he's a fundamental part of the equation, Tonya."

"Yeah, too bad." Her lips curved up as she strolled down the hallway. "The Lord might have to perform a miracle, although I have a guy in mind."

*Poe.* He ambled by her side, aching feet notwithstanding. What if he ended up marrying Tonya in four short months? Now *that* would be a miracle.

They approached her room, and she stopped to face him. "Tell me, Murray. Do guys care about big, fancy weddings? Wouldn't most men rather elope?"

"Not necessarily." He looked down into her beautiful eyes as she stared up into his. "A wedding is an important occasion since it marks an important beginning—the marriage of two lives into one. Most men want to make it a big day."

"I'm glad to know that." She knocked on the door of her room. "Thanks, Murray. Good night."

He took a step back. "See you tomorrow."

Walking back down the hallway, he heard the door to her room open and close. If only he could reveal himself as Poe. But was Tonya ready to accept him for who he was? What if she rejected him and shut him out of her life?

That scenario scared him. All correspondence would stop. The entire town would discover the identity of her secret admirer—and her dismissal of him. He would be a failure in everyone's eyes.

He paused in front of room 127 as a verse of scripture popped into his mind—something about the Lord holding the king's heart in His hand and turning it whichever way He willed.

God held Tonya's heart. Murray would leave their relationship in the Lord's capable hands. He was thankful he had followed his impulse to apologize. At least he and Tonya were friends once more. For now, that would have to be enough.

∽

Surrounded by other single girls, Tonya lifted her arms, ready to catch Molly's bouquet during the reception the next afternoon.

"Okay, ladies, squish together!" Molly, dressed in Melissa's creamy white bridal gown, turned her back to them and flipped the bouquet over her shoulder.

Watching it spiral toward her, Tonya gave a little basketball-player-like jump and grabbed it. "I got it!" She grinned as the other girls congratulated her. Despite all the weddings she had attended, this was the first time she had caught the bridal bouquet.

Callie ran up and hugged her, their fuchsia dresses blending together. "Congrats, baby sis! Remember how I caught Melissa's bouquet and ended up getting married the next year?"

"I sure hope that happens to me." Tonya giggled. "But my wedding will take place this June, and my groom will be Poe."

"Maybe." Callie glanced around the reception room and then lowered her voice. "You know, I think Murray likes you. He's certainly been attentive to you today."

Tonya shrugged. "He's making up for the disastrous date we had last Tuesday."

Callie's eyebrows shot up. "You guys are dating?"

"No!" Now Tonya glanced around. Murray stood by the punch bowl talking to Derek. She looked at her sister. "It's a long story, but he apologized last night. We're friends, nothing more."

"I think it's more." Callie leaned closer. "I've seen the way Murray looks at you. He's interested romantically."

Tonya rolled her eyes. "Oh come on. Murray and I never got along, you should know that. We argue all the time." She shook her head. "It would never work. Besides, he's not very handsome. When I get married, I'm going for a hot guy." Tonya's conscience struck her as she thought of her impromptu Bible study Tuesday night. What happened to not looking at the outward appearance? "Well, someone who's pleasant to look at and has a nice personality, too."

"Don't write Murray off, Tonya. He's a good Christian guy. Remember, he wanted to marry me before Lane came along."

Tonya gazed at her sister. "So why didn't you marry Murray?"

"He wasn't the one for me." Callie glanced toward the men. "But he might be the right one for you."

"Thanks a lot." Tonya pursed her lips. Certainly she could do better than Murray Twichell. On the other hand, no one was banging on her door right now, begging to marry her. If she didn't have Poe in her life, she might consider Murray.

Maybe.

# Chapter 16

On Sunday morning, Murray walked into the crowded church auditorium. The service had already started, and he hated being late, although it wasn't his fault. After Sunday school, George Whitmore had buttonholed him, wanting to know the laws concerning domestic violence. His daughter was in a bad marital situation, and Murray had taken fifteen minutes to enlighten the man. Now he needed to get his mind off other people's problems and onto the Lord.

The organ and piano reverberated through the auditorium as Wayne Holland led the singing and the standing congregation belted out the words to "Power in the Blood."

The tempo was much too fast.

Murray wandered down the side aisle, looking for an empty seat. He smiled a greeting to several singing people as he passed the crowded pews. Finally he found an empty spot at the end of the second row just as Wayne seated the congregation.

Murray settled on the pew. Straight ahead he had a perfect view of Tonya Brandt. She sat at the piano, replacing the hymnbook with another music book.

His heart stirred as he gazed at her profile and thought of their instant messaging last night. He had arrived home at five minutes to nine and immediately went to the computer. After all, *Poe* wouldn't have been at a wedding in Douglas all weekend. Sure enough, Tonya's comments showed up at nine o'clock, and they wrote back and forth until midnight.

Pastor Reilly stood behind the pulpit. His shoulders seemed a bit more stooped than usual, but his voice was strong. "Welcome to our church service this morning. We have a lot of announcements, so listen carefully."

*Announcements.* Murray tuned him out and went back to pleasant thoughts from last night. He kept his eyes on Tonya as he reviewed some of their conversation.

Tonya: *I want to know your identity, Poe.*
Poe: *Sorry.*
Tonya: *Just tell me what you look like.*
Poe: *Picture a fat, bald guy who wears Bermuda shorts.*
Tonya: *Poe! You're not Horace Frankenberg, R U?*

Poe: *Ha! You caught me!*

Tonya: *Tell the truth. R U Horace?*

Poe: *(We had this same conversation over Reed Dickens.) What if I am Horace?*

Tonya: *Just say yes or no.*

Poe: *Well, um. . .no.*

Tonya: *Whew! (Big sigh of relief here.) That man is old enough to be my father, plus he has a strange personality—unlike you. You're so much fun.*

Poe: *We do get along well, don't we?*

Murray had to laugh at that bit of sarcasm.

With the announcements over, the ushers stood in the center aisle, passing the offering plates down each row. Murray pulled two fifty-dollar bills from his wallet, folded them, and threw them into the plate as it went by. Then he centered his attention on Tonya, who played "How Firm a Foundation" for the offertory. Could that arrangement be from the piano book he had given her?

While she played, she kept her eyes glued on the music, and he kept his eyes glued on her. She played flawlessly, weaving around on the piano bench like a cobra to a snake charmer's music.

*That girl is so proud.* She never moved around like that when she played hymns for the congregation, but as soon as the spotlight was on her, so to speak, she became a drama queen. As the music intensified, so did her hands. She raised them higher and higher, crashing them down perfectly on the right chords every time.

Murray folded his arms. That music must not be as difficult for her as she pretended.

When she finished, the congregation broke out in ardent applause, but Murray didn't clap. Smiling, Tonya glanced around the auditorium. Her eyes stopped at his, and her smile disappeared. Raising her chin a fraction of an inch, she left the piano and walked past him to her seat without so much as a glance his way.

A silent sigh escaped Murray's lips. He picked up his Bible as the pastor approached the pulpit to give the message. *Lord,* he prayed, *I need a word from You today.*

Maybe he should forget Tonya. He loved her on the computer, but in person their relationship was an emotional roller coaster. Of course, it didn't help when he gave her speeding tickets and pointed out her faults.

Pastor Reilly's white hair touched the back of his suit collar as he looked out over the congregation. "Since this is the Sunday after Valentine's Day, we will center our thoughts on love. Our text is taken from 1 John 4:19, 'We love him, because he first loved us.'"

*That's your answer.* As if the Lord had spoken directly to Murray's heart, he saw the love of Christ to himself—a sinner who didn't deserve God's love. *"While we were yet sinners, Christ died for us."*

And that was the exact love he needed to show Tonya. Love that gives and doesn't expect anything in return. Love that wouldn't be turned off by any angry retort, a cold shoulder, or a proud look. Love that keeps on loving, no matter what.

Murray closed his eyes. *I'll try, Lord.* He would show Tonya the love of Christ, and deep down inside he hoped she responded because now he knew...

As crazy as it seemed, he was falling in love with her.

❧

Tonya : *I'm going to a cooking show this Friday in Denver.*

Tonya hit RETURN on her computer and sat back to wait for Poe's reply. It was Monday evening, and even though it was only nine o'clock, she was completely ready to go to bed. She and Poe usually kept IMing until midnight, when she could barely keep her eyes open.

Poe: *What is a cooking show?*
Tonya: *From the brochure—"a two-hour showcase of cooking demonstrations and creative meal ideas, plus handy cooking tips and fresh seasonal recipes." Sounds fun, huh?*
Poe: *Joyous. R U going by yourself?*
Tonya: *Cheyenne Wilkins, Laurie Smullens, and Gretchen Hughes are also going. We're planning to drive down in my car early Friday morning. I'm so excited. Not only will we take home a dozen recipe cards, but also everyone will receive a set of measuring cups as a gift.*
Poe: *Woo-hoo! Measuring cups. Every woman's fantasy dream.*

She huffed out a breath. Men!

Tonya: *You could at least be happy for me.*
Poe: *JK—it sounds like your kind of thing, and I hope you have a great time.*
Tonya: *Here's another secret—I'm compiling a cookbook of recipes I created. Since my brother-in-law, Lane Hutchins, is a famous author, I hope he can help me get my cookbook published.*
Poe: *Wow! Sounds great, Tonya. Go for it!*
A warm feeling filled her. Poe was so encouraging.
Tonya: *At the cooking show they're giving away three prizes—an electric mixer, a new stove, and a trip for two to Hawaii! That grand prize is my fantasy dream.*

Poe: *Don't get your hopes up.*
Tonya: *I know.*

She sighed. It would be amazing if she won anything. On the other hand, it really didn't matter. The cooking show would be exciting enough.

Poe: *What kind of recipes are you putting in your book?*

She shared her ideas with him, dominating cyberspace for half an hour. His comments were few and short.

Tonya: *Am I boring you?*
Poe: *No way. I'm interested in anything that interests you. I want to know all about you.*
Tonya: *Really?*
Poe: *Yes. I have to admit—I'm falling in love with you, Tonya Brandt.*

Drawing in a sharp breath, she sat back. Poe was falling in love with her? But did she love him? She didn't even know who he was!

Tonya: *Are you serious?*
Poe: *I wouldn't tell you I love you unless I was serious. Since we've been IMing, I feel I know your heart—the real Tonya.*
Tears pricked her eyes.
Tonya: *Thank you, Poe. That means a lot to me.*
Poe: *Hey, let's pick out a poem. It will be "our poem."*
Tonya: *My favorite is "How Do I Love Thee?" by Elizabeth Barrett Browning.*
Poe: *Good choice.*
Tonya: *How about a song? Most couples have their very own song.*
Poe: *I'm in favor of "When I Fall in Love, It Will Be Forever."*
Tonya's heart took a leap.
Tonya: *I love that song! But I haven't heard it for years. Do you remember the words?*
Poe: *I'll write out the chorus for you. Hang on, it will take a few minutes.*
Tonya: *OK, I'll wait.*

She couldn't believe this was happening. Poe actually said he loved her! But who was this faceless, nameless guy? Lifting her heart to heaven, she prayed. "Lord, You know who Poe is. Should I tell him I love him?" She rubbed her temples. *I just want to meet him.*

But what if he was "seven shades of ugly"?

Tonya stood and paced to the door. Did it really matter what he looked like? His heart was more important—she could see that now.

*"We love him, because he first loved us."* The verse from the pastor's Sunday sermon jumped into her mind. The Lord had loved her first, before she loved Him. It was the same with Poe. He became her secret admirer and loved her first, and now she was loving him back.

Poe's reply came on screen, and she leaned forward to read the words of the song, letting the tune run through her mind. With a wistful sigh, she prayed that those words would be true for them—falling in love forever, giving their hearts to each other completely. Yes, that was what she wanted.

> Tonya: *That's a great song, Poe, with a message of commitment. But how can we be committed to each other if we never meet? Our relationship can only progress so far on the computer.*
> Poe: *I know, but if you met me, you'd be disappointed.*
> Tonya: *Disappointed? I'm disappointed you don't want to get together in person.*
> Poe: *I'll think about it. So, we have a poem and a song. How about our very own scripture verse? Do you have a suggestion?*

"Man looketh on the outward appearance. . ." Tonya shook her head. That wasn't a good "couples" verse. Besides, she didn't even know what Poe's appearance looked like.

> Tonya: *Well, my favorite verse is Proverbs 3:5, "Trust in the LORD with all thine heart; and lean not unto thine own understanding."*
> Poe: *OK, and let's add verse six because the Lord needs to direct our paths.*

If only the Lord would direct their paths to each other! But Tonya would have to wait and do what verse five said: Trust in the Lord. Where would she find another man who humbly stayed in the background, wanted to know her heart, and loved the Lord?

Poe was definitely the one for her.

# Chapter 17

On Tuesday morning, Tonya sat at the kitchen table in her favorite blue-flowered pajamas and lilac robe and concentrated her thoughts on a devotional magazine.

It was her only day off this week, but instead of being able to sleep in, Dad had stuck his head in her bedroom at five thirty. "Tonya, get up and make breakfast for Derek and me. We want a hearty breakfast. You know, bacon and eggs—the works."

She did not appreciate her dad waking her, but Mom was in Casper at Grandma's house for a few days, and of course, Dad and Derek could not be satisfied with a simple bowl of cereal.

But now she was awake, thanks to a cup of coffee, and she had everything ready for omelets. She glanced at the counter. Diced onions and green peppers rested on the cutting board along with two tablespoons of cooked bacon bits. Eight large beaten eggs waited in a bowl. Four pieces of bread stood in the toaster, ready for her to push them down. She even had the stove's electric burner on with the skillet sitting nearby.

Now she had to wait for the men, who were out in the barn finishing their chores.

She sipped her coffee as she read the devotion. Today's verse was from Proverbs 31. "Favour is deceitful, and beauty is vain: but a woman that feareth the Lord, she shall be praised."

That was the same verse on the bookmark that her secret pal—Murray—had given her.

The outside door opened, and she heard Dad's voice in the mudroom. Two pairs of boots stomped off snow as the male voices carried on their conversation.

Standing, Tonya walked to the stove. She placed the skillet on the hot burner and whipped up the eggs.

The back door opened. "I'll get that information for you." Dad strode through the kitchen and into the dining room. "Be right back."

Tonya poured the eggs into the pan.

"Good morning, Tonya."

At the baritone voice, she almost dropped the bowl. "Murray?" What was he doing here? She glanced around, and then, realizing she had on no makeup and her hair was a mess, she turned her back on him.

209

He walked up beside her, and she could feel his eyes on her profile. "Tonya? Are you all right?"

She turned her face away. "Don't look at me! I look awful."

"Awful? Why?"

Tonya tilted the pan. "I don't have any makeup on."

Murray reached out his hand and gently tugged her chin so she had to look at him. He met her eyes—those eyes that were devoid of any mascara or eyeliner. Then his gaze roamed her face a second before he let go. "You don't look awful. Remember when I said you're probably just as beautiful without any makeup?" He grinned. "I was right."

Heat rose in her face, and it wasn't from the stove. "Thanks, Murray." Why did she feel so nervous around him this morning? Callie's words came back to her. *"I've seen the way Murray looks at you. He's interested romantically."*

That couldn't be true, could it?

The back door opened, and Derek entered the kitchen. "Hey, Twitch! Want to eat breakfast with us?"

Tonya held her breath. She'd never survive if she had to sit across the table from Murray with her makeup-less face. *"Beauty is vain."* The Bible verse entered her thoughts and pierced her soul. She bowed her head. *I'm sorry, Lord. Help me not to be vain.*

She turned her head slightly to peek at him. "There's plenty of food here, Murray. You're welcome to stay."

He looked at his watch—the one she had given him at the Valentine's party. "Thanks for the invite, but I have to drive down to Cheyenne this morning."

Dad walked in from the dining room. "Here's that information, Murray." He handed him several sheets of paper. "Let me know what you think."

"I'll do that, Jake." Murray took the papers and moved toward the door. "See you guys later. Bye, Tonya."

"Uh, Twitch." Derek followed Murray into the mudroom. "I'll walk you to your car. I have a question for you."

"Sure."

The men's voices faded as the back door closed. Tonya heaved out a sigh. Why did she care what he thought? Murray—of all people! It shouldn't make one bit of difference. After all, Poe was the one for her.

◆

Through the snow, Murray clomped beside Derek toward his SUV by the side of the house. Tonya's face stayed in his mind, and what he said was true. She was just as beautiful sans makeup, although he had to admit—with makeup, she was a knockout.

He glanced at Derek. "So what's your question, Brandt?"

"I'm just curious." Derek stuck his hands in his pockets. "Are you interested in Tonya?"

THE THING ABOUT BEAUTY

Murray stopped in his tracks. "That's your question?"

"Yeah." Derek grinned as he stopped beside him. "Callie and I were talking the other day, and she thinks you're interested in our little sister romantically. I just wondered if it was true."

Murray looked up at the tall, dark-haired guy. He and Derek had been good friends since childhood, so why not spill his feelings? "Yeah, it's true. But who wouldn't be interested? *Tonya Brandt* is the definition of the word *beautiful*." Murray's breath formed a cloud in the cold air. "But she never pays any attention to me—not romantically. I'm not handsome enough." He grimaced. "She's Beauty, and I'm the Beast."

Derek folded his arms. "Sometimes Tonya's the beast. You should try living in the same house with her."

Murray laughed. "I'd love to, but I doubt if she'd marry me."

"Although, come to think of it. . ." Derek knit his brows together. "She seems to be changing for the better. Writing to that Poe guy has really affected her. Kind of strange, if you ask me."

"That is strange." Murray hid a smile as he turned toward his car. "Well, I guess time will tell, as the old saying goes." He opened the driver's door.

Derek took a step back. "I'll keep this in prayer—about you and Tonya. Wouldn't it be cool if we ended up as brothers-in-law?"

*Wow.* Murray had forgotten they would be related if he married Derek's sister. "That would be awesome, Brandt."

"We'll pray that way. Tonya could use a steady guy like you." He lifted his hand in a wave before jogging back to the house. "See you later."

Murray got in the car and started the engine. Now both Derek and Callie knew he wanted to marry Tonya. He had always wanted to belong to the Brandt family, but that didn't matter so much anymore. What mattered now was whether Tonya—the woman he loved—would marry him.

At least no one had guessed that he was Poe.

Leaning over, he pushed the buttons on the CD player, hitting the SELECT button until he came to number seventeen. He drove out to the end of the Brandts' driveway before he pushed PLAY. The music of the Hollywood Bowl Orchestra filled the car, and he sang along.

"When I fall in love, it will be forever—or I'll never fall in love. . . ."

# Chapter 18

O n Thursday evening, Murray left George Whitmore's house on Bighorn Avenue and trudged to his SUV, which was parked on the street. He had spent the past hour talking to George's daughter, Sandra, about domestic violence and the type of things she could legally do to protect herself.

He ran a hand over his face. *Lord, I feel wrung out!*

Gaining the sidewalk, he glanced down the street. The tall, thin spire of his church pointed toward the sky. *That's what I need.*

Leaving his car, he strode toward the white clapboard building. The side door was unlocked, as usual. Pastor Reilly kept it open for the very reason Murray wanted to enter the sanctuary tonight—to have a quiet place to pray.

Walking through the back hallway, he entered the darkened auditorium from the pulpit area and ambled down the middle aisle. He knelt at the last pew on the piano side.

*Father, I come before You tonight, lifting up Sandra and her family in prayer.*

After he prayed for the Whitmore situation, his prayers turned toward Tonya and himself. Why had he told Tonya he was falling in love with her? That was stupid, even though it was true. But her relationship with "Poe" would never go anywhere. What Murray really wanted with Tonya was a regular man/woman dating relationship. He wanted to marry her.

But would she accept him?

A noise at the front of the auditorium put his senses on alert. Before he could get off his knees, a light came on. Turning, he peeked over the pew in front of him.

Tonya stood at the piano, shuffling some music. The light illuminated her, causing her dark hair to shine as she took a seat on the bench. A few seconds later, the sound of the piano filled the auditorium.

Murray eased onto the pew and let the music flow over him.

*When peace, like a river, attendeth my way,*
*When sorrows like sea billows roll;*
*Whatever my lot, Thou has taught me to say,*
*It is well, it is well, with my soul.*

Closing his eyes, he felt God's peace fill him. And suddenly he knew God's will—he should pursue Tonya. He should ask her out, let her know he loved her. God was directing his path, just as Proverbs 3:6 stated.

# THE THING ABOUT BEAUTY

Now if only he could convince Tonya.

*Lord, I need some confirmation from her.* Even though he had peace about this decision, how did she feel about him?

The hymn ended, and she played another. As Murray watched her, he frowned. Tonya was weaving around on the bench just like she did on Sunday morning. Maybe it wasn't all for show. Maybe it wasn't from pride—unless she was practicing her weaving just as she practiced her playing. He grinned. Yep, that had to be it. Tonya was practicing her pride.

When she finished the song, he stood. It was time to make himself known.

~∞~

Tonya lifted the damper pedal as the last chord faded away, and someone began clapping at the back of the auditorium. Startled, her hand flew to her throat, and she jumped to her feet. Walking toward her, a man emerged like a phantom from the shadows.

"Who's there?" Her voice sounded squeaky.

"It's just me, Tonya." Murray came into the circle of light.

She breathed out her relief. "Oh Murray, you scared me." She slid back to the bench as a prick of annoyance hit her. "What are you doing here?"

"Do you know how many times you've asked me that question?" He took a seat on the front row and looked up at her. "Sorry, I didn't mean to frighten you. Actually, I had a heavy burden on my heart, and I came in to pray."

"Oh." With a twinge of conscience, Tonya averted her eyes. Murray had just as much right to be here as she did, but here she was, judging him. Again. *Lord, forgive me.*

Suddenly she didn't want him to leave. "Let me play a song for you." She turned the pages of the hymn arrangement book. "I'm playing through this book you gave me, Murray. I love these arrangements."

"Good." Sitting back, he stretched his arms out on either side of the pew. "Uh, Tonya, I have a question."

She raised her eyebrows at him. "What is it?"

"Just wondering. . .why do you weave around on the bench when you play a piano solo? You never do that when you play for the congregation."

She thought a moment. "Do you remember Janet Oliver, my piano teacher?"

"Sure. She and her husband moved to Kansas a few years ago, didn't they?"

"Nebraska. Mrs. Oliver told me my piano playing should be visual as well as auditory. She was very outgoing, and she *really* moved around when she played the piano." Tonya laughed. "She played according to her personality. So when I play a piano solo, I try to get into my music and be expressive. I don't want to look like a stick with two hands."

He smiled. "You would never look like that, Tonya."

Her face warmed, and she creased the pages of her book. She'd better start

213

playing before he said something romantic, although she was beginning to like his attention. "This hymn is called 'To God Be the Glory.'"

She played the marchlike opening, trying not to think about Murray sitting on the pew. But after a few measures, all she could do was concentrate on the music—the running eighth notes in the bass, the chords an octave higher in the treble, the juxtaposition of soft and loud measures that climaxed in a crashing fortissimo chord.

Keeping her fingers on the keys on that last chord, she let the music die away. She lifted her hands and turned to Murray.

He leaned forward, his arms resting on his knees and his hands clasped. She gazed at his auburn hair, and her heart stirred. Murray was really a great guy.

He looked up. "That was beautiful, Tonya. You have a wonderful gift."

"Thank you."

He walked to the piano. "Reminds me of something Edna Beazer told me when I was seventeen years old." His eyes met hers. "I sang a solo one Sunday morning, and afterward everyone said what a great job I did and what a good voice I had." He gave a little laugh. "I believed them. I was so proud—and not in a good way. Then Mrs. Beazer said, 'That's a wonderful talent the Lord has given you.'" He paused, tapping his fingers on the piano case. "That really made me think. God had given me my talent, and He could easily take it away. It was a humbling lesson. Since then I've tried to use my talent for God's glory, as the hymn says."

His eyes held hers for a moment before Tonya looked down. She was often proud of her piano ability—and not in a good way. She was proud of her beauty, too. What if God took those gifts away from her?

Murray glanced at his watch. "Guess I'd better get going. It's eight forty-five already."

"Oh!" Tonya hopped up. Poe would be IMing at nine, and she didn't want to miss him. "I didn't realize it was so late."

Murray grinned. "Is it your bedtime?"

"Well, no." She felt her face flush again. What was wrong with her? "I have something to do at nine." She threw on her coat.

"Let me kill these lights, and I'll walk you out to your car."

She gathered her music together. "You don't have to do that, Murray." He would just slow her down, and she might not get home in time.

"I insist." He followed her out the door.

As it was, Tonya didn't get home until nine fifteen. She immediately ran to the computer and booted it up.

Tonya: *Poe? R U there?*
Poe: *Hi, Tonya! Where've you been?*

With a smile, she settled on her seat.

Tonya: *Sorry. I was practicing the piano at church and lost track of time.*

Pausing, she wondered if she should explain more, then decided against it and hit the RETURN button. She wasn't going to tell Poe about Murray.

Murray settled in front of the computer. Good thing he lived in town and beat Tonya home. He frowned as he read her explanation about being late. She didn't mention anything about seeing Murray Twichell. They had stood at her car for ten minutes talking.

Poe: *So, tomorrow you'll be at the cooking show in Denver.*
Tonya: *Yep. We plan to leave before seven in the morning, go to the show from ten to twelve, then spend the afternoon shopping.*
Poe: *When will you return?*
Tonya: *Don't know. We're shopping at the Park Meadows Mall in southern Denver, so it might take a couple hours to drive back to Fort Lob.*
Poe: *Four hours, at least—an hour just to drive through the big city. BTW, don't rush home to IM with me. I have to work Friday night until eleven.*
Tonya: *OK, but I can't IM on Saturday either. The Single Servings are visiting the Pine River Nursing Home in Douglas that evening.*

Murray had forgotten. A few weeks ago Derek announced the activity in Sunday school. Later Murray discovered it was Tonya's idea, which surprised him. He didn't realize she liked to visit old people.

Poe: *Hey, I'm off work on Saturday. Maybe I'll come along.*
Tonya: *Yes! Please do! BTW, where do you work?*
Poe: *Ha! Classified info.*
Tonya: *Why won't you tell me who you are?*

With a sigh Murray sat back. Tonya was certainly persistent. He thought back to their conversation tonight at church and knew that Tonya was thawing out toward him. But was she ready to find out that Poe was Murray?

Poe: *You're not ready to meet me.*
Tonya: *Yes I am! If you really loved me, you would do it.*
Poe: *Well. . .I'll think about it.*
Tonya: *You said that before.*
Poe: *I'm still thinking.*

As Murray typed those words, a plan formed in his mind. On Saturday evening, he could sit beside Tonya in the church van on the way to Douglas, stay near her side at the nursing home, and then—as Murray—ask her to attend a play with him at the Cheyenne Playhouse next week.

Their date would be an experiment. He would show her the love of Christ, as well as his own love for her, and gauge her reaction. If they could get through the evening without arguing, and if she seemed romantically inclined toward him, maybe he would reveal himself as Poe.

Maybe.

# Chapter 19

On Friday morning, Tonya picked up Cheyenne, Laurie, and Gretchen in town, and they began their trek to the cooking show in Denver. Although it was only seven o'clock, all four were wide awake and chatting. Not only were they looking forward to the cooking seminar, but they also couldn't wait to go shopping.

"I need some new clothes," Gretchen said from the backseat.

"Me, too." Tonya glanced down at her jeans. The blue was fading at the knees.

Cheyenne, on the passenger's seat, glanced back at the other girls. "I only brought a hundred dollars in cash, so I can't buy too much."

"I'm using my debit card, and I just got paid." Laurie laughed. "The sky's the limit for me. I want to buy something special for Corey, too."

Tonya rolled her eyes. "I can't believe you're dating Mr. Hands-on-Me, Laurie."

"Hey, he's been a perfect gentleman. Besides, our names rhyme."

"Corey and Laurie." Cheyenne grinned. "Maybe you two will fall in love."

"I hope so." Laurie giggled.

The conversation swirled around Tonya as she thought back to IMing with Poe last night. Now there was a perfect gentleman, and someone who loved her for herself. As she drove down Highway 270, his words lingered in her mind.

Poe: *Have a great time tomorrow. Win that trip to Hawaii!*
Tonya: *OK, I will!*
Poe: *I'm sending my love with you, and you wouldn't believe how much I love you, Tonya. I'll keep you in prayer, too.*

She gave a wistful sigh. She still hadn't told him she loved him, but she knew she did. If only she knew who he was. *Lord, please let me meet this guy!*

But what if he really was Reed Dickens? Poe said he had to work until eleven tonight, and a three-to-eleven shift was common for hospital nurses. Could Poe be Reed? If so, he was certainly different on the computer than he was in person. At church Reed barely acknowledged her, and he wasn't the sensitive, poetic type. No, Poe couldn't be Reed.

At least she hoped not.

But what if she ended up marrying someone else, and Poe just faded from her life? What if she never found out his identity? What would happen to all his talk about love?

Well, she wouldn't give up! She'd keep praying and trusting God to bring them together.

In the distance, Tonya heard a siren. She glanced in the rearview mirror. A Wyoming highway patrol car, lights flashing, rushed up behind them.

"Oh no!" Tonya's shoulders drooped as she pulled over to the side of the road.

The other three girls craned their necks toward the back window.

"Don't worry, girlfriend." Cheyenne touched Tonya's shoulder. "Maybe that cop received a dispatch, and he's going around."

"No such luck," Laurie said. "He's stopping behind us."

Tonya hit the button to roll down her window. "If that's Murray, I'm going to kill him."

Cheyenne laughed. "Murray wouldn't give you a ticket."

"Are you kidding? He's already given me two."

Laurie leaned forward. "Guess what? It *is* Murray."

Tonya tried to quell her irritation, but getting a ticket would take twenty minutes of their time, not to mention another bite out of her paycheck and another spike in her car insurance.

He strode up to her open window and looked inside the car. "Hello, ladies."

"Hi, Murray!" came the reply in three voices.

Tonya didn't greet him. "Murray, I wasn't speeding, was I? I was really trying to stay within the speed limit, and besides that, we're going to a cooking show. We don't have time for this. I don't want to be late."

"Whoa!" He held up his hands. "I'm not giving you a ticket, Tonya."

She looked up into his blue eyes. "You're not?"

He smiled. "You were going four miles over the speed limit, so I stopped you—but just as a warning. The WHP is out in full force on I-25."

"What's the WHP?" Gretchen asked.

Murray glanced at her. "Wyoming highway patrol." He looked back at Tonya. "They're watching for speeders today on the interstate, so I thought I should warn you. Be careful, and keep your eye on the speedometer." He took a step back and winked at her. "I don't want you to get a ticket."

Her heart fluttered at his wink. "Thanks, Murray."

"Sure. Have a good time, ladies." He strode back to his patrol car.

"That was nice of him." Cheyenne settled back in her seat. "But how did he know you'd be driving on I-25?"

⌘

The cooking show was more awesome than Tonya could have imagined. When the girls arrived, they were each given a tote bag full of recipe cards, coupons, and the free measuring cups. The four of them took seats in a large auditorium among several hundred participants, mostly women. A fully functional kitchen was set up on the stage, and one of the cooking masters named Jessie demonstrated a recipe step-by-step. Tonya and the other girls followed along on a recipe card, watching Jessie's hands in a huge mirror hanging above her head and tilted toward the audience. An hour later, they stood in line to fill up on free food samples set on long tables.

With a half hour of the show left, Tonya took her seat in the auditorium. "I guess we won't have to eat lunch."

"I'm stuffed." Cheyenne sat down beside her. "This is so much fun, Tonya. I'm glad we came." She pulled the schedule from her tote bag. "The prize giveaways are the last thing before we leave."

Tonya grinned. "I'm sure we won't win anything, although Poe and I are both hoping for the trip to Hawaii. You know, that would make a great honeymoon package."

Cheyenne raised her eyebrows. "Poe asked you to marry him?"

"No, but I'm trusting the Lord. Someday I'm going to marry that man."

"If I were you, I wouldn't be too quick about that decision. You'd better find out who he is first."

"But he's a Christian, and he's so sweet." Tonya sighed. "Do you know why he's holding off on meeting me?"

"No, why?"

"He says I'll be disappointed. He's 'seven shades of ugly,' or so he says."

"Maybe he's the hunchback of Notre Dame."

Tonya laughed. "I don't think so."

But her smile faded as she thought on Cheyenne's words. Could there be something physically wrong with Poe? Some type of deformity? Maybe that was why he didn't want to meet her.

Tears edged her eyes. Someone as wonderful as Poe should not have to suffer like that. *Lord, no matter what Poe's problem is, I will continue to love him.* She would accept him as he was, deformed or not.

The auditorium began filling up again. Laurie and Gretchen came back and took their seats next to Cheyenne. Tonya stowed her purse and tote bag between her feet, ready to go when they were dismissed. She looked forward to spending the rest of the day shopping at the Park Meadows Mall in southern Denver.

When the audience settled, one of the cooks came to the mic. "Hi, my name is Marcie, and it's time to give away our prizes!"

The audience went wild, clapping and screaming. Tonya screamed with the best of them. She would forget about Poe and enjoy herself.

Marcie waited for the noise to die down. "First, we have a surprise giveaway." She held up a book. "We have twenty cookbooks to award before we choose winners for our three main prizes."

Tonya glanced at Cheyenne. "I'd love to win a cookbook."

Marcie continued, "Open the tote bag you received when you first came in. Everyone has a number posted under the inside flap."

Along with the rest of the attendees, Tonya picked up her bag and looked inside. Sure enough, a small square of paper was wedged under the flap. She pulled it out.

Cheyenne leaned toward her. "My number is 136. What's yours?"

Tonya glanced at the paper. "It's 224."

"My number is 118." Laurie looked at both of them from the other side of Cheyenne. "And Gretchen's is 104."

Tonya smiled. "Let's hope one of us wins something."

On the stage, Marcie turned the handle on a big see-through barrel that was filled with small slips of paper. The other cook, Jessie, joined her as Marcie spoke into the mic. "Jessie is going to pick out twenty numbers for the cookbooks. If I call your number, please come to the front."

The hushed audience waited as Jessie plucked out a paper from the barrel and handed it to Marcie. "Seventy-two."

With a little scream, a woman in the middle jumped up and made her way to the front.

Marcie and Jessie kept the numbers coming, with a steady stream of participants moving forward. Finally Marcie said, "Here's our last one—number 104."

Gretchen gasped. "That's me!" Her wide eyes glanced at the other three girls.

"Go, Gretchen!" Cheyenne gave her a thumbs-up before Gretchen stood and walked down the aisle. "At least we won something!"

"I'm glad." Tonya grinned. "I wanted to see what kind of recipes they put in their cookbook."

After the participants took their seats, Jessie picked a number for the winner of the electric mixer. Amid the applause, a stout woman claimed the prize. Marcie chatted with her for a few minutes in front of the audience before the lady took her seat.

Marcie looked out over the crowd. "Now Jessie will pick a number for the new stove."

"That would be nice to win," Cheyenne whispered.

But someone else claimed it—a man! Everyone laughed and applauded as he went to the front. Marcie chatted with him for a few moments before he took his seat.

Tonya slipped her number back into her bag. *I knew I wouldn't win anything.*

"Now for our grand prize—a trip for two to Hawaii!" Marcie waited while

Jessie picked a number, and then she stepped to the microphone. "The winning number is 224."

Tonya's jaw dropped.

Cheyenne grabbed her arm. "Tonya! You won!"

She met Cheyenne's eyes. "I can't believe it!"

Amid thunderous applause, Tonya jumped up and almost ran down the aisle. She couldn't stop smiling. *Poe will be shocked!*

Marcie welcomed her with the microphone.

"Congratulations! What's your name?"

"Tonya Brandt." She took a deep breath and glanced out at the audience. A blur of smiling faces greeted her with more clapping.

Marcie waited a moment for the applause to die down. "So, tell me, Tonya—who do you plan to take with you on this trip to Hawaii?"

Poe was the only person who came to mind. "Well, last night I was IMing with my...my boyfriend, and he told me to win the trip to Hawaii, and I told him I would. But I really didn't think it would happen."

Marcie laughed. "So now you can show your boyfriend a wonderful time in paradise."

"Well..." She didn't want these people to get the wrong idea. "Maybe this will entice him to propose marriage. After all, a trip to Hawaii would make a great honeymoon package."

"It certainly would!" Marcie turned to the audience. "Give our winner another hand."

Tonya smiled as she walked back to her seat. Imagine winning the grand prize out of hundreds of names! Deep in her heart she knew it wasn't a coincidence. Maybe God was providing the motivation for Poe to reveal himself.

⁓

At ten o'clock that evening, Tonya passed the WELCOME TO WYOMING sign on I-25. Her passengers were quiet—probably as exhausted as she was. After the cooking show, she had filled out a couple of papers for the Hawaii trip, which was good for an entire year. Then the four of them spent the afternoon shopping. On their way north to Wyoming, they stopped for a late supper at an Olive Garden restaurant.

A half hour later, she exited the interstate at Highway 20. The freeway hadn't had much traffic, but this road looked deserted. After a good twenty miles, she passed the town of Lost Springs, which was more like a building than a town. After all, the sign said it all—LOST SPRINGS, POPULATION: ONE.

She mused on who that one person could be as she drove past a farmhouse off to the left side of the road. A solitary light shone through a window. *Those people are probably getting ready for bed.* Tonya wished she could do the same, but from here it might take her another hour to get home. She had to drop off the three girls in town at their respective houses, then drive the seven miles out to the Brandt family ranch.

The orange lights from the dashboard illuminated the inside of the car, and soft classical music from the radio accompanied the hum of the engine. With a sigh she rubbed her left eye. That heavy Italian meal made her sleepy.

Suddenly two coyotes dashed across the road in front of her car.

With a gasp Tonya swerved to the left. The car plunged into the roadside ditch. Tonya's left arm smacked against the window, and her face hit the glass.

Then everything went black.

Murray received the dispatch at 10:48—twelve minutes before he was scheduled to go off duty. An accident on Highway 20? *Must be a drunk wrapped around a telephone pole.*

Turning on his siren, Murray left the town of Fort Lob and sped down Highway 270. As his speedometer reached eighty miles per hour, he thought about Tonya speeding. She was never far from his thoughts.

He turned west on Highway 20. Glancing in his rearview mirror, he spotted Fort Lob's only ambulance far behind him, the lights flashing. Murray turned right and floored the accelerator for fifteen miles until he neared the Whartons' ranch. Ken Wharton had made the call to 911. As Murray slowed down, he vaguely made out a car in the ditch. Four or five people stood on the road above the vehicle.

Stopping in front of them, he killed the siren and switched on the patrol car's floodlights. His heart almost stopped when he saw Tonya's red Hyundai. It tilted into the ditch, the passenger door open.

Breaking away from the others, Cheyenne ran toward him.

He got out of his car. "What happened?"

"I don't know." Cheyenne looked at him with wide eyes. "I was half-asleep, and then all of a sudden we were in this ditch."

"Is anyone hurt?" Murray surveyed the others as he strode toward them. Ken Wharton, his arms folded, stood beside the car. Gretchen and Laurie stood in the middle of the road together, their arms around each other. Dorothy Wharton, a faded nightgown peeking beneath her coat, stayed beside the girls, her arm around Laurie's shoulders.

Murray's scalp prickled. "Where's Tonya?"

"She's unconscious, Murray. We tried to wake her. . . ." Cheyenne's voice trailed off as she twisted her hands together. "The rest of us are okay."

*Tonya.* . . . Murray stared at the car. He wanted to run to her side, but his feet wouldn't move.

The wail of the ambulance grew louder, snapping him out of his mental fog. The siren stopped as the vehicle pulled up beside Murray's car. Davin Traxler climbed out of the driver's side. "How can we help?" He walked toward them as Joe Fonsino exited the passenger side of the ambulance.

"We have one unconscious." Murray strode to the car and thrust his head inside the open door. Tonya lay slumped against the driver's door, her seat belt lying useless in her lap. "Tonya? Can you hear me?" He reached across the seat and grabbed her wrist. Feeling a steady pulse, he breathed a sigh of relief as he backed out of the car.

Davin glanced inside. "Looks like her seat belt broke."

Murray looked from Davin to Joe. "Are we going to have to drag her out from the passenger side?"

"Let me look." Joe walked down the ditch and surveyed the car. He tried the driver's door.

"There's no way to get her door open on this side."

"I'll get the gurney." Davin walked backed to the ambulance.

"Please hurry." Murray muttered the words, almost to himself. His heart twisted as he glanced at her still form. What if he lost her?

His determination kicked in. If Tonya lived through this, he was going to tell her he was Poe. He would declare his love for her—whether she accepted him or not. And it didn't matter if the whole town knew.

He would keep pursuing her until she married him.

# Chapter 20

On Saturday morning, Tonya opened her eyes to stare up at a white ceiling. She blinked. *Where am I?* A headache pounded in her temples. A middle-aged woman in a white uniform came into view above her. "Hi, Tonya. My name is Carrie. You were in an accident last night, and now you're at the county hospital in Lusk. You have a concussion, so the doctor wants you to stay here a few days where he can keep an eye on you."

"An accident?" Tonya licked her lips. "What about Cheyenne? And Gretchen and Laurie?"

The nurse smiled. "Your friends are fine. You were the only one who was hurt. Evidently your seat belt broke with the impact, and you hit your head against the window."

"Oh." Tonya suddenly noticed her left arm in a blue sling. "Did I break my arm?"

"You have a hairline fracture just above the wrist. When the swelling subsides, your arm will be put in a cast. It will take at least six weeks to heal."

*Six weeks?* A numbness filled Tonya as Carrie pushed a button to raise the head of the bed. She helped Tonya reposition herself into a sitting position and get comfortable.

Carrie lifted a plastic cup from the small table beside the bed. "Here, drink some water." She waited as Tonya sipped through the straw. Then she left, promising to send in the doctor.

But that was an hour ago, and no one had come. Tonya had plenty of time to think, especially about the fact that she wouldn't be playing the piano for six weeks. She wouldn't be able to work at the Beauty Spot either. It was a good thing Aggie had hired Connie.

The events of last night were hazy. Her mind reached back, trying to remember. Something had cut in the path of her headlights, but what was it? Then—nothing. What happened after that?

The door opened, and her parents walked in.

"Mom! Dad!"

"Oh, Tonya!" Her mom leaned over and hugged her tight. "We were so concerned." She stood back and gazed at Tonya, her eyes bright with tears.

Tonya looked up at them as tears filled her own eyes. "I'm so glad you came."

"Wild horses couldn't keep us away." Dad hugged her, then plopped a little brown teddy bear on her lap. "Here's someone to keep you company."

"Oh, it's cute. Thanks, Dad." Tonya picked it up, admiring the bear holding a red heart with the words GET WELL SOON embroidered on it.

"So tell us, honey. . . ." Mom gazed at her with concerned eyes. "How did your car end up in a ditch by the side of the road?"

Tonya blinked. "Is that what happened?"

"You don't remember?" Dad raised his eyebrows. "The other three girls were asleep, and Murray thought perhaps you had fallen asleep at the wheel also."

Tonya's lips parted. "Murray was there?"

Mom nodded. "Cheyenne said he was very concerned about you. I guess it took a while to get you out of the car."

"Then Davin and Joe took you to the hospital." Dad folded his arms. "Murray called a tow truck, waited for it, then drove the other three girls up to the hospital."

"Dorothy Wharton insisted on it." Mom sat down on the chair beside the bed. "She thought the girls were in shock, but by the time they arrived at the hospital, it was one o'clock in the morning." She shrugged. "They were okay by then."

"So Murray took them home?"

"No." Mom scooted the chair closer. "Murray called us and the other parents around midnight. We all drove to Lusk as fast as we could. The others left with their daughters, but Dad and I stayed here until three in the morning, hoping you'd wake up."

"I woke up about an hour ago—with a splitting headache."

Dad leaned against the wall. "When we left, Murray was still here. He said he was off duty at eleven last night, and he didn't have to work today, so he didn't mind staying."

*Eleven.* Tonya frowned. Was there something significant about *eleven?* She lifted her right hand and touched her forehead. *Why is it so hard to think?* "I must look awful."

"The left side of your face is bruised." Mom took a closer look. "It's swollen, too."

"Really?" Tonya wished her head would stop pounding. "Do you have a mirror, Mom?"

Opening her purse, Mom pulled out a compact and handed it to Tonya.

She gasped at her reflection. Her face was puffy, all her makeup had been washed off, and deep purple bruises reposed under both eyes. Her left cheekbone was highlighted with purple, too. She groaned. "I look horrible."

"You're beautiful to us, Tonya." Dad smiled at her. "Things could have been worse."

Mom took back the compact. "Get some rest, honey." She leaned over and kissed her. "We'll be back later."

"Okay." Tonya did feel sleepy.

She closed her eyes, and when she opened them again, her parents were gone.

∽

Saturday afternoon Murray exited the hospital elevator on the fourth floor, thankful Tonya was awake now. He had called the hospital on the way over, just to make sure.

Last night he had stayed until five in the morning, but she was still unconscious. He finally left, but only after the nurses promised to sit by her bedside and keep an eye on her every second. Now, after a six-hour sleep and a good hot shower—and a visit to the florist—he felt rejuvenated.

He glanced down at the miniature rosebush in his hand, knowing Tonya would like the tiny pink roses. A plant would be something she'd have to take home and care for. Hopefully it would grow and thrive.

Like their relationship.

He paused at the nurse's station, surprised to see Reed Dickens sitting behind a computer. "Hey, Reed. Is it okay to visit Tonya?"

He looked up. "Oh hi, Murray. Yeah, go ahead. Tonya's had a flood of church people come by. Seems like the whole congregation." He grinned as he motioned down the hall. "Room 415."

"Thanks." Murray strode down the hall. The door was already open, but he knocked before he walked into the room.

"Come in." Tonya raised her eyebrows when she saw him. "Murray."

"Hi." He gazed at her face as she reclined at a forty-five degree angle on the hospital bed. She looked worse now than she had last night. Her left arm sported a sling. Plenty of flower arrangements filled the small room, and a couple of teddy bears kept vigil over them.

He walked to the bedside. "How are you feeling?"

"A little better. I've had a headache all day, but the doctor has me on all kinds of medicine, so it's not as bad as it was."

"Good." He set the plant on the little table. "I brought you some roses."

"Thank you." She picked up the plant and gazed at the flowers. "They're so tiny."

He nodded, thinking he'd have to start "tiny" with their relationship and keep a lid on his feelings for now. "I was really concerned about you last night."

"I heard." Her eyes looked up into his. "Thanks for all you did for me, and for the girls, too. You really went the second mile."

*Because I love you.* He shrugged. "When you know the people involved in an accident, it's different than business as usual."

A smile lifted her lips. "I guess so."

"Did the doctor say when they'll release you?"

"I have a concussion, so Doctor Kessler wants me here until Monday." She pointed to a chair against the wall. "Why don't you sit down?"

She wanted him to stay! Hiding a grin, he pulled the chair up to her bedside.

Tonya looked down at her sling. "I also have a broken arm. I won't be playing the piano for six weeks at least."

Murray raised his eyebrows. "That's too bad. I'm glad I was able to hear you play on Thursday night."

"I've been thinking about that. Do you remember our conversation? You said God gave you your voice talent, and He could easily take it away." She sighed. "I guess God is punishing me. He's taken away the two things I care about the most—my piano playing and my looks."

"He's not punishing you, Tonya."

"So many people from church visited me today, and they all saw my ugly, swollen face. The doctor won't let me wear any makeup at all until I go home." A tear ran down her cheek.

Murray's heart twisted at her pain, and he grabbed her hand. "Hey, don't cry."

"I can't help it." Pulling her hand away, she covered her face. "I look so horrible." Tears fell between her fingers.

"Tonya. . ." Startled, Murray moved to the edge of the bed and pulled her into his arms.

Grabbing his jacket, she buried her face in his shoulder and sobbed. He tightened his grip, wishing he could hold her forever. He hadn't realized her beauty meant so much to her.

Finally she pulled away with a sniff. "Sorry. I'm so embarrassed."

Reluctantly he let go. "You've just gone through a rough ordeal. Maybe you've been in shock all day, and you're just starting to realize what's happened."

"Maybe." She pulled a tissue from the box by the bed and wiped her eyes. "But it's so hard to let people see me like this."

"Tonya, it's okay. No one is thinking less of you." Gently he ran his hand down her left cheek. "This isn't permanent. It will heal."

"I know." She sniffed again.

He gazed at her, wishing he could tell her how much he loved her. For the first time in his relationship with Tonya, Murray was jealous of Poe.

He stood. "Guess I'd better move along. The Single Servings are going to the nursing home in Douglas tonight, and I want to go with them."

"Oh, that's right." Tonya looked down. "I was looking forward to that."

"I usually visit my mom twice a week. Why don't you go with me next week?"

She looked up at him. "I'd like that. Thanks, Murray."

His heart stirred as their gazes held. "You know, you're still beautiful, Tonya, even with your face all banged up. The thing about beauty is that it's only skin deep. The real person is inside." He spread out his hands. "Just as the Bible says in First Peter, it's more important for a woman to have a meek and quiet spirit than outward beauty."

She sighed. "I know that on paper, but it's hard to put into practice. I guess I just want to keep up my *image*." She gave a little laugh at her pun.

He grinned, thankful she was in a better mood. "Before I go, may I pray with you?"

Her lips parted, but then she nodded.

Bowing his head, Murray captured her fingers in his. "Father, I lift Tonya up to You. Thank You that she wasn't killed in the accident—it could have been much worse. But now we ask for Your healing. Please heal her physically and emotionally, and thank You that You freely give us all things in Christ because You love us, more than we could ever realize. In Jesus' name, amen." He squeezed her fingers before letting go.

"Thank you, Murray." She wiped away another tear. "And thanks for listening to me blubber."

He backed toward the door. "Remember what I said. The real person is inside, and your inward beauty is shining through." With a little salute, he walked out.

Striding toward the elevator, he heaved a sigh that turned into a prayer. *Lord, I love that girl!*

❧

Tonya blew her nose. She couldn't believe she had cried all over Murray's shoulder. But it felt good to cry, and it felt good—unbelievable as it was—to be embraced in his strong arms.

She shook her head. Murray, of all people!

If only he were still here, talking to her. *"I wish we could talk all night and then watch the sun come over the horizon together."* She frowned. Those were Poe's words, not Murray's.

*Poe!* She hadn't thought of him once today!

Of course, he had not expected to hear from her. Last night Poe worked until eleven, and this evening she had planned to go to the nursing home.

She drew her brows down. *Eleven.* That's what she'd been trying to rack her brain about. Poe had to work until eleven, and when Dad said. . .

What had he said?

With a groan, she lay back on the pillow. *Dear Father, please help me get well so I can think.* Her thoughts wandered back to Murray's prayer, and her heart warmed. Murray really was a great guy, a wonderful man. She closed her eyes. *Wonderful. . .man. . .wonderful. . .*

He stayed in her thoughts as she drifted off to sleep.

❧

Murray booted up his computer at 8:55 on Monday night, then paced the room as he waited. He couldn't sit still, and neither could he keep the smile from his face.

Tonya had gone home from the hospital that morning, and he hoped she was planning to IM with Poe tonight. When the computer was ready, he typed his first instant message.

> Poe: *Hey, Tonya! I heard about the accident—obviously. My heart just about wrenched out of my chest when I found out, and it made me realize how very much I love you. I've been keeping you in my prayers.*

In a few minutes he was rewarded with her response.

> Tonya: *Poe! I could not believe the gifts waiting for me when I got home. Thank you so, so much!*

Murray grinned. He had sent her not only a huge bouquet of flowers, but also a card, a poem, and a sapphire bracelet to match the necklace he had given her.

> Poe: *You're welcome. It's a pleasure to buy gifts for you.*

He waited for a few minutes. What was taking Tonya so long? Oh, her broken arm, which he heard was now in a cast. She was probably typing with one hand.

> Tonya: *Guess what? I won the trip to Hawaii!*

"Whoa!" Murray stared at the monitor. With all the concern about the accident, not one word had been mentioned about the cooking show in Denver.

> Poe: *Are you serious, Tonya?*
> Tonya: *Yes!*
> Poe: *I can't believe it. Congratulations!*
> Tonya: *Thanks.*
> Poe: *So, when are you planning to go to Hawaii?*
> Tonya: *Not sure, but it's good for a year. It would make a great honeymoon (hint, hint).*

Murray sat back. *Wow!* A honeymoon in Hawaii.

He raised his eyes to the ceiling. "Lord, if this is Tonya's confirmation that I should marry her, You certainly aren't sparing any expenses!" He laughed. "Thank You, Lord!"

# Chapter 21

Late Saturday afternoon Tonya sat on the passenger seat of Murray's SUV as they made their way to the Pine River Nursing Home. Since Murray wasn't on duty, he wore jeans and a button-down shirt with a blue jacket—the same jacket she had cried on a week ago. She took a deep breath, thankful her bruises were healed and she could wear makeup. Tonya glanced at Murray's profile, admiring the dark beard beneath his skin. Was he getting more handsome?

As he drove, Murray told her about the Single Servings visit to the nursing home the week before.

"Twelve people showed up, including me, and we visited all the residents in their rooms." He glanced at her. "Then one of the nurses asked us to sing, even though our piano player was hospitalized. We gave an impromptu concert in the hallway."

Tonya sighed. "I wish I could have come. What did you sing?"

"Some oldies. 'Red River Valley' and 'Bicycle Built for Two.' Songs like that." He grinned. "Then Corey Henning and I hammed it up with 'Who Threw the Overalls in Mistress Murphy's Chowder?' Corey knew the words better than I did, and he's not even Irish."

"Corey sings?" Tonya couldn't imagine that.

Murray shrugged. "He's pretty good. Wayne should enlist him in the choir."

She didn't reply. Laurie claimed that Corey was a perfect gentleman. Tonya couldn't imagine that either, but maybe she shouldn't be so quick to judge people.

It began snowing as they exited the interstate and entered the town of Douglas. Murray turned the car onto the main street, and they passed a shopping center with a string of stores.

She pointed. "There's the Facial Boutique."

Murray glanced out her window. "What kind of store is that?"

"It's a makeup outlet, and I love that place. I haven't visited it for months." He slowed the car. "Do you want to stop?"

Tonya hesitated. A week ago she would have insisted they stop. But now thinking about buying new makeup didn't thrill her as it once had. Since the swelling had gone down and her face was back to normal, she was thankful for her looks instead of being proud of them.

Perhaps God let the accident happen for that very reason.

"No, I have enough makeup." She glanced at Murray. "Let's go visit your mom."

He shrugged. "Okay."

With a few turns, they entered the heart of downtown Douglas.

Murray cruised by an empty spot at the edge of the curb between two cars. "Guess I'll park here." He threw his right arm across the back of the seat as he parallel parked. "Hope you don't mind walking a couple blocks. The nursing home has a small parking lot, and I can never find a space. I always park on the street."

"This is fine." She watched several people strolling down the sidewalk. "I guess Douglas has a nightlife."

He chuckled. "Yeah, all the restaurants and bars do a hopping business on Saturday night, even in the winter." He cut the engine. "Let me get your door."

Tonya waited while he circled the car. She thought of the easy camaraderie they shared. She was beginning to like Murray—way more than she should. Wasn't Poe the one for her?

He helped her out, and the cold air smacked Tonya as she exited. She wore her winter coat over her jeans and T-shirt, but she couldn't get her left arm in the sleeve with her cast, so her coat was unbuttoned.

"This sidewalk is icy, so be careful." Murray breathed out white clouds in the frosty air as he spoke.

She smiled. "I'll be fine, Murray. My arm is broken, not my leg."

"I know." He grinned. "I just don't want any more accidents."

As they began walking, Tonya reached to pull her coat closed with her right hand. "It's freezing out here." Thick snowflakes floated down and landed on her hand. If only she'd thought to wear gloves.

Murray stuck his hands in his jacket pockets. "I'm sorry, Tonya. I should have dropped you off at the door. I didn't think about it."

"Neither did I, but that's okay."

On the sidewalk, a tall, thin man ambled toward them. His old overcoat was two sizes too big, and Tonya felt sorry for him.

As he approached, he leered at her with bloodshot eyes. "Hey, gorgeous. How 'bout my place?"

She gasped.

Murray's arm encircled her waist. "She's with me, buddy. Move on."

"Oh yeah, shorty?" A string of profanity spewed from the man's mouth, along with the foul smell of liquor.

Tonya quickened her steps, hoping the drunk man didn't follow them.

Murray kept his arm around her waist as he glanced back between them. "Too bad I'm not in uniform. That guy might have thought twice. . . ." He pulled her closer. "I'm sorry you had to go through that, Tonya."

"It's all right." She shivered. "I always thought Douglas was a pretty decent town."

"Drunks are everywhere. Sin abounds, unfortunately."

They reached the nursing home, and Murray's arm slipped off her waist as he opened the door for her. She felt the loss as they entered the warm building.

A tiled walkway led directly to a receptionist's desk, but on either side were two sitting rooms. The one on the left was decorated as a Victorian parlor, complete with blue-flowered wallpaper and long blue drapes at the windows. A baby grand piano sat in the corner.

Wishing she could play it, Tonya gave a sigh. "That's a beautiful room."

Murray raised his eyebrows. "You've never been here before?"

"No, and my sister works here. I wonder if she's working tonight."

"I'll ask." Murray stopped at the desk and nodded a greeting at the dark-haired receptionist. "Hi, Kate. We're here to see Priscilla Twichell."

"I just talked to your mom an hour ago." The woman smiled as she handed Murray a clipboard. "Please sign in. She'll be glad to see you."

He signed his name, then handed the clipboard to Tonya. She glanced at his neat, blocky printing, reminding her of those speeding tickets. But for some reason she couldn't conjure up one spark of anger. She signed her name below his.

Murray handed back the clipboard. "Is Molly Brandt working tonight?"

Tonya leaned toward him. "Molly Hunt."

"Oh, that's right." He grinned at her, and she once again noticed his straight white teeth. He looked back at the receptionist. "This is Molly's sister, Tonya."

Kate adjusted her glasses. "I see the resemblance." She opened a folder and perused the paper inside. "No, Molly left at three o'clock, and she won't be working until Tuesday."

"Thanks, Kate." Murray turned to Tonya. "Ready to visit Mom?"

❧

Tonya hadn't seen Mrs. Twichell for five years, since the woman became a resident at Pine River. Murray's mom had always been short with red hair. Now her hair was snow white, and her tiny frame was as thin as a skeleton. When they entered her small room, she was sitting on a rocking chair near the bed.

"Hi, Mom!" Murray bent over and gave her a kiss on her cheek.

"Murray, I didn't know you were coming over this evening." Mrs. Twichell's head quivered as she spoke.

"Well, here I am." Murray motioned toward Tonya. "I brought a visitor."

Tonya leaned over the older woman and took the fragile hand in her own. "Hi, Mrs. Twichell. Do you remember me?"

"Of course I do, Tonya. Murray told me about the accident. I'm so sorry, dear."

"Thank you." As Tonya gazed at the watery blue eyes, she thought of Aggie saying that Murray was the spitting image of Priscilla, and it was true. Same close-set blue eyes, same large nose. Mrs. Twichell was really rather homely, but Tonya had not remembered that. She just remembered the woman's kindness. Murray's words pierced her thoughts. *"The thing about beauty is that it's only skin deep. The real person is inside."*

Tonya smiled. "I'm so glad Murray brought me to visit you."

"I'll get a couple chairs." He disappeared into the hallway.

Mrs. Twichell kept a grip on Tonya's hand. "Molly keeps me up to date on your family. I was so sorry I couldn't attend her wedding, but she shared her pictures with me. It was a beautiful wedding."

"Yes, it was."

Murray came back with two folding chairs. "Have a seat, Tonya." He set up a chair for her, then sat on the other one.

Mrs. Twichell watched them get settled. "Molly is the best nurse here, in my opinion."

"All the nurses here are good." Murray clasped his hands between his knees. "This is a great nursing home."

"Yes, but I wish the Lord would just take me home to heaven." Mrs. Twichell turned to Tonya. "I'm such a burden to Murray."

"That's not true, Mom." He placed his hand on her shoulder. "Don't talk like that."

Tonya nodded. "I'm sure he's thankful you're still here for him."

"That's right. If it wasn't for you, Mom, I wouldn't have any family at all except for the Hunts. But I don't see them very often."

Tonya thought about Murray living alone in his parents' big, drafty house. Poe lived alone, too. She had such a big family; she couldn't even imagine living alone.

An hour passed quickly as they talked about Tonya's family, the church at Fort Lob, and years gone by. Several times Mrs. Twichell's thin knee would begin to shake, slowly at first and then more violently. The first time it happened, Tonya was alarmed. But Murray put a restraining hand on his mother's knee, and the shaking slowed.

Finally Murray glanced at his watch. "We'd better go, Mom. Why don't we pray with you before we leave?"

"Please do." Mrs. Twichell reached out her left hand and grabbed Tonya's good hand. She slipped her other hand in Murray's.

He glanced at Tonya, then looked down at her cast. "Okay. Let's pray."

As Tonya bowed her head, she felt Murray place his arm around her shoulders, pulling her into an intimate circle. Listening to his baritone in her ear gave her a feeling of peace and protection. Tears touched her eyes. Murray was a good son to his mom. A good son and a wonderful man.

Murray relaxed as he drove Tonya home. Besides that miserable drunk excuse of a man, this had been a good visit. He hoped Tonya was by his side many times when he visited his mom. Hopefully she'd be by his side the rest of his life.

"I'm surprised you didn't want to stay longer." Tonya smiled at him. "I really enjoyed getting to know your mom again."

"You can come with me anytime, Tonya. I just figured you'd want to get home at nine o'clock so you can instant message."

She frowned. "How did you know about that?"

*Oops! Just blew my cover!* "Um, don't you IM every evening with your secret admirer?"

"Did Derek tell you that?"

Murray wished he could blame Derek, but he couldn't. "No. . .Poe told me."

Tonya gasped. "Murray! You know who Poe is?"

He shrugged. "Maybe."

Leaning across the seat, she placed her right hand on his arm. "Who is he, Murray? Please tell me."

Murray glanced into her beautiful dark-blue eyes. Her face was only inches away, and he wished he weren't driving. If only he could take her into his arms. If only he could tell her who he really was. If only she would respond ecstatically.

With a sigh, he looked back at the road. "Sorry, only Poe can tell you who he is. It wouldn't be fair to him if I told you."

She moved back into her seat, and he felt the loss of her warmth. "Okay then. If you can't tell me who he is, can you tell me what he looks like?"

He glanced at her. "What does that matter?"

"Murray. . ." She leaned toward him again. "Is Poe deformed in some way?"

*Deformed?* "Not that I know of. Why would you ask?"

"Well, he said. . .oh never mind." She sat back. "He looks normal?"

Murray grinned. "As normal as anyone else I know."

She sat back with a sigh. "That's good. I was willing to accept the hunch-back of Notre Dame if necessary, but I'm thankful he's not deformed."

*Hmm. . . Must have been that "seven shades of ugly" description.* Murray glanced at her. "So you really like this guy?"

She smiled. "Poe and I are of one heart and mind. We love each other."

"You love him?" Murray's head spun. Tonya had never said those words to Poe.

"I think so, but I want to find out who he is before I say anything." She frowned at him. "Please don't tell him."

"I won't, but how can you fall in love with someone just by exchanging e-mail letters over the Internet?"

"It can happen. Like Elizabeth Barrett and Robert Browning." Tonya turned toward him. "You've heard of the Brownings, haven't you?"

"Uh, poets?"

She laughed. "Murray, you're so clueless. Yes, of course they're poets. Poe and I both love poetry and music. We picked out our very own song, and now I'm composing a song for him."

"You are?" Murray raised his eyebrows.

Tonya placed her finger over her lips. "Shhh. Keep it to yourself. I want it to be a surprise."

*It won't be now!*

She looked down at her cast. "Unfortunately, I won't be able to play it for a few weeks, so I'm taking my time with the composition."

"So what's your 'very own song' that you two picked out together?"

"It's called 'When I Fall in Love, It Will Be Forever.' Have you heard of it?"

"Yeah." Murray motioned toward the radio/CD player. "I have an orchestra version of it on CD."

"You're kidding!" Tonya stared at the radio. "Could you play it for me?"

"Sure." Leaning over, he pushed the SELECTION button to number seventeen. "This is just the music. Want me to sing it for you?"

"Yes please! That would be wonderful." With a smile Tonya settled back in her seat and closed her eyes. "I haven't heard this song in years."

*Good thing I practiced!* Murray glanced at her beautiful face as the orchestra played the introduction. If he weren't driving, he could gaze at her during the entire song. But a glance now and then would have to suffice.

He waited for the intro, then began to sing. "When I fall in love, it will be forever. . ."

Tonya gave a happy sigh.

If only that sigh were for him.

# Chapter 22

Tonya: *I found out that Murray Twichell knows who you are.*

She pushed the RETURN button, wishing she could type with more than one finger.

> Poe: *What? That bonehead! Did he give away my identity?*
> Tonya: *NO, he refused to tell me.*
> Poe: *Good. OK, I take back the name-calling. Actually, Murray's a good guy.*
> Tonya: *I agree. We visited his mom and had a nice time.*

But their visit to the nursing home that evening was beginning to bother her. Not the long drive with Murray, and not the visit with his mom. Even their discussion about Poe didn't bother her. What bothered her were the emotions that pierced her heart when Murray sang.

It would be so easy to fall in love with that man.

Murray had a magnificent voice, but that wasn't the only thing Tonya now loved about him. She loved the way he prayed. She loved his strong hands with the square nails, and she loved the dark beard beneath his skin and his straight white teeth. She even loved his blue eyes.

But what about Poe?

She loved his strength of character, the way he encouraged her, the funny things he said. She loved his Christian principles and humble attitude. And he loved her—the real Tonya. He knew her inmost thoughts and desires, unlike Murray. But how did she know Poe was the one for her when she was developing feelings for someone else?

There was only one thing to do—she *must* discover Poe's identity.

Murray reread Tonya's sentences. *Whew!* She hadn't guessed. That was rather amazing, considering all the hints she'd had.

Poising his fingers over the keyboard, he hesitated. Maybe he should take advantage of talking about Murray and find out what she really thought about him.

> Poe: *I'm glad you had a good time with Mrs. Twichell. I was*

236

*wondering—do you really, really like Murray? Is there anything about him you don't like?*

He sat back. This would be enlightening.

Tonya*: If you're jealous, don't be. He cracks his knuckles.*

Murray raised his eyebrows.

Poe: *That bothers you?*
Tonya: *Yes.*
Poe: *Why? Cause it makes his knuckles big? (haha)*
Tonya: *It makes him seem arrogant.*

Murray fell back in his seat. Arrogant? Cracking his knuckles was a sign of self-confidence. At least that's how he always felt. He'd better change the subject before she brought up something he didn't want to hear.

Poe: *Hmm. . .interesting. Now, tell me your hidden thoughts. What are you contemplating right now?*

Figuring it would take her a few minutes to write back, he entered the kitchen, rummaged around in the fridge, and found a can of cola. He carried it back to the computer and took a swig.

He almost choked when Tonya's IM appeared.

Tonya: *Poe, you MUST tell me who you are. NOW! I've waited patiently, and patience is not my virtue. WHO ARE YOU?*

"Great," he muttered.

Standing, Murray walked to the window and gazed out at his snowy front yard. The skies were clear and several stars winked at him. "Lord, I love Tonya and want to marry her. I know You gave me peace about our relationship, but I'm still scared."

As strange as it seemed, Poe had become a problem in Murray's developing relationship with Tonya. She wanted Poe, not him. It seemed she had built this fantasy man up to godlike proportions. When she found out he was Murray, she would be disappointed.

He slipped back into his seat at the computer.

Poe: *Give me a couple days to pray about it, OK?*

Just thinking about revealing his identity made Murray's palms sweat.

∂෨

On Sunday afternoon, Tonya walked down the stairs from her second-floor bedroom. Hopefully she could find some luncheon meat in the refrigerator to make a sandwich before she attended the evening church service. She glanced at her cast. Maybe Mom could help her make the sandwich. It was hard to do anything with one hand.

Murray, dressed in his green patrol uniform, walked through the living room on his way to the front door. "Hi, Tonya."

"Murray, what are you doing—" She stopped. Murray was right—she always asked him that question. "Never mind."

He grinned. "Your dad had a computer problem. Didn't you know I was over here?"

"No." She finished walking down the stairs.

"Uh, Tonya. . ." Taking a couple of steps back, he positioned himself in front of her. "I got a couple tickets to the Cheyenne Playhouse for Tuesday night. Want to go with me?"

A date with Murray Twichell? What about Poe? If she kept spending time with Murray, she might put her heart in grave danger—as far as Poe was concerned. "I don't know, Murray. I'd really like to, but I feel an obligation to Poe. He's my soul mate, after all."

"Oh." Murray looked down. "Um, I didn't want to mention this, but Poe gave me the tickets." He met her eyes. "He asked me to take you to this play for him."

"What?" Tonya's ire rose, along with her voice. "Why doesn't he just ask me out himself, for goodness' sake?"

Murray shrugged. "He's a big chicken."

"Aargh!" Her right hand curled into a fist. "What is wrong with that man? I wish he would just tell me who he is."

"Give him time. Now how about that play on Tuesday? It's *Singing in the Rain*."

Tonya's lips parted as her anger dissipated. "Really? That's one of my favorites." She sighed. If Poe wouldn't take her out, it would serve him right if she dated someone else. "Okay, I'll go with you."

"Great!" Murray brought his hands together like he did when he cracked his knuckles, but then his hands dropped to his sides. "I forgot, you don't like me doing that."

She raised her eyebrows. "Poe told you?"

"Uh, yeah. We're good friends, remember?"

Her anger seeped back—against Poe! Why was he telling Murray things that she had told him in confidence?

Murray opened the front door. "I'll pick you up around six thirty Tuesday evening, okay?"

"Sure." She waited for the door to close behind him, then sank down to the second stair. What was the big deal about Poe not revealing himself? And why was he sharing their private correspondence with Murray? Didn't he know Murray liked her romantically? After all, he was asking her on dates, not wearing aftershave because it made her sneeze, not cracking his knuckles because she didn't want him to. . . .

Tonya sighed. Murray was just too nice.

On Monday night, Tonya was completely ready for bed as she IMed with Poe. She decided to test the truth about the squeaky wheel getting the oil. Every evening she would bug Poe and nag at him, no matter how long it took, until he agreed to reveal his identity.

> Tonya: *Still waiting, Poe. When am I going to meet you?*
> Poe: *Uh, well, let's see. Tomorrow's out. How about never? Is never good for you?*
> Tonya: *NO! I want to meet you ASAP. Who R U?*
> Poe: *OK. I once heard a preacher say, "faith takes risks," and I guess it's time for the big reveal. I'll take you up on dinner with your family.*

She almost jumped out of her seat.

> Tonya: *Woo-hoo! I can't believe it!*
> Poe: *Yeah, well, you might be singing a different tune once you meet me. I hope you're not disappointed.*

They kept IMing, and a decision was reached. Poe had other plans for Tuesday night, and he was working on Wednesday. But Thursday night was free, so he would reveal himself then. Tonya invited him over for dinner with the Brandt family that evening.

Now Tonya wished she didn't have to go out with Murray tomorrow night, but she wasn't about to stand him up. One more date with Murray, and then Poe would be hers forever.

Murray drove his SUV up the Brandts' drive on Tuesday night at the end of their date. It was now after midnight. On the way home, all Tonya could talk about was the play and how great it was. He enjoyed the animated conversation. Now she was quiet, probably tired from the late hour, but he didn't want her to fall asleep.

"Um, Tonya, I heard that Poe plans to reveal himself on Thursday."

She turned a smile on him. "Yep. He's coming over for dinner with the family."

"The entire family?" He could just imagine a huge family reunion with all her sisters and brothers gaping at him. Sweat broke out on his hands as he drove.

"No, just my parents and Derek." She held up her broken arm. "Since I'm not working right now, Mom and I will take all day Thursday to get ready. I'm planning to make my brownies for dessert." She grinned at him. "You know—Tonya's Terrific Brownies?"

"That's great." His hands started sticking to the steering wheel.

"I'm so excited." She gave a little laugh. "Can you imagine? I'll finally discover who's been writing to me all this time."

"Yeah, if he doesn't chicken out."

"He'd better not!" Tonya leaned toward him. "Keep his feet to the fire, okay, Murray?"

*Fire.* That's what it would feel like. He wiped his left hand on his pants.

Parking the SUV, he glanced at the house. The porch light was on, but besides that the house looked dark. Probably Jake, Yvette, and Derek were all in bed. "I'll get your door, Tonya."

Together they walked up the three steps to the porch. Murray's mind was still on the big unveiling. What if Tonya rejected him?

That would be a true identity crisis!

She opened the front door, then turned to him. "Thanks so much, Murray. I loved that play."

"Yeah, me, too. Thanks for going with me."

"Bye!" Leaning toward him, she brushed a quick kiss along his jawline, then ran into the house.

His eyes widened. "Tonya! Come back here!" If he had known that kiss was coming, he would have grabbed her and kissed her back—on the mouth!

He heard her laugh on the other side of the closed door.

"Tonya!" He wanted to shout her name at the top of his lungs, but he might wake up the rest of the household.

With a sigh, he trudged back to his car. Thursday would come way too soon.

❧

Tonya lightly ran up the stairs, then entered her bedroom on tiptoe. What had gotten into her? She had kissed Murray Twichell! But she had to admit that the beard under his skin fascinated her. As the evening wore on, she watched it grow darker. She couldn't resist seeing if his skin was as scratchy under her lips as it looked.

It was.

Murray had seemed rather preoccupied until she kissed him. What had they been talking about before that?

Poe.

───────── THE THING ABOUT BEAUTY ─────────

Poor Murray. He didn't want her to meet her secret admirer. He must figure that Poe was going to marry her. Maybe Murray and Poe had even discussed it.

She sank down to the bed. Wow! She couldn't wait for Thursday to come.

# *Chapter 23*

O n Thursday evening, Tonya paced the living room, stopping in front of the big picture window to gaze out at the driveway. Nothing. She took another turn around the room.

"Why don't you sit down, sis?" Derek relaxed in the blue chair.

She stopped in front of him. "I'm too nervous." In fact, she couldn't believe how nervous she was. Her legs were actually shaking.

He stood. "Here, you can sit in this chair. Then you'll have a perfect view of the driveway."

"I can't sit." She held her left elbow with her right hand, supporting the cast. She had dressed up for Poe's big night and was wearing the sapphire necklace and bracelet he had given her. A light-blue dress swirled around her knees as she paced, and a navy cardigan completed her outfit. She had actually managed to get her casted arm in the sweater sleeve.

She glanced out the window again. *Where is he?*

Mom walked into the living room. She had also dressed up for the occasion, although a yellow-checked apron covered her green print dress. "Derek, could you come to the kitchen? I need your help."

"Okay." Derek glanced out the window. "Hey, I see a car."

"Really?" Tonya ran to the window and peered out. Her shoulders sagged as she watched Murray's SUV slowly drive closer. "Oh, it's only Murray."

"Ha!" Derek fisted his hand in the air. "I knew Twitch was Poe!"

Tonya faced him. "But he's not. Murray said he knows who Poe is." She bit her lower lip. "I bet Poe chickened out, and Murray came to break the news to me."

"Are you serious?" Derek stared at her. "Murray's been in love with you for weeks. I think he got the idea from Mrs. Yvette Brandt the Matchmaker." He winked at Mom. "Remember the secret pal thing?"

Mom's face tinged pink as she turned around. "I need to check the potatoes."

Tonya placed her right hand on her hip. "Murray is not Poe. I asked him point-blank, and he said Poe had to tell me himself who he was." She cocked an eyebrow at her brother. "It's someone else."

"Tonya," Mom called from the kitchen. "You may as well invite Murray in for supper. And Derek, are you coming? I need your help in here."

"I still think Twitch is Poe," Derek muttered as he left.

# THE THING ABOUT BEAUTY

Tonya glanced out the window, and a sigh escaped her lips. She wasn't going to find out who Poe was after all. Murray parked his car a few yards back on the driveway, but he didn't get out. She waited. Still he didn't move.

*What is keeping him?*

She opened the front door and walked outside. As she descended the porch steps, a cool breeze lifted her hair. Fortunately, they were in the middle of a warming trend, and all the snow had melted.

Murray stepped out of his car and slowly closed the door.

She walked down the driveway toward him. *Why is he just standing there?* But as she walked closer, a sense of relief replaced her disappointment.

And it suddenly hit her.

Murray had the exact same qualities she loved about Poe, and Murray was a flesh-and-blood person. The last few weeks ran through her mind. When she had cried, Murray held her in his arms. When threatened by a drunken man, he pulled her close. When he prayed with her, he took her hand in his, squeezing her fingers.

And now she knew. She didn't want to marry Poe, that nameless, faceless guy, that man who said he loved her but was too chicken to come out of hiding.

She had fallen in love with Murray Twichell—of all people!

As she walked closer, gazing at his wonderful, in-person face, she knew she loved him. And deep down in her heart, she knew Murray loved her, too. That must be why he looked so nervous. He didn't want her marrying Poetry Lover Guy. He wanted to marry her himself. And she wanted to marry him.

But how could she tell him?

⊶≫

Murray's heartbeat drummed in his chest as he watched Tonya walk toward him. She was beautiful with her dark hair swirling around her in the nippy air. She had dressed up for Poe, and Murray felt underdressed, even though he wore slacks with a button-down shirt and his blue jacket.

He kept his clammy hand on the door handle, ready to escape as soon as Tonya discovered his identity. She would be disappointed, perhaps even angry, when her bubble burst.

"Murray, it's okay." Tonya put up her right hand like a stop sign as she paused in front of him. "I know Poe chickened out, but it doesn't matter."

He raised his eyebrows. "It doesn't?"

"No, really, it's all right." She took a deep breath. "You see, I've fallen in love with someone else, so Poe is off my short list. Another man has stolen my heart."

His lips parted. She had fallen in love? With someone else? He knew everything going on in her life. Who was this other person?

"Murray. . ." She took a step closer and gazed into his eyes. "These last few weeks have shown me what real love is. It's not just IMing on a computer and sharing secrets; it's everyday living, spending time together, talking face-to-face." Reaching out, she straightened the lapel of his jacket. Her hand lingered there as she continued. "I know we've had our differences, and we've argued. Most of the time it was my fault, and I'm sorry. But Murray, you loved me anyway, even when I had an ugly spirit. You loved me, even when I had an ugly face."

Murray's jaw dropped. "You're talking about me? I'm the guy you've fallen in love with? I'm the guy who stole you from Poe?"

She nodded, and tears glimmered in her dark eyes. "I love you, Murray."

*Wow!* With a whoop, he threw his arms around her and pulled her close. "I can't believe this, Tonya. I love you, too! I love you—warts and all."

Her eyes widened. "Poe told you about my warts?"

"Haven't you guessed by now, Tonya?" He hesitated. "I am Poe."

"What?"

"Yes. Poetry Lover Guy and Murray Twichell are the same person." He shrugged. "I figured you wouldn't date me, so I became your secret admirer. I wanted to discover the real Tonya Brandt."

❧

Tonya could not shut her mouth. She stared at Murray's close-set eyes and got lost in the blue. Why did she ever think he was homely? "You are Poe? The person I've been writing to all these months?"

"One and the same." He gazed at her. "How do I love thee? Let me count the ways; I wish we could talk all night and watch the sun come over the horizon together." He raised his eyebrows, looking a bit unsure. "I hope you're not disappointed, but it was me all along, Tonya. I can't believe you didn't guess."

"I didn't!" She threw her arms around his neck, resting her cast on his shoulder, and hugged him. "I'm so glad it was you."

"You are?"

She pulled back and looked deep into his eyes. "Yes, I am, Murray. There's so many things I love about you."

His gaze dipped down to her lips. "You wouldn't believe how much I love you."

Tonya had been kissed by a lot of guys, but Murray's kiss was indescribably the best she had ever received. When they parted, they were both a little breathless. For a long moment, they stared into each other's eyes until Murray spoke.

"You will marry me, won't you, Tonya?"

She raised her eyebrows. "You're asking already?"

Murray shrugged. "We've known each other all our lives, and you wanted to get married in June, remember? That's only three short months away. Then there's that honeymoon trip to Hawaii." He shook his head. "I can't believe how the Lord provided that."

"I know!" *Thank You, Lord!* "Guess I'd better get busy with the wedding plans."

"I'll ask you more formally later, with a ring, and it will have to be somewhere romantic. I'm quite the poet, you know." He grinned before glancing toward the house. "But first I'll ask your dad for your hand in marriage. Should I be nervous about that? He might say no."

"Are you kidding? Dad and Mom love you. They'll be so happy."

Murray nodded. "I think you're right. In fact, they're smiling at us right now."

"What?" Tonya whipped around to look at the house. Sure enough, Dad, Mom, and Derek stood at the window. Mom had the phone pressed to her ear.

"Great!" Tonya turned back to Murray. "Mom is on the phone. She's probably inviting everyone to our wedding."

"That's good. We won't have to send out invitations." He grinned. "I've already spent a ton on postage this year."

Tonya laughed and grabbed his hand. "Come on, Poe. I'll introduce you to my family."

As they walked hand in hand to the house, peace filled Tonya. The Lord had given her a great gift, a man who exemplified the beautiful spirit of Christ's love. A man who loved not only her outward appearance but also her heart.

Yes, Murray was the man for her—the man who had taught her the thing about beauty.

# TUMBLEWEED WEDDINGS

## Recipe for Tonya's Terrific Brownies

*Chocolate Layer:*
>    6 ounces semisweet baking chocolate
>    ½ cup canola oil
>    ¾ cup sugar
>    1½ teaspoons vanilla
>    3 eggs
>    ¾ cup flour
>    ¼ teaspoon salt
>    ¼ cup semisweet chocolate chunks

*Cream Cheese Layer:*
>    8 ounces cream cheese
>    ¼ cup sugar
>    1 egg

Preheat oven to 325 degrees. Lightly grease an 8-inch square pan; dust with flour.

Melt baking chocolate in a double boiler over boiling water, stirring until melted. Remove from heat and whisk in oil, sugar, and vanilla. Whisk in eggs, one at a time. Stir in flour and salt until just blended. Fold in chocolate chunks.

In another bowl, beat cream cheese with sugar and egg. Spread ⅔ of the chocolate mixture in the baking pan; spoon the cheese mixture over the chocolate layer; spoon the remaining chocolate on top. Drag a knife through to swirl.

Bake for 40 to 45 minutes. Insert a toothpick to test. Let cool in pan for 20 minutes for warm brownies that you can eat with a fork, or cool completely for terrific finger-held brownies. Enjoy!

# NO ONE BUT YOU

# Dedication

This book is dedicated to my Savior, Jesus Christ, who called me to write according to His own purpose, and also to my daughter, Holly Marie Robinson Armstrong, who is a great "first editor." Thanks for all your help, Holly!

# Chapter 1

Cheyenne Wilkins perched on the edge of the red leather chair in the law office of Mr. Barton Griggs, her heart beating an erratic tempo as she listened to the lawyer read her grandmother's will. Since Grandmother Ingersoll's death seven months ago, she had been hoping she would inherit some money, but she didn't expect this.

Mr. Griggs laid his reading glasses on the mahogany desk. "So that's it." He raised bushy white eyebrows as his gray eyes glanced from Cheyenne to her dad, Jim Wilkins.

She lifted her hands, palms up. "I have to be married? And have a child?" She exchanged a glance with her dad. He looked just as stunned as she felt.

The lawyer nodded. "I tried to talk your grandmother into putting the money in a trust fund for you, but she had her own stubborn ideas." Mr. Griggs gave her a sad smile. "She wrote this will shortly after your grandfather died and long after your mother had died. You were a teenager, Cheyenne."

Dad gave a grudging nod. "I'm sure she thought you'd be married and have two or three kids by the age of thirty."

"Yes." Mr. Griggs steepled his fingers. "And even though Florence turned eccentric toward the end, she was in her right mind when she made the will. I can't find any loopholes to change it."

Cheyenne's shoulders drooped. "I'll never inherit that money. My birthday is next week, and I'll be twenty-eight."

The lawyer leaned back in his chair. "You have two years, Cheyenne. Surely you'll find someone to marry before then."

"What happens to the money if Cheyenne doesn't meet the conditions of the will?" Dad folded his arms.

Mr. Griggs straightened the papers on his desk. "All the recipients in Florence Ingersoll's will are dead, except for Cheyenne and George Sommers."

Cheyenne willed her pulse to slow down. "Who is this George Sommers?"

Dad's blue eyes met hers. "A distant relative of your grandfather's. I believe he was in the restaurant business." He waved a beefy hand toward the lawyer. "Florence must have liked him to include him in the will. Either she really liked someone and couldn't do enough for them, or she didn't like them at all." He grimaced.

Lowering her eyes, Cheyenne felt a stab of pain for her dad. Bitterness laced his words, and her mind went back to a conversation she once had with her grandmother. Cheyenne had only been seventeen, but she remembered every word.

*"Jim Wilkins was not good enough to marry my daughter, and he's still not good enough."* Grandmother's blue eyes flashed, and her white hair quivered as she ranted. *"If it hadn't been for your grandfather intervening, Lynn would have married William Thorndyke. He would have taken care of her."*

Cheyenne still recalled the shock she felt. Grandmother had always been kind to her, maybe because she was her only grandchild, but evidently her kindness didn't extend to Jim Wilkins.

Mr. Griggs donned his glasses. "Sommers is the only other relative of Mrs. Ingersoll's who is still living." He shuffled some papers. "Ah! Here's the information. The man lives in Reno, Nevada, and has expanded his restaurant to include a hotel and a casino."

"A casino?" Dad frowned as he glanced at Cheyenne. "So if my daughter doesn't fulfill the requirements of her grandmother's will, Sommers will get the four million dollars?"

Mr. Griggs nodded. "That is correct."

"Without any stipulations on his part?"

"None whatsoever."

*I can't believe this!* Cheyenne sighed. "So if I'm not married in two years, with a child, all of Grandmother's money will go to this casino owner?"

Mr. Griggs shrugged. "I'm sorry, Cheyenne."

"Don't give up yet." Dad's eyes met hers. "A lot can happen in two years." She looked down. *But will it?*

# Chapter 2

On Saturday, June 20th, Cheyenne stood in the church lobby, waiting her turn to walk down the center aisle of the auditorium. *Always a bridesmaid, never a bride.* But she hoped to be a bride soon, and in this very church in Fort Lob, Wyoming.

If only she had a groom.

The white carnations in her bouquet shook slightly, and she took a deep breath before smoothing down the sky-blue satin of her long bridesmaid gown. She glanced around at the other bridesmaids dressed in different shades of pink, yellow, green, and violet. Cheyenne was thankful she had been given a blue dress since it brought out the blue in her eyes.

"I can't believe my little sister's getting married," Callie Hutchins whispered. She was wearing a light-green dress, which didn't do a thing for her dark eyes.

Cheyenne smiled at her best friend. "I love weddings, and this one's going to be so pretty." She glanced at the front of the auditorium. The men stood on the platform, waiting for the ten attendants in Tonya Brandt's wedding. There were only four men, two standing on each side of the groom. Four women would join them on the platform, and the other six girls would stand below, forming a circle of pastel "flowers"—as Tonya described it.

Callie leaned toward her. "By the way, happy birthday."

"Thanks!" That was all Cheyenne had thought of today. A pang of apprehension stabbed her. She had exactly two years to fulfill the conditions of Grandmother's will, which was never far from her mind.

No use thinking about that during Tonya's wedding, although she wished she could tell Callie about the will. But Mr. Griggs was adamant that she and Dad keep that info to themselves.

She turned to Callie with a smile. "Dad already gave me a present this morning at breakfast."

Callie raised her eyebrows. "What was it?"

"A ruby necklace he had given Mom when they were dating. I never saw it before, and I love it!"

"That was thoughtful of him. It's something you can remember your mom by."

"Yeah, I'm planning to wear it to church tomorrow."

Evelyn Seymour, the wedding coordinator, hushed them as she walked by. She adjusted her black-rimmed glasses. "Be ready for your turn, girls." She waved her sheaf of papers toward the auditorium.

Cheyenne glanced behind her at the bride. Tonya stood beside her father Jake Brandt, with her arm laced through his. She looked beautiful, as always with her perfect complexion and dark hair and eyes. A tiny tiara crowned her head, and a veil flowed down her back. Jake stood tall and confident, as well he should be. He'd already given away three daughters—Melissa, Callie, and Molly. He must be a pro at this by now.

With a last glance at Tonya, Cheyenne held in a sigh. The tiny sequins sewn on the lace of Tonya's bridal gown, which she had designed herself, glinted in the overhead lights as she moved. But it was the bride's figure that Cheyenne envied. The dress had a fitted waist, and Tonya's waist must have a smaller diameter than one of Cheyenne's thighs.

*I haven't been that thin since I was ten!*

The organ music changed, and Evelyn waved her papers. "That's your cue, girls." She corralled the first six girls to the door, and they walked down the aisle, two by two, and then fanned out across the front of the auditorium as they rehearsed last evening.

Cheyenne moved into place and stepped into the aisle at Evelyn's prompting. Sucking in her stomach, she smiled and slowly walked down the aisle feeling curious eyes on her from every crowded pew as she moved past.

As she neared the platform, she glanced ahead at the groom. Murray Twichell smiled back at her as he stood beside Pastor Reilly. Her glance flitted to Jon Hunt, the best man, and then landed on Derek Brandt. He was her destination.

Pinching the satin skirt of her gown, she pulled up the fabric a couple of inches and ascended the three steps of the platform. She raised her eyes to Derek's handsome face as she drew nearer. He smiled at her, his dark-blue eyes holding hers.

If only that look and smile meant something! But it had been rehearsed last night, as per Evelyn's instructions. With an inward sigh, Cheyenne turned to face the audience, standing as close to Derek as she dared.

Melissa walked the length of the aisle and ascended the platform on the other side, sharing a smile with her husband, Philip, before stopping at his side. Then it was Molly's turn. After walking up the stairs, she stood beside Jon, near Cheyenne. Callie came down the aisle last, as the matron of honor. Her husband, Lane, smiled at her as she took her place between him and the pastor.

The music changed once again, and the congregation stood to turn and watch the bride. Tonya seemed to float down the aisle on her father's arm. A beautiful smile lit her face as she gazed at her groom.

Tears crept to Cheyenne's eyes, and she sent up a silent prayer. *Oh Lord, this is what I want.* She had been in love with Derek since high school, ever since he asked her to the prom when he was a junior and she was a senior. But for the past ten years, their relationship had deadlocked into being nothing more than good pals. He seemed to enjoy spending time with her, but they always hung out in a group. Would he ever view her as more than a friend?

And now with Grandmother's will hanging over her head. . .

She glanced across the platform as Tonya and Jake stopped in front of the pastor. All the couples in the bridal party were married to each other—except for her and Derek. Melissa and Philip, Callie and Lane, Molly and Jon, and now, of course, Tonya and Murray. They were all part of the Brandt family, too.

*Is that a sign, Lord?*

Derek didn't plan to get married until he was forty. At least, that's what he told his sisters. Evidently he enjoyed living at home, letting his mom make his meals and do his laundry, and working on that huge sheep ranch with his dad.

But Cheyenne wasn't about to let him remain single, not with the Last Will and Testament of Florence Ingersoll pressing her into marriage. As the ceremony progressed, her determination increased at the same time. She would lose weight and make a concentrated effort to win Derek's hand.

Win *his* hand? That would be a role reversal, but she couldn't depend on Mr. Laid-Back to win *her* hand. If she left it up to Derek, she would be forty-one years old before they married, if they married at all.

And that would definitely invalidate Grandmother's will.

Tonya and Murray repeated their vows, gazing into each other's eyes. Cheyenne could only see Tonya's face, but she envied the look of love the bride held for her bridegroom. A wistful sigh escaped Cheyenne's lips. Maybe someday. . .but not too far into the future.

Next week would be good.

∽

Derek relaxed on the blue chair in the living room, thankful the wedding was over and he was now wearing comfortable clothes. Why did people have to make such a big fuss about weddings anyway?

After the cake-only reception at the church, all the Brandt relatives had descended on the house en masse, and the noise level drifted up to the ceiling and bounced back to Derek. He laid his head back on the chair and watched the ceiling fan turn in lazy circles. His eyes began to close when a commotion roused him.

"Hey, everybody." Tonya, dressed now in a classy skirt and blouse, stood in the middle of the living room, her dark eyes shining. "Before Murray and I leave, we all have to sing 'Happy Birthday' to Cheyenne." She nodded to her husband. "Ready?"

Murray started the song, and everyone joined in.

Easing out of his chair, Derek rumbled in on the third line. He glanced at Cheyenne, standing near the fireplace. Her round face sported a smile, and Derek thought the two deep dimples in her cheeks made her cute.

When the song ended, she nodded at the crowd. "Thanks, everyone! I've had a wonderful birthday."

Derek kept his eyes on Cheyenne as she hugged a few well-wishers, and something stirred deep inside him. He and Cheyenne had been best buddies for years, but sometimes it hit him how pretty she was.

"Okay, folks." Dad strode through the living room. "Time for the happy couple to leave. I'll get my car keys."

Tonya and Murray followed him but stopped every few seconds to receive hugs from the many aunts, uncles, and cousins, not to mention brothers and sisters, who lined the room.

Derek waited until Murray stepped in front of him. "Is Dad driving you guys to Denver?"

"Yep." Murray looked up at him. "We're staying at the Brown Palace Hotel tonight. Our flight leaves Denver International Airport at one o'clock tomorrow afternoon."

"Stay safe, Twitch." Derek shook Murray's hand. "I hope you two have a great honeymoon in Hawaii."

"We will." Murray cocked an eyebrow at him before he smiled.

Derek grinned. Twitch got the girl he wanted.

"Bye, Derek!" Tonya threw her arms around his shoulders.

He hugged her. "Have fun, sis. We'll be praying for a safe trip."

"Thanks."

The crowd followed the happy couple to the door and flowed outside behind them. Everyone waved as they drove off, with Mom and Grandma waving handkerchiefs, and then they all tramped back into the house.

Above the din of the noisy relatives, Lane tapped Derek on the shoulder. "Callie wants to eat at Mama's Kitchen in Lusk for a nice quiet dinner. Want to go with us? I'm paying."

"Sure. I'm always game for a free meal at a good restaurant."

Lane grinned. "I'll let her know. Most of the relatives are leaving, and Mom is going to Casper with Grandma for a week. Callie wants to say good-bye to everyone. Then the four of us will go out to eat."

Derek frowned. "The four of us?"

"Callie invited Cheyenne."

"Oh." Derek watched Lane wend his way past several uncles out to the kitchen. Was this date Callie's idea? His sisters were always trying to throw Cheyenne and him together.

Not that there was anything wrong with Cheyenne. He glanced around the crowded living room, but she was gone. If he ever got married, Cheyenne Wilkins would be the kind of wife he would choose—godly, vivacious, pretty.

But for the past several years, Derek felt the Lord wanted him to stay single in order to serve Him. And the Lord was keeping him busy. Besides his regular volunteer work at the orphanage in Casper, he planned to help build a church in Honduras in October. Then there was the soup kitchen that requested volunteers during the holidays.

The last thing Derek needed was a dating relationship. He knew that dating a girl took time and money. But it wouldn't hurt to go out on this impromptu date with Cheyenne.

Besides, it was her birthday.

✎

"Don't tell the waiter it's my birthday." Cheyenne whispered the words to Callie, using her tall menu to not only guide her words across the table but also keep Derek and Lane from hearing. "All the servers will sing to me."

"But they'll give you a free cake." Callie spoke so softly that Cheyenne had to read her lips.

Cheyenne lowered her own voice to almost nonexistent. "That's the problem. I'm trying to lose weight."

"You don't have to eat it." Callie motioned sideways with her head. "Give it to Derek."

"But if it gets too close to me, I won't be able to help myself."

Derek cleared his throat. "What are you girls whispering about?"

"Nothing." Cheyenne laid her menu on the table as she glanced at Derek sitting beside her. "I think I'll order the soup and salad." She took a sip of her water.

He looked back at his menu. "I'm getting the lasagna."

"Sounds good to me." Across the table, Lane closed his menu and looked at his wife. "What about you, Callie?"

She was hidden behind her menu. "I'm still deciding."

The waiter, a short man with a mop of black hair and a thick mustache, stopped at their table. "Are you ready to order this evening?" He had a charming Italian accent.

Derek motioned toward Cheyenne. "She'll have the soup and salad, and I'll take the lasagna."

"Very good." The waiter pulled a pad from his white apron pocket and wrote it down.

Cheyenne's heart swelled. Derek had ordered for her, like they were on a real date! She had been apprehensive about how he would react to this double date, but now she relaxed, leaning a little closer to him.

An hour later the waiter came to collect their dirty dishes. Cheyenne could have eaten more, but she wanted to leave hungry, hoping it would make her a pound or two lighter.

The waiter glanced around as he picked up the salad bowl. "Did you save room for dessert?"

Callie shook her head. "I'm too full."

"So am I," Cheyenne agreed, even though it wasn't quite true.

Like a common hitchhiker, Derek pointed his thumb at Cheyenne as he addressed the waiter. "It's her birthday today."

Cheyenne gasped. "Derek! You would have to bring that up!"

He grinned at her.

The waiter inclined his head toward her. "It will be our pleasure to sing to such a beautiful woman."

*What a flirt!* Cheyenne smiled at him. "Thanks."

In a few minutes, seven people surrounded their table, all dressed in white aprons. Instead of singing the traditional birthday song, they sang some other ditty, accompanied by hand clapping and feet stomping. When they finished, the waiter set a tiny cake in front of her, complete with piped frosting and a red rose in the center.

"Thank you." She smiled at the servers as they offered their congratulations before leaving.

Derek threw his arm around her shoulder and squeezed. "We got you good, Cheyenne."

She smiled back at him, his face only inches away. If only they were a bona fide couple! But in another second his arm lifted, and she felt the loss.

The waiter stood at the end of their table. "Would you like anything else for dessert?" His dark-brown eyes glanced between Lane and Derek.

Lane frowned. "Don't you have some type of cream puffs on the menu?"

"Ah yes, the cannoli." The waiter wrote it down and turned to Derek.

He shrugged. "I'll have the same."

When the waiter left, Cheyenne forced her fingers to slide the cake in front of Derek. "You can have this, too. I'm"—*on a diet*—"too full to eat it."

"Thanks." Derek picked up his extra fork then looked at Lane. "Want a bite?"

"Nah." Lane eyed the cake. "It's only big enough for one person."

"A single serving." Derek raised his eyebrows. "Just like my Sunday school class, the Single Servings. Too bad you two aren't in my class anymore. We miss you."

Callie looked at her husband with a sly smile. "I'd rather be married."

Lane waggled his eyebrows at her. "We're not single servings anymore, are we, Callie? We're double portions."

Derek laughed.

"I just realized. . ." Cheyenne looked at Derek. "Tonya and Murray won't be in the Single Servings anymore either. If your class members keep getting married, you soon won't have a singles class."

"I'll be there." He leaned toward her, a pleading expression in his dark-blue eyes. "Don't leave me, okay?"

Before she could reply, the waiter brought two plates of cannoli to the table.

Cheyenne glanced at Callie, who hid a smile behind her water glass. Cheyenne smiled back, a little thrill running through her.

Someday she and Derek would be double portions—and by the end of this year, if she had anything to say about it.

# Chapter 3

On Sunday morning, Cheyenne adjusted the waistband of her black skirt as she opened her bedroom door. Dad's collie ran down the short hallway of their one-floor home and jumped on her, his nails scratching against her favorite gray blouse with silver hearts. He barked out a greeting as his tail wagged.

"Marshal! Get down." Cheyenne brushed her hand across her skirt. "Oh great. Now I'll have dog hair on me when I go to church." Her fingers slid across something wet. "Yuck! Dog slobber is even worse."

The collie sat down and panted, his almond-shaped eyes gazing up at her.

Cheyenne's heart melted. "Okay, I forgive you—especially when you smile at me like that."

Marshal came from a litter of collies from the Rocking B Ranch. The Brandt family always used collies as their sheepdogs, and Jake and Yvette had given Marshal to Dad as a birthday gift three years ago. Patting the dog on his head, Cheyenne walked past him and entered the kitchen. Her dad sat at the table, reading the Sunday paper. She perused her father. Jim Wilkins was dressed for church in a dark-green shirt with the cuffs rolled back, exposing his meaty hands and thick wrists.

*Why did I have to inherit a Wilkins body?* All her dad's brothers and sisters had big bones. On the other hand, her mom, who had died from leukemia when Cheyenne was eight years old, had been of average height and weight.

Opening a cupboard, she pulled out a coffee mug. "Good morning, Dad."

Glancing up, his blue eyes met hers. He ran his hand over his full head of gray hair. "Morning, baby girl." His booming voice echoed in the small kitchen. "Sleep good?"

"I guess so." Cheyenne poured herself a cup of coffee. Dad had called her "baby girl" ever since she could remember.

Folding the paper, he laid it on the table and stood. A pink-flowered tie blossomed on his barrel-like chest. What decade had that tie come from? "Dad, why aren't you wearing the tie I picked out for you last night?"

Frowning, he lifted the end of the tie. "I like this one." He glanced at the clock on the stove. "I need to leave. I'm the greeter at church this morning."

She sighed. "Okay, Dad. I'll see you when I get there."

He pulled her into a quick bear hug before grabbing his keys. "See ya."

Dad was tall—six foot five. At least Cheyenne hadn't grown to *that* height.

It was bad enough being almost six feet tall. And she was thankful she hadn't inherited his loud voice.

As she sipped her coffee, she glanced out the kitchen window. Dad backed his Town Car out the short driveway and roared off down the street toward church. Cheyenne fingered the ruby necklace Dad had given her yesterday—the necklace that had belonged to her mom. A melancholy feeling swept over her. She missed her mom. Dad had been a widower now for twenty years.

In the quiet, she heard her cell phone ring. Taking a quick walk back to her bedroom, she pulled the phone from her purse and glanced at the number. Marshal padded to her side as she flipped it open. "Hi, Callie!"

"Cheyenne, I need your help." She sounded agitated.

"What's up, girlfriend?"

"Lane is really sick this morning."

Cheyenne raised her eyebrows. "He was okay last night at the restaurant."

"That's the problem. I talked to my dad this morning, and Derek is sick, too. It was those cannoli. They must have been spoiled."

"Oh no." Cheyenne sank down to her bed, and Marshal laid his head in her lap. She stroked his tan fur. "What can I do to help?"

"Lane could use some ginger ale, but your dad's store is closed today. Could you possibly go over and get me a can? I'll pay him tomorrow."

"Don't worry about paying. I'll get a two-liter bottle for you." Cheyenne stood and grabbed her purse. "In fact, I'll give one to your dad for Derek."

"That would be great. Thanks, Chey."

They said their good-byes, and Cheyenne locked up the house, leaving Marshal inside. She walked back to the detached one-car garage. Dad let her park in the garage since her car, an olive-green Dodge Dart, needed to be babied. It broke down at least once every six months, but she'd bought it sec-ondhand in high school and couldn't imagine getting rid of her classic antique.

After picking up two bottles of ginger ale at Wilkins Grocery and drop-ping off one at Callie's house, Cheyenne drove to the Brandt home and knocked on the back door.

Jake opened it. "Hi, Cheyenne." He adjusted his wire-rimmed glasses as he stepped back. "Come on in."

"Thanks." With a smile, she followed him through the mudroom. He was tall but not big like her dad, and he looked dignified in his Sunday suit.

Cheyenne stepped into the kitchen. "I got a call from Callie this morning. She said Lane and Derek are both sick." She held up the bottle of ginger ale. "I thought this might help Derek."

"Callie called me, too." Jake lifted a large black Bible from the kitchen table. "Derek wants me to teach his Sunday school class. Since Yvette's in Casper this week, I'm glad you came by." He took a set of keys from his pocket. "Would you mind staying? I really don't want to leave Derek alone all morning."

Cheyenne's lips parted before a thrill buzzed through her. "Sure! I'd love to stay and help Derek out if he needs anything."

"That's great!" Jake motioned toward the living room. "He's out there on the sofa. Don't know if he'll want any ginger ale, but you can ask." He walked to the door. "I appreciate it, Cheyenne. See you later." He entered the mudroom, closing the door firmly behind him.

She grinned, reveling in the turn of events. *Thank You, Lord!* Maybe God let Derek get sick so they could spend another day together. Perhaps she could meet the conditions of Grandmother's will sooner than she thought.

Opening the ginger ale bottle, she poured some into a glass and added ice from the freezer. Then she walked through the dining room and into the living room. Derek lay on the sofa, dressed in sweatpants and a blue T-shirt. Dark circles rested under his closed eyes, and his face looked pale—except for the dark stubble on his jaw.

"Derek?"

His eyes opened and focused on her face. Her heart fluttered.

"Oh, Cheyenne," he murmured. "Why are you over here?"

"Callie told me you were sick." She held up the glass. "I brought you some ginger ale."

He moaned. "No thanks." Closing his eyes, he tightened his arms around his stomach. "I'll be okay."

Cheyenne set the glass on the end table. "Your dad asked me to stay with you this morning. I hope you don't mind." She held her breath, hoping he wouldn't tell her to leave.

"Yeah, whatever." He shivered.

"Are you cold?" Leaning over him, she placed her palm on his forehead. His skin wasn't burning, but it was warm. "You might have a fever. I'll get you a blanket."

She ran upstairs to the second floor, knowing she'd find extra bedding stashed in the hall linen closet. Pulling out a soft yellow blanket, she headed back downstairs. She covered Derek with the blanket and tucked it around his shoulders.

"That's better," he murmured. "Thanks."

"Are you sure you don't want some ginger ale?"

He screwed up his face. "Won't be able to keep it down. I found out at breakfast this morning—must have thrown up the last three days' worth of food in ten minutes."

"Oh." His words made Cheyenne a bit queasy herself. "I'm sorry those cannoli were spoiled."

"Yeah. They tasted a little strange, so I only ate one." Derek closed his eyes. "Good thing."

"Why don't you rest, Derek? I'll be out in the kitchen if you need me."

"Okay, thanks." He closed his eyes, his dark eyelashes lowering on his pale cheeks.

Cheyenne gazed at his handsome face. The day's growth of beard made him look like a pirate. With a wistful sigh, she turned toward the kitchen.

∼

"Cheyenne?"

At Derek's voice, she jumped up from the kitchen table. She had spent the past hour looking through Yvette's cookbooks and had decided to test a soup recipe. Turning to the stove, she lowered the burner before walking into the living room. Derek still lay on the sofa, but the color had returned to his face. "Do you need something?"

"Since we're missing church today, I wondered if you could read some scripture to me."

"I'd love to, but I left my Bible in the car." She glanced around. "Where's yours, Derek?"

"Upstairs. Next to my bed."

Again she climbed the stairway to the second floor, puffing a little as she reached the top. *I'm going to get rid of these extra twenty pounds!*

She walked down the hallway, knowing exactly where Derek's room was. He used to share it with his older brother until Ryan got married and moved to Denver. Both single beds were neatly made with navy comforters. A brown leather Bible sat on the nightstand. She picked it up, then took a moment to breathe in his scent. This was Derek's domain—a masculine room with a braided gray rug on the polished wood floor and an oak dresser between the windows. She glanced outside, catching a glimpse of the backyard that ended at the white barn. Beyond that was nothing but open fields. In the distance, a flock of sheep dotted the hillside.

Walking downstairs, she mentally compared all the acreage the Brandt family owned with the small parcel of land her dad had in town. Hundreds of houses like theirs could fit on the Brandts' property. But if she inherited Grandmother's money, she would share it with Dad. He had always wanted to have a bigger house on a couple acres of land.

She pulled a dining room chair near the sofa, sat down, and opened the Bible. "What do you want me to read?"

Derek's eyes opened to slits. "Psalm 23. 'The Lord is my shepherd.' Isn't that what you read when someone is dying?"

Cheyenne raised her eyebrows. "You're not that bad, are you?"

He rewarded her with a lazy grin. "Just kidding."

With a smile, she shook her head. Leave it to Derek to tease her, even when he was sick. "So do you want me to read the twenty-third Psalm, or do you have something else in mind?"

"Read John chapter 10."

Cheyenne turned the thin pages to the New Testament. "This is a shepherd passage, too."

"Yeah, well, I'm a shepherd." He cracked another smile.

Cheyenne's heart swelled. She loved being with Derek, talking to him, getting teased by him. "You must be feeling better."

He nodded. "I feel a lot better than I did this morning."

"Good." Looking down, she began reading. When she finished, she and Derek discussed the chapter for a few minutes.

He motioned toward the Bible. "Read verse 10 again."

She found the place. " 'The thief cometh not, but for to steal, and to kill, and to destroy: I am come that they might have life, and that they might have it more abundantly.' "

He gave her a weak smile. "Love that verse—my favorite in the whole book." He stared at the ceiling. "The abundant life. That's a great concept— what Jesus wants to give Christians in this life, but so many want to go their own way."

"That's true." Cheyenne chewed on her lower lip. *He's so godly, Lord!*

"The Bible says if we abide in Christ and keep God's commandments, He'll bless us. He'll give us exceeding abundantly above all we can ask or think." He grinned. "That was your Sunday-morning sermon, Miss Wilkins, and I'm sure it blessed your heart beyond measure."

She laughed. "It certainly did."

"Kind of basic, actually." Derek sat up and sniffed. "What's that wonderful smell?"

"I made you some soup. It's simmering on the stove right now." She raised her eyebrows. "Are you ready to eat? It might make you feel better."

❧

Derek's stomach felt empty. "That would be great, Cheyenne." Throwing the blanket aside, he stood and wobbled a moment. He rubbed his chin, hoping she wouldn't notice how weak he was. "I should make a pit stop in the bathroom first. I probably look like three-day pond scum."

She laughed. "No you don't. You look. . .good."

"Only good?" He grinned at her.

"Well. . .I was going to say 'handsome,' but you always look handsome."

He folded his arms. "Are you trying to flirt with me?"

"Maybe." Giving him a wink, she turned toward the kitchen.

Derek watched her go. For the first time, he noticed that she was dressed for church, and her black skirt swished as she walked away. He'd always liked hanging around with Cheyenne, and he loved to tease her, but he had to be careful. There was a fine line between teasing and flirting, and she seemed to want to cross it. He couldn't do that. He had to remain single—single for the Lord's work. Wasn't that God's will for him?

When he emerged from the bathroom, the smell of the soup drew him into the kitchen. He took a seat at the table.

Cheyenne turned from the stove. "How do you feel—now that you're up?"

"Hungry." He smiled at her. "What's for lunch?"

"Chicken noodle soup." Picking up a large spoon, she stirred it around in a pan. "I found some carrots and celery in the fridge, a package of egg noodles, and some chicken in the freezer." She turned to him. "I hope your mom doesn't mind if I used the chicken. She might have been saving it for something."

"She won't care." Cheyenne was making homemade soup? For him? He would have just opened a can and heated it up. As Derek watched her ladle the soup into two bowls, it struck him that Cheyenne had a servant's heart. "Hey, um, thanks for coming over and taking care of me. I really appreciate it."

"It was your dad's idea, but I didn't mind helping out." Setting the bowls and two spoons on the table, she took a seat across from him. "I didn't have anything to do at church this morning besides warm the pew. Sometimes I work in the nursery, but I wasn't on the schedule today."

He cocked an eyebrow at her. "You ended up taking care of a big baby anyway."

She laughed, a musical sound he enjoyed hearing. "Oh Derek, you're not hard to care for at all." Folding her hands, she raised her eyebrows at him. "Would you ask the blessing?"

"Sure." He bowed his head. "Father in heaven, thank You for providing all our needs, especially for healing me. Thank You for this good soup Cheyenne made. Bless her for coming over to help me. In Jesus' name. Amen."

Cheyenne tucked a strand of blond hair behind her ear as she took a napkin from the holder on the table. Derek watched her. He had always liked that little trait she had—tucking her hair behind her ear. He lifted a spoonful of soup to his lips. The warm liquid felt good as he swallowed. "Hmm, this is great."

"Glad you like it." She took a sip.

"I hate missing church." Derek stirred his soup then lifted the spoon for another bite. "It doesn't seem like Sunday morning if I'm not teaching Sunday school."

"I'm sure your dad's doing a fine job." Cheyenne glanced at her watch. "Of course Sunday school's been over for an hour or so."

"True." Derek swallowed another spoonful before he spoke. "I hope Dad didn't forget to announce our bowling activity in two weeks, although he must not have had many students. Tonya and Murray are out of the picture now."

Cheyenne smiled, creasing her dimples. "And you and I weren't there either."

He rubbed the stubble on his chin. "Makes me wonder what people thought. They might start a rumor that we ran away together." As soon as the words left his mouth, Derek frowned. *Why did I say that?* He didn't want to give her any ideas.

But it was too late.

Cheyenne laughed. "Yeah! Let's run away! We'll give the ladies in this town some fuel for their gossip."

Derek didn't share her smile. "I was just kidding." He took another bite.

"I'm sorry." Cheyenne's smile lingered as she stirred her soup. "I guess we shouldn't give people things to gossip about. That's just wrong."

Despite his concern about her flirting, Derek grinned. Some girls were hard to talk to, but not Cheyenne.

Being with her was like putting on a pair of comfortable old shoes.

# Chapter 4

Almost two weeks later, Cheyenne drove up Highway 270 on her way back from Lusk. She had just finished her Thursday class, and tomorrow evening would be the last one. For the past week and a half, she had attended a class on the art of applying makeup, something she had always wanted to learn. Tomorrow evening was her test—applying makeup to another person's face.

The engine of her Dodge gave a sudden cough, and the front end rattled and shook violently.

"Oh no!" Cheyenne let up on the gas. With a wheeze, the engine died. Her shoulders slumped as she pulled over, letting the car roll to the side of the road. Getting out, she lifted the hood. Steam poured from the engine, and she jumped back.

"Oh great!" She really should invest in a new car, but her Dart was a familiar old friend. Emphasis on *old*.

Leaning against the side of the car, she folded her arms. The sun had already set over the Laramie Mountains, and her cell phone was useless out here in the boonies. The highway stretched out on either side of her, deserted, not a vehicle in sight.

Maybe Murray Twichell would drive by in his patrol car. This road was part of his section for the Wyoming Highway Patrol, and he and Tonya were back from their honeymoon in Hawaii. In fact Cheyenne had asked Tonya to come to her class tomorrow night for the makeup demonstration. The new bride had agreed to be her model, and Cheyenne couldn't have asked for a prettier face.

She glanced up and down the road again. Nothing. She looked up to the darkening sky. "Lord, help!"

Maybe she should try to start the car. The steam was gone, so perhaps the engine would start up. She got in and turned the key.

The engine started then sputtered and died.

Cheyenne dropped her head on the steering wheel. Would she be here all night? *Lord, please send someone!*

A few minutes later, she heard the hum of a vehicle approaching. *Praise God!* She jumped out of the car and waved her arms at the two headlights, hoping it wasn't a serial killer.

A red pickup truck slowed down, pulled behind her car, and stopped.

The headlights glared in her eyes as she ran back to the truck. Myriads of people in Wyoming drove pickup trucks. Hopefully this person lived in Fort Lob, someone she knew.

The driver's door opened, and Derek Brandt stepped down from the cab. Wearing a Western shirt, jeans, and a white cowboy hat, he looked like an authentic cowboy. "Hi, Cheyenne. Need help?"

Relief poured through her, and she hadn't realized until that moment how tense she was. "Oh Derek, am I glad to see you!" She laughed. If she had to be stranded, at least she was rescued by the most handsome man in the West. "My car died. Could you give me a lift into town?"

"Sure." He pulled a flashlight from under his front seat, then walked around to the front of her car. "What's wrong with it?" He leaned over to peer down, shining the light on different parts of the engine.

"A lot of steam poured out when I opened the hood." Standing beside him, a quiet peace filled her. *Thank You, Lord, for sending Derek!*

"Must be the radiator." He straightened and snapped off the light. "Guess you'll need to be towed."

"Could you tow my car, Derek?"

He tapped the flashlight in his palm. "I would, but I lent my chains to Miguel, one of our hired hands. Call Tom Shoemacher when you get home. He'll tow it to his garage." Derek walked back to his truck and motioned for her to follow. "Hop in."

Cheyenne grabbed her purse and notebook from her car, then got in on the passenger side of his pickup. "Thanks for the lift." She closed the door.

"Not a problem. Why were you way out here tonight?"

She settled on the seat as he pulled around her car and headed down the road. "I'm taking a class in Lusk."

Derek frowned. "What for?"

"Well. . ." How could she tell Derek she was trying to learn beauty tips to go along with her weight-loss program? "I'm learning the art of applying makeup." Stopping, she pressed her lips together. *I'm doing this for you, mister!*

His eyes roved her face before his gaze caught hers. For a brief moment, a sudden chemistry arced between them.

Clearing his throat, Derek looked back at the road. "Your makeup looks good enough to me."

"See? I'm doing it right."

He chuckled.

She sank back against the seat. *What did that look mean?* A touch of nerves hit her stomach. Here they were, alone in Derek's truck, but he didn't seem to want to deepen their friendship. A tiny sigh escaped her lips. "Tomorrow evening is my makeup test, and Tonya agreed to be my model, although she said she might be late."

"How are you gonna get there? I doubt if Tom will have your car fixed by tomorrow night."

"Oh." Cheyenne bit her lower lip. She hadn't thought of that. "Maybe I can borrow my dad's car if he doesn't mind being stranded at the store all evening."

"Hey, no worries. I'll drive you to Lusk."

Cheyenne raised her eyebrows. "But that's way out of your way."

"My schedule is flexible. Besides"—he grinned at her—"you went out of your way when I was sick last week, so it's the least I can do to pay you back."

"You don't have to pay me back, Derek, but I do need a ride." And it would be more time spent with him. She hadn't seen much of him lately. "Okay, I'll take you up on your offer."

He nodded. "What time should I pick you up tomorrow night? Six thirty?"

"Sounds good." In fact, the whole plan sounded better than good.

Now if only Tom Shoemacher would keep her car for a while!

⬲

On Friday evening, Derek sat on a folding chair beside Cheyenne at the Maximum Cut in Lusk. He watched a girl with a brown ponytail apply makeup to the pasty face of another girl, but she wasn't the only student taking the makeup test. All five beautician chairs in the room were occupied, with each student industriously applying makeup to her model.

The teacher, with fluffy brown hair piled on top of her head and shaved up the back, walked around and wrote notes about each girl's demonstration on a clipboard.

With a sigh, Derek folded his arms. Too bad he hadn't brought a book to read.

Sitting next to Cheyenne, he could almost feel the tension radiating from her. Tonya had not shown up yet. Cheyenne had tried to call her several times, but her cell phone wouldn't connect.

Leave it to Tonya to be late.

Cheyenne's phone chirped. "Finally!" She flipped it open. "Tonya, where are you?" She listened for a few minutes.

The girl with the ponytail finished her test, and she and the other girl took seats on the folding chairs. Derek had to admit, the model's pasty face had been transformed.

Closing her phone, Cheyenne turned to him. "Tonya can't come. Murray's mom had a setback at the nursing home, and they're on their way to Douglas right now."

Derek frowned. "That's not good."

"Yeah, I hope she's okay. But now I don't have a model."

The teacher turned toward her. "Cheyenne, are you ready? We have an empty chair."

Standing, Cheyenne twisted her hands. "I'm sorry, Mrs. Bartlett. My model won't be able to make it, so I guess I can't take the test." Her shoulders drooped.

Derek glanced around. In the quiet room, the other girls had all stopped their work to stare at Cheyenne with their painted eyes. Had he and Cheyenne driven all this way for nothing?

He stood. "I'll be your model."

Cheyenne's jaw dropped, and several of the students tittered.

He turned to the group. "Hey, I have a face, don't I?" He rubbed his chin. "I even shaved this morning."

His words caused more giggles, and the teacher smiled.

Cheyenne placed her hand on his arm. "You wouldn't mind, Derek?"

He shrugged. "Why not? Let's get this show on the road."

"Thanks." Her dimples creased as she smiled up at him.

He nodded, thinking once again how pretty she was, then took a seat in the chair. Cheyenne threw the cape around his shoulders and snapped it at the back of his neck.

She selected a small brown bottle from the counter under the mirror. "I have to test the foundation shade underneath your jawline first and blend it into your neck to see if it's the right color." Opening the bottle, she dumped some tan liquid on a wedge-shaped sponge.

Derek lifted his chin as she dabbed his neck.

"This color is perfect." Cheyenne dabbed some more on the sponge. "Now I'll apply it evenly to your face. I have to blend it carefully so there's no smudge line." Her voice dropped to a whisper. "That's the hard part."

He tried to relax, closing his eyes as she swabbed his face with even strokes. He was only doing this for her. But one thought kept running through his mind.

*I'm going to look like a girl.*

⌒⌒

Cheyenne stepped back. "That's the last step, and your makeup is complete." She smiled at Derek, who now looked more beautiful than handsome with his outlined, dark-lashed eyes and pink cheeks.

A smattering of applause echoed through the room from the other girls. They had finished their tests, and for the past five minutes they surrounded Cheyenne. It was a little nerve-racking, but Cheyenne had a feeling they wanted to see what this hot guy looked like in makeup.

Derek glanced back at the mirror and then pinned Cheyenne with his gaze. "Now we need a demonstration of how to take makeup off."

Everyone laughed, and Mrs. Bartlett nodded. "That's a good idea, Cheyenne. I'll give you a bonus point for showing us how to remove it."

"Okay." She smiled as she picked up the bottle of oil-free makeup remover from the counter. "First I'll remove your eye makeup."

"Amen to that," Derek muttered as he closed his eyes.

Cheyenne applied the remover carefully, not wanting to get any in his eyes. She'd be forever grateful to Derek for volunteering to be her model. But the bonus for her was being able to touch every millimeter of his face—smoothing foundation over his skin, outlining his dark eyes, gazing at his handsome features.

She was going to keep working and praying to win his hand—by the end of this year.

~

"I appreciate the ride." Cheyenne touched the passenger door handle of Derek's truck as it idled in her driveway. She wished she could sit here and talk with him awhile, but it was getting late, and he always got up early to care for the animals at the ranch. "Thanks for being my model tonight. You really went the second mile—literally on the road as well as for my makeup test." She laughed at her own joke.

He grinned. "Glad to do it. We make a good team."

"Yes, we do." Smiling, she pulled the handle. The door popped open, and the truck's inside light came on.

"Hey, if you need a ride to the bowling activity on Tuesday night, let me know."

"Okay, thanks." She looked back at him then frowned. "You still have a spot of mascara under your eye."

"I do?" He studied his reflection in the rearview mirror. "Yeah, so I do."

Cheyenne rummaged in her purse. "Let me clean that off." She pulled out a tissue.

Derek threw his arm across the back of the bench seat and leaned toward her.

She dabbed the tissue under his eye, feeling his gaze on her. Their faces were so close—a little tingle went up her spine at his nearness. She wiped the tissue under his lashes one last time, wishing she could stay a few more minutes, but her job was done. "There, that's better." She looked into his eyes.

His gaze held hers. "Much better." His eyes dipped down to her lips.

Cheyenne caught a quick breath. He was going to kiss her!

But Derek suddenly cleared his throat and sat back. "Thanks." Placing a fist against his mouth, he coughed. "Uh, guess I'll see you Sunday at church."

"Yeah." She fumbled to push the door open. "See you later." Jumping out of the pickup, she closed the door.

He backed out of the driveway then took off down the road. An aura of sadness enveloped her like a shroud. *He almost kissed me!* But something stopped him.

What was it?

*Whew! That was close.*

Derek hit the steering wheel with his fist as he drove out of town. If Cheyenne hadn't given that little gasp, he would have pulled her in his arms and kissed her. Whatever had possessed him? He knew God's will. *Single for the Lord.*

He huffed out a breath. He would not mess up again.

But he had already offered Cheyenne a ride on Tuesday night to the bowling alley, so he'd have to give her a lift if her car was still in the shop.

He thought back to those few moments in the truck as she wiped the tissue under his eye. She was so close he could actually feel her softness. And some type of awareness crackled between them. But why had he suddenly turned into a love-struck teenager?

*Crazy.*

With a shake of his head, he stepped on the gas and roared down the road. He had to make sure that didn't happen again.

# Chapter 5

O
n Tuesday afternoon, the bell over the door to the Fort Lob Post Office signaled a customer.

Cheyenne put down the mail she was sorting and walked out from the back room to stand behind the counter. "May I help you?"

A tall, thin cowboy removed his black hat, revealing a thatch of brown hair. His tanned face had a weathered look. "Hello there, ma'am. I'd like to secure a post office box."

"Okay." Cheyenne pulled a form from under the counter. "Just fill this out." With a smile, she handed it to him.

He pulled a pen from his inside jacket pocket and leaned over the counter to fill in the boxes.

She waited a few minutes, watching his large, tanned hands. Those hands were definitely used to work. "You must be new in town."

"Yep." He had a deep voice. "Just bought the ranch that was for sale on Antelope Road."

"Oh—the old Dudley place." Cheyenne's memory conjured up images of the elderly couple who had died. Their children had been trying to sell the ranch for years. "That ranch is next to the Rocking B, owned by Jake Brandt. Have you met the Brandts yet?"

"Nope." Leaning over the counter, he glanced up at her with his brown eyes. "I haven't met a single soul in Fort Lob. Even the Realtor was from out of town."

Cheyenne grinned. "Well, you've met me." She held out her right hand. "I'm Cheyenne Wilkins. Welcome to Fort Lob."

He straightened and shook her hand. "Glad to meet you, Mrs. Wilkins."

"It's *Miss*, but please call me Cheyenne. Everyone does."

A slow smile spread across his face, crinkling the corners of his eyes. "Cheyenne. A pretty name for a pretty lady."

Her heart skipped a beat. "Thank you." She looked down, rather embarrassed to be called a "pretty lady." But she couldn't help noticing how his smile transformed his features. He looked around forty years old and his skin looked like tanned leather, but that smile made him handsome.

He pushed the form toward her. "Rex Pierson. Moving from Montana, and I'm gonna pepper my new ranch with beef cattle and buffalo."

Cheyenne glanced up. "So you're raising them for meat?"

271

"Yes, ma'am. I mean, *Cheyenne.*" Rex grinned.

She smiled back then looked down at the form. "Would you rather pay for your post office box for six months or for a year?"

They transacted business, and Cheyenne showed Rex where his box was located along the wall. When they were finished, he thanked her and turned toward the door. She walked back to the counter.

"By the way. . ." Rex stopped. "Is there a good restaurant in town where I could have supper?"

"We have two good restaurants." She joined him at the glass door and pointed outside. "The Cattlemen's Diner is located across the street. That would be my first choice for supper." She pointed to the left down the road. "Then there's the Trailblazer Café. That's a good choice for breakfast or lunch."

With a nod, he squinted as he looked out the door. "Another thing I'm looking for is a good church." His brown eyes turned to her. "Any around here? I'm looking for one that has a Bible study or prayer service on Wednesday night."

Cheyenne's lips parted. "You must be a Christian!"

"Yep." His smile deepened the wrinkle lines on his face. "Blood-washed, bought, and on my way to heaven."

*Wow.* "That's great! My church has a prayer service on Wednesday, and services on Sunday, too."

"Where's it located?"

She gave him directions, pointing out the door.

"Thank you, Cheyenne. You've been most helpful." He donned his cowboy hat.

She watched him amble across the street and enter the diner. Her heart warmed at the thought of meeting another Christian, one who wasn't afraid to share his testimony. Then she thought of what he had called her. *Pretty lady.* With a smile, she shook her head. Her thoughts wandered to Grandmother's will and Derek Brandt. Did he think she was a pretty lady?

All weekend she had ruminated on that intimate moment with him in his truck.

The near kiss that turned into a near miss.

She didn't tell anyone what happened, not even Callie. Now if Derek had actually kissed her, Callie would have been the first person to find out.

*What went wrong?*

A definite chemistry had hung between them in that moment, and he must have felt it, too. Why had he suddenly gotten cold feet?

She would probably never know.

⌒≈⌒

That evening Cheyenne leaned over to tie her bowling shoes, then cuffed the bottom edges of her jeans and flattened them out. The noise of conversation and laughter, along with the clatter of bowling pins, surrounded her. Only seven members of the Single Servings showed up for the bowling activity, and they claimed two lanes. Cheyenne was on a lane with Matthew Werth and Derek.

Sitting up, she glanced around the bowling alley. In the next lane, Corey Henning already stood behind the line and released his ball down the lane with a tight spin. The pins crashed in a strike. With a whoop, Corey turned toward the three people sitting behind him—Laurie Smullens, whom he was dating, Reed Dickens, and Horace Frankenberg.

Derek sat to Cheyenne's left in a plastic chair, tying his shoes. He stood. "Now to find a good ball. It's times like this when I wish I owned one." He grinned at Matthew who stood by the ball return.

"Yep." Matthew pulled a red bowling ball from his bag. He held up his gloved hand. "I'm trying this Super-Flex 3000 wrist support glove. I'm hoping it will add a few points to my game." He bent over the hand dryer.

Cheyenne rolled her eyes as she stood. "I'll go with you, Derek." Since her car was still at Tom's shop, Derek had driven her to the bowling alley and acted as if nothing had happened between them on Friday. But she wanted something to happen. Tonight.

*I'll stick to him like gum on his shoe!*

The conditions of Grandmother's will lingered. She needed to make every day count.

Behind him, she ascended the three steps from their lane. "I didn't even know they made bowling gloves."

Derek turned. "Of course they do. That's why the two middle fingers are missing." He walked beside her to the ball rack. "What kind of ball do you want?"

"I need a light ball, but I can never find one that fits."

He hefted a blue ball then put it down. "Are you a good bowler, Cheyenne?"

"No!" She laughed. "My highest score of all time is 83. I'll be lucky if I can stay out of the gutter."

He grinned. "Just so your life doesn't end up in the gutter."

"Oh thanks a lot." She smiled, loving it when he teased her.

Derek hefted a yellow ball then handed it to her. "Try this one—it's light."

Cheyenne glanced at the tiny finger holes and shook her head. "My fingers will get stuck." She sighed as she set the ball down. "That's my problem. The bigger the finger holes, the heavier the ball. I suppose the reasoning is that a bowler with big fingers must be strong." *And how am I supposed to lose weight in my fingers?*

Derek twisted a purple ball on the rack so the holes were on top. "Here. Try this one."

As she took it, the door to the bowling alley opened. Bruce MacKinnon and Aggie Collingsworth walked in.

*It must be true that opposites attract.* Cheyenne hid a smile as the pair walked toward them. Bruce, a dignified Scotsman whose speech still held a slight brogue, was dating Aggie, an overweight down-home gal from Texas, complete with southern accent.

A short young woman walked beside Bruce. A pair of jeans clung to her thin hips, and long red hair flowed over the shoulders of her jade T-shirt. With bright eyes and a pretty smile, she was cute.

*And tiny.*

That girl would never get *her* fingers stuck in a bowling ball.

Aggie nodded at Derek and Cheyenne. "Howdy, y'all. Having fun at this bowling shindig?"

Cheyenne smiled. "Hi! Are you guys joining us tonight?" Aggie was in their Sunday school class, but Bruce taught an adult class, and the girl looked like she might be in high school.

Bruce motioned to the women beside him. "Agatha wants to go shopping in Lusk, but my granddaughter, Kandi, would like to join you in the activity." He looked at Derek. "Is that all right?"

Derek shrugged. "Sure. The more the merrier." He extended his hand toward the girl. "Derek Brandt. Glad to meet you."

She shook his hand. "I'm Kandi MacKinnon."

Since Cheyenne held a bowling ball, she just nodded at the girl. "I'm Cheyenne. Welcome to the party."

Kandi had obviously mastered beauty secrets. The makeup on her smooth face was perfect, with the green eye shadow bringing out the green in her eyes. Her eyelashes were thick.

Bruce smiled at his granddaughter. "Kandi attends a Christian college in California, but she's staying with me this summer. She'll be in your Sunday school class, Derek."

"That's great." Smiling, he took a step toward her. "What year in college?"

She looked up at him, returning his smile. "I'll be a sophomore in the fall."

Derek thumbed back at their lane. "You can bowl with me. There's only three on our lane."

"Thanks."

Cheyenne cocked an eyebrow. Derek seemed entirely too interested in Kandi MacKinnon. The girl couldn't be more than five foot three—a whole foot shorter than Derek—but she gazed up at him with a dazzling smile as they walked back to the lane. Bruce and Aggie departed, which left Cheyenne standing alone by the ball rack.

Derek was just being friendly. Yeah, that was it. After all, he was the teacher of the Single Servings. He had to be friendly.

*As long as he's not too friendly.*

Derek relaxed in the plastic chair as he watched Kandi release her ball into the lane. She was so pretty! And he couldn't believe how athletic she was, with perfect bowling form. Already, on the seventh frame, her score was 149. Derek only had 116, and Cheyenne trailed behind with a mere 52 points. Of course Matthew, the pro, had a leading score of 218.

Kandi waited as her ball quickly spun down the lane. Upon impact, all the pins succumbed with a crash, and she whirled around, raising both hands in the air. "Strike!"

Derek grinned. "Great job!" He glanced at her lithe figure as she walked toward him. *She's so small!* He loved her red hair, and he'd already christened her *the little red-haired girl*, like Charlie Brown's girlfriend in *Peanuts*.

He wanted to get to know Kandi MacKinnon.

For a moment his conscience struck him. What about remaining single to serve the Lord? But was that what the Lord really wanted him to do?

"I thought that was going to be a split." She took the seat beside him.

He grinned. "You're a good bowler, Kandi."

She returned a shy smile. "Thanks."

He gazed at her pretty green eyes, her soft red hair. *She's so pretty.* Maybe he should ask her out.

On the way home from the bowling alley, Cheyenne stared out the passenger window of Derek's pickup, even though it was pitch-black, and tried to tune out Derek's voice. *Please give me patience, Lord!*

This night had not turned out as she had hoped.

When Bruce and Aggie came by to pick up Kandi at the beginning of their third game, Derek volunteered to take her home—which meant, of course, that Cheyenne had to ride with them. Now they bumped along in his truck, with Kandi in the middle of the cab sandwiched between Cheyenne and Derek. The girl didn't say much, but she sure smiled a lot, mainly at Derek who had never talked so much in his life. All Cheyenne could do was sit there and grit her teeth.

He pulled into her driveway. "Here you are, Cheyenne."

Of course he would drop her off first.

She opened the passenger door, and the inside light popped on. *Déjà vu.* Was Derek thinking about what happened between them last Friday night? She climbed out. "Thanks for the ride."

"Anytime, Cheyenne."

She looked back as she closed the door. Kandi, who had barely moved two inches away from him, smiled at her.

Cheyenne trudged to the house, not looking back as the truck pulled out and roared down the street. With a sigh, she crossed the porch to the front door, which was illuminated by the porch light.

Stopping at the door, she bowed her head until it touched the wood. For ten years she had thought she would someday marry Derek Brandt. He was perfect for her—calm in every situation where she was emotional, staying in the background when she liked to be out front.

*Well, he's not the only man in the world.* Perhaps God had someone else in mind—someone who would be even more perfect. Someone who would complete her.

"Lord," she whispered. "Please show me who that someone is. Show me Your will."

She took a deep breath. God already had her future all worked out. But would it happen in time? Would she be able to fulfill the conditions of Grandmother's will?

She walked to the edge of the porch and looked up at the shiny white moon high above. "All I need is a man, Lord!"

❧

On Wednesday afternoon, Cheyenne walked from the garage to the house, glad her Dart was back from Tom's shop and thankful she didn't have to depend on Derek Brandt to cart her around. Now to get out of her postal uniform and eat something before the prayer service at church. Dad wouldn't be home until after eight o'clock when he closed the store for the evening.

Entering the house, she pushed the back door shut. Marshal greeted her with a bark.

"Hey, Marsh!" She patted the collie's tan head then bent down and let him lick her face. She relished his affectionate greeting. "Okay, Marshal. That's good." She laughed. "I guess you missed me today, huh?"

He answered her question with another bark then turned in a circle and sat down by the back door.

Cheyenne placed her hands on her hips. "Sorry, I'm not taking you for a walk. That's Dad's job. I'm planning to eat something and go to church."

Dad always took Marshal out around ten o'clock at night, and Cheyenne was glad she didn't have to walk the dog. She hated exercise in any form, even walking.

She strolled back to her bedroom and stopped in the doorway. *What a mess!*

A corner of her tiger poster, which had been hanging between the windows since high school, peeled away from the wall. Piles of clothes littered the chair, and her bed had not been made since she changed the sheets three days ago.

With a sigh, she walked inside, mentally comparing this room to Derek's. *Why can't I keep my room neat?*

She plucked her jeans from the pile on the chair. They were still cuffed from bowling last night. With a sigh, she sat down on her bed, reliving those memories. If only Kandi MacKinnon hadn't shown up! She was such a good bowler.

*And my bowling was awful!*

But what really bothered Cheyenne was Derek's reaction to Kandi. He seemed more infatuated with her as the evening wore on. "Well!" Cheyenne shook her jeans at Marshal, who had padded into the bedroom. "I don't need him! I'm going to lose weight, and just maybe I'll find another man."

*Yeah right.* Her shoulders slumped. Maybe God did have another man for her, but Derek had always been her number-one candidate for marriage. After all these years, it was depressing that another girl had caught his attention. And a tiny, cute girl at that.

Marsh sat down and thumped his tail against the floor. His almond-shaped eyes gazed at her as his tongue hung out in a pant.

Grabbing a women's magazine from her nightstand, Cheyenne leaned back against the pillows. She glanced at the thin model on the cover and read the titles of the articles listed there. Her eyes stopped at one. "Walking Off the Pounds."

Biting her lower lip, she glanced at Marshal. What better way to lose weight than to take the dog for a walk every day?

With a sigh, she looked at the clock on the dresser. It was only 5:22.

She had plenty of time.

# Chapter 6

After the waiter took their order, Derek gazed across the table at Kandi MacKinnon. The elegant Four Seasons restaurant in Cheyenne, Wyoming, was bustling with customers on this Friday evening, but he only saw her. They sat at a small table for two at the back of the dining room, and Derek couldn't have asked for a more perfect spot.

He raised his eyebrows. "All you ordered was a salad? You're not watching your weight, are you?" He winked, letting her know he was kidding.

"No." Her face tinged pink, adding to the blush that blended in perfectly with her foundation. Thanks to Cheyenne, Derek knew all about makeup.

She shrugged. "I guess I'm not that hungry."

*Is she nervous?* Derek had to admit he was nervous himself. This was only the second time in his life he had purposely asked a girl on a date because he wanted to. The moment he saw Kandi in church Wednesday night, he asked if she would go to dinner with him on Friday.

Tonight she had dressed up in a green sleeveless dress, and her freckled arms looked athletic with firm muscles. It was amazing how attracted he was to *the little red-haired girl.* Maybe Mom was right—he should get married.

That thought *really* made him nervous.

He glanced around at the other patrons of the Four Seasons, other couples at other tables having intimate conversations. Looking back at Kandi, he gazed at her pretty green eyes. "So. . .you have three more years in college. What are you majoring in, Kandi?"

"English literature." She smoothed the napkin lying beside her plate.

"So. . .English." He cleared his throat. Why did he keep saying *so*? "What are you going to do when you graduate?"

"I might go on for my master's degree."

"You're not going to become one of those professional students, are you?" He grinned.

That pink hue crept to her face once more, and she shook her head. "No." Her fingers started picking at the edge of the napkin.

Derek drew in a silent sigh, wishing Kandi would expand her short English sentences. On the way to the restaurant, he had done most of the talking, telling her about his degree in range management from the University of Montana and about his family. She just listened. How could he get to know her if she didn't talk?

"My sister, Callie, majored in English. She worked as a librarian until she got married. Now she and her husband are building a museum for our town."

"Oh."

"Would you be interested in becoming a librarian someday?"

"I don't know." She looked down at the tablecloth. "I might."

Taking a deep breath, he tried again. "Tell me about your family, Kandi." He sat back. *I've got you there!* She couldn't tell him about her family in a three-word sentence.

"I have a mom and dad, a sister, and a brother." She leaned forward. "We've lived in Salt Lake City since I was four years old. My dad was transferred there."

"I see." He nodded, hoping it would encourage her to keep talking. "What does your dad do?"

As she answered, Derek felt like he was playing Twenty Questions. Was Kandi always this quiet? Maybe she was shy.

Cheyenne's face popped into his mind. Now there was a girl who could talk! For a moment, he wished she was the one sitting across from him. But why was he even attempting to date a pretty girl? Didn't the Lord want him to remain single in order to serve Him?

No wonder this date with Kandi was going nowhere.

≈

Cheyenne tried to control her breathing as she opened the back door. "Okay, Marshal, that was our exercise for tonight." She was panting more than he was.

The collie waited while she unhooked his leash. Then he lay down on his doggy bed by the back door.

"My sentiments exactly, Marsh." Heaving out a breath, she walked into her bedroom and threw herself across the bed, facedown. *I must have lost fifty pounds!*

She'd been walking Marshal every evening for three days, and she'd eaten nothing but fruit and salads, plus some egg whites for protein. So far, according to the bathroom scale, she had lost exactly two pounds. Two pounds! So on her "walk" with Marshal tonight, she started jogging.

*Mistake!*

She was still trying to catch her breath when her cell phone rang.

With a groan, she sat up and swiped her phone off the dresser. She glanced at the caller's number before flipping it open. "Hi, Callie." She sighed. "What's up?"

"Hi! You sound kind of down."

Cheyenne flopped to her back. "I just got back from jogging with Marshal."

"Jogging? You?" The sound of a chuckle escaped over the phone.

"It's not funny! Marshal and I are trying to lose weight, you know."

"Hmm. . .I didn't realize he was overweight."

"He's not." Cheyenne sighed. "But you know what? I've lost two pounds in the last three days."

"That's great! I'm proud of you, Chey. Keep up the exercise with Marshal, and someday you'll be thinner than Tonya."

"Oh sure." Cheyenne laughed. "What can I do for you, girlfriend?"

Callie paused. "I hate to give you bad news when you're tired, but I thought you should know about this."

"Bad news?" Cheyenne sat up. "What happened? Did someone die? It's not Murray's mother, is it?"

"No, nothing like that. In fact, his mom is doing a lot better."

"Oh, that's good." Cheyenne breathed out. "So what's the bad news?"

"It's about Derek. I was talking to Mom on the phone just now, and she told me Derek took Kandi MacKinnon to the Four Seasons tonight."

"What!" Cheyenne jumped to her feet. "He asked her out? You've got to be kidding!"

"Would I joke about a thing like that?" Callie paused. "Derek is finally dating someone of his own volition, and to be honest, I'm brokenhearted. I had high hopes for you and him."

With a moan, Cheyenne sank down to the bed. "I've lost Derek for sure. How can I compete with that teeny-weeny girl who has zero fat on her teeny-weeny body?"

"Chey. . ."

"It's true! There is no way I can compete with her." Cheyenne walked to the full-length mirror. Looking at her almost-six-foot pudgy self decked out in sweats, she grimaced. "If I ever succeed in getting married, it will be to a man whose sole passion is to fall in love with a big, fat woman."

"Chey, Derek likes you. He's comfortable around you."

"But not in love." She dropped down to her bed. "I'm thinking of doing something different, Callie. Something radical."

"Oh?"

"Yep. I'm moving to Colorado."

"What? You can't move! You've been my best friend since first grade."

"Life changes, Callie. I'm thinking about Loveland." She smiled. "Isn't that a great name? That's where I'll find the love of my life." She lifted up a quick prayer, asking God to make it so.

"But that's so far away."

"Not that far, Callie. I already put in for a transfer at the post office, but I'm also looking at other jobs."

"You're really serious, aren't you?"

Cheyenne ignored the question. "Remember that makeup class I took a couple weeks ago? I'm applying for a job at Hallie's Beauty Supply Shoppe in Loveland. It's a new store, and their grand opening is next month." Her heart leaped. "Can you imagine? I took that class just for myself, but the Lord knew that certificate would help me get this job. It looks like He's working everything out for good."

"Please don't move, Cheyenne." Callie's voice had a whine tucked inside it. "Don't give up on Derek yet. You two would make such a great couple. You're perfect for each other in every way. And besides, I've always wanted you to be my sister-in-law."

A tiny flicker ignited in Cheyenne's heart, but she snuffed it out. Why should she hold out for Derek Brandt? "It's no use, Callie. I'm just one of Derek's many friends—no one special."

"That's not true. You two are the best of friends."

"Give it up, Callie. Derek has his eyes on Kandi, and the Lord has some-one else in mind for me. At least, I hope so." *And I need to meet him soon!*

If only she could tell Callie about Grandmother's will.

"Well. . .okay. But I'm going to keep praying about you and Derek." Callie paused. "Remember how you encouraged me last summer when I was ready to give up on Lane?"

Cheyenne thought back. "You said you didn't have peace about dating him."

"I didn't! But you thought we were perfect for each other, and you told me to trust the Lord to work things out. And He did!"

A lone tear rolled down Cheyenne's cheek, but she brushed it away.

"The Lord can do the same for you and Derek." The sound of static filled the phone. "I have to go, Chey. Talk to you later."

"Bye, Callie."

Dropping her phone in her purse, Cheyenne closed her eyes. She *was* excited about moving, but if Derek gave any indication that he wanted to marry her, she would rather stay in Fort Lob. Her shoulders slumped as all the air escaped from her lungs. She couldn't believe Derek had asked Kandi out.

So much for trying to win his hand.

~~~

The stars shone in the dark sky as Derek drove his pickup to the front of Bruce MacKinnon's house. He stopped beside the front porch, where the porch light cast a warm glow. "Here we are."

Kandi touched the handle of the passenger door. "Thanks, Derek."

"Let me get that for you." He walked around the front of the truck and opened her door then grabbed her elbow to help her down.

The front door of the house opened, and Bruce stuck his head outside. "I wondered when you two would get home. I'm glad it's not too late."

Derek grinned at him. "I brought her right home, Bruce."

"That you did." He opened the screen door wider as Kandi ascended the porch steps. "Why don't you come in and set a spell, as Agatha would say."

"Okay." Derek climbed the porch steps and walked into the house, where the air-conditioning made a noticeable difference. He didn't want to "set a spell." Kandi had barely said two complete sentences on the hour-long drive home from the big city, so he had talked for both of them.

It was exhausting.

Bruce motioned toward the blue and white plaid sofa where his grand-daughter was sitting in the middle. "Have a seat. Can I get you something to drink?"

"No thanks." Derek eased down next to Kandi and sank into the comfort-able cushions. He hadn't been to Bruce MacKinnon's house for years. A blue braided rug partially covered the polished wooden floor, and several light-houses decorated the fireplace mantelpiece.

Bruce faced them as he took a seat in a wooden rocking chair. "It certainly was warm out today."

Derek nodded. "It hit 101 degrees this afternoon. Hope it cools off, espe-cially during the last week of July. Dad and I plan to be in Cheyenne for the rodeo."

"Ah! You must be referring to Cheyenne Frontier Days."

"Yep." Derek grinned. "Time for cowboys to get down and dirty."

"Cowboys?" Beside him, Kandi perked up. "What rodeo is this?"

He glanced at her. "Cowboys call it 'The Daddy of 'Em All.' It's been held every July since 1897. They do cattle roping, barrel racing, and bull riding, among other things. They even have pancake breakfasts and parades. It's a huge event, lasting ten or twelve days."

"Wow." Her pretty eyes stared into his. "Are you doing any cattle roping?"

"No." He grinned. "I'm a sheep rancher, not a cowboy."

Bruce leaned back in his rocker. "How many days are you going, Derek?"

"Dad and I go every day except Sunday. We love watching the cowboy contests. My mom and sisters only attend one day. They like to see what people are wearing." Derek laughed. "You can tell a city slicker in cowboy getup a mile away."

"Aye." Bruce chuckled. "That's one reason I don't go. I feel out of my element."

Derek raised his eyebrows. "You're not going this year?"

Bruce shook his head. "I never do. Once, about fifteen years ago, I attended the rodeo. That was enough for me."

Kandi folded her arms. "Well you'll have to go this year, Grandpa. I want to see it, especially the cowboys roping cattle. I'd really like to see a parade, too. Sounds awesome." She smiled at Derek.

*That's the most I heard her talk all night!* "The parades are held three or four days in downtown Cheyenne."

"Do they have floats?"

"Yep. Floats, marching bands, antique cars. It's great, especially if the weather is good."

"And what about the pancake breakfast?"

"They have three free breakfasts on Monday, Wednesday, and Friday during the last week."

"Awesome." She turned to her grandfather. "You have to take me one of those days, Grandpa."

Bruce stopped rocking. "Sorry to disappoint, dear girl, but I can't stand out in the hot sun all day. Your grandfather is too old for that kind of thing."

"You can go with our family, Kandi." Derek hastened to emphasize the others. "My mom and sisters hang out together, and they would love to show you around." Looking at Bruce, he frowned as a thought popped into his head. "I assume Callie and Tonya will go with us. This is the first summer that both of them are married."

Bruce nodded. "They'll drag their men with them, I'm sure, although Murray was on patrol duty last July. He might be on duty again this year."

Derek rubbed his chin. "Yeah, I remember seeing Twitch in his uniform."

"Twitch?" Kandi raised her eyebrows.

"My brother-in-law, Murray Twichell."

"That's his name?" She shook her head. "Poor guy."

Derek frowned. "I never thought a thing about Murray's name. I've known the Twichells since I was born."

"Aye, a name becomes familiar." Bruce looked at his granddaughter. "Of course, not everyone has a great last name like MacKinnon."

"It's the best!" Kandi laughed. "I'm proud to have Scottish blood running through my veins."

Derek glanced at her, thankful she was finally contributing to the conversation. Perhaps shyness had been the culprit on their date. But it didn't matter. He should have listened to his conscience in the first place.

*Dating and I just don't get along.*

# Chapter 7

At nine forty-five on Monday night, Cheyenne glanced up from the book she was reading as Dad's voice filled the house.

"Come on, Marshal. Time for our walk, boy."

Marshal barked several times by the back door.

"Cheyenne!" Dad bellowed. "Marsh and I are leaving!"

"Okay, Dad." She had read the same paragraph three times and still didn't know what it said.

She waited to hear the back door open, but it didn't happen. Instead Dad walked to the living room, leading Marsh. "Hey, do you want to go with us?"

She raised her eyebrows. "On the walk?"

"Yeah. It's a beautiful evening. You could get some exercise."

With a sigh, she laid aside her book. Even her dad was telling her she needed to lose weight. "Sure, I'll go with you."

"We can talk. Seems like I never see you anymore, baby girl."

They left the house, and Cheyenne fell into step beside him on the smooth sidewalk. For a big man, he walked fast. Marshal trotted at his side with the leash limp in Dad's hand.

Cheyenne breathed in the warm night air. Every minute or so, they passed under a street lamp, the light spreading a yellow circle around them before they entered the darkness again. A thin sliver of moon peeked through the trees.

"Where are we going?" *I can't believe I'm not winded yet.* Maybe she was in better shape than she thought.

"I always go to the park." Dad looked down at the dog. "It's peaceful at this time of night, and Marshal enjoys the scenery."

She grinned. "Marsh would enjoy the slums of Calcutta."

They turned right on Pronghorn Avenue and passed the Elks Lodge, which was dark. Soon the houses ended, and a glow of lights signaled the park's entrance. Inside, a maze of sidewalks skirted around trees, benches, and light posts. Several other people strolled the sidewalks, and they greeted them as they passed.

"You're right, Dad. This is peaceful." Cheyenne took in a deep breath. "I should do more walking at night."

"Not without Marshal or me." Dad cocked an eyebrow at her. "A young woman shouldn't be out by herself, even in a safe town like Fort Lob."

"I'll remember that, Dad, especially when I move."

He grabbed her arm, forcing her to stop and face him. "You're moving, baby girl?"

*Oops!* How had she let that slip? She looked up into his blue eyes, knowing she had to tell him eventually. "I guess I didn't tell you my plans."

"No."

"I need a change in my life, Dad." She began walking at a more leisurely pace. "I'm thinking of moving out of the house."

Dad strolled beside her. "It's about time you became independent. I suppose you want to buy your own place in Fort Lob."

They passed a park bench illuminated by a lamppost. "Not in Fort Lob. I'd like to move to Loveland."

"In Colorado?" He stopped again, and his voice echoed through the park. "That's crazy!"

"Dad!" Holding up her hands, Cheyenne almost whispered. "Keep your voice down."

"I am keeping my voice down," he said, just as loud as before. "Why do you want to move to Colorado?"

She sighed. "I feel stuck, Dad. Maybe if I settle somewhere different, I can meet a new guy."

Rex Pierson's handsome face popped into her mind. He came to the post office every day to check his box, and he always greeted her. Sometimes they talked for ten or fifteen minutes before he left, and she enjoyed the conversation. But he was just being friendly.

*Besides, he's too old for me.*

Dad pursed his lips, then turned and strode down the sidewalk with Marsh trotting beside him. Cheyenne caught up, knowing better than to interrupt Dad's thoughts. She prayed he wasn't offended that she wanted to leave but would instead give his blessing.

After circling the park and coming back to the same spot, Dad motioned to the bench under the lamppost. "Let's sit down."

They settled on the bench with Marshal sitting at their feet. He panted as he surveyed the area, and Cheyenne reached down to fondle his ear. *No worries for you, Marsh.*

Dad placed his hefty arm on the back of the bench behind her. "I assume you've prayed about this?"

She nodded. "I already applied for a couple jobs in Loveland, and I feel good about it. Maybe this is God's will for me."

"When do you plan to move?"

She lifted one shoulder in a shrug. "As soon as I get a job."

Dad grunted then looked her in the eye. "You'll have to join a good church when you move."

He was giving his blessing! *Thank You, Lord!* "I know the Lord will lead

Dad squeezed her shoulder. "We'll have to keep praying, baby girl." He paused. "God's ways are not our ways. Maybe He doesn't want you to have that money."

"But Dad. . ." Her eyes widened. "Four million dollars!"

He gave her a sad smile. "We've lived without it all these years, and the Lord has always provided." A muscle in his cheek jumped. " 'Course, I'd hate for George Sommers to inherit that money. He'll just sink it into his casino."

She grit her teeth. "That will not happen, Dad. But that's why I have to move and meet someone different. No one in Fort Lob is standing at my door begging to marry me."

"Truth to tell, I always figured you'd end up with Derek, but I guess your interest in him died out."

"I'm still interested. *His* interest is the one that died." Admitting it out loud was like twisting a knife in her heart.

"Are you sure? Remember when Derek was sick a few weeks ago? Jake told me Derek was impressed by your help."

"Big deal, Dad." She grimaced. "Last Friday night Derek took Bruce MacKinnon's granddaughter out on a date."

"Bruce's granddaughter? Was she in church yesterday—that pretty girl with the red hair?"

Cheyenne nodded. "Kandi." *The girl with the cute face, perfect figure, and impressive bowling ability.* "There's no way I can compete with her."

"What do you mean?" He pulled his arm from the back of the bench. "You're every bit as pretty as that girl."

"She's tiny—just naturally thin, unlike me." Cheyenne huffed out a breath. "Derek seems crazy about her."

A minute passed before Dad spoke. "When you were a little girl, your mother would pray for you every night before we went to bed. Sometimes she prayed for a good husband for her daughter. I thought that was strange when you were so young. But Lynn was right. The years have gone by quickly, and now you're a young woman." He glanced at her, and Cheyenne was surprised to see a tear in his eye. "I'll miss you, but God will take care of you."

"Thanks, Dad." Tears crept to her own eyes, but she blinked them away. "Somehow, if I keep trusting the Lord, I know everything will work out."

Dad patted her knee. "Yep—even if you don't inherit Florence Ingersoll's money."

A sigh escaped under her breath. Why couldn't she marry the right man *and* inherit the money?

"Dad, how did you know that Mom was the one for you? Were you super attracted to her, and you just knew she was the one?"

"No, not really. Actually I was dating another girl named Noreen. I met her at my job, and I thought *she* was the one I would marry. One Saturday our church group went ice-skating, and I invited Noreen to come along. Everything was going great until I skated into one of the girls, and she fell and broke her leg." He looked her in the eye. "That girl was your mom."

"Mom was ice-skating? I can't even picture that." Cheyenne grinned. "Are you sure *she* didn't run into *you*?"

Dad laughed. "She wasn't the most athletic person."

"Just like me." Cheyenne rolled her eyes. "So what happened? How did you and Mom get together?"

"I felt so bad for knocking her down that I volunteered to take her to the hospital. So I carried her to my car—"

"The big Wilkins body came in handy that time, huh, Dad?"

"Sure did." He grinned. "We talked all the way to the hospital, even though she was in pain. Then I hung around until her parents got there." He shook his head. "Noreen was so mad at me for leaving her."

"Well. . .you really can't blame her."

"Except for the fact that Noreen harped at me for a week. She was so jealous, and she wouldn't get off my back! Your mom was so different. The next time I saw her in church—hobbling around on crutches—she apologized for ruining my date with Noreen. Right then I realized who I wanted to marry. Your mom and I dated for three months, and I proposed to her on Valentine's Day."

Cheyenne gave a wistful sigh. "That's so romantic, Dad. I wish Mom was still here to tell me her side of the story."

"I can fill you in. Lynn had been secretly in love with me. She called it 'unrequited love.' It hurt her to see me dating Noreen."

*Like me with Derek.* Cheyenne sighed again, but it wasn't wistful this time.

"But Lynn bided her time and prayed a lot. Deep in her heart she knew I was destined to become her husband." He cocked an eyebrow at her. "Maybe you shouldn't give up on Derek."

"I've wanted to marry him for a long time." Why was she telling Dad this? Yet at the same time, it made her feel closer to him to share her heart. "But how do I know if he's God's will for me or if the Lord has someone else in mind?"

"Pastor Reilly says God's will is revealed through His Word. Keep studying the Bible and praying, and God will let you know. I'll pray, too. Derek's a great guy, and he'd make a wonderful husband for you." Dad glanced at his watch. "It's almost eleven. We'd better get back."

Cheyenne stood. She had a lot to pray about when she got home.

～

Derek swung his flashlight around as he walked over the acres where the sheep had been feeding that afternoon. Shep, his collie, bounded over the hilly terrain beside him. Derek was thankful it was a warm evening, but his heart became heavier as the toll of dead bodies mounted.

Shep gave a sudden bark.

"Did you find one, boy?" Derek strode to where Shep stood, and his light passed over a small white lump. Leaning over, he trained the beam on it.

A lamb lay under the sagebrush.

He straightened. "Found another lamb, Dad," he yelled. Squatting down, he brushed his hand over the animal's tiny back. *Broken neck.* A pack of wolves must have killed all these sheep. Coyotes would have eaten what they killed, and they didn't break their necks.

Dad walked toward him, a rifle cradled in his arm. "Fourteen so far—three ewes and eleven lambs." He squinted off across the field. "We'll have to take care of the carcasses tomorrow when we can see what we're doing. Hector and Miguel will help." Dad shook his head. "Just don't know how they got past the electric fence."

Derek adjusted his cowboy hat. "We'll have to ride along the borderline tomorrow and see if there's a break. With two thousand acres of land, anything could have happened to the fence."

"That's true." Taking off his glasses, Dad rubbed his eyes. "It's almost eleven. Let's get back to the house. At least the rest of the flock are safely penned for the night."

"Yeah, too bad." Derek stood. "It's such a warm evening. I wish they could stay outside."

Falling into step, they strode together over the uneven ground back to Dad's Jeep with Shep trotting beside them. Removing his hat, Derek glanced up at the sliver of moon and the millions of stars that created a bowl above their heads. Nothing could be heard but the crunch of their footsteps until Dad spoke.

"Mom and I are thinking of turning over the ranch to you in the fall."

Derek's eyebrows shot up. "Already?"

"We saw a good deal on an RV last week, and I'm tempted to buy it. Mom wants to start traveling."

Derek slipped his hat back on. "I thought you were going to wait until you turn sixty-five."

"Why wait? That's ten years away, and Mom said she doesn't want to travel when she's decrepit." Dad laughed. "She loves traveling, and she wants to visit the states she's never seen, especially in the South." He looked at Derek as they strode side by side. "You'll have the house to yourself, son. Might as well get married and have a passel of kids. Maybe you'll end up marrying that MacKinnon girl you took out to dinner last Friday."

Derek shook his head. "Not Kandi." He turned to his dad. "To be honest, I'm confused. Every time I pray about my future, it seems that God is telling me to stay single in order to serve Him. But I'd like to get married someday." Cheyenne's pretty blue eyes entered his thoughts. "I'm just not sure what

God's will is right now."

Approaching the Jeep, they both climbed in, and Shep jumped into the back. Dad started the engine.

A cool night breeze hit the brim of Derek's hat, and he removed it. "Dad, how did you know Mom was the right one for you? Did the Lord strike you with a lightning bolt, and you just knew she was the one?"

"No, that's not what happened at all." Dad shifted gears, and the Jeep rolled over the uneven ground. "Your mom was the prettiest girl in high school, but she was dating my best friend, Kyle. The three of us hung out together, and the more I got to know your mom, the more I liked her. She was a lot of fun." He paused. "Then during our senior year, I realized I was falling in love. I wanted to spend the rest of my life with her."

Derek grinned. "So you stole her right under Kyle's nose, and she willingly ran into your arms."

"I wish. Unfortunately I didn't have the gumption to do that. But Kyle was always starting arguments with Yvette, and I would get so mad at him for yelling at her." Dad looked at him. "She would yell right back."

"Yep, that's Mom."

Dad stared out the windshield as they slowly bumped along. "Somehow I always managed to calm them down, and they would get back together time after time."

"You missed your calling, Dad. You should have been a marriage counselor."

"Ha! I'm more suited for sheep. They don't argue with you."

"That's why I like sheep." Derek grinned. "So how did you and Mom finally start dating?"

"She and Kyle had another fight, a real humdinger. When I confronted Kyle, he asked me to talk to Yvette for him. To plead his case, so to speak."

"Sounds like *The Courtship of Miles Standish*."

Dad glanced at him. "That's exactly what happened! I took your mom to this little diner that evening and told her Kyle wanted to get back with her." A half smile shadowed his face. "She laid her hand on my arm and said, 'Jake, I'm tired of fighting with Kyle. I want someone who's more easygoing—like you.' I was stunned!"

"That was a bold move on Mom's part."

"Later she told me she had wanted to date me for months. She tried to break up with Kyle, but he wouldn't let go. When I took her to the diner, she knew this was her one and only opportunity to let me know how she felt."

Derek nodded. "She seemed to know what the Lord had for her. But how am I supposed to know God's will?"

"Keep it in prayer, son. God will make the way clear." Dad parked the Jeep in back of the house and opened the driver's door.

Derek climbed out of the passenger's side. He had a lot to pray about.

# Chapter 8

Cheyenne smiled at the elderly woman on the other side of the post office counter. "Here's your change, Mrs. Hochstetler." She dropped a few coins into the outstretched hand.

"Thank you, dear." The thin lips curved into a smile, revealing straight dentures. Mrs. Hochstetler slowly turned, and the bell over the door jangled as she walked outside.

Glancing out into the customer area, Cheyenne noticed some crooked mailing boxes in the display. She walked around the counter, and the bell over the door rang again. A tall, middle-aged woman dressed in a yellow pantsuit walked in. Her short brown hair was smoothly styled, and Cheyenne gazed at her pretty face, thinking she looked familiar.

The woman stopped and put her hands on her hips. "Why, Cheyenne Wilkins!"

Cheyenne gasped. "Mrs. Oliver!" She reached out to give the woman a hug. "I almost didn't recognize you with that different hairstyle." Janet Oliver and her husband had been members of their church since Cheyenne was a little girl, and Janet had been a close friend with Cheyenne's mom. But the couple moved away several years ago.

Janet hugged her then gripped Cheyenne's forearms so she could look at her. "It is awesome to see you again! You look absolutely wonderful." She shook her head. "I can see your mother in your face. You look just like her, and she was such a beautiful woman."

"Thanks." Cheyenne smiled. "It's great to see you again, Mrs. Oliver."

The bell jingled, and they both turned in time to see Agatha Collingsworth walk in.

"Why, Aggie!" Janet left Cheyenne to give her a hug. "Don't you look good!"

"Oh my word!" Aggie hugged her back. "Janet Oliver! It's been so long."

Janet stood back. "It's only been four years since we moved away. You're still doing business at the Beauty Spot, I presume?"

Aggie nodded. "Yep, still at it. Why are you in town, Janet?"

"I'm moving back to Fort Lob." Her light-brown eyes flitted over to Cheyenne, and she touched her arm. "Remember when you took piano lessons from me? Do you still play the piano?"

"Never." Cheyenne laughed. "We still have the piano at our house, but no one has touched it for years."

"That's a shame." Janet's thin eyebrows dipped into a frown. "I'll have to come by and tickle those ivories."

Aggie perused Janet's hairstyle. "Why are you moving back?"

"You probably heard that Fred died last year. My cousin, Adelaide, lives in Fort Lob, and we only have each other now. No one else in the whole world. So I thought I might as well move back."

"Adelaide is your only relative?" Cheyenne couldn't imagine that.

"The only one. Fred and I never had any children, and Adelaide's husband and son died years ago."

"I'm sorry to hear that."

Janet's voice softened. "Thank you, dear."

She turned back to talk to Aggie, and Cheyenne studied the woman. She was almost as tall as Cheyenne, but she certainly had a better figure. *I am going to firm up this flab!* Maybe a new wardrobe would be good, too.

If Janet Oliver could look like a million bucks, so could she.

❧

Cheyenne glanced at the clock. *Almost five.* Janet and Aggie had stayed for an hour, but fortunately the post office had not had any customers while they were shooting the breeze. *And we probably won't have any more.* She entered the back room and took the door key from the hook on the wall. *Might as well lock up for the day.*

The bell rang as the door opened.

*Then again, maybe not.*

She walked out from the back room. Carrying a medium-sized Priority mailing box, Derek Brandt approached the counter.

His eyes met hers, and her pulse quickened.

"Hi, Cheyenne." He set the box on the counter. "Mom wants to mail this box to Grandma in Casper." He pulled his wallet from his back pocket.

"Do you need any insurance or delivery confirmation?" She lifted the box to the scale.

"Nah, just send it."

She glanced at the readout. "That will be four dollars and eighty-three cents."

Derek handed her a five-dollar bill. "Glad I made it to the post office. Wasn't sure if you would still be open."

She dropped the change in his hand. "I was just about to lock up when you—"

The bell jangled again. Cheyenne glanced at the door, and Derek turned his head. Rex Pierson walked inside. Cheyenne frowned. He had already come in this morning to check his post office box and stayed to talk to her between customers.

"Hey, neighbor!" Derek stuck out his hand as Rex strode to the counter.

Rex shook it. "Howdy, Brandt," he drawled. "Good to see you."

Cheyenne eyed the two men. They were the same height, so Rex must be six three, although Rex was thinner than Derek. And he looked a lot older. She listened as they talked for five minutes about a cattle auction next week. Finally she moved to the door, key in hand, and waited.

Derek glanced at her. "Guess it's time to leave, Rex." He winked at her as he walked to the door. "I think Cheyenne is giving us a subtle hint."

Her heart fluttered at his wink. "Well. . .it is past five o'clock."

Rex stepped toward the wall of post office boxes. "I need to check on my mail. See you around, Brandt." He thrust a key in one of the boxes.

"Later, Rex." Derek moved past Cheyenne as he exited. "Bye, Cheyenne." He didn't look back as he walked outside.

A cloud of disappointment hung over her as she turned and waited for Rex. Derek wasn't paying her much attention. He must be serious about Kandi MacKinnon. Or maybe he was going back to his no-marriage-until-forty policy.

Well, no matter. She would move to Loveland and find someone else.

"No more mail." Rex closed his box and turned the key.

Cheyenne grinned. "I could have told you that. Bernie and I fill the post office boxes every morning before we open. Once you get your mail for the day, that's it. No more until tomorrow."

Rex turned to her, and that slow smile curved his lips. "I knew that. Just waiting for Brandt to leave." He frowned. "What's his first name?"

"Derek." Cheyenne bit her lower lip. Why was Rex hanging around?

"Oh yeah—Derek. And his dad's name?"

"Jake."

Rex nodded. "Derek and Jake. Good family. Mrs. Brandt made me a pie when I first moved in. Apple."

Cheyenne smiled. "That was nice of her."

"Yeah. I'm not much of a baker, so it was appreciated." Rex cleared his throat. "Uh, Cheyenne, I was wondering. . .uh, if you'd like to go to supper with me tonight."

Her lips parted. *He's asking me out?*

She met his brown eyes and saw uncertainty there. It made her heart melt. She'd heard through the grapevine that Rex was a widower, and he must be lonely. "I'd love to eat with you."

He visibly relaxed. "Great! Um, the Cattlemen's Diner?"

The pros and cons of that eating establishment sprinted through her mind. It was close—a walk across the street—so she wouldn't have to ride with him to a restaurant, but their dining experience would fuel local gossip. Certain people in Fort Lob would have her married to Rex Pierson by sunset.

But who cared what other people thought? She and Rex were just friends.

"The Cattlemen's Diner is fine." She turned and locked the door. "You can go out the back way with me."

Together they walked outside and crossed the street. Rex held the door for her as they entered the restaurant. Within ten minutes they were seated across from each other in a booth by the front window, and Sara Stine, a high school senior, took their orders. Rex requested a steak with mashed potatoes. Cheyenne ordered fish with rice pilaf.

As Sara left, Cheyenne glanced around the busy restaurant. "I haven't been to the Cattlemen's Diner for years, but not much has changed." In the corner, the jukebox crooned an oldie, and the sounds of clashing silverware and loud conversation filled the room.

Rex's brown eyes met hers. "I'm starting to recognize a few faces. Seems like the same people eat in here every night."

Cheyenne raised her eyebrows. "You eat here every evening?"

He nodded. "So far."

Opening her mouth, she was about to issue him an invitation to eat at her house tomorrow night. But the way his eyes stared at her clamped her lips shut. For more than a week, he had talked to her every day at the post office, and now he had asked her out.

Most likely, Rex Pierson's end goal was matrimony.

Cheyenne's stomach clenched. She studied his tan, weathered face with new eyes, remembering that she had asked the Lord to send her a man. If she was going to inherit Grandmother's fortune, she needed to get married—and soon.

Was Rex the one?

Obviously Derek was not interested in a relationship with her, especially with Kandi MacKinnon hanging around.

But did Cheyenne want to marry this old rancher?

*I don't have to decide that tonight.* She would be a good friend to Rex—and see where their relationship led.

She took a deep breath. "Why did you move to Wyoming, Rex?"

"Always wanted to own a ranch." He steepled his work-worn, knobby fingers in front of his face. "For years I worked for my brother on his ranch 'cause my wife wanted to live in town." His eyes darted around the restaurant before reconnecting with hers. "When she passed on a couple years ago, I thought I'd see what ranches were for sale." He shrugged. "Looked at ranches in four different states, finally settlin' on the one here."

With a smile, she nodded. "The old Dudley place. My mom and I visited Mr. and Mrs. Dudley several times when I was a girl. The house is quite small, as I remember."

Folding his arms on the table, he leaned forward. "Just a little one-floor bungalow. I'd like to expand it after I get married. Might even have some kids someday. That's why I'm looking to marry a younger woman. A good Christian woman."

His eyes held hers, and his left eyebrow hiked up slightly, as if asking what she thought about that.

Cheyenne drew in a quick breath. Forget the local gossip! In Rex's mind, they were already destined for the altar.

❦

"This is our house right here." Cheyenne pointed to the right, and Rex pulled his rattling truck into the driveway.

He glanced at the house. "Looks dark, except for the porch light."

"Dad left that on for me. He's probably in bed."

It was Saturday night, and Rex had taken her to a movie in Lusk. Now it was after midnight, and Cheyenne felt a twinge of nerves clench her stomach. Would Rex kiss her good night?

Did she want him to?

On Thursday evening, after they'd eaten at the Cattlemen's Diner, he had walked her back across the street to the post office parking lot, opened her car door for her, and wished her a pleasant evening. She thanked him for the dinner and drove away. But now. . .

Rex shifted the gears into Park and switched off the key. With a shudder, the engine gave up the ghost. "I'll get your door." He exited the truck and walked around it.

As she waited, her mind replayed the evening. She could barely recall what the movie was about after Rex put his arm around her in the darkened theater. With slight pressure from his fingers, she moved closer to him until her head rested on his shoulder. After the movie, they got ice cream at the local Dairy Queen, sitting across from each other at a tiny two-person table. Rex leaned in as they ate, his eyes gazing into hers, his attention never waning. She gazed back, but nothing stirred inside her.

The truck door creaked open. "Let me help you down, Cheyenne."

"Thanks." She took his rough hand to climb out of the cab, and a soft breeze lifted her hair. "It's a warm night."

"Sure thing." Rex didn't let go, and they walked hand in hand toward the house.

Cheyenne felt the need to keep talking. "This is late for you, isn't it? I'm sure you get up early every morning to take care of your animals."

"Yeah." His calloused fingers squeezed hers. "But I don't need much sleep. Four or five hours will do me."

"Really?" They crossed the porch to the front door. "I need at least seven."

Rex dropped her hand and faced her. "Guess I'd better let you go then." He smiled, and his eyes gleamed in the porch light.

Cheyenne's stomach clenched a little tighter, and she took a small step back. "Thanks so much for taking me out, Rex. I had a nice time."

"Me, too." He opened his arms. "Let me hug you 'fore I go."

*A hug.* Okay, she could handle that.

Stepping into his embrace, she draped her arms around his thin frame. It wasn't like hugging her dad, who was hefty, but Rex was closer to her dad's age than he was to hers. Dad had just turned fifty-two. How old was Rex? Was he old enough to be her father?

After a prolonged squeeze, he stepped back. " 'Night, Cheyenne."

"Good night."

Opening the door of the house, she stepped inside and softly closed the door behind her. In the dark she waited until she heard Rex's truck wheeze to life. He revved the engine a couple times, and she could just imagine how those fumes permeated the air. Then the gears shifted, and the vehicle rattled down the road, the sound becoming fainter until it was gone.

Cheyenne closed her eyes and leaned against the door. *Lord, is Rex really the man You sent me?*

With a sigh, she walked through the darkened living room and sank down to the sofa, not bothering to turn on the light. Her attraction to Rex Pierson was just as dark as the room. When he gazed into her eyes, there was no electric spark, no tingle, no jolt of awareness.

Nothing like the chemistry she had with Derek.

*Why don't I have any passion for Rex, Lord?* Certainly the God who made her could change her desires so she would swoon in Rex Pierson's presence.

But maybe this would be a different kind of romantic relationship—the kind where love sneaks in silently, after years of marriage, and one day she would wake up to discover that she loved her husband.

With a groan, she laid her head back on the sofa. "I don't want that kind of marriage, Lord!" She had felt more passion for some of the boys she dated in college, even the ones she knew she would never marry.

*Enough of this!* Standing, she walked to her bedroom. She passed Dad's bedroom and heard soft snoring. At least she hadn't awoken him.

Closing her bedroom door, she flipped on the light switch, blinking in the brightness. Then she dropped to her knees beside her bed.

"Heavenly Father, all I can do is put this relationship in Your hands. I don't know if Rex is the one for me or not, but he's a good Christian man, and I'm willing to give him a chance."

She still wanted Grandmother's millions, but money was a poor substitute for love. The important thing was to marry the right man.

As soon as possible.

# Chapter 9

On Sunday morning, Derek walked into the church auditorium after his Sunday school class. He couldn't believe it was the third week of July already. It seemed the summer had just started, and now it was half-finished.

*Time flies when you're getting old.*

As he ambled down the center aisle toward his usual spot, he glanced ahead and saw Cheyenne sitting with Rex Pierson in the third row. Rex had his arm draped on the pew behind her.

Derek stopped. *What in the world?*

Kandi MacKinnon stepped in front of him. "Hi, Derek." She smiled.

It took him a moment to focus on her. "Oh hi, Kandi. We missed you in the Single Servings this morning. I'm glad you made it to church."

She moved closer. "Grandpa wasn't feeling well this morning so he decided to skip Sunday school. But after a while he felt better, and we decided to come. Can you sit with us?"

*Amazing—three sentences!* "Uh. . ." He hesitated as musical laughter reached his ears, and he glanced toward Cheyenne. She was looking at Rex, an angelic smile on her pretty face. If he sat in his usual spot, he would be sitting right behind them. He turned to Kandi. "Sure, I'll sit with you." He followed her to a pew down front on the right—the opposite side from where Cheyenne and Rex were sitting.

Bruce MacKinnon stood to let them slide into the pew. He shook hands with Derek then sat down beside him.

Kandi smiled up at him. "I haven't seen you since last Sunday. What have you been doing all week?"

"Just working on the ranch." He leaned back in the pew. "Dad and I had to fix the fence. It took us two days to find the spot where wolves broke in. They killed fourteen sheep last Monday."

Her eyes widened. "Oh?"

"It was just senseless killing." He grit his teeth. "It still wrenches my heart out to think about those wolves killing poor defenseless ewes and lambs."

Frowning, she looked down. "Oh."

*She must be all talked out.* Derek turned to Bruce. "I hear you're not feeling well."

"It's just my arthritis. Some days are—"

"Why, Bruce MacKinnon!"

The female voice caused both men to look up. A tall woman in a light-blue suit, whom Derek recognized as Janet Oliver, stood beside the pew and beamed down at Bruce.

"Well, my goodness!" Bruce jumped up and pumped her hand. He didn't seem to have any trouble with his arthritis now. "So good to see you, Janet. Welcome back to Fort Lob."

She laughed. "Thank you, Bruce. I feel like I've come home."

Kandi leaned toward Derek. "Who's that?"

"Janet Oliver—my sister's piano teacher. She and her husband moved away a few years ago."

"Oh." Kandi gazed at her grandfather and Janet as they continued their animated conversation.

Derek lowered his voice. "She has an outgoing personality, as you can see, and she was always quite a showman on the piano."

He turned back to watch, and Janet caught his eye. She leaned into the pew. "Now you look familiar."

He stood and held out his hand. "Derek Brandt, Mrs. Oliver."

"Derek!" Her mouth dropped as she squeezed his hand. "I can't believe how tall you are! And how old are you now? Twenty-three? Twenty-four?"

"Twenty-six." He didn't glance around, but the auditorium was quiet. He figured the entire congregation must be witnessing this exchange.

"No!" Janet gave his hand a shake before she dropped it. "Why Derek, you make me feel so old!"

He grinned, not sure how to answer that declaration. Fortunately he was saved by Aggie, who made a sudden appearance. The two women gabbed a minute before Aggie invited Janet to sit with them. They got settled in the pew as Wayne Holland, the song director, announced the first hymn. The congregation stood.

Sharing a hymnbook with Kandi, Derek sang out on "Amazing Grace." Beside him Janet belted out the words, almost covering Aggie's southern twang. Derek couldn't hear Kandi's voice at all, although she seemed to be singing. Must be because he was way up here in the stratosphere and she was a foot lower. He glanced down on her red hair. It shone in the overhead lights, looking soft. But it didn't make his heart beat any faster.

He glanced across the auditorium at Cheyenne. Singing, she smiled as she stood next to Rex. *What does she see in him?* Rex Pierson was nothing but an old wizened cowhand. He looked about fifty.

Derek sat down with the rest of the congregation as Pastor Reilly stepped to the pulpit.

"We have an unusual announcement this morning." The pastor's aged gray eyes squinted as he gazed over the auditorium. "A Christian organization is hosting a trip to Yellowstone National Park. They have asked several churches, including ours, for volunteer counselors to accompany elementary-age children."

Derek raised his eyebrows. *I would love to do that!*

"The dates are Friday, August 7, through Sunday, August 9." The pastor motioned toward the left side of the auditorium. "Ralph Little is taking down the names of the volunteers, so please see him after the service if you're interested."

Derek made a mental note to talk to Ralph. This was exactly the way he wanted to spend his life—serving the Lord through mission trips. He still had his eye on that trip to Honduras, where a missionary needed help building his church. So how could Derek get married? His wife would want him to stay home all the time.

Unless she had a servant's heart and accompanied him.

He glanced at Cheyenne. Rex had his arm around her, and a prick of jealousy hit Derek. Why had he always thought of her as nothing more than a good friend—the girl his sisters hung out with? She was a beautiful woman, but it looked like she had found someone else.

*Cheyenne is out.* He glanced down at the girl beside him. *Kandi is definitely out.*

But why was he even thinking about a relationship? His original idea to get married after he turned forty was looking better all the time.

❧

As the church service ended, Cheyenne turned to Rex. "I'm going to sign up for the Yellowstone outing." Her heart gave a little leap.

"Okay, whatever." Rex glanced at his watch. "I need to get back to the ranch and check on Bessie. If she don't start rallying, I'll have to call the vet." He looked at Cheyenne. "How about you sign up for the Yellowstone thing, I'll go check on Bessie, and then I'll pick you up at your house, and we'll go out for lunch."

She smiled. "Okay. Let's do that."

Rex smiled back—that slow smile that made him look handsome. "I'm taking you to a steak and potatoes restaurant I found in Douglas."

"Mindy's Diner?"

With a little grunt, he folded his arms. "You already know the place?"

Cheyenne laughed. "I've lived in this area all my life, Rex. I know every restaurant within a two-hundred-mile radius."

He chuckled. "If you say so, pretty lady. Pick you up in an hour, okay?"

"Sure."

He winked at her before walking down the aisle toward the church door. Cheyenne watched him, and a small sigh escaped. That wink should have raised her heartbeat or her blood pressure—something!

Ralph Little stood at the back of the auditorium, and she made her way toward him. "Ralph, I'd like to sign up for that Yellowstone outing."

"Thanks for volunteering." He handed her a clipboard and a pen. "Just fill out this information."

Cheyenne glanced down the page-long application. "What organization is hosting this?"

"The Bolton Creek Children's Home near Casper. It's run by Mr. and Mrs. Frank Lindley." Ralph raised his thin gray eyebrows. "Ever hear of them?"

She shook her head. "Can't say that I have."

"The Lindleys have been the houseparents there for thirty years. They've seen hundreds of kids go through their place. Right now they have eighteen orphans."

*Hmm. . .an orphanage.*

Ralph motioned to her application. "This is a field trip for the children. Frank told me they wanted to give the staff a weekend off."

What would it be like to work in an orphanage? She had never thought of that before.

By the time she finished filling out the form, most of the congregation had left, except for Bruce and Aggie, who were conversing with Janet Oliver. Derek stood nearby talking to Kandi. The girl gazed up at him, her green eyes shining as she listened. Cheyenne's heart took a dive.

She clenched her teeth. *Why am I still pining after him?* Old habits die hard, and she needed to kill this one. Rex was part of her life now. So what if she wasn't super attracted to him? He was a great guy, and she could learn to love him.

Couldn't she?

She turned to Ralph and handed him the clipboard. "Here you go."

"Thanks." He tucked it into a soft-sided black leather case. "Looks like you might be the only volunteer from our church."

Cheyenne raised her eyebrows. "But this is such a great opportunity. I'm surprised no one else—"

"Ralph, wait!"

Cheyenne turned at Derek's voice.

"I want to sign up for Yellowstone." Derek's glance cut to Cheyenne. "You going, too?"

She nodded. "It sounds like fun."

"It does, doesn't it?"

Ralph thrust a clipboard under Derek's nose. "Here's an application, Derek."

"Okay." Derek took the clipboard and glanced at the paper. "Who's sponsoring this trip?"

"The Bolton Creek Children's Home." Ralph raised his eyebrows at

Derek. "Have you ever heard of them?"

"The orphanage in Casper?" Derek smiled. "I've known the Lindleys for years."

Kandi stepped toward Ralph. "I'd like to sign up, too."

"Certainly!" He pulled another clipboard from his briefcase and handed it to her.

Cheyenne bit her lower lip. Kandi didn't seem like the outdoor type. She must be following Derek to Yellowstone. Or maybe he talked her into going with him.

Taking a step back, Cheyenne gave a little wave. "Thanks, Ralph. See you all later."

Derek glanced up. "See you around, Cheyenne."

For a brief second, their eyes locked before he looked back down, and her heart tripped at his piercing gaze. She turned away, her thoughts in turmoil. *Why does he still affect me like that and Rex doesn't affect me at all?* Obviously Derek was falling in love with Kandi. And Cheyenne had Rex.

*No, Rex has me.*

As much as she hated to admit it, her heart still belonged to Derek Brandt. Maybe she should stick to her original plan and move to Loveland.

⌒⌒

Derek pulled his truck out of the church parking lot. He glanced across the bench seat and gave Kandi a tight smile. She had asked him to take her to the Cattlemen's Diner for lunch since Bruce and Aggie had invited Jim Wilkins and Janet Oliver out to eat, and the four of them planned to catch up on old times.

Kandi could have gone with them.

*Ah, well. . .Christian charity.* He had to eat somewhere since Mom and Dad were in Denver visiting Ryan and his family, and he might as well have someone to eat with, even if his dinner partner was almost mute.

At the end of Bighorn Avenue, he braked at the STOP sign and glanced to his left. Cheyenne stood on the corner, waiting to cross Main Street.

Derek rolled down his window. "Hey, Cheyenne! Need a lift?"

She looked up at him before smiling. "That would be great!" She stepped off the curb to walk around the front of the truck.

Derek nodded to Kandi as he rolled up his window. "Move over."

She slid over to the middle. "Is Cheyenne coming to the restaurant with us?"

He hesitated. *That would be awkward.* "No, I'll just give her a ride home."

Kandi frowned. "Why? She can walk."

"Christian charity," he whispered.

Cheyenne climbed into the cab and sat down. "Thanks for the ride, Derek." She closed the door then turned to him with a smile. "Rex wanted to check on a sick cow before we go out to lunch. He told me to wait for him at home."

*Rex.* She was really falling for that guy. "But where's your car?" Derek turned right on Main Street.

Cheyenne sighed. "The old Dart finally bit the dust."

"So it's at Tom's shop?"

"No, Dad wants me to junk it."

"Really?" Raising his eyebrows, he glanced at her.

She nodded. "Dad wants me to buy a good used car at Skinny's."

Kandi turned to Cheyenne with a frown. "Skinny's?"

Derek laughed. "Skinny Olander. The slickest car salesman in the West."

Cheyenne nodded. "Did you know that Dad grew up with Skinny? They attended the same high school in Bismarck."

"No joke?" Derek grinned. "Was he always trying to pawn something off on other students? Maybe a good piece of swampland in Florida?"

She laughed. "Probably. Dad has bought all his cars from Skinny." She fell silent a moment as Derek rounded the corner of her street. "I wanted to go there tomorrow since it's my day off, but Dad has to mind the store. Both Harold and Dale are taking vacation this week."

"I'll take you." The words were out of Derek's mouth before he thought. But why shouldn't he drive her to Douglas tomorrow? His dad would be back from Denver tonight, which would free up Derek at the ranch.

"That's all right, Derek. Dad and I can go next Monday."

He pulled the truck into her driveway. "I don't mind, Cheyenne. Besides, I want to look at the kind of cars he's selling now. I haven't been to Skinny's in years." He paused. "I'll pick you up tomorrow morning, say, nine o'clock?"

"Okay. Thanks." She opened the door and climbed down. "And thanks for the lift."

"You're welcome." He smiled as she closed the door and walked to the house. Shifting gears, he backed out the driveway.

Kandi stayed in the middle next to him. "I suppose that's Christian charity, too?"

Derek glanced at her. "What? Taking Cheyenne to Douglas tomorrow?"

She nodded.

"I suppose it is." He shrugged. "She needs a ride, and I can take the day off. Why shouldn't I volunteer to help her out?"

Kandi said nothing, and Derek bit back a sigh.

Their lunch was going to be very short.

# Chapter 10

"Cheyenne, have you been to Yellowstone before?"

"Once, when I was little." She looked at Derek as he drove her to Douglas the next morning. Under her breath, she gave a wistful sigh. He was so handsome. Too bad he was dating Kandi.

Of course, she was dating Rex. She thought about their lunch yesterday. It was...nice, but not thrilling. And he had yet to kiss her. Maybe once he kissed her, she would feel like they were a real couple. Maybe she would start falling in love with him.

"You've only gone once?" Derek's dark-blue eyes met hers. "Yellowstone is so close, Cheyenne."

She shrugged. "It must be true what they say about having a tourist place in your backyard. You never visit it."

"That's not true for me. I've been to Yellowstone so many times I've lost count. And I love mountain climbing. I'm glad we have the Rockies in our backyard."

She shook her head. "You're so athletic. If I went mountain climbing, I'd end up in the hospital."

"How about skiing?" He glanced at her before looking back at the road. "I bet you went skiing last winter. Maybe in Vail or Aspen?"

Her eyes widened. "Me? Miss Klutz? You've got to be kidding!"

He grinned. "Okay, no skiing. But wouldn't you like to try it?" He waggled his eyebrows.

Cheyenne's defenses weakened considerably. Derek was just too handsome, and he was so easy to talk to. "You don't understand. Walking Dad's dog on the sidewalk is almost beyond me. How would I ever be able to ski down a mountain?"

"It's fun. I could teach you."

"Oh sure." She pictured herself trying to ski—and falling. Of course, if she fell into Derek's arms, that wouldn't be such a bad thing.

"Here we are." He pulled into the parking lot full of new cars. The sign read SKINNY'S QUALITY NEW AND PRE-OWNED VEHICLES. "Looks like a quality place."

Cheyenne glanced at all the triangle flags that decorated the lot, and her stomach cramped. "I hope he has a good used car for me. Dad called him on Saturday and told him my price range."

"Since Skinny knows you, I'm sure he'll give you a good deal."

She cocked an eyebrow at Derek. "Actually, I've never met the guy. I bought my Dart from Horace Frankenberg."

Five minutes later, she stepped into the showroom. Derek walked in behind her.

"Welcome to Skinny's Vehicles!" A rotund man dressed in a tight-fitting brown suit approached her. Tufts of gray hair surrounded his bald head. He stuck out a large hand. "I'm Skinny. And you're Jim Wilkins's daughter, right?" Barely waiting for a nod from Cheyenne, he continued. "You look just like your mother—an extremely beautiful woman."

*Hmm. . .a flattering car salesman.* Cheyenne smiled as she shook his hand. "I'm Cheyenne Wilkins."

He raised bushy eyebrows. "Cheyenne? Like the city? Wow, that name fits you! Beautiful name!"

Derek coughed and turned toward the nearest car model. He studied the sticker price in the window.

Cheyenne wanted to poke Derek in the ribs. She smiled at the salesman. "My dad asked you to show me a good used car."

"Right. I have so many good vehicles that I picked out a couple to show you." Skinny held the outer door open for her and followed her outside.

As they walked down a row of cars, Cheyenne noticed that Derek had come outside, too. She motioned to him. "Derek, come over here."

He joined them, and Skinny thrust out his hand. "You must be the significant other."

Derek shook his hand, not correcting Skinny's impression. "Derek Brandt."

"Glad to meet you! Now." Skinny turned to a dark-green car. "Here we have a 1997 Saturn. Runs like a top." He opened the driver's door. "Sit down here, Cheyenne. I'll show you the controls."

She took a seat, and he pointed things out on the instrument panel.

Skinny straightened. "Would you like to take this one for a spin?"

Derek opened the passenger door and leaned inside. "You don't want this one, Cheyenne. There's hail damage on the roof."

"Really?" Cheyenne stood and looked at the roof. Sure enough, the entire thing was pockmarked. "Skinny, can I look at another car?"

"Hey, I'll subtract a hundred dollars for the damage."

Cheyenne glanced at Derek. With a frown, he gave a slight shake of his head. She turned to the car salesman. "I think I'd rather look at another one."

"Okay." He gave Derek a dark look. "Let's walk down here."

She followed him to a wine-colored car, and Derek walked by her side.

"You'll like this one, Cheyenne." Skinny placed his hand on the roof. "Wonderful car! A 2003 Cavalier with low mileage." He tapped the sticker price in the back window. "It's a little higher than your dad wanted to pay, but a real steal at this price."

Derek looked at the sticker before walking around the car.

Skinny opened the driver's door. "Take a seat, Cheyenne. We'll take this one for a spin."

Within five minutes, they were on the road. Skinny sat in the passenger seat, talking the entire time. Derek sat in the back. After riding around the streets of Douglas, she drove the car back on the lot.

"Nice, huh?" Skinny smiled at her. "Let's go inside, and we can fill out the paperwork."

Cheyenne got out and whispered to Derek. "What do you think?"

"Looks like a good car." He raised his eyebrows. "Do you want it?"

She studied the sticker price. "I like it, but it's so much money—about a thousand more than I can afford."

Derek turned to Skinny. "Take off a thousand dollars, and she'll take it."

"A thousand?" Skinny shook his head. "Five hundred is all I can afford to subtract on this beauty. It's such a good car. A real steal at this price already."

Derek turned to Cheyenne. "I saw a couple other used car places when we were—"

"Okay!" Skinny turned to the office. "A thousand off. Let's do the paperwork."

Cheyenne smiled at Derek as they walked together. "Thanks, Derek. I couldn't have done this without you."

"Hey, that's what friends are for." Placing his arm around her shoulders, he gave her a squeeze.

She looked up at him. For an instant their gazes held, and then he opened the door for her.

Cheyenne walked inside, her heart thumping.

Would she ever have that kind of chemistry with Rex?

❧

On Thursday afternoon, Derek walked into the mudroom and pulled off his boots. The good smell of fried chicken wafted out from the kitchen. His stomach growled, and he glanced at his watch. Mom would have supper ready in twenty minutes, and that would give him just enough time to take a shower.

Wiping his shirtsleeve across his forehead, he entered the kitchen. His mom and Tonya sat at the table talking. They both turned to him.

"Oh good, you're here." Mom stood and lifted a pan lid on the stove. "Is Dad coming?"

"Yeah, he was cleaning up." Derek raised his eyebrows at Tonya. "Hey, sis. What are you doing here?"

"Murray is working a two-day shift, so Mom invited me over for supper." She glanced at his dirty jeans. "Hard day with the sheep?"

He shrugged. "Normal day. I spent all afternoon checking for cuts and cleaning them." He walked to the dining room door, ready to go upstairs.

"Derek, guess what?"

He turned back.

Tonya's dark eyes took on a sudden shine. "This morning I signed the contract to get my cookbook published!"

"Wow, congratulations!" She had been working on writing her own cookbook for years. "So when are we going to see the published book?"

"It won't come out until next year. But this never would have happened if Lane Hutchins wasn't my brother-in-law. He got me in with his agent."

Mom laid her hand on Tonya's shoulder. "You don't know that, honey. You might have been published without Lane's help. God works in mysterious ways."

"Maybe." Tonya gave a happy sigh. "I'm just glad the Lord let it happen."

Derek grinned. "Another published author in the family. Congrats again, sis." Turning, he ambled through the dining room. As he entered the living room, he heard Tonya ask Mom about their new neighbor.

"His name is Rex Pierson," Mom said. "He's dating Cheyenne."

Derek stopped beside the piano and glanced back the way he had come.

"Yeah, I noticed them sitting together at church." Tonya's voice sounded far away, but Derek could hear her clearly. "What do you know about him?"

"Dad and I went over to his ranch last week." The sounds of a drawer opening and silverware clinking competed with Mom's voice. "That place has been vacant for so long, it was a mess. But Rex is a hard worker."

"Is he raising sheep?"

"Cattle. He brought eight cows with him from Montana then went to auction yesterday and bought ninety-two head. So now he'll have an even hundred. They're supposed to be delivered on Friday."

Derek already knew all that, so he continued to the stairway. He shouldn't be eavesdropping anyway. But as he stepped on the first stair, Tonya's voice stopped him.

"I heard that Rex is in the market for a wife. Gloria Schutzenhofer says he has his sights set on Cheyenne."

"Well, she deserves a good husband." Mom's voice softened, and Derek crept back to the dining room. "We had always hoped she'd end up as Derek's wife, but I guess that wasn't to be."

"That's what Callie and I were hoping." Tonya sighed. "Don't know what's wrong with that guy."

A chair scraped on the kitchen tile. "Derek thinks the Lord wants him to remain single so he can serve Him."

"What? That's crazy. He doesn't have to remain single to serve the Lord."

"I know, but that's what he wants to do." Mom sighed. "Did Gloria have anything else to say about Rex?"

"He and his wife were married for eighteen years, but they didn't have any children." Tonya paused. "I guess she was a sickly woman, and Rex took care of her. She died two years ago."

"That's sad. I hope he gets a good wife."

Derek walked to the stairway, not waiting for Tonya's reply. *Cheyenne would make a fantastic wife.*

He thought of the sparks of electricity that often arced between them. Did she have that kind of chemistry with Rex? Did he appreciate her? Her beauty, her friendliness, her kindness?

A frown pulled at his mouth as he climbed the stairs. *I should steal her away from that guy.*

Startled by the thought, he stopped. His mind drifted back to the conversation he'd had with his dad last week.

*"So you stole her right under Kyle's nose, and she willingly ran into your arms."*

*"I wish. Unfortunately I didn't have the gumption to do that."*

Derek continued on his way upstairs.

*Gumption.*

Did he have the nerve, the courage to win Cheyenne? Or was he just jealous?

*Lord, what is Your will?* Maybe the good Lord brought Rex Pierson to Wyoming just to marry Cheyenne Wilkins. And maybe Derek would remain single for life.

*Is that what I really want?*

Reaching the top of the stairs, he said a silent prayer. He was more confused than ever.

# Chapter 11

Early on the last Monday of July, Cheyenne drove her car under the Rocking B Ranch archway and down the long driveway to the Brandt home. Callie had invited her to join their family for the pancake breakfast at Cheyenne Frontier Days and spend the rest of the day at the rodeo.

Last year Cheyenne had gone with the Brandt family, spending the entire day hanging around with Derek. She looked back on that day with fond memories, but it hadn't changed their relationship much.

This year she thought she would go to Frontier Days with Rex, but he was busy getting his ranch settled. The cattle he bought at auction had arrived, plus he was interviewing several men today for "hired hand" positions.

*Five dates.* That was the extent of their relationship, plus sitting beside him in church, and Rex had yet to kiss her good night. But he always hugged her, and she enjoyed talking to him, getting to know him. He entered her thoughts more often, and she was beginning to view him as her future husband. If they could get married by the end of this year and have a child next year, that would take care of Grandmother's will.

She gave a little shiver. When her thirtieth birthday rolled around, she would be a millionaire—with her husband and child. The thought made her head spin.

But today Cheyenne would forget about Grandmother's will. She would relax and enjoy some "girl time" with Callie.

Exiting the car, she took a deep breath of warm Wyoming air. A few birds twittered in the large oak tree by the two-story farmhouse. Besides that, the place was quiet. Peaceful. She looked up at the expansive sky, still streaked with pink and orange from the sunrise. Cheyenne gazed at the rolling hills spreading to the east as far as her eye could see. Rex's ranch was over there somewhere. Someday, hopefully soon, she would live on that ranch, and the Brandts would call her "neighbor."

The front door of the house opened, and Yvette Brandt walked out carrying a light jacket. "Hi, Cheyenne!" Her slim figure sported jeans and a green T-shirt. Even in her fifties, Yvette was a beautiful woman. She descended the three porch steps. "I think you're the first one to arrive. We're going to take the family minivan so we have plenty of room."

"Sounds good." Cheyenne smiled. "Thanks for inviting me."

Jake Brandt walked out of the house, pulling the front door shut behind him. "Looks like a beautiful day." He rounded the house toward the detached garage. "I'll pull out the minivan so you ladies can climb in easily."

"Thanks, honey." Yvette turned to Cheyenne. "I'm glad it's not raining. Jake and Derek got soaked last Friday afternoon at the rodeo."

"But the show goes on—rain or shine."

"Yes it does." Yvette placed her hand on Cheyenne's arm. "Oh, I wanted to tell you—this Friday is Tonya's birthday. We're planning a surprise party for her at our house at five o'clock. Can you come?"

"I'd love to. I know Tonya likes surprises."

"She does. We're planning it for five o'clock because she thinks she and Murray are just coming for dinner." Yvette smiled, creasing the crow's-feet by her eyes. "But the dinner will expand into a party, and the biggest surprise is that all her siblings will be here. We're turning it into a family reunion."

"Wow." *And I've been included!* "I'm sure you're looking forward to having all your children at home."

"Yes. I'm counting the days."

Jake pulled the minivan into the sunshine and parked. When he cut the engine, Cheyenne heard the sound of another car heading down the driveway. She recognized Lane's Mazda as it approached.

"Oh good. Callie and Lane are here." Yvette waved to them as they pulled up. "Now we just have to wait for Derek and Kandi." She walked to the minivan.

Cheyenne raised her eyebrows. *Kandi?* Derek must still be dating her.

A tiny pinprick of jealousy stabbed her, but she reminded herself that she had Rex.

Callie got out of the car and hugged Cheyenne. "I'm so glad you're coming with us, Chey. We're going to have so much fun today."

"I can't wait!" Cheyenne grinned. "I hope Lane doesn't mind if we run off to buy souvenirs."

"Yay for souvenirs!" Callie laughed. "That's the most fun thing about CFD to me. And don't worry about Lane. He wants to write a book about rodeos in America, so he'll be busy taking notes."

They walked together to the minivan.

"Hi, Mom." Callie hugged her. "Where's Derek?"

"He left about an hour ago to pick up Kandi." Yvette looked at her watch. "They should have been here by now. I hope they won't be too late."

Cheyenne ignored the clenching of her stomach as she followed Callie into the minivan. Lane was already sitting on the backseat in the corner, jotting a few thoughts in a small notebook, and they took seats next to him.

*Girl time.* That's how Cheyenne would frame this day, and Derek would be out of the picture.

⁂

Derek drove his pickup under the archway. As he crested the hill on the driveway, he noticed Mom and Dad, along with Lane, Callie, and Cheyenne, already sitting in the minivan.

*Great!* How long had they been waiting for them? He had been annoyed when Kandi called this morning at five thirty and asked him to pick her up. Bruce was supposed to drive her over, but Kandi claimed that Bruce's arthritis was bothering him. So Derek raced over to the MacKinnon ranch, only to discover that Kandi wasn't ready. He sat in their living room for twenty minutes trying to make small talk with Bruce.

Pulling over to the side of the driveway, Derek killed the engine. "Can you get your own door, Kandi? We need to hurry."

Without waiting for an answer, he grabbed his hat from the middle of the seat and strode toward the van. Kandi ran to his side. He paused to let her get in first. Amid a flurry of greetings, they sat on the empty middle seat. Lane, Callie, and Cheyenne sat in the back.

"Sorry we're late." Derek pulled the sliding door shut.

"That's okay." Dad threw the gears into DRIVE, and they started rolling. "We'll get some pancakes, no matter how long we have to wait in line."

≈≈

Derek adjusted his cowboy hat as he stood in line beside Kandi. He glanced at his watch. Almost seven. They had been standing for a half hour in the middle of the long line. Cheyenne Frontier Days claimed that ten thousand people ate at one of these free breakfasts, and as Derek looked back at the line that stretched four or five blocks, he figured they were right.

Mom and Dad stood beside him, with Kandi sticking to him like a burr under his saddle. She looked pretty today in jean shorts and a white peasant blouse, and her makeup was perfect. Most likely she had been painting her face while he waited for her at Bruce's house this morning. Derek folded his arms, no longer infatuated with her. If only he hadn't invited her to attend CFD with their family.

His glance bumped ahead about a half-dozen people to where Callie and Lane stood with Cheyenne. Somehow the three of them had gotten ahead in line. They laughed, and Cheyenne's musical laughter floated back to him. Derek grimaced, wishing he were standing with them—sans Kandi.

A few minutes after seven, the line began moving. Within fifteen minutes they were at the front, and Derek was handed a plate filled with pancakes and ham. He had to give credit to all those volunteers. They knew how to handle a crowd.

"Oh look at that!" Kandi pointed to the men who cooked the pancakes. They flipped them over their shoulders when they were done, and several boys ran behind the cooks, catching the flapjacks on large platters. She laughed. "I hope those kids don't miss."

A smile touched Derek's lips as he watched the boys. "I'm sure they'll throw away the ones that land on the ground."

"I hope so." Kandi turned to follow Mom and Dad.

Derek followed her, wishing he could somehow signal Mom to keep Kandi company. But she probably thought Kandi was his date. Obviously Callie and Cheyenne were going to hang around together all day, so that left Derek as Kandi's sole companion. He sighed.

It was going to be a long day.

In the arena, amid hundreds of other spectators, Cheyenne sat next to Callie on a white seat in the grandstand. "Those were good pancakes, and I'm actually full!" She gave a little laugh. "I hope my stomach's shrinking."

Callie lowered her voice. "You're doing great on your diet."

"Nine pounds so far." Cheyenne shook her head. "Just doesn't seem like much." She glanced down the row to her right. Lane sat on the other side of Callie. He pointed something out to Jake and Derek. All three men wore cowboy hats, and Yvette sported a pretty one made of straw. On the other side of Derek, Kandi listened as Yvette talked to her.

Cheyenne sighed. *What does Derek see in her?* Of course she was pretty and tiny, but Kandi didn't seem to have much of a personality.

*But it doesn't matter. Today is girl time.* With a smile, she inhaled deeply, smelling all those great smells of a rodeo—horses, leather, and the bodily scents, both good and bad, of the fans. She didn't need Derek to have a good time. *"This is the day which the Lord hath made; we will rejoice and be glad in it."*

"They're having barrel racing this morning." Callie motioned toward the center of the arena, where three fifty-five-gallon barrels formed a large triangle on the mud of the arena floor. "When I was a little girl, I always dreamed of being a barrel racer. But I didn't have enough passion to be a good horse rider. I would rather sit in a corner and read a book."

Cheyenne looked at her. "I've only been on a horse one time. Remember?"

Callie laughed then covered her mouth with her fingers. "Sorry."

"It was your fault!" Cheyenne tried to hide a smile. "Why'd you let me ride bareback? I slid right off that animal, and it was a long way to the ground."

Callie giggled. "We were only ten years old, Chey. I didn't know you couldn't stay on a horse."

The announcer interrupted their memories, and the arena grew quiet as he announced the competition. A minute later, a brown horse thundered from the arena's alley. The female rider was dressed in jeans and a Western shirt, complete with cowboy boots and hat. The audience seemed to hold their collective breath as the cowgirl rounded the first barrel, raced over to the second one, rounded it, and galloped up to the third. Rounding that one, she raced back toward the point where she started.

Cheyenne leaned toward Callie. "That girl is skinny."

"Barrel racers have to be skinny. Think of the poor horse trying to race around the barrels with a big heavy person weighing him down."

Cheyenne laughed. "That's why I'm not a barrel racer, even if I could stay on a horse."

Derek sat forward, leaning his arms on his thighs as he watched the barrel racer cross the finish line. Sitting back, he looked at his dad. "She almost nicked that third barrel with her foot."

"Yep. She needs to tighten her inside leg against the horse's flank."

The score flashed on the electronic board at the end of the arena.

"Nineteen point sixty-three seconds." Dad shook his head. "She's not going to win."

Derek glanced at Kandi, who was looking down at her hands. Was she bored? *How can anyone be bored at a rodeo?* Mom talked to her sometimes, but Derek wasn't being fair to his mom if he let her carry the conversation. Since he had invited Kandi, he was responsible to see that she had a good time.

He sighed. "Ever see barrel racing before?"

"No." Her eyes met his. "It looks hard. When she rounded those barrels, the horse was almost sideways."

Derek adjusted his hat. "The faster, the better. It's actually dangerous, both for the horse and the rider. But those girls know what they're doing." He stopped as another cowgirl raced around the barrels.

When she crossed the finish line, Dad leaned toward him. "She was faster than that first gal."

The score flashed on the board.

"See there." Dad smiled. "Seventeen point ninety-eight seconds. She just might win."

Kandi cleared her throat. "How many barrel racers are there?"

Derek shrugged. "They usually have over a hundred."

"That many?" Her shoulders slumped.

He nodded. "This competition will last all morning." He pointed toward the arena. "Here comes another one."

The girl rounded the first barrel but was thrown from her horse as she rounded the second one. In unison, the crowd rose to its feet. Several workers helped the girl up as the horse pranced off to the side.

Derek sat down with a relieved sigh. "She was going way too fast."

"Yep." Dad took his seat. "That little gal should have been more careful."

A half hour later, as another cowgirl successfully finished her race, Kandi leaned toward him. "Is there anything else we can do, Derek?"

He glanced at her. "Are you bored?"

She nodded, her mouth forming a little pout.

Derek glanced at his mom, but she had her eyes glued to the arena as

311

another cowgirl galloped around. Barrel racing was Mom's favorite sport at the rodeo.

He waited until the score flashed on the board. Then he turned to Kandi. "Do you want to see the Old West Museum? They sell souvenirs there. Or we could wander around Wild Horse Gulch. That's like an old Western town. They sell merchandise, too, and even have people walking around dressed in nineteenth-century clothes."

She smiled. "Souvenirs first."

He stood, holding in a sigh. "Okay. Let's go."

She followed him down the grandstand and out into the sunshine. Dozens of people strolled along the sidewalk.

Derek took her to the museum, wishing he were back at the rodeo. He'd attended CFD since he was a boy, and he wasn't really interested in the museum or the town. But he would try to be interested for Kandi's sake.

At noon, after Kandi bought salt and pepper shakers shaped like a pair of boots as well as a CFD T-shirt, they met the others at the Oasis for lunch. Derek's mom, Callie, and Cheyenne placed food and bottles of water on a picnic table that was shaded by a huge red-and-white umbrella.

Mom looked up as they approached. "We bought hamburgers at the concession stand for everyone." She set a large box in the middle of the table. "Let's sit down and say grace."

Derek waited for Kandi to sit on the bench at the table then sat beside her. Dad asked the blessing. The table was quiet as everyone grabbed a hamburger and started eating.

Dad swallowed his first bite. "You two missed some excitement, son. One of the barrel racers really got hurt. I think they took her to the hospital."

Kandi shivered as she glanced at Derek. "I'm glad we weren't there."

Derek wished they *had* been there. "Who won the competition?"

"Some little gal way down the list." Dad grinned. "Her score was seventeen point four. She was fast! And she sure knew how to handle her horse."

"Oh man! I wish I could have seen that." Derek took a few more bites as the conversation drifted around him. He glanced down the table. Lane and Callie sat across on the other side with Cheyenne at the end. Derek nodded at his sister. "Did you stay for the entire competition?"

Callie leaned forward. "Most of it, but Cheyenne and I spent an hour at the Indian village. I bought some turquoise jewelry, and she bought an arrowhead necklace."

Kandi perked up. "I love Indian stuff! Where is the village?"

Callie pointed off in the distance. "It's over on the southeast corner of the park. We even saw a little show they put on by their dance group. They were decked out in their Indian garb and feathers, and their costumes were very colorful."

Kandi looked up at Derek. "Let's visit the Indian village after lunch."

He cocked an eyebrow. "You can visit it if you want to, but I'll be in the arena for the rest of the day to watch the cowboy contests."

"Oh." Kandi looked down.

Callie reached out to touch her hand. "I can take you over there. They have something special going on every hour. We'll go to the arena first so we know where the family is sitting."

Kandi smiled at her. "Thanks."

With a relieved breath, Derek added his smile of thanks to his sister. Hopefully that would take care of Kandi for the rest of the afternoon.

∾

In the grandstand, even though a lot of people conversed in the rows in front of her and behind her, Cheyenne sat in the Brandt row by herself. Jake and Lane had decided to get some soft drinks, and Callie had just left with Kandi and Yvette for the Indian village. Cheyenne should have gone with them—the walking would have helped her lose weight. But she would rather sit and watch the cowboy contests.

Feeling someone sit down beside her, she looked to her left. Her eyes met Derek's, and her pulse quickened.

"Hey, Cheyenne. Sitting here all by yourself?" He held a can of cola and took a quick swig.

She leaned away from him. "I already spent all my money on souvenirs, so I plan to stay in the arena and watch the cowboys all afternoon."

He grinned. "Good choice."

Cheyenne looked out at the arena. She wasn't going to let her heart beat a second faster over the guy sitting next to her. "How's the ranch doing, Derek?"

"Right now things are going well, but did you hear what happened two weeks ago?" When she shook her head, he continued. "Wolves broke through our fence and killed fourteen sheep."

She gasped. "Oh that's terrible!"

He nodded. "Three ewes and eleven lambs. Dad and I found the break in the fence where they got in, but we've never caught the wolves."

"How do you know they were wolves? They could have been coyotes."

"No." Derek adjusted his hat. "Those lambs were brought down by dispersers—young males trying to establish their own territory. And they didn't eat the sheep, they just broke their necks." He sighed. "That's the way wolves operate."

"Those poor little lambs." Tears crept to her eyes. "I'm so sorry that happened, Derek. That's a loss of income for you, isn't it?"

"Yeah, but we'll recover." Derek eyed her a moment then looked up beyond her.

Cheyenne turned her head as Jake took the seat next to her. Lane sat down beside him.

"Howdy." Jake held a large cup of cola in his hand. "Did the other girls already leave for the Indian village?"

"Yep, they're sightseeing." Cheyenne twirled a strand of blond hair between her fingers. "I think they'll be gone most of the afternoon."

Jake grunted. "Why would they want to miss the rodeo?"

Derek leaned over her to talk to his dad. "Kandi's not into rodeos, even though she told me she wanted to see the cowboy contests." With a little shrug, he sat back and slid down a few inches in his seat.

Cheyenne glanced at him before looking out at the arena. Evidently Derek was disappointed that Kandi wasn't sitting beside him right now. *He really must like that girl.* Instead here he was, sitting next to Cheyenne.

*I'll treat him like I would treat my brother.*

She'd never had a brother, but she could pretend, couldn't she? *Call me Callie.*

Derek's shoulder bumped hers. "Saddle bronc is next. It's one of my favorites."

"I like saddle bronc and bareback bronc, but not bull riding."

"You've got to be kidding!" He stared at her as if she were crazy. "Everyone loves bull riding."

"That's *my* favorite." Jake nodded. "Those bull riders are really talented—and fearless."

"They have to be." She frowned. "It's dangerous to hop on a live bull!"

They both laughed, and Jake turned to Lane with a comment.

Derek sat up and leaned toward her. "That's true, Cheyenne, but all of these events are dangerous. Even barrel racing."

"Yeah. I saw that girl go down." She shook her head. "Why would anyone want to risk her life? But the cowboys are the real daredevils. Did they start bronc riding for the challenge? Man against animal?"

"Bronco busting started when cowboys had to break in wild horses. They competed with each other to see who could ride with the most style." Derek motioned toward the arena. "Now they have all kinds of rules, and they have to stay on at least eight seconds, or they'll be disqualified."

"Why would anyone want to do that? It's so dangerous."

He grinned. "I'd have to agree with you there. The life of a cowboy is not as glamorous as some people think, but it sure is fun to watch the competitions."

The announcer's voice came over the loudspeaker, introducing the event. In a few minutes, the first rider jumped out of the chute on the back of a bucking bronco. The man held to a rope with his right hand, and his cowboy boots pushed out the saddle's stirrups as he bounced up and down.

Derek placed his arm around the back of her chair, his eyes never straying from the cowboy. "Notice how he waves his left hand in the air." He spoke in a hushed voice as if he didn't want to break the cowboy's concentration, although the man would never hear him. "He can't touch anything with his free hand."

Cheyenne already knew that, having attended quite a few rodeos during her lifetime, but her heartbeat took off at Derek's nearness. She glanced at his profile, just inches away, as he watched the rider. His dark eyes, his straight nose, his perfect lips—a face that must be twenty years younger than Rex's weathered one.

His straight, slim fingers pointed to the arena. "Leaning so far back in the saddle helps him stay on and keeps his feet in the stirrups. If either foot slips out or he drops the buck rein, he'll be disqualified." The cowboy fell off the bucking horse into the mud, and Derek turned to her. Their gazes locked, and Cheyenne's scalp prickled. His gaze dropped to her lips, just like it did more than three weeks ago in his truck, before he looked back at her eyes.

The hint of a smile touched his lips before he pulled his arm from her seat and sat back. "I think he made the eight seconds. We'll see what his score is."

A small sigh escaped as Cheyenne's pulse returned to normal. Why didn't she have that kind of emotional interaction with Rex? She had tried to gaze into his eyes and work up her emotions, but the chemistry just wasn't there.

But why was Derek acting like this? Wasn't he dating Kandi? Was he two-timing her?

*"If you can't be with the one you love, love the one you're with."*

The old saying popped into Cheyenne's head. She remembered some girls at college spouting off those words and laughing about it, but Cheyenne never thought it was funny.

Now she was experiencing it with Derek Brandt! And she didn't like it, not one bit.

# Chapter 12

On Friday evening, Derek sat in the living room along with the entire Brandt family. They watched collectively as Tonya tore the birthday paper off her last gift.

Derek had purposely taken a seat beside Cheyenne on the sofa, and she had looked startled when he sat down—the same look she gave him at CFD when he sat next to her in the grandstand. He grinned to himself. He certainly enjoyed sitting next to her during the saddle-bronc contests, and he couldn't believe that "electrical moment" they shared.

But Cheyenne had seemed distant. She frequently conversed with Dad and Lane during the rest of the competition, and she seemed relieved when the women arrived later to sit with them. Then, for the remainder of the day, she paid absolutely no attention to him.

She must really like Rex Pierson.

Derek's brother, Ryan, pulled a straight-back chair from the dining room and set it beside the sofa. Derek was thankful he had someone to talk to. After Cheyenne's initial reaction, she turned her back on him and talked to Callie, who was sitting next to her.

Across the room, Tonya sat in the blue chair with Murray perched on the arm. Mom and Dad sat on the love seat, and most of Derek's siblings sat beside their spouses on chairs they had pulled from the dining room. His two little nephews played with building blocks on the floor.

Tonya held up a DVD. "Oh! *The Quiet Man*. I love old movies. Thanks, Callie." She turned to her husband. "Do we have this one, Murray?"

"Nope." Twitch grinned. "Callie asked me last week."

Tonya smiled as her glance swung around the room. "I can't believe you guys planned a surprise party behind my back. Thank you so much for all the presents. This has to be the greatest family in the world."

"It is." Dad glanced at Mom. "God has been good to us, hasn't He, honey?"

"He certainly has." Mom smiled as she looked around. "The Lord gave us six wonderful children, five children-in-law, and two grandchildren."

Melissa leaned forward. "With more on the way."

This announcement precipitated an outburst of exclamations. Melissa was quickly surrounded by the women of the family. Most of the men stood and shook Philip's hand.

Since Cheyenne stayed seated, Derek kept his seat beside her, but he caught his brother-in-law's eye. "Congratulations, Phil."

"Thanks." Philip smiled as he took a step toward Derek. "Would you believe—her due date is two days after her birthday. Melissa is hoping the baby's early so they'll be exactly thirty years apart."

"Thirty years." Derek nodded. "Wow."

Philip turned away as Ryan claimed his attention.

Derek heard a quiet sniff beside him, and he turned in time to see Cheyenne wipe a tear from her eye. Compassion filled him, and he leaned toward her. "You okay?"

She nodded, but a tear rolled down her cheek. She covered her face with her hands.

"Cheyenne?" Barely thinking what he was doing, Derek put his arms around her and pulled her close to him. "What's wrong?"

With her face still in her hands, she just shook her head, but after a few seconds she leaned toward him, and a few quiet sobs escaped between her fingers. He tightened his grip, smelling the sweet fragrance of her hair, and a surge of protectiveness swept through him.

Ryan came back to claim his seat. Frowning, he glanced at Cheyenne in Derek's arms. "Is she okay?"

Suddenly she straightened, causing Derek's arms to slip away. "I'm fine." She wiped her fingers under her eyes as she stood. "Excuse me."

Derek watched her walk out of the room before turning to Ryan. "I have no idea what's wrong with her."

Ryan lowered his voice. "That happens with women sometimes. Puzzling, if you ask me." Raising his hands, he gave a little shrug.

Derek just nodded, still concerned. Should he follow Cheyenne? See if she was all right?

"Well." Ryan motioned toward Melissa. "It's about time someone else in the family has kids besides Holly and me."

"Mom and Dad will probably have a bunch of grandkids in the next few years." All Derek's siblings were married now—everyone except him.

He glanced at the door where Cheyenne had disappeared. If only she was still in his arms.

❧

"Let me grab some clothes for tomorrow." Derek poked his head in his closet and pulled out a pair of jeans and a T-shirt.

Holly, his sister-in-law, smiled up at him as she changed her younger son's clothes. "Thanks for giving up your bedroom for us, Derek. We appreciate it."

"No problem. I can sleep on the sofa for one night."

He stepped over his nephew Peter. The three-year-old pushed Matchbox cars across the wooden floor as he made motor noises.

Ryan entered the room, pulling one suitcase behind him and carrying a duffel bag. "I have to make another trip out to the car for that stuff in the backseat." His brown eyes glanced at his wife. "Do you need anything else?"

"No." Holly picked up Paul. "Just the diaper bag and that box of things for your mom."

"I'll help you." Derek laid his clothes on the bed and descended the stairs behind his brother.

They walked out the front door and into the warm night air.

Ryan opened the back door of his car. "I can't believe tomorrow's August first."

"I know." Derek took the large diaper bag he was handed. "This summer is whizzing by. Next weekend I'm scheduled to go to Yellowstone."

"Really?" Ryan straightened and closed the car door. "Are Mom and Dad going, too?"

"No, it's for the children's home in Casper. They're sending the kids on a field trip with volunteers so the staff can have the weekend off." Derek turned toward the house and fell in step beside his brother. "We have three going from our church—Cheyenne, Kandi, and me."

"Who's Kandi?"

"A girl I dated. She's—"

"You? Dating?" Ryan stopped. "Get out of here! You've never dated a girl in your life."

Derek leaned against the porch rail. "Is there some rule that I can't go out with a girl?"

"I'm not saying it's bad." Ryan set his box on the porch floor. "I'm just surprised. Ever since you were fifteen, you said you weren't getting married until you're forty. And I happen to know that you don't like change."

"I don't." Derek dropped the diaper bag down to the floor. "Actually, I'm not dating Kandi anymore."

Ryan frowned. "Why not?"

Derek gave a shrug. "She's not my type. I'm not sure about marriage anyway. That would be a huge change in my life, and I don't know if I'll ever be ready for it."

"It is a big adjustment and a big responsibility, especially when you have kids. But I wouldn't trade it for anything. I love my family." Ryan quirked an eyebrow at him. "What about Cheyenne? You two looked rather cozy. Did she ever tell you why she was crying?"

"No." Derek folded his arms. "Cheyenne's not interested in me. She's dating Rex Pierson, our new neighbor, and it looks like they're headed toward marriage."

"Too bad. You and Cheyenne would make a great couple."

Derek grimaced. "I know, although to be honest, I've been struggling with God's will. Sometimes I think God wants me to remain single so I can serve

Him." He spread out his hands. "Next weekend I can go to Yellowstone to help out without worrying about leaving a family back home."

Ryan shrugged. "If that's what the Lord wants you to do, that's great. But don't forget the old saying, 'Charity begins at home.' I want to raise my children to be the next generation of Christians for Christ's kingdom. I get to have an impact on my own family, which is a lot more than just a once-in-a-while charity thing for strangers."

"I suppose that's true."

"I'll keep you in prayer." Ryan laid his hand on Derek's shoulder. "Whatever you do, make sure that it's God's will, not your own."

"Thanks, bro." Derek picked up the diaper bag and followed Ryan into the house. He liked the thought of raising the next generation of Christians.

But he couldn't think of one girl he wanted to marry—at least not one *available* girl.

# Chapter 13

Cheyenne walked in the back door and released Marshal from the leash. "Dad? Are you home?"

That was a dumb question since his car was parked in the driveway. But it was only six o'clock on Saturday evening. Usually he wasn't home from Wilkins Grocery until eight thirty.

He walked into the kitchen. "Hi, baby girl. I'm on my way out again."

She raised her eyebrows at her father's attire. "A dress shirt and slacks?"

He turned to face her and patted his stomach. "Does this look okay?"

"Well, you can't go wrong with blue and tan. Where are you going, Dad?"

He lifted his keys from the hook by the door. "Didn't I tell you?"

"Obviously not." Cheyenne folded her arms as she leaned against the counter.

"Well. . ." A smile crept to his face. "I have a date tonight."

Cheyenne's jaw dropped. "A date? You?"

"Yes, me." He dropped his keys and stooped to retrieve them. "Don't you think a woman could find your old man attractive?" He straightened up with a grunt.

"It's not that, Dad." She rolled her eyes. "What woman could resist you? I'm just surprised, that's all." *Stunned* would be a better word. "Uh, who is she?"

"Janet Oliver."

Cheyenne's right eyebrow hiked up on its own accord. "Mrs. Oliver? Uh, that's great, Dad." *I can't believe it!* "She's. . .a nice lady." *My dad is dating Janet Oliver!*

He just grinned. Jiggling the keys in his hand, he turned toward the door. "Guess I'll be off."

"Wait! How did this come about? When did you ask her out?"

He turned back. "Janet dropped by last night when you were at Tonya's party. She played the piano, which she said is badly out of tune, and then we had a good talk." Leaning against the door, he sighed. "I don't know if you remember this, but your mom and Janet were the best of friends when she lived in Fort Lob."

Cheyenne thought back. "I do have a distinct memory of her being here when I was little. We were eating lunch, and Mrs. Oliver and Mom were talking about me starting kindergarten soon."

He nodded. "After you started school, Janet came over for lunch almost every day, or your mom would go to her house. Sometimes they went shopping." His eyebrows pulled into a frown. "A couple years later when your mom got sick, Janet sat with her and read the Bible, especially toward the end. When Lynn died, she really grieved." He shook his head. "She was really good to Lynn, and I'll always be grateful for that."

With his gaze on the floor, Dad seemed to have forgotten that Cheyenne was standing there.

She cleared her throat. "So you're just taking Janet out as an old friend? I mean—this is just a friendship date, right? Not a serious looking-for-a-spouse date?" She bit her lip, hoping she hadn't overstepped some imaginary boundary.

Dad cocked his head. "It might turn into something serious. I need to find God's will for my future just as you do for yours."

"I know, Dad." She placed her hand on his arm. "Well. . .whatever happens, I hope you and Janet have a good time tonight."

He smiled. "Thanks. We will." Turning, he pulled open the door and walked out.

Cheyenne watched as he got in the car and drove away. She looked down at Marshal, who was resting in his doggybed. "Do you think Janet will end up as my stepmother?" She took a deep breath. "That would be so weird."

On the other hand, maybe Janet could spice up Dad's wardrobe. At least she'd never let him wear a pink-flowered tie with his brown plaid suit coat.

*Hmm. . .Janet and Dad.* "That might be good. Dad won't be alone after I get married."

Her goal was to marry Rex by the end of the year—a December wedding, or January at the latest. That would leave a year and a half to have a baby before her thirtieth birthday.

And Grandmother's millions would be hers.

She sank into a chair at the kitchen table. "I feel so. . .greedy!"

Marshal cocked his head at her.

"Do I really want to get married just to get that money? I could be miserable my whole life!" Folding her arms on the table, she laid her head down with a sigh.

In the quiet, she heard her cell phone ring in the bedroom. Walking back, she picked it up and looked at the ID. *Rex.*

She opened her phone, anticipating his deep voice. She hadn't seen Rex since Thursday evening when he waited for her to lock up the post office and took her to supper at the Cattlemen's Diner. That date was becoming a common occurrence in their relationship.

"Hi, Rex!"

"Howdy, darlin'. How've you been?"

"Great! How is the ranch coming along?"

"Well now, I just about have everything squared away. Got the ol' bunkhouse cleaned out and have three hired hands livin' there. One of 'em is a really good wrangler, but I don't have no horses." He stopped to chuckle. "My hundred head of cattle seem content with their new place. Had to get the plumbing fixed in the house, but the pipes are in good shape now." He took a deep breath. "Anyways, I feel like I can finally breathe."

She smiled. "That's good." She never noticed before how much he sounded like a country bumpkin.

"Yeah. I'll probably be tied up here all next week workin' the ranch, but ya wanna go out on Friday? It'll be kinda like a celebration."

"Not on Friday, Rex. I'll be at Yellowstone next weekend."

"Oh yeah. Forgot about that." He paused. "How about Thursday then? We can make a night of it in Lusk with a dinner and movie."

*Yes! Somewhere besides the Cattlemen's Diner.* "I like that idea. There's a restaurant in Lusk called Mama's Kitchen. They serve Italian food, and it's really good."

"Okay, we'll go there. How about I pick you up at the post office at five on Thursday?"

She smiled. "I'm looking forward to it. And I'll see you tomorrow morning in church, right?"

"Yep, church tomorrow morning." He paused. "Night, darlin'."

"Good-bye, Rex."

With a sigh, she closed the phone. *Darlin'.* At least Rex liked her, and he was taking things slow, not rushing into an intimate relationship. But it still bothered her that they had no chemistry.

Her thoughts shot back to Tonya's birthday party last night. Melissa's announcement hit her so hard. She suddenly realized how much she wanted to have a baby.

Whether she got the four million or not.

⊷

Cheyenne stopped at the front door and turned to Rex with a smile. "Thanks for the great time. I really enjoyed that movie."

"Me, too." The reflection from the porch light pricked his eyes, and his face wrinkled up with his smile. "But I enjoyed going out with a pretty lady more."

Before Cheyenne could reply, he cupped her face in his calloused hands. His lips met hers in a kiss that lasted for a few seconds. He lifted his head then kissed her again.

He stepped back. "Night, darlin'." He winked.

"Bye." Cheyenne waited as he walked off the porch. He got in his truck and started it in a cloud of fumes, then waved to her. She waved back.

*This is not good.* Not only was there no passion, but she didn't even enjoy his kisses.

Cheyenne blew out a breath. What could she do?

She only had two choices—give up the inheritance or try to fall in love with Rex Pierson.

# Chapter 14

Behind the wheel in his pickup, Derek was thankful when the orphanage in Casper came into view. It was Friday, August 7, the weekend for the Yellowstone National Park outing. Early this morning, he met Cheyenne and Kandi at the church in Fort Lob and gave them a ride to Casper. Kandi had scampered up into the truck cab first, beating out Cheyenne, whom Derek wished was sitting beside him. As usual Kandi didn't say much, so Derek and Cheyenne ended up carrying on the conversation around her.

"Here we are, ladies." In the orphanage driveway, he pulled up behind two fifteen-passenger vans, threw the gears in PARK, and turned off the engine.

Cheyenne gazed up at the huge house. "Wow, it's a mansion. The columns in the front make it look so stately."

Derek leaned forward to look at her across Kandi. "You've never visited the children's home before, Cheyenne?"

"No. I've never even heard of it." Her blue eyes met his. "And it's been here for thirty years?"

"Yep. Started by Frank and Grace Lindley. I usually come once a month and do some activities with the children as a volunteer."

"Oh, I'd love to do that." Cheyenne smiled. "Let me know the next time you come."

He grinned. "I will."

Kandi sat silently during this exchange, turning her head to look at each speaker as if she was at a ping-pong match.

Derek glanced out the windshield. "Here comes Mr. Lindley." He opened the door and exited the truck, looking forward to the day at Yellowstone.

Cheyenne watched a tall, bearded man descend the porch steps. He held a piece of paper in one hand and was dressed in a short-sleeved gray shirt and dark slacks. Cheyenne opened the passenger door and climbed out of the cab. Kandi followed her. They joined Derek in front of the truck.

Mr. Lindley stretched out his right hand. "Derek! Good to see you again."

Derek shook his hand. "Hi, Mr. Lindley." He turned and motioned to the girls. "This is Kandi MacKinnon and Cheyenne Wilkins."

"Thanks for volunteering to go with us." Mr. Lindley's handshake was firm as he took Cheyenne's hand, and his dark eyes twinkled when he smiled. He reminded her of Professor Bhaer in *Little Women*.

She returned his smile. "This trip sounds fun. I'm looking forward to it."

"Um, me, too." Kandi nodded.

"Good, good." Mr. Lindley took a pair of reading glasses from his shirt pocket and looked at his paper. "You will each be in charge of two children. Let's see. Kandi, you will have two girls." He glanced at her over his glasses. "Madeline is eight years old, and Rayna is six. They're good children. I'm sure you'll have no problem with them."

Kandi just nodded.

He looked back at the paper. "Cheyenne, you'll be in charge of two boys."

"Boys?"

Mr. Lindley shrugged. "We have more boys than girls, and we have a lot of women volunteers." He looked down. "These two are both five years old. Arthur and Noah."

Cheyenne frowned. "Will I share the same cabin with them overnight?"

The director looked at her over his glasses. "If you were the boys' mother or housemother you could, but since you're not. . ." His over-the-rim gaze switched to Derek. "I'll have them stay overnight with you, Derek. You'll also be in charge of Nathan and Joshua."

"Nathan, huh?" Derek pursed his lips.

Mr. Lindley placed a fatherly hand on Derek's shoulder. "You can handle him. Besides, Nathan likes you, whether he shows it or not."

Another car pulled into the driveway, and Mr. Lindley waved at them. "More of my volunteers. We'll leave for Yellowstone in about fifteen minutes." He walked to the other car.

Placing his hands on his hips, Derek looked at Cheyenne. "I guess I'll end up with four boys."

"Only at night. I want to watch my two during the day."

Kandi sidled up to Derek. "We can all hang out together, can't we?"

"Yeah, we can do that." He walked to the back of his truck.

Cheyenne glanced at Kandi, who looked lonely standing by herself. Suddenly she felt sorry for the girl. "Don't worry, Kandi." She smiled at her. "We'll all stick together and have a good time this weekend."

"Okay." Kandi smiled back, and that smile transformed her entire countenance.

*She really is a pretty girl.* No wonder Derek was taken with her.

∽≈∾

That afternoon, Cheyenne breathed in the warm air as a "covered wagon" bumped along the uneven ground toward the Rosey cookout near Tower Falls. She sat on a padded bench seat between Arthur and Noah. The orphans, as Mr. Lindley unabashedly called them, filled the long yellow wagon. A cowboy named Mitch held the reins of the two horses, and the wagon had canvas awnings tied up against the roof. The murmur of conversation surrounded them.

"When are we gonna eat?"

Looking down to her right, Cheyenne met the blue eyes of Arthur. "When we get to the cookout, we'll eat. I hear they're serving steak. That sounds good, doesn't it?"

"Yeah. I'm hungry. Can we have seconds, too?"

She raised her eyebrows. Arthur didn't fit her perception of a poor orphan. Although he was taller than most five-year-olds, he probably weighed fifteen pounds more, with a roly-poly body and chunky arms and legs. A thatch of blond hair topped his chubby face.

Cheyenne cleared her throat. "Are you sure you need a second helping?" She lowered her voice. "Did you know that I'm on a diet, Arthur? I want to lose a few more pounds. At the cookout, I'm only going to eat what's on my plate. Maybe you should do that, too."

"But why?" His light-blond eyebrows formed a V in the middle of his forehead. "Just 'cause I'm fat? I'm not worried about being fat. 'Big is beautiful.' My mom always used to say that. She was a fat person, too."

"Was she?" Cheyenne tried to hide her smile.

Arthur frowned. "What does it mean, Miss Anne?"

"My name is *Cheyenne*, not Miss Anne."

"But what does 'big is beautiful' mean?"

"Well. . ." Cheyenne thought a moment. "Maybe your mom was trying to accept herself the way she was instead of trying to change."

"I like myself just the way I am." He grinned. "Big is beautiful, right?"

"Right!" With a laugh, Cheyenne put up her hand. "Give me five!"

Arthur smiled as he slapped her hand.

She glanced down to her left at her other little charge. Noah's small brown head bent over two round magnets. He concentrated on keeping as little space between them as possible before they snapped together.

Amid the hum of conversation in the wagon, she heard Derek's voice way in the back. "Hey, everyone! Bison on the left!"

The heads of counselors and children turned that direction. A hundred yards away, five humpbacked shaggy animals ate grass like cows.

"Wow! They're big!" Arthur leaned against Cheyenne. "What are they?"

She glanced down at him. "Bison. Some people call them buffalo."

"Oh." Arthur nodded. "I know what a buffalo is."

Derek's strong voice reached over the wagon. "A herd of deer! Over on the right!"

Everyone's head turned that way.

"Look at that." Cheyenne pointed to the three deer that were leaping away from the wagon. "Don't they run fast?"

Arthur nodded. "They're cool."

"More bison!" Derek's voice again.

With a grin, Cheyenne turned around and raised her voice. "Are you the self-appointed tour guide, Derek?"

From the back bench he gave her a thumbs-up. "Hey, I've been to Yellowstone before."

Cheyenne turned to the front, wishing she hadn't looked back. Derek's two boys sat on his left, and on his right Kandi MacKinnon stuck to his side. She seemed to be paying more attention to him than she was to the two little girls who sat beside her.

A sigh slipped between Cheyenne's lips. She thought of her date with Rex last night, and his good-night kisses. If that man had been Derek. . .

*Lord, help me to accept my circumstances as they are.* She would learn a lesson from Arthur's mom.

Noah lifted his brown eyes to meet Cheyenne's blue ones. "Are we almost there?"

"I'm not sure." Taking his small hand in hers, she gave it a quick squeeze. Noah hadn't said more than a few words, and she wondered if he had lost his parents recently. "But we'll be at the Rosey cookout soon enough. Then we can eat."

Arthur leaned against her. "I really am hungry."

"You told me." She smiled at him as she tucked a strand of hair behind her ear.

"Hey!" Arthur jumped up. "I think I see the cookout place. We're almost there, Miss Anne."

"It's *Cheyenne.*" She looked ahead. Between the trees, she spotted several long picnic tables. "Yep. Looks like we've arrived."

She smiled, determined to forget about her relationship woes this weekend. She would "mother" these two sweet boys God had placed in her care.

❧

It was dark that evening when Cheyenne unlocked the Lake Lodge cabin and opened the door. "Okay girls, here we are." She flipped the switch inside, and the overhead light came on.

Stepping over the threshold, she glanced around as she set down her duffel bag. The small room was furnished with a double bed and a table with two chairs. Through the thin wall on the left, she could hear the exclamations of their neighbors—another group of girls.

Kandi walked inside and frowned. "How. . .primitive." Her two charges, Rayna and Madeline, dropped their sleeping bags on the floor.

Rayna smiled, showing the gap in her teeth. "Cool."

"Yeah. I like it." Madeline's ponytail bobbed as she nodded her head.

"That's good." Cheyenne walked to a small window. "The room is clean, but it's a little stuffy in here. Let's open the window." After a couple of tugs, she succeeded in sliding it open. A cool evening breeze brushed past her. "Ah!

That feels good." She turned back to the room.

The little girls knelt on the wooden floor to spread open their sleeping bags, but Kandi still stood by the door. Her hand rested on the handle of her suitcase, and a frown rested on her face.

Cheyenne took a deep breath. She *would* get stuck sharing a room with Kandi MacKinnon—with a double bed of all things! *Lord, help me to have a good attitude.* She smiled at the two girls on the floor. "You girls have the right idea. We might as well call it a night and get ready for bed."

With a sigh, Kandi rolled her suitcase to the double bed and opened a narrow door in the wall. "At least we have a bathroom. I hope the shower has plenty of hot water. I feel grimy after being outdoors all day."

"Um. . .Kandi, why don't you let the girls use the bathroom first? Then they can get to sleep."

Kandi plunked down on the bed. "Okay."

Cheyenne raised her eyebrows. "Uh. . .are you going to help them?" She didn't mind helping the girls, but they were supposed to be in Kandi's charge, not hers.

"We can do it ourselves." Madeline pulled a pair of pajamas from her backpack. "When Mrs. Lindley tells us to get ready for bed, we know what to do."

Cheyenne smiled at her. "You are very grown-up."

With a sigh, Kandi took off her left shoe and rubbed her foot. "I'll be glad when we can get back to civilization."

Cheyenne unzipped her duffel bag. *Give me patience, Lord!*

∽

Cheyenne shifted on the mattress, turning on her side away from Kandi. Outside the window several crickets chirped. She listened to the even breathing of the two little girls on the floor. Her eyes drifted shut.

"Cheyenne."

At her whispered name, she startled awake. "Yes?"

"I have a question about Derek."

*Great!* Cheyenne turned over to face the middle of the bed. "What's your question?"

"I was just thinking about when Derek and I get married."

*When!* Cheyenne's heart thudded. "I didn't know the two of you were engaged."

"We're not." Kandi gave a high-pitched giggle. "But I'm sure it will happen. Woman's intuition, you know."

Was that all Kandi was going on?

"Anyway, do you know how many children Derek wants?"

In the dark, Cheyenne rolled her eyes. "Uh, knowing Derek, he would say children are cheaper by the dozen. He'll probably adopt twelve."

"Did you say *adopt*?"

Cheyenne tried not to laugh at the incredulous sound in Kandi's voice. She cleared her throat. "He volunteers at the orphanage every month, doesn't he? I bet he'll have two or three orphans living with him by the time you guys get married."

"All right. Now I know you're kidding." Kandi gave a little grunt. "I hope he doesn't want to adopt. I sure don't. I want to have my own kids."

"Yeah, so do I." *By the time I'm thirty!* "But there's nothing wrong with adoption. I already love those two boys I watched today. That little Arthur is so cute. I would adopt him in a heartbeat."

"Are you serious?"

Arthur's round face popped into her mind, and she realized it was true. "Yes I am. I would love to adopt him."

"That is crazy."

*Arthur.* What would it be like to be his mother? He had blond hair and blue eyes, as she did. He was tall for his age, as she had been. He was chubby, as she still was—unfortunately.

Kandi yawned. "We'd better get to sleep. Good night, Cheyenne."

" 'Night." Cheyenne rolled back on her side. She smiled to herself as she thought of Arthur saying "Big is beautiful." But then her smile faded. Rex said he wanted children, but what if he didn't want to adopt Arthur? Adoptions were expensive. Of course, they could wait until Cheyenne inherited her grandmother's money in a couple of years. But what if Rex said no? Or what if someone else adopted Arthur?

*Lord, I would love to adopt that little boy.* She prayed for a few more minutes, asking God to place that desire in her future husband's heart, too. A gentle peace filled her soul, and she drifted off to sleep.

# Chapter 15

The next afternoon, Derek stood in the back of the group beside his two boys, and Joshua, the ten-year-old, leaned against his left side. Derek threw his arm around the boy and squeezed his shoulder. "Ready to see Old Faithful blow its top, Joshua?"

The hazel eyes looked up into his. "I've never seen a geyser before."

"There's a first time for everything." Derek glanced beyond Joshua to Nathan, his other charge. Nathan was a typical twelve-year-old—rebellious. But beyond that, Nathan seemed to be jaded by life. That boy's attitude had been a problem since Derek met him a year ago.

Cheyenne stood in front of Derek with Arthur and Noah. Kandi's two girls stood with them as Cheyenne pointed at the steam from the geyser that floated off in the wind. Instead of standing next to her girls, Kandi planted herself beside Derek. He wished she would take her duties as a counselor more seriously. She didn't seem to care about the kids at all.

The crowd quieted as the geyser started, and the water went up a foot then stopped. The steam wafted off to the right.

"False start." Derek looked to his left. "Do you know what makes the geyser blow, Nathan?"

The boy gave him a dark look before he shrugged. "Is this like science class or something?"

"No, it's like me asking you why a geyser shoots up." He glanced from Nathan to Joshua, who looked at him with interest. "Do you know, Joshua?"

He shook his head.

Derek pointed toward the geyser. "Deep underground the water is heated—"

"Skip the science lesson." Folding his arms, Nathan looked away.

"Hey, buddy. You might need to know this someday."

Nathan turned back with a frown. "Why?"

"Well. . ." Derek lowered his voice. "Let's say you started liking a really pretty girl, and your class went on a field trip to Yellowstone. What if you wanted to impress her?"

Derek reached out and tapped Cheyenne's shoulder. She turned around, her clear blue eyes meeting his. *And she sure is pretty.*

He glanced back at Nathan. "If I wanted to impress Cheyenne with how smart I was, I would tell her that water heats deep below the surface by very hot rocks to a boiling temperature." He looked around, realizing he had an audience.

Not only were Nathan and Joshua listening, but Cheyenne and the other children stared at him with rapt attention. Kandi folded her arms, as if she didn't like him using Cheyenne for the pretty-girl illustration.

Kandi would just have to get over it.

"That boiling water soon changes to steam. And steam rises. Right?" He glanced around, and several heads nodded. "Okay. Then the steam pushes the water above it up toward the surface. When the steam suddenly expands, it pushes the water out the geyser with great force." Clapping his hands together, he lifted them as he made a whooshing sound.

Cheyenne's blue eyes widened. "Oh! So that's how it happens." She looked at the children surrounding her. "Isn't Mr. Derek smart? I'm impressed."

He grinned at her before turning to Nathan. "See? I knew I could impress a pretty girl."

Nathan actually smiled. Derek squeezed his shoulder before glancing around. His eyes met Kandi's.

She wasn't smiling.

"Look, everyone!" Cheyenne pointed toward the geyser.

A column of water, cloudy with steam, shot up about 120 feet in the air.

"There she blows!" Derek looked down at Joshua. "Now you can say you've seen Old Faithful in action."

The children were silent as the geyser held their attention. When the show was over, Mr. Lindley walked in front of the group.

"That was awesome, wasn't it?" With a smile, he raised his bushy eyebrows as he nodded at several children. "There's a lot of power in that water, and it's really hot." He motioned toward the wooden boardwalk behind them. "Right now we're going to stroll along the boardwalk. You'll see all kinds of geysers and boiling pools in this area. Stay with your leader, and don't step off the walkway."

"Hear that, men?" Derek smiled at Nathan and Joshua. "Let's go."

The two boys followed the others as all the children and counselors turned and started down the path. Derek brought up the rear.

Kandi stayed by his side. "I'll walk with you, Derek."

He frowned. "You're supposed to be with your girls."

"Cheyenne has them." Kandi motioned up ahead. Sure enough, Cheyenne strolled along the boardwalk with Kandi's two girls as well as her two boys. Cheyenne talked to the children, holding the hand of one of the girls. They didn't seem to miss Kandi.

Derek shook his head. "I think you'd better go up there."

"But I need to talk to you."

He sighed. "What do you need to talk about?"

"Did you like your cabin last night? I thought ours was kind of primitive."

*Is this what she needs to talk about?* He blew out a breath. "Were you expecting a five-star hotel?"

"No, but it was so. . .basic."

"You don't know what *basic* is, Kandi. Camping in tents is basic. Those cabins were nice, I thought."

She walked beside him in silence for a moment. "Cheyenne and I had a good talk."

He hesitated, but curiosity got the best of him. "What did you talk about?"

"Well. . .we were talking about children, and she said she would adopt one of those orphans in a heartbeat if she could." Kandi frowned. "She meant Arthur."

"Wow." *Good for you, Cheyenne!* "That's cool."

"I think it's crazy. When I get mar—" She shook her head. "Never mind. But then we talked about someone else." Leaning toward him, she grabbed his hand and squeezed. "You."

"Me?" With a frown, Derek disengaged his hand and thrust it in his pocket. Kandi was coming on a little too strong. "You know, I really think you should walk with Rayna and Madeline. Mr. Lindley put you in charge of those two girls."

Her lips formed into a pout, but Kandi turned and jogged ahead to join Cheyenne and the children. Derek slowly let out a sigh. Why couldn't that girl take a hint and leave him alone?

Nathan turned around and grinned at him. "I guess you told her, huh, Derek?"

*Great!* He should have figured the two boys in front of him would hear every word of their conversation. "Girls are hard to figure sometimes, Nathan." *Which is why I should remain single.*

Derek looked out at the barren land as they walked. The wooden boardwalk cut a path through the sedimentary deposits on the land, and a dead tree spread its spindly branches toward the sky. A heavy sulfur smell hung in the air.

This area was just as barren as his love life.

≈

That evening, Cheyenne sat on a split log with Arthur on her left and Noah on her right, and they watched the sparks of the campfire ascend into the evening sky. The group had left the geysers in the early afternoon and had spent an hour wading in Yellowstone Lake. After a picnic supper, Mr. Lindley and Derek built the campfire in a cleared space. Now the orphans and counselors sat around it.

Derek had taken a seat beside Arthur, along with his two charges, and Kandi was off to his left with her two girls.

Cheyenne looked down at Arthur, aware of Derek's presence on the other side. "I like how the sparks go up from the campfire. Do you see them?" She pointed above the fire, watching the little orange sparks ascend into the evening sky.

Arthur watched. "There's so many."

"That fire is hot. I wish we had some marshmallows to toast over the fire. Wouldn't that be good?"

"Yeah! Marshmallows!" Arthur's blue eyes lit up. "Why can't we have some, Anne?"

Derek turned to the boy. "Her name is Cheyenne, buddy."

"My name's not Buddy—it's Arthur."

Derek spread out his hands. "See there? You don't like it when you're called by the wrong name. It's the same way with Cheyenne."

Arthur gave her a puzzled glance before looking back at Derek. "But why is Anne so shy?"

Derek burst out laughing. "Oh, I get it!" He caught her eye. "Shy Anne!"

She laughed with him. "No one's ever called me *shy* before."

"Nope. This girl is not shy at all, Arthur." Derek continued laughing as he reached his hand over Arthur's head and grabbed her shoulder, pulling her toward him and bringing the three of them into an intimate circle.

Cheyenne's heartbeat pulsed into high gear, and she automatically placed her arm around his waist. Their hug only lasted a few seconds before Derek let go.

She glanced into his eyes, and he winked, causing her heart to race again. *Talk about sparks!*

Arthur looked up at her, a puzzled expression on his sweet face. "What did he mean, Anne?"

She put her arm around him and gave him a hug. "Let me spell my name for you." Bending over, she found a short stick and carved out the letters in the dirt at their feet as Arthur watched. "That's how you spell Cheyenne. It's the same name as the capital city of Wyoming."

Derek leaned toward her to whisper in her ear. "He probably can't read."

She glanced into his eyes, and a little smile shadowed his face.

Mr. Lindley walked in front of the group and raised his voice. "We can't have a campfire without singing." He motioned toward a cowboy who had a guitar strapped around his back. "This is Jonas. He's going to lead us in some songs."

"Hello, ladies and gentlemen, boys and girls." Jonas had a deep voice that reminded Cheyenne of Rex.

*Rex!* She had completely forgotten about him. How could she do that? She certainly didn't want to cheat on him.

"Our first campfire song is an old classic—'Kumbaya.' Ya'll know that one? The words go: 'Kumbaya, my Lord, kumbaya. . .'"

Cheyenne raised her eyebrows. *That song was way before my time.* How would these kids know it? She looked over Arthur's head at Derek.

He rolled his eyes.

She grinned. Derek was just a good friend, right?

Too bad he was the one who made her heart zing.

# Chapter 16

On Sunday morning, the orphans and volunteers filled the two vans and took off for a ranch located near Cody, Wyoming. Reaching their destination—a white farmhouse with a huge red barn—Derek helped Mr. Lindley herd everyone inside the barn. Bales of hay lined one side of the long, dusty room.

Mr. Lindley pointed. "Take a seat on the hay bales." He watched the children file by him. "Everyone sit down, please. Be sure you have your Bibles."

Other people from nearby ranches entered the building. The bale "seats" were soon filled to capacity.

Derek stood by the door, waiting for the children to settle down. Nathan and Joshua waited beside him. He placed his hand on Nathan's shoulder. "This is an authentic cowboy church, Nathan. What do you think about it?"

The boy looked around, an interested look in his eyes. "Cool."

*Praise God!* Derek had been praying for Nathan's attitude all weekend. "Let's sit back here, guys." He gestured toward the fourth row of bales since the first three were filled.

Nathan and Joshua sat down, and Derek settled next to them.

A moment later, Kandi plunked down beside him. "Is this where we're having church?" Frowning, she glanced around the barn.

Derek cut a glance toward her. *I cannot get rid of this girl.* "It's called a cowboy church." He raised his eyebrows. "Isn't it great?"

She lowered her voice. "But it's so. . .rustic."

"Take a deep breath, Kandi." He demonstrated, breathing in the faint smell of manure. "The *pews* are here." He grinned.

She didn't even smile.

*Cheyenne would have laughed her head off.* "Uh, you need to sit with your girls." He motioned toward the first row where Cheyenne was sitting beside Madeline and Rayna.

Kandi grimaced but stood and walked to the front. She sat beside Rayna.

Derek released a sigh. *She is really getting on my nerves.*

⁓

A half hour later, after several guitar-playing cowboys sang hymns with the congregation, one of the men opened his Bible. "My name is Pastor Wes. Let's look in God's Word this morning for a few minutes. God has a purpose, a will for your life. That's what we'll be talking about." He removed his cowboy hat.

"But first, we'll begin our message with prayer."

Bowing his head, Derek prayed that the Lord would speak to his heart. He wanted to know God's will for his life.

Pastor Wes concluded his prayer and donned his hat. "If you have your Bible, open to Colossians chapter 1." He waited as the rustle of pages filled the room.

Derek pulled a New Testament from his shirt pocket. Beside him, Joshua and Nathan both opened their Bibles to Genesis and began to page through every book.

Leaning toward them, Derek whispered, "Let me help you." By the time he found Colossians in both Bibles, the pastor was reading verse 9.

" '. . .that ye might be filled with the knowledge of his will in all wisdom and spiritual understanding.'" Pastor Wes looked up. "God has a will, a purpose, for every Christian. If you have to struggle with what you feel is God's will in your life, then it might not be God's will." He paced the dusty floor in front of his congregation. "Before God calls you to do something, He will first give you the desire to do that very thing He wants you to do."

Derek stared at the pastor. *A desire.*

His eyes shifted to Cheyenne. He had a perfect view of her profile from where he sat. She kept her attention on the pastor, nodding her head slightly at what he was saying.

*She is so pretty.*

Another realization hit him. He couldn't go back to what he was before—a bachelor who didn't want to marry until age forty, or maybe never. He wanted what his brother had. He wanted a wife to love, children to raise for Christ's kingdom.

Did that involve Cheyenne?

It wouldn't be a *struggle* to have a relationship with her. His mind traveled back to that intimate moment in his truck, the time he held her in his arms at Tonya's party, the closeness at the campfire last night. He raised his eyebrows before a grin stole to his face.

No, it wouldn't be a struggle at all. Unless. . .

What if Rex wouldn't give her up without a fight? Or what if she really wanted to marry him?

Pastor Wes concluded his message. "Let's all stand for a closing prayer."

Derek stood as the congregation rustled to their feet. Bowing his head, he didn't hear the pastor's prayer. He had his own petition.

◇∾◇

Cheyenne was stuffed. The entire "church" had shared a huge dinner on the grounds, and now she sat on the grassy banks of the Shoshone River that ran through the rancher's property. The orphans played together, hiding behind the trees or wading in the river. She smiled at Arthur and Noah as they played near some large rocks at the river's edge.

"Be careful, boys," she called to them. "Don't fall in the water."

Arthur wielded a thin stick. "We're looking for snakes!"

"Yeah." Noah's thin face broke into a smile.

Cheyenne shook her head. *Boys will be boys.* "Don't let them bite you."

"We won't." Arthur turned back to a crevice between the rocks.

A few yards away, Derek stood on the river's bank, demonstrating how to skip stones across the water. A group of kids surrounded him, each one trying to ricochet a stone along the water's surface. Kandi stood by Derek's side.

Closing her eyes, the pastor's sermon entered her mind. Was Rex really God's will for her? Was she destined to get that inheritance, or would Mr. Sommers sink the money into his casino? How long before she would know?

A scripture verse penetrated her thoughts. *"Wait on the LORD: be of good courage, and he shall strengthen thine heart: wait, I say, on the LORD."*

*Wait.* Cheyenne would wait—for the Lord's plan, not her own. Strangely, she had more peace about adopting Arthur than she did about marrying Rex. If she legally adopted Arthur, that would take care of the child part, but she still needed a man.

A scream pierced the air.

Cheyenne's eyes flew open.

Noah ran toward her. "Miss Cheyenne!" His face was pale. "Arthur fell."

Cheyenne jumped up and followed him to the other side of the rocks. Arthur lay at the base of two large rocks, his right leg twisted at an odd angle. "Arthur!" Her heart pounding, she knelt beside him.

His blue eyes looked up into hers, his face wet with tears. "It hurts!"

"What happened?" Derek hunched down beside her.

"I don't know." Cheyenne clasped Arthur's hand as he whimpered.

"We were jumping on the rocks." Noah's voice quivered. "And Arthur fell."

"I'll take him to the house." Derek examined Arthur's leg before carefully lifting him.

Cheyenne stepped back, wiping a tear from her eye. *I should have been watching more closely!* All she could do now was pray.

❧

By the time Derek walked the five hundred feet to the house, the entire group of children and counselors followed en masse. Arthur cried softly in his arms, and Derek shifted him to a more comfortable position, trying to keep his voice calm. "You'll be okay, Arthur. You're very brave."

Mr. Lindley ran out of the house. "What happened?"

"We have a casualty." Derek nodded to Arthur's leg. "It might be broken."

"I'll take him to the hospital." Mr. Lindley looked at the crowd. "The rest of you get in the vans. It's time to go back to Casper anyway."

Amid a murmur of conversation, the counselors and children turned toward the vehicles.

"Mr. Lindley?" Holding Noah's hand, Cheyenne looked up at the orphanage director. "Could I go with Arthur? I feel so responsible."

Mr. Lindley shook his head. "These things happen, Cheyenne. It wasn't your fault. You need to go back with the others." He turned to Derek. "Take Arthur to Wesley's car." He nodded to a late-model Chevy on the driveway before striding toward the house. "I'll be right back."

Derek took a step to the car, but Cheyenne stopped him. She gazed at Arthur, who had stopped crying. His eyes were closed. She brushed back a lock of his blond hair. "I think he fainted, Derek."

"Looks like it." Derek kept his eyes on Cheyenne. If only he could pull her into his arms and comfort her. "Don't worry. He'll be okay."

"I hope so." She looked up, and her blue eyes held tears. "I wish I could stay with him." Looking down at Noah, she pulled on his hand. "Let's go, Noah." They slowly walked away.

Turning toward the Chevy, Derek bumped into Kandi, who lingered by his side. A prick of annoyance hit him, and he used his head to motion to the van they came in. "Go with the others, Kandi."

A little pout formed over her lips before she left. Derek strode to the car, carrying Arthur in his arms.

"Derek." Mr. Lindley walked up with Pastor Wes. "Wesley will drive Arthur and me to the hospital. I'm putting you in charge of getting the orphans back to Casper. You'll have to take my place driving one of the vans."

"Okay."

Wes opened the back door of his car. "Lay him on the backseat." Derek did so, clicking a seat belt around the boy's middle. Pastor Wes got behind the wheel and started the engine.

Mr. Lindley walked around to the other side of the car. "Thanks, Derek. I called my wife, and she and the staff will be waiting for you when you arrive."

Derek nodded, relieved that his only responsibility would be driving the orphans back to the children's home.

∽∾

Two hours later they neared Casper, and Derek was thankful. The noise level from the nine orphans in the van had reached a peak when someone suggested they sing. With help from Jean and Leslie, the two counselors in the back, the van exploded with renditions of "Father Abraham" and "I'm in the Lord's Army."

At least they didn't sing "Kumbaya."

Kandi insisted on sitting in the front, replacing Nathan in the passenger seat. That annoyed Derek, but she didn't even attempt to talk to him. He spent the time praying for Arthur. Poor kid. Did he break anything besides his leg?

When the children finally expended their energy, the van became quiet. In the seat behind him, Cheyenne talked to Noah. Derek heard snatches of their conversation.

"Will Arthur be okay, Miss Cheyenne?"

"The Lord can make him better, Noah. We'll just have to pray and trust God."

*Pray and trust God.* That's what Derek would have to do concerning Cheyenne.

In the stillness a cell phone rang.

"That's mine." Kandi turned around to look back. "Chey-enne, could you get my purse?" She pointed. "It's under your seat."

"Here you go." Cheyenne handed it to her.

Pulling out her phone, Kandi flipped it open. "Hello?" She listened for a few moments then turned wide eyes on Derek. "Really? Oh that's terrible."

He frowned. "What happened?"

"My grandfather had a heart attack."

Derek raised his eyebrows. "Bruce?"

With a gasp, Cheyenne leaned toward Kandi. "Is he going to be all right?"

Kandi listened intently on the phone. "Yes, we're on our way to the Bolton Creek Children's Home. . . . I'll let you talk to Derek." She handed him the phone. "It's my dad. He wants to know how to get there."

Derek took the phone. After giving directions and then talking for several minutes, he closed the phone and handed it back to Kandi.

Cheyenne touched his shoulder. "Is Bruce going to be okay, Derek?"

"They don't know. He's at the county hospital in Lusk. Kandi's parents are driving in from Salt Lake City, and they're almost to Casper. We should get there about the same time that they arrive."

Kandi nodded. "I'll go with them to the hospital." Her eyes filled with tears. "What if Grandpa dies?"

Cheyenne reached out and touched Kandi's arm. "Let's pray for him." Without waiting for a response, she bowed her head. "Father in heaven, we lift Bruce up to You right now. Please heal him, Lord. Keep him on earth for a few more years. Comfort Kandi's parents, and keep them safe as they travel. And comfort Kandi, too. In Jesus' name, we ask. Amen."

"Amen!" Looking into the rearview mirror, Derek caught Cheyenne's eyes. "Thanks, Cheyenne."

"Yes, thank you." Kandi whispered the words before she turned back to the front.

Derek glanced at Kandi and saw her lower lip quiver. Without thinking, he grabbed her hand and squeezed it. "We'll trust the Lord. Your grandfather will pull through."

She just nodded.

He dropped her hand and concentrated on his driving. That was certainly nice of Cheyenne to pray for Kandi.

Cheyenne's heart dropped as she watched Derek squeeze Kandi's hand. *They certainly have a strange relationship.* Turning to the children sitting around her, she attempted to smile. "Let's sing another song."

Noah perked up. "Can we do the army song?"

"Yeah." Joshua smiled. "I like that one. Let's sing it loud."

Cheyenne glanced behind her at Jean and Leslie. "Are you guys going to join us?"

"Sure." Jean looked at the girls beside her and gave them a motherly smile. "We can sing loud, can't we?" She started the song, and everyone joined in, singing at the top of their lungs.

Within fifteen minutes, Derek parked the van in front of the orphanage. Cheyenne gazed up at the large house. She would pray about adopting Arthur someday. Maybe that was God's will for her.

# Chapter 17

Cheyenne threw her duffel bag in the back of Derek's pickup, then opened the passenger door. Climbing in the cab, she pulled the door shut and rolled down the window. Kandi was still waiting for her parents, and Derek sat beside her on the front steps of the orphanage. The low murmur of his voice floated on the breeze. Kandi just sat there, staring at the ground.

Closing her eyes, Cheyenne leaned back against the seat, and Rex's face entered her mind. She would call him when she got home. At least he had a predictable, steady personality. Derek's behavior confused her. All weekend he had teased her and gazed into her eyes and often ignored Kandi. But since they received word about Bruce's heart attack, Derek showed a tender side toward her.

Derek had never seemed so unpredictable before.

A car drove up the driveway and stopped next to Derek's pickup. The car doors opened, and an overweight, bald man exited from the driver's side as a thin woman emerged from the passenger's side.

Kandi jumped up from the porch and ran to them. "Mom! Dad! I'm glad you're here!" While her parents hugged her, Derek slowly stood. Kandi turned to him. "This is Derek."

"Good to meet you." Mr. MacKinnon shook his hand.

"Oh Derek!" Mrs. MacKinnon threw her arms around his shoulders. "I'm so glad to meet you at last. Kandi's told us so much about you." She stepped back. "And look at you! Such a tall, handsome man! I can see why Kandi is totally smitten with you."

Derek's face colored slightly, but he smiled. "Thanks."

From her spot at the window, Cheyenne's lips parted. It looked like Kandi's mother had already pegged Derek as her son-in-law.

Derek cleared his throat. "How is Bruce, by the way? Have you heard any further news?"

Kandi's dad opened his mouth, but her mom answered. "He's not out of the hospital yet, but they think he'll be all right. Agatha Collingsworth called us. I guess she's staying by his side, and we're so thankful for that."

Mr. MacKinnon turned to his wife. "We'd better get on our way."

"Yes, we need to go." Mrs. MacKinnon turned to Kandi. "Where's your suitcase, honey?"

While they got everything settled, Jean walked out the front door of the orphanage. "Derek?" She stopped in front of him. "Could you possibly drive me to Douglas? My husband's car won't start, so he can't pick me up."

"Sure, I can take you. It's right on the way." Derek motioned toward his truck. "I'm driving Cheyenne back to Fort Lob, but we have room for one more."

Cheyenne moved over to the middle of the seat. She wasn't sure if she was glad or disappointed that Jean would be going with them, then decided she was glad. At least she wouldn't have to talk to someone else's boyfriend all the way home.

&

Derek tuned out the ladies' conversation. Cheyenne asked Jean a lot of questions, and Cheyenne got a lot of answers—the inside story about Jean's husband and teenaged kids. His mind drifted back to the MacKinnons. What had Kandi told her parents about him? Well, it didn't matter. When the MacKinnons went back to Salt Lake City, Kandi would forget all about him.

At least he hoped so.

Exiting the freeway, Derek drove his truck through the streets of Douglas as Jean gave him directions to her house. In another minute he was pulling into her driveway. He got out to retrieve her suitcase from the back.

" 'Bye, Jean!" Cheyenne leaned out the passenger window. "It was great to talk to you."

"Same here." Jean smiled as Derek set her suitcase down. "Thanks so much for the lift, Derek."

He nodded. "Anytime."

He climbed back in the cab, almost nervous that he and Cheyenne were finally alone. This ride back to Fort Lob could be a turning point in their relationship. Leaving the town of Douglas, he got back on the freeway.

Cheyenne leaned back against the seat, her eyes closed.

He glanced at her, and his heart stirred. "Tired?"

She opened her blue eyes and smiled at him. "A little." She sat up. "I'll be glad to get home. I'm going to call Rex and see how his weekend went."

Derek tightened his grip on the steering wheel. "So. . .you really like that old cowboy, huh?" *That was a stupid thing to say!*

Cheyenne's smile faded. "He's a very nice person, Derek, and a good Christian, too."

His cell phone chirped. *Saved by the bell!* He pulled it from his pocket and glanced at the number but didn't recognize it. He flipped the phone open and pulled it up to his face as he drove. "This is Derek."

"Hi, Derek." A loud male voice spoke in his ear. "Frank Lindley. I wanted to update you about Arthur."

"Oh good." Derek looked at Cheyenne. "It's Mr. Lindley. I'll put it on speakerphone so you can listen."

"Thanks." She leaned toward him.

Derek pressed a button and spoke into the phone. "How is he, Mr. Lindley?"

"It was a bad break, close to his knee. The doctor said he'll need to perform surgery and secure a pin to hold the bones in place."

Derek's pulse quickened. "Surgery? When are they doing that?"

"The hospital here in Cody is taking him to the Greenbrier Hospital in Casper. It's close to the orphanage. They'll move him tomorrow morning and then perform surgery on Tuesday or Wednesday." Mr. Lindley paused. "Arthur also has a slight concussion."

With a gasp, Cheyenne sat back. "A concussion?"

Derek spoke into the phone. "How bad is it?"

"I don't know, but they want to make sure that's cleared up before they do the surgery on his leg."

"I see." Derek glanced at Cheyenne. She turned away to the window, but not before he noticed a tear roll down her cheek. His heart clenched. "Thanks for the update, Mr. Lindley. We'll keep Arthur in prayer."

"I'll call later if there's any more news."

Derek bid him good-bye and cut off the call. He turned to Cheyenne. "I guess that's all we can do—pray."

"That's the best thing." She looked at him, her eyes bright with tears.

A strong urge to pull her into his arms and comfort her came over him. But he was driving, and besides, she belonged to Rex.

≈

Cheyenne smiled as Derek pulled into her driveway. "Thanks for the ride." She climbed out of the pickup's cab and shut the door; then waited as he grabbed her duffel bag from the back.

He handed it to her. "Here you go. And if Mr. Lindley calls about Arthur, I'll let you know."

"Thanks." She turned and trudged to the house. She needed to eat something. It was almost seven o'clock, and she hadn't eaten since they had lunch in Cody.

Stepping inside the house, she heard Derek's truck leave the driveway. She closed the door, and another sound penetrated her hearing. The television? Dad never watched TV.

She walked to the living room and stopped short. On the sofa, Dad sat beside Janet Oliver, his arm around her. She leaned her head on his shoulder.

Cheyenne's mouth dropped open. Taking a deep breath, she stepped into the living room. "Hello."

Both turned to her, an identical look of surprise on their faces. Dad jumped up. "Hey, baby girl. How was Yellowstone? We didn't realize you were back."

*We?* Obviously Dad was not expecting her to arrive home this early.

Cheyenne forced a smile to her face. "It was great! Uh, but I'll tell you about it later. I'm kind of tired. Finish your movie." She turned and walked down the hallway.

In the safety of her bedroom, she closed the door and set down her duffel bag. *Wow! They sure looked cozy.* She plopped down on her bed.

*Dad and Janet.* Well, she was happy for them—two widowed people who had gone through tough times and deserved a "happily ever after" with each other.

From her purse, her cell phone rang. Sitting up, she glanced at the number before flipping open the phone. "Hi, Callie."

"You sound discouraged. Are you okay?"

A smile crept to Cheyenne's face. "You know me too well, girlfriend. Yeah, I'm discouraged. . .and tired. . .and hungry. Give me some good news. Please?"

"I do have good news. In fact, I have two pieces of good news."

"That's exactly what I need to hear." Cheyenne moved the pillow and sat back against the headboard. "I feel better already. What's the first thing?"

"The James Thomas Lob Museum is almost finished. Lane hopes to have the grand opening in October sometime."

"Oh Callie, that's wonderful." Cheyenne smiled, feeling her depression steal away. "Now you'll have the bookstore you always wanted. I know you're going to enjoy reading all those new books."

"I'm really looking forward to it. But we've been so busy, carting all that stuff over from the third floor of the library. Then it had to be cleaned and cataloged." She gave a little laugh. "Running the bookstore and souvenir shop will be easy compared to the last few months."

Cheyenne relaxed. "I can't wait to visit the museum."

"Hey, why don't you come out to the building site sometime? I'll show you around."

"I'll do that." Cheyenne tucked a strand of hair behind her ear. "Now what's the other good news you have for me?"

"Very few people know about this, so you're one of the first." Callie paused. "Lane and I are expecting a baby."

Cheyenne squealed. "Callie! Congratulations! When is the little bundle of joy due?"

"In April." Callie gave a happy sigh. "Do you realize that I met Lane just a year ago? And now we're married and we're going to have a child. Time goes by so fast."

"It does." Cheyenne brushed a tear from her eye. *That's exactly what I want!* "I'm so happy for you, Callie. That is just wonderful."

"God has been so good to us." A moment passed before Callie spoke again. "But I'm worried about you, Chey. Why are you so discouraged?"

She let a sigh escape her lips. "I don't know. It just seems that life is passing me by. Everything is working out for other people, but nothing is working out for me. I'm praying for the knowledge of God's will for my life, but I'm just not sure of anything."

"How are things with you and Rex? I thought you guys were really hitting it off."

"Oh, everything's fine with Rex, although. . ." Cheyenne rolled on her side. "Maybe I'm looking for the wrong things, but I don't think my feelings for him are as deep as they should be." She sighed. "And then this little boy I was supposed to be watching broke his leg. . . . It's a long story."

Callie paused. "That's too bad. I'll pray for the little boy. What's his name?"

"Arthur. He's five and so cute! A little roly-poly."

"Arthur," she repeated. "And listen, about Rex—the Lord won't let you make a mistake. He might even be the one. I'll keep praying for you two."

Cheyenne sighed. "Thanks." *I think.*

## Chapter 18

Derek rounded the corner in the Greenbrier Hospital corridor on Monday afternoon, looking for Room 116. His heart beat a little faster as he approached the door and pushed it open. Maybe he should have told the Lindleys he was coming instead of arriving unannounced.

Stepping into the room, he stopped short. Arthur lay on the hospital bed, hooked up to some machines, and sitting by his bedside was...

"Cheyenne?" Derek walked to the bed. "I didn't realize you were coming over here today."

A hint of surprise flitted across her face before she smiled. "Since I'm off work today, I thought I'd pay Arthur a visit."

He gazed at her pretty face. "We could have come together and saved some gas."

"Thanks, but my new Cavalier is working great." She turned to the little boy in the bed. "And you're doing great, aren't you, Arthur?"

"Yeah." Arthur's round face was pale, but he grinned. "I'm glad you came, Miss Anne."

Derek's lips twitched. "I hope you're not feeling too *shy*, Anne."

Cheyenne laughed. "I'm getting used to my new name, Mr. Derek." She nodded her head sideways toward Arthur. "But I don't think we can convince a certain someone that my name is actually C-h-e-y-e-n-n-e." Standing, she pulled another chair next to hers. "Have a seat."

"Thanks." Derek walked around the bed and sat down beside her.

"Look what Miss Anne brought me." Arthur held up a pack of crayons with a long, thin coloring book. A cartoon character grinned from the cover.

"Cool." Derek smiled at him. "How are you feeling, Arthur?"

"Okay." Arthur thumbed through the book.

"He's on a lot of pain medicine." Cheyenne lowered her voice. "The concussion is gone, so the doctor wants to do surgery tomorrow morning."

Derek leaned toward her, relishing their closeness. "I'm surprised the Lindleys aren't here."

"Mrs. Lindley stayed by Arthur's bedside all night." Cheyenne tucked a strand of hair behind her ear. "I told her to go home and get some rest. I'm staying with Arthur until she gets back."

Derek raised his eyebrows. *Talk about a servant's heart.* "Want some company, Cheyenne? I'll stay with you until Mrs. Lindley returns."

"That would be. . .nice. Thanks, Derek." Cheyenne turned back to Arthur, who was leaning on his pillows, a listless look on his face. She walked to his side and smoothed his blond hair back from his forehead. "You need to sleep, honey. Mr. Derek and I will be right here if you need us. Okay?"

Arthur nodded before closing his eyes.

Cheyenne looked at Derek. "Let's sit over there." She pointed to some vinyl-covered chairs by the wall. "We can talk, and we won't bother him."

Derek stood and waited for Cheyenne to sit down before he took a seat beside her. He looked forward to being with her for a while.

His cell rang, and he glanced at the number. "Sorry, Cheyenne. I'll be right back." He stood and headed for the door. "Hello, Kandi."

"Hi, Derek. How are you?" She sounded a little breathless.

"Good." He pulled the door closed behind him and walked down to the end of the hospital corridor. "I heard that Bruce is recovering now, and your family left this morning for Salt Lake City. You made it back okay?"

"Yes."

He waited a beat, knowing she wouldn't expand that one word into an explanation. But he wasn't about to carry the conversation. "Why did you call?"

"Well. . .I haven't heard from you, and. . .I just thought I'd call. To talk."

He smirked. Kandi talking in a phone conversation? "Okay. What do you want to talk about?"

"I—I want to keep our. . .relationship going, you know? We need to call each other every day or e-mail."

With a sigh, he looked out the window at the end of the hallway, viewing the hospital parking lot. *Lord, help me here!* He didn't want to hurt her feelings. "Um. . .a long-distance relationship usually doesn't work out, Kandi."

"We can make it work. I have Skype on my laptop. We could see each other every evening and get to know one another."

He shook his head. "I've been praying a lot about my future, trying to discern God's will for my life, and I feel—"

"There's another girl."

Derek's lips parted as Cheyenne's pretty face popped into his mind. "Uh, yeah." It was true, wasn't it? "There is another girl I'm interested in."

"I knew it." Kandi sounded grim. "I knew you were involved with someone else. You were so mean to me at Yellowstone, and I went just because of you!"

He raised his eyebrows. "I didn't ask you to go."

"Well, I thought you wanted to spend time with me. I was enjoying our relationship, and all of a sudden you changed. Now you like Cheyenne."

His eyebrows shot up. Was it that obvious? "We're good friends—"

"I saw the way you looked at her. Why were you leading me on?"

"I wasn't leading you on."

"Were you just using me to make her jealous? Obviously you're in love with her."

*In love?* "No, Kandi—"

"I don't want to talk to you again."

He breathed out a relieved sigh. "Okay, if that's the way you feel."

A faint *click* followed.

"Kandi? Are you still there?" When she didn't answer, Derek closed his phone. *Strange conversation!* But he was glad Kandi had ended their "relationship." Glancing out the window at the blue sky, he spent a few moments in prayer. Was he in love with Cheyenne? Slowly he walked back down the hallway.

Pushing open the door to Arthur's room, he heard a soft feminine voice as he stepped inside. Mrs. Lindley sat beside Cheyenne on the vinyl chairs. Both women's heads were bowed, their hands clasped together, as the older woman prayed.

". . .and we not only pray for Arthur, Father, but for Cheyenne here as well."

Derek stayed near the door, bowing his head as he listened.

"She has expressed an interest in adopting Arthur someday, Lord, and we would love to see her become his mother. But she needs a husband. I pray that You might provide, as You have promised."

Derek's eyes opened. *Should I be standing here?*

"She has someone in mind, Father, but she's not sure if he would welcome Arthur into their home." Mrs. Lindley hesitated. "You know who he is, Father. Speak to his heart. . . ."

Derek stepped back into the corridor. *"She has someone in mind."* Rex Pierson, of course.

He frowned. *I would welcome Arthur into our home.* If he were married to Cheyenne, Derek would be more than happy to adopt Arthur and raise him as the next generation for the Lord. But it looked like Cheyenne wanted Rex for that job.

Derek clenched his jaw. He was going to end up as an old bachelor.

⌒⌒⌒

The next Sunday after the first hymn, Cheyenne started to replace the hymnbook in the pew rack in front of her, but Rex's knobby fingers reached out.

"Allow me," he whispered as he grabbed the book.

"Thanks." She smiled at him.

He returned her smile with a wink before placing his arm on the pew behind her. Cheyenne leaned toward him. If only she loved him! She had a sinking feeling that she never would.

Pastor Reilly began making the announcements. "Don't forget about our Sweet Memories banquet this Friday night. We'll have a potluck dinner, so you ladies need to bring your favorite dish."

Cheyenne tucked a strand of hair behind her ear. Now was not the time to dwell on her problems. What should she make for the banquet? Maybe she could debut the new enchilada recipe she had invented, inspired by an assortment of damaged cans and boxes from her dad's store. She had volunteered to help serve coffee and punch at the banquet and help with the cleanup afterward.

"After the dinner," Pastor Reilly continued, "we'll have a PowerPoint presentation from the past forty years. Forty years of ministry in this church for the wife and me." He smiled. "And I expect to be your pastor for the next forty."

Everyone chuckled. In forty years, Pastor Reilly would be more than a hundred years old.

Cheyenne looked at Rex and grinned. "He just might make it," she whispered.

⌘

On Monday Cheyenne parked her Cavalier in front of the orphanage in Casper. She patted the dashboard before she got out. *Thank You, Lord, for this car.* It was great not to worry about an old car breaking down. She should have replaced the Dart months ago when it started falling apart.

It had been a week since she'd seen Arthur in the hospital—too long for her. If only it wasn't such a long drive to Casper. Now he was recovering at the children's home, and his leg was in a cast. She thought of Mrs. Lindley's prayer from last week. Would she ever be Arthur's mom?

As she walked up the front steps, the door opened and Mr. Lindley stepped outside.

"Cheyenne! I suppose you're here to visit Arthur?"

She nodded. "Is that okay?"

"More than okay—it's great!" His dark eyes twinkled. "I think Arthur views you as his surrogate mother already."

"Really?" She dropped her voice. "Have you told him I want to adopt him?"

"No, of course not. My wife and I are keeping that secret to ourselves—and praying about it, too." He grinned. "The Lord has a plan."

"I've been wondering about Arthur's background. I was going to ask your wife about it last week, but I didn't have the chance. Has he been living here a long time?"

Mr. Lindley shook his head. "His mom just died four months ago from a blood clot. She was a single mother—never married as far as I know. But she was a Christian and attended our church."

Cheyenne raised her eyebrows. "So you knew Arthur? When his mom died, I suppose you offered to take him in."

"Actually, she had listed the children's home in her will." He folded his arms. "If anything happened to her, she wanted the home to take care of her son, with the request to find a Christian couple to adopt him."

Cheyenne's heart picked up its beat. "That was in her will?" She shook her head. "Unbelievable."

"The Lord is working in that boy's life." Mr. Lindley smiled. "We'll take good care of Arthur for you, Cheyenne." He walked down the steps. "Maybe someday, when you marry. . ."

She sighed. *Yeah, maybe someday.*

On Thursday Cheyenne relaxed on a chair at the Beauty Spot as Tonya cut her hair. She would be glad when her hair was back to shoulder length with the split ends cut off.

"Bruce is finally getting out of the hospital tomorrow." With a broom, Aggie swept some hair into a dustpan from another customer. "His son's wife calls us every day. I really like them, and of course Kandi is so cute. She's just the sweetest thing."

Closing her eyes, Cheyenne let a small sigh escape. *Kandi again.* She remembered Derek getting a phone call from Kandi at the hospital. Since that day, Cheyenne had not seen much of him.

Tonya sectioned off a strand of hair and pinned it to the top of Cheyenne's head. "You won't be working tomorrow, will you, Aggie?"

"Nope." Aggie put the broom in the closet. "I'm driving Bruce home from the hospital in the morning, and I'm going to pamper him all day."

"Is your famous fried chicken on the menu for supper?"

"Are you joking?" Aggie sat down on the other beautician chair. "The doc gave me a list of foods Bruce can't eat, and fried chicken is right at the top. It's going to be spinach and fish for the next few months." She gave a little laugh. "But it will be the most delicious spinach and fish he's ever had." Aggie touched the yellow butterfly barrette in her hair. "I'm not working for the rest of the week, but Connie will be here to help you out, Tonya. And don't call me. I'll be taking care of my man—cooking and cleaning."

"You'll be like a regular wife to him." Tonya grinned.

"A wife?" Aggie grunted. "More like a housekeeper. I'll just be the servant girl. Bruce will never see me as wife material." She pursed her pink lips. "Don't know why, but I just can't please that man. I still don't see anything wrong with that tangerine lipstick. Always liked the orange color myself, but Bruce is more comfortable with my makeup toned down." She sighed.

Tonya picked up a comb from the counter. "I'm thankful Murray loves me the way I am. He's so sweet."

"But did ya'll notice what happened?" Aggie frowned at Tonya. "You and Murray are the ones who got Bruce and me together in the first place, and then you two up and marry while we're still floundering in friendship." She turned her frown on Cheyenne. "Now isn't that just the way it goes? Bruce will never propose to me. It's like I told Murray that day he came in to get his hair cut—Bruce and I will be friends forever, and only friends, if someone don't nudge that man toward me. And even after I asked Murray to put a bug in his ear—"

"Aggie!" Tonya cocked an eyebrow at her. "That was my idea, and Murray and I had to push you into it."

"But it did no good! All those changes I made for Bruce, and we're still only friends. It will be unrequited love for the rest of my days."

*Unrequited love.* Derek's face popped into Cheyenne's mind. She had loved him for all those years. "I know how you feel." As soon as the words left her mouth, she regretted saying them.

Aggie leaned toward her, interest sparking in her dark eyes. "I've seen you with that handsome Rex Pierson. I bet you have a case on him!"

Cheyenne smiled. "We have a date tonight at the Four Seasons."

"Ooh!" Tonya snipped at a section of hair with professional panache. "That's exciting, Cheyenne. I hope you guys have a great time."

"Thanks." If only the Lord would answer her prayers. Something had to change tonight in their relationship.

❧

Walking into the kitchen, Derek answered the phone on the fifth ring. "Derek here."

"It's about time you picked up the receiver, son."

He grinned. "Hi, Mom! How are the RV travelers?"

"Oh I love traveling and seeing the beauty of God's creation. Right now we're staying at the Lakes in Kentucky. This is a beautiful area. So many trees, so much water. . ."

"You sound like a travel brochure."

She laughed. "I can't believe we won't be home for a couple of months. I'm taking notes on all the places we're visiting, and we've met so many interesting people." She paused. "Now Derek, you're keeping the dishes washed up, aren't you?"

"Uh, sure." He eyed the stack of dirty plates and bowls in the sink. *I need to buy some paper plates!* "Don't worry, Mom, you'll come back to a clean house."

"You need to keep up with it, Derek. Be sure to dust and vacuum every week."

He rolled his eyes. "Yes, ma'am."

"How is everything going on the ranch?"

He glanced out the kitchen window and caught sight of Hector's overalls as he disappeared into the barn. "Good. Miguel and Hector are helping run everything, but we haven't had any problems. No wolves. No coyotes." He shrugged even though Mom couldn't see him over the phone.

"That's good. I know you're taking good care of those sheep. Don't forget to watch out for my favorite little lamb."

"Snowflake?" He grinned, remembering how Mom had bottle-fed the tiny lamb, turning her into a pet. "She's a happy camper, Mom. Just like you. I think Snowflake knows she's not destined for the slaughterhouse this fall."

Mom laughed. "None of the lambs know that, but Snowflake is going to be a big fluffy ewe someday." The sound of static filled the phone. "I need to go, son. This cell phone needs to be recharged. We love you, Derek."

"Love you, too, Mom."

Hanging up the phone, he gazed out the kitchen window. He could barely see the flock of sheep resting on a hillside. *I should go out there and see how Shep is doing.*

As he opened the back door, a feeling of loneliness overwhelmed him. He missed Mom and Dad being here. There was no one to talk to in this big old house.

Maybe staying single was not such a good idea.

# Chapter 19

That evening, Cheyenne folded her napkin next to her plate and looked across the table at Rex. He was dressed up for this date, wearing a dress shirt with a Western tie and black jeans. And he had actually shaved. "Should we order some coffee, darlin'?"

"That would be nice, Rex."

He signaled the waiter. "Two coffees. And please bring a lot of creamers for the little lady."

She raised an eyebrow. "The 'little lady,' Rex? I've never considered myself little."

Reaching across the table, he took her hands in his work-worn ones. "You are one pretty lady, Cheyenne, and you're pretty special to me."

The waiter set two cups and saucers on the table then poured steaming black coffee from a silver urn. He set the pot down along with a small pitcher of cream.

She smiled at the man. "Thank you."

Rex let go of her hands, and she poured cream into her cup. As she stirred her coffee, she thought of how romantic this evening should be—a handsome cowboy, a gourmet dinner, a perfect atmosphere.

*And I feel nothing.*

They sipped their coffee for a few moments, and then Rex set down his cup and once again took her hands in his. He cleared his throat.

"There's something I've been meanin' to ask you." His brown eyes held hers. "Would you do me the honor of becoming Mrs. Pierson?"

Cheyenne drew in a sharp breath. *He's proposing?*

Rex tightened his grip. "I would provide well for you, darlin'. Even that little bungalow feels lonesome. It's too big for just me. We could have a passel of kiddos someday or even adopt that little boy you like."

Cheyenne's mind raced. Wasn't this what she had been praying for? She could get married and adopt Arthur in time to fulfill all the stipulations of her grandmother's will.

*Lord, is this what You want for me?*

She looked across the table into Rex's eyes and knew what her answer had to be.

Taking a deep breath, she looked down at their hands. "I've really enjoyed getting to know you these last few weeks, Rex, but I can't marry you." She glanced up at him. "You are a wonderful man, and you deserve a woman who really loves you." She paused. "I'm not that woman."

Rex let go of her hands and leaned back in his chair.

Tears crept to her eyes. "I'm sorry."

He sighed. "If that's the way you feel, then we'll part as friends."

Relief flooded through her. "Thank you, Rex." She now had no prospects for a husband, she might not get to adopt Arthur, and she probably wouldn't inherit Grandmother's millions, but the decision was made.

And she knew it was the right one.

❧

Derek was late.

On Friday night he entered the fellowship room in the basement of the church for the Sweet Memories banquet, hoping he could find a seat. Long tables stretched the length of the room, and all the seats were filled with talking, eating people.

As his eyes swept the room, he noticed Janet Oliver sitting next to Jim Wilkins. Derek raised his eyebrows. *Interesting.* Jim and Janet had been sitting together in church last Sunday, too.

Next to Janet, Aggie and Bruce sat side by side. Bruce had been out of the hospital for a few days, and he seemed to be doing well. Derek was glad Kandi was back with her family. Their relationship had been a good learning experience, as his mother would say.

What he learned was that he needed to stay away from quiet, possessive girls.

With a coffeepot in her hand, Cheyenne walked up to him, sporting a jean jacket and a long pink skirt. "Hi, Derek! Did you just arrive?" Her blue eyes gazed up into his as she smiled.

*What a knockout!* "I like your haircut—and your outfit, too."

"Thanks! Tonya did my hair, and this was my favorite outfit in high school. I thought it would be appropriate for the Sweet Memories banquet." She grinned. "I can't believe I fit into it after ten years!"

He returned her grin, enjoying her bubbly personality. This was the girl he loved to be around. "You look really pretty tonight."

A look of surprise skittered across her face, and their eyes locked. Derek was a little surprised himself that he had blurted out his thoughts.

Someone called Cheyenne's name, and they both turned to look at a nearby table. A man raised his coffee cup. "Refill?" he asked.

"I'll be right there." She turned back to Derek and motioned toward a long table of food by the wall. "Help yourself to the food. I'll find a chair for you."

"Thanks." His eyes followed her as she walked away. Then he looked around. Where was Rex?

He passed his sister Callie, who was filling water glasses.

Walking to the table, he picked up a paper plate and dished a spoonful of green bean casserole on his plate. *Why am I so hung up on Cheyenne?* He added a chicken leg. *Does the Lord really want me to stay single?* The scalloped potato dish was almost empty, but he scraped out a spoonful. *What do I really want?* He threw a dollop of baked beans on his plate. *Even if I want Cheyenne, will she want me?* Glancing at the scanty dessert section, he added two squares of cake to his plate. *I might not have the chance to find out.*

Turning from the table, he glanced around. Cheyenne motioned to him from the end of the room. He made his way toward the back, greeting several people on the way.

"You can sit here, Derek." Cheyenne laid her hand on a folding chair at the end of one of the long tables.

"Thank you." Derek took the seat.

"You're welcome." She glanced at his plate. "You didn't get any of my enchiladas."

He looked at the food on his plate. "Did I miss something?"

She smiled. "I'll get some for you."

As Cheyenne left, Derek greeted the Newmans, the young couple on his right. They had two children who kept their attention, so they didn't say much.

Edna Beazer sat on his left. She leaned toward him and smiled, showing off her straight white dentures. "Derek Brandt! I haven't seen you for ages."

He glanced at the older woman as he dug the plastic fork into his food. Her thin hair was tinted blue. "How are you doing, Mrs. Beazer?"

"Oh, my arthritis is acting up something fierce, but besides that, I'm better than middling."

A drop of her spit landed on the table, and Derek deftly moved his plate to the right.

Cheyenne came back and set a small plate beside his arm. "They were almost gone. Here's the last of it. This recipe is making its debut tonight since I made it up."

"Thanks." Derek glanced at the small square of layered tortillas, meat, and cheese. "Looks good." He pulled the plate toward him and took a bite.

Mrs. Beazer looked up at Cheyenne. "What are you calling the new recipe, dear?"

Cheyenne shrugged. "Ten-Layer Enchiladas."

"Wow, this is really good, Cheyenne." Derek took another bite.

"Glad you like it." With a smile, Cheyenne picked up a coffeepot from the table and moved away, refilling cups.

"Where are your parents, Derek?" Mrs. Beazer sucked in her dentures. "I didn't see them Wednesday night in church, and they aren't here tonight."

"Mom and Dad are traveling. They purchased an RV and left town on

Monday. They're planning to travel around the southern states during the next few months."

Edna's thin eyebrows raised. "So you're all alone in that big old house of yours?"

Nodding, Derek swallowed another bite of enchiladas. "Until November. They plan to be home for the holidays."

She placed a bony hand on his arm. "You must be lonely."

"I'm doing fine by myself, thanks." He wasn't about to let Mrs. Beazer or anyone else know how lonely he really was. He finished eating and headed for the nearest trash can to throw away his plate. Callie struggled to pull a full trash bag out of the can.

"Hey, let me help you do that."

"Oh thanks, Derek." Callie stood back as he took over. "You wouldn't believe how intense smells can be when you're pregnant."

He quirked an eyebrow at her. "I've never been pregnant, so I'll take your word for it."

She laughed. "Just put the full bag by the back door. I'm going to sit with Lane."

"Hey, Callie."

She turned back to him.

He lowered his voice. "I noticed Rex Pierson isn't here. I thought Cheyenne would be sitting with him."

"Didn't you hear?" Callie's eyes widened. "They broke up."

He stared at her. "What?"

"Yes." She glanced around before moving closer to him. "Rex proposed to Cheyenne last night, and she turned him down."

The pastor walked to the front of the room and stood behind a small lectern.

"We'd better take our seats," Callie whispered.

"Welcome to our Sweet Memories banquet." Pastor Reilly glanced around the tables. "Most of you are finished, so we'll begin our program."

His head still spinning, Derek reclaimed his seat. *Cheyenne is available!* He couldn't believe it. This changed everything.

As the pastor spoke about the history of the church, several ladies who had helped in the kitchen took seats with their families. Cheyenne came out from the kitchen also, but she didn't sit down. Clasping her hands in front of her, she stood by the wall near the food table.

The pastor motioned behind him to a large white screen. "Since a picture is worth a thousand words, we have a PowerPoint that Ralph Little put together. These are slides from the last forty years—from the very first year my wife and I came to Fort Lob until the present." He smiled. "But first we'll listen to a number from our own men's quartet—the Four Methuselahs."

Derek folded his arms on the table. He loved to hear the "Methuselahs" sing. All four men were over sixty years old, but they harmonized perfectly.

The men walked to the front, all sporting minty-green blazers with yellow handkerchiefs in the front pocket. A quiet hum was heard, and then the men broke out into a rousing a cappella rendition of "Joshua Fit de Battle of Jericho." When they finished, Derek joined in the applause.

"Thank you, men." The pastor moved the lectern to one side. "If someone douses the lights, we'll watch our PowerPoint presentation."

The pastor took a seat in the front, and the lights went out. Derek glanced over at Cheyenne, whom he could barely see. Was she going to stand during the entire program?

*I am going to take care of that girl.*

Grabbing his chair, Derek walked to where she stood. "Cheyenne." He kept his voice low as the presentation started with music. "Here's a chair." He unfolded it next to her.

She glanced down. "But that's your chair," she whispered.

"No, it's yours." He motioned toward it. "Sit."

She smiled as she took a seat. "Thanks, Derek."

Folding his arms, he leaned against the wall next to her. The room was quiet as the photos faded in and out with the music. The first pictures were before Derek's time, although he saw photos of his parents as young people. Aggie, Bruce MacKinnon with his first wife, Edna Beazer and her husband, Fred and Janet Oliver. . . All were captured in the prime of life. As the years moved along, Derek began to appear as a little kid with his brother and sisters.

At one picture, Cheyenne turned and looked up at him with a smile. "Remember that?" she whispered.

A group of elementary children smiled for the camera. As a ten-year-old boy, Derek stood next to Cheyenne and Callie, who were both eleven. All three of them held up colorful award ribbons.

Derek hunkered down next to Cheyenne's chair. "Neighborhood Bible Time, wasn't it?"

"Yes." She grinned. "I loved that summer. We had so much fun." She turned her attention back to the slides.

Cheyenne had always loved fun, and Derek had always loved being around her, even when they were kids.

He glanced at her profile. Could they have a future together?

At the end of the PowerPoint, Derek stood and leaned against the wall.

Pastor Reilly came back to stand behind the lectern. "You have just witnessed the last forty years of this church's history. The Lord has been so good to us, faithfully guiding us, leading us to people who need Him, and strengthening our members in the faith." He motioned toward the front table. "But I couldn't have accomplished the work of this ministry without my dear wife by my side. We have served the Lord together all these years. She's been such a blessing to me." He turned to her. "Honey, stand up."

Someone started clapping, and the audience joined in. Mrs. Reilly smiled at her husband and then at the church people.

Derek didn't clap. He stared at the Reillys. *"We have served the Lord together."* Tonya's voice flitted through his mind. *"That's crazy. He doesn't have to remain single to serve the Lord."*

He glanced at Cheyenne. He knew that she cared about him. She even cared about his sheep. Maybe she even loved him.

*And I love her!* Kandi had been right about that.

The pastor was winding down his comments. "Thank you for attending this banquet. It has certainly been sweet memories for my wife and myself. Now let's close—"

"Pastor?" Bruce MacKinnon stood. "Before we dismiss, could I give a short testimony?"

The pastor nodded. "Certainly, Bruce. Go right ahead."

Bruce swung around to face most of the crowd. "You all know that I had a heart attack almost two weeks ago. Being confined to the hospital, flat on my back for a week, I had a lot of time to think about my life. I'm so thankful God spared me, and I want to use my remaining years to serve Him." He glanced down at Aggie, who smiled up at him. "I also realize that life is short. Therefore, in front of all my friends, I'd like to ask you, Agatha Collingsworth, to marry me."

Aggie's mouth dropped open, and several gasps could be heard around the room.

But Aggie recovered quickly. Pushing back her chair, she jumped up to stand beside him. "Why Bruce, you old codger, you! In front of all these people, I can't say *no*!"

Everyone laughed as Bruce drew her into his arms and hugged her.

Pastor Reilly raised his voice. "Congratulations to the happy couple! You are all dismissed."

Chairs scraped against the tile floor as everyone stood, and the noise level grew to a joyous din. Derek wanted to talk to Cheyenne, but she rushed off to join the crowd of well-wishers surrounding Bruce and Aggie.

Perhaps now was not the time to talk to Cheyenne.

*Life is short.* Derek turned and walked out the door to the parking lot. He would go home and spend the next hour on his knees, praying that someday his house would be filled with his wife's laughter and the happy voices of their children.

# Chapter 20

On Saturday Cheyenne hooked the leash to Marshal's collar. "Okay, Marsh, we're ready to go." Opening the door, she walked out into the early evening.

*I'm not jogging!* She would take an easy-paced walk and pray. She hadn't even donned her sweats, opting instead for jeans and a blue T-shirt.

It had been raining that afternoon when she got home from work, and now a fresh scent hung in the air. She took a deep breath as she walked down the sidewalk with Marshal by her side.

*Life is short.* That's what Bruce had said last night at the Sweet Memories banquet. Cheyenne couldn't believe he asked Aggie to marry him in front of everyone! Of course Aggie loved the attention, and she finally got what she wanted—the promise of marriage to Bruce MacKinnon. Cheyenne was so happy for her.

*And I'm happy that I'm not going to marry Rex.*

A horn honked, making her jump. She glanced at the Town Car driving by and waved at her dad. He was coming home from work.

Crossing the street, she made her way toward the park. Walking Marshal had become an everyday habit for her. Since her birthday, she had lost nineteen pounds. She even had to buy some new clothes. But the best thing about going to the park was the time she spent in prayer as she walked.

She couldn't imagine any man more perfect for her than Derek Brandt. But maybe the Lord had other plans. She sighed.

It was sad that a casino owner would be getting all of Grandmother's money.

⁓

Derek lifted his truck keys from the hook by the door. For a moment, his heart beat a hard staccato, and he almost put the keys back. But after spending time in prayer last night, he knew Cheyenne was God's will for him.

"Don't be a coward!" he admonished himself.

Leaving the ranch, he drove the seven miles to Fort Lob. It only took a few turns from Main Street to arrive at Cheyenne's house. He drove up the driveway and parked behind Jim's Town Car. His hands shook slightly as he climbed out of the truck and approached her house.

He couldn't believe he was so nervous. *This is Cheyenne, for goodness' sake.* Taking a deep breath, he knocked on the door.

A moment later the door opened, but it wasn't Cheyenne.

"Hi, Derek!" Jim boomed out. "What can I do for you?"

"Is Cheyenne here?"

"No, she's on a walk with Marshal. I passed her on my way home. She probably went to the park."

"Oh." A sense of relief spread through him, yet at the same time, Derek knew exactly what his next step should be. "Uh, could I come in and talk to you a minute?" He didn't want to talk at the door. With Jim's loud voice, the whole neighborhood would hear their conversation.

Jim stepped back. "Sure. Come on in."

"Thanks." Derek followed him inside to the living room.

"Have a seat." Jim motioned to the sofa. "Can I get you something to drink?"

Derek shook his head. "I just have a question to ask you."

Jim took a seat across from him in a La-Z-Boy recliner, and his blue eyes—the exact color as Cheyenne's—stared at him. "So what's the problem?"

"It's not really a problem." Derek tapped his fingers on the arm of the sofa. Where should he start? "Well. . .I've loved your daughter for a long time." *Whoa!* He couldn't believe those were the first words out of his mouth.

A look of surprise passed over Jim's face, but then he smiled. "I'm glad to hear that, Derek. Cheyenne thought you weren't interested in her. I understand you were dating someone else?"

"Kandi MacKinnon, but she's out of the picture now, and I hear that Cheyenne is not dating Rex anymore."

"That's true." A hint of a smile touched Jim's lips.

With a kick of determination, his nervousness vanished. He would tell Jim the truth. "I wish I had started dating Cheyenne years ago, but I thought the Lord wanted me to remain single to serve Him. But then at the banquet last night, Pastor Reilly said he couldn't have accomplished the work of his ministry without his wife. They served the Lord together all their lives." Derek spread out his hands. "Something hit me. I realized I've loved Cheyenne—for years. The Lord showed me that if I want to serve Him, I need a wife by my side." A little warmth crept up his neck. "Does that make sense? Cheyenne has a servant's heart, and she's a lot of fun, and she's pretty, and. . .and I love her."

Jim raised his eyebrows. "Uh, so, are you asking for her hand in marriage?"

"Yes!" Derek nodded. Didn't he make that clear? "Sorry. I don't do well at explaining things, but I do want your permission and your blessing to marry your daughter—if she'll have me."

"I'm more than happy to give my blessing to your marriage. In fact, this is an answer to prayer—not only my prayers, but Cheyenne's mom's prayers as well. As far as Cheyenne's answer. . ." He shrugged. "All you can do is ask." Then he grinned. "But I doubt that she'll turn you down."

"That's good." Derek got to his feet. "Thanks, Jim. I'll drive over to the park and see if I can find her."

Jim stood and thrust out his hand. "Welcome to the family, son."

With a laugh, Derek shook it. "Aren't you being a little premature? Cheyenne hasn't agreed to marry me yet."

"She will." Jim's smile faded. "Oh wait a minute. Before you leave, I want to give you something."

∽

Cheyenne took a seat on a park bench—the same bench next to the lamppost where she and Dad had their discussion several weeks ago. "Let's rest awhile, Marsh. I can see you're tired."

Marshal sat down on his haunches and panted.

The twilight deepened, and the light above her turned on. Two boys whizzed by on their bikes. Then all was quiet. Taking a deep breath of warm summer air, she rubbed Marshal's ear.

"It's just you and me, boy." Her thoughts drifted back to last night at the banquet when Derek had given her his chair. *That was so sweet of him.*

Closing her eyes, she felt a tear creep out from her lashes. *Why am I crying?* Pulling a tissue from her jeans pocket, she wiped the tear away. *I will wait, Lord.* Once again, she closed her eyes and breathed in the warm air, spending several minutes in prayer.

Someone sat down on the bench beside her. "Cheyenne?"

Her eyes flew open. Derek gazed at her from under the brim of his cowboy hat. He wore a Western shirt, and his long legs were clad in jeans.

"Hi." He smiled at her. "Glad I found you."

Her heart leaped. "Um, hi!" What was he doing here? He had such a strange look on his face. "Do you need something?"

"Well. . .I went to your house, but your dad told me you were walking the dog. He figured you were at the park."

She shrugged. "Here I am."

Derek removed his cowboy hat and held it in his hands a moment before setting it on the bench. He cleared his throat. "I've been thinking a lot about my life lately—you know, relationships and stuff."

She frowned. "Relationships?"

He met her eyes. "I learned a few things, Cheyenne. In fact, I learned a lot through dating Kandi—a real trial-and-error relationship."

She stiffened. Why was he talking about this? She didn't want to hear about his relationship with Kandi. What did he want? Advice?

He cleared his throat. "I really don't have much experience in relationships."

*That's obvious!* She sniffed. "I'm sure you and Kandi will be very happy—"

"Kandi?" He placed his arm on the back of the bench. "Is that what you think? I'm planning to marry her?"

She frowned. "It sure looked that way at Yellowstone. The two of you were together every second. And then her mom said—" *Oh! I'm really putting my foot in my mouth!* "Never mind." She looked away.

"Cheyenne." Derek gently placed his fingers on her chin and pulled her face toward him. "I had nothing to do with that closeness at Yellowstone. Kandi is a very possessive person, I found out." He dropped his hand but looked deeply into her eyes. "I learned two things through my short relationship with Kandi."

She gazed up into his eyes, trying to blink away the tears that insisted on appearing.

Derek curved his arm around her shoulders. "I learned that God does not want me to remain single in order to serve Him, and I learned that. . ." His gaze dropped to her lips before it came back to her eyes. "I love you, and I've loved you for a long time."

Cheyenne's head spun. "Me? You—you love *me*? Not Kandi?" Was that what he'd been trying to tell her with all his talking in circles?

A smile flitted across his lips. "Yes, you, Cheyenne. There's never been anyone else. No one but you."

Her lips parted. Was this really happening? Was she actually sitting on a park bench on a warm summer night with Derek Brandt? Had he just said that he loved her? The moment seemed surreal as she gazed into his eyes.

But in the next moment, her senses flooded back. God was answering all her prayers in a single moment of time!

"Oh Derek," she whispered. "I love you, too."

He lowered his head, and her hands seemed to slide around his neck of their own accord. His arms tightened around her as his lips touched hers.

That same surreal feeling flew through Cheyenne as Derek kissed her, but at the same time, she felt an aura of peace. God's peace.

*This is where I belong.*

In another moment Derek raised his head. He gave her a little half smile then leaned in to kiss her again. Cheyenne didn't mind. This time she kissed him back with all the passion she'd been saving up for him.

Finally he sat back. "Wow, Cheyenne. If I had known you kiss like that. . ." He waggled his eyebrows.

She giggled. "You could have kissed me in your truck. Remember—the near kiss that turned into the near miss?"

He laughed. "Is that what you call it?"

She gazed at his handsome face. "Why didn't you kiss me, Derek? I think you wanted to."

"I did." His smile faded. "Back then I thought the Lord wanted me to remain single." Looking down, he took her hand in his. "I didn't want to get involved in a relationship, but I know I hurt you." He looked up. "Will you forgive me?"

Cheyenne thought a moment. "Yes, but there's only one way I'll forgive you."

He raised his eyebrows.

"I'll forgive you if we simulate that moment in the truck again." She lifted her tissue to his face. "First I wipe off the mascara. . . ."

He burst out laughing. "This is why I love you so much."

Her eyes widened at him. "Why?"

"You're so much fun." He grinned then cleared his throat. "Okay, so you're wiping off the mascara."

"Right." She tried not to laugh. "Then I say, 'That's better.'"

"And I say, 'Much better.' And then. . ." His gaze dropped down to her lips, and he leaned in to kiss her.

Cheyenne kissed him back with more passion than before. *I still can't believe this is happening!* But knowing Derek, he would take his time to propose marriage. He might be forty years old before he got around to it.

They were both a little breathless when their kiss ended. Derek sat back and gazed into her eyes. Cheyenne could feel the chemistry between them, and she gave a contented sigh.

Breaking their gaze, Derek looked down. With his free hand, he fumbled in his shirt pocket. "When I was talking to your dad, he gave this to me." Derek pulled out a small velvet box and opened it to reveal two rings, one with a large diamond surrounded by sapphires in a yellow gold setting.

She gasped. "That was my mom's wedding set."

Derek nodded. "Your dad wanted you to have it. He gave it to me when I asked his permission to marry you."

"What?" She looked up at him, and his face blurred as fresh tears clouded her vision. "Are you asking to marry me?"

Raising his eyebrows, he looked a little unsure. "I am. . .if you'll have me."

"Yes, I'll have you!" Laughing, she threw her arms around his neck. "Yes, yes!"

He kissed her again. Then he took the rings out of the box. "Let's try these on." Slipping them on her finger, he held up her hand. The rings fit perfectly.

Her eyes widened. "I can't believe they fit."

Derek took her hand and squeezed it. "I think it was meant to be. The Lord made this ring for your finger, just like He made you for me and me for you." He looked at her and winked. "We'll celebrate by going bowling—after I teach you how to ski."

"Derek!" Laughing, she leaned against him.

He kissed her forehead. "Do you realize how God designed us to complement each other? You're outgoing, and I like to stay in the background. You like adventure, and I like the rut I'm stuck in. But we both want to serve the Lord." He dropped his voice. "And now we can serve Him together."

"Yes." She could barely squeak out the word as tears rushed to her eyes.

She cleared her throat. "Do you think we could get married by the end of this year?"

With a shrug, he grinned. "Sure, the sooner the better. But what's the reason?"

She took a deep breath. "I have four million very good reasons. . . ."

# Epilogue

*Two years later*

Derek couldn't wipe the smile off his face. He strode through the hospital corridor and passed the nurses' station.

One of the nurses looked up. "Congratulations!"

"Thanks!" His smile grew bigger as he hit the automatic-door button. The two wide doors swung outward. He stepped out and rounded the corner.

The door to the waiting room was closed, and he peered through the small window. His parents sat in the sturdy padded chairs. Dad looked down at an open Bible on his lap. Evidently he was having his morning devotions, and no wonder. It was only seven thirty. Mom sat next to him, knitting something small with yellow yarn.

*I know who that's for.* The thought made him grin.

Across the room, Cheyenne's dad read a newspaper. His wife, Janet, sat beside him, reading a children's book to Derek's seven-year-old son. Arthur had slimmed down quite a bit since Derek and Cheyenne had adopted him, and he'd grown four inches.

Derek opened the door, and Arthur jumped to his feet. "Hey, Dad! Did Mom have the baby?"

"Yep!" He paused, looking at the five pairs of wide eyes that stared at him. "It's a girl!"

His announcement was met with an outburst of exclamations. Everyone rushed forward and surrounded him. Dad pumped his hand, and Jim slapped him on the back while Mom and Janet both tried to hug him at the same time.

Arthur hopped up and down beside him. "I bet she looks like me, huh, Dad?"

"Not exactly." With a laugh, he motioned for them to follow him. "Cheyenne is waiting for all of you to come visit her—and our daughter."

Mom turned to Janet as they walked out of the room. "We finally got a granddaughter—not that I don't love our little grandsons, mind you."

Janet smiled. "She'll be fun to shop for. I just love looking at little girl dresses."

Derek entered Room 333. He stopped short to gaze at his wife and daughter while his son, his parents, and his parents-in-law surrounded the bed.

Cheyenne sat up with the baby in her arms and gave him a tired smile. Then she took turns hugging everyone. The room echoed with talking and laughter.

"Look at all that dark hair!"

"Her fingers are so little!"

"We'll have to buy some girl's clothes right away."

Mom picked up the baby and cuddled her. "What's her name, Cheyenne? I remember that you and Derek were waffling back and forth on names."

Cheyenne tucked a strand of light-blond hair behind her ear. She glanced up at Derek and smiled before she answered. "We've decided on Arianna."

Janet smiled. "Ooh—that's pretty."

Derek stepped behind Arthur and placed his hands on his son's shoulders. "Since we have one A name, we decided to go for two."

Arthur looked up at him. "Really, Dad? You named her Arianna because of me?"

"Yep. And Arianna's middle name is Lynn, after Cheyenne's mom."

"That's so nice." Janet looked up at Jim as she looped her arm through his, and they shared a smile.

"That reminds me." Derek placed his hand on Cheyenne's shoulder. "The Lynn Wilkins Memorial Wing of the Bolton Creek Children's Home is scheduled to open next week. You're all invited to the grand opening."

Jim raised his eyebrows. "You've done a lot of good with that money, Derek. I'm proud of you two."

"Knock, knock."

Everyone turned to the door at Callie's voice. She and Lane walked into the room with Lane carrying their little son, Cody, in his arms.

After initial greetings by everyone, Callie walked up to Mom and gazed at the baby. "Oh, she's so pretty."

Cheyenne grinned. "She looks like Derek, so of course she's pretty."

He shrugged. "She got my black hair, Cheyenne. Who knows who she'll look like."

"Yeah, Mom." Arthur leaned against the bed. "I look like you, so Arianna has to look like Dad."

Everyone laughed.

Lane turned to Derek. "Just wait until she's the same age as Cody." He looked down at his son. "This boy gets into everything."

Callie nodded. "And he'll be two years old in six months. The terrible twos. I'm dreading that."

Still holding Arianna, Mom smiled. "Enjoy him while he's little, Callie. Children grow up way too fast." She glanced around the room. "I can't believe we have six grandchildren already."

"And I'm the oldest." Arthur smiled up at her. "Right, Grandma?"

"That's right, Arthur. You'll probably be our first grandchild to get married and start the next generation."

Cheyenne laughed. "Now that's too fast, Mom. I haven't even thought that far ahead."

"That's right. Hold your horses." Derek grinned. "Arthur's only starting second grade this year."

An hour later, the family said their good-byes, and Derek's parents took Arthur with them. He would stay with them in their RV for the next week. But Derek and Cheyenne kept getting visitors, mainly friends from church. The small hospital room began to fill up with flower arrangements, teddy bears, and gift bags of little clothes.

After supper, Tonya and Murray came by. Tonya was still working at the Beauty Spot, but she wouldn't be for long. In two months she would have her own bundle of joy.

Tonya gazed at Arianna. "She is so pretty!"

Murray nodded. "Yep. She looks like a Brandt with the black hair."

"Do you want to hold her, Tonya?" Cheyenne motioned to the chair by the bed. "You can sit there."

"Sure." Tonya took little Arianna in her arms and sat down, her giant belly pushing out her maternity shirt. "You know, I don't think I'm the right shape to hold a baby." She laughed. "I can't wait until ours is born."

"Me, too." Murray turned to Derek and rolled his eyes. "She makes me rub her feet every night."

"Well, they hurt!" Tonya shared a smile with him then cooed to the baby.

Cheyenne lay back against her pillow. "The last month is the worst, Tonya. You'll be ready to have that little one."

"How are your cookbook sales going, sis?" Derek asked.

"Great! Since Lane mentioned it in his newspaper column, sales have boomed."

Murray grinned. "We have so many famous authors in our family."

"We have one." Tonya laughed. "Lane is the only famous person I know."

"You might become another Rachael Ray, Tonya." Cheyenne gave her a tired smile.

⤳

After Tonya and Murray left, they had a few more church people come by. Cheyenne was thankful when everyone was gone. She wanted to spend time with her husband and little daughter.

Derek set Arianna in the bassinette by the side of the bed. Then he pulled Cheyenne into his arms and kissed her. "You are really tired, baby. You need some sleep."

"I know." She gazed into his eyes. "But I've enjoyed this day. Isn't God good to us?"

"He sure is. Let's thank Him." Derek took her hand in his. "Father, thank You for the many blessings You've given us. We especially praise You for our daughter's safe arrival into this world. Please save her at a young age. May she grow up to know You and serve You with her whole heart."

Cheyenne wiped a tear from her eye. *Lord, thank You for giving me such a wonderful husband.*

She had waited, and God had worked out His plan for both of them.

God's plans were always worth waiting for.

# NO ONE BUT YOU

## Cheyenne's Ten-Layer Enchiladas

4 cups cooked chicken or turkey, shredded
1 (14.5 ounce) can diced tomatoes
1 (10 ounce) can black beans, rinsed
1 box Rice-a-Roni Mexican-style rice, cooked
1 cup nacho cheese (queso)
3 (10 ounce) cans enchilada sauce
1 package (24 count) yellow-corn tortillas
1 (4 ounce) can chopped green chilies
2 cups cheddar cheese, shredded
1 carton (8 ounce) sour cream

Mix first five ingredients together. In a 9x13-inch pan, make ten layers:

1. Pour 1 cup enchilada sauce in pan to cover bottom.
2. Put 6 corn tortillas on sauce.
3. Spread half of meat mixture on top.
4. Put on another layer of 6 tortillas.
5. Spread 1 cup enchilada sauce mixed with chopped chilies.
6. Put on another layer of 6 tortillas.
7. Spread second half of meat mixture on top.
8. Cover with another layer of 6 tortillas.
9. Pour 1 cup enchilada sauce over all.
10. Top with both cups of shredded cheddar cheese.

Cover with aluminum foil, and bake at 350 degrees for 45 minutes. Uncover and bake for 5 more minutes or until cheese is melted. Serve with sour cream and tortilla chips.